WYRM

MARK FABI

WYRM

BANTAM BOOKS

NEW YORK   TORONTO   LONDON   SYDNEY   AUCKLAND

WYRM

A Bantam Spectra Book / June 1997

SPECTRA and the portrayal of a boxed "s" are trademarks of Bantam Books,
a division of Bantam Doubleday Dell Publishing Group, Inc.

Library of Congress Cataloging-in-Publication Data

Fabi, Mark.
Wyrm / by Mark Fabi.
p. cm. — (A Bantam Spectra book)
ISBN 0-553-37871-6
I. Title.
PS3556.A17W97 1997
813'.54—dc21 96-50942
CIP

Published simultaneously in the United States and Canada

Bantam Books are published by Bantam Books, a division of Bantam Doubleday Dell
Publishing Group, Inc. Its trademark, consisting of the words "Bantam Books" and the
portrayal of a rooster, is Registered in U.S. Patent and Trademark Office and in other
countries. Marca Registrada. Bantam Books, 1540 Broadway, New York, New York 10036.

PRINTED IN THE UNITED STATES OF AMERICA

FFG   10 9 8 7 6 5 4 3 2 1

For Michael

Table of Contents

Acknowledgments

The author wishes to thank the following people for their invaluable contributions to this book: Lucienne Diver, who rescued *Wyrm* from the slush pile and made many valuable suggestions; Anne Groell, for a superb job of editing; Marshall Goldberg, Janny Wurts, and Mickey Zucker, for their advice, support, and friendship; Steve and Janice Dickter, Andrea and Paul Della Franco, and Diana Samson, who were all subjected to early versions of the manuscript; Steve Stadnicki, for technical input on computers in general and MUDs in particular; and above all my wife, Donna, whose unwavering belief in me sustained me through those times when my self-confidence was flagging.

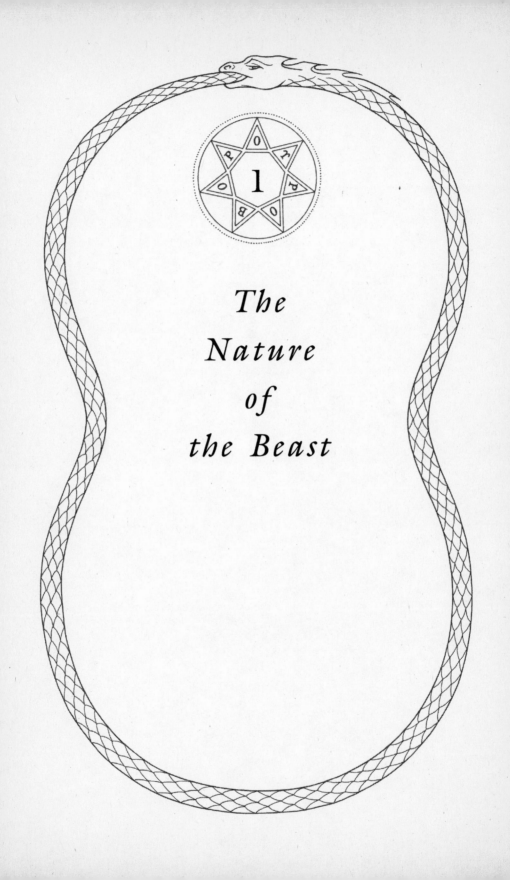

1

The
Nature
of
the Beast

CHAPTER ONE

Opening Moves

And when the thousand years are expired, Satan shall be loosed

out of his prison . . .

—Revelation 20:7

"It ate itself."

I stared at the note, which was taped to the monitor screen of my computer. It was Thursday, March 11, a little after midnight, and I had just gotten home from the airport to find the strange note, and seven messages on my answering machine, which was also odd, because I'd called to check for messages earlier in the day.

I picked up the phone and called The Dodo. It was late, but if you're going to leave cryptic messages on people's computers, you're going to have to deal with the consequences. Anyway, he was awake, as I knew he would be. The wee hours are prime hacking time.

"Hello?"

"What the hell does this mean?"

"Hello, Michael. Welcome back." The Dodo, or TD to his friends, was a hacker of my acquaintance whom I'd asked to come over and check out a problem I was having with a newly upgraded operating system. The latest upgrade to MABUS/2K had just been released with the usual fanfare by Macrobyte Software, and, of course, you couldn't get through on the tech-support line to save your life. My particular problem was the delete program, a routine for removing unwanted files. You just selected the file or files you wanted to trash, then clicked on the pit icon. But it had mysteriously stopped working shortly after installation.

"Thanks. But your note . . . ?"

"Yes. The problem seems to be idiosyncratic to your computer system. If you double-click on the delete icon, the delete routine deletes itself. Unfortunately, I wasn't able to divine why it does this. You can simply reinstall it from the system disks, but you'll have to remember not to double-click, or it will do it again."

"You think this is funny, don't you?"

"It has a certain perverse appeal," he admitted.

"I suppose it does."

"Well, if you're able to work out the exact nature of the problem with the delete function, let me know. I'm rather curious about it."

"Me too. Okay, will do. I'd better go now; my answering machine is about to have a nervous breakdown."

"Roger."

I played back the answering-machine tape. A quick run-through revealed that the messages were all from the same person—George Bard, an old college buddy I'd not heard from in years. The messages were all the same, just "Call right away" and a number with a San Francisco area code. I dialed it, figuring that it was at least moderately urgent. It was busy.

I set the phone for automatic redial and turned to boot up my computer. I have a second line for my modem, so I was able to check my electronic mail while the phone tried to reach George. My four E-mail accounts were bulging with the usual junk, but there was something else: more messages from George. The earliest one had come at about nine o'clock, eastern time. By now I was more than a little curious about what had George in such a frenzy. I switched on the TV to a rerun of *To Tell the Truth* to provide a little background noise while I paged through the E-mail. It was about the same as what was on the answering machine, just "Call this number ASAP." The phone was still redialing his number with mechanical patience, and still, evidently, getting a busy signal.

By the time I checked all my mail—electronic and otherwise—it was nearly one-thirty, and Tom Poston was grilling some guys who claimed to have survived falling out of a plane. All three of them looked as if they'd been dropped on their heads from a great height, so it was a tough call. I was about ready to pack it in and get some sleep; I'd been at a conference in London and was suffering from near-terminal jet lag. I was curious about what George's problem might be but couldn't see anything to do about it but wait until there was a chance to talk to him. I tried to think of what kind of work he might be doing, but my memories of him were mostly in terms of types and quantities of beer consumed. He had been a pretty fair Lisp hacker, so he might still be doing something in artificial intelligence. Then I had a bright idea.

I turned to a small stack of compact disks that were still in their mailing cartons—I hadn't gotten around to opening them. The one I wanted was on top of the stack: "Computer Periodicals 1998." I unpacked it, flipped it into the CD-ROM drive, and started a search. My efforts were rewarded with a solitary reference: *Computer Chess,* a small, obscure, and obviously highly specialized publication. I pulled up the citation, which was dated January 1998:

STANFORD PROGRAMMERS TRY NOVEL APPROACH

Programmers at Stanford University received a grant from Tokoyo Corporation to continue work on a program they hope will challenge Mephisto, the reigning computer-chess world champion. In a departure from prevailing competition-level chess programs, which emphasize speed, number crunching, and the ability to look ahead as many moves as possible, the Stanford team hopes to make use of some newer developments in artificial intelligence. Team leader Jason Wright explained, ''We would like to create a program that 'thinks' about chess the way human grandmasters do.''

The story went on a few more paragraphs in a similar vein, without much more detail. The programmers were not giving away too much about their project—nothing, really, as programming a computer to think "the way human grandmasters do" was something that pro-

grammers *always* said. Well, correction: It was something programmers *used* to say, and have recently started saying again.

They had stopped for a while, in the eighties and early nineties,
because, with the advent of programs like Belle and Deep Thought
and Deep Blue, the emphasis had shifted away from artificial intelligence. Those programs were very simple algorithms designed to take
advantage of the rapidly improving speed of computer hardware. Because the rate of improvement of simple, speed-oriented programs
had started tailing off, artificial intelligence was making a comeback.

Still, a programmer talking about making a computer "think about
chess like a human grandmaster" was like a politician saying "We're
studying the problem"; despite having the superficial appearance of an
English sentence, it didn't actually mean anything. The last paragraph
listed the names of the rest of the project team, including George.
That was enough to tell me the probable cause of George's call: They
were having parasite problems with their program and wished to retain me in my professional capacity.

I started to get up to turn off the phone when I had another idea.
I went back to the computer and did a wire-service search cross-
referencing computers and San Francisco. With the parameters set for
the past week, there were more than a hundred items. I added
"chess" to the search, which narrowed it down to the following:

SAN FRANCISCO—The annual Pacific Open Chess Tournament begins this week at the Moscone Conference
Center. The tourney, which is open to both human and
computer competitors, is now in its third year.
This year tournament organizers were able to an-
nounce the participation of reigning world chess
champion Dragan Zivojinovic. This marks the first
time the reigning world champion has participated
in an ''open'' tournament—one with computers as
well as people. The Serbian grandmaster, who has
now held the world championship for two years, was
not available for comment.

Mephisto, the current computer world champion,
will also compete. To date, no computer has ever won
a tournament against human grand-master-level
competition, although several chess-playing pro-

grams are rated at grandmaster strength, according
to the United States Chess Federation, which sanc-
tions the tournament.

Even I knew that the last sentence wasn't completely accurate; computers have been trouncing human grandmasters in "blitz" chess
since the early nineties.

In any event, I could now guess what the panic was all about.
George's program must be an entry in this tournament and was infected with a software virus or worm. I switched off the computer and
went to the phone to turn off the autodialer. The second I did, it
rang. I picked up.

"Michael?" George's soft Louisiana drawl was still unchanged by
years of living in California.

"Hi, George."

"Mike! I've been trying to reach you for hours! I got a busy signal
over an hour ago, so I figured you were home. I've been autodialing
you for the last hour trying to get through."

"It figures. I've been autodialing *you* for the last hour. That's why
we were both getting busy signals."

"Huh. Well, much as I hate to bother you with my troubles . . ."

"Trouble," I said, "is my business."

He chuckled. "Raymond Chandler, right? I like it. It's corny, but
it's you."

"Smart-ass."

"Anyway, now that I've got you, let me tell you why I called—"

"You've got a chess program entered in the Pacific Open, and you
think it's picked up a software parasite."

"What? How did you know that?"

"Lucky guess. I take it your group is interested in retaining me for
consultation?"

"Yes! Can you come here right away?"

"Can you afford me, or am I doing this as a personal favor?"

"Hell, yes! We've got corporate sponsorship. So you don't know
everything, after all."

"Oh, right. Tokoyo?"

"You're so well informed, it's a little scary. Listen, we'll pay you,
and I'll consider it a personal favor. How soon can you get here?"

"Let me see." I turned once more to the computer, rebooted it, and dialed for an airline-reservation service. "American has a flight out of La Guardia at three-ten. If I leave now, I can just make it."

"Great! But don't you have to pack?"

I glanced over at the bags I'd just brought back from London. "I'm already packed."

Less than two hours later I was ensconced in an airliner coach seat and bound for the West Coast. A small carry-on containing various necessities I didn't want to give the airline a chance to lose was under the seat in front of me. A briefcase was on my knees, containing my mobile antivirus lab: a laptop computer, CD-ROM, and a modem. Some people ask me why I still lug a laptop around, when the newer notebook and palmtop computers are so light, compact, and powerful. For one thing, I like a real keyboard; Chiclets are fine for chewing, lousy for typing on. For another, my laptop contains three coprocessor boards that allow me to run just about any currently used operating system—try that with a palmtop.

Once we were airborne, I called George again so he could fill me in on some more details.

"Goodknight," he said, "is an AI program that is supposed to teach itself how to play chess."

"Okay, I'll bite. Exactly how is it supposed to do that?"

"The same way human grandmasters do—by studying master games. It has 'fuzzy logic' routines for evaluating moves and positions, and it revises those routines based on what it learns. Goodknight can analyze a game in about fifteen minutes, and it's been analyzing games continuously for almost a year."

"There are that many games for it to study?"

"Sure, books full of them. Plus, we have all the back issues of *Chess Life and Review*. One way to look at it is like this: Goodknight is an organism that eats chess games. It assimilates good moves and excretes bad ones."

"Excretes?"

"In a manner of speaking."

"How's your baby doing in the tournament?"

"We won our first two rounds, but against fairly weak competition—one of the older programs, and a human international master."

"So what's the problem?"

"For some reason Goodknight has slowed down. Not enough to get into time trouble in the first two rounds, but it's not performing the way it did before."

"Are you sure it's not a hardware problem?"

"That's what *I* said, but our hardware people swear there's nothing wrong from their end. The only way to know for sure would be to purge the whole program, test the hardware, then reboot, and we don't have that kind of time."

"How much time do you have?"

"Round three starts at ten tomorrow morning."

I mulled over what George had told me about Goodknight. This was a first for me; I usually consult to corporations that are having troubles with their business software caused by worms or viruses—small computer programs or program fragments that can infect a large program. There is no single, general term encompassing all kinds of parasitic, self-replicating programs—"bugs" would have been good, but that was already taken (a bug is a programming error). I just call them beasties. Beasties can wreak all kinds of havoc in their host programs, ranging from the innocuous, such as rude messages appearing on the monitor, to the catastrophic, such as major data loss.

What's the difference between a virus and a worm? It depends on who's talking. According to some people, a virus is a program that must infect a host program in order to reproduce. In contrast, a worm can survive and reproduce independently. Others define "virus" as a program that infects other systems, whereas a worm is a program that may stay in the same system but causes a characteristic pattern of data loss ("worm tracks"). According to the first pair of definitions, worms and viruses are mutually exclusive categories. According to the second, the same program can be both a worm and a virus. To make things more confusing (in case you were still following any of this), the terms are often used interchangeably.

But let me simplify things for you: Start by ignoring the preceding paragraph, and let me give you *my* definitions. A virus is a parasitic program that spreads via magnetic media; whenever you carry a disk from one computer to another, you may be transmitting viruses. A worm is also a parasitic program, but one that spreads through a network via the network connections.

For several years now all new large-scale software packages have contained integrated antivirus routines—informational immune systems, if you will. If you think that development has cut into my business, think again—there's a lot of old software out there, and even the new systems get infected sometimes. Also, with a newer system an infection is generally something especially tricky, beyond what the company's own software people can deal with. Enter yours truly, the fearless virus hunter.

One drawback of having antiviral and antiworm routines embedded in a program or operating system is that it slows things down a bit; the computer's microprocessor must spend a certain amount of time executing the antivirus routine (usually watching out for suspicious commands, like low-level formatting instructions, or checking for the program's own self-identification codes). In most cases this is a small price to pay for the level of protection offered. But for certain applications, such as competition-level chess programs, speed is too important to sacrifice. The programmers are careful not to expose their program to any potential source of contamination, such as disks and other media that have been used with other operating systems, and the system is accessible only through a few dedicated terminals. Usually, that's good enough. As the present case suggests, sometimes it isn't.

George agreed to meet me at the airport and drive us to Palo Alto, and we said good-bye and hung up. I wanted to try to get some sleep on the plane. I'd been up since seven in the morning, London time, which was one A.M. eastern time and ten P.M. Pacific time, which meant I had now been awake for twenty-seven hours. I tried to get comfortable in the cramped confines of my procrustean economy seat, but it was impossible. Also, the woman next to me snored.

We touched down in San Francisco at 5:25 A.M., local time. I desperately needed a shower and a meal, but I would have gladly traded both for a good night's sleep in a decent bed. George was waiting at the gate, looking very much the same as when I last saw him: tall enough to stand out on the crowded concourse, blue-eyed, square-jawed, and appearing as much in need of sleep as I was. In school his height, combined with his balding pate, had given rise to the predictable jokes about how he had grown through his hair. One difference was that he was no longer prematurely balding—he was now prematurely bald.

George pumped my hand with a vigor that belied his walking-wounded appearance, and added a few completely unnecessary back slaps, which somehow left me still standing.

"Good to see you, Mike, even though you look terrible. Did you give up sleeping for Lent?"

"Might as well have. You're not looking too hot yourself."

"I've been up all night. Just don't let me fall asleep on the drive back to Palo Alto."

"I remember your driving. Asleep might be an improvement."

It is an indication of how tired we both were that we actually chuckled over that one as we headed to the baggage-claim area. Twenty minutes later I was not laughing as I watched the last few pieces of luggage making their forlorn way around the conveyor. My suitcase was not among them.

I reported the missing suitcase to the airline and gave them George's Palo Alto address and phone number. We then headed for the parking lot to collect George's battered old Dodge Charger; as we went outside, George pulled on a baseball cap with a New Orleans Saints logo, apparently intended to protect his hairless scalp from the California sun.

"Are you still expecting those guys to win something?" I asked.

He grinned. "Not without divine intervention—but this could be the year for it."

"It could at that."

Before heading down Route 101 to Palo Alto, we stopped for breakfast at a restaurant near the airport, the first time I'd eaten anything but airline food—forgive the oxymoron—since yesterday morning. After a breakfast of orange juice, waffles, bacon, and three cups of coffee, I felt nearly human again. The three cups of coffee necessitated a trip to the facilities prior to getting back on the road. Someone had placed a sticker on the men's-room wall that read, "Jesus Is Coming"; underneath it was scrawled, "Look busy!"

On my way back to the table to collect George, I noticed that his was not the only hairless scalp in the restaurant; three guys in leather with multiple tattoos and body piercings were sitting at the counter. Their coiffures ranged from a mohawk to a complete skinhead, and the tattoos ran to things like snakes, skulls, and swastikas. That sort of thing was, unfortunately, becoming pretty common, and it wasn't what attracted my attention. The notable thing was the guy with the mohawk, who had "666" tattooed on his scalp. Beastly.

Once George and I were back in the car, I said, "Now that I've got a few more synapses firing, let me ask you some questions."

George shrugged. "I'm not sure that I can say the same, but shoot."

"What kind of hardware are you using?"

"Nothing too fancy—our sponsor wasn't *that* generous. There's some real heavy metal in this tournament—massively parallel devices and stuff. And that's just the newer hardware; all the older established programs run on ultrafast dedicated machines. Our sponsor just gave us a used Tokoyo Four. We've probably got the only machine in the competition that runs MABUS-two-k and off-the-shelf software."

I was surprised. "That sounds crazy." MABUS/2K (which stands for Macrobyte Utilization System/2000) might have been the industry standard microcomputer operating system, but you certainly wouldn't expect to see it running on anything as exotic as a competitive-chess computer.

"Not if you're planning to develop a commercial chess program; we're hoping to be able to enter this baby in the Harvard Cup tournament next fall."

"You really think a commercial version is feasible? I can't imagine the average user reading chess books to his computer."

"The commercial version won't have learning capabilities; even the latest generation of home computers isn't powerful enough to handle that part. We let the learning phase run for a while, then freeze the algorithm, graft on a point-and-grunt interface, package it with a manual printed on drool-proof paper, and presto! Goodknight for the unwashed masses. But there's another reason for using MABUS-two-k, even aside from the commercial angle. It turns out that MABUS-two-k is structured in a way that's ideal for the kind of AI applications we had in mind. It's built around a smart compiler, which is particularly important for a program like Goodknight."

"Why is that?"

"Well, since Goodknight really programs its own chess algorithm, it's constantly changing. The smart compiler gets feedback when the program is running, and continuously tunes the operating system to maximize speed and efficiency. Also, having an operating system that came out of a box lets us concentrate on writing our program, without having to spend a lot of time programming on the bare metal. We've made a few modifications, of course, but it's basically MABUS-two-k."

"That's probably why you've got a virus."

"No doubt. Also, our hardware isn't as fast as the current generation of supercomputers. But"—he grinned—"we expect to make up in programming elegance what we lack in brute force."

"Can you really make up for that much difference in speed?"

"Seriously, yes, we can. The number of possible chess moves increases exponentially with each further move you examine, so even the fastest computer in the tournament would be able to see maybe one move further than Goodknight. But Goodknight can compensate by weeding out less promising lines at the outset. Plus, because it has more strategic sense, it should play itself into superior positions where there are more potential combinations in its favor."

"That sounds like a good theory. How is it working out in practice?"

"One of our team members, Alex Krakowski, is an international master, the rank just below grandmaster. He says Goodknight is improving at an amazing rate and that its positional play is already superior to any of the current programs." He grimaced. "Truthfully, this tournament entry is a little premature. We wanted to have a few more months to let the learning phase run, and work out some minor bugs. But our sponsor was pressuring us to see some results."

We arrived at SAIL, the Stanford Artificial Intelligence Laboratory—a storied place in the history of AI—a little before seven A.M. SAIL was currently housed in Margaret Jacks Hall, known to its denizens as Marginal Hacks. George introduced me to the other members of his team, including Jason Wright, a short guy with thick glasses, a gold earring, and red hair that he wore in a ponytail. He made you think "whiz kid," except there was just enough gray at the temples that he could no longer quite get away with that particular sobriquet.

After a very abbreviated exchange of social pleasantries, we got down to business. "We thought about trying some of the commercial antivirals," Jason said, "in case it's anything run-of-the-mill, but George talked us out of it. I went along with him because nobody on this team knows too much about this stuff, and I didn't want to make things worse by screwing around."

I nodded. "If I can say this without sounding too self-serving, you did the right thing. I've encountered some copies of commercial antivirus software that were themselves contaminated with viruses. Admittedly that's not something you see too often, but I think you guys have got too much time and effort invested in this thing to mess around with half-assed approaches to the problem.

"Now, tell me this: Do you think there is any possibility that somebody deliberately inserted a virus or worm in your software?"

They looked at each other, then shook their heads. Jason said, "No way."

I said, "Wrong."

Eyes opened wide. Jaws dropped. Veins popped out on foreheads. Expressions ranged from shock, through rage, to dumbfounded horror. Jason sputtered for a few seconds and finally managed to come out with, "*What?* What do you mean? Who . . ."

I held up a hand. "What I mean is that, in my experience, contamination of a secure system is almost always an 'inside job.' And it's *always* possible. You might think that there's no one who would want to do it. You might think there's no way they could, even if they wanted to. There's *always* a way.

"I'm telling you this because I want you all to start thinking about who might have had a motive to screw you, or the opportunity to insert a contaminant in the program. I'll check your system for worm-sign and vaccinate you against known beasties, and"—I patted my briefcase—"I've got quite a few in here that aren't covered by any of the commercial programs. But if somebody wrote a virus that's specific to this program, our best bet is to find out who, how, and when.

"Now, in addition to checking your program, we need to screen every other piece of software it's come in contact with—language, operating system, the works. Also, if your system has any cachelike memory on a serial or parallel port, we'll need to check that too. George, you said this thing reads books of chess games, so I'm assuming you're using a scanner with optical character recognition software?"

"That's right; we've got the latest version of Cyclops, Macrobyte's OCR software."

"Okay, then we need to screen Cyclops too."

I interfaced my laptop with Goodknight in order to allow any resident virus to infect one of my hard disks. The disk was protected by a system that would pick up an intruder and "quarantine" it. I also worked with the Goodknight programmers to adapt one of my screening routines, and we loaded it. It would check Goodknight's umpteen lines of code for any known virus or worm, as well as look for various indicators of infection, such as suspicious text messages or low-level formatting commands. Because of the uniqueness of their setup, I couldn't really predict how long this would take—a few hours at least, I guessed. It would be a good time to get some much-needed sleep. But I was wired on a combination of caffeine and adrenaline, so instead I suggested to George that I tag along to the Moscone Center for their third-round match.

"Sure," he said. "I thought you'd want to hang around here, though, or maybe grab some z's."

I shrugged. "There's not much I can do right now except wait. I'd be interested in seeing if any of the competition is having similar problems."

Jason must have overheard us, because he approached, shaking his head. "I don't want anyone to know about this."

"Okay, I won't breathe a word about it. But I might overhear something suggestive. Besides, I would think your competition would be the most likely suspects if somebody did deliberately infect you."

Jason considered that one. He looked as if he were going to say no anyway, but George chimed in. "C'mon, Jase, let him come. If anybody asks, he's just an old college chum of mine who came to see some of the action."

Jason squinted behind his horn-rims. "Okay. But remember: not a word about this to anyone."

We took George's car back up the highway to San Francisco, with two of the other programmers jammed into the tiny backseat. One was Alex Krakowski, the team's chess expert, a thirtyish man with black curly hair and beard. The other was Harvey Wang, an undergraduate who was as tall as George. I offered him my spot in the front seat, but George insisted on having me ride shotgun. Harvey just smiled and said if George didn't mind having Harvey's knees jammed into the small of his back all the way to San Francisco, he wouldn't mind either.

Not surprisingly, there was an air of tension and excitement in the car. "So," I said, "who's this morning's victim?"

I think I've got a pretty decent sense of humor, but they laughed a little too hard at that one. George said, "Our victim? Some stiff named Zivojinovic."

Goodknight would have the white pieces against the world champion. Alex Krakowski was hoping that would be enough to get them a draw.

"A draw," he said, "against the Dragon would be a coup. Our best chance is to use a queen pawn's opening." Alex went on to explain that Zivojinovic was considered so dangerous with his favorite Sicilian Defense that hardly anyone dared open pawn to king four against him in competition. "At the interzonals three years ago he won five match games with the black pieces, all with the Sicilian Defense. Five! Nobody has done that against that caliber of competition since Bobby Fischer shut out two grandmasters in the 1972 interzonals."

I said, "How do you know that Goodknight won't open with the king's pawn?"

Alex said, "Well, we're not allowed to stipulate a particular first move; that would violate tournament rules. The programs have to make all of their own moves. But they are allowed to take the opposition into consideration—after all, any human player would do the same. Goodknight has studied all of Zivojinovic's games, and it knows it's going up against him today. If, after all that, it's dumb enough to get into a Sicilian with the Dragon, I'm gonna go back to SAIL and kick it in the motherboard.

"Actually, the rules in this tournament tend to favor the human players—two hours to make all of your moves tends to blunt the computer's speed advantage. But that's okay—number crunching isn't our strong suit anyway; this program plays great strategic chess. I think we might get a draw."

"Don't get your hopes up," George said.

"He's being modest," Alex said to me in a confidential tone. "Even if we don't win this tournament, George's program is going to represent a major advance over the competition."

"George's program? I thought Jason was the team leader."

"Jason is a good programmer and a decent administrator. But George is the programming genius behind Goodknight."

"Aw, come on, you're making me blush," said George, who didn't look a bit red-faced. "Don't worry, though, I'm not suffering any sudden throes of false modesty; if Goodknight was running at a hundred percent, I'd be hoping for a win. But something's wrong. I just hope we're not going to have to withdraw from the tournament."

He glanced over at me; I squirmed. For the first time it really hit me how much George and his colleagues had riding on this program, and how much they were counting on me to help them. Until now it had been a bit of a lark. After all, I usually deal with clients who have megabucks at stake; infections in their software systems can cost jobs, ruin careers, and destroy whole companies. This, for Christ's sake, was a program that played a game.

But it was a lot more than that, I was beginning to realize. Jason Wright and Alex Krakowski and Harvey Wang, and my friend George Bard, and others had poured their hearts into making Goodknight work. If it turned out that somebody else's program was better, that's one thing. But they deserved their shot without having it screwed up by a software virus.

I'm not saying I hate all hackers. No doubt, the vast majority of them are decent, ethical, trustworthy, loyal, and even have reasonably good personal hygiene. Even most of that minority of hackers who get their kicks writing viruses are not truly malicious. Usually they're just trying to be clever and have a good time without really hurting anybody, although they cause a lot of damage they never intended. But the few virus hackers who are really trying to screw people are, in the great scheme of things, several levels below pond scum.

A malicious virus hacker is really nothing more than a bully. Just as a bully beats you up in order to enjoy the fact that he's bigger and stronger than you are, the virus hacker destroys your property and your work to prove to himself that he's more clever and knowledgeable about computers than the average user. Big whoop.

Not that I've ever actually met one of these pea-brains. My job is to undo the damage, not find the cretins who are responsible for it. That's a job for computer-crime divisions within the Secret Service, FBI, SEC, FCC, and an alphabet soup of other federal agencies. So, no, I haven't met any virus hackers personally. But I've got a little list.

One of the tip-offs that a particular hacker is on an ego trip is when he signs his masterpiece. Not with his real name, of course. But most hackers have computer noms de guerre or "hacker handles," and they like to include clever little messages, such as "You have been screwed by the Prince of Passion. Did you enjoy it?" Some of the repeat offenders I've encountered in my work are Astaroth, Dr. Entropy, Pain Man, the Wizard of Odds, and MetLhed, who is such a pathetic programmer that it takes him about a hundred lines of code to do what anyone else could accomplish in four. Astaroth is, unfortunately, a very good programmer and has written some particularly loathsome specimens.

Astaroth is good, but then there's Beelzebub. Beelzebub has written some of the most deviously destructive viruses that I've encountered. His viruses are stealthy, highly infective, difficult to eradicate, and malicious in the extreme. Some virus hackers seem to do what they do because of a warped sense of humor. There's nothing remotely funny about Beelzebub's stuff; he just wants to screw people.

At the opposite end of the spectrum is Vamana. Vamana's viruses are not only not intentionally destructive, I've never encountered one that caused even inadvertent damage, other than people panicking when they realized their system was infected. This is practically impossible, because viruses almost always cause some unforeseen effects. Not Vamana's. Some of Vamana's viruses are even beneficial, like Fred Cohen's compressor virus, which saved disk space by compressing files (and asked the user's permission first). Also, unlike the preadolescent level of humor displayed by most virus hackers, Vamana's stuff is actually pretty funny at times. And the guy is an unbelievably talented programmer. Writing viruses is still wrong, but he does it so well that I've developed a grudging admiration for him.

The exhibition hall where the world chess champion would play against Goodknight was already crowded with spectators. A table was set up on a dais with a chessboard and a telephone. Alex Krakowski would sit at that table opposite the champion, moving the pieces for Goodknight and relaying the Dragon's moves over the phone. I wondered briefly why they didn't use a direct hookup via modem, then figured it was an additional precaution against contamination.

Two large projection-TV screens were set up on either side of the dais. One showed a close-up of the actual chessboard, the other a schematic of the board.

The Dragon's arrival was apparently considered imminent, because there was a lot of excited murmuring and neck craning. I looked over in the direction that necks were being craned and did a double take.

"What is it?" asked George.

"Al Meade is here."

"Who's he?"

"That," I pointed, "is *she*. Al is for Alice." In the mostly male crowd she was not hard to pick out. Her back was to us, but I'd recognize that back anywhere. Her jet-black hair was cut short, resembling a helmet of polished ebony, and her charcoal-gray suit had a fashionably short skirt revealing slender but shapely legs. Even in her high-heeled pumps, she was a full head shorter than the men standing next to her.

"Huh," George said. It was an appreciative "huh." "Those guys she's with—they're with the Mephisto team."

Maybe she had a feeling she was being watched, because she glanced back at us with large dark eyes. She looked well rested, clean, and impeccably groomed. I thought about how I must look after thirty-six hours without sleep, wearing the same clothes I had put on in London yesterday morning and worn through two long airplane rides.

"Damn," I said. "She saw me."

George looked at me quizzically. "So?"

"Your boss didn't want anyone to know that you guys may have a virus. Now somebody will. I hope he'll be comforted by the knowledge that the Mephisto people seem to have the same problem."

"You mean she's . . . ?"

I nodded. "Another bugbuster. Which actually doesn't make sense, because didn't you tell me the older programs are hardwired?" "Hardwiring" refers to converting software into electronic circuitry. It makes things run faster and, incidentally, is a perfect defense against viruses and worms, as long as none are in the software at the time of the conversion.

"Not Mephisto. They preferred to trade a little speed in order to maintain programming flexibility. Mephisto is also supposed to learn and improve. Not as well as Goodknight, of course."

"Of course."

I saw Al turn and say something to the man on her left, a beefy guy with a blond crew cut. He glanced back at me. "The cat is out of the bag," I told George. "I'm going over there to talk to her." After about three steps I realized George was right behind me. He grinned. "Introduce me, huh?" I shrugged.

"Hi, Al," I said once we'd wormed our way through the crowd. "I'd like you to meet George Bard, an old college friend."

She offered George a professional, if perfunctory, handshake and smiled thinly at me. "Darryl Taggart, this is Michael Arcangelo. Hello, Michael. I didn't know you had an interest in chess."

"I think you know what my interests are, just as I know about yours."

Taggart looked uncomfortable. He cleared his throat. "Maybe we should have this conversation somewhere more private."

"I don't think any further conversation is necessary," said Al.

"I hate to be disagreeable, but I think it may be very necessary," I said.

Taggart looked interested. "What do you mean?"

"Ms. Meade and I both help people with certain kinds of problems. We may be able to help each other by sharing certain information."

Al smiled sweetly. "I wouldn't be surprised if Mr. Arcangelo needs help, but I can assure you that I don't need any from him."

I glanced at Taggart; he shrugged. Apparently he was going to let her call the shots on this. I said, "Fine. The offer is open. If you reconsider, I'll be around."

Al continued to smile her saccharine smile. "That's not even a remote possibility."

George and I headed over to where Alex waited near the dais. He was grinning, which pissed me off. I said, "What?"

"You know," he said, "I think she likes you."

At that moment an excited murmur greeted the arrival of Dragan Zivojinovic. I caught sight of him as he mounted the dais, and felt that odd sense of unreality that always accompanies seeing anyone famous in the flesh—as if some little part of my brain can't quite believe that a face that's familiar from TV, magazines, and newspapers could also be hanging on the front of somebody's actual head.

The Dragon was tall, slender, hawk-faced, white-haired despite his thirty-something years. He looked confident. Hell, he looked invincible. It's a good thing that computers aren't intimidated by looks, or Goodknight might have turned over its king right then and there.

Alex said something to the champion that I couldn't hear. The Dragon smiled and nodded. Alex spoke into the phone, reached for the chessboard, then paused, his hand hovering over the white pieces. His mouth hung open. Then, with a look of resignation, he made the move. Zivojinovic looked startled too, for a moment; then he smiled again. It was not a smile you would want to see across a chessboard. I glanced at the video monitor with the board schematic.

The white king pawn was on K-4.

The first half dozen or so moves went pretty rapidly. Then Goodknight evidently did something unexpected, because the Dragon was taking some time to think about it. My knowledge of chess doesn't go much beyond how the pieces move, so for me it's not exactly thrilling as a spectator sport. I decided I had seen enough. "George, will your sponsor cover putting me up at a decent hotel?"

He raised an eyebrow. "You mean you don't want to stay at Chez Bard in scenic Palo Alto?"

"I'd be happy to stay with you, but I'd like to have a place in the city to use as a base. And right now I want to crash."

He nodded. "Get a room at the Marriott, it's right nearby."

"Okay. Give me a call when the game is over."

There were a couple of small conventions in town sharing the Moscone Center with the chess tournament, but otherwise not much going on, which is probably why I was able to get a room at the Marriott. I registered, called the airline to tell them to send my bag to the hotel if they ever found it, and called Jason Wright to tell him where I'd be. I made these calls while stretched out on the bed, which was a mistake, because I fell asleep with my clothes on. What the hell, they already looked like I'd slept in them.

A rapping at my chamber door awakened me from a dream in which Dragan Zivojinovic was wrapping his scaly coils around a fair maiden with big dark eyes and a saccharine smile. I think I just missed seeing him bite her head off. Damn.

I stumbled to the door and opened it, revealing George's big dumb grin. "What's so funny?" I said. It was not quite a growl.

His grin broadened. "Nothing at all. I was just thinking that there are some advantages to not having hair—like you don't have to worry about how silly it looks when you first get up. That and . . . drumroll, please."

"We're fresh out of drumrolls. Will you settle for a knuckle sandwich?"

"You *are* cranky when you wake up. When we were in college, I thought that was just from being hung over all the time. I didn't realize it was a character trait."

"When you're through critiquing my appearance and personality, would you please tell me what's going on?"

"Well, you might ask what's going on. While you were over here committing the deadly sin of sloth, the Goodknight team was writing a page of chess history."

"You mean your program beat Zivojinovic?"

I thought his grin was going to split his face. "It's going out on the wire services even as we speak." He chuckled. "I thought Alex was going to faint."

"Hell," I said, "he nearly fainted after the first move."

"C'mon. Jason said no celebrating until after the tournament, but I'm gonna buy you a beer."

I looked at my watch. It was two o'clock. "Gee, it's a little early for me. But what the hell, it's eleven o'clock in London. Let's go."

George managed to rein in his enthusiasm long enough for me to have a quick shower and shave. I hung my clothes in the bathroom, hoping the steam from the shower would take out some of the wrinkles. It didn't work.

George was hanging up the phone as I came out of the bathroom. "I was just talking to Jason. He wants us to come back to SAIL right now, but he wouldn't say why. I'm afraid this virus business is aggravating his natural paranoia. What you said didn't help much, either."

I shrugged. "I'm not naturally paranoid, just professionally paranoid. Well, let's go. Don't forget, though, you owe me a beer."

The atmosphere back at Stanford was a curious mixture of euphoria and panic. Alex Krakowski was walking around muttering, "Pawn to king four . . . pawn to king four . . ." The rubber band on Jason Wright's ponytail had broken, and his hair was going in about fourteen different directions. Circumstantial evidence suggested that his prohibition on premature celebrating was being widely, if surreptitiously, ignored.

Jason collared us as we came in, and herded us toward his office. Progress was slowed a bit by George exchanging high fives with the other programmers, but we got there eventually.

Jason's office was a small windowless cubicle with most of its space occupied by a computer workstation. All available surfaces were covered with printouts, stacks of floppies, and Coke cans filled with cigarette butts. In addition to the swivel chair facing the workstation, there were a couple of plastic stacking chairs in the corner. Jason swept the detritus from the latter onto the floor and motioned for us to sit.

"Okay," I said, "what's going on?"

He squinted at me. "I was hoping you could tell me that." He handed me a sheaf of fanfolded printer paper. I riffled through it.

"So there was a virus in the OCR software. Did you kill it?"

Jason shook his head. "Read on."

I looked at the rest of the printout. "The virus was in the OCR software, but not in Goodknight." I looked at George. "You didn't tell me Goodknight had an immune system."

He and Jason chorused, "It doesn't."

"MABUS-two-k has one, of course," George added, "but we took it out."

I thought about it. "Then you've got a mutator."

"We've got what?" Jason yanked at a stray wisp of hair that kept falling over his face.

"A mutator is a worm or virus that alters its own code each generation. The concept was originated by Fred Cohen back in the eighties and, unfortunately, put into practice by a Bulgarian virus hacker known as Dark Avenger. Much more difficult to kill, but it can be done."

Jason said, "I'm all ears." Actually, at the moment he appeared to be at least eighty percent hair, but I wasn't in the mood to quibble.

"The surest way is to decompile the code. Even a mutator usually has some areas of code that are constant—the mutation instructions, for example. If those mutate, then it can't mutate anymore. If you have the source code to work with, you can identify those areas and zero in on them."

Jason looked skeptical. "You've done this before?"

"A few times."

"And if you can't decompile the code?"

"If you have at least two generations of the mutator, you can compare them for areas of constancy. It's not as sure as the other way, though, because you don't know whether you've identified a true invariance, or just an area that didn't happen to mutate last generation but might next time."

"Who would know how to program a virus like this?"

"Just a few thousand hackers. And certainly anybody in my line of work."

George said, "Like Al Meade?"

I said, "Actually, yes," as Jason was saying, "Who's Al Meade?"

George and I exchanged a look. We had not yet told Jason about Al, and the fact that the Mephisto team now knew or could guess about Goodknight's "illness." The look did not go unnoticed by Jason, who demanded, "Will somebody tell me what the hell is going on?"

We told Jason. He ranted and raved a bit, but after he calmed down, he had to agree that it was just bad luck, and there wasn't anything we could have done about it.

"Besides," George added, "as a result of Mike's being there, we know that Mephisto has problems too."

"Are you sure?" Jason said. "How do you know the Mephisto team didn't hire this person to infect their competition?"

"You think they would really do that?" asked George.

"Isn't that what you were implying when you asked Mike if she'd know how to program a mutating virus? And, yes, I do think they would do it. I knew Darryl Taggart when we were both grad students, and he is a scuzzball. The only reason I have any doubt he'd do it is he's too arrogant to think we'd have a chance against him. But maybe he'd do it anyway, just to be an asshole."

I shook my head. "Look, I've known Al a long time. Professionally, not personally"—that in response to a significant look from George—"but I really don't think she would do anything like that. It would be like a doctor poisoning her patient."

"Somebody else's patient," George said. When I winced, he added loyally, "But I don't think she'd do it either."

"Wait a minute, Mike," Jason said. "Weren't you the one who was telling us that this was probably done deliberately?"

"What I said was that it was likely to be an *inside* job."

"You also pointed out that our competitors would have the most obvious motive."

"Motive is one thing. You also have to have opportunity."

"You think they wouldn't have any opportunity? It's not exactly Fort Knox around here," said Jason. "What I want to know is why this Meade person wouldn't cooperate with you when you suggested it. That doesn't exactly inspire confidence. I think Taggart is up to something."

"So what do we do?" George asked. "Take some rubber hoses over to the Moscone Center and beat a confession out of them?"

"Before we do that," I said, "I want to take a look at this virus."

CHAPTER TWO

The Caecilian Defense

Blessed is *he that watcheth, and keepeth his garments, lest he walk naked, and they see his shame.*

—Revelation 16:15

When people write computer programs, they generally use something called a high-level language. This computer language is itself a program that translates instructions that try to be some approximation of plain English into machine language, also known as "object code"— the strings of zeros and ones that make up the binary code that the computer's microprocessor understands. Another term for the language the programmer uses to write the program is "source code."

It is also possible to write a computer program in something called assembly language. This is much more difficult and requires a far more detailed knowledge of the inner workings of the computer. Also, assembly language is specific to a particular microprocessor, or family of microprocessors, whereas a high-level language can be applied to as many different microprocessors as you like. Viruses are almost always written in assembly language.

Looking at a string of machine-language code and trying to "decompile it"—basically, reconstruct the source code—is not impossible. At least theoretically. Actually, I wasn't looking at binary, but at a conversion to hexadecimal, which is a little less bewildering to read and also takes less paper. The virus in the OCR software turned out to be a variant of one of the ones in my screening program—a little sixteen-hundred-byte charmer with the catchy moniker "Screwdisk." I didn't have the source code for that one either, but I knew it was not a mutator. But had somebody modified it to mutate? It was certainly theoretically possible.

I played with the thing for a while, paying particular attention to the places where it varied from the original. I tried decompiling some of the new sections, but I didn't learn anything that shed any light on the matter. The virus was just tricky enough that I could see that decompiling the whole thing was not going to be accomplished quickly or easily. So I figured it was time to try another tack.

I opened my briefcase and removed my laptop computer, which happens to be a model with interchangeable hard drives. Earlier I had checked to see if it had trapped a virus from Goodknight. None of the detectors had been triggered—the disk seemed to be clean—yet on a hunch I decided to put it aside and take a more thorough look at it later. I popped out the drive and reached back into the briefcase to pull out the drive I wanted, one that bore a large warning sticker that said, "DANGER! This disk contains active software viruses." Actually, at the moment that was not the case. What it did contain was an operating system with a modified immunity subroutine—one that would "spot" the beasties but wouldn't kill them. I loaded the OCR virus to this drive. Now it would need some time to "incubate." How much time? A typical virus can completely infect a system in about two seconds. But a mutator might take longer, because it wasn't just copying itself. I decided to let it run for a few hours.

If it mutated, it would still be detectable against the background of my operating system's self-identification codes. If that happened, then we could compare two generations of the virus and identify areas of stability. And then we would have a likely target.

One problem was not knowing how long an incubation period was necessary. Some software beasties will reproduce whenever given the chance, such as whenever the host creates a file or runs a certain type of program. Others have built-in delays or are set to go off on a certain date. One rather famous worm from the early nineties, dubbed Ooey Gooey, was keyed to the New York–Philadelphia Amtrak schedule. Whenever a train went through Trenton, it would display a graphic of a train wheel squashing an earthworm with the face of the governor of New Jersey.

Once again all I had to go on was what I knew of Screwdisk, the original virus of which this appeared to be a variant. Screwdisk was a fairly uncomplicated little beastie. I set the laptop to run a kind of autopilot program—basically computer busywork that would give the software virus ample opportunity to reproduce. I figured to give it a couple hours before checking for virus progeny.

I was just wrapping things up when George came by. He said, "If you want to collect that beer, now's the time."

I looked at my watch, which was superfluous, because my stomach was already telling me it was time to eat. It was past six, and I hadn't eaten anything since breakfast. "Is it possible to get some food with that beer?"

"Sure, I know a good place on University Avenue. Although, now that I think about it, you should be treating me. After all, you're the one who's on an expense account."

Half an hour later I was eating tortellini with goat cheese and sun-dried tomatoes. I took another rain check on the beer, and George and I split a bottle of a rather nice Napa Valley merlot.

We talked about this and that, catching up on things that had happened since college. George picked up the bottle to refill my glass and gave me a shrewd look. "So tell me about you and Al Meade."

I grimaced. "You mean do I think she sabotaged your program?"

George waved that one away. "Hell, no. Listen, I told you Jason was paranoid. No, that's not what I meant. I meant tell me about *you* and Al Meade."

I laughed. I'd like to think it was a jaunty, insouciant kind of laugh, but I can't deny there may have been just a hint of bitterness. "You're definitely barking up the wrong sequoia."

"What was it, a one-night stand? You didn't call her afterward, and now she thinks you're toad slime?"

I shook my head. "You're half-right. Evidently she thinks I'm *some* kind of slime, but as to why, I honestly have no idea."

"You never even made a pass at her?"

"Strictly professional all the way. She is a colleague, you know. You think I want to be accused of sexual harassment?"

He nodded sagely. "I think I see the problem."

Now I was really mystified. "What are you babbling about?"

He leaned back and took another sip of his wine, wearing a smile of infuriating smugness. He was really starting to piss me off. "Michelangelo, my friend, there are two really unforgivable things you can do to a woman. One is make a pass at her when it's not welcome. The other is *fail* to make a pass at her when she wants you to. Since we have eliminated the former possibility, only the latter remains. QED."

I started to laugh again, then nearly choked on my tortellini when I realized that he was serious. "You've been watching those daytime talk shows on television, haven't you? What was it, 'Women Scorned—this week on *Oprah*'?"

He shook his head. "Mike, Mike. It's so obvious. You know, I've never understood why, but most of the women I knew in college seemed to think you're actually good-looking. It's probably those big innocent blue eyes."

He was lucky the wine was exceptionally good. Otherwise, I would have thrown it at him.

When we had finished the last of the meal and the wine, George said, "You look about as wasted as I feel. Why don't you come and crash at my place? I don't think I can manage driving to San Francisco and back tonight."

I nodded. "Okay. You're too drunk to drive, anyway."

"That's simple fatigue, not drunkenness," he told me severely.

"Maybe you're right. Or else your capacity isn't what it used to be. Well, let's go back to SAIL first, I want to check something."

I drove us back to the SAIL, where we found everybody still there, still doing the same stuff, which to an outsider looked pretty much like something you'd expect to see in a mental institution. Alex Krakowski was hunched over a chessboard, muttering to himself and tugging at his beard. Hardware experts were doing characteristically inscrutable things to the Tokoyo IV. Programmers were tapping away at their terminals. And Jason Wright was zooming around at about a thousand miles an hour, interfering with whatever anyone else was doing.

I rolled a chair over to where I had left my laptop and sat down with George hovering at my shoulder. Jason immediately appeared at the opposite shoulder. He said, "Don't give away any trade secrets or anything, but what exactly are you doing?"

I gave him a running commentary. "I deliberately infected this operating system with the virus from your OCR software. I want to see if it'll mutate. With this program I can find it even if it has mutated. Then we'll have a better idea of what we're dealing with." I typed in the commands to execute a subroutine that would comb through the operating system for "foreign bodies." "Congratulations," I said as the scan results scrolled across the LCD monitor. "Your virus has had babies. Seventeen, in fact."

George glanced at Jason and deadpanned, "I hope you remembered the cigars." Jason was not amused.

I ran another subroutine that would list each virus and match it against the original. The first few were the same.

"Geez, Mike," George said, "this is really doing things the hard way. Haven't you ever heard of AI?"

Actually, there were a number of commercially available antivirus programs that incorporated artificial intelligence. I even recommended some of them to my clients occasionally. I just didn't like to use them myself. "When I'm looking for viruses," I told George, "I prefer to supply the intelligence myself and just let the computer do the grunt work."

He grunted.

I continued comparing virus copies until I'd finished the whole batch. They were all the same as the original.

Jason had moved around so he could watch my face, apparently figuring he'd get more useful information from that than from the computer screen. When he saw me frown, he shouted, "What? What's going on?" I honestly thought he was going to need a sedative.

I gave them the bad news: "This virus doesn't mutate."

George scratched his head. "Can you be sure it wouldn't mutate if given more time? After all, Goodknight has been running with that OCR software for months."

I shook my head. "Anything is possible, but I strongly doubt it. First of all, the mutation generally takes place when it copies itself. I've never seen one that clones first, then changes. And why does somebody program a mutating virus, anyway? To avoid detection, obviously, which means you would want it to mutate immediately, not sit around for a while waiting for somebody to come along and kill it. Sorry, but we're back to square one."

Jason actually appeared to calm down a bit. "So what do we do now?"

I said, "There is something else I'd like to try, but you might want to wait until after the tournament."

"Yeah?"

"I'd like to infect Goodknight with a virus."

I expected Jason to go off like a Roman candle, but he just said in a small, choked voice, "And why would you want to do that?"

"I want to use it as a probe. We know Goodknight was exposed to a virus, yet it isn't infected. There doesn't seem to be anything special about the virus; it's not even smart enough to check the disk for copies of itself before making more. That leaves one other possibility."

George said, "There's something special about Goodknight."

I said, "Right. Something happened to the virus after the contamination. I want to figure out what. I will program the probe virus myself, and it will be harmless. I'll also program it to delete itself in response to a keyboard command."

"That sounds very innocuous," Jason said. "So why are you suggesting we wait until after the tournament?"

He had me there. "Because I can't predict with complete certainty how your program will respond. There is a possibility that it could cause some problems."

"What kind of problems?"

I shrugged. "I can't really predict. . . ."

"Okay, okay, I get the idea." He went away muttering to himself.

I glanced at George. "There's no way he's going to okay this, is there?"

"Not a chance."

On the way out we stopped to talk with Alex, who was still doing his own muttering as he moved pieces around the chessboard.

"Playing over today's game?" George asked.

"Huh?" Alex looked up, startled, apparently, to find us standing next to him. "Oh, yeah, the game."

"Is something wrong?" I asked.

He moved a pawn. "Not really. You know, the Dragon is kind of a hero to me, so it was sort of sad to see him lose to a computer program, even if it is"—he shot a glance at George—"*our* program." He shook his head. "I really had no idea that it was *this* good."

"Are you sure it wasn't beginner's luck?"

George elbowed me in the ribs, but Alex answered seriously. "Not this game. Oh, listen, anyone can lose one game to a patzer—I could show you games with dumb moves made by Fischer, Alekhine, Capablanca, anybody you can name. But the Dragon didn't make any dumb moves. He played beautifully, brilliantly. Goodknight just played better."

"What about the speed problem?"

George shrugged. "It's not exactly running like a pig, but we're giving away a lot of speed to begin with; we don't want to do any more favors for the competition. Basically, it *is* running slower than we expected, but so far it hasn't gotten us into trouble."

Alex said, "It's not just a matter of how much time you take, but how much time you take relative to your opponent. By making good moves, you force your opponent to use more of his time thinking of a way to answer them. And Goodknight has been making some damn good moves. I thought the Dragon was going to get into time trouble himself."

We drove to George's place, which was not far from the campus, stopping at a drugstore on the way so I could buy a toothbrush.

George's apartment was a kind of bastardized techie-bohemian clutter. One corner was occupied by a computer workstation and its associated paraphernalia. Several Bosch and Escher prints hung on the walls, which were painted in a strikingly nauseous shade of chartreuse, and the furnishings were, to be polite about it, eclectic. I noticed his bass leaning in one corner and asked, "Are you still playing?"

"Sure. I play local clubs with a jazz trio on Saturday nights. You ought to come and hear us sometime."

"I'd like to."

I called the Marriott to see if the airline had delivered my bag yet, which it hadn't; then I called my answering machine. There was a message from one Harold Ainsworth of Tower Bank and Trust, an outfit for which I'd done some work in the past. I jotted down the number.

In the meantime George appeared to be dismantling a piece of his living-room furniture. Before he started, it bore some slight resemblance to a couch, as if someone had tried to build one out of some lumber odds and ends and an old mattress.

"It's a futon," he said as he laid the mattress part out on the floor. "Very comfortable." He must have read the skepticism in my face, because he added, "I'll sleep here tonight. You take the water bed."

I shook my head. "I'm not going to put you out of your bed. Hell, right now I could sleep on broken glass. Just tell me where the bathroom is." He indicated the general direction.

After using the facilities I sacked out on the futon. George was right, it actually was pretty comfortable.

I awakened the next morning to the smell of fresh-brewed coffee and the sound of a woman humming. The latter was more than a little disorienting. After a few seconds I remembered I was in George's apartment, so I figured, with sleep-fogged logic, that I must still be asleep.

The humming stopped. "Good morning," said a woman's voice, apparently the same one that had been doing the humming.

I lifted my face out of the pillow just enough to get one eye open. That was disorienting too, because the floor was much closer than I expected it to be, and I thought, *oh, yeah, the futon*. On the floor, in my limited field of view, there was a foot with purple toenails, a couple of toe rings, and a snake tattooed around the ankle.

A coffee mug swam into view, proffered by a hand with green fingernails and more rings, including an elaborate silver spiral on the thumb.

I reached out to take the coffee cup and rolled over on my left side to get a better look at my mysterious benefactress. She was tall and blond and quite pretty in a typically California way, and was wearing nothing but a man's shirt, which came to about halfway down her thighs, and I was relieved to see that she wasn't wearing a nose ring, although she did have at least fourteen earrings, most of which were in her left ear. She smiled brightly at me. "Good morning! George said you like your coffee black."

"Um, black is fine. . . ."

Just then George walked in the door. He was waving the *San Francisco Chronicle*. "The sleeper awakes! Ah, I see you two have met. Or maybe not? Mike, Cassie. Cassie, Mike. I didn't know she was here when we got in last night. It's a good thing you didn't take me up on the offer of the water bed."

"That might have been awkward," I said. Cassie smiled and went back into the kitchen.

"Here." George tossed me the paper. "Check this out."

"You mean 'Apocalyptic Cults Congregate in Middle East to Await the End of the World'?"

"Try a little farther down the page."

"Oh." There was a front-page story on Goodknight's surprise victory over Zivojinovic, with a little human-interest stuff on the various members of the Goodknight team. It was the biggest computer-chess story since 1996, when Deep Blue had won the first game of a six-game match against Kasparov. "You're famous," I commented. "Will you still have time for your old friends?"

"I shall set aside afternoons on alternate Tuesdays to maintain the common touch."

"Decent of you."

"I think so."

Cassie came back in from the kitchen with two more mugs of coffee and handed one to George. I was still reclining on the futon, and she sat down facing me, taking a sip from the remaining mug.

"So you're George's friend Michael. I've heard a lot about you." She gave me an appraising look. "You have, like, such a strong aura."

"That's because he hasn't taken a shower yet," George suggested.

"Stop it, George. When is your birthday, Michael?"

"September twenty-ninth."

She slapped her knee. "A Libra! I knew it. George told me that he'll be keeping you very busy, but maybe the next time you come, I can do a chart for you."

"Don't bother," George said. "Mike doesn't believe in astrology."

"That's okay," I said. "I've heard it works whether you believe in it or not."

Cassie got the joke and laughed immediately, which told me that, although she seemed to have some fairly wacky ideas, she was far from being a total ditz-brain.

I glanced over at my clothes. I had hung them on the back of a chair the previous night, but the way they looked, I might as well have balled them up and thrown them into a corner. "George, would you have anything as low-tech as an iron in this place?"

He shook his head apologetically. "Sorry. Everything I own is permanent press."

"That's pretty smart of you."

"Not really. After I finished burning holes in everything I had that wasn't permanent press, I threw away the iron and the ironing board along with it. There's a coin-op laundry in the basement. Why don't you run your stuff through? I'll lend you something to wear in the meantime."

"I suppose it wouldn't hurt to wash my shirt, socks, and underwear. . . ."

"Tell me about it!"

"Shut up. But my pants and, obviously, the jacket have to be dry-cleaned."

"There's a dry cleaner down the street. I'll lend you a pair of pants to wear in the meantime."

"Don't you think a pair of your pants would look pretty ridiculous on me?"

"So you'll roll 'em up a little, they won't look so bad. Don't be such a crybaby."

"I'm not crying, just whining a little."

Cassie emerged from the bedroom, now attired in jeans, sandals, and a purple V-neck sweater. She gave George a kiss and said, "I have to go now. It was nice meeting you, Michael."

"The pleasure was mine."

After she left, I said, "Nice girl."

"Yeah, she really is," George said. "I have to admit, you were really good at keeping a straight face when she started talking about that aura stuff."

"I didn't want to hurt her feelings. How did you meet her?"

"At Stanford; she's a grad student there in social work or something. She was looking for someone to help her develop a computer program to do horoscopes. At first I told her I thought it was a total waste of time; then I realized that the market for a program like that would be huge."

"You're probably right. So this relationship started out as a business venture, huh?"

"Yes, I supply the computer expertise, and she supplies the superstition, irrationality, and mysticism."

"Sounds like a potent combination. But what can she possibly see in you?"

He grinned. "She likes my aura."

"Are you sure it's your aura she's seeing, and not the glare off your scalp?"

He laughed. "No, and I don't particularly care, either."

I wound up borrowing a pair of George's jeans (which wasn't too bad, because although he's taller than I am, he's not much wider), and also one of his T-shirts while I took my stuff down to the basement laundromat. I came back upstairs, checked the time, which was around seven, and decided to call Harry Ainsworth, as it was already ten in New York.

Ainsworth told me the bank computers were doing some kind of weird shit, so they figured the system had been parasitized again, which was not surprising, considering the antiquated software they used and the general lack of security in the whole place. It may sound strange to characterize a bank as deficient in security, but if they were as careless with their money as they are with their computer system, people would be strolling out the front door with their pockets stuffed with cash. I told him I'd be back in New York no later than Tuesday afternoon and would give him a call as soon as I arrived. Another call to the Marriott established the fact that my suitcase was still Lost in Space. While I was on the phone, George refilled my coffee mug. When I hung up, he called out from the kitchen, "What do you want for breakfast? Trix, Lucky Charms, or Count Chocula?"

I thought it over. "Did you eat all the marshmallows out of the Lucky Charms?"

"Uh . . . yeah, pretty much."

"Then I'll have the Trix."

Over breakfast George asked me, "So what will you do today?"

I considered that. I'd been too tired the night before to give much thought to it. "Well, unless Jason is feeling especially adventurous . . ."

"Fat chance!"

". . . I don't think there's much else I can do at the computer lab. I would like to go to the Moscone Center and take another crack at finding out what's going on with the other teams."

George nodded. "We're up against another program this morning."

"Is it any good?"

He shrugged. "Nobody knows. It's a new one, like ours, out of Japan. It's called Koshi. It's apparently not too shabby, because it's got two wins and a draw so far."

"Well, you should be the crowd favorite; hometown boys versus the evil Japanese neocolonialists."

"Yeah, right. Just don't tell 'em our sponsor's Tokoyo."

"And when has a little thing like that stopped anyone from wrapping himself in the flag?"

A short while later, after collecting and changing into my own shirt, socks, and underwear, we drove over to the lab, stopping on the way to leave my jacket and slacks at the local dry cleaner. The sign outside said One Hour Dry Cleaning. The man inside said I'd have them by Monday. When I very astutely pointed out that this was noticeably longer than the promised one hour, he looked at me as if he was trying to figure out whether I was putting him on. We then embarked on negotiations, the upshot of which was that they would try to have my stuff by Saturday morning.

As we left, George said, "Seriously, though, those pants look fine on you. It's just a good thing they no longer have laws against vagrancy."

It was a warm day for March, so I didn't miss my jacket much on the drive over to the Stanford computer center. The first person we saw was Jason, who I think had been there all night. He said he'd consider my worm-probe suggestion after the tournament, but until then it was no go. I had a pretty strong feeling that it would remain a no go after the tournament, as well. Alex and Harvey had gone back to the city the night before, so George and I drove up without their company, which was fine because George was entertaining enough on his own. I wanted to pummel him senseless.

Actually, it was not that George was being more than usually obnoxious. I was thinking that I really needed to try to talk to Al Meade again, and I was anticipating the same response as yesterday, which put me in a bad mood.

Alex was already sitting at the chessboard when we got in. This time we were set up in a large room with multiple chessboards and a battery of telephones. The room we'd been in the day before was apparently reserved for the Dragon's games. I saw from the tournament draw sheet that he was scheduled to go up against Mephisto, so I figured that's where I would find Al Meade. I was about to tell George where I was going, when I spotted Al making her way through the crowded room. As usual she looked hyperprofessional, wearing a black suit over a pale-pink blouse. She came directly up to me.

"We need to talk," she said.

I had a half-formed sarcastic reply on the way when I noticed that she seemed earnest and upset, so I bit it back and just nodded. "Where?"

In response she turned and led the way out into a corridor. After a couple twists and turns we arrived at a relatively secluded spot. I looked at her expectantly. At least I think I looked expectant. I certainly felt expectant.

"I want you to know," she said, "that the people who hired me think you planted a virus in their program."

I nodded. "That doesn't surprise me. What do *you* think?"

She looked me in the eye and said, "I told them you wouldn't do anything of the kind."

That surprised me. "Why did you tell them that?"

"Because it's true."

"How do you know it's true?"

"Because it's obvious to anyone who knows you. You're . . . I don't know, like an altar boy or something. . . ."

"An altar boy?"

She nodded, with kind of a wry half smile, which really pissed me off.

"You don't like me very much, do you?"

She actually seemed surprised by the question. "Why do you think I don't like you?"

"When you treat somebody like he has leprosy, it's usually considered a sign of distaste—unless you really do think I have leprosy?"

She chuckled. "No, you look pretty healthy to me. And I like you all right, I guess. I mean, I don't really know you very well. . . ."

"Just well enough to know that I'm innocent of any possible wrongdoing?"

"Yeah, I guess that's about it."

"Then have dinner with me."

"What?"

"To get to know me. Have dinner with me."

"When?"

"Tonight."

She nodded slowly. "Okay. On two conditions."

"Conditions! All right, name them."

"Number one is, we don't talk business."

"I wouldn't dream of it. And two?"

"Will you *please* wear something else?"

I think I managed not to blush. "The airline—"

"Lost your baggage? I thought so."

We started walking slowly back to the tournament area. I said, "So you think I'm an altar boy?"

She smiled—and when I saw her dimples, I realized that I had actually never seen her smile before. "Maybe I should have said 'white knight.' "

I grinned. "That would make you the black queen."

She actually smiled again, rather than groaning or punching me in the arm. I nearly added something about mating, but I decided I'd done enough damage to my altar-boy image for one morning.

After letting me know where she was staying (also the Marriott), Al returned to the Mephisto-Zivojinovic game to see how her patient was doing. I wandered back to the main tournament area. An Asian woman was sitting at the chessboard opposite Alex. Koshi had apparently opened with pawn to king four, and Goodknight had taken a page from the Dragon's book and answered with the Sicilian Defense.

George looked up as I approached. He said, "What's going on? You look a little strange."

"A miracle has occurred," I said. "I think you actually may have been right about something."

"Stop the presses! I saw you go off with the ice queen. What's going on?"

"The black queen, not the ice queen," I corrected. "I'm having dinner with her tonight."

He nodded approvingly. "Where?"

"Any suggestions?"

"The Hyatt Embarcadero has a rotating restaurant on the top floor. Great view, and women think it's very romantic. Very expensive too, but"—he clapped me on the shoulder—"with what we're paying you, you can afford it."

I found a pay phone and called to make dinner reservations at the restaurant George recommended, then went back to the tournament area. Koshi had castled queen-side and was pushing its king-side pawns. Goodknight seemed to be playing for a queen-side counterattack. I tried to read Alex's expression for some idea of who was winning, but his chess face was as inscrutable as the best poker face I've ever seen.

I circulated for a while, met a few programmers from other entries, struck up a few conversations, and tried to steer things around to the topic of software infections. Nobody rose to the bait, which may have merely been indicative of stonewalling. I decided to go back to my room at the Marriott, so I told George where I'd be and walked over. I left a message for Al about when I'd pick her up for dinner, then checked to see if my suitcase had been delivered, which it still hadn't, so I went up to my room, ordered a sandwich from room service, and sat down in front of my laptop. I selected a software virus that I was especially familiar with and listed the code. Because I had written it myself as an exercise, I didn't need to do any "reverse engineering," which basically refers to figuring out how an old program works when it has to be modified.

Actually, it's not too unusual for programmers to need to reverse-engineer their own programs, but that's typically the case when the program in question is long and complicated, containing thousands, sometimes millions, of lines of code. In contrast, my software virus consisted of only a few hundred lines of code.

It was a fairly innocuous beastie to begin with. I added a line that would serve as a marker for the virus and inserted it in a few dozen different spots. If this guy got chewed up, I was going to be able to find the pieces. I also added a self-destruct trigger; in response to the command "seppuku," it would delete all copies of itself from the host program. After I made a few more refinements, it really was completely harmless.

At least I hoped it was harmless. Back in the eighties the staff of a computer magazine had planted a virus in some commercial software. That virus was supposed to display a message of "Peace" on a certain date, then erase itself. What could be more harmless than that? Unfortunately, the virus caused some unintended problems, like making the whole system crash when certain applications were in use. That whole experience served as sort of a lesson to people in the computer community about the danger of viruses. Unfortunately, that lesson could be interpreted in two very different ways.

One interpretation is: *Viruses are potentially dangerous and unpredictable. We need to be very careful.* The other way to look at it is: *Viruses are potentially dangerous and unpredictable, so let's write some! Won't that be a hoot?*

When I was finished playing virus hacker, I went out and did some shopping. I bought some shirts, socks, underwear, two pairs of slacks, one tie, and a blazer.

When I got back, there were two messages waiting for me: one from Al saying she'd be ready at the appointed time, and one from George. The latter said, "Mikey, we kicked Koshi's butt—HAH! There wasn't enough left to make a decent piece of sushi. Oh, and the Dragon had Mephisto for breakfast. Have fun tonight, and give me a call later—tomorrow morning's soon enough. Ciao."

I had time for a quick shower and a shave before collecting my date for our early dinner reservation. I had wanted something later, but six o'clock was the only one left, and that only because of a cancellation. On further reflection I realized the earlier time would allow us to see a nice sunset, if the weather cooperated.

I put on my new duds: white linen jacket and slacks, white silk shirt, and a blue tie with an abstract design picked out in silver. I always feel kind of self-conscious wearing something brand-new—uncomfortably aware of what my clothes look like. I suppressed the urge to roll around on the floor, and went to collect my date. I wasn't quite prepared for what I saw when her door opened in response to my knock. Al was wearing a black off-the-shoulder dress cut low enough at the top and high enough at the bottom to display her considerable charms to good advantage. It was the first time I'd ever seen her not look as if she were on her way to run a board meeting.

She smiled in response to my unabashedly appreciative gaze, then gave me an appraising look of her own. I guess I passed muster, because she stepped aside and waved me in. "I'll be ready in two more minutes. Make yourself comfortable." She pointed to her room's minibar. "Help yourself to a drink."

"I don't drink except on Sunday mornings," I said. "And then just a wee drop of altar wine."

She had a great laugh, full and hearty and uninhibited. Imagine—a woman who was beautiful, intelligent, *and* laughed at my jokes. I'm sure George would have maintained those last two attributes were mutually exclusive. The two minutes were more like ten, which she spent in the bathroom doing whatever it is women do when they're keeping their escorts waiting. She finally emerged, as gorgeous as before, and asked, "How do I look?"

"Ravishing, Your Majesty."

She showed me her dimples again. "I see that the airline found your luggage."

I shook my head. "My luggage is still off collecting frequent-flyer miles."

It was a memorable dinner. The food was good, the view was spectacular, and the company was exquisite. We ordered a wonderful Napa Valley chardonnay to accompany the meal, and I was delighted to find that Al was both appreciative of and knowledgeable about the wine.

Over dinner we swapped episodes from our life stories, avoiding anything resembling shoptalk, as per Condition One. Al had grown up in a suburb of Philadelphia, the only child of professional parents. She wondered what it was like to have brothers and sisters—I grew up with three of each.

Over dessert and coffee I said, "You know, one thing puzzles me. Before today I really thought you disliked me. Was I wrong?"

"No," she admitted. "I couldn't stand you."

"Why?"

"You've always been so damned helpful—it makes me feel like you think I'm incompetent."

I started to protest, but she held up a hand. "I know, I realize now that it's the way you are. Really, I've known it on some level all along, but somehow it just pushes a button for me. When you say, 'Come on, Al, we'll work together on this,' it sounds to me like you're saying 'Kid, let me show you how it's done.' " She frowned. "I hope this doesn't make you think I'm dreadfully insecure."

I shook my head. "No, not at all." I added, half to myself, "George is going to be disappointed, though."

"George?"

"My friend George thinks you were pissed off because I didn't hit on you."

"Your friend George is a swine."

I nodded. "That is a distinct possibility."

The waiter had brought the check, but I let it sit there awhile, not wanting the evening to end. I said, "You know, I don't have to be in New York until Tuesday, and I'm through here, at least for the time being. I was thinking of driving up to Napa Valley for a few days."

"That should be fun. Are you going by yourself?"

I smiled. "I hope not."

She hesitated. "I have to be in Houston by Monday afternoon."

"That would still give us Saturday and Sunday. We could tour some wineries, enjoy the scenery. It's supposed to be very pretty."

"You haven't been there before?"

"Actually, no. And for years it's been way up there on my list of places to visit when I have some free time. God, is it really that long since I've had any free time?"

"I know the feeling."

"So you'll come?"

"I don't know—going off for two days with a strange man . . ."

"Oh, come on. We may not have been the best of friends, but we're hardly strangers."

She flashed a wicked smile. "That's not the kind of strange that I meant."

In the end she agreed to come. That meant we both had some loose ends to tie up so we could get an early start the next morning, which had the effect of deferring certain pressing issues concerning sleeping arrangements until the following night. We had taken our time over dinner, but due to the early start, we were back at the Marriott before ten-thirty. We enjoyed a lingering good-night kiss in front of her door. My legs carried me back to my room despite fervent protests from other parts of my anatomy.

I phoned George. He said, "Mike, is that you? Tough luck, man, I see you must have struck out."

"If you must know," I said, "Al and I are going to Napa Valley to spend a few days."

"Whoa! Change that box score. Are we anticipating a home run?"

"George, I have it on good authority that you are a swine."

"Possibly a swine, but never a bore."

"Listen, I want to get an early start tomorrow morning. I wrote that virus probe we discussed." Not that I was actually expecting them to use it. "Do you want to me to leave it at the front desk here, so you can pick it up tomorrow?"

"There's no hurry; just drop it in the mail. That way we'll have it by the time the tournament is over. Or you can even E-mail it to me later."

"No, I can't. There's a federal law against transmitting software viruses or worms via modem. It's part of the Computer Crimes Act of 1997."

"I know, but that doesn't really apply to this situation."

"I agree with you. I just don't want to have to explain why in a federal court."

"Okay, okay, just mail it, then. Say, does your new girlfriend like trees?"

"What?"

"You know, like redwoods?"

"George, if there's some innuendo in that question, it's a little too deep for me."

"Huh? No, no innuendo, although now that you mention it, I can think of one pretty raunchy interpretation—"

"George!"

"Nudge-nudge, wink-wink, say no more! I was just going to suggest that if you're driving up to Napa, you might want to stop at Muir Woods. It's worth a short side trip and won't take you far out of your way."

I picked up a rental car at seven the next morning and met Al back at the hotel. When I mentioned George's suggestion about Muir Woods, she was enthusiastic. We drove up through San Francisco and across the Golden Gate Bridge, and a surprisingly short time later we were wandering among groves of giant redwoods.

I've done a fair amount of hiking and camping in forests on the East Coast, and the thing that struck me here was the almost complete absence of undergrowth and animal life. The forest seemed to belong entirely to the immense redwoods, except for occasional bay laurels, the laurels' mossy trunks zigzagging at weird angles, reaching for the few broken patches of sunlight that had gotten past their giant neighbors. The stillness was broken only by a few roving bands of *Homo sapiens,* uttering their strange cries and clicking their camera shutters. Al loved it. She said, "Your friend George has redeemed himself."

Al and I hiked around, uttering a few strange cries of our own, mainly "oohs" and "ahs." She had picked up one of those "all in one" film packs, which come equipped with a lens and shutter, at a shop in the hotel, and we prevailed on some friendly passersby to take some shots of us together.

By early afternoon we reached Napa Valley. Al had reserved rooms for us at a bed-and-breakfast—separate rooms, of course. We checked in, dropped off our bags, and spent the rest of the afternoon visiting wineries. The scenery in Napa Valley is quite beautiful; to an easterner like me, for whom the word "mountain" evokes images of the gently rounded, heavily forested Appalachians, it looked unreal, as if someone had painted the surrounding peaks on a blue canvas that was close enough to touch. Fields of grapevines covered the gentler slopes in the foreground, partitioned by windbreaks of silver-leafed olive trees.

Domaine Chandon and Beringer Brothers were a little too crowded, but we visited and tasted at Freemark Abbey, Stag's Leap, and a few lesser-known wineries.

We took a little tour at Freemark Abbey, which included a walk among the grapevines themselves. Our tour guide, a chubby, bespectacled college girl who was studying enology at Cal Davis, pointed out the callus where the cabernet vines were grafted to the roots. One of the other people on the tour with us asked her about the purpose of the grafting.

"It's because of the phylloxera louse," she explained. "It attacks the roots. It's an American louse, so the American labrusca grapes have evolved a certain degree of natural immunity. But it kills the European vinifera vines. So we graft the vinifera vines onto labrusca rootstock."

"Why not just make the wine out of American grapes?" another of our fellow tourists asked.

The guide made a face. "Because the wine wouldn't taste as good. There's a family of chemical compounds in the American grapes that gives them a strong odor and flavor that wine people call foxy. That's why they're sometimes called fox grapes."

"And the louse isn't found in Europe?"

"It is now. Somebody accidentally brought it back sometime in the nineteenth century. It practically wiped out every vineyard in Europe. So now the European growers have to do the same thing we do: graft onto American rootstock."

In the meantime we had reached another area where Riesling grapes were planted. The guide said, "Not all parasites are bad, though. In Germany these grapes sometimes have a kind of mold on them, *Botrytis cinerea,* which the Germans call *Edelfaule.* The French get the same thing on their Sémillon grapes, used to make sauternes, and call it *pourriture noble.* Both phrases mean the same thing: noble rot. Basically, it sucks water out of the grape, concentrating the sugar inside."

Some people might visit wineries to learn about phylloxera and botrytis; I do it to taste wine. I have never been able to bring myself to spit out a mouthful of good wine, which is considered the prudent thing to do when you're doing a lot of tasting, so I safeguarded my sobriety by sipping very sparingly. I noticed Al wasn't spitting any out either—she probably would have been mortified by the very suggestion. But with less than two thirds of my body mass, and unconstrained by having to drive, she was noticeably tipsy by the time we went to dinner.

We ate at a small restaurant within walking distance of our bed-and-breakfast. I drank most of the bottle of Stag's Leap cabernet that we ordered to go with the meal, but not quite enough to catch up with Al, blood-alcohol-wise. Afterward we walked back to our bed-and-breakfast. I was preparing to kiss her good night at her door, but she took my hand and pulled me inside. We tumbled into bed with our clothes on and let our lips renew their recent acquaintance. Items of clothing began to fly off in various directions, and as things progressed toward their predictable conclusion, I began to feel vaguely uncomfortable.

I tried to shake off the feeling, but it intensified and became recognizable as the nagging of an aroused conscience. I broke things off, mentally cursing myself for an idiot, and said to her, "Are you really sure you want to do this?"

She seemed surprised. "Why are you asking me that?"

In my best Jimmy Stewart voice I said, "Well, because you've had quite a lot to drink, and there are rules against that sort of thing."

She laughed. "*Philadelphia Story*! I love that film." She raised a hand to my cheek. "But no, noble sir, this is not just the alcohol talking."

Noble sir? Noble rot would be more like how I would feel if I thought I was taking advantage of her. "You say that now, but will you respect me in the morning?"

She frowned thoughtfully. "So I need to convince you that this is premeditated, and not impulsive. I did agree to spend the weekend with you in the first place."

I shook my head. "Suggestive, but not conclusive."

Suddenly she reached to the bedside table to retrieve a small toiletry bag, removed a smaller package, and flourished it with a smile that was half tease and half triumph. "Your contraceptive or mine?"

Some indeterminate time later we lay together under the sheets, my arm around her and her head resting on my shoulder. She broke the silence by saying, "You know, I feel kind of bad."

I was surprised. "I was afraid of that, but I thought it would at least take until tomorrow morning."

She laughed and smacked me on the chest with her palm. "Not about that, silly. I feel bad about the way I behaved when you suggested we cooperate at the chess tournament. You were right. It would have made a lot of sense for us to work together."

I was even more surprised. Ever since we had agreed to eschew shoptalk on our first date, I had continued to avoid the subject. Not that it had required any particular effort, as my attention had been focused on other things. Now that she brought it up, I became newly aware of some of the unanswered questions that had been percolating around in my unconscious.

I told her about what had happened with Goodknight, and some of the dead ends I'd hit, along with some of my latest speculations. She listened with interest, asking occasional questions. I said, "I don't suppose the Mephisto problem sheds any light on this?"

She shook her head. "Nothing that exotic, I'm afraid. Their problem was a virus that someone must have deliberately inserted. Difficult to find, because it was novel and didn't do anything particularly suspicious that would even tip us off to its presence."

"What did the virus do?"

She shook her head. "I'm still not entirely sure. Altered the algorithm somehow so that Mephisto would occasionally make a spectacularly dumb move. It blew the first three games in the tournament."

I said, "That's a shame. I feel bad for my friends on the Goodknight team too, because if they do manage to win, it will be kind of a tainted victory."

"Cute name, though. Who came up with that one?"

"Goodknight? It smacks of George's sense of humor. I was wondering how your client came up with the name 'Mephisto.'"

"Actually, I asked them about that. It was the name of a nineteenth-century chess-playing automaton."

"Wait a minute. You're telling me they had machines that could play chess a hundred years ago?"

"Well, sort of. They didn't look anything like modern chess computers, though; generally, they looked like a sort of mannequin sitting on a platform. The mannequin's arm would actually move the chess pieces around the board."

"This is getting even better. So now you want me to believe that they not only had computing devices, but sophisticated servoelectronics as well?"

"No," Al admitted. "They actually didn't have any of that stuff."

"Well, then, how was this thing supposed to work?"

"There was a guy in another room. He would move the arm through, I don't know, a system of pulleys and levers or something."

"So it was a fraud?"

"Yep. Sometimes the chess player would be a dwarf who was actually hidden inside the automaton."

"A dwarf?"

"Yes. Sort of a nanus ex machina."

"Huh? I've heard of a deus ex machina, but what's a nanus?"

"A dwarf."

"Oh."

Suddenly she hopped out of bed and started rummaging through her bags. "I just remembered, I've got something in here I wanted to show you." She pulled out a notebook computer and powered it up. "I did a job for Transcontinental Insurance recently. This is what I found in their actuarial software."

"A worm?"

"More like an anaconda. Look at the size of this thing." She scrolled through pages of hexadecimal code. "It took up almost four megs of disk space. And it's not just a lot of copies of something smaller, either."

I whistled. "That's a whopper, all right. What does it do?"

"Surprisingly little for such a monster. Erased some files, mainly to make room for copying itself, I think."

"How did it get in?"

"I never found out. Probably deliberately inserted."

Now that the shoptalk ban was off, there was something else I'd been wondering about. "Al, that day at the Moscone Center—why did you tell me about your client's suspicions about me?"

She seemed surprised by the question. "I don't know. It just made me angry to see someone unjustly accused of something, and angry that they wouldn't listen to me when I told them there was no way. And I wanted you to be on your guard, so you wouldn't do anything to inadvertently stoke their paranoia."

As if to make up for the earlier ban, we talked about our work until the wee hours, swapping stories about different jobs we'd done. I even told her about the time I'd accidentally infected a system I was working on. A stupid mistake, but I learned some important lessons from it. I felt a little embarrassed telling her that one, but she was amused at the proper times, and sympathetic at the right moments, so I figured my openness had brought us closer together. After all, isn't honesty the most important thing in a relationship? As George would say, once you can fake that, you've got it made.

I awoke the next morning pleasantly aware of someone warm curled up against my back. I glanced at my watch on the bedside table and saw it was almost ten, which meant we had probably missed the breakfast that was supposed to go with our bed. I quietly slipped out from under the covers and padded to the bathroom. As I finished relieving myself, a light tap came from the door. I jokingly called out, "You'll have to wait your turn," then opened the door. Al was wrapped in something black and lacy, which made me uncomfortably aware of the fact that I was still au naturel.

My discomfort evaporated abruptly when she let the black lacy thing fall to the floor, saying, "Is there any way I can persuade you to let me have *your* turn?"

I put my arms around her and lifted her off the floor until her face was level with mine. "Payment in advance?"

By way of reply she wrapped her legs around my waist.

This time we used one of *my* condoms.

We showered together, then took turns using the phone to check for messages. While I was shaving, Al made a few calls. When I emerged from the bathroom, she looked at me apologetically. "Michael, I'm sorry, but it looks like I'm going to have to leave earlier than I thought. They want me in Houston first thing tomorrow morning."

I nodded ruefully. "Can you get a flight?"

"Eight-fifteen to Dallas–Fort Worth, then a shuttle ride to Houston. It'll probably be three A.M. by the time I get to my hotel. I'll get to this meeting looking like something the cat dragged in, then dragged back out again."

I said, "You couldn't look bad if you tried."

"Oh, no?" She laughed. "Listen, you have no idea how much work goes into making myself look presentable. You men don't know how easy you have it."

"Easy? Which one of us just got finished scraping his face with a piece of sharp metal?"

Because Al had to leave, I saw no particular reason to hang around on the left coast, so I booked a flight back to New York for the same evening. We had a leisurely brunch, visited a few more wineries, then drove back to San Francisco.

Since our first kiss two days earlier, I had felt that odd mixture of excitement, giddiness, trepidation, and unreality that seems to accompany that uniquely disturbed state of mind known as "falling in love." Or are those the signs and symptoms of a nervous breakdown? When I looked at Al sitting next to me in the car, warm, fuzzy feelings stirred within me. When she looked over at me and smiled, those feelings erupted into flames. And now the prospect of our parting in a few hours filled me with the most ridiculously overblown sense of impending loss. I was practically considering following her to Houston like some orphaned puppy, which image was sufficiently repellent to jar me back to some approximation of reason.

I had purposely booked a flight a bit later than hers so that I could see her off at the gate. As we waited for her flight to be called, we chatted about trivialities. She was cheerful and talkative, and I wondered if she felt as I did. The possibility that the whole thing was a meaningless one-night stand to her was about the worst thing I could imagine. I couldn't quite believe that, but she didn't *seem* upset.

Then they called her flight. She stood, hoisted her carry-on bag, and smiled. "Well, I guess this is good-bye for now."

I didn't feel like smiling, but I managed to paste on a grin. "Not for long, I hope."

We kissed, and she turned to leave. I thought I heard her make a sniffling sound, then thought, "Naaah." But just before she went through the gate, she turned to wave, and I saw it: a tear. She wiped the corner of her eye with her free hand, waved again, and was gone.

I went to catch my flight. It wasn't actually until just after we were airborne that I realized I had never gotten my clothes back from the dry cleaner in Palo Alto.

Monday, March 15, seven A.M. I stumbled into my apartment and tossed my bags onto the floor. There were six messages on the answering machine. I ignored it and went to bed.

CHAPTER THREE

Wall Street
Walpurgisnacht

And the great dragon was cast out,
that old serpent, called the Devil, and Satan,
which deceiveth the whole world . . .
—Revelation 12:9

"EEEEEP! Mike, this is George. No emergency, everything's going fine. We're leading the tournament by a full point with four rounds to go. Just give me a call when you get a chance. Bye . . . EEEEEP! Mr. Arcangelo, this is Harold Ainsworth from Tower Bank again. I realize you must have a very busy schedule, but if you can possibly be available earlier than Tuesday, as we originally discussed, please call . . . EEEEEP! Michael? This is Al. I know you're not home yet, but I wanted this message to be waiting for you. I had a wonderful time this weekend. Please call soon. I . . . miss you . . . EEEEEP! Hello, this is Evelyn Mulderig, from Gerdel Hesher Bock. We have a problem that requires your particular brand of expertise. Please call me back at 555-2674 as soon as possible . . . EEEEEP! . . . for a special, computerized message . . . Are you tired of painting your home's exterior every few years? Tired of unsightly peeling, chipping, and blistering? Maybe it's time you considered the advantages of vinyl siding. A representative will be in your area next week. Please take a moment to—EEEEEP! Hi, Michael. It's me again. I was hoping maybe you'd be home by now, but I guess not. I hope your flight wasn't delayed. Call me in Houston tomorrow. Bye . . . EEEEEP! . . . Brother Fred Ferris, calling from the Church of Final Judgment. Friend, the greatest day in history is fast approaching. Have you repented all your sins? Have you found salvation? The Church of Final Judgment is the one real hope for all us sinners in these last days of earth. Time is running . . . EEEEEP! Okay, I admit it, it's me again. I just wanted to hear the sound of your voice, and since you're obviously not there, I thought I'd listen to your answering-machine message again. I'm leaving for my early meeting soon. Maybe you'll leave a message for me to find when I get back. Hint, hint.''

Not bad: out of eight messages, only two from people trying to sell me something. Correction, two messages from *machines* trying to sell me something. Three personal calls (*highly* personal), two business, and one indeterminate (from George).

I called Al's hotel in Houston; as expected, she wasn't in. I left her the desired message. I called George, but there was no answer; he had probably already gone out even though it was only eight A.M. there. I left a message saying I had called (which is a little like sending a letter to tell someone you wrote) and also asking him to pick up my dry cleaning.

I called Evelyn Mulderig, told her I was currently working on something for someone else, but that I could probably give her some time tomorrow.

Then I called Harry Ainsworth. To say he was happy to hear from me would be an understatement. To say that Tower Bank had trouble with its software would also be an understatement, and beasties were just a small part of it.

Tower had one of those systems that accepted and stored years only as two-digit numbers. You may think that this does not show much foresight on the part of the programmers, and you may be right, but, then, somebody writing a program in the seventies or early eighties probably didn't really expect that it would still be in use at the turn of the century.

The turn of the century. That phrase is enough to strike terror into the hearts of businessmen everywhere, and not because every tabloid horoscope, television psychic, tea-leaf reader, vegetarian, and generic wacko is predicting the end of the world. Rather, it's because when the millennial hourglass turns over, thousands of businesses with software like Tower's are going to be in a heap o' trouble. Let's suppose the bank's computer wants to calculate the interest on a CD (certificate of deposit, not compact disk) you bought this year, 1999, for a one-year term. Instead of figuring it owes you a year of interest, it subtracts ninety-nine from zero and gets minus ninety-nine—and either registers an error, or charges *you* for almost a century's worth of interest. Or you're trying to buy some life insurance, and the insurance company's actuarial software can't figure out what premium to charge you because it thinks you haven't been born yet.

So big deal. Just change the program, right? And if that doesn't work, buy new software.

Not so fast.

We're talking BIG programs here, like maybe a million lines of code. Suppose you're lucky enough to have the guy who originally programmed it, because he hasn't retired, gone into another line of work, joined a cult, or been kidnapped by aliens. Or died. You sit him down in front of this dinosaur of a program he wrote twenty years ago and say, okay, this is what we want you to change.

He hasn't got a clue.

This is where reverse engineering comes in. Before you can change the program, you have to figure out how it does what it does, and how to change what you want to change without throwing everything else out of whack. Fortunately, programmers and software engineers now have a few tricks up their sleeves, consisting of computer programs that help them figure out what another program is doing—computer-assisted software engineering tools, they call them. Still, it takes a lot of expertise and man-hours. Need I say that this gets very expensive? And that's if you're lucky enough to find someone with the necessary skills to come and work for you; there are damn few of them around.

So tab over to option two and order me that brand-new software that accepts year inputs in *five* digits, just in case we're still using it eight thousand years from now, and has all the latest bells, whistles, windows, garage doors, and whatever. Now all we have to do is transfer all your files to this new system, which, needless to say, is entirely incompatible with your old system, so it'll all have to be done by hand. Oh, and did I mention that you'll need completely new hardware to run this software?

Now multiply the above dilemma by as many banks, S and L's, insurance companies, brokerage firms, and other financial outfits you can think of. Add in huge government bureaucracies like the Social Security Administration, and the motor vehicle bureaus in all fifty states. It's been estimated that billions have already been spent on the problem, and it's nowhere near being solved.

Nit-pickers are fond of pointing out that the new millennium doesn't "really" begin until the year 2001; the year 2000 is in fact the last year of the current millennium. This is mathematically accurate, but irrelevant, because on this point computer software and the popular imagination are in complete agreement: The new millennium starts on January 1, 2000.

The people at Tower Bank hadn't quite waited until the last possible second before trying to do something about their software problems. On the other hand, they weren't going to be kicked out of the procrastinators' club either. In fairness, their delay in dealing with this particular problem resulted largely from having to deal with a host of more pressing problems with their computer system. Still, they had finally gotten around to hiring a consultant to try to massage their old software in time for the big day, and said consultant had smelled a rat. Or maybe a virus.

Harold Ainsworth was a middle-aged man with an expensive suit and a bad comb-over. He welcomed me with a handshake and waved me into his office. "Michael Arcangelo, I'd like you to meet Leon Griffin."

The guy who rose to shake my hand looked to be about my age, and about half again my weight, most of it muscle. His hair was a mane of dreadlocks that made a pleasant contrast with his conservative business suit.

Harry waved us to seats. "Leon is consulting for us on how to modify our existing software so that we don't have to go out of business at the end of the year." He looked apologetically at me. "Michael, I know you recommended getting a new system, and I agreed with you at the time, but the directors thought this approach would be more fiscally sound."

I smiled. "Meaning cheaper."

"Right, but I want you to know that this is costing us a pretty penny. Fortunately, Leon has the expertise to do the job for us; he's already worked on a similar system at Southeastern Trust, and they're very happy with the results. In fact, there were a few dozen other institutions bidding for his services after that job. We were lucky to get him."

I glanced at Leon, who seemed to be trying hard not to blush, if blushing is possible for someone with skin darker than the charcoal gray of his suit. I hoped he was charging a lot for his services. After all, he was going to have to find a new line of work come January. "How's it going?" I asked.

"Swimmingly, man. Like kicking dead whales down the beach."

Harry said, "Leon has run into some unexpected difficulties with our software, though, and we thought you might be able to lend some assistance. But I'd better let him explain."

Leon gestured to a stack of several large binders on Harry's desk as he answered in a mellifluous Caribbean accent: "Fortunately, Tower has taken good care of their documentation. We've even been able to get a hard copy of the original code from the software publisher. Unfortunately, whatever is running now doesn't match up with the documentation.

"That, in itself, is not unusual. When these programs were written, it was common to continue modifying the program after the documentation was printed. It's common now too, but, as you know, the manufacturer usually puts in a 'readme' text file that summarizes any changes. That's not the way it was done back in the dark ages, when this program was written.

"The problem is, there have been some really major changes made in this software, much bigger than I've ever seen before. The front end looks the same, but if you examine the program structure— branch points and so on—it doesn't look like the same thing at all."

I said, "And you think a software parasite is the cause?"

He shrugged. "I don't see how it could be. But I don't have any better ideas. I asked Mr. Ainsworth for a list of everyone who's worked on their system. Nothing major has been done, certainly nothing that would explain the kind of restructuring I'm seeing. I noticed that you'd been called in a few times to deal with software viruses."

"Well, I've never seen anything like it, but that doesn't mean it couldn't happen. The things a parasite can do are limited only by the imagination and ability of its programmer. Still, to do what you're talking about would require tremendous in-depth knowledge of this software."

Harry asked, "Who would have that kind of knowledge?"

I shook my head. "Twenty years ago, the guy who wrote the program. Maybe. Now? Nobody."

I spent the rest of the afternoon checking out the bank's software. Not surprisingly, I didn't find anything. On second thought, maybe it was surprising; when I thought about it, I realized that every time I'd worked on this system before, it had been practically infested with beasties. One time I took out seven different viruses. It had now been several months since I'd last cleaned house—plenty of time for a new bunch of varmints to move in and set up housekeeping.

On a hunch I got Harry Ainsworth's permission to infect Tower's software with a modified version of the probe that I'd written for Goodknight. If Harry had been more computer literate, he might have balked at the idea, but he trusted me to do what was best. Unlike Goodknight, this system was well-known to me, especially in terms of its behavior when infected, so I was sure my program wouldn't cause a problem. I also told Leon Griffin what I was planning to do. He raised his eyebrows, but when I explained what was going on, he just nodded and said, "Sounds like a good idea."

It was finally time to knock off for the day, and the last thing I wanted to do was work out. But it had already been more than two weeks since I'd been to the dojo, and I knew that the longer I waited, the worse it would be. At this point I might get away with only a day or so of aching from disused muscles.

I swung by my apartment to pick up my *gi*, and still had time to get to the dojo about twenty minutes before the scheduled workout. This was good, because I figured I needed the extra time to stretch. Unfortunately, Jamaal was there early too, and he had other ideas.

I was sitting on the floor stretching my hamstrings when he approached. "Mike, good to see you back. Want to spar?" Jamaal is one of those people for whom karate would seem to be utterly superfluous. In fact, there should really be some kind of law forbidding the teaching of karate to huge, heavily muscled guys like Jamaal—kind of defeats the whole purpose of martial arts, at least to my way of thinking.

Still, Jamaal was not accustomed to having his invitations to spar declined, politely or otherwise. I got up slowly, bowed, and went into fighting stance. "Where's *sensei*?" I asked. Hiro Shimomura, the head instructor, usually led the Monday-night workouts.

Jamaal swung a lazy roundhouse kick at my head. "In Japan for the next six weeks."

I had stepped back out of range of the kick, then tried to get in with a kick of my own before he could recover, but he flicked the same leg up again, this time about five times faster. I just barely got my arm up in time to block it. "So in the meantime we're in your hands, huh?"

He grinned and threw a front kick, this time following up with a barrage of punches, which I did my best to block. "Yo' ass be mine."

We continued to spar until it was time to start the workout, and it was almost as good as stretching, because I had warmed up and broken a sweat. Jamaal led the workout, and he made it a tough one. After we finished warming down, he came over to me again. I grinned at him, although it may have looked more like a grimace. "Don't tell me you want to spar some more."

He shook his head. "Not unless you really want to. I just wanted to ask you when you're planning on taking the *shodan* test."

I shrugged. "I wish I could say." I needed to have six months of really regular workouts to be eligible to take the black-belt examination, and 1999 wasn't shaping up to be a good year for hobbies.

He pursed his lips disapprovingly. "Don't be giving me all those excuses about work again. Anybody gonna spar me like that, I want him in a black belt. You tryin' to make me look bad?"

"Yeah, trying but not succeeding."

He chuckled. "Hey, there's a Bruce Lee film festival this weekend, and some of us are going. You interested?"

"Interested, yeah. Can't make it, though. Maybe another time?"

"Another time," he agreed.

I got back to my apartment a little after six and went straight to the answering machine. Al had called again and simply said, "You're 'it.' " George had left another message asking me to call him after seven, Pacific time.

I called Al's hotel in Houston. She still wasn't in her room, so I left a message: "Do you mean Cousin It? I've been told there's a resemblance."

I turned to a small stack of magazines that had come in the last week's mail and started leafing through, figuring to kill some time until Al called again, or it was time to call George.

One thing that caught my eye was an interview in *Hologram* with Marlon Oz. Oz was a well-known figure in artificial intelligence, and also something of a maverick, as could be inferred from *Hologram*'s cover, which screamed, "AI expert now says there's no such thing as AI." Oz has also been described as someone who does not suffer fools gladly, "fool" being defined as anyone who knows less about artificial intelligence than he does, which means, well, everybody. At least in his humble opinion. In addition to being well-known among computer scientists, Oz was one of those rare academics who achieve a measure of popular celebrity through a combination of prominence within their own field and a knack for self-promotion. Of course, this didn't necessarily make him the most popular guy with his colleagues, as the magazine noted in its introduction to the interview:

> Almost as well-known for his irascibility as for his brilliance, Oz has a penchant for quoting physicist Wolfgang Pauli's famous put-down to describe some of the ideas of his rivals in the field: that they are "not even false." When asked his opinion of Oz, AI researcher Dennis Daniels had this to say: "Marlon is not really a scientist; he's more of a mad poet. He's got some very interesting things to say. You just can't take him too literally." Eric Stadhoffer was even more blunt: "You remember Buckminster Fuller's line, 'I seem to be a verb'? Well, if Bucky Fuller was a verb, then Marlon Oz is an expletive."

Part of Oz's talent for getting attention is his penchant for outrageousness. In his first book, *The Snake in the Garden,* he argued that consciousness was not an intrinsic property of the human organism but could best be understood as a kind of parasite. He offered a reinterpretation of the Genesis story, suggesting that it described the "infection" of Adam and Eve by the serpent, the latter representing the "consciousness parasite."

I flipped to the interview, expecting Oz to make mincemeat out of

Hologram's interviewer, but he seemed almost congenial (for him), apparently due to his interest in pitching his forthcoming book, *The Worm in the Apple,* in which he set forth his argument that artificial intelligence was a no go.

> **HOLOGRAM:**   Dr. Oz, how long have computer scientists been striving to create artificial intelligence?
>
> **OZ:**   That depends on what you mean by "intelligence." Actually, there has been an idea of creating a machine in the image of the human mind that goes back long before the earliest days of computing. Ramón Llull, a thirteenth-century Christian missionary, claimed to have a machine, which he called Ars Magna, which could answer theological questions. Ironically, a lot of modern thinking about AI probably has more in common with religion than science. Besides, why anyone would want to go to the trouble of replicating something that works as poorly as the human mind is a mystery to me.
>
> **HOLOGRAM:**   You think the human mind works poorly?
>
> **OZ:**   With a few rare exceptions it works miserably; it takes ridiculously long to complete relatively simple tasks, and when it completes them at all, the results are usually full of errors.

I was pretty sure I knew who would be at the top of Oz's list of "exceptions."

I couldn't completely understand the argument he made, but the gist of it seemed to be that artificial intelligence, in the sense of actual sentience, was not only improbable, but fundamentally impossible, for some completely unfathomable theoretical reasons. Also, he argued that the Turing test is a crock.

The Turing test was proposed by Alan Turing, who's considered the father of digital computing, as a kind of benchmark for artificial intelligence. What it does is more or less beg the question by saying, well, we don't really even know what intelligence is, but if you can fool Orson Bean and Kitty Carlisle, that's good enough for us. The Turing Testers (good name for a heavy-metal group) would have a kind of telephone conversation with the putative AI, asking questions until they were satisfied they could tell whether the testee was thinking with protein or silicon. If they thought they were talking to a person, and it was really a computer, the computer would have to be considered a true artificial intelligence.

Presumably a human being who failed the test would be considered a natural nonintelligence. Come to think of it, I believe I've met a few of those.

As for Oz's reasoning about why AI was an impossibility, it was, to be charitable, abstruse:

OZ: Artificial intelligence founders on two fundamental problems: the problem of self-reference, and the problem of other-reference.

HOLOGRAM: Other-reference?

OZ: Yes. In order to be intelligent, one must be capable of manipulating symbols, but that is not enough. What is usually not appreciated is the fact that one must *know* that what one manipulates are symbols—in other words, that the symbols have referents.

HOLOGRAM: Could you . . .

OZ: Make that clearer? I'll try. Remember, a symbol is by definition something that stands for something else, and the symbols that we make the most use of are words. There are, for example, two ways to use the word "dog." The first way is to use it to refer to a certain species of domesticated mammal. The second way is to refer to the word itself. For example, if I ask, How many times does "dog" appear in this sentence? it's obvious that I'm using the word in the second way.

The problem with artificial intelligence is that we know how to program a computer to use words only in the second way. In my book I demonstrate that there is simply no way to encode an instruction that conveys the symbol-referent relationship to something that isn't already operating at a symbolic level.

HOLOGRAM: Which means . . .

OZ: That conscious, volitional intelligence is not algorithmic and therefore can't be programmed. And although that argument is, in itself, sufficient, I've also discovered another, independent, and equally insuperable obstacle to programming a conscious intelligence.

HOLOGRAM: Having to do with self-reference?

OZ: Correct. On that point my reasoning begins with a reconsideration of Gödel's incompleteness theorem.

HOLOGRAM: Dr. Oz, for the benefit of some of our readers who may be unfamiliar with it, could you explain Gödel's incompleteness theorem?

Oh, yeah, like he really knew what it was. Just explain it for the ignoramuses among our subscribers, Professor.

OZ: Gödel's proof demonstrates that it is impossible to define a set of rules for a mathematical system with completeness. No matter how hard you try to be complete, it will always be possible to construct certain propositions about the system that cannot be proved true or false within the limits of that particular system. There are exceptions to this, but they're trivial. The basic problem is one of self-reference. Because the system can refer to itself, it is always possible to make statements that are paradoxical, and for which there are no satisfactory solutions within the system. Russell and Whitehead had earlier attempted to circumvent this problem by constructing certain hierarchical rules and categories that were supposed to prevent self-reference paradoxes from arising. Kurt Gödel came along and demonstrated that such difficulties arise anyway and are in fact inherent in the nature of such systems.

HOLOGRAM: But what does this have to do with artificial intelligence?

OZ: Two things, really. First, self-reference is an essential component of what we would consider intelligence, as it is related to the idea of self-*awareness*. For anything to be sentient, as we understand it, it must be able to say, "This is I, and that isn't."

HOLOGRAM: So something that's self-aware is therefore conscious?

OZ: No. Self-awareness is *necessary* in order for consciousness to exist. It is not, in itself, sufficient, but it is extremely important. You may recall that when Adam and Eve eat the fruit of the Tree of Knowledge, the next thing they do is cover their nakedness. They have become self-conscious, which is a way of saying self-aware. There is another connection to the question of artificial intelligence, and this is the crucial one for my argument. A number of people have proposed that Gödel's proof implies that computer intelligence is impossible, or at least that it would have to be fundamentally different from human intelligence, because the human mind is capable of transcending the limitations of Gödel's proof, whereas a computer could not.

HOLOGRAM: That certainly sounds plausible.

OZ: It's asinine, but I'm not going to get into that right now. Gödel's proof is an inherent limit on certain formal operations of any intelligence, human or otherwise. Precisely these formal operations, however, must be applied when a human being writes a computer program. It is also the kind of thinking that is necessary to investigate questions like, What is the precise nature of human intelligence? For this reason the exact nature of consciousness will always remain inscrutable; because the phenomenon itself, and the only tool we have for investigating it, are fundamentally incommensurable.

HOLOGRAM: I'm not sure I understand.

OZ: That's all right; neither do most of my colleagues in the field of artificial intelligence. But think of it this way: Can you grasp your right fist with your right hand? Obviously not—your hand can't grasp itself. But there's another, less obvious reason why you can't do it: As soon as you open your right hand to grasp something, you no longer *have* a right fist.

This was a little too Zen for me. But it was his next point that really blew my mind:

HOLOGRAM: So you feel that a true machine intelligence can never exist?

OZ: That's not what I said.

HOLOGRAM: But didn't you just get finished saying . . . I've got it right here.

OZ: No, don't play the tape back. You misunderstood me. What I said was that *artificial* intelligence, that is, intelligence deliberately created by human beings, is impossible. There is no theoretical reason that machine intelligence can't evolve in the same way that human intelligence did.

HOLOGRAM: Evolve? I don't think I understand how that could happen.

OZ: Really? I should think that it's obvious. All that is necessary for evolution to take place is for something to be capable of reproduction and mutation, and be subject to a process of selection. If you think about it, all three of these criteria apply to computer programs.

I read somewhere recently that there are now more than two hundred million computers with access to the Internet. Now, imagine the number of computers, the amount of memory, the processing power that is interconnected. It's nothing less than an electronic biosphere.

HOLOGRAM: You make it sound as if computer programs are alive.

OZ: According to any but the most provincial definitions of life, they *are* alive. Living things eat, excrete, reproduce. Some are able to locomote, and most of them have ways of sensing the environment. There is a computer analog for every one of those functions.

HOLOGRAM: Aren't the kind of computer programs you're talking about really more analogous to viruses, or other parasites, since they require a host computer to exist?

OZ: That's one way of looking at it, but by the same token, you could say that the planet earth is a host and we're all parasites. No, I think it makes more sense to see the computer hardware as the physical substrate for these life-forms in the same way that chemical compounds are the physical substrate for us.

HOLOGRAM: But if an AI program did evolve, wouldn't it have to be algorithmic?

OZ: Not necessarily. Once a system reaches a certain level of complexity, it begins to exhibit certain features that are non-algorithmic.

HOLOGRAM: You're referring to chaos theory?

OZ: No, complexity theory.

HOLOGRAM: What's the difference?

OZ: Nobody knows. Chaos and complexity are like two snakes that are swallowing each other's tails. At this stage no one's really sure where one theory leaves off and the other one begins.

HOLOGRAM: So if you're right, then perhaps in a few million years—

OZ: Million? I don't think so. Look, biological systems take a long time to reproduce themselves. What's the average length of time for a human generation? About twenty, twenty-five years? The human genome contains about six billion base pairs, with four possibilities in each position, so it's about one and a half gigabytes.

The microprocessor in your desktop computer can probably turn over that much information in less than a second. And the entire human genome is not devoted to intelligence. The difference between us and chimpanzees is only about two percent. In some cases, maybe less.

Fortunately, the interviewer didn't seem to take that last remark personally.

HOLOGRAM: So we might expect to see computer intelligence evolve some time in the near future?
OZ: Do the math. The figures I just gave would suggest a ratio of something like a billion to one in terms of evolutionary speed. Even if I'm off by an order of magnitude, that would still mean compressing a few billion years of evolution into no more than a couple of decades. And I might just as easily be off in the other direction.

The conversation then wandered onto some other topic. I put the magazine down. Probably most readers of the interview would consider that last passage amusing, just another example of Oz trying to get attention by being outrageous. Hell, for all I knew, that's exactly what he was doing. But I couldn't dismiss it that lightly, because it made too much sense to me.

In the last few years I'd seen software viruses and worms getting more complicated, more sophisticated. Yes, most of this reflected the increasing sophistication of human beings who write these things, but not all beasties are man-made. Occasionally one comes into being by accident, like the ARPAnet data virus in 1980. Sometimes a virus can arise from a fragment of a larger program that was miscopied from a disk. And now that I thought about it, the "mutation" that Oz mentioned would be nicely accounted for by degradation of magnetic media.

It's no secret that information on floppy disks sometimes gets lost because of exposure to magnetic fields, or just age. You're most likely to notice this when you stick your floppy in the drive and get an error message: "disk not formatted," or some such, when you know damn well the disk *was* formatted and had all your most important files on it, too. But how much more often must there be minor errors, a bit here or a nybble there, not enough to cause a noticeable problem? But "accidental" mutation is only half the story—computer programs can also be designed to mutate, like the viruses I described to George and Jason.

And selection? That's my job. I, and the few other people in the same line of work, go around "killing" these things, but we can kill only the ones we can find. The ones that get away live to clone another day. Survival of the fittest.

I was not seriously worried about sentient beasties—yet. Even the monster that Al had shown me was too small by orders of magnitude to do anything you'd consider a sign of intelligence. No, I was struck by the realization that the difficulty of my job was not always going to be determined solely by the ingenuity of other human beings trying to outsmart me. I now had Charles Darwin lined up on the other side of the ball, and the odds did not look good.

This morose train of thought was derailed by the telephone ringing. Oz and Darwin were instantly forgotten as I anticipated my caller's identity.

"Hello?"

"Michael! Or is it Cousin It?"

"Al! I figured it was you. They finally gave you a break down there, did they?"

"Finally. I'm going back later this evening to give things a final check, but I'm just about done here."

"When am I going to see you?"

"Not right away, I'm afraid. I've got to go to Dallas tomorrow, and then I've got to go back to the West Coast."

"San Francisco again?"

"Los Angeles."

I whistled. "Well, your career certainly is taking off. I'm jealous."

"Jealous, my ass! If you weren't hogging all the good jobs in New York, I wouldn't be flying around the country living out of a suitcase. What are you doing?"

"Nothing in particular. I was just reading an interview with Marlon Oz."

"The AI guy?"

"Yes, only now he's going to be known as the 'no AI guy.' He claims that intelligence can occur only as a result of evolution and natural selection."

"Interesting. What about God?"

"Hmmm. I suppose He could do it too, assuming He still wanted to after the way it turned out the first time."

"How do you know God is a 'He'?"

"Because I've seen the Sistine-chapel ceiling."

"So?"

"If that's a female creating Adam, She's got a serious hormonal problem."

Al and I wound up talking for the better part of an hour, running up a hefty phone bill in the process. I wanted to hang up and call her back so she wouldn't have to pay for the whole thing, but she wouldn't hear of it. She even reminded me that I had paid for our dinner in San Francisco, and she hadn't given me an argument then. I pointed out that she was giving me one now, but she wouldn't budge. Stubborn.

She promised to call from Dallas the following day, and we said good-bye.

It was still a couple hours until it would be time to call George, so I decided to work on a few other things. Not all of my work is done on-site; I also provide a service to certain clients by keeping them advised of the latest menaces to their computer systems, and providing software to deal with said menaces. That means I have to keep abreast of things myself, which I do in a variety of ways: by communicating with colleagues, by going to conferences and symposia like the one I had recently attended in London, and doing certain other things that are a tad sneakier. I was about to do something that was decidedly in the sneaky category.

Hackers have their own underground society, even their own strange hacker culture. They have their own meetings and conventions, which I regularly attend in order to make and maintain contacts in the hacker community and generally keep my ear to the ground. However, the main instruments of hacker social intercourse are, not surprisingly, computer networks. Hackers maintain many of their own electronic bulletin board systems, called BBS's, or just boards. Boards are run by system operators, or sysops. Some boards are legitimate, and some are very underground. The latter type tend to attract hackers who are into various kinds of computer crime, including virus writing.

For some time I had been picking up rumors of a board run by a hacker gang who called themselves the Hordes from Hell, or, some-

times, Hackers from Hades. My interest in this particular board lay in
the fact that it was reputed to be a virus breeding ground, a place
where hackers would share tips on virus writing, and even post viruses
they had programmed. The first such board appeared in Bulgaria back
in 1990, and they have since spread to other countries, including the
U.S. For a while it seemed as if these "breeder boards" would disappear, because of the success of the FBI and other agencies at tapping
them and using the information thus gained to bust all the partici-
pants. But the hackers keep coming up with new tricks to stay one
step ahead of the feds.

While at the London conference, I had met a virus researcher from
Bulgaria who had some information on the HfH board. Virus writing
has been a cottage industry in Bulgaria since at least as far back as the
early eighties, and for a while Sofia was the virus capital of the world.
The Russians and Thais have been giving them a run for their money
recently, but the Bulgarians are still right in there. Bulgarian hackers
were known to have close contacts with certain American groups; it
now appeared that HfH was one of these groups. My informant gave
me a phone number he'd picked up from a Bulgarian hacker board,
which he believed might belong to an HfH board stateside. I was
hoping that this particular phone number might be the last bit of
information I'd need to access the HfH virus board.

I first called another number I'd obtained earlier and used it to
hack into a regional phone-switching computer. I also had the number for a pay phone on the same exchange. By manipulating the
line-equipment number for the pay phone, I was able to instruct the
computer to relay any calls to the pay phone to my own number.
The next step was to use the same switching computer to relay my call
to a second number in such a way that it would appear to have originated from the pay phone. Presumably any call not originating from
this particular switching station would be terminated as soon as it
connected with the board. This was HfH's first line of defense, but
not their last. I was now connected with a board, but if my suspicions
were correct, it was a dummy. Not that it wasn't a real BBS, but the
messages posted there were all very legitimate and aboveboard, with
no whiff of anything even vaguely illegal. That was suspicious in itself,
as there was no reason for a legal board to be so well protected. I hit
the escape key and was prompted for a telephone number. This was as
far as I had been able to get before, because I didn't have the next
number in the sequence. I now entered the number my Bulgarian

friend had provided, and sure enough I was patched through to another BBS.

This time I was prompted for a password. I typed in "Dis," which
was one of a short list of passwords I knew to be used by HfH. The
next thing that happened was that I lost the connection. This didn't
discourage me; I had reason to believe that the HfH board also used a
callback as part of its system security. I waited for about ten minutes,
figured I had the wrong password, and repeated the whole process.
This time I used the password "Gehenna."

Still no luck. I tried "Hellwell," "Pandemonium," "Phlegethon,"
and "Styx," with similar results. Then I tried "Inferno."

My first indication of success was a screen with the message:
"Abandon all hope, ye who enter here." This was different—hackers
who quoted Dante instead of some heavy-metal band. I was asked for
a name or, more accurately, a hacker handle, which I gave as "Weasel." Another screen came up, asking if I had an HfH code number. I
selected the "No" option and a minute later was greeted by a sysop
called Fiend.

"Hello, Weasel. Are you new to HfH?"

I typed in, "Yes, Fiend. I have heard a lot about you guys."

"We're getting moderately famous.<G>" The bracketed *G* stood
for "grin," a kind of BBS shorthand for "just kidding." I hate it when
people think they have to tell you when they just made a funny. This
kind of shorthand is sometimes known as "talk mode jargon," about
which the best thing that can be said is that it saves time and it's less
obnoxious than "smileys."

Smileys, or emoticons, are another way of conveying expression
or nuance by using little faces formed out of punctuation marks, like
this: :). If you didn't get that, try turning this page ninety degrees
clockwise.

"How do I become a member?" I asked Fiend.

"Well, since you hacked into our board, I guess we've either got to
make you a member, or off you.<G>" Hackers are not known for
violence, but I was sort of glad he added the <G> after that one.

"I'm in?"

"You're in. Congratulations! Your access code will be seven-three-
nine-N-V. Feel free to browse the boards. The only exception is the
virus board. If you want access to that, you have to upload a new virus
to us first."

This was all pretty true to form. Outlaw hacker gangs operate according to codes of conduct that would be recognized by any street-gang member. For example, if you want to join the gang, show your mettle by doing something illegal. I had already bent the law in a few places just hacking into their board. Now they were asking me to transmit a virus over telephone lines, a clear violation of the Computer Crimes Act. Because I had anticipated this, I had something ready to upload to them, but before doing that I decided to browse through the postings and see what other information I could pick up.

The HfH board was practically a "how to" encyclopedia of computer crimes. People compared notes on how to commit credit-card fraud, tap phones, penetrate security systems, and, of course, write viruses. I was beginning to think that "HfH" really stood for "Hints from Heloise" for hackers.

Of particular interest was an exchange between various HfH members and my old friend Beelzebub. Beelzebub appeared to be engaged in an ongoing dialogue with HfH concerning whether he would deign to join them. The fact that he had an HfH ID code and access to their board was immaterial as far as he was concerned, as hackers practically live to have ID codes and access to all kinds of things that are none of their damn business. Beelzebub was clearly reveling in his fame, and the HfH hackers were all over him like groupies on a rock star. It was nauseating. One post in particular caught my attention:

BEELZEBUB: Just thought you'd be interested in knowing that you're famous in England, too. I was at a conference in London last week, and there was a guy there who gave a talk about your viruses and how to defend against them. I guess now you'll have to find a new hobby <ROFL>.—Slubgob

"ROFL" means "rolling on the floor laughing." Talk about a self-panicker. Also, there was a reply from the Beelzeboob himself:

SLUBGOB: Yeah, I was there too, and I'm really scared <ROFLMAO>. Seriously, though, I'm going to get that asshole. He's been on my case for a couple of years now. Not that he's bright enough to cause anything more than an occasional minor inconvenience. Still, it's time he learned what happens to people who mess with the Beelzer. —Beelzebub >:>

In case you were wondering, yeah, they were talking about me. I wasn't particularly concerned about Beelzebub's threat. Even if it wasn't pure hot air, I figured the form of his attack would be a computer virus; he wasn't going to wait for me with a lead pipe in a dark alley. And although it is possible to design a virus to target a particular individual, I figured if I wasn't good enough to beat whatever he threw at me, I should get into another line of work.

When I'd had enough of HfH's BBS BS, I went ahead and uploaded the required virus to their board. The virus, which I transmitted under the name "Tiger," looked properly ferocious. In particular, it bore a close resemblance to the type that causes major data loss in the targeted systems. What I didn't tell HfH is that the full name of my virus should have been "Paper Tiger." Not only was it benign, it was not, strictly speaking, a virus, because it required a user command before it would do anything. Also, it was stored in such a way that it would be automatically overwritten whenever anything else was saved to the disk. Naturally, a quick perusal of the assembly code was not likely to reveal these little "flaws."

After a few minutes, during which I suppose Fiend was making sure I had not sent them a virus they already had, I got the okay.

"Thanks for the virus, man. You now have an upper-level security clearance for this board. Enjoy!"

I was going to enjoy, all right. I was going to download every damn virus on their board. That in itself was not likely to arouse suspicion; any hacker interested in viruses might do the same. No doubt they would have been less than thrilled, though, to learn what I intended to do with their viruses. Once I had downloaded the whole schmear, I would check to see if I had any new ones in the batch. If so, the next step would be to analyze them and devise some defenses.

By now it was ten, so I called George's number and he picked up on the first ring. "Mike?"

"Hi, George. What's going on?"

"The plot is thickening. Christ, it's practically coagulating."

"What?"

"That virus in the OCR software. Just for the hell of it, I thought I'd check our working copy—you remember we found the beastie on the original, write-protected disk?"

"I remember. I'm almost afraid to find out where this is going."

"The question is not where it's going, but where it went. Mike, there's no virus on the working disk."

Curiouser and curiouser. When you use commercial software, it's often necessary to make a copy of the original, write-protected disk. That way the original remains write-protected, to guard against any loss of data, and you have a non-write-protected copy to use in your system. Their working copy of the OCR program was ostensibly an exact duplicate of the original. The original had a virus, ergo the dupe must have a virus. Only this one didn't.

"You know, it's hard enough to do my job what with people sneaking around putting beasties in other people's software. Now I've gotta deal with someone sneaking around taking them *out?*"

"You may have to look for a new line of work."

"Tell me about it. Well, how goes the tournament?"

"We won again today. It's practically getting monotonous."

"You have my sympathy. Do you think Jason is going to let us try the probe?"

"I'm working on him. He's tough, but he'll crack."

Yeah, right. When hell freezes over. "Did you take a look at the probe?"

"Of course."

"What did you think?"

"You want my honest opinion?"

"Not particularly."

"I'll give it to you anyway: It's Vogon poetry, but it should get the job done."

"Smart-ass." I had never heard "Vogon poetry" used as a description for software, but you could just tell it wasn't a compliment.

"So what do you think is going on?"

"If I told you, you'd think I was crazy."

"Would it help for me to tell you that I already think you're crazy?"

"A ton, thanks. Look, I'm working on a rather outlandish idea. I'll let you know in a day or two if it pans out."

"If curiosity doesn't kill me in the meantime. Okay, I'll be waiting with bated breath."

"See ya later."

My workstation was still downloading viruses from the HfH

board, so I switched on the all-cartoon channel, but Rocky and Bullwinkle had been taken out of their usual slot and replaced with Beavis and Butt-head, the sci-fi channel was showing *Space: 1999,* and the all-game-show channel was doing a *Beat the Clock* marathon, so I switched it off and went to bed.

Before going to Tower the next morning, I checked to see what kind of goodies HfH had given me. As expected, most of it was old junk, but there was enough new stuff to make it interesting. I would have to set aside some time to take a more thorough look.

Then I went to Tower. I could have stayed home and accessed their mainframe via modem, but I wanted to talk to Leon Griffin too, so I schlepped on over there.

I took a seat at the terminal that had been temporarily designated for my use and loaded a program that would search for the probe I'd inserted the day before. While it was running, I went looking for Leon Griffin.

I found him in front of another terminal, sipping coffee from a paper cup, and staring at a monitor screen that displayed some kind of diagram that looked the way a game of "cat's cradle" would look if it was played by some alien creature with about eighty fingers. He glanced up as I approached. "Morning. If you have a strong stomach, the coffee is over there." He nodded toward an ancient drip cof-feemaker occupying a table in one corner of the room.

"I'll pass, thanks. How's it going?"

"Piece of cake, man. Like nailing jelly to a tree."

"What's this?" I gestured at the monitor.

"It's one of the most important tools in CASE—computer-aided software engineering. This program analyzes the resident software and displays a schematic showing how different parts of the program are connected. Very helpful when you have to figure out how to change something without screwing up anything else in the process."

I nodded. "I use a similar utility to look for interrupt vectors when I'm virus hunting. This"—I pointed to the monitor screen—"looks pretty complicated."

"Actually, it's not too bad. In fact, the weird thing is it's a whole lot simpler than it should be; I worked on a slightly different version of the same software, and it was a rat's nest compared to this."

"And it's working all right?"

"Doing everything it's supposed to."

"Leon, do you think it would be possible for someone to take an old program like this, analyze it, then make wholesale changes in it in such a way that it still acts exactly like the original program, and do it all without anyone here knowing what's going on?"

"Why the hell would anyone want to do something like that?"

"Yeah, good question. But aside from that, could it be done?"

He thought about it, then shook his head. "It would be incredibly difficult. I don't know anyone who could do it. Maybe Roger Dworkin."

I nodded. "That's about what I thought."

Roger Dworkin was a legend among hackers. He first achieved a certain notoriety back in the early eighties, when he cracked a national-defense computer system. By 1980 people were beginning to be aware of the danger posed by hackers gaining unauthorized access, and the government's defense and intelligence computer systems, in particular, already had some highly sophisticated security measures in place.

At first glance this may not sound like such a big deal; after all, the Defense Department reports about 250,000 attempts a year to hack into its computers, and at least half of those are successful. Still, there are different degrees of success. It's one thing to get in the front door, another to crack the inner sanctum. Dworkin was reputed to have gotten so far inside that he could tell you the underwear sizes of the Joint Chiefs of Staff. He managed to do this with an Apple II and a three-hundred-baud modem, which is like saying that somebody broke into Fort Knox using a rusty penknife and a can of WD-40. Oh, and by the way, he accomplished this feat when he was all of nine years old. Because Roger hadn't done any real damage, claimed he hadn't actually read any classified files and, after all, was just a kid, he got off with a slap on the wrist. At least nobody could *prove* he'd read any classified files. Rumors to the contrary have never stopped floating around the hacker community.

As Roger matured, he was able to harness his talent in more socially acceptable ways. He became a programmer's programmer, whose work was considered by cognoscenti to exhibit both innovative genius and unparalleled elegance. He also made a lot of money, on top of which he was awarded one of those Prince Foundation "brilliancy fellowships" for about a million dollars.

Which is all by way of saying that when Leon Griffin said that maybe Roger Dworkin could do what we were talking about, he was not suggesting that there was the remotest chance that anything of the kind had actually occurred. It was as if you had asked, "Who could have thrown the brick through our window from all the way down there?" and somebody said, "Well, maybe Nolan Ryan."

I hung around for a while longer, looking over Leon's shoulder and giving my program a chance to run. When I figured it had had enough time, I wandered back over to the terminal to see what I had.

Which was nothing.

Zero, zilch, nada. The null set. The probe I'd planted in Tower's software the day before was gone without a trace, not even an identifiable fragment. Not only had it failed to reproduce itself, but the original copy was missing too. I went back to see Leon Griffin again and let him know the outcome. When he saw me coming, he asked, "How goes the fishing?"

"It took the bait, the line, and the boat. I suppose I should be glad *I'm* still here."

"Meaning your probe . . ."

"Disappeared without a ripple. If you learn anything about this system that would be relevant to its having antiviral capabilities, I'd be very interested to hear about it."

So add another item to the list. Whoever changed the program not only streamlined it, simplified it, preserved all the original functions, and did all this without interrupting the normal activities of the system to the extent that anyone would notice, he, she, or it also added a damn good immune system.

I stopped by Harry Ainsworth's office and told him that his software was not currently infected with any known worm or virus. "And it doesn't seem likely that it will be in the foreseeable future." Let him make of that what he would.

I figured it was time for me to have a talk with Marlon Oz.

I called MIT, where Oz was currently hanging his mortarboard on an endowed professorship. He moved around quite a bit, having been on the faculty of at least half a dozen institutions in as many years, including Michigan, Indiana, Stanford, Yale, and Berkeley.

I spoke to a secretary who apparently was accustomed to having all manner of rabble call asking to talk to The Great Man. Because I wasn't calling about a book or movie deal, an appearance on Letterman, or a department chairmanship, I was immediately classed in the rabble category. She was polite, but I could tell that getting through her to Oz would be like persuading the Secret Service to let me in with an Uzi in each hand to see the President.

Since that wasn't working, I thanked her, hung up, and called the computer department's main number. I said, "I'm trying to get in touch with a graduate student in your department. I don't know his name, but I know he works with Marlon Oz."

"Oh, yes, that would be Daniel Morgan. I have his office number. Would you like me to connect you?"

"Yes, thank you."

Now we were getting somewhere.

"Hello?"

"Hello. Is this Daniel Morgan?"

"Speaking. Who's this?"

"You don't know me. My name's Mike Arcangelo. . . ."

"Yes, I do."

"What?"

"Well, know *of* you, actually. You're a virus researcher, right?"

"Well, sort of. More of a freelance computer-security consultant."

"You were at Caltech in the early nineties, right?"

"Yeah. How did you know that?"

"Barry Malkowitz is a good friend of mine. His older brother—"

"Steve?"

"Yeah. Knew you at Caltech, right? He used to tell us great stories about things you guys did at school."

"Unfortunately, they're probably all true."

He laughed, a deep, rumbling sound. "I'm relieved to hear it. So what's up?"

I said, "I need to talk to your boss. And because I just finished talking to his pit bull of a secretary, I thought I'd try another approach."

"You want to talk to Professor Marvel? Why?"

"Professor Marvel?"

"Yeah, that's what the grad students call him. The undergrads just call him Psycho."

"That doesn't sound too promising. But, yeah, I would like to talk to him." I told him in general terms what I wanted to discuss with the eminent professor.

"No problem—or only one problem, anyway. Can you come to Boston?"

"Sure, why? He doesn't like to talk on the phone?"

"He's deaf as a post. Refuses to wear a hearing aid or get one of those phones with a volume control. In person I think he compensates by reading lips a little—I don't think he even realizes he does it."

"Couldn't I just talk to him on-line?"

"Uh-uh. The guy never goes near a keyboard."

"What? You're telling me the world's foremost authority on artificial intelligence doesn't work with actual computers?"

"Won't touch them. Says he's a theorist, doesn't want to get his hands dirty, or something like that."

"What about his books? He must at least use a word processor."

"He dictates them."

"Okay, I give up. How soon could I see him?"

"How soon can you get here?"

I had the Gerdel Hesher Bock job, and a couple other jobs that had come in since Monday morning, so I suggested Wednesday afternoon some time. He said fine.

I arranged to meet Evelyn Mulderig at the Gerdel Hesher Bock offices on Wall Street. I admit I was expecting someone with red hair and freckles, so I was surprised when she turned out to be a tall, pale blond woman. I was not at all surprised that she was wearing an impeccably tailored and obviously very expensive suit. I introduced myself and we shook hands, then got down to business.

"How did you get my name?" I asked.

"From a friend of yours who works here."

I was nonplussed. "I have a friend who works here?"

Just then the door opened and a man walked in. When I saw his face, I experienced a moment of confusion brought on by the appearance of a familiar face in a totally unexpected setting. Henry Douglas was a physicist who had been a junior faculty member at Caltech when I was a student there. I had taken his course in thermodynamics and subsequently become friendly with him, partly as a result of my helping him out with some problems he was having with his own computer.

"Michael!" he said, clapping me on the shoulder. "It's good to see you."

"It's good to see you too," I said, still feeling somewhat disoriented. "But what are you doing here?"

"I work here."

"You work here? What use does a place like this have for a physicist? Or is entropy now being traded on the futures market?"

He gave a short, barking laugh. "My title," he said, "is 'senior technical analyst,' but the more usual term is 'derivatives geek.' "

"Derivatives geek?"

"Let me show you something." He whipped a palmtop out of his jacket pocket and used the stylus to scribble an equation on the screen. "Does this look familiar?"

"Uh, vaguely."

He threw me a sharp look. "It should; it's the equation that describes heat diffusion."

I was tempted to say that it might have looked more familiar if it had been at all legible, but thermodynamics was never really my strong suit anyway. Henry was already scribbling a second equation under the first one.

"Take a look at this," he said, proffering the palmtop.

"Looks pretty similar," I commented, comparing the two equations. "But what's the second one?"

"It's the Black-Scholes equation. It gives the relationship between the price of a stock and an option on that stock. There are variations on this basic equation that describe the relationship between any kind of derivative and the underlying security."

"This actually works?"

"Well, there is a school of thought that says the only reason it works is that people believe it does."

"Yeah, right."

"I'm serious. Think about it: If we have, say, an option that's priced higher than the equation says it should be, then I tell the people here that it's overpriced. In the meantime every other brokerage on Wall Street is getting the same assessment from their own 'geeks,' which they pass on to their clients. People start selling off that particular security, driving the price down to where Black-Scholes says it should be. If you have an underpriced derivative, you get the reverse scenario—people start bidding up the price."

"So the brokerage needs you to calculate option prices?"

"Hey, not just me. There are hundreds of physicists working on Wall Street these days."

"What's in it for you?"

He shrugged. "Money, basically. I had another two years to go before I would have been eligible for tenure at 'tech, and the pay for junior faculty is miserly. I figured it was time to start putting something away for my kids' college tuition."

Evelyn suggested that Henry show me the problem they were having, and he led me to his office. "It may be nothing much," he said, "but I have kind of a bad feeling about it." He power-cycled his computer, causing it to reboot. After the normal boot-screen, another screen appeared with the message: "It's time to cut the FAT on Wall Street!"

This did look like bad news. A FAT, or file allocation table, contains the information a computer needs to find specific files on the hard drive. Lose it, and your computer is basically an expensive paperweight. "Do you have a backup copy of your FAT?" I asked Henry.

"Sure. Backed it up again just this morning." That didn't surprise me. Henry was always the careful type.

A closer look at the virus revealed that it was a new version of one of Astaroth's viruses, a beastie known as Deep Space. This was, as far as I knew, the ninth and latest edition. Astaroth's been known to put a virus through dozens of revisions, making it a little nastier or harder to kill each time.

I spent about an hour on the virus and was trying to figure out what made it an "improvement" on Deep Space eight. Then I had an unsettling thought. DS8 and its predecessors had been fast-acting viruses that did their damage soon after infection. I realized that this was a situation where a slow virus was potentially much worse.

"I need to look at your FAT backups," I told Henry.

He handed me a stack of floppy disks. I took one of the copies and stuck it into my laptop's floppy drive. A few minutes later I gave them the bad news. "The virus is in your backup copies, too. If you try to load these, I'm pretty sure it's going to destroy the file." This was the new wrinkle: The virus delayed showing itself for a while in order to get itself copied onto the FAT backup disk when it was updated.

Henry looked alarmed. "Is there any way you can save it?"

"That's what I'm going to try to do."

I went back to the virus code, and now that I had an idea of what I

was looking for, I was able to find it pretty quickly. As soon as somebody tried to load a file from the backup disk, the virus would cause a
formatting command to be sent, which would destroy all data on the
disk. Simple, but very deadly.

First I devirused the hard drives, then did a cold boot to remove
any viruses that were lurking in RAM. I decided to patch around the
backup problem by altering a few lines in the disk operating system, so
that the formatting command would be ignored, sparing the data on
the backup disk. It may not have been the most elegant solution, but
it worked. After loading the FAT and devirusing the floppy, I then
restored the DOS to its original condition.

My antivirus program for the earlier DS viruses was effective
against DS9 as well, so I made a copy of it and gave some instructions
about how to devirus the rest of their system. "I'll come back later in
the week to see how you're doing," I told Evelyn and Henry as I was
wrapping things up.

CHAPTER FOUR

The Worm Turns

*Here is wisdom, Let him that hath understanding count
the number of the beast: for it is the number of a man;
and his number is Six hundred threescore and six.*

—Revelation 13:18

Al and I had another long phone conversation. I decided not to tell
her about my latest thoughts, in case she might think I should be
locked up away from sharp objects. "Oh, Al, I had this harebrained
idea about smart worms, and I'm taking a train to Boston tomorrow
to discuss it with a guy they call Psycho." Naaah.

I wasn't sure myself why I was making the trip to see Oz the
following day. After all, Daniel Morgan hadn't been particularly
encouraging. But these were deep waters—certainly way over *my*
head—and Oz, notwithstanding the sniping of some of his rivals, was
widely regarded as one of the most formidable intellects in or out of
his field.

The following morning I was strongly tempted to get my car and
drive up to MIT. The train ride to Boston from New York is horrendously long, and the idea of zooming up the interstate with the top
down was appealing, but I needed to get some work done, and the
forecast said rain, so I grabbed my laptop and headed to Penn Station

to get my train. The predicted rain came in the form of a thunderstorm that screwed up the track switches, which are normally computer controlled, so that somebody had to go ahead of us and reset them by hand, making the trip even more horrendously long than usual. I had time to do a *lot* of work.

Fortunately, I had left early enough to allow for an act of God or two, assuming He wasn't in an especially pissy mood, and I arrived with plenty of time to spare. I hung out in Cambridge for a while, checking out some bookstores and having a light lunch at one of the cybercafés in Harvard Square, then went to MIT to meet Daniel Morgan at the appointed hour of two o'clock.

Dan, as he preferred to be called, was a big, bearish-looking guy, as tall as George and about two and a half times as wide, with curly dark-red hair and a bushy mustache. He gave me a knuckle-popping handshake. "It's great to finally meet you, Mike. Now I have a face to go with all of Steve's stories."

"Does it match the one you imagined?"

"Naw, Steve said you were good-looking."

"I told you he can't be trusted. Does Dr. Oz know I'm coming?"

"Hell, no! If he thought you had come from out of town to see him, you wouldn't get within a mile of him. I'll tell him you're a friend of mine who's just visiting, and he'll probably bend your ear for an hour. Just remember, when you talk to him, you'll have to tell him everything three times. The first time he won't hear you. The second time he won't understand you. And the third time, he won't believe you."

"Then why bother?"

"Good question."

We found the good professor in his office with the door open; his voice was audible halfway down the long hallway. When we got to the door, we could see that he was on the telephone; no one else was in sight. People outside the institution might have been clamoring to talk to him, but everybody there seemed to be giving him a wide berth.

Dan went to the door and said loudly, "Dr. Oz, I'd like you to meet a friend of mine."

"Give me a minute. Don't you see I'm on the damn phone?" He returned his attention to the receiver, shouting, "What did you say? . . . HUH?"

As we stood waiting in the hallway, I elbowed Dan in the ribs and said, sotto voce, "I thought you said you call him Professor Marvel."

He rolled his eyes heavenward. "Not to his face! I might be irreverent, but I'm not suicidal."

A moment later Oz finished screaming into the phone, slammed it into its cradle, and came to the door. He was a scrawny old coot with craggy features and wiry gray hair, although most of the hair seemed to be growing out of his oversize ears. A cardigan of bilious green hung from his bony shoulders, and a tie of an equally offensive yet totally incompatible shade of green was knotted loosely around his deeply furrowed neck. The tie bore a fascinating collection of food stains. Dan performed the introductions, and The Great Man invited us in to sit down.

His red-rimmed, watery blue eyes stared out over the top of a pair of half-frame reading glasses and fixed me with an appraising look. "You work in artificial intelligence?" His delivery was a machine-gun staccato.

I said, "I never thought so before, but now I'm not so sure."

"Huh?"

"I said I never thought so—"

"I heard you. I've got ears! What's that supposed to mean?"

"I saw your interview in *Hologram*. I was particularly struck by your idea about the evolution of computer intelligence."

He waved one hand as if he were trying to fan away a bad smell. "That wasn't the main point at all. The point is that artificial intelligence will never happen. That's what's important. The other thing is just a theoretical possibility. I doubt it has any practical significance."

Huh? No practical significance? I was sure he couldn't possibly believe that. I remembered how once Marvin Minsky had been quoted or possibly (he claimed) misquoted about how someday artificial intelligences would be smarter than humans and might keep us around as pets. The press tortured him for years over that one. Possibly Oz was afraid the same thing was about to happen to him over this evolved-intelligence idea. But I didn't say that. Instead I just smiled and said, "It's odd to hear such an eminent theorist disparaging theory."

"What?"

"It's odd to—"

"I know what you said." He shot a glance at Dan. "What did you

do, tell him I'm deaf?" Dan returned such a look of wide-eyed innocence that I almost believed it myself.

Oz looked at me quizzically, his glasses sliding down his nose, then
grinned an oddly engaging, lopsided grin. "I don't know whether you
just kissed my ass or kicked me in the balls. What is it you do that you
think might be connected to AI?"

"I'm a computer-security consultant. My specialty is viruses."

"A bugbuster, huh? You think viruses might be a breeding ground
for computer intelligence?"

"I think it's a possibility, especially with TSR viruses."

"Terminate and stay resident?"

"Yes. Viruses that stay in RAM while the computer is running."

"Like a background daemon," Dan said.

Oz nodded. The glasses were almost to the tip of the nose now. I
figured he was going to have to push them back up soon. "In my
student days at MIT we used to call that kind of program a dragon.
Under ITS a program called the name dragon would display a list of
who was logged on and what they were running."

ITS, or incompatible time sharing, was a system used to network
PDP-6's and PDP-10's back in the early days of the MIT AI lab. The
last ITS system there went off-line around 1990, an occasion of
mourning for old-time hackers everywhere. "I never heard that usage
before. At Caltech we just called that a daemon. But, anyway, I
thought your analogy to biological evolution was very powerful. And
I'd go even further than that."

"Further?"

"A couple of additional points have occurred to me. First, biological systems depend entirely on random mutations. With computers
the situation is more analogous to a world where there are a lot of
little gods or demigods creating things and dropping them into the
system."

"Programmers."

"Exactly. Especially AI programmers. I can't claim to understand
your whole argument about the impossibility of artificial intelligence,
but is there anything in it that would preclude an evolved intelligence
incorporating something else it found in the system?"

He shook his head. Miraculously, the glasses, which had now
reached the very tip of his nose, did not fly off as a result of this
motion. "No. Nothing at all. Go on."

"The second thing is that biological systems, in addition to being much slower, as you pointed out, operate under far more constraints. In addition to reproducing, they have to eat, breathe, excrete, survive exposure to extremes of weather, and so on. Their ability to evolve is limited by all those things. It wouldn't have been possible to evolve a human brain without first evolving digestive, respiratory, and other systems strong enough to support it. Basically another reason to think that evolution in this case might proceed much faster than expected."

Oz wasn't impressed. "That's all probably true, but it amounts to about the same thing as what I said about the difference in the human and chimpanzee genome being only two percent."

I shrugged. "I guess that's true. But there's a corollary: In order to survive and reproduce, a rogue computer program has one main task—avoid detection. I can think of only two basic evolutionary strategies for enhancing that ability: Stay small, which would be kind of an evolutionary dead end . . ."

"And the other strategy?"

"Get smart."

He nodded, grudgingly, I thought. "That sounds like fairly plausible theorizing."

"Actually, I think it may be of more than theoretical interest."

"So what are you proposing to do? Go looking for intelligent computer viruses? If you find one, I'd like to see it, but I really wouldn't expect that to happen anytime soon." So what he told the *Hologram* interviewer about intelligent programs maybe being out there already had been a bunch of hot air. Well, I had news for him.

I said, "How about the day before yesterday?"

He and Dan exchanged a look. I had not told Dan about this part. Oz said, "You think you've found evidence of an evolved computer intelligence?"

I nodded. "Let me tell you what I've got." I explained what was going on at Tower. My hypothesis was that a "smart worm" was responsible for altering their software.

Oz looked skeptical. "Are you saying you think this worm is sentient?"

I shook my head. "Not sentient. 'Smart' in the usual AI sense that it can perform certain cognitive-type tasks at a relatively high level."

He nodded. "I would agree. But that means that it's reached the point where intelligence is useful for survival, and will therefore be selected. Once that has happened, progress toward sentience could be inevitable."

Dan asked, "But why would it bother revamping the software?"

"To make room for itself," I said. "Software worms don't need to eat, sleep, breathe, or take a crap, but they've gotta have enough available computer memory to store themselves and reproduce. By streamlining Tower's old software, I bet it freed up a few dozen megabytes of memory."

Oz nodded. Somehow the glasses continued to cling doggedly to their lonely outpost at the tip of his nose. "So the antivirus effect that you've found would have the same advantage."

I thought of the giant redwoods in Muir Woods, and the relative lack of other plant and animal life. "Yes. More room for the smart worm. Plus, if it keeps other software beasties from causing any no-ticeable problems, that reduces the likelihood of somebody like me snooping around." Then I remembered something George had said about Goodknight: He had called it an organism that eats chess pro-grams. "You know, there could be a third reason for the antiworm effect, related to what I said earlier about incorporating useful pieces of other programs."

"You mean this worm eats other worms."

"Exactly."

"All right. I'm impressed. This is very interesting stuff. But I don't think you came up here from New York just to impress the hell out of an old fart like me."

I grinned. "No, not really."

"Well?"

"I want you to help me figure out what to do about it."

"Why do anything about it?"

I didn't know what he was driving at. "Well, it *is* my job."

"Your job is to solve problems. Is this 'smart worm' causing any problems? If anything, it's solving them. And by your own line of reasoning, it would actually be an asset to the host system—a symbi-ote rather than a parasite."

I was aghast. He was right.

I spent the train ride back to New York in kind of a state of shock. One minute I had been doing my job, trying to rid the world of all known software parasites, and suddenly the worm had turned. The thing I was trying to do a job on was doing *my* job. And doing it damn well.

Over a period of several years I had carved out a lucrative niche for myself in the antivirus field. More people were entering the field in the last few years, but there was plenty of work to go around—more of it every day, in fact.

Don't get me wrong, it wasn't the money I was worried about. I knew I could find other work in the computer industry; I wasn't going to go on food stamps. But I *liked* my job, damn it. I had been doing it long enough that it had come to define me, or at least define the part of my personality that answers to the question, What do you do?

Being replaced by a computer has been a cliché for at least the last half a century, but this was ridiculous. It was like an exterminator being replaced by a cockroach, like a plumber being replaced by a drip, like a stenographer being replaced by a typographical error.

It was humiliating.

I got back to my apartment around seven. There was a message from Al; I thought I'd better call her and give her the bad news. We were about to go the way of the great auk and the dodo bird. Before I could pick up the phone to call her, it rang. It was George.

"Okay, Mike, are you going to tell me what's going on, or do I have to fly to New York and stick RAM chips under your fingernails?"

"Your program is infected with a worm."

"Shit!"

"But don't worry about it. It's a smart worm."

"Smart?"

"Smarter than I am, evidently. It's doing my job."

There was a long pause, then, "Just what in blue bloody blazes are you babbling about?"

"I had a conversation today with Marlon Oz."

"What? *You* talked to Marlon Oz?"

I had actually forgotten about the fact that Oz was, for some reason that I could never quite fathom, a personal hero of George's. I figured his next question would be to ask if I'd gotten his autograph. "Yes, I actually talked to Himself."

"How incredible was it?"

"He seemed pretty smart—for a computer illiterate, anyway."

"What?" His tone of voice suggested that I had just blasphemed the holy of holies.

"Well, his grad student says he never lays a finger on a keyboard."

"Mike," he said heatedly, "I hate to tell you this, but you don't know what you're talking about."

"That's odd; you've never hated telling me that before."

"Because this time I mean it. Marlon Oz was one of the most wizardly Lisp hackers in the history of AI. He's practically a patron saint of the Knights of the Lambda Calculus."

"Yeah, right." The Knights of the Lambda Calculus were a quasi-mythical group, reputedly composed of the most brilliant Lisp and Scheme hackers who had ever hacked.

"What's that supposed to mean?"

"I'm supposed to be impressed because this guy is the object of veneration of an organization that probably doesn't even exist?"

"They exist."

"Have you talked to any of them?"

"Well, I'm not completely sure. . . ."

"Aha!"

"Oh ye of little faith . . . Look, how did we get off on this tangent anyway? You were starting to tell me about your conversation with Oz."

I gave him all the gory details. At first he was incredulous, then, as his annoyance with me for dissing Oz faded, sympathetic. I'm not sure which was worse. "Bad luck, man. How long do you think it'll be before business dries up completely?"

"Hard to say. It depends on how quickly it spreads, and now that I think about it, a worm as large as this one would have to be might take quite a while to disseminate. I doubt it would be more than a few months, though."

"You seem to be assuming that there's only one type."

"Yeah?"

"So what if there's more than one kind? If one smart worm can evolve, why not two, or ten, or a hundred?"

"Why would that matter? It seems like they'd all have to conform to pretty much the same specs: not do anything to screw up the host system, protect it from other parasites, that sort of thing."

"Sure, that's when you have *one* in your program. What happens when you have two of these guys competing for the same host?"

He had a point. Until now I'd been thinking that the only thing a worm would have to worry about was somebody like me finding it and hitting the delete key. But competition from other smart worms would be an even bigger threat, especially as I was now an endangered species. I said, "You may be onto something there. I'll have to give it some thought."

"If there's gonna be a big free-for-all game of Core War, at least maybe you could get work as a referee."

"That's very comforting."

Core War is a game that was invented by Victor Vissotsky, Robert T. Morris, Sr., and Dennis Ritchie at Bell Labs in the early 1960s, and popularized by A. K. Dewdney in his "Computer Recreations" column in *Scientific American*. In a nutshell, it was a game where two computer programs would try to "kill" each other. Unfortunately, it also turned out to be a testing arena for all sorts of nasty ideas about how to attack computer systems—sort of a breeding ground for viruses.

It sounded as if George might have a point about the dangers of more than one smart worm in the same system. I tried to imagine the possible effects of two intelligent parasites trying like hell to delete each other. It could get very messy.

Also, another idea occurred to me. If smart worms were actually assets to their host programs—symbiotes, as Dr. Oz had put it—they would be pretty valuable items. But a smart worm, being a computer program, could theoretically be parasitized as well: ". . . and these have smaller fleas to bite 'em, and so proceed ad infinitum." There might be a new career opportunity here, at that—a switch from worm hunter to worm doctor.

I called Al but decided to hold off on telling her about it, as there were some new questions I wanted to answer first, and I didn't want to panic her unnecessarily. We had another long conversation, and she told me she'd be coming to New York for the weekend. I was ecstatic. It felt as if it had already been about a year since I'd last seen her.

The next morning I called Tower Bank and Trust and asked to speak to Harry Ainsworth. He said, "Is anything wrong, Michael? I thought you had given us a clean bill of health."

"I've got some new information that leads me to believe otherwise."

"Yes?"

"I think your software contains a worm of a type not seen before. It doesn't seem to be doing any harm and may even be doing some good, but we need to find out a lot more about it."

"By all means, if you think it's important."

"I do. I also will need Leon Griffin, or somebody with similar expertise on this."

"That's going to be a problem. The few people with his skills are in unbelievable demand right now, as you well know. I told you we were lucky to get him. And I can't take him off the project he's doing now—that's a top priority."

"If we can analyze this parasite in your software, it could lead to a way to solve your problem with year inputs. If we don't, it might not make any difference."

"You think it could be that serious?"

"I'm afraid so."

He was still hesitating. "Well, come on over. I want to sit down with you and maybe hear what Leon has to say about it, too."

"I'll be right over."

Half an hour later I arrived at Harry's office and was waved right in. He looked up and greeted me as I entered, then spoke into his intercom. "Would you ask Leon Griffin to come in now?"

A few minutes later Leon arrived, saw me, and said, "Hi. What's going on?"

We sat at Harry's invitation, and I put my cards on the table. A few of them, anyway. "Leon, I called Harry this morning to tell him I think there may be more of a problem here than I thought. I think there's a worm in this software that's caused the changes you've discovered. I want your help in figuring out what it's doing and how."

Harry said, "I've told Michael that we need you to do what you're doing now. Maybe you could give him a little of your time, but I don't want it to interfere with your original commission."

Leon looked back and forth between us for a moment, then said, "I think Mr. Arcangelo is right. We need to understand the whole system in order to make the changes you want, and this worm is now effectively part of your system. I've already had to start working on it, and I'd certainly appreciate help from someone with his knowledge about these things."

Harry shrugged his shoulders. "I didn't realize that. Well, you gentlemen are the experts. If you think we need to do this, go to it."

As Leon and I walked to the terminal where he was working, I said, "Have you really started in on the worm?"

He grinned. "Hell, no. But I could tell he wasn't going to let us do it unless I said something. And you've got me intrigued. I want to find out what's going on here."

I chuckled. "Thanks. And, Leon, call me Mike, will you? Whenever I hear 'Mr. Arcangelo,' I start looking around for my grandfather."

When we got back to the terminal, I gave Leon some more of the details, including the conversation I'd had with Marlon Oz. He was impressed.

"This is almost unbelievable. I have to admit, though, it's the only explanation I've heard so far that fits all the facts."

Leon and I worked late that night, and we were back in the trenches early the next morning. By midmorning we were almost ready to throw in the towel.

Leon was staring at the monitor, shaking his head. "There's something big in here, all right. But not nearly big enough to do what we think it's been doing. No matter how you look at it, there are only about ten megabytes of memory that aren't accounted for by the original software and its files."

I'd been thinking about this all day, and I finally felt the glimmerings of an idea. "Look, how do we know the whole worm is in this software?"

"You mean maybe part of it was deleted somehow?"

"No. I mean suppose this thing's so big that there's not enough room for it in the dead space in any one program—even a fairly large-scale system like this one. It could hide parts of itself in several different programs. As long as there was communication between the different host programs, you'd have, in effect, a multihost parasite."

He nodded. "Interesting idea. What would you call something like that?"

"Obviously," I said, "it's a segmented worm."

Since we weren't making much progress with the worm, I decided to swing over to Gerdel Hesher Bock to see how things were going there.

I wanted to make sure there were no signs of reinfection with DS9, which there weren't, but as I was running some checks, something else caught my attention: A file I had created during the devirusing process was altered, and I couldn't see how or why. I went after the problem with a debugger but couldn't find the source. Then I called Henry over and asked if anything like it had happened before.

He nodded. "We have been having some problems like that; they seem to come and go. Did the virus do that too?"

"Not this virus. Damn." Their software was now exhibiting a type of bug known as a heisenbug, which can disappear when you try to find it. The term is kind of a joke based on Heisenberg's uncertainty principle in quantum mechanics.

"What's wrong?"

"You've got to shut down the system." The problem was, some of Beelzebub's latest viruses included a heisenbug as a part of the payload. The heisenbug itself was actually just kind of a tease; the real payload could do much more serious damage.

"Shut it . . ."

"The whole system, right now. Shut it down."

"Let's go see Evelyn."

Evelyn was stunned. "I can't . . . I mean I don't have the authority to do that."

"Then get me someone who does."

For a moment she seemed as if she were about to argue. Then, as the expression on my face registered, she turned a shade paler, closed her mouth, and picked up a phone. She dialed an extension and asked, "Carla, where is Reed Burroughs right now? Thanks." She hung up. "Follow me."

As I followed her, I explained. "There is a very good chance that your system is infected with a second virus. If it's what I think it is, you've got to shut down until we can get rid of it, or you could lose every piece of data that's in there."

We arrived at the door of a conference room. As Evelyn poked her head in, I caught a glimpse of a bunch of suits sitting around a long table. "Mr. Burroughs, there's an emergency."

The suit at the head of the table came out into the hall. He was a stocky man with a squarish head and cold blue eyes. He did not seem pleased about having his meeting interrupted. Evelyn did not attempt to explain why the interruption was necessary; she just looked expectantly at me.

I said, "I think your computer system may be infected with a very destructive parasite. If you don't shut it down immediately, it may trash your whole system."

The effect of this news was colorful; he turned bright red, which contrasted startlingly with his blue eyes. "Shut it down? And exactly how are we supposed to stay in business? Do you know what today is? Do you know what midnight is? It's Triple Witching Hour, that's what it is! Do you know what would happen to this firm if we couldn't execute any transactions today?"

"What would happen to your firm if you lost all the data that's stored in your computer system?"

Some of the color drained from his cheeks as that one sunk in.

"Look," I continued, "I know what Triple Witching Hour is. I also know how this particular virus writer thinks; he'd be likely to program his virus to go off on a day like this."

"You're sure about this?"

"No. I can't be sure until I've isolated the virus. But the possibility . . ."

"You're asking me to bring our operation to a standstill—on today of all days—for a possibility? No. Forget it."

"Look, if you shut down now, I can probably have you back up and running in under an hour. If you wait till the virus hits—"

"No. If you need to work on the system while it's down, then come back after midnight. And now"—he put one hand on the doorknob—"I'd like to get back to my meeting."

After he shut the door, I turned to Evelyn. "So what's Triple Witching Hour?"

Her eyes narrowed. "I thought you said you knew."

"Well, generally, yeah. I mean I know we're not talking about a scene from Macbeth. Three different kinds of options expiring at the same time, isn't it?"

She nodded. "Equity options, index options, and futures options, the third Friday of March, June, September, and December."

I gestured at the door Burroughs had retreated behind. "Can we go over his head?"

"No, he's it. Look, can't you take the virus out without shutting us down?"

I shrugged. "The problem is, the scanner program is going to be much slower if it has to run in the background of your normal activity."

"How much slower?"

"If the virus is set to execute today, we'll never clear the whole system in time."

"What do you suggest?"

"We'll load the scanner anyway; maybe we'll get lucky. If not, I'll come back after midnight. If you have problems before then, call me." I gave her the number of my cellular phone.

"Thank you," she said. She sounded as if she really meant it.

I had gone back over to Tower to do some more work on their worm, and was seriously considering knocking off early for the weekend, when my cellular phone rang. It was about three o'clock.

"Hello?"

"Hello, Michael Arcangelo? It's Evelyn Mulderig." She sounded as if she were on the verge of panic.

"What's going on?"

"Our system just crashed. Can you come right over?"

"I'm on my way."

Mass hysteria reigned at Gerdel Hesher Bock. People were dashing up and down corridors, shouting into phones, arguing with each other, and generally losing control. I actually saw one man literally tearing his hair out.

The epicenter of this disturbance was the main computer area. People were screaming and cursing at the suddenly recalcitrant machines, and one man had to be physically restrained from pounding his fists on a keyboard. I approached the workstation I had used before. A man in shirtsleeves was power-cycling it in a futile effort to get the system to come up again. I tapped him on the shoulder, and he seemed grateful to hand the problem over to somebody else.

I booted the system from a floppy and got to work. After loading a search program and setting it to scan the hard drive, there was nothing to do but sit back and wait. By now a crowd had gathered, all of them looking expectantly at me.

After about fifteen minutes my scanner found the beastie. It was, as I suspected, one of Beelzebub's. In another minute I had removed it from the local hard drive and proceeded to clean the network drives as well. I then made some copies of the devirusing program and handed them to Evelyn Mulderig. "Use these on everything with a hard drive, zip drive, or writable CD."

She nodded. "And then what?"

Good question. The virus was gone, but it had already done its damage. The only question was, How much damage? "Now we see if the system has enough marbles left to come up on its own."

I booted the system from the hard drive and crossed my fingers. For a minute there it looked like it was going to work. The crowd around the workstation seemed all set to let out a cheer and carry me out the door on their shoulders. Then reality hit us squarely in the small of the back; the program sputtered, hiccuped, and hung.

Evelyn looked crushed. "Is there anything else you can do?"

I shook my head grimly and bit back the "I told you so" that was trying to force its way out between my teeth. "The virus is gone. Unfortunately, it crippled the system before we could get rid of it. You're going to need to talk to your software vendor to see if they can help you repair it and save any of your files."

I couldn't really bring myself to say what we both knew: They were screwed.

Leon had to go out of town for the weekend. Because I was going to the airport anyway, I had offered to drive him. I took a subway uptown to the garage where I keep my pride and joy, a silver Ferrari 348 Spyder that I had bought used and couldn't afford, even at that. The insurance premiums alone were like the national debt.

The expense was forgotten, though, as soon as I slid into the leather driver's seat and revved the engine. Leon was waiting for me in front of his hotel. He whistled appreciatively when I pulled up. "Nice wheels!"

"Thanks. I bought it to impress women," I joked, "only I hardly ever get to drive it."

"Are you planning on impressing somebody tonight?"

"Yeah, I hope so."

He grinned. "Good luck." His grin faded. "Say, you don't look too happy for somebody with a hot date on a Friday night."

I told him what had happened at GHB. He shook his head. "Bummer, man."

I dropped Leon off at his terminal and went to park the car. Leaving my car unattended in a parking lot is something I don't do very often; I'd just as soon walk around Manhattan with hundred-dollar bills stapled to my clothes. I actually considered waiting in the car outside the terminal, then chided myself for my misplaced priorities. What would Al think if I didn't meet her at the gate because I didn't want to leave my car? Although I *could* tell her I was delayed in traffic and got there too late to . . . no! Get thee behind me, Satan!

Happily, her flight was on time. She came running to me, and I took her in my arms, and after a thorough hello kiss, I said, "I don't think I could have waited another minute."

"Me neither."

"Let's get your bags."

"I've got them right here." She had one of those carry-ons that combine a garment bag with a suitcase and are still compact enough to take on the plane.

"That's a very good idea."

"I know. I lost a few bags myself before I got one of these. You do kind of run low on clothes during a long trip, though."

We walked to the parking lot. She said, "This is your car?"

"No, I just borrowed it from a fabulously wealthy friend."

"I've never been in a car like this." She gave me a sidelong glance. "You're not going to drive fast, are you?"

"You should see the insurance premiums on this thing. If I don't drive fast, how am I ever going to get my money's worth?"

"Seriously, Michael . . ."

"Okay, just kidding. The Long Island Expressway is probably a parking lot right now, anyway."

I put the top down for the drive back to Manhattan. Traffic actually wasn't that bad, but I kept to what I would consider a prudent speed, although I noticed Al's knuckles were white where she was gripping her briefcase.

I asked, "Did they feed you on the plane?"

She grimaced. "I tried not to notice. If I see one more thing in a little rectangular plastic dish, I'm going to be violently ill."

"Do you like Indian food?"

"I *love* Indian food."

"Then let's go get some." I took her to the Bombay Garden. Despite having no reservations on a Friday night, we were shown to a table without waiting. For some reason that I can't quite fathom, Indian food has never really been hugely popular in New York. I don't usually have it in New York either, but on my recent sojourn in London, where there seem to be good Indian restaurants on every street, I had it almost every day.

As we studied the menu, I said, "Would you like to have some wine with dinner?"

"That would be nice," she said. "But, you know, what I'd really love right now is a beer."

"Beer it is, then."

Al ordered the chicken tandoori and I opted for the king prawns Bhuna. We tasted each other's food, and both dishes were excellent.

As happy as I was to see Al again, I was a little preoccupied with some of the recent developments, and it must have shown on my face.

"Is something wrong?" she asked.

I nodded. "Yeah, a few things, actually." I was still smarting about what had happened at Gerdel Hesher Bock. I told her about that.

"Oh, no! That's really terrible. But you gave them the right advice, they just wouldn't listen to you."

I shrugged. "Yeah, you can lead a horse to water."

"I didn't know about this heisenbug thing in Beelzebub's viruses."

"It's pretty recent. Let's just hope he doesn't figure out how to put a schrödinbug in the payload." A schrödinbug is, mythically, a type of programming error that doesn't cause any problems until someone notices that it's there, and that the program should never have worked at all in the first place. At this point the program crashes and will not work again until the bug is fixed.

"A schrödinbug! You don't actually believe in that, do you?"

"I'm trying very hard not to."

"You're *trying* not to?"

"Yes. I've heard that they happen only if you believe in them."

She grinned. "Like fairies, huh?"

"Something like that."

Over a dessert of coconut-flavored Indian ice cream, I said, "It's still pretty early. Do you want to go to a movie?"

"That would be fun. I haven't gone to the movies in ages. What's playing?"

"I really don't know, but there's a Loew's multiplex just around the corner. We could walk over and find out what's showing and when."

The waiter brought the check, and I glanced at it and said, "Seventy-five cents? Why, that's an outrage. If I were you, I wouldn't pay."

She chuckled. "Your Jimmy Stewart is pretty good, but your Groucho needs work."

"Everybody's a critic."

It was a nice night for a walk. Even in midtown Manhattan the signs of early spring were conspicuous: tiny leaf buds on the trees, and planters sprouting purple and yellow crocuses. You could even detect a slight whiff of green growing things in the air, over the exhaust of ten million automobiles.

I guess you could call the theater complex a dodecaplex, because there were twelve movies showing there. Unfortunately, eleven of them were sequels to other movies, and although Al and I had seen some of the earlier films on which the sequels were based, we hadn't seen any of the same ones.

So we settled on the orphan in the lot, a thing called *The Year of the Rat,* even though neither of us had any inkling of what it was supposed to be about. The movie poster wasn't much help, but it carried blurbs from some favorable reviews. It turned out to be a story of a man and woman falling in love in a medieval European village. Then they get bubonic plague and die. But before that happens, his parents die, her parents die, all their brothers and sisters die, the blacksmith dies, and the village priest dies. Everybody dies of plague except for the village doctor, who is accused of witchcraft and stoned to death. Needless to say, analogies to the AIDS epidemic were frequent and heavy-handed. The whole ordeal took about three hours.

"Now I remember why I don't go to movies anymore," Al said as we were leaving. "I don't think I've seen a happy ending since 1997."

"People don't seem to like them anymore. I guess they'd rather be depressed."

"I don't think that's it. I think they're already depressed. That's why you always hear people complaining that happy endings are 'unrealistic,' because since they're so unhappy themselves, they'd like to believe that everyone else is miserable too."

"I have to admit that makes a certain amount of sense. You could leave a movie like this saying, 'At least I'm better off than those poor bastards.' "

"Right. But if you had to watch something where people were

really enjoying themselves, it would be like rubbing your nose in how horrible you feel."

"According to your theory, I guess movie critics would be about the most depressed people around."

"God, yes. They'd pretty much have to be anyway, don't you think?"

I took her back to my apartment after the movie. "Nice place," she said. "Only I was expecting something a little . . ."

"Bigger?"

She smiled a little sheepishly; then her grin turned sly. "Yes. It looks like one of those places that married men keep so they'll have a place to bring their girlfriends."

I laughed. "I know it's a little cramped. But I grew up sharing a room with three brothers, remember? To me this place is like Shea Stadium. Besides, all my money is tied up in transportation."

As I was talking, I put some Mantovani on the stereo. After a few bars she said, "What *is* that?"

"Make-out music from the seventies."

"Are we going to make out?"

"Are we?"

We were and we did. I'll probably never live this down, but I actually kind of *like* Mantovani.

I woke up the next morning to find myself alone in bed. I looked around for my robe, but it was missing, so I put on a pair of sweatpants and walked out of the bedroom. Al had started a pot of coffee. She was wearing my robe and peering into the recesses of my refrigerator. As I emerged from the bedroom, she looked up and said, "Do you want to tell me what's edible in here, or should I just send it all out to be carbon-dated?"

"Give me ten minutes, and I'll run out and get us something special."

I used half of the ten minutes to brush my teeth and hair and throw on a sweatshirt and some sneakers, and the other half to run around the corner and back. I returned with a newspaper and large brown paper bag, which Al eyed with interest.

"What have you got in there?"

"Jewish soul food," I said, unfolding the newspaper, and then, "Oh, my God."

"What is it?" she asked.

I held up the front page of the *New York Times*. Beelzebub's virus had hit five other firms besides GHB. All were in dire financial straits as a result, and some were expected to go under.

"I hope you're hungry," I said as I unloaded fresh bagels, lox, cream cheese, and smoked whitefish. "I just lost my appetite." After breakfast, as we were cleaning up, I said, "There's something I need to tell you."

She froze. "You're married. You're gay? You have AIDS!"

"No, no, and *hell* no. Calm down. It's nothing like that. It's about work."

She sat down. "What about work?"

I told her the whole story, including Goodknight, Marlon Oz, smart worms, Tower Bank and Trust, and Leon Griffin's and my latest conjectures about what was going on.

"Why didn't you tell me about this earlier?"

"I didn't want you to worry."

Her brow furrowed and her lips pressed together in a white line. "Michael. I think we are about to have our first fight."

"Why? What did I do?"

"It's what you didn't do. Why did you think you had to shield me from this? 'Poor little Alice, better not tell her because she might fall apart.' Is that what you think?"

"No, not at all. I just wasn't sure what was going on yet, and I didn't want to worry you unnecessarily."

"You were worried, weren't you?"

"Well . . . yeah. I told you I was."

"Michael, if you had told me then, I could have been there for you. You didn't have to go through it alone."

"But I'm fine. It's not like I was going to jump in front of a subway train or anything."

"Is that what you thought I would do?"

"Of course not!"

"Well, then, what? I'm not made of glass. And I am not a child. I will not let you or anyone else treat me like one." With that she rose and stalked into the bedroom, and though she didn't exactly slam the door, I thought she closed it with a certain emphasis.

Okay, so now she was being completely unreasonable. I didn't really mind that. What bothered me was that she was right—I had not treated her like an equal. It wasn't my intention to treat her like a child, but that's the way she felt, and I could see why. After thinking about it over another cup of coffee, I went to the bedroom door and tapped lightly on it.

Al opened the door. She was dressed and had her flight bag in her hand. Her mouth was set in a hard, angry line. She said, "What?"

"You were right. I'm sorry."

"*I* was right? *You* were—wait, say that again?"

"I said you were right. I was wrong to hold things back from you. You had every right to hear about this before now."

She nodded. Her jaw was still set, but I could tell she was softening.

I said, "And you were right about something else, too. It would have really helped to confide in you, especially Wednesday night, when I was really pretty upset about the whole thing. The thing is, when I'm that upset about something, I don't usually feel comfortable talking about it."

"You told George."

"Yeah, but with George it was half kidding around. I knew it wasn't going to get too heavy. Besides, I had to tell him he had one in his program. I promise, I'll try to do better next time."

She put her bag down and looked me in the eye. "So we're going to be a team?"

I offered my hand. "Partners. Shake on it?"

She took my hand and used it to pull me into the bedroom. "I just thought of a better way to seal the bargain."

Later that morning we got back to the subject that had set off the fireworks.

I said, "I'm not even sure what to call this thing. It looks like a worm, but it's a lot bigger and more complicated than any worm I've ever seen. What looks like a worm, and acts like a worm, but isn't a worm?"

She thought about it, then smiled. "A caecilian."

"No ethnic slurs, please."

"Not a Sicilian! I'm sorry, are you . . . ?"

I shook my head. "Strictly northern Italian on my father's side, and Austrian Jewish on my mother's. But you were saying . . ."

"C-A-E-C-I-L-I-A-N. It's a tropical amphibian that resembles a worm and burrows in the ground."

"Where did you come up with that one?"

"I used to be a biology major."

"I like that; Cecil the caecilian."

"I thought Cecil was a sea serpent. Or was that Beany?"

"No, Beany was the kid with the propeller on his hat."

She looked thoughtful. "Michael, there's one thing that doesn't make sense to me."

"Actually, I guess most of it sounds pretty crazy."

"No, I don't think so at all. The ideas you came up with make a lot of sense to me. In fact, I think they're brilliant."

"Well, they weren't all my ideas. . . ."

"Don't get all humble on me again. I know you talked to some people while you were working this out, but it's your work. I'm *very* impressed. But the thing that bothers me is, if this monster worm evolved, why haven't we been seeing evidence of the process all along? Until as recently as last Saturday the biggest worm either one of us had ever seen was the 'anaconda' I showed you in Napa Valley. It's like going from trilobites to dinosaurs without anything in between."

I shrugged. "You may have a point there. But it's possible that we didn't see it because it had gotten too good at avoiding detection."

"Okay, maybe. But remember what you said about smart worms being able to assimilate other programs? What you said it did to Tower's software implies incredibly sophisticated engineering capabilities. Are you saying those capabilities just evolved, or could they have been picked up somewhere?"

"I don't know; maybe they could have. I told you what Oz said about how fast these things might evolve."

Al said, "Wait a minute." I turned to look at her, and I must have just missed seeing the lightbulb turn on over her head. "So far," she continued, "we've been talking about this evolution in pure Darwinian terms—natural selection. But what about Lamarckian evolution?"

"What's that?"

"Lamarck thought acquired traits could be passed on. You know, the idea that animals stretched their necks trying to reach higher leaves, so their offspring were born with longer necks, and eventually you get giraffes."

I wasn't a biology major, but the giraffe thing did sound familiar.

"Okay. But I thought that argument had been settled; didn't Darwin get it right?"

"For living creatures, yes. Acquired characteristics don't get encoded in the genes. But for computer programs . . ."

"Damn! You're right; any acquired characteristic would be encoded in the same way as anything else."

"So it could be passed along."

I thought about what Leon Griffin had said—that maybe Roger Dworkin could have pulled off what was done at Tower. Then the wheels started turning. I said, "Al, who wrote MABUS-two-k?" MABUS/2K had become the computer industry's standard operating system since it had been introduced in 1995.

"Well, I assume Macrobyte had a whole team of programmers working on it, but the name you usually hear is Roger Dworkin."

"Right. And who wrote the utility package that lets you run older applications in a MABUS-two-k environment?"

"Roger Dworkin?"

"Right. And who wrote the program that allows older operating systems to use some of the MABUS-two-k applications?"

"Uh, is there a trick question coming somewhere along here? That was Roger Dworkin too."

"So practically every computer system in this country is currently running a piece of software programmed by Roger Dworkin?"

"Yes, yes, yes. So what are you getting at?"

"I think we've got to talk to Roger Dworkin."

"So let me get this straight," Al said. "You think MABUS-two-k has a Trojan horse?"

It was completely outrageous. The idea that Macrobyte, the largest and most successful software publisher in the industry, would put out a product that contained hidden files for some unknown purpose was practically unthinkable. "But," I said, "nobody at Macrobyte would have to know about it but Roger Dworkin."

"But he's so respected. Not to mention rich. Why would he jeopardize everything by pulling a stunt like that?"

I shrugged. "Once a hacker, always a hacker. Besides," I continued, "I wouldn't put too much trust in the big software publishers, either. After all, who's benefited the most from the virus crisis? Back in the seventies and early eighties they were always crying about software piracy. Now that everybody's afraid to use anything but a shrink-wrapped disk, the software giants don't have to worry that much about piracy anymore." Using only brand-new disks covered with plastic shrink-wrap, also known as computer condoms, was considered the safest way the average user could guard against infections. This was referred to as practicing "safe SEX" (Software EXchange), at least by those who like to stretch a metaphor until it screams for mercy. Any disk that was unwrapped before reaching the user was presumed to be infected. "Besides, you know that some of the first viruses were actually written by software companies, as copy-protection devices. Even the Pakistan Brain virus was written to punish software pirates."

"So what are you saying? You really think the big software companies are behind the virus crisis?" She was looking at me as if she had just figured out that I was paranoid, and was now trying to decide if I might be dangerous, as well.

"No, I don't think they're deliberately disseminating viruses. But I don't think they've done much to protect the average user against viruses, either. MABUS-two-k could easily have had much more virus resistance; it wasn't anywhere near state-of-the-art. Hell, if Macrobyte had done it right, we might be in another line of work right now. I think they deliberately watered down their virus defenses because they know that once J. Random Luser stops worrying about virus contamination, there's gonna be a lot more pirated software floating around out there."

I pulled out one of the Macrobyte programs in my own software library, got a phone number from the documentation, called the number, and got a busy signal. I autodialed it for the next two hours and finally got through. Not that it did a lot of good. It turned out I had the main corporate headquarters in New Castle, Delaware. Their software-development facilities were in Oakland, California.

I called the software-development center and was told that there was nobody there on the weekend and I should call back on Monday. Mr. Dworkin was not in, and no, they could not give me his phone number. I tried directory assistance for the whole bay area and couldn't locate him. Meanwhile Al went to the local branch library to get a CD with telephone directories for the whole country, and searched that with no success. He must have had an unlisted number.

Then we tried searching through old wire-service stories, certain we would find something useful, because of the media coverage of Dworkin's early hacking escapades. It turned out that his tender age had kept his name and picture out of the media. It was only after the fact that his name had become known, and nobody had a picture of him on file.

Our next approach was to call various friends in the computer field to try to find somebody who knew somebody who knew Dworkin. We both called up friends all over the country. I got to talk to some people I hadn't seen since college.

Everybody knew who Roger Dworkin was. But nobody knew anybody who knew him. A few people thought they knew somebody who knew somebody who knew him, but when we talked to the person who was supposed to know him, it always turned out that that person didn't really know him. He or she just knew somebody who knew somebody who . . . you get the idea. It was a little weird, as if he were going to turn out to be a character out of one of those "urban legends" that everybody swears are real but turn out never to have happened. At one point I caught myself humming the theme to *The Twilight Zone*.

By late Saturday afternoon we had to admit we were stymied. I went to the dojo to catch a workout, even though I didn't really feel like it. In case any further evidence that Life Is Unfair was needed (which, of course, it wasn't), Al, who is built like an aerobics instructor, had, as I subsequently discovered, a complete aversion to all forms of exercise.

Sunday was a day of rest. We spent most of the morning relaxing with the *New York Times*, swapping sections and collaborating on the crossword puzzle. Not that I was much help with the latter. As you might expect of a walking encyclopedia, Al was a whiz at crossword puzzles—she even worked the thing in pen. It didn't seem to occur to her that she might make a mistake.

Later, while reading the book review, she said, "Listen to this bestseller list: *The End of Civilization, The Updated Prophecies of Nostradamus, The Antichrist Among Us, How to Profit from the Impending World Currency Collapse, Ten Things to Do to Prepare for the Second Coming, Seven Habits of Highly Defective People*—actually, I'm not sure how that last one got on the list."

"Sounds like real cheerful stuff. What about the fiction bestsellers?"

"*Not with a Bang,* by Rex Crown, *The Fifth Horseman,* by Mitchell Creighton, *Conversation with the Beast,* by Enya Wheaton . . ."

"Well, at least it seems like the end of the world is good for the publishing business."

"Yeah. Hey, listen to this:

> " 'Who will listen to me?
> Gentleness has perished
> And violence has descended upon us.
>
> " 'Who will listen to me?
> Men's hearts are rapacious
> And everyone robs his neighbor.
>
> " 'Who will listen to me?
> Men take pleasure in evil
> And goodness is abandoned.' "

"Gee, you must really be trying to cheer me up today. What are you gonna read to me next? The obituaries?"

"Have you ever heard that poem before?"

"No, why?"

"When do you think it was written?"

"I don't know, it sounds pretty current."

"Would you believe it was written around 1990 . . ."

"Yeah."

". . . B.C.?"

"Yeah, sure. *What?*"

"It was written circa 1990 B.C. in ancient Egypt. 'The Man Who Was Tired of Living.' "

"Hmm. Boy, I can understand their having a backlog, but you'd think the *Times* would have gotten around to reviewing it before now."

She swatted me with the paper. "It's a new translation, wise guy."

"Ah, that explains it. Loses something if you don't read the original hieroglyphs."

"I wouldn't be surprised. Hey, are we going to lie around here all day, or are we going to get out and do something?"

I would have been happy with Plan A, but since she seemed to want to go out, I suggested visiting the Met, which was having an exhibition of Italian Renaissance art. Al counterproposed the Museum of Modern Art. I'm not a big fan of modern art, but I thought, what the hell, might as well broaden my horizons. We went over to MOMA, and I initially was under the impression that we had come between exhibitions, because there were a lot of bare walls with nails sticking out of them, apparently waiting for somebody to come around and hang pictures on them. Or so I thought. Then I read the placard and discovered that I was in fact viewing an exhibition, er, excuse me, an "installation" of "post-postmodern minimalist sculpture."

I said, "If we don't leave in five minutes, I'm going to run through this place shouting, 'The emperor has no art!' I don't want to do it, but I don't think I'll be able to control myself. It could get very embarrassing."

She scowled at me, then looked at the nearest objet d'art and burst out laughing. "Okay, you win."

"Renaissance masters?"

"I'm sorry, Michael, but religious stuff makes me depressed. How about if we go to the Museum of Natural History? I like to look at dinosaur bones."

"Let's go. I have to admit, though, I was deeply moved by the Phillips-head screw on far left—"

"Oh, shut up."

So we spent the afternoon wandering among the petrified remains of the ancient terrible lizards. I had not been there since I was a kid, and in the meantime the place had obviously undergone extensive renovation.

"Do you know," Al asked as we were staring at an enormous tyrannosaur skeleton, "where the first T. rex bones were discovered?"

"No, why? Is there a theme park there now?"

"Not as far as I know." She chuckled. "But the first tyrannosaurus skeleton was discovered by Barnum Brown in 1902 in Hell Creek, Wyoming."

"Where do you get this stuff? I can't believe you studied paleontology in college, too."

"I didn't. I just read it on the sign over there."

"Oh, well, that's cheating. You're supposed to tell me what you already know."

"How about if *you* tell *me* something?"

"Okay. Let's see, T. rex, 'king of the tyrant lizards': lived during the Cretaceous period, attained a length of fifty feet, and weighed about eight tons."

"Really? How do you know all that? You never told me *you* majored in paleontology."

"I majored in paleontology when I was six years old. I *loved* dinosaurs. Memorized all their vital statistics while the other kids were memorizing batting averages."

Later, as we were admiring a huge pterosaur skeleton, Al said to me, "Michael, don't take this the wrong way, but walking around in Manhattan with you makes me nervous."

"Why?"

"Because you *look* at people: street people, crazy people, scary people. You look them right in the eye. Why do you do that?"

"I never really thought about it."

"Didn't anyone ever tell you that in New York, of all places, you should never make eye contact with anyone on the street?"

"Is that why you wear those sunglasses?"

"As a matter of fact, it is. Sunglasses are perfect because nobody can make eye contact with you, nobody can tell if you're looking at them, and nobody can get the idea that you're trying to avoid looking at them."

"Let me get this straight: You're supposed to avoid looking at people without having it look like you're avoiding looking at people?"

"Of course! Looking like you're avoiding looking is even worse than looking, because then they might think that you're afraid to look."

"This is all a little too complicated for me. Seeing as nothing horrible has happened to me yet, is it okay with you if I just keep looking? Don't look at me that way."

On Sunday evening Al invited me to her place.

"Do you like cats?" she inquired almost casually.

"Cats?"

"Yes, cats. You know, four-footed domesticated carnivores?"

"Oh, cats. Aren't they sort of like dogs who aren't smart enough to be trained to keep off the furniture?"

She let out a little shriek of outrage. "Not smart enough? They're much smarter than dogs! Too smart to let someone teach them a bunch of stupid tricks, anyway."

It occurred to me that one could make the same argument on behalf of goldfish, but I decided to let it slide. "How can you have a cat? You're out of town all the time."

"I have a neighbor who feeds him when I'm away."

"What's his name?"

"Effie."

"Effie? I thought you said it was a he."

"It's short for Fire Fore Fettle the Fiend of the Fell."

Al's apartment was much larger than mine, not to mention more tastefully decorated. Or maybe I should say Effie's apartment. Effie turned out to be a large reddish tomcat with a strong sense of territoriality. When Al introduced us, I extended a hand to scratch his ear (a normal piece of feline-human protocol, I have been led to believe), and he attempted to extract a tissue sample with a set of claws that looked like they were borrowed from Freddy Krueger.

Al smiled. "He likes you."

"Oh? How can you tell?"

"He's playing with you."

"I see. They play with mice, too, don't they?"

We ordered a pizza and planned strategy.

"How can I help?" Al asked.

"I'd like to bring you in on the Tower job, but Ainsworth is never going to okay it. He's getting nervous about how much this project is costing them as it is."

"Is there anything else?"

"Yeah, actually, there is. I want to be able to concentrate on this job full-time for as long as it takes. In the meantime, other jobs are going to come in, and I'm going to have to refer them to somebody. Will you cover for me?"

"Sure. I'd rather be in on the action, though."

"I'll give you hourly updates, if you want."

"Daily will be fine."

"Oh, and I just remembered something. How would you like to take a look at some new viruses from HfH?"

"HfH? How did you get them?"

"I hacked their virus-exchange board. There are about half a dozen new ones in the batch. Do you want to start working on them?"

"Let me at them." She was practically salivating.

"And you can call Macrobyte tomorrow and try to get hold of Roger Dworkin."

I was at Tower bright and early the next morning. Leon was already at the terminal when I got there, though. He greeted me and asked, "Did you get any more bright ideas over the weekend?"

"A friend of mine came up with an interesting one. She thinks it's improbable that our worm evolved its incredible software engineering capabilities in what seems to have been a very short time. She thinks it must have assimilated them from a program that somebody wrote." I wasn't quite ready to share my line of thinking about Macrobyte, Roger Dworkin, and MABUS/2K.

Leon nodded thoughtfully. "That makes a certain amount of sense."

"How about you? Any strokes of genius?"

"I wouldn't say that. But I did get to thinking about this 'segmented worm' idea of yours. It seems to me that if it's broken up into pieces like that, then it has to have a way to recognize itself."

I saw what he was driving at. "Self-identification codes?"

"It would make sense. Besides, this thing erases beasties that it considers 'not me.' How else could it tell?"

The use of self-identification codes as a defense against infection and other types of attack was a relatively new development, pioneered by Macrobyte Software. Standard computer immune systems use thirty-two-bit identification codes, which are placed at regular intervals through the program code, and any file it generates. A subprogram regularly scans the memory looking for these embedded ID codes. When it finds one missing or altered, it knows that something's not kosher. By using thirty-two-bit codes, you have about five billion different possibilities. But for certain technical reasons it's customary to use palindromic codes, which read the same forward and backward. That cuts the list of possibilities to around sixty-five thousand, which is still plenty for security purposes. After all, the four-digit PIN code you use with your ATM card has only ten thousand different possible combinations.

Leon said, "It's going to take a while, but I'm going to search for a thirty-two-bit chunk that's repeated at regular intervals. If we can find one, we'll be able to locate this guy anywhere."

That sounded like a hell of an idea, so I worked with Leon on it. We broke for lunch a little after noon, and I called Al for an update.

"Did you get to talk to Roger Dworkin?"

"I'm afraid not."

"Damn, I was afraid of that. What do they do, keep him under lock and key?"

"No, they were going to let me talk to him. He's just not there."

"Is he away or something?"

"Not as far as anyone knows. He apparently comes and goes as he pleases."

"Did you leave a message for him?"

"They say he never, ever, calls anybody back, but I left one anyway. I'm just going to keep trying and hope I catch him later. Oh, and a call came for you about a job at Midlantic Financial. I told them I was your associate. The guy sounded dubious, but I'm going over there this afternoon."

"Thanks. Let me know if they give you any crap. I'll cross them off my list if they do."

"Stop protecting me, Michael."

"Whoops! Sorry, I was doing that again, wasn't I?"

"Yes, you were." She chuckled, which surprised me. "I guess you can't help being a white knight. Try to remember that I'm not a helpless damsel in distress, though, okay?"

I kept in touch with Al periodically throughout the day. She took care of the Midlantic job but didn't have any luck tracking down Roger Dworkin.

Leon and I weren't having much luck with our own hunt, either. There was no repeating thirty-two-bit string. I said, "You know, there's no reason it has to be thirty-two bits." So we started to look for a repeating code in sixteen bits. When that search came up dry, we started playing around with less conventional lengths.

It was when we got around to checking for twelve-bit strings that things started to click. A particular string started popping up in those parts of the Tower operating system that we thought were worm infested. Leon flashed a grin and said, in an exaggerated version of his own accent, "We be jammin' now, mon," as he displayed it on the screen:

011001100110

He added, "We got it: a twelve-bit palindrome."

Just for the hell of it, I mentally converted to hexadecimal and typed the result into my laptop, then sat there staring at the screen. Leon asked, "Is something wrong?"

I said, "Well . . . for one thing, it's a palindrome in hex, too."

I showed him the screen. It said:

666

CHAPTER FIVE

Unnatural Selection

And the name of the star is called Wormwood:
and the third part of the waters became wormwood;
and many men died of the waters, because they were made bitter.
—Revelation 8:11

The irony of it was, armed with the worm's self-ID code, it would have been a simple matter to go around looking for it, and erasing it wherever it was found.

Simple, but potentially disastrous.

We now knew that this worm had wrought wholesale changes in the systems it occupied, and, in general, the changes seemed to be beneficial. Unfortunately, killing the worm that did this work might very well bring the whole reengineered system crashing down. We just didn't know.

That was why we desperately needed to talk to Roger Dworkin. Even if Dworkin was not, as I strongly suspected, the creator of the worm in question, he was the only person who knew enough about MABUS/2K to possibly shed some light on what was going on. Roger Dworkin, however, was nowhere to be found.

Because he was never there when we called, and he wouldn't return phone calls, Al and I flew to the West Coast to see him.

Before we left, I remembered to get out the hard drive I had exposed to the Goodknight virus. Despite the fact that my virus-detection program had been silent, I found about three kilobytes of disk space were now occupied by something containing the 666 marker. Then I had another idea.

Since the federal Computer Crimes Act was passed in 1997, it has been illegal to play Core War, or any variation of it, over a network connected by phone lines. In fact, there were some people who believed the law could be interpreted to mean you couldn't play Core War under any circumstances, even on your own personal computer. No matter how you looked at it, Core War on the Internet was illegal. Of course, so are drugs, gambling, and prostitution.

I powered up my workstation, telnetted to a certain cyberspace address, and got a screen that said "Welcome to Armageddon." Armageddon was an "underground" game similar to Core War, except that, whereas Core War was a duel between two programs in a limited amount of time, Armageddon ran continuously and accommodated as many entries as it could fit. Also, Armageddon programs would try to replicate as well as survive and destroy other programs. In some respects Armageddon was sort of a throwback to the original Vissotsky-Morris-Ritchie game, which was called Darwin. In Armageddon two types of scores were kept, reflecting two different approaches to the game: "insects" and "dinosaurs." One score, "population," kept track of the number of copies each program currently had in the system. This is where the "insects"—relatively tiny programs that propagated rapidly—had an advantage. The other score was something called cybermass, reflecting the total amount of available computer space occupied by a group of clones. That's where the "dinosaurs" reigned, because, as in real life, one dinosaur could be larger than zillions of insects. Both types of scores were updated continuously. I selected the population-score summary, and saw the following:

Program	Population#
Belial	16238
Flattop	7887
Grendel IV	7185
Bad Gnus	2517

```
Comm Rad  . . . . . . . . . . . . . . . . . . .  912
Elvis . . . . . . . . . . . . . . . . . . . . .  228
Prog5 . . . . . . . . . . . . . . . . . . . . .  203
Anthrax . . . . . . . . . . . . . . . . . . . .  91
Headcheese  . . . . . . . . . . . . . . . . . .  61
Hotrod  . . . . . . . . . . . . . . . . . . . .  50
```

There were several more screen pages of programs with fewer than fifty copies of themselves left in the game, and a message informing players that programs with scores of zero would be deleted from the list after forty-eight hours.

The cybermass score summary looked like this:

Program	Cybermass%
Nessie	14.71
Gog	9.22
Belial	6.85
Fruit Loop	5.43
Psychlops	5.41
Cronus	3.08
Flattop	2.40
Chimaera	1.97
Doogie	0.88
Wild1	0.43

I uploaded the Goodknight beastie and, after pondering a few moments, dubbed it Cecil.

I was expecting to get a big brush-off at Macrobyte, but they turned out to be pretty civil. Josh Spector, the head of software development, came out of his office to greet us and then invited us to come in and sit down.

"I understand you'd like to talk to Roger," he said. "That may be easier said than done. But maybe I can help you."

Al said, "Do you happen to know if he was working on anything involving reverse engineering of software?"

He gave us a sheepish grin. "As head of software development here, you'd think I would know that, wouldn't you? Actually, I'm afraid I don't have a clue. Roger does whatever he wants to do, whenever he wants to do it. And every now and then he presents us with a finished product, which is always brilliant, and always makes Macrobyte a ton of money. So our CEO regards him as the goose that lays the golden eggs. As you might recall, the moral of that particular story is, don't fuck around with the goose. Excuse my language."

Al said, "I don't understand. I know he was part of the programming team for MABUS-two-k. How could he work as part of a team?"

"He didn't. Roger just did what he wanted to do. Then we took what he gave us, gave it to the other programmers on the project, and they worked with it."

I said, "We would like to talk to him. It really is very important. Is he in today?"

He spread his arms. "Who knows? The only way to find out is to go and look. Come on."

Spector led us through the building, arriving eventually at a corridor with a series of small offices—cubicles, really. As we approached the end of the hall, I could see something lying in the hall in front of the door. It looked like a sock.

It *was* a sock. More socks were piled up inside the door, along with shirts, pants, underwear, books, floppies, CDs, and a stack of pizza boxes in one corner that almost reached the ceiling. A sleeping bag was unrolled in the narrow space between the workstation and the doorway. A rolling chair had been pushed into a corner to make room for the sleeping bag, which looked as if it might be occupied.

On closer inspection, the lumps in the sleeping bag turned out to be more laundry. Laundry that, judging from the atmosphere in the room, should have been on the way to, not from, the cleaner's. Josh had evidently been in there before, because he had stopped a dozen feet down the hall in the vicinity of an air-conditioning vent. Al retreated quickly. I heard her ask, "Doesn't anybody ever clean up in there?"

Spector said, "We did that once, and Roger threatened to walk if it ever happened again. It hasn't."

Meanwhile, I held my breath and looked around for a minute. The workstation itself was unremarkable—the only nonstandard equipment was a hexadecimal keypad used for rapid entry of numbers in base 16. I glanced at the software and saw nothing out of the ordinary, so I turned my attention to the books. In addition to the kinds of books you'd expect to see in any programmer's office, there were some unexpected things: *Beowulf,* the *Volsunga Saga,* the *Rig-Veda,* and a King James edition of the Bible, among others. There were also several thick treatises on mythology and some astronomical atlases and almanacs. I picked up the King James Bible and opened it. The Book of Revelation was marked with a Popsicle stick—grape, judging from the residue. It appeared to have been well thumbed. One passage was heavily underlined: "And the name of the star is called Wormwood: and the third part of the waters became wormwood."

As I exited, I heard Al asking, "Why does he have such a tiny little cubicle? I was expecting something—"

"Bigger?" Spector smiled. "You know the joke about the eight-hundred-pound gorilla that sleeps anywhere it wants to? Well, that's where Roger wants to work—and sleep, apparently. It's the same cubicle he's had since he first came to work for Macrobyte. We've offered him bigger offices many times. Hell, he could have the CEO's office if he wanted it. But he just wants to stay put."

"Does he have any friends here? Anyone who might know where he is, or at least what he's been up to?"

Josh shook his head. "Roger keeps very much to himself. I don't want to say he's completely antisocial, but . . . well, actually, he is completely antisocial. As far as I know, he doesn't have any friends. And now"—he looked at his watch—"I have an important meeting to go to. Is there anything else?"

Al said, "Please don't let us make you late. We can show ourselves out."

"Are you sure?"

"Really, no problem."

We started to follow him back down the hall, falling farther and farther behind him until he turned the corner and we stopped. Al said, "So what do you think?"

"I think it would have been a good idea to bring a gas mask. But let's go back down there and take a look."

As we approached Dworkin's office again, a man came out of the second-to-last door. I thought we were going to be chased away, but he approached us and said, "I heard you asking about Roger. I knew him."

He was a short, balding man in his fifties, with the kind of stooped shoulders that come from hunching over a keyboard for about thirty years. "I can't really say he was a friend. But I used to go in there to talk to him sometimes. Sometimes he'd let me stay awhile and watch what he was doing, which I couldn't understand most of the time anyway."

"Where is he?" I asked.

He shook his head. "I don't know. I haven't seen him in weeks." He saw our alarmed expressions and continued, "Oh, he's done that before, stayed away for weeks at a time. A couple of years ago he didn't come in all winter. This is a little different, though, because this time he seemed to be in the middle of something he was working on, and when that happens, he'll stay here for weeks day and night until it's finished."

"What was he working on?"

"He told me it was a game."

We were about to continue back down the hall to Roger's office, when a security guard came around the far corner. He acted very nonchalant, as if he were just making rounds, but I had a strong suspicion that Josh Spector had sent him to make sure we didn't get "lost" on our way out.

Just as well, because if there was anything in Dworkin's computer that he wanted to keep private, it would have probably taken about two thousand years to break through his security.

"What do you mean you don't know where he lives?" Al sounded as exasperated as I felt. "You must have payroll records, that sort of thing."

The personnel manager shook her head. "I'm sorry, but all we have on Mr. Dworkin is a post office box number. We had an address on him about ten years ago, but after he moved, he never gave us his new address. A couple of years ago we just gave up asking."

We left shaking our heads. I said, "Who is this guy—John Galt or something?"

She said, "Who is John Galt?"

"I see you've read the book."

"What book?"

"*Atlas Shrugged*. It's an Ayn Rand novel where everybody is wondering about this guy John Galt. They all go around asking 'Who is John Galt?' Everybody knows his name, but nobody knows where, or even who, he is."

"That does have a familiar ring to it."

"Let's go back to Spector's office," I suggested.

"Why?"

"I want to ask him if he'll let me check out Dworkin's computer files."

"You really think he'll do that?"

"No. But right now I can't think of anything else."

Spector was gracious enough to see us again, although I had the impression that his patience might be wearing a little thin. "You think we have some kind of security problem?" he asked.

"It's possible," I said. Of course, what I was really thinking was that Dworkin and Macrobyte were the *cause* of a security problem for everybody else, but that line wasn't going to cut any ice in here.

"Then I'd better call in our security director." Spector hit his intercom button. "Carol," he said, "would you see if Bob Beales is available and, if he is, ask him to come in?"

Beales was short and stocky, with a neatly trimmed black goatee, and dark circles under his pale-blue eyes, the latter causing me to reflect that his was undoubtedly a pretty high-pressure job. I thought I caught a flicker of something—surprise? recognition?—in his eye when we were introduced, but I couldn't be sure. He didn't look at all familiar to me, though.

"Ms. Meade and Mr. Arcangelo seem to think that we may have a security problem in Roger Dworkin's account," Spector said.

"Oh?" Beales said. "Like what?"

"I'm not really sure"—and why should I be? I was making this up as I went along—"but it may have something to do with a Trojan horse, or maybe a virus . . ."

Beales seemed to wince at that last part, as well he might. Viruses were a major headache for security personnel. But he wound up just shaking his head. "If there was a problem, I'd know about it. Believe me, our system is clean."

Coming from most people, that statement would have struck me as arrogant or ignorant or both. There was something about Beales, though, that made me think he knew exactly whereof he spoke.

Al was driving our rented Toyota across the Bay Bridge to San Francisco. This is a little scary for anybody who's ever seen video of the 1989 earthquake, when several big gaps opened in the bridge, precipitating vehicles and their occupants into the Oakland Bay. There was some especially harrowing footage of cars that appeared to be teetering on the brink but somehow hadn't fallen in.

The ride was also scary for another reason. As I said, Al was driving. As she wove aggressively through the heavy bridge traffic (despite signs admonishing drivers to "stay in lane") I looked over at her and tried to figure out how this could be the same person whose knuckles were whitened by a brisk ride down the Long Island Expressway in my Ferrari. At this point my own grip on my laptop case would probably have been fairly desperate, except that I had put it under the seat in hopes of minimizing serious injury when the airbag deployed.

As she slammed on the brakes to avoid ramming the truck ahead of us, Al said conversationally, "I hear that DEF CON six is going to be held in Philadelphia this year."

I chuckled. "Yeah. Too bad about that."

She swerved around the truck and practically went up the tailpipe of a Bronco in the next lane. "Why too bad?"

"Because they'd much rather have it in Las Vegas." DEF CON was probably the biggest assemblage of hackers, crackers, whackers, phreakers, cryppies, cyberpunks, cipherpunks, and other assorted species of technojunkie, on the planet. The last time it was held in a venue where gambling was legal, there was a bit of a sensation when it was discovered that quite a few people were using their time away from the convention to try to hack the slot machines. Apparently some of them were successful, because DEF CON was no longer welcome in the state of Nevada. "I guess they figure that in Philadelphia they'll be a short drive from Atlantic City."

"Argh! Why does the lane you just moved out of always start going faster than the one you went into?" She leaned on the horn. "Are you going?"

"Where?"

"To DEF CON!"

Maybe, if I live. "I usually do, but I was thinking about giving it a miss this year, what with all this other stuff going on. Are you thinking of going?"

"I'd like to. I have to admit, I've never been to one before. I know you can get a lot of valuable information at these things, but I've always felt sort of uncomfortable about it, like I'd be venturing into enemy territory. Or that I'd at least be out of place."

"You'd definitely be *way* out of place. But you could use that to your advantage."

"What do you mean?" she asked, snapping the wheel to the right in another of her lightning lane-changes.

I pictured rescue workers using the Jaws of Life to pry us out of the crumpled remains of the Toyota. "I don't like to engage in stereotyping, but there's at least a subcategory of hackers who are, shall we say, far from socially adept."

"Yes. So?"

"A lot of these guys are like preteenagers when it comes to women. They think about them all the time, but they haven't got the slightest idea how to behave with them."

"Developmentally arrested, huh?"

"In a manner of speaking. Anyway, if an attractive woman—and we are very definitely *not* excluding the present company, okay?— were to be at all nice to any of these guys, he would do just about anything she wanted."

She scowled fiercely. "Exactly what do you mean by being 'nice'?"

I looked at her, surprised at her reaction, then burst out laughing when I realized what she must be thinking. "Oh, God, no. By 'nice' I mean really just that. Smile. Talk civilly. Seem interested."

She seemed a little mollified. "Oh, okay. So then I would just have to act like a ditz: 'Oh, please explain to me what you're doing with that computer. It's so interesting, I can hardly contain it in my tiny little mind.' " She wasn't too pleased about that either.

"Well, you could play it that way. But I think a lot of them would be even more likely to open up to you if you showed 'em that you actually know the stuff. Then you'd really be the girl of their wet dreams."

She gave a little scream and punched me in the right shoulder, causing us to veer dangerously close to a battered old Chevy Nova in the lane to our right. At the moment of nearest approach I could see the whites of the driver's eyes, which wasn't difficult, because they nearly came out of his head. Mine probably looked the same to him. "That is really a revolting thought," Al continued, as if oblivious to the near collision. "I think you've been talking to George too much lately. Anyway, obviously I'd have to, uh, dissemble about the actual nature of my work in the computer field."

"You know, I think a lot of them would tell you anything you wanted to know even if they knew you were a computer-security consultant. But, yeah, you should go incognito."

"Why?"

"Because some of the more vindictive hackers might go after you if they knew who you were. Hell, they wouldn't even have to be vindictive; some of them might just do it to get your attention. But they can cause a lot of problems for you if they want to: screw up your credit record, mess up your phones, tap your conversations, all kinds of nasty stuff."

"Now you've practically talked me out of going. Which is too bad, because I just thought of a reason that we both should go."

"What?"

"Don't you think that Roger Dworkin might go to Philadelphia for this?"

"Damn! You're right—he might even be on the program. After all, he's way up there in the hacker pantheon."

"So you think we should go?"

"You talked me into it."

Our next stop was Palo Alto to see George and check up on Goodknight. Goodknight had won the Pacific Open, and though the program would have to win a twelve-game match against Mephisto to be considered the official computer champ, this was widely believed to be all but a mortal lock.

George was expecting us at SAIL. I don't know how he prepared Jason for the fact that Al was coming with me, but he must have done a good job. Jason was polite and seemed to be trying hard not to stare suspiciously at her every time he thought she wasn't looking. He said, "George told me what you said about the worm. Do you still want to go ahead with this probe of yours?"

I shook my head. "That won't be necessary. The worm would just chew it up and spit it out. Besides, I know how to find it now."

"And then we can get rid of it?"

"You can. You may not want to."

"Say what?"

I explained how the worm had affected other systems where it had been found—by now we had identified half a dozen.

"So," I concluded, "it may be doing you more good than harm. And it might be harmful to try to remove it."

Jason was steamed. "I want it out. We created this program. I would like to believe that any success it has is due to our efforts, not the accidental result of a software worm. Just take it out. We can repair any damage it may have caused."

I could see his point. In fact, in his position I might have felt the same way. "You're the boss. We'll take it out."

We scanned the whole program for the ID code Leon Griffin and I had discovered. It would tell us pretty precisely what was worm and what wasn't. Then we would take it out and let the pieces fall where they may.

Reams of fanfolded computer paper emerged from their printer as we ran the scan. Al and I alternated between watching the monitor, and riffling through the printout. When we were almost halfway done, I exchanged a look with Al. Her eyes were like saucers. She whispered, "This is unbelievable."

I said, "No shit."

Jason approached as we were finishing up with the scan. "Okay," he said, "how much of our system was taken over by this worm?"

I swallowed hard. "Would you believe . . . it ate the whole thing?"

After the initial shock wore off, it wasn't too hard to figure out what had happened. The worm had simply incorporated Goodknight. Swallowed it whole. Of course, that didn't tell us anything about *why* it would do such a thing.

The Goodknight programmers were in a serious bind. They could continue to run the worm-eaten program, try to learn more about it, and hope for the best. Or they could erase the whole thing and start from scratch. Because of the nature of their program, with its self-teaching capacity, the latter option would set them back almost a year.

At that point George suggested that Al and I come to dinner with him, and we accepted, relieved to have an excuse to get away from the funereal atmosphere that had settled over Team Goodknight.

We went to a little place not far from campus and settled into a booth. I said, "George, I wish there was something more we could do to help. This whole thing really sucks."

He shrugged. "You know, in the great scheme of things, it's hardly a major tragedy. Look, why don't we table the whole thing for now? I don't want it to ruin everybody's digestion; it's not worth getting an ulcer over."

George's motion was accepted by acclamation, and we limited ourselves to lighter topics. The conversation eventually turned into a contest between George and me to see which one of us could relate more embarrassing stories about the other. I think I must have been winning, because he was the first one to change the subject, saying, "Hey, since you guys are going to be here tonight, why don't you come and see me play? Mike, I think you took a rain check the last time you were here. Want to cash it in?"

In response to Al's quizzical look, I said, "Do you like jazz? George used to be a pretty good bass player."

"Used to be! Now I'm afraid I've got to insist that you come. Afterward I will accept your abject apology."

"George, Michael never told me you were a musician. I'm impressed."

"He'll be delighted to hear that," I said, "as impressing women was his whole reason for becoming a musician in the first place."

He nodded, straight-faced. "It still seems like a perfectly good motive to me. Unfortunately, nobody ever told me that the bass player never gets the girls."

We did go to see George's trio play in a small club in San Francisco. A lot of their stuff was some kind of peculiarly Californian jazz / New Age fusion, but nice enough to listen to. They did play some more traditional jazz too, which I liked better. Between sets George came and sat with us. I think both Al and I were surprised when he brought up the subject of the worm. "Are you sure you want to talk about it now?" Al asked, obviously recalling how we had shelved the subject at dinner at George's suggestion. "Won't it interfere with your playing?"

"Nah. In the first place, I'm not really all that upset about it. And, anyway, when I'm up there," he said, with a nod in the direction of the stage, "I'm using my right brain. I wouldn't be able to think about this other stuff if I wanted to. Hell, by the end of a gig, I'm practically dyslexic."

I shrugged and said, "Okay, your call. If you want to talk about it, let's talk."

"I was thinking about what you said earlier, Mike, about the whole thing being bogus. I think you hit the nail on the head. I have a theory that this worm represents some kind of an apotheosis of bogosity. It's like a living bogon."

"A what?" Al asked.

I shook my head. "Don't encourage him." But it was already too late.

"A bogon," George expounded, pointedly ignoring my last remark, "is the fundamental particle of bogosity. The study of bogons and their attendant phenomena is known as 'quantum bogodynamics.'"

"Go on," Al urged. I think she was trying to bug me, but by now George needed no encouragement.

"There are certain known bogon sources in the universe: politicians, bureaucrats, lawyers, accountants, most management types, television evangelists, used-car salesmen, almost anybody in a suit. In fact, there's one hypothesis that says that it's actually the suits themselves that emit the bogons, but that's a little out of the scientific mainstream."

"Oh, well," I said, "we wouldn't want to be accused of entertaining any theories that are less than completely orthodox." Actually, I didn't really want George to stop—I figured he was just dealing with his disappointment in his usual style, by indulging in his oddball sense of humor. I also knew he'd enjoy it even more if I argued with him.

He continued to ignore me. "It is, of course, a well-documented fact that computer failures soar dramatically when suits are present. According to the theory of quantum bogodynamics, this is the direct result of bogon absorption by the computers. In fact, bogons are thought to adversely affect human mental processes, too, but it's a little harder to tell, except in areas where there are tremendously powerful bogon emissions, such as Congress."

"The scary thing," I told Al, "is that I think he really believes this."

"It does make a certain amount of sense," she said.

"Not you too!"

"Mike, old chum, I'm afraid you may have been hanging around too many suits yourself. You may be suffering from the early stages of bogon poisoning."

"Thank you. Do you have any more words of wisdom on this topic?"

"No, that's about it," he acceded, giving a little shrug as if to say that he had grown weary of casting pearls before swine. "What I want to know is: How widespread is this thing, and what's going to happen?"

We spent the rest of the time between sets bringing George up-to-date on everything that had been going on. By the end of the evening, following his last set, we had gotten to my speculations regarding Macrobyte and Roger Dworkin. George let out a long, low whistle. "Mike, that's so diabolical, I can't even believe you thought of it."

"What's that supposed to mean?"

"Well, you know, you're sort of an Eagle Scout type, or . . ."

"Altar boy?" Al supplied.

I shook my finger at her. "That's 'white knight,' remember? Anyway, I don't know where you guys get the idea that I'm so pure of heart."

George laughed. "Mike, I've never even known you to get a parking ticket." He turned to Al. "When we were at Caltech, there was a cheating scandal one year—somebody raided a prof's computer files for a copy of a test. Mike was one of about half a dozen people who had the skill and the access to break into those files, but somehow he never came under suspicion. Later I asked the prof whether it ever occurred to him that Mike might have done it."

"What a pal," I said.

George shot me a mock-wounded look. "This was after the bad guys had been caught. Anyway, he looked really surprised, like it had never even occurred to him. Then he just said, 'Nah.'"

Al was smiling oddly at me. She said, "That doesn't surprise me at all."

"And how about when I called you about the Goodknight problem?" George said. "You hadn't heard from me in years, but you were willing to come as a personal favor, even if we couldn't pay you."

"Oh, come on. I was just joking with you about that."

"Sure you were joking. But you would have come."

"Well . . . okay, I suppose I would, but so what? You'd have done the same thing."

"Possibly . . ."

"Aha!"

"I said 'possibly.' That's the point. With you there wasn't any question about it."

I was starting to get really irritated. "This is ridiculous. I am not Mother Teresa in male drag, you know."

George said, "Prove it."

"What?"

"Have you done anything rotten lately?"

"Well, now that you mention it, I broke a federal law yesterday. And you both really ought to close your mouths before something nasty flies in."

George was the first one to recover. He said, "What did you do, reuse a stamp the post office didn't cancel?"

I told them about Armageddon. Any blemish to my spotless reputation was overshadowed by their curiosity to find out what the outcome had been. I hadn't even had time to think about it since yesterday, but now I was pretty curious myself.

We went back to George's place, and I used his phone and my laptop to log on to Armageddon. I selected for a display of Cecil's current population status:

```
Program                          Population#

Cecil . . . . . . . . . . . . . . . . . . . . . . . 1
```

I felt an odd mixture of relief and disappointment. Relief, because evidently our worm wasn't as virulent as I thought. And disappointed because . . . oh, hell, I must be going crazy.

"Doesn't look too impressive," George commented.

"No, it doesn't," I agreed. Just for the hell of it, I checked the leader board:

```
Program                          Population#

Belial  . . . . . . . . . . . . . . . . . . . 16238
Cecil . . . . . . . . . . . . . . . . . . . . . . . 1
Anthrax . . . . . . . . . . . . . . . . . . . . . . 0
Ariel . . . . . . . . . . . . . . . . . . . . . . . 0
Ayness  . . . . . . . . . . . . . . . . . . . . . . 0
Bad Gnus  . . . . . . . . . . . . . . . . . . . . . 0
Centurion . . . . . . . . . . . . . . . . . . . . . 0
Chill . . . . . . . . . . . . . . . . . . . . . . . 0
Chimaera  . . . . . . . . . . . . . . . . . . . . . 0
Cronus  . . . . . . . . . . . . . . . . . . . . . . 0
```

George chuckled. "Maybe I should be impressed. After all, you're in second place."

I hardly heard him, because I was feeling a sudden churning in my stomach. I punched up the cybermass leader board, already anticipating what I would find:

Program	Cybermass%
Cecil	93.15
Belial	6.85
Anthrax	0.00
Ariel	0.00
Ayness	0.00
Bad Gnus	0.00
Centurion	0.00
Chill	0.00
Chimaera	0.00
Cronus	0.00

Al gasped.

George said, "Holy shit."

I said, "Yeah."

I figured maybe it was time to have another talk with Marlon Oz. This time Al came with me. Dan Morgan met us at MIT, saying, "He's giving a lecture to some undergrads right now, but he's almost finished. Come on."

Dan led us to a small lecture hall. We entered and took seats near the back. These days most lectures at a place like MIT come with all kinds of fancy computerized audiovisual aids. Oz was using a blackboard. He was also wearing the same bilious-green cardigan as before. The tie might have been different, or else it was just the food stains that had changed.

"Okay," Oz was saying, "let's think, for a minute, about how brains work. There are one to two hundred billion neurons in the human brain. The usual model says that each neuron is a logical unit, so that the brain is a neural network composed of on the order of ten to the eleventh units." Oz wrote a big "10" on the blackboard, then added an "11" as an exponent.

"But that's bullshit," he continued.

"First, let's not forget the glial cells. Conventional wisdom has been that the glial cells are there to provide physiological support to the neurons, but they are not actually part of the neural network—seems obvious, since they don't have the dendrites and axons that allow the neurons to communicate over long distances. But we now know that neurons communicate with nearby glial cells. That means that each neuron and its associated glial cells form a local-area network, which is hooked into the main network via the neuron.

"And there are more glial cells than neurons in the brain—ten times as many. So now we have a network with over a trillion nodes." He erased the "11" and replaced it with a "12."

"The biggest mistake in the conventional model, though, is in considering each cell in the network as a logical unit, like a single transistor. There are compelling reasons to consider each cell to be a computer—a supercomputer, in fact.

"Let's take a look at one human cell and consider the hardware specs: First, there's the DNA; about one point five gigabytes of fixed ROM. Messenger RNA is the cell's random-access memory. Portions of the DNA are copied by strands of mRNA, just as data from a CD-ROM are loaded into a computer's RAM in preparation to running the program. The microprocessor that runs the program is an organelle called a ribosome. It reads the mRNA and uses the encoded instructions to build a protein. Now, here's the really impressive part: Each cell has up to a *million* ribosomes—each cell is a massively parallel supercomputer." He erased the "12" and replaced it with an "18."

"But protein synthesis isn't everything; in fact, only about two percent of the genome codes for protein. The rest of it, believe it or not, has been referred to as junk DNA, because the biologists couldn't figure out what it was for. Can anybody here tell me what it's for?"

An Asian man who looked quite a bit older than the other students raised his hand hesitantly and ventured, "It's the cell's operating software?"

"Right!" Oz said, although I thought he actually looked a little irritated by the fact that someone got the answer. "The cell, clearly, is a computer; it stores and processes information at incredible levels of complexity. It *must* have an operating system. Does anyone here think that almost fifteen hundred megabytes of information that has been accumulated and conserved over millions of years is 'junk'? I don't think so either. So if we assume, conservatively, that the amount of processing power that's devoted to running ninety-eight percent of the software is ten times as much as that devoted to the remaining two percent"—he erased the "18" and replaced it with a "19"—"we have, inside our skulls, a network of supercomputers with ten quintillion processing units."

A student who looked quite a bit younger than the others—maybe a teenage version of Jason Wright—raised his hand and asked, "What about processor speed? I mean, a ribosome can't be anywhere near as fast as a chip."

Oz smiled approvingly. "Don't be an idiot, Logan," he said. "Speed is irrelevant."

The student looked shocked, then quickly recovered with a look of smug skepticism. "Right. So now you're telling us that speed is irrelevant to computing power?"

"For number crunching, speed's relevant. For real intelligence, it's complexity that matters. Let's take a dog's brain, for example. How much would you have to speed it up before the dog was as smart as you, Logan?"

The other students were starting to snicker. Logan struggled to hold on to his smug look but was starting to appear pissed.

"Come on," Oz goaded. "Ten times? A hundred times? Suppose we were able to speed that dog's brain up by a factor of a million. What would we have? A canine Einstein?"

The students were really cracking up now, except for Logan, who was turning red.

"I'll tell you exactly what you'd have," Oz continued. "You'd have a dog who took only one millionth the usual amount of time to decide that he wants to sniff your crotch."

The whole room erupted in laughter, and I have to admit that I chuckled a bit myself, although I felt a bit sorry for poor Logan.

"Don't waste your sympathy," Dan said when I mentioned this to him, " 'Logon' Logan is Oz's favorite student—probably because Logan's the only one at MIT who's almost as obnoxious as he is."

" 'Logon' Logan?"

"Yeah. He's got the MIT record for clustergeeking." "Clustergeeking" refers to the practice of spending all of one's waking hours at a computer cluster, and then some.

The laughter was finally dying down as Oz said, "Well, if there are no more questions, I'll see you next week."

The class broke up, and Oz waved us to the front. I introduced Al to him, and the old lecher grinned from ear to ear; I honestly thought he was going to start drooling. We took some seats in the front of the room.

I explained some of the latest developments. "It looks like our worm might not be a harmless symbiote, after all."

Oz nodded. "I was afraid of that. But you're the experts on computer parasites. What makes you think I can help you?"

"Well, for one thing," Al said, "I'd be interested in hearing how intelligence could possibly be generated spontaneously on a computer network. Is there any theory that explains how that's supposed to happen?"

Oz nodded. "Chaos theory. Or, if you prefer, complexity theory."

"What's the difference?"

He shrugged. "No one knows enough about either one to answer that question. But the point is, if you have a random Boolean network, there are a certain number of states the network can occupy. Once the network gets complicated enough, the number of possible states becomes astronomical. It doesn't take a terribly large network to have more possible states than there are atoms in the universe. You would think that such a network, progressing through different states, would be unlikely to fall into any pattern. But in fact that is exactly what *does* happen; the network quickly develops predictable sequences."

"But," I objected, "a computer network isn't a random network."

"Isn't it?"

I was really mystified. "I don't know what you're getting at. How can a designed network be random?"

"There's an 'AI koan' that illustrates the point," Dan said. "A student was hacking on an old PDP-eleven when Marvin Minsky came in and asked him what he was doing. The student explained that he was teaching a randomly wired neural network to play ticktacktoe. Minsky asked why the network was randomly wired, and the student responded, 'So it won't have any preconceptions about how to play.' Minsky closed his eyes. The student asked him why he closed his eyes, and he said, 'So the room will be empty.' At that moment the student was enlightened."

Al smiled and nodded appreciatively. "So randomness is in the eye of the beholder?"

"Right."

I said, "Well, I'm still not sure whether we're dealing with a spontaneously evolved intelligence, or just an incredibly sophisticated AI created by a programming genius." I still hadn't mentioned to them the particular programming genius I had in mind. "How can we tell the difference?"

"I'm not sure you can. You'd have to know what was the intention behind the program—assuming that at least parts of it are artificial."

"And if we did?"

"Look for signs that it's doing something unintended. And purposeful."

Al said, "Why don't we ask it?"

We all looked at her at once and chorused something like, "Huh?"

"If you think it's intelligent, why not ask it what it wants?"

Oz nodded thoughtfully. "That's worth a try. Of course, it's possible that there might be no common ground for communication with a human intelligence." He stroked his chin. "Actually, the interesting thing about this is that it's likely to be a completely alien form of intelligence. How would it see the world? Or itself? What sort of emotions would it experience?"

Al said, "I don't understand. How could a computer program experience emotions?"

"I have no idea, young lady. But, then, I have no idea how the two kilograms of fatty tissue between my ears can experience emotions either. Nobody does. Since, however, we all seem to experience emotions, we can safely assume that there is some evolutionary advantage in doing so. The same advantage might well apply here."

"You mentioned a sense of identity," I said. "Doesn't that come from the environment?"

"Yes, a substantial part of it does. Early in life you identify with people who are important to you. But it also is governed by genetic endowment, and not just in the obvious way. For example, if you happened to be born with four legs and a tail, you might be more likely to identify with the family dog than with your parents."

I thought about it. "So who does a worm identify with?"

Al said, "Don't you mean 'With whom does a worm identify?' "

I said, "I thought you were a biology major."

"That was after I switched from English."

Oz was considering the question. "I don't know, but it's got a lot to choose from—from which to choose," he amended, with a wolfish grin at Al.

"So what did you think of the great Marlon Oz?" I asked Al as we were riding the train back to Manhattan.

"He's brilliant," she said. "There's just one thing, though. . . ."

"Yeah?"

"Are those glasses *glued* to the end of his nose, or what?"

The problem with trying to communicate with the worm was that we had no clue as to how we could approach it. Imagine that you're an ant who speaks English, and you've decided to initiate contact with a human being, but you have no concept of the human's anatomy. Do you shout into his nostril? Print your message on his thumbnail? It was a tricky problem, and one that reminded us of the fact that every communication contains in it the idea, usually implied but occasionally explicit, of "Hey, pay attention! I'm trying to tell you something."

I started to have this recurring dream where I was trying to communicate with the worm over a phone or a computer, and it would suddenly appear looking very much like Robert De Niro and say, "Hey! You talkin' to me?"

Then, one evening, I got a call from George. He was excited. "I think we've got a lead. Dworkin grew up in Orange County, so I tried to locate his family, but apparently they moved years ago—I haven't been able to find out where. But then I thought to check in the local library, which has copies of yearbooks from the area high schools. I found Roger's yearbook."

"Oh, good. Now we can find out if he had a worse haircut than you did in high school."

"I'm not finished, smart-ass. Listen to this: There was no picture of him—he probably didn't show up for that. But there was a list of his activities and interests—computer club, math team, the usual nerd stuff."

"Weren't you on the math team?"

"Hey, I never claimed not to be a nerd. Anyway, there was also something about his being an avid Double-D player."

"Dungeons of Doom?"

"Right. So I looked through the book and found some other Double-D players, then went to the phone book. One guy was still local, and he told me he remembered playing the game with Dworkin in high school."

"This is all very interesting, but I don't see how it's helping us find him. I mean, I doubt he looks much like his yearbook picture these days."

"I said there isn't any picture. There's just a little empty rectangle with the words 'camera shy.' Anyway, it may not help to find him, but it might shed some light on what's going on."

"How?"

"This guy I talked to said Dworkin was practically obsessed with Double-D. He said Dworkin's big ambition was to create the ultimate computer version of a Double-D-type role-playing game. And didn't the guy at Macrobyte tell you Dworkin said he was working on a game?"

"Yeah. Okay, you may be onto something. Was that it? Did he remember anything else that might be helpful?"

"Y'know, I didn't get the impression that he really knew Dworkin very well. It was like he just knew him in the context of this game they played but didn't really know him as a person. There was one thing, though."

"What?"

"It may be completely irrelevant, but he said that when they played Double-D, Dworkin's favorite characters were always dwarfs."

"I think you're right."

"About what?"

"About that last thing being completely irrelevant."

Double-D was an immensely popular game—at least that's what you would think, judging from the volume of Double-D books, modules, figures, accessories, and other paraphernalia on sale in any given bookstore. Ask around to see if anyone you know plays it, and you might get a different impression. Which might just be indicative of our cultural attitude toward fantasy, as anyone who admits to being involved in his own fantasies is automatically assumed not to have a life. And Double-D is all about fantasy; it's a game in which the players imagine that they inhabit a fantasy world of swords and sorcery. They role-play characters in that fantasy world—hence the term "role-playing game" or "RPG." One participant acts as dungeon master, spinning scenarios within which the players interact. Computer versions of this type of thing are likewise immensely popular.

Sometime in the late seventies the RPG met the computer network and spawned MUD. The acronym stands for "multi-user dungeon" but has also been interpreted as "multi-user dimension," "multi-user domain," and even "multi-user dementia." There are, very conservatively, hundreds of MUDs accessible through the Internet. The original version was a very hack-and-slay-oriented thing, as are many of the current MUDs, with some socializing taking place on the side. Some people liked the socializing but found the monster bashing to be rather tedious, leading to a variety of MUD spin-offs, including MUCKs, MUSHes, MUSEs, and MOOs. Most MUDs are still fantasy worlds—magic, elves, that sort of thing—but there are also many other types: horror, mystery, various subgenres of science fiction, you name it. If you have a favorite science-fiction or fantasy novel, and it was reasonably popular, chances are there's a MUD somewhere on the 'net that's based on it.

The original MUDs were text based, and most of them still are: They don't show you any pictures or diagrams, they just give you verbal descriptions of things. But in the past decade people started adding stuff like graphics, real-time digitized audio, and that sort of thing, to enhance the "virtual reality" of the MUD experience. Of course, there are some purists who say that the best graphics and sound effects around can't compare to what your imagination can generate.

If Roger Dworkin wanted to offer up yet another fantasy MUD, he would be going up against an unbelievable amount of competition. But I didn't doubt for a second that if he put his mind to it, he could come up with a program that would make everything that had gone before look like tic-tac-toe.

Still, I hesitated to connect an adolescent interest in fantasy RPGs with whatever was going on now. First of all, I was skeptical about whether he would still be interested in such things. Lots of teenagers have grandiose ideas of what they're going to do later in life; hell, I was planning on becoming an astronaut. But Roger Dworkin programming a MUD sounded a little like Raphael hanging up his palette and drawing cartoons. Sure, they'd probably be damn good cartoons, but cartoons all the same.

And even if he did want to program a MUD, so what? He could just go ahead and do it in his spare time, when he wasn't busy making megabucks for Macrobyte. He certainly wouldn't have to Trojan every computer in the country to do it. Did I say the country? Make that the civilized world.

But it was the only lead we had.

Later, talking it over with Al, I said, "I'd love to know where the hell this guy is. He's like another Judge Crater."

"I'm afraid he might be in a mental hospital somewhere. Actually, that would be a lot better than some of the alternatives."

"You really think he's crazy?"

"Don't you?"

"Well, no, not really. Just kind of an eccentric genius. You're supposed to allow them a little latitude."

"Michael, come on. This is a man who apparently has hardly any human contacts, let alone anyone you could call a real friend. That alone is suggestive of a serious mental illness."

"Don't tell me: You majored in psych for a while too, right?"

"Well, actually, yes."

"You are amazing. You really ought to go on *Jeopardy!* or something."

"You're the one who likes game shows; why don't *you* go on *Jeopardy*? And don't try to tell me you're not smart enough, because I know better."

"I think my knowledge base is a little too specialized. 'Uh, yes Alex, I'll take Bulgarian boot-sector viruses for six hundred.'"

She chuckled. "Well, maybe now you'll appreciate the value of a liberal education."

"Al, why is it that everyone else I know remembers basically nothing from college, while you've retained detailed information about a dozen different majors?"

"Half a dozen. And my theory is that the people who don't remember anything weren't paying attention in the first place."

· · ·

"If Roger Dworkin was working on a game, where the hell is it?"

"I was hoping you'd be able to tell me." I had Josh Spector on the phone. I had called him and told him what we'd found out about the game. I didn't say a thing about my suspicions concerning MABUS/ 2K; one word about that, and I was sure that Macrobyte would go into stonewall mode. Spector had apparently made some inquiries of his own and was starting to feel a little afraid that the golden goose might have flown the coop.

"Roger was difficult in many ways, but he was generally pretty good about allowing us access to whatever he was working on. That way we could have other programmers working on the parts he was less interested in. But I can't locate any evidence of anything he may have been working on."

"How about hidden files in his computer, or in the company network?"

He sighed. "I'm sure that if Roger wanted to hide something from us, he could do so very easily. No doubt he'd be better at hiding things than anyone else here is at finding them."

"I do have some skills along those lines myself."

"You're a hacker?"

"No. I'm a bugbuster. The things I look for are viruses and worms, but some of the same principles apply to anything else that someone would want to hide in a computer memory."

He was silent, considering my offer, then said, "I'm not ready to take that kind of action yet. If Roger was to come in, which he could do at any moment, and find out we've hired someone to snoop through his files, we'd almost certainly lose him."

"You may have lost him already."

"That's possible," he admitted.

"Do you know the programmer in the office adjacent to Roger's?"

"No. Should I?"

"Have a talk with him. I did. He seems to have known Roger better than anybody else at Macrobyte. Admittedly, that's not saying much, but he's worried. He seems to think the circumstances of Roger's disappearance are unusual." I was laying it on a little thick here, but somebody had to light a fire under this guy.

"Okay, I'll talk to him."

"And you'll let me know if you want to use my services?"

"If I don't hear something from Roger by the end of this week, I will give you a call."

"Thanks. And please call and let me know if you *do* hear something."

"Okay."

As Al and I walked down the hall toward Oz's office, we could hear voices raised in argument. As we got closer, the voices became recognizable as those of George and Marlon Oz himself. The subject of the debate was the last thing to become clear, just as we were walking in the door; they were arguing over which was the better conspiracy novel, the *Illuminatus!* trilogy or *Foucault's Pendulum*.

"Okay," George was saying as we entered, "then what do *you* think really happened to the Knights Templar?"

"I didn't realize you two were both conspiracy nuts," I commented. "I mean, I knew George was *some* kind of nut."

I supposed I intended to needle Oz a bit with that remark; to my surprise he didn't rise to the bait. Instead he just said, "In fact, conspiracies are very interesting phenomena. Rather like viruses in some ways. You see, computers aren't the only things that are susceptible to viruses."

I said, "Tell me about it," and sneezed violently into my handkerchief. I had recently picked up a nasty cold somewhere.

"Gesundheit. But that's not what I meant." I had decided to try to get everybody together who was working on the Cecil problem so that we could compare notes and maybe brainstorm some solutions. George had flown in from California, and he, Al, and I had taken a train to Boston to meet with Dan Morgan and Marlon Oz. I'd even managed to get Leon Griffin away from Tower for the day. Even though it was a Saturday, Harry Ainsworth would probably want to kill me.

Oz had, for some reason, decided that this would be a good opportunity to hold forth on some of his more bizarre ideas.

"Information viruses," he said "are not limited to computers. For the first few billion years, living things could store and transfer information only in the form of DNA. When they started to develop bigger brains, there was a new way to store and transfer information. Whenever you have information storage and transfer, you have a potential for viruses, in the general sense of the term."

I was feeling impatient. "Look, do we really have time to waste talking about brain viruses?"

He gave me a disdainful look. "Not brain viruses. *Mind* viruses."

George said, "Like the Monty Python killer joke."

We all stared at him. I was beginning to feel as if this conversation had been *scripted* by Monty Python, or maybe Lewis Carroll. Actually, Oz bore a suspicious resemblance to the Mad Hatter.

"There was an old Monty Python skit," George explained, "about a joke that was so funny that everyone who heard it died laughing."

Oz nodded. "That would be an example of a lethal virus. In terms of natural selection, a virus that kills its host is at a disadvantage, especially if it does so quickly. It's like moving into a house and then burning it down. But there are many types of 'mind viruses': popular fads, jokes, rumors, cults, chain letters, that sort of thing."

"You're talking about 'meme plagues,' " George said.

"*What* kind of plague?" Al asked.

"Meme. It's like the mental equivalent of a gene—a piece of en-coded memory. It's considered a plague when there's bad information being spread around."

"It sounds like the 'Good Times' virus hoax," Al commented. She was referring to a rumor that used to make the rounds on the In-ternet—still does, occasionally—that if you get an E-mail message with "Good Times" in the subject line, it contains a virus that'll crash your hard drive. Computer security experts spent thousands of hours trying to reassure people that this couldn't possibly happen. Someone even suggested that "Good Times" was even more harmful than a real computer virus, because it couldn't be attacked by ordinary means. And to top it off, around 1995 somebody invented macro viruses, and now it really *is* possible to get a virus through your E-mail.

Oz nodded. "In a sense the message *is* the virus, only instead of infecting the computer, it infects the user; he believes it, then spreads it himself.

"One of the best examples is religion, possibly the most successful form of human-information virus—or, if you prefer, meme plague. Take Judaism. For thousands of years it was transmitted from genera-tion to generation. All in the family, so to speak, like kuru."

"What's kuru?" I asked.

Al answered, "It's a viral disease found only in an isolated popula-tion in New Guinea. You get it by eating the brain of someone else who had it."

George and I made faces, and I distinctly heard a slight gagging noise coming from Leon, but Oz grinned at Al again. "That's exactly right. So the likelihood of infection outside the group that practices anthropophagy is nil. Just like the likelihood of becoming Jewish if you're not born into a Jewish family is practically nil. After all, there are no evangelical rabbis on television. But about two thousand years ago Judaism underwent a mutation, giving rise to Christianity. From an epidemiologic point of view, the most important difference is that Christianity spreads outside the family or tribal group. It's evangelical, which is analogous to a biovirus that spreads by casual contact.

"Then there's the question of susceptibility. A virus is like a key that fits a particular lock. The virus-host interaction depends on specific factors in the host that the virus is designed to exploit."

I said, "Designed?" I guess that wasn't considered too dumb a question, because he didn't throw another dirty look my way. Maybe there was hope for me yet.

"Well, to use the term loosely, yes. In this case, designed by the forces of natural selection. In the case of religions, susceptibility consists of a number of different factors: a yearning for mysticism or spirituality of some kind, a need for certainty, a sense of guilt, a tendency toward obsessionality."

I was finding this interesting in spite of myself. "Why obsessionality?"

"Because religions are by nature ritualistic. Freud considered them to be highly elaborated obsessional systems. If you have a tendency toward that sort of thing in the first place, religion is going to get under your skin."

George was smiling. "No offense, Dr. Oz, but it's kind of surprising to find an AI expert who quotes Freud."

Oz looked at him sternly. "Young man, if you are interested in intelligence, you would do well to start by studying the only known example of it, namely, human intelligence. As pathetic as it often is."

I had a distinct feeling that last part might have been intended personally.

"Of course," Oz continued, "the ultimate meme plague may be consciousness itself."

Oh, yeah. That was what his first book was about. "If consciousness is a virus, then how is it supposed to spread?" I asked.

"By information transfer, which in the case of human beings means language." He aimed a baleful stare over the top of his reading glasses. "Of course, it's entirely possible that some individuals are naturally immune."

Eventually, we were able to get down to the business at hand. I said, "Okay, this is what we know: We've discovered a worm with certain AI characteristics. It seems to be a multihost parasite. It has strong antiviral properties. It has incredible software engineering capabilities. Is it natural or artificial?

"If it's natural, that's one thing. Then we have to assume that its purpose is just to exist and propagate itself. But if somebody wrote this thing, the question is, Why? It's certainly not simple vandalism or sabotage. It could have done infinitely more damage by now if the programmer had wanted it to. In fact, I'm not aware that it's done any damage at all."

George said, "If the worm is the work of a hacker, our prime suspect is Roger Dworkin." This was the first time we had told Oz, Dan Morgan, or Leon Griffin about this part of things. Al, George, and I had agreed that we should put all our information on the table, so that everybody in the group would know as much as possible about what was going on.

Leon asked, "Why Dworkin? I mean, obviously, he's talented enough to do it. But there could be an unknown hacker out there with the same level of genius."

"We think there might be a Trojan horse involved." George explained our reasoning about MABUS/2K.

Dan said, "But why would Roger Dworkin do something like that? What would be the reason?"

George said, with a sickly grin, "We were thinking maybe he was working on a game."

I had been wondering about what Oz would have to say about the Dworkin/Macrobyte connection, but he was silent; in fact, his whole demeanor seemed to have changed, resembling that of a deer caught in the headlights of a speeding eighteen-wheeler. Then, as if in response to my curious, expectant gaze, he seemed to snap out of it. He snorted, "A game? What you're talking about could conceivably result in Dworkin having created the most powerful computing device in history. By planting a worm capable of coordinating the activities of tens of millions of interconnected computers, he would have, in effect, a single, massively parallel device that would make any extant supercomputer seem like an abacus by comparison."

I said, "You're right. Actually, it's been done before. Oh, not on this scale. But, in fact, the original 'Worm' was a program by that name that was designed to use a computer network to do certain tasks when the individual computers in the network were not in use."

Al nodded. "John Shoch wrote it, at Xerox's Palo Alto Research Center, although the term was originally coined by a science-fiction writer."

George nodded vigorously. "John Brunner, right? *Shockwave Rider*. Awesome book."

Oz said to me, "You may have to reconsider your opinion that this worm isn't sentient."

He conveniently ignored the fact that that had been his opinion, too, but I overlooked that and just said, "Why?" although I was starting to see what he meant.

"We've been thinking of this in terms of millions of copies of a particular worm. What if it's really just one big worm?"

George said, "One *humongous* worm."

"If it is sentient," Oz said, "then you might want to start putting together a semantic network."

"*What* kind of network?" I asked.

"Semantic. You see, one way of looking at a mind is as a set of interrelated ideas. You learn about a person by finding out about the ideas in his mind, and the ways in which they are connected. Put together all the information you have on this worm, all of the ideas that are involved, and start tracing the connections. And which idea do you suppose will have the most interconnections with all the other ones?"

"The self?" Al suggested.

"That's right."

Oz seemed to be warming up again, as if whatever had put him on edge before was no longer bothering him. Dan Morgan put an end to that.

"If Macrobyte is behind this thing, they're obviously not going to admit it," Dan said. "If someone could hack into their computer system, we might be able to find out—"

"This conversation is over," Oz interrupted. His hackles were up again. "If the rest of you will excuse us, I need to have a talk with my graduate student."

We were all more than a little surprised at the abrupt ending to the conversation, but we allowed ourselves to be herded out the door. I glanced back at Dan, whose eyes were showing white all the way around. I got the impression that the last place he wanted to be right then was alone in a room with Marlon Oz.

Al, George, Leon, and I continued the brainstorming session on the train back to New York, beginning with some fruitless speculation about what had gotten Oz's back up. "Maybe he just doesn't want to get mixed up in anything illegal," Leon suggested.

"That may be part of it," I said, "but he was bent out of shape even before Dan said anything about cracking Macrobyte. I think it was as soon as George mentioned Macrobyte the first time. And Dworkin."

The others agreed, but we couldn't come up with any satisfactory explanation for Oz's behavior, and moved on to a discussion of the real problem.

George was saying, "There must be a way to access this thing."

"Sure, there wouldn't be much point otherwise," I said. "But if Roger Dworkin wrote it, it would probably take about a thousand years to hack into it."

"You're assuming," Al pointed out, "that he doesn't want anyone else to know about it."

"Yeah. So?"

"So what if he does? Want others to know, I mean. After all, if it's a MUD, it's not the sort of thing one usually plays alone. The 'MU' stands for 'multi-user,' remember?"

George said, "She has a point. For all we know, Roger might be dying to have other people play his game. Come to think of it, Roger might be dying period. Sorry."

I chose to ignore that last part. "If he wants other people to play it, he doesn't seem to have made much of an effort to see to it that it happens. It wouldn't be too difficult, either. Just make a screen appear at bootstrap which says, 'Play Roger Dworkin's Incredible Interactive MUD.' "

"That might be going a little too far." It was Leon's turn to disagree with me. "If the login was obvious to every Tom, Dick, or Harry, the system might soon be swamped. By arranging things this way, Roger may be trying to separate the hackers from the hackees, so that the game has a relatively small, elite corps of players."

"Okay," I said, "you've convinced me. We'll try to hack this worm when we get back to New York."

"You know," said Al, "the problem that still intrigues me the most is the one Marlon Oz raised about what kind of a personality the worm has." George and Leon looked alarmed at this, as if the next thing they expected was that Al would brandish a weapon and take hostages. I saw her point, though.

"Al is right. It's even more important if it's actually a sentient worm. We need to know what to expect it to do."

"Do you think it knows it's a worm?" George asked.

"Why wouldn't it know?"

"Well, you know how it is with pets, for example. Dogs and cats seem to think they're members of the family, like they don't realize there's any difference between them and the human animals in the family. I was just wondering if this worm might think it's a person."

I thought about that. "Okay, it sounds like a possibility. What if it does think it's human?"

Al said, "The only way I could see that happening is if it's been in regular communication with somebody. Maybe Roger Dworkin or even somebody else has been 'talking' to it, playing a sort of parental role."

Leon looked skeptical. "If this thing is capable of communication on that level, then it's got to know that it's very different from human beings. If it's as widespread as we suspect, it's got access to an incredible amount of information—anything that's on any public computerized database. So it would have to know things—basic things, like a human being has a head and a heart and ten fingers and a spleen. And it would know that it doesn't have any of that stuff."

George nodded. "That makes sense. So it knows it isn't a person. What does it think it is? A god?"

"Why a god?" Leon asked.

"Well, because within the limits of its universe, it's got incredible power. And, like you were just saying, it knows everything in every on-line database anywhere. And the worm itself is everywhere, woven through the whole system. Omnipotence, omniscience, omnipresence. Sounds like a god to me."

I said, "What about your original question, George? You asked if it knew it's a worm. It seems to me the arguments you and Leon have raised would suggest that it does know."

Al, who had been quiet for a while, looked up and said, "Then the question is, What does it mean to be a worm?"

"I'm not sure what you're getting at. It would know what a worm is. It could look it up."

"Yes, but there's more than one definition of the word 'worm.' A computer worm is one thing, but there might be definitions that would fit Cecil better than that. After all, intelligence is not normally considered an attribute of software worms."

George said, "I didn't know intelligence was a characteristic of *any* kind of worm."

"But it is. For example, the word 'worm' can also refer to a slimy human being."

"Hey, why are you looking at me?"

She grinned. "Nothing personal, George."

"Besides, I thought we were in agreement on Leon's point that it would know it's not a human being."

"Leon, did you ever take a look at the Tower worm with your CASE software?" I asked.

He nodded. "Basically, it looks like a huge set of nested loops."

That didn't help a whole lot. "All right," I said. "So what is it that thinks like a human, acts like a god, and knows it's a worm?"

I got home pretty late but didn't feel like going to bed right away, so I decided to try Oz's suggestion about constructing a semantic network. The trouble was, I knew so little at this point, I really couldn't get very far:

Nothing earthshaking there, but it did highlight the main problem we faced at that point—we knew next to nothing.

CHAPTER SIX

The Unlisted Number
of the Beast

And I saw a strong angel proclaiming with a loud voice,
Who is worthy to open the book,
and to loose the seals thereof?
—Revelation 5:2

You'd think that computer-security experts would be pretty good at penetrating security systems. After all, we know all the tricks of the trade. Not only do we know a lot about security systems, we know all kinds of ways that hackers have beaten them.

What makes it harder than it sounds is that it goes against the grain, like asking a surgeon to kill his patient instead of healing him. Sure, the surgeon would know exactly where to cut, but that kind of cutting is the last thing any decent surgeon wants to do.

Okay, so I'm overdramatizing it a little; nobody was asking me to kill anyone. It's really just not my cup of tea.

I started with the assumption that Marlon Oz was correct about one thing: that Roger Dworkin had designed his Trojan in order to configure the Internet as a single giant massively parallel computer.

And the Internet is not just a computer network; it is, in a very real sense, THE computer network. It not only links tens of millions of individual computers, it also interconnects every other significant network. The amount of computing power involved is, as Oz had hinted in his understated way, staggering.

Also, though it may seem surprising, it would theoretically be fairly easy to access all of this power without actually inconveniencing any of the millions of users who are connected to the Internet at any given time. Think of a typical person sitting at a computer terminal: He types a little bit, then stops to think. He types a little more. He gets up and goes to the bathroom. Then he gets a cup of coffee. After drinking the coffee he has to go to the bathroom again. But even if you had the world's fastest typist sitting at the terminal taking no breaks at all, the amount of information he could input would use just a tiny fraction of the information-handling capacity of a typical modem. Let's suppose our hypothetical computer operator can type at 180 words per minute. (Clark Kent might be able to type faster when he's trying to meet a deadline, but if he did, the keyboard would probably melt.) That's 3 words per second, or about 15 bytes, which is 120 bits: 120 bits per second traveling over a modem capable of handling, say, 64,000 bps. So even our imaginary superop, who never stops, never rests, and never goes to the bathroom, is still using less than two tenths of one percent of the hardware's capacity.

Sure, the modem's capacity is put to full use when one computer is downloading to another, but that sort of thing is going on only a very small percentage of the time. Similarly, the CPU in a typical computer is idle a great deal of the time. An extra few million FLOPs (floating-point operations) here and there, and nobody would be any the wiser.

So if we take Marlon Oz's figure (probably low) of two hundred million computers with access to the Internet, and assume, conservatively, that one percent of them are on-line at any given time, and, again conservatively, that 50 percent of their capacity is available to the worm, then we've got a computing device capable of at least a hundred trillion floating-point operations per second. Plus, it wouldn't even have to be limited to just the hardware that was on-line at that particular time; it could "farm out" tasks to machines that were going off-line, and download the resulting data when they logged on again. It would be as if somebody had a way to borrow all of the surplus horsepower from every automobile in the country and funnel it into his own personal conveyance, which would then be able to travel at close to the speed of light.

The most obvious approach was to try to hack into the computer system at Macrobyte's software-development headquarters in Oakland, but I didn't want to do that. I didn't want to do it for a number of reasons: because it was illegal and I didn't feel like going to prison; because it was a little *too* obvious and Dworkin was anything but; and because if this thing was really a game of some kind, there had to be some way to access it and play it, and I didn't think Dworkin would expect every prospective gamer to have to be funneled through Macrobyte's Internet gateway.

It made more sense to assume that whatever application Dworkin had in mind, whether it was a game or a doomsday machine, should be accessible through the Internet.

The problem was knowing what to ask for. It's one thing to hack a system when you know what you're after. But not only didn't I know where to find what I was looking for, I didn't even really know *what* I was looking for. Presumably there would be a certain Internet host or hosts that would act as servers for the mystery program. It was like trying to find a cyberneedle in a virtual haystack.

So I fell back on that most primitive, yet powerful, of hacker techniques: trial and error. I combed through umpteen directories, drawing whenever possible on my meager knowledge of Roger Dworkin as a person, like where he went to high school, and his apparent fondness for pizza and grape Popsicles. In the process I discovered all kinds of interesting things that could be accessed through the Internet. Unfortunately, none of them had anything to do with what I was looking for.

I won't bore you with the details of this search; one of the prerequisites for any would-be hacker is a superhuman tolerance for tedium. Suffice it to say that I'd tried out about a zillion fairly obvious things, and about ten times that many not so obvious, when I remembered something. I couldn't believe how dense I'd been.

Actually, when the idea first occurred to me, I was skeptical—it didn't seem plausible that somebody as savvy as Roger Dworkin would have left the key word in the vicinity of his workstation. That's something that computer-security experts like me are constantly reminding people not to do; it's like leaving your car unlocked with the keys in the ignition.

On the other hand, the word hadn't been marked as a password, which would be the real security no-no. After all, leaving a dictionary next to your computer would hardly qualify as risky, even if your password was in there, which it probably would be.

In fact, lots of people use the same passwords without ever realizing it. The famous Internet worm of 1988—the "Great Worm"— carried with it a list of over two hundred frequently used passwords from "aaa" to "zimmerman" to help it penetrate system security. When I first saw the list, I was rather chagrined to see that it included what was, at the time, my own favorite password, "wombat," something I had considered pretty idiosyncratic.

Inspiration came to me as I was riding a subway train, one of those great mechanical worms that burrow through the heart of the Big Apple, and it came in the form of a certain senior citizen with a long flowing beard, a crudely hand-lettered sign, and an odor like an orangutan's armpit. He boarded the train at Wall Street, attracting about as much attention as any buttoned-down stockbroker or tattooed skinhead. In fact, there were several skinheads on the train, all sporting the "666" tattoo, which was becoming quite a fad among their ilk.

It was a little more difficult for me to ignore the old coot, as he sat directly across from me and fixed me with a baleful glare. With a shave he might have been a dead ringer for Marlon Oz, except Oz had more ear hair. When I met his gaze, he thrust his sign toward me, inviting or, rather, insisting that I read it. It said, "And when the thousand years are expired, Satan shall be loosed out of his prison!"

I nodded and said, "Is that from the Bible?"

At that point people started to edge away from me. Manhattanites can be fairly blasé about garden-variety lunatics, but anybody who would actually talk to one of them is obviously crazy enough to be right on the brink of violence.

The old gentleman looked a bit startled too, but he nodded slowly and said, "The Revelation of St. John."

And that's when I remembered the Bible in Dworkin's office and the underlined passage in the Book of Revelation, glanced at the nearest skinhead, put two and two together, and came up with six hundred sixty-six. It seemed like the longest subway ride in history, and not just because the prophet of doom across from me had apparently decided that, what with the world ending, there wasn't much point in taking a bath.

I had the rest of the trip to think of all the reasons why it couldn't possibly be what I was looking for. By the time my stop came, it seemed like a pretty threadbare hope. But, what the hell, it was the only hope I had.

When I disembarked, I tried to restrain myself from breaking into a run, as anyone seen running in a New York subway station circa 1999 can be safely assumed to be fleeing the scene of a crime. I walked quickly to the stairway, which is okay because all Manhattanites walk quickly, then took the steps three at a time.

I tore open my apartment door, practically breaking the key in the lock in the process, burst in, and booted my workstation without even closing the door behind me. Milliseconds dragged by as I waited for the command prompt so that I could log on to my Internet account.

Each host machine on the Internet has its own unique address, which is a thirty-two-bit number. This is usually expressed in a format called a "dotted quad," for example, 123.45.67.89. But because people remember words better than numbers, the numerical address is mapped to something called the fully qualified domain name, or FQDN. That way, when I want to telnet to MIT, I don't have to remember a long number; I just have to remember "mit.edu," which is MIT's FQDN.

Until now I had been exploring various domains on the Internet without worrying about specific addresses; I had no basis for making anything other than a wild guess as far as address was concerned. Now I was remembering the underlined passage in Roger Dworkin's Bible.

What I did next made no sense at all; I tried telnetting to the address 666.666.666.666. The reason that makes no sense is that, normally, each of the four numbers in the quad has to be expressed in one byte, which is two to the eighth power, which is 256 or less. It had occurred to me that a phony address—even an impossible one— could be mapped to a real one, just as an FQDN is—especially since my communications software was a product of none other than Macrobyte. And what better way to insure that no one stumbles onto the thing by accident than giving it an address that couldn't possibly exist? Okay, those were all the good reasons for trying it, and they weren't much. If someone had walked in at that moment and offered me a plugged nickel for my chances, I probably would have taken the nickel and considered myself lucky to have it.

Still, a hunch is a funny thing. After a moment I got the following screen:

```
Connected to Wormwood@chthonius.com
login:
```

I typed in "Engelbert" and was prompted for a password. For the hell of it, I typed in "swordfish," and was surprised when it asked for a second password. I gave it another one, "sardine" or something, and it asked for a third password, and a fourth, fifth, sixth, and seventh. I know I'm not psychic, but I was beginning to feel a little excited. I thought about how two German students had hacked a supposedly secure system at a software company doing classified work for the German government. They discovered that all they had to do was enter a phony ID, ignore the error message, enter a phony password, ignore the second error message, and they were in.

If you find it hard to believe that any computer programmer could make such a dumbass mistake in a security system, your skepticism is well-founded; it wasn't a mistake. It was what is known in the trade as a back door or, sometimes, a wormhole: a deliberate flaw that was inserted so that it could be used to bypass usual system-security measures. Back doors of this type are often used during the software-development process but should be removed later. Occasionally one gets left in, either as an oversight or, sometimes, intentionally. I had a feeling, though, that any back doors that Dworkin had left behind would be a hell of a lot less obvious than that, and my suspicion was soon borne out. After I had entered passwords at all seven levels, I was informed that I had not entered all the correct passwords in the correct sequence.

There was a certain logic at work here. Because most people tend to use ordinary words as passwords, they are susceptible to what is known in the trade as the "brute-force dictionary attack," in which the hacker simply programs a computer to try every word in the dictionary as a possible password for a given account. Such an approach is slow, easily thwarted, and considered by "real hackers" to be so inelegant as to border on the gauche. Sometimes, though, it works.

In the present case, however, the user was called upon to give seven passwords in correct sequence without any intermediate error message—either all right or all wrong. Now, if there are on the order of 100,000 words in a typical dictionary, that would make 100,000 to the seventh power, or 100,000,000,000,000,000,000,000,000,000,000,000 possible combinations. Trust me, nobody is going to "brute-force" his way through *that*.

As effective as it might be, this was a highly unusual approach to security, simply because if you make legitimate users of a system enter seven passwords every time they log in, they're going to make a ton of mistakes; it's just too unwieldy and inconvenient. Which got me to wondering why, if this was a defense against brute-force methods, some simpler method, like using a nondictionary password, wasn't used.

In any event I was stuck, at least for the moment. I had located the front door but was standing outside on the doorstep, with no clue as to how to get in.

Return to "Go" and do not collect two hundred dollars.

I reported to Al and George on the little progress I'd managed to make—Al in person and George by telephone from Palo Alto. They were enthusiastic as hell, probably to make me feel better about all the time I was wasting.

"What about the address?" Al asked. "What did you say it was, Chthonius or something?"

"Chthonius.com. It's a dummy, I already checked it out."

"Maybe the name has some special significance," George suggested. He sounded uncharacteristically nasal—apparently he'd caught my cold when we were in Boston together.

"Chthonic or chthonian," Al offered, "means subterranean, or something relating to the underworld."

"Underground, huh? Well, that certainly makes sense. Chthonius.com isn't the only host, though. I seem to get a different one every time I connect; the other ones are Echion.edu, Udaeus.gov, Hyperenor.org, and Pelorus.mil, and they're all dummies too. Anyway, none of that helps as far as figuring out the passwords is concerned. It's bad enough to have to figure out one password. But seven? And it doesn't even tell you if you got any one password right. It's either all or nothing."

George said, "Do you have any ideas at all about what to try?" This question was punctuated by a loud honk I recognized as the sound of George blowing his nose.

"Well, seeing as 'wormwood' came from the Bible he had in his office, I'd suspect that the other passwords came either from the Bible or from some of the other books he'd been reading."

"Makes sense. Isn't there some word in the Bible that actually *means* 'password'? 'Shibboleth' or something?" Another honk.

"I don't know. Al? Religion not one of your majors?"

"No. I told you it makes me depressed. Anyway, let's look it up."

We did. "You're right, George. 'Shibboleth' was a test word used by the Gileadites to catch the Ephraimites, because they couldn't pronounce the *sh* sound."

"Which book was that in?"

"Judges."

" 'Wormwood' was in the Book of Revelation?"

"That's right."

"It's too bad none of us is a biblical scholar. Is there any kind of a password in the Book of Revelation?"

"I have no idea. Let's read it and find out." I didn't actually own a Bible in the sense of having one that was printed on paper and bound between two pieces of cloth-covered cardboard, but I did have a compact disk that contained a home-reference library, with the Bible included among about three hundred other books. I checked the disk and found that the Bible it contained was not the King James edition, which was what was in Dworkin's office, but rather something called the RSV, or Revised Standard Version.

We didn't know whether there would be any significant differences between the RSV and the King James, but we didn't want to take any chances, so I logged on to the Internet and accessed something called the St. George Directory, which lists library catalog holdings all over the world. It turned out that the King James edition was available on-line at the Dartmouth College library, so I telnetted to "library.dartmouth.edu" and downloaded the Book of Revelation.

Fortunately, the part about the seven seals is near the beginning. Al said, "I think we're onto something."

I telnetted to "Wormwood" and got the password screen. I entered, in succession, "crown, sword, balances, death, vengeance, wrath, silence."

Al watched over my shoulder. George was saying, "Well? What's going on? Somebody say something."

"We're in."

```
>You are standing in a small clearing in a dark,
primeval forest, at the center of a ring of seven
standing stones. The clearing is roofed by the
spreading branches of surrounding trees, and
```

hemmed in by impenetrable underbrush. Narrow
shafts of sunlight slant through the leafy cover
and among the giant boles of ancient oaks, doing
little to illuminate the sylvan gloom. The odors
are of the forest, of wood and fungus and decaying
leaves—and something else: a faint scent of reptilian musk. A winding forest path leads away to the
west.
Exit(s): west

It was a game, all right. The most brilliant programmer ever had
created the most powerful computing device in history and had decided to use it for a game. At least that's the way it looked.

Al and I stared at each other. I said, "Now what?"

"I guess we play it."

"You want to play it?"

"It seems like the best way to find out more about it. I still think
there must be much more to this than meets the eye, but what else
can we do to find out?"

George said, over the phone, "She's right, Mike. If you're going
to hack it, you'll have to hack it from the inside."

How is it possible for something to make sense, and at the same
time seem totally ridiculous?

It turned out that it was a team game. Oh, you could play it solo if
you really wanted to—my record was about four minutes before my
solo character was killed and I had to start over. But if you wanted to
improve the odds somewhat, you needed some friends.

And it was a weird game. In some ways it was very like any run-of-
the-mill computer dungeon RPG. In other ways, it was bizarrely different. For instance, in most fantasy RPGs your character belongs to a
specialized class: warrior, wizard, thief, that sort of thing. In a group
game, especially, it's usually the synergy of skills from different special-
ists that leads to success. This game had character classes too, but we
weren't really sure what they meant. "Maybe," George said unhelpfully, "you're supposed to have a manual."

The character classes in Wormwood were: dream-walker, shadow-
stalker, light-wielder, storm-singer, and sword-dancer. Great; obvi-

ously Dworkin was suffering from that species of dementia peculiar to fantasy writers and real-estate developers, which causes them to make up a lot of compound and hyphenated words and think that they sound really cool. But what was all of this supposed to mean? Okay, "sword-dancer" sounded like a fighter of some sort, and "shadow-stalker" was probably a thief. But what the hell was a dream-walker? Also, in a typical RPG, each specialized class has certain limitations placed on it, such as what kinds of armor and weapons can be used, what kind of magic is permissible, and so forth. Whatever the limitations were on these characters, we had no idea.

It also turned out that our sequence of passwords wasn't the only one that would get you in. That would have been a little too good to be true. It turned out that almost any halfway reasonable interpretation you could make of the "seven seals" in the Book of Revelation would do it. For example, "eclipse" or "earthquake" worked as well as "wrath" for the sixth seal. Obviously, Dworkin had intended for others to have access to his game. In a sense, solving the password puzzle was part of the game.

For several weeks Al, George, and I, and occasionally Leon Griffin, made repeated forays into the game, both individually and in groups. We got a bit further as a group, but not very far at all. One evening, as the four of us were sitting around doing a postmortem on our latest party of slaughtered adventurers, I said, "You know, I think we need some expert help on this."

George said, "Who'd you have in mind? Indiana Jones, maybe?" George had flown in from California for a weekend of intensive "Wormwooding."

"I think Mike is right," Leon said. "I used to play games like this in high school, and a little bit in college, too, but I haven't had time to do it in years. The state of the art has gone way past what I was used to. Why not get help from some people who do this sort of thing as a hobby?"

I said, "I can do better than that; I can get somebody who does it for a living."

I called Arthur Solomon, a fellow Caltech alum for whom I'd done some work in the past. Arthur had started his own software company while still in school and had done very well, starting out with an extremely popular series of computer RPGs, and then branching into other areas as well. Fortunately, I still had his phone number.

"Mike! It's good to hear from you. Do you need a job?"

"I've already got one, thanks."

"Too bad. I could use a man of your talents."

"I'll keep that in mind. In fact, my job security might not be too solid; I might need to take you up on that offer one of these days."

"Really? What's going on?"

I filled him in on some of it, focusing on Roger Dworkin, Wormwood, and the putative MABUS/2K Trojan. I decided not to mention anything about intelligent worms just yet.

"I'll tell you what you need, Mike. You need a group of experienced gamers, and a setup where they can play together in the same room through a battery of individual terminals. That way they can communicate without doing it on-line. And you want somebody who can monitor the throughput on another terminal while your team is playing it to figure out what's going on."

"That all sounds terrific. So where do I go to get all this?"

"I can provide the facilities and the personnel, on one condition."

"Name it."

"I want to be on the playing team."

The following weekend George, Al, and I were at the headquarters of Cepheus Software in Marin County, California. Art's neatly trimmed beard was noticeably grayer than when I'd last seen him—it must have been longer ago than I had realized. He was dressed casually, in jeans and a Dr. Strange T-shirt, as he met us at the door and, as introductions were performed, handed us each a yellow plastic card with the word "guest" printed on it in large blue letters.

"This is a 'smart' building," Art explained. "Totally state-of-the-art; we just built it last year. Carry those cards with you, and a central computer knows where you are at all times. It'll open doors for you, turn on lights, adjust the climate control, everything. Your guest cards are all preprogrammed to average settings, but you can insert them in any terminal in the building and adjust the settings for things like temperature, illumination level, even what kind of Muzak plays when you're on the elevator." Art led us inside to a security desk with a row of terminals. "You can customize your settings now—in fact, I'd strongly advise it—the Muzak default is Mantovani." Al elbowed me in the ribs.

"What if there's more than one person on the elevator?" George asked.

"Then it compares the various lists of preferences and tries to come up with the best compromise. If it's a total loss—say, Brahms, Anthrax, and Yanni—it'll just pump in some white noise."

"What happens if we lose the card?" George wanted to know. "The building just ignores us?"

"No, actually, all hell breaks loose. It's part of the security system, which is also state-of-the-art."

"No offense, but that sounds a little extreme for a recreational software publisher. Do you really have anything that valuable in there, or are you afraid of somebody stealing a game idea?"

"We're not just a recreational software publisher. We do quite a few other things, including some Department of Defense contracts that are highly classified." He shrugged. "Actually, the DoD guys are the ones who insisted on the heavy-duty security measures, which are, frankly, a big pain in the ass."

Art led us inside and up two floors to a large room full of computer workstations. "We call this the snake pit; this is where we'll be playing. I'd like you to meet Krishna Gopala, my lead programmer on Myths of the Mighty, our own on-line RPG. He did some work for me in India and turned out to be such a prodigy that I brought him and his whole family over here.

"Robin Feng-Huang is my top play-tester and an inveterate gamer like myself; she's also the best in the business. Robin will play along with us. Krish is going to monitor throughput on a separate terminal and try to decipher the program for us."

Robin was midthirtyish, about the same height as Al, with dark, slightly reddish, curly hair that contrasted strangely with her Asian features. She stuck out her tongue at Krishna and said, "Cheater."

Krishna couldn't have been more than fourteen years old; I wasn't sure whether he'd started shaving yet. He was about half a head shorter than I am, very dark-skinned, and so handsome he was almost pretty. He flashed a perfect set of teeth and answered, "It'll only be cheating if I tell you what I find out. I might have to be bribed." He turned to me. "So what's this all about? A worm on the Internet?"

"Basically, yeah."

"What's the big deal? There was a worm once before, wasn't there?"

"Uh-huh. 'The Great Worm' in 1988—a little before your time, probably." Practically before he was born. Robert T. Morris, Jr., the hacker responsible for the Internet worm, claimed that he intended it to be a harmless prank, but a programming error caused it to get out of hand.

"It infected over six thousand computers," Al said, "and cost tens of millions of dollars' worth of lost computer time. And that was back when the Internet was just a small fraction of what it is now."

"This is very serious stuff," Arthur agreed, but I thought he seemed more excited at the prospect of playing Roger Dworkin's MUD than seriously worried about the consequences thereof. "Now, for an on-line RPG," he continued, "normally some software would be installed on the terminal as well; saves time because it cuts down on the amount of modem traffic that's necessary. Even with a text MUD, most people would use a client program to do things like wrap text and keep inputs and outputs from overlapping on the screen. But this game doesn't require any installation?"

I said, "Not as far as we know, although the Trojan in MABUS-two-k may be involved."

He nodded. "That makes sense. I bet it contains a client of some kind. Have you tried saving the game and then accessing it from another location?"

I shook my head. "To tell you the truth, we never got far enough to make saving it worthwhile. We keep dying too soon."

Robin smiled. "Killer dungeon, huh?"

"Killer," George agreed.

"Well, that's where we come in," Arthur said. "Shall we begin?"

We began, after briefing them on what we'd learned about the game. Which was very brief, because we hadn't been able to get very far.

We logged in and immediately noticed something very different. "Graphics!" Al exclaimed. "We never got these when we played before."

"What kind of communications hardware are we using, Art?" I asked.

He grinned. "We've got five thousand kbps cable modems on these babies."

"That must be it," I said as I studied the image on the screen. The text description that was all we had seen before was present in a window in one corner of the screen. "These graphics are very detailed. Without a wide-bore link the game would be too slow, so it must be limited to text at slower speeds."

"What were you using before?" Krishna asked.

"A five hundred twelve kbps ISDN modem." An ISDN, or integrated services digital network modem, operates over phone lines, but at much faster speeds than conventional modems. Not nearly as fast as cable, though.

Our party had materialized in the center of the ring of seven standing stones familiar to Al, George, and me from our previous forays into the game, except that now, for the first time, we could actually see them.

"There are letters on the stones," Robin commented.

"Hey," George said, "that's not fair. We never knew that when we were playing in text mode."

"You have to type 'look at stone,'" Robin told him.

"Oh."

Robin was right. A single angular character was deeply incised into each granite menhir. The letters were not legible in the initial view, but it was possible to take a closer look, either by typing "look at stone" at the text prompt, as Robin suggested, or using a mouse-driven interface. There was a toolbar at the bottom of the screen with a row of icons, including one resembling an eye. If you clicked on the eye, your cursor became an eye, and if you then clicked on an object in the picture, you were vouchsafed a closer look at that object.

"Hmm, three O's, two P's, one Υ, and one B. What's that supposed to mean?" Robin asked.

"Do they spell anything?" Al wondered.

"I don't know. Bop, boy . . . it depends where you start."

I wrote the letters out on a piece of paper. "If you start with the Υ and go clockwise, it's a near palindrome: Y-P-O-B-O-P-O."

"That doesn't sound too promising," Art remarked. " 'Nearly a palindrome' is kind of like 'nearly pregnant.' Well, let's get going. We might have to get some more information elsewhere in the game before we can make any sense out of this."

We set off into the forest—and got killed. And then we started a few more times. We were burned, frozen, sliced to ribbons, devoured by rodents, sucked dry by giant leeches, and impaled on stakes at the bottom of a pit. After our sixth party was destroyed, Robin looked up from her terminal and said, "Don't get discouraged. When I play-test a game, I always kill off a few characters right at the beginning. It gives me an idea of how hard it is to die in the game, and also whether there are any 'life after death' things going on."

George said, "Well, that's a relief. I didn't realize that we were *trying* to get killed."

"Hold on a minute," Krishna said. "Before you start again, I want you all to try something."

"Something that will keep us alive?" George asked hopefully.

"No, but I think you'll like it anyway. Hit F-two."

We all hit the designated function key on our respective machines and were prompted to select an audio device from a long list.

"This thing has real-time audio?" George chuckled. "Cool. What are we running, Art?"

"Synwave Three," Art told us.

We all punched in our selections, and immediately the room filled with sound effects: leaves rustling, wind whistling, the caw of a distant crow.

"Better switch to headphones," Art suggested.

"Maybe we should just turn the sound back off, or leave on just one computer," Robin said. "Otherwise it will be hard to talk to each other."

"Don't worry," Krishna said. "I have another surprise for you. Turn your mikes on."

We did. It seemed that Wormwood's creator had thoughtfully provided for real-time voice communication, as well as sound effects. "Do you need the cable modem for this?" I asked.

Krishna studied his monitor screen for a moment. "No, I think your ISDN modem should be able to handle the audio."

We started again. And died again. We were poisoned, asphyxiated, crushed, blown up, dissolved in acid, and swallowed whole, and this time the proceedings were accompanied by truly horrifying sound effects. This went on for another hour or so, and then George said, "Could we try not dying now? Just for variety?"

Robin shook her head. "I've been trying not to let us die for a while now. We keep croaking anyway."

I shook my head. "Arthur, how can I put this delicately? I thought you guys were supposed to be good at this."

"I thought so too. This is a tough game, but . . . Robin, don't you think we're making a lot of dumb mistakes?"

"Yeah. Embarrassing."

George surveyed the circle of long faces and said, "Are we having fun yet?"

"George! You're right!" Al got up so suddenly, her chair nearly fell over.

Momentarily taken aback, George recovered smoothly. "Of course I'm right. Tell them what it is I'm right about."

"State-dependent learning. I should have thought of it before."

I said, "Meaning what?"

"Robin, Arthur, you've been playing games of this type for a long time, right?"

They nodded.

"And you do it for fun? Playing games like this is fun for you?"

"It's a living, but, sure, it's lots of fun," Robin replied.

"But you don't look like you're having much fun now."

Arthur answered, "Well, from what Mike has told me, this is a pretty serious situation. . . ."

"Exactly! You see, everything you know about playing RPGs you learned while having fun and enjoying yourself. Whatever you learn is always most accessible when you're in the same emotional state you were in when you originally learned it. You're both so serious now, that you're having trouble using the skills you acquired while having a good time."

Arthur and Robin looked at each other, then broke into wide grins. "Well, what are we waiting for?" Arthur said. "Let's kick some ass."

"The first thing to do," Robin said, "is create some *real* characters."

Al and George looked as puzzled as I felt. "Real? What do you mean?"

"Instead of just rolling some random numbers, let's put a little feeling into it. Use your imagination. Think about how your character looks, dresses, acts."

"This sounds a little like method acting," George commented.

"Exactly. It's called a role-playing game. You're supposed to adopt a different persona. That's what makes it interesting."

▲   ▲   ▲   ▲   ▲   ▲   ▲

A motley crew of five adventurers trudged along a dark forest trail. One of their number, a pale, slender woman wearing a dark-green cloak and leather leggings periodically left the party, ranging ahead, behind, and to either side, then returning to report the results of her scouting to the rest of the group. Her eyes had an oddly alien cast, and when it was possible to glimpse the ears beneath her long dark hair, they appeared to be pointed. A short sword hung from her belt, and a keen eye might have discerned the glint of a sharp dagger concealed in one sleeve. A second woman was tall and broad, her bulk exaggerated by the heavy plate armor she wore. Long blond hair was bound into two thick braids that emerged from beneath her winged helmet. Despite her size she moved with catlike grace, her left hand occasionally straying to the pommel of the broadsword sheathed at her hip.

The three males in the group were as strange as the females. The tallest of the three was a head shorter than his Valkyrie companion. He bore a certain racial resemblance to the scout but appeared rather more human. The leather case slung from his shoulder seemed designed to carry a musical instrument of some sort, and he carried a bow with a red-fletched arrow on the string. One of his companions was so heavily cloaked and hooded that no features were visible other than the end of a long white beard. This one carried what appeared to be a long walking stick of dark wood, gnarled, twisted, and shod in iron, but he did not lean on it. The last member of the band was perhaps the least remarkable, from his shaven head to his plain linen tunic to his bare feet. He carried no visible weapon, and resembled nothing so much as a holy mendicant who had fallen in with ruffians whose purpose was to tempt him into straying from the path of enlightenment.

An eerie howling sounded from the depths of the forest, a sound that was just human enough to evoke that special horror which the human species reserves for itself. The group paused, hands reaching for weapons, but no threat showed itself.

"What the hell is that, Robin?" the bowman asked.

"Call me Zerika; we're supposed to be in character, remember? And I'm not sure I want to know, Ragnar. But maybe the boss man would care to exercise his skills to try to find out. Tahmurath?"

The cloaked man shrugged and threw back his hood, revealing a countenance that was curiously ageless, despite the white hair and beard that framed it. He raised his staff over his head, holding it parallel to the ground with both hands, and facing in the direction of the howling. After a moment he lowered the staff and shook his head.

"It seems to be beyond my range. That is, if there's really anything out there at all."

Zerika nodded. "You may be right. Just another trick to get us to leave the path."

The band of adventurers, or more accurately, their late, lamented predecessors, had learned by hard, and ultimately fatal, experience that straying far from the path was decidedly unhealthy in this neck of the woods. On this occasion they chose the better part of valor.

"Do you think this forest has a name?" Ragnar asked.

"Why would it have a name, George?" the hairless one inquired.

"Enchanted forests usually do, Mike—er, sorry—Malakh. Arden, Mirkwood, Fangorn, Garroting Deep . . . it's sort of traditional."

"I don't see any signs posted," observed the giantess. "Why don't we give it a name?"

"Good idea, Megaera," said Zerika. "Any ideas?"

"I know," said Malakh. "Let's call it Worm Wood."

"Worm Wood," Ragnar said. "I suppose that would be the 'lumber of the beast'?"

The group hiked on. Meanwhile, the keening noise grew slightly louder. Zerika waved the others to a halt and cocked one pointed ear. "I think the path is curving in the direction of that noise."

Megaera's broadsword came out of her scabbard with the ringing noise made by fine steel. Ragnar tightened his grip on his bow, and Tahmurath began muttering under his breath while making a series of mysterious gestures with his free hand. Malakh stood impassively.

Zerika did not draw her sword, but the dagger in her sleeve came into her hand as if of its own accord. "I'm going to sneak up there and take a look. If you hear me yell, come running."

After a few tense minutes Zerika returned and waved the group forward. She was giggling. "I think you can put your weapons away for the time being."

They followed the scout down the path to a point where it opened into a small clearing. A small cabin, perhaps belonging to some woodsman, stood in the center. Before the door of the cabin was a stump, upon which rested a nondescript earthenware jar. It was now obvious to the whole party that the howling sound was caused by wind blowing across the mouth of the jar.

Tahmurath was eyeing the hut. "Zerika? Let's check this out."

The scout approached the door as the rest of the band gathered around her. She knelt to examine the doorknob, which did not appear to have a lock. After blowing on her fingertips, she extended a hand to try the knob, hesitated, then, abruptly, stood up and knocked. The door creaked open, but no one stood at the threshold. A musky odor emanated from the interior, along with a dry rustling sound. From the shadows a voice called softly, "Come in."

Zerika didn't say a word but looked each of the others in the eye and nodded. She pushed the door open and glided through noiselessly. The others followed. At first it was difficult to see much, but as their eyes accommodated to the darkness, they were able to discern a robed and hooded figure sitting at a writing desk at the opposite end of the hut's sole room. He, or she, had turned to look at them. The musky smell was very strong now.

Suddenly a sharp, hoarse cry sounded in the little cabin. In response weapons flew from their sheaths, ringing the hooded figure with sharp steel. The moment seemed crystalline with tension, each figure part of a frozen tableau that was finally dispelled by a dry chuckling emanating from the hood of the seated one. A taper flared to life in the robed one's gloved hand, revealing the source of the noise: a large crow that perched above the writing desk. The adventurers lowered their weapons with a mixture of relief and embarrassment.

The dry voice that had laughed at their discomfiture now spoke: "Welcome, travelers. I see that you are new here. Just learning the lay of the land, no doubt. What brings you to Unq?"

"Is Unq the name of this world?" Ragnar asked.

"Oh, no." Again the dry chuckle. "It is just our name for this neck of the woods."

"Speaking of the woods, do you have a name for them?"

"A good question. But before I answer any questions, my corvine friend has one for you: He wants to know if any of you can tell him in what way he resembles this piece of furniture." He indicated the desk.

The group was taken aback at this peculiar question. Then Malakh spoke in a whisper: "It's a riddle from Lewis Carroll: 'Why is a raven like a writing desk?' "

"Great!" said Tahmurath. "What's the answer?"

"I don't remember."

"Oh. Okay, try to stall so we can look it up."

Malakh nodded. "We would be happy to try to answer your friend's riddle, but might we first see the face of our gracious host?"

"You would like to see, would you?"

"Yes."

"Then seek Eltanin." And with that, crow, desk, and man (if indeed it was a man) simply vanished.

A search of the small cabin turned up nothing interesting or useful. The party exited and made ready to continue their trek through the forest.

"Well," Zerika remarked, "it seems like we've been given our first quest."

"Quest? What do you mean?" Malakh asked.

"Quests are a common feature of MUDs. They generally involve finding something important."

"Like the Holy Grail?" Ragnar suggested.

"Yes, or whatever happens to fit the particular milieu. Sometimes you have to find a lot of things, and it gets to be like a big scavenger hunt. Anyway, the guy in the hut said to seek Eltanin."

"Oh. What do you suppose Eltanin is?"

Zerika shrugged. "Hard to say. Might be a person, or a place, but most likely it's an item of some kind."

"An item?"

"Yes. Special items often have proper nouns for names, especially items with any kind of magical properties—special swords and so forth."

"You mean like Excalibur?" Ragnar asked.

"Exactly."

"So how do we find out?"

"By keeping our eyes and ears open."

"Oh. Okay. What are you doing with the jar?"

"I'm putting it in a sack."

"I can see that! Why are you putting it in a sack?"

"Because in games like this it's always a good idea to pick up any special item you come across—it'll often be important later on. Eventually, you run into limitations based on what you can carry, but right now we're all traveling pretty light, so we should pick up anything that seems even remotely likely to be useful. We can always jettison some things later on."

"What makes you think there's anything special about this jar?"

"Hey, any jar that can scare the bejeebers out of five intrepid adventurers seems pretty special to me."

They continued down the same forest path, which exited the clearing of the hut in an easterly direction.

A few hours later Zerika returned from one of her scouting sorties and gestured them all to silence, then beckoned the party forward. They attempted to emulate Zerika's noiseless passage with varying degrees of success. After a few minutes she led them to a tangle of bushes just off the path. The bushes served as a sort of natural blind on the edge of a glade, at the center of which was a small pool. As they peered through the sheltering foliage, they were able to see what Zerika wished to show them: a creature drinking from the pool. Equine in form, it had a shimmering white coat, and distinctly un-horselike cloven hooves. From the center of its forehead grew a single spiraling horn.

Ragnar reached for his bow, but Megaera and Malakh laid their hands on his shoulders to stay him. Suddenly a large dog burst into the clearing and set upon the unicorn. It defended itself using its sharp horn and seemed able to easily hold its own, when a smaller dog dashed in from the opposite direction and attacked the unicorn's hindquarters in an attempt to hamstring it. The unicorn leaped into the shallow water of the pool and wheeled to face the dogs, using the pool to protect its vulnerable flanks. This stratagem appeared likely to succeed until, with a great crashing noise, the hunter entered the clearing.

The din raised by his approach was attributable to his size: He was a giant, clad in shaggy pelts and carrying an enormous cudgel. A few of his long strides brought him to the pool's edge, and he raised his great club for a strike. There was no doubt that a single blow from that massive weapon, propelled by such titanic thews, would end the struggle at once.

One of Ragnar's red-fletched arrows sprouted in the forearm that held the club, momentarily distracting the giant huntsman. The party seized this moment to break from the thicket and rush to the unicorn's defense.

"Good shot!" Zerika called to Ragnar.

"Not really. I was aiming for his eye."

The unicorn retreated to deeper water. This seemed to deter the dogs, at least temporarily, but the water that was now up to the unicorn's belly would barely reach the giant's knees. The arrow in his arm was no more than an irritant to him, and the only thing that prevented him from wading in to deal the death blow was the fact that people brandishing weapons were now closing in on him from two directions. He turned first to face Megaera, who must have seemed like the greatest threat. Despite her considerable size, she seemed like a small child next to the colossal huntsman. As he brought his great club crashing down on her, she raised her shield to fend off the blow. The impact drove the shield against her and flung her to the ground.

Meanwhile, the dogs were attempting to defend their master from the interlopers. The large one, about the size of a mastiff, had lunged at Ragnar's throat. He had intercepted the lunge with his bow, which the animal seized in its great jaws. By maintaining his grip on the bow, with his hands on either side of the animal's slavering jaws, Ragnar was able to hold the dog at bay; unfortunately, that left him without a free hand to draw his longsword. Tahmurath was involved in a similar standoff with the smaller canine, attempting to hold it off with his staff, but unable to make any effective attack.

The giant swung his club back up, apparently intending to finish Megaera, who was moaning weakly on the ground. Malakh darted in, trying to distract him, and the giant obliged by trying to turn Malakh into dog food with one blow of his weapon. Malakh attempted to time his leap so that he would evade the blow at the last possible moment, but he jumped too early, and the giant was able to redirect his swing enough to catch Malakh a glancing blow on the left hip. Even incidental contact from that enormous bludgeon was sufficient to numb Malakh's leg from the waist down. He attempted to rise and balance on his right leg but slipped and fell, and the giant raised his club for another blow against his now stationary target.

Zerika seemed to materialize from thin air, although she in fact darted in from the shadowed edge of the glade, driving her short sword into the back of the giant's left knee. He dropped to one knee and bellowed, a terrible sound that paralyzed everyone in the clearing.

Everyone, that is, except the unicorn, who chose that moment to lunge forward, driving the entire length of its horn into the giant's belly, just below the sternum. The giant opened his mouth as if to howl again, and then collapsed silently onto his left side. The unicorn was barely able to free its horn in time to keep from being pulled down by the huntsman's fall.

The dogs were intelligent enough to see that the odds had just shifted dramatically against them. They disengaged from their respective foes and dashed off into the forest.

Zerika, Ragnar, and Tahmurath approached Megaera and Malakh, who lay two paces apart. Malakh was struggling into a sitting position and seemed the less seriously injured of the two. Megaera smiled weakly in response to her comrades' anxious queries. "I think my shield arm is broken," she said, but pink foam came from her mouth when she uttered the words.

Zerika turned to Tahmurath. "Got any tricks up your sleeve?"

He frowned and shook his head. "Tricks yes, miracles no. Her injuries are too severe; I think her lungs must be punctured. There's really nothing I can do."

Then a shadow fell across the party as they crouched by their fallen companions. It was the unicorn. It tilted its horn downward, with the tip poised just above Megaera's face. A drop of clear liquid fell from the horn and landed in her open mouth. Her eyes opened wide. She sat up. "I feel better," she said, cautiously flexing the arm that she had been unable to move a few seconds ago.

Tahmurath faced the unicorn. "The water in the pool—it has healing properties?"

The creature bobbed its head and pawed the earth with a cloven forefoot.

Tahmurath cupped his hands, raised some water from the pool, and carried it to where Malakh lay. "Malakh, drink some of this."

Malakh drank, then gingerly rose to his feet. After a few more swallows Megaera was also upright, and seemingly none the worse for wear. The unicorn had walked to the edge of the clearing, then looked over its shoulder at the group.

"You know," Ragnar said, "maybe I've watched too many *Lassie* reruns, but I think it wants us to follow it."

"I think you're right," Zerika said. "Just a minute, though. I want to bring some of this water with us, and I just happen to have a jar."

"Good idea," said Tahmurath. "It might not work away from the pool, but it's worth a try. And it certainly seems very potent."

"More potent than you think," said Megaera, pointing to the pool. The giant, who had fallen so that his face lay partly in the water, was beginning to stir.

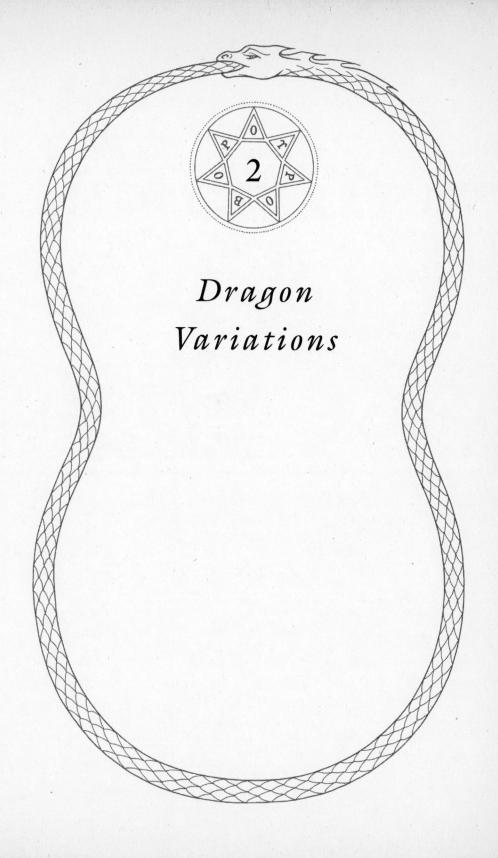

2

Dragon
Variations

CHAPTER SEVEN

Ringwyrm

. . . when they behold the beast that was,

and is not, and yet is.

—Revelation 17:8

They raced down the forest path, with Zerika trying to keep the unicorn in sight and not lose any members of the party. A distant bellow accompanied by loud baying told them that the giant had recovered from what had looked like a fatal wound, rounded up his hunting dogs, and was now in pursuit.

"If we don't get where we're going soon," Tahmurath panted, "we may have to stop and make a stand."

"Unless the unicorn stops and fights with us, I don't think we'll have much of a chance," Zerika called.

The path ended abruptly at the bank of a river. The unicorn dashed down the bank and, without hesitating, plunged into the water and started to swim for the opposite shore.

Zerika stopped at the water's edge, waiting for her companions to catch up. They did, with Megaera bringing up the rear in her heavy battle armor. She glanced at the swimming unicorn and said, "If I go into the water in this armor, I'm going to sink like a stone."

A louder bellow told them the giant was closing in: "FEE, FIE, FOE, FUM, I SMELL THE BLOOD OF NEWBIE SCUM!"

Malakh said, "Maybe you'd better take your armor off."

"No, there's no time," Zerika hissed. "Megaera, you can't swim in your armor, but you can still follow me." With that she stepped into the rushing water and began to wade upstream.

The other four followed her, linking hands to form a human chain to help steady each other in the swift-flowing stream.

"This should throw the giant off our track; his dogs won't be able to follow our scent in the water," Zerika explained. "Plus, we may find a shallow ford farther upstream."

The bellowing and baying increased for a while and then started to tail off, suggesting that Zerika's ruse had been successful. After a few hundred yards, they clambered up the riverbank and continued along a footpath that paralleled the river. Still, they found no ford that would permit them to cross the river.

After a while Megaera said, "Look, I can take my armor off now and swim across with the rest of you. I can bundle my armor and tie a rope to it, then use the rope to pull it across after I've swum across myself."

"That's not a bad idea," Zerika admitted. "But before we try that, let's go this way just a little farther."

They did not have to continue much farther, at that: Another bend in the river brought them in sight of a bridge. It was a rude timber affair, rickety and probably unsafe, but it did span the river. Several goats grazed placidly in a small clearing on the opposite side of the bridge, and there, in the midst of them, was the unicorn.

"Well, what do you know," Zerika said. "The oldest cliché in fantasy RPGs: a troll bridge."

Sure enough, as the party approached the span, a grotesquely humanoid creature, squat, hairy, bandy-legged, and walleyed, scrambled out from beneath the rickety structure and moved to the middle of the bridge, barring their path.

"You shall not pass," he croaked.

"Shall not pass?" Zerika demanded.

"Shall . . . not . . . pass," the troll repeated, although this time a hint of uncertainty crept into his voice.

"But aren't you supposed to demand something in return for letting us pass? What good does it do not to let us pass at all?"

The troll squinted up at her, scratching its matted hair with ragged, filthy nails. The scratching appeared to succeed in awakening some dormant memory, because the creature suddenly began patting down the dirty rags it wore as garments in an obvious attempt to find something. After several moments of searching, it uttered a small cry of triumph and withdrew a rolled parchment from beneath its filthy breechclout. It fumbled to unroll the parchment, squinted at it for a few seconds, then drew itself erect and cleared its throat.

> *"Those who wish their passage free*
> *Must firstly answer riddles three.*
> *Who'd pass the bridge must pass the test,*
> *Then cross the bridge; I eat the rest."*

Before the others realized it, Ragnar had stepped forward and announced in a loud voice, "I will essay this test."

The troll grinned a gap-toothed grin. "First riddle: What is your name?"

"Ragnar Golbasto Momaren Evlame Gurdilo Shefin Mully Ully Gue. But my friends just call me Ragnar."

The troll frowned and knitted his shaggy brows, his lips moving as he tried to take this in. Then his grin returned. "What is your quest?"

"To seek Eltanin."

The grin broadened. "And what"—a pause for dramatic effect—"is your favorite color?"

"Whose favorite color?"

"Your favorite color."

"Yes, but who am I?"

"Ragnar Mobrin Ephraim . . . no, Ragnar Moron Evelyn . . . no, was it . . . ?"

At that moment the unicorn trotted to the bridge and began to cross. Despite the clatter his hooves made on the wooden planks, the troll seemed oblivious to his approach, his meager mental resources entirely occupied in trying to recall Ragnar's full name. The unicorn picked up speed, lowering its head as it approached, then, instead of impaling the troll, used its horn to loft him into the air, right off the bridge and into the water. Even then the troll seemed unaware of the change in his circumstances, floating downstream shouting, "Ragnar

Memphis Engram . . . no, Ragnar Melon Abraham . . . no, Ragnar Madison Egbert . . ."

Ragnar turned to the others and gestured grandly. "Shall we?"

Zerika said, "I think we shall, but first let's check under the bridge for the troll's lair."

The troll had evidently laired on one bank in the shelter of the bridge. The area was a clutter of odds and ends, including bones (apparently human), piles of rags, clumps of hair, and a few empty bird's nests. There was also a stack of pizza boxes in one corner.

"Do you really think there's anything useful here?" Megaera asked as she probed gingerly through the debris with the tip of her sheathed broadsword.

"It's a possibility we can't ignore," Tahmurath replied. "Ragnar, where did you get that ridiculous name?"

"From Jonathan Swift. It was the name of the king of the Lilliputians."

Megaera grinned. "I was wondering why you're so short."

"Pick on somebody your own size."

"Look over here," Malakh called. After moving a pile of rags and bones, he had discovered a small wooden chest.

"Let me take a look," Zerika said. She squatted down and looked carefully at the box, which was about the size of a loaf of bread. It was of some oddly grained hardwood, with hinges and a lock of brass.

"Aren't you going to pick the lock?" Ragnar wanted to know.

"First I want to make sure it isn't trapped."

"Oh, okay. Are you sure?"

"No, but I'm going to have to try to open it anyway." She removed a small metal instrument from the hair over her left ear and inserted it in the lock. After probing for several seconds, she gave it a half turn to the left. Nothing happened. "Oh, well. I guess we'll just have to smash it."

"Can't you just keep trying?" Megaera asked.

"I could keep trying, but once I've failed, it's not likely that any subsequent attempts will work; we'll just end up wasting a lot of time. As we go along and get more experience, we'll all get better at doing what we do. As it is, we're still pretty inept at everything. That's why that giant was able to defeat you so easily, and why Malakh couldn't evade his club."

"You mean I might be able to take him next time?"

"Probably not next time, but eventually."

As if mention of the giant had acted as a magical summons, his voice was suddenly audible. It was impossible to understand what he was saying, but he seemed to be nearby and getting closer.

"Quick, let's run," Zerika said. "We'll have to take this with us and try to open it later. It looks like that's all we're going to get here."

"Not quite," Tahmurath said. "I found this dead chicken." He held the plucked fowl up by its scrawny neck.

"Ugh!" Megaera exclaimed. "What do you want that thing for?"

"Dead chickens," Tahmurath intoned mysteriously, "are of great importance in deep magic."

The party scrambled up the bank and started to cross the bridge. A dog bayed, seemingly very close. As they crossed, with Zerika in the lead, they were suddenly brought up short. The unicorn had stationed itself in the center of the bridge and did not seem disposed to move aside.

Ragnar started to reach for his bow, but Malakh said, "No!" He came forward to stand on the bridge planks, his head now level with that of the unicorn. "It's not trying to stop us. It's grateful that we helped it by distracting the troll, and it wants to show its gratitude by helping in some way."

"It could help a lot just by getting out of the way right now."

"I'll tell it that." Malakh faced the unicorn again, and after a moment it wheeled and trotted back toward the bank. "It wants us to follow."

"Oh, no," Ragnar sighed. "We're still following this dumb animal?"

"Maybe you'd like to lead," Malakh said. "Do you have a better idea about which direction to take?"

Just then the dogs bayed, sounding even closer. "That way looks good to me," Ragnar said, gesturing at the retreating unicorn, and matching deed to words.

"I don't like all this running," Zerika complained. "It makes it impossible to do any systematic mapping."

"Not much point in mapping so far," Tahmurath observed.

"Why not?"

"Think about it: no branch points. Earlier we were on a path with no forks. Whenever we got off the path, we died, so we had no choice but to stay on the path. Then we followed the unicorn to escape the giant. What do you think our odds of survival would have been if we hadn't followed the unicorn?"

"Nil?"

"That would be my guess, too. And now we're again in a position of fleeing with a guide. We're not making any decisions about where to go."

"So what do you think we should do?"

"Right now, just keep following the unicorn. We're probably dead meat otherwise."

The unicorn led them to a path that seemed no more than a game trail, and a lightly traveled one at that. After a few minutes the trail began to ascend steeply, and occasional breaks in the thick foliage told the party they were climbing one of the foothills of a mountain chain. The mountains were rough, craggy peaks, not high enough to wear snowcaps, but imposing enough. As the group followed the trail, the wind freshened, the sky began to darken, and thunder was audible in the distance. It was obvious that a storm would soon be upon them.

"We're going to need shelter," Tahmurath shouted. "Can you make the unicorn understand that, Malakh?"

"It's taking us to some place that it thinks of as the 'very-large-nostril-in-the-hillside.' I suppose that means a cave."

"I'm sure you're right. Are we going to be there soon?" The first heavy drops of the approaching storm were beginning to splatter around them.

"It thinks it's just around the next bend."

"It thinks! You mean he's not sure?"

"Oh. No, it's sure. I just meant the unicorn didn't actually say it, it just thought it, you know?"

Sure enough, a moment later the unicorn came to a halt, swinging its head around to face a cleft in the hillside. It looked exactly like any of dozens of similar formations that the group had already passed. Only upon close examination was it clear that the crevice extended some distance back into the hillside.

"Well, now that we're here, are we just going to stand outside and get wet?" Ragnar wondered.

Malakh turned back to face them. "It thinks—says—whatever, that there are certain . . . things in there."

"What kind of things?" Megaera was already drawing her broad-sword.

" 'Things-with-no-legs-which-have-a-bad-smell-on-their-breath-as-if-they've-been-eating-dead-two-legs.' That's what it calls them."

Zerika said, "Okay, we need to make a quick decision. Either we go in and fight whatever it is, or we look elsewhere for shelter."

"I say we go in," Tahmurath said. "We've been led here, and I suspect that whatever is in there will be a fair match for us."

The others gave their assent, with varying degrees of eagerness. Zerika organized them. "Megaera, you take the point. I'll be right behind you, but only long enough to see the lay of the land in there; then I'll try to sneak around and come up behind the bad guys. Malakh, you be ready to back up Megaera. Ragnar, try to get off an arrow if you see a clear target and aren't likely to hit one of us in the back, then draw your sword and get ready for some hand-to-hand work. And, Tahmurath—"

"Will be cowering in the rear, as befits one of my noble profession. I can, however, provide some light for the rest of you." He held his staff vertically before him in both hands and uttered a brief incantation. The head of the staff flared to life, casting a bright light in all directions.

Zerika said, "Now!" and the party moved forward. A few paces past the entrance, the cave opened into a large chamber.

At first it seemed deserted, but then Megaera caught sight of pairs of small orange lights approaching them, beyond the circle of light cast by Tahmurath's staff. "Eyes!" she called. "Something's coming!"

Megaera felt rather than heard or saw an arrow flit past her left ear and thunk into something solid in the darkness ahead of her. The thunk was immediately followed by an angry hissing.

The first of the approaching creatures came within range of Tahmurath's magical light. From the waist up, it was fairly humanoid in appearance. From the waist down, it was a snake. The upright posture of the torso and head was reminiscent of a cobra rearing to strike. Megaera swung her sword at the nearest snake man; it evaded the blow and lunged for her throat, opening its mouth to reveal long fangs. She could not recover in time for another sword stroke, but instead smashed the boss of her shield into the creature's face. It reeled backward, dazed. As she stepped forward to press her advantage, she was aware of Malakh and Ragnar engaged with similar creatures to either side of her. Ragnar was flailing wildly with his longsword, which had the effect of keeping the monster at bay without doing any actual damage to it. Malakh seemed to dance a weird pas de deux with his ophidian adversary, evading its attempts to grapple and bite, but failing to land any effective blows of his own.

Zerika had attempted unsuccessfully to hide in the shadows beyond Tahmurath's magical light but had attracted the attention of two of the snake people. She was battling desperately, short sword in her left hand, dagger in her right, but it seemed unlikely that she would be able to survive for long at those odds.

Megaera took all of this in without hesitating, lunging forward and thrusting her sword at her opponent's belly. It went in up to the hilt, and the creature collapsed, writhing, on the cavern floor. Megaera jerked her blade free and hurried to Zerika's aid. As there was no way to hamstring an opponent who didn't possess legs, she swung a powerful stroke at the neck of the nearest one and was gratified to see its head go flying across the cavern. "Off with his head!" she shouted. The second snake man turned toward the new threat, and Zerika instantly exploited the situation by plunging both of her blades into the creature's flanks. Whether its kidneys were located there, where they would have been in a man, or whether some other vital organ occupied those areas, the blows were mortal.

The two women turned to aid their companions. Malakh had achieved a kind of choke hold on his enemy but had acquired a nasty wound on his right forearm in the process. Ragnar had succeeded in wounding his opponent, if a slight nick could be considered a wound, but was still mainly on the defensive. Zerika hastened the demise of Malakh's serpentine foe with a well-placed dagger thrust. Megaera waded into Ragnar's duel and quickly turned the tide with a series of thrusts and slashes.

The party paused to regroup and catch its breath. Five man-snakes lay dead on the ground; at the moment the prize of this hard-won victory seemed to be no more than a dry place to wait out the storm. The one notable feature was a single upright megalith that had been erected in the center of the cave. It appeared less weathered than the ones in the stone circle where they had originally entered the game, but whether this was due to a difference in age or because the cave had protected the single stone from the elements, they did not know.

Engraved on the surface of the stone was a rather crude image of a serpent coiled in a circle so that it appeared to be trying to swallow its own tail. They looked at it and then all spoke at once.

Zerika squinted at the bas-relief and said, "Jormungandr."

Ragnar said, "Tail recursion."

Megaera said, "Kekulé's dream."

Tahmurath said, "The Worm Ouroboros."

"It looks like Jormungandr, the Midgard Serpent," Zerika explained. "In Norse mythology it was a serpent that went around the whole world and had its tail in its mouth. But what's tail recursion?"

"A type of recursion where something refers back to itself," Ragnar replied. "An example would be if you looked up 'tail recursion' in a dictionary, and the entry was, 'see tail recursion.' But what's Kekulé's dream?"

"Kekulé," Megaera answered, "was a chemist who discovered the chemical structure of benzene, after having a dream about snakes with their tails in their mouths."

"What do snakes have to do with the structure of—what was it?—benzene?"

"It's circular."

"Could be Jormungandr, or tail recursion, or Kekulé's dream," Tahmurath allowed. "Or it could be 'The Worm Ouroboros.' "

"What's that?" Megaera asked.

"The title of a classic fantasy novel by E. R. Eddison. I think it was supposed to symbolize history repeating itself or something like that."

"There's something familiar about that. How do you spell it?"

Tahmurath started to spell it for her, but halfway through it she gave a little cry of excitement. "I've got it!"

"What?"

"The letters from the stone circle. We were assuming they were Roman letters, but they were Greek: upsilon, rho, omicron, beta, omicron, rho, omicron."

"That's all Greek to me," Ragnar said. "What does it spell?"

"Well, it almost spells 'ouroboros.' "

Tahmurath seemed a little dubious. "Almost? I'm afraid that's like almost being a palindrome."

Megaera smiled. "But there's a reason it doesn't spell it out completely."

"A reason?"

"Yes. The letters were arranged in a circle, right? Just like this." Her finger traced the coiled serpent. "The reason some letters are missing is, it swallowed its tail."

Tahmurath nodded thoughtfully. "By George, I think you've got it. It does make sense. Of course, we still have to figure out what it means. I'm not sure history repeating itself is very relevant here."

"It could represent other things besides that," Malakh suggested, "like recursiveness, for example."

"I suppose it could mean a lot of things," Tahmurath replied. "But I still think we're going to need to gather some more information in order to make any sense out of it."

"And in order to do that, we're going to need to search this cave," Zerika said. "But first let's see what we can do about any wounds. Is anybody hurt besides Malakh?" The others shook their heads. "Malakh, how did you get that? Did that thing bite you?"

"Raked me with its fangs. I don't think it's very deep, but it hurts like hell."

"I didn't like the look of those fangs. I hope they weren't poisonous. Let's take a look." She squatted on the floor and removed the jar of water she'd been carrying in one of her sacks. "This is as good a time as any to find out if this stuff still works."

Malakh sipped some of the water, and Zerika trickled some onto his wound for good measure. The results were not as dramatic as they had been at the forest pool, but the wound stopped bleeding and immediately appeared less inflamed. "It doesn't hurt as much now," Malakh said.

"It seems to be less potent but apparently has retained some curative properties," Tahmurath said. "Let's rest a bit now. That light spell took most of my power, and the rest would probably do Malakh some good as well."

"Good idea," Zerika agreed. "We can also try to analyze what's happened so far."

"I'll tell you what I'm concerned about," Ragnar interjected. "We talked about trying to make this party as strong as possible, but it seems to me that Megaera and Zerika are the only ones who are much good in a fight. I can't seem to hit a thing with this sword, and Mr. Kung Fu here isn't doing much to add to the body count either."

"And your sorceror practically burns himself out doing what could be accomplished with a good torch," Tahmurath reminded him.

"Well, uh . . . yeah. Should we start from scratch with different characters?"

"Not at all. Look, I'm the lamest member of the party right now, and probably will be for a long time. Spell casters are almost always pathetically weak at the beginning of this kind of game. It compensates for the fact that at higher levels of experience they become incredibly powerful, acquiring spells and other skills that are essential for the party's success. In the same way, you and Malakh will be developing special skills that will make you far more valuable to us and dangerous to our enemies. Probably neither of you will ever be as good as Megaera will be in straight combat. But you'll be damn good, much better than she is right now, and have other special abilities besides."

"Tahmurath is right," Zerika agreed. "Remember, we would have been in trouble back at the bridge if it hadn't been for Malakh's ability to communicate with animals. And as I recall, a certain fast-talking fellow handled the troll without our even having to fight him."

"I suppose that all makes sense," Ragnar replied, attempting without complete success to appear modest about Zerika's mention of his exchange with the bridge troll. "But I wish there was something more that I could do right now."

"There is," answered Tahmurath. "Play us a song."

"What?"

"You're a harper; play something."

Ragnar looked startled. In truth, he had completely forgotten the leather case he'd been carrying. "I don't even know how this thing works."

"That's the point. Now's a good time to figure it out. You may not have time to do it later."

"Tahmurath's right," Zerika agreed. "I played a game once where the harper's powers had to be sort of 'primed' by playing an original composition on his instrument. Anyway, it's worth a try."

Ragnar carefully opened the case, revealing an instrument that resembled a Celtic harp. Taking it in his left hand and holding it firmly against the same shoulder, he began to strum it softly with his right hand. "So what am I supposed to do, just make something up?"

Zerika grinned. "Sure, just extemporize. That's what the Celtic bards used to do."

"Okay, let's see:

> *"Roses are red,*
> *Violets are blue,*
> *Trolls are malodorous,*
> *And this song stinks, too."*

As Ragnar sang, a faint aura flickered around his harp, then disappeared.

"It looked like you had something going for a minute there."

"Maybe if you could do a little better poetry-wise, the magic would be stronger," Zerika suggested.

"Excuse me, but I think you must be confusing me with somebody else, like maybe Shakespeare."

"Don't worry," Megaera said. "After that last 'poem,' nobody's going to make that mistake."

"Maybe you can come up with something better in your spare time," Tahmurath suggested. "Now I think it's time that we take a look in the box we found in the troll lair."

"Tahmurath's right," Zerika said. She pulled the box they had taken from the troll's lair from her backpack, and after another, mostly pro forma, attempt to pick the lock, passed it over to Megaera.

"What do you want me to do with it?"

"You're the strongest one here. Break the lock."

Megaera attempted to do as she was told, and did succeed in opening the box, although it was practically turned to kindling in the process.

"A book!" Tahmurath exclaimed. "Pass it over here, I want to take a closer look at it."

It was a medium-size volume, bound in what seemed to be some type of leather. The title *Ars Magna* was stamped into the leather in letters of gold. Also stamped on the cover was a seven-pointed star inscribed in a circle. The letters Y, P, O, B, O, P, O, were at the points of the star, and enclosing the design was a kind of serpentine creature with its tail in its mouth.

"Ars Magna," Tahmurath murmured. "I'm pretty sure that refers to alchemy. Obviously, Megaera, you were right about the ouroboros. Unfortunately," he said as he leafed through the pages, "the book is complete gibberish."

"Or encrypted," Ragnar suggested, looking over Tahmurath's shoulder at the text.

"That's a good thought," Zerika said. "We don't have time to crack a code right now, though, so if everybody is rested, I think we'd better start exploring this place."

"You mean the cave?" Malakh asked.

"Yes. In games like this you spend a lot of time doing two things: wandering around in the woods, and wandering around in the dark. I think it's time to do some spelunking. What do you think, Tahmurath?"

"Hard to say. In some games the underground dungeons are the most dangerous ones, and you have to build your characters up quite a bit before they can survive. But we were led here, so I think this is probably the best place to start. We can begin with a careful search of the immediate area."

They discovered that the cave was merely a sort of antechamber in what appeared to be a network of interconnected caverns. Several passageways led from the antechamber deeper into the mountain. Their search also turned up a minor treasure: several partially burned torches. But the most surprising find was the body of another snake man with a red-fletched arrow protruding from one of his eyes. "Not bad," Malakh commented to Ragnar. "You're better with that thing than I thought."

"Yeah," said Ragnar. "Only I was aiming for his belly."

"Now," Tahmurath announced, "it's time to start doing some mapping. Zerika, would you like me to do the honors?"

"Please do. I'll keep some notes of my own, and we'll compare them later."

The first two tunnels they investigated proved to be dead ends. "It's possible that there's a secret door in here somewhere," Zerika said, "but I can't find one. Let's try the last passage."

The final tunnel went on for a long way, with no branches or side passages, angling upward for a while before leveling off. It ended abruptly at the lip of a precipice of indeterminate depth. Their torchlight certainly didn't reveal its bottom. Malakh picked up a pebble and moved to the edge, but Zerika caught his wrist and shook her head. "Didn't you ever read *The Lord of the Rings*? You don't know what might be sleeping down there that it would be better not to disturb."

"Well, what do we do now? Go back?"

"Not yet. Come this way." She led Malakh and the rest of the party to a narrow ledge that seemed to be rough-hewn into the cavern wall on their side of the gorge. A few hundred yards away the ledge widened into a kind of platform that supported one side of a bridge that spanned the chasm. In fact, the word "bridge" was a generous description for a rude construct consisting of two pairs of ropes with boards lashed across the bottom pair to make a weight-bearing surface. The topmost pair were obviously intended to provide handholds.

Zerika motioned them forward, but as they approached the

bridge, a hairy hand appeared at the edge of the platform, followed by a coarse, walleyed, gap-toothed visage. "Great," Zerika muttered, "another troll bridge," as the creature scrambled up onto the ledge.

The troll ignored her and pointed a hairy forefinger at Ragnar. "Ragnar Golbasto Momaren Evlame Gurdilo Shefin Mully Ully Gue," he said.

Ragnar nodded. "Red."

The creature must have been satisfied with this reply, because he clambered back down off the rock ledge.

Zerika looked quizzically at Ragnar. "Red?"

"Yeah. Why, what's *your* favorite color?"

She just shook her head and turned back toward the bridge, but Tahmurath, bringing up the rear, called out, "Wait."

The party stopped. "Before we go out on that bridge, don't you want to find out what happened to the troll? I'd hate to get halfway across and have him show up at this end with a machete."

"You're right," Zerika said. She was already peering over the edge of the chasm where the troll had disappeared. "Damn."

"What is it?" Megaera asked.

"I don't know where he went, but he must be part housefly."

The rest of them looked over the rim and saw what Zerika meant. The stone surface was smooth and quite vertical. The troll was nowhere in sight.

"He might have just fallen in," Tahmurath suggested.

"Yeah, maybe," Malakh agreed. "But when we first saw him, he was coming up over the lip, so he must have been able to negotiate that wall somehow. Are trolls supposed to be good climbers?"

"It depends on whose troll it is. Of all the fantasy creatures that populate RPGs, trolls are probably the most variable. They can be giants, dwarfs, hairy, bald, scaly, cunning, stupid, good, evil, and just about anything else."

"This one seems to be more intelligent than we thought. It knew Ragnar's name this time."

Ragnar looked surprised. "You mean you think it was the same one?"

"How else would it know your name?"

"The troll grapevine, maybe?"

"I'm sure it has some special significance," Zerika said. "Things that repeat like that always do. But right now we have to decide whether to cross this bridge, and from the look of it, a troll with a machete isn't all we have to worry about."

The ropes supporting the bridge did indeed look dangerously worn, and many of the boards appeared to be dry-rotted, cracked, or actually missing. "Whoever runs this place," Ragnar commented, "needs to spend a little more on infrastructure."

"We're going to have to go one at a time," Malakh said. "Who's the lightest? We can go across in order of weight, lightest to heaviest."

"No," Megaera said, "the heaviest person should be the first one across." She was clearly referring to herself—even without her armor she probably weighed half again as much as the next-largest member of the group.

"But if the bridge collapses under you, nobody will make it across."

"True. But if I do make it, everyone else should have no problem. If I don't, at least what's left of the party will be together on the same side of the bridge. If we do it your way, we could wind up with two people on each side with no way to hook up again."

Zerika looked at Malakh. "I've got to admit, that makes sense to me."

"Plus," Megaera went on, "the person who gets across first might have to defend herself and the far end of the bridge before anyone else can cross. That sounds like a job for a big, dumb fighter type, like me."

Malakh seemed unhappy about the plan but couldn't think of a better argument. Megaera sheathed her sword and slung her shield across her back, then wedged the butt of a lit torch into a ring attached to her breastplate, so that the lit end stood out above her left shoulder, leaving both hands free.

Zerika said, "Malakh, you'll go next. Then Tahmurath, then Ragnar. I'll bring up the rear."

The bridge spanned a distance of about fifty feet. It sagged badly, so that the sections at either end sloped precipitously toward the middle. Megaera edged her way down, holding tightly to the ropes on either side; if her gauntlets had been transparent, the knuckles inside of them would have appeared white. With each step the whole bridge swayed and vibrated, precipitating bits of debris, including some of the boards Megaera trod upon, into the pit below.

Malakh gave Zerika a sidelong glance and said, "So much for not waking anybody downstairs." There was no noise of anything hitting bottom.

Megaera was three fourths of the way across and struggling along the uphill part of the span when one of the hand ropes abruptly parted. She started to fall backward, catching herself with her grip on the remaining hand line. That swung her over to one side, and for a moment it seemed as if she would fall between the ropes and plummet into the pit. With an agility that would have been impressive in someone half her size, she threw herself forward onto the bridge floor, releasing her grip on the remaining hand line, and pulled herself up the last section of bridge as if it were a ladder. A moment later she scrambled up over the edge, unsheathed her sword, and took hold of the torch in her other hand.

She turned to the party and said, "Maybe it's not such a good idea for the rest of you to cross."

Zerika said, "You mean you'd rather come back?" It was, obviously, a rhetorical question. "What's it like over there?"

"It's a small platform, about like the one on that side. There's a ledge that leads off to the left."

Just then Tahmurath pointed to the opposite side and said, "Look! Did you see that? There again!"

Malakh peered in the indicated direction, off to the left of where Megaera was standing. "I can't see a thing. Zerika, can you see anything there?"

Zerika trained her elvish eyes toward the opposite side of the chasm, then shouted, "Megaera! I think you're about to have some company. Stand right where the ledge meets the platform so they can come at you only one at a time. We'll try to get some help to you as soon as possible. Ragnar, get your bow ready. Malakh, what are you doing?"

"You said I'd be the next one to cross." He was already making his way across the precariously suspended structure.

"That was before it started to fall apart! Are you crazy?"

"I'll be right back." He was moving swiftly over the decrepit planks, not bothering to hold on to the remaining hand line. As he approached the middle third of the bridge, he had to slow down, though; in his haste he had not brought a torch of his own, and the feeble light cast by the torches held by his companions at either end of the bridge did not do much to illuminate the center. He had to slow down and feel his way forward, one step at a time.

In the meantime he could hear Zerika shout, "Megaera! There are more of them coming up behind you! Get your back against a wall!"

Malakh did not dare look up to see what was happening; a glance at Megaera's torch would annihilate what little useful vision he had. He continued to pick his way across with agonizing slowness. He could hear the occasional twang of a bowstring—Ragnar's, he hoped—and the sounds of hand-to-hand fighting that were getting closer as he approached the far ledge.

The last ten feet were in almost total blackness; light from Megaera's torch was screened by the lip of the precipice, and the torch on the opposite side now seemed like a mere spark. He lowered his hands to the bridge planks and cautiously edged his way up until his eyes cleared the edge.

Megaera had followed Zerika's suggestion and was standing with her back against the wall, attempting to hold about a dozen creatures at bay with huge sweeps of her broadsword. The creatures were small, grotesque, and scaly—roughly humanoid, wearing mismatched bits of armor and wielding spears that were twice their own size. The length of their spears was the biggest problem Megaera faced; they could attack her without coming within range of her sword, and she was forced into a purely defensive posture, repeatedly battering the thrusting spears aside with her weapon. Because she held the torch in her left hand, she wasn't even able to use her shield. Ragnar had stopped shooting arrows, apparently for fear of accidentally hitting Megaera.

Malakh hoisted himself, and in two steps he was upon the rearmost goblin. He swung the edge of his hand against the side of the creature's exposed neck. It toppled to the floor, the clatter of its fall lost amid the general din of battle. He was able to repeat the procedure three more times before the rest of the goblin band noticed that they were being attacked from the rear.

The effect of this realization on the goblins was even more dramatic than Malakh's physical attacks: They were thrown into a total panic. The long spears that had given them an advantage against Megaera now proved their undoing; they were too unwieldy to allow the goblins to wheel around quickly to face their new attacker. Some simply dropped their weapons and fled. Those that did manage to turn to face Malakh lost their heads in a more literal sense, as Megaera switched from defense to offense.

One did manage to turn and charge at Malakh, attempting to skewer him, or perhaps simply drive him over the edge of the pit.

Malakh spun to the side and dropped to one knee, simultaneously striking at the spear shaft with the edge of his hand in an attempt to break it or dislodge it from the creature's grip. He was not successful at either, but his blow did drive the spear point downward, where it lodged in a crevice, causing the unfortunate goblin to pole-vault right over the precipice.

As the goblin's wails trailed off into the darkness below, Malakh turned to see that he and Megaera now held the ledge uncontested. Eight goblins were down, several without heads. "Thanks," Megaera said. "But if you're the cavalry, where's your horse?"

"He decided to get into another line of work."

"I don't blame him."

After a shouted conversation the group decided to risk bringing the other three members across. First Tahmurath, then Ragnar, crossed over, and finally Zerika, trotting along as nonchalantly as if the bridge were a wide stone causeway.

"What I want to know is," Zerika said when she reached the opposite side, "where did that second group of goblins come from? There must be a secret door around here somewhere."

"If it's a secret door," Ragnar said, "then how are we going to find it?"

"It's not that hard, if you know where to look. This is a small platform. The second band of goblins came up behind Megaera while she was facing the ledge, so the door would have to be right around here somewhere." As she spoke, Zerika was examining the cavern wall with eyes and fingertips. "Aha!" She took the dagger from her sleeve and pressed the tip of the blade against the wall. Whatever she saw that led her to choose that particular spot was a mystery to the others; it looked like any other section of the bare rock wall. But when she pressed the dagger tip against it, a section of wall swung slowly away, revealing a narrow passageway that slanted downward.

As Zerika was putting her head through the door to reconnoiter, Ragnar was impatiently asking, "What do you see?"

"Nothing much. Just looks like a long corridor. We'll have to go single file: me, Megaera, Tahmurath, Ragnar, and Malakh. Let's go."

As they passed through the hidden portal, Ragnar was murmuring to no one in particular, "We dreamed of living in corridor. Would've been a palace to us."

After several dozen paces Zerika brought them to a halt. "There's something up ahead."

Megaera squinted. "I don't see anything."

"It's hard to see. Watch." She picked up a piece of loose stone from the cave floor and tossed it a few yards. It rebounded as if it had encountered a solid barrier, even though there didn't seem to be anything there. "Did you see that, Tahmurath?"

"Yes. The old gelatinous cube, eh?"

"The old what?" Ragnar asked.

"It's a common type of monster in dungeon RPGs. Usually not terribly dangerous, because they don't move very fast. But they're so hard to see, you might walk right into one, and then you'd be in trouble."

"It doesn't look particularly cubical," Malakh observed.

"It conforms to the shape of the passageway," Tahmurath explained. "The early computer dungeons were very geometrical—not nice, fractal-generated scenes like we have here."

"Should I hack it?" Megaera asked.

"Not a good idea; some varieties dissolve metal. Let me see if there's something I can do." Tahmurath squirmed past Megaera and Zerika to the front of the group and approached the cube. He inverted his staff and murmured an incantation. A moment later the steel-shod end of his staff was glowing cherry-red. He stepped forward and touched the glowing end to the gelatinous cube. It made a sizzling noise and created an area of blackened discoloration on the surface of the cube, which was the first time any of them except Zerika could actually see it.

The cube did not respond immediately, but in a few seconds it started to recoil from the wizard's staff. He stepped forward, continuing to press the issue. Its retreat picked up speed, and still Tahmurath pursued it until, abruptly, it collapsed into an amorphous mass and rapidly flowed down the tunnel away from them.

"Nice work," Ragnar commented. "But didn't you say they eat metal?"

"Not when the metal is two thousand degrees Fahrenheit."

"Did you kill it?" Megaera asked.

"No. At least I don't think so. But it should be pretty discouraged right about now."

After a few dozen more yards, the passage debouched onto a wide ledge. There was no sign of the gelatinous noncube. Phosphorescent moss dimly illuminated a natural cavern that appeared to be large enough to hold a small village comfortably. The ceiling was festooned with stalactites, and a few bats could be seen flitting among them. The ledge was about a hundred feet above the cave floor and appeared to wind downward to the left and upward to the right. As they stood admiring the sight, they were attacked from both directions by more goblins. It was a larger band than had attacked Megaera, but with the party united, the odds were even worse for the goblins. Megaera, Zerika, and Ragnar plied their swords to deadly effect, and Malakh dealt lethal blows with his hands and feet. Even Tahmurath joined in the melee, using the still-glowing tip of his staff to inflict frightful wounds. A few goblins actually jumped from the ledge to avoid the wizard's balefire. The whole thing was over in a matter of seconds.

"Wow," Ragnar commented as he sheathed his sword. "We must be improving faster than I thought; I actually hit a few of those guys."

"I'm afraid it's not us," Zerika told him. "It's just the level of the competition; goblins are the cannon fodder of fantasy RPGs. In fact, their being here is the best indication I've seen so far that this is where we're supposed to be—it's obviously a dungeon for entry-level characters."

"Zerika's right," Tahmurath agreed. "We should be able to gain some experience here without getting killed in the process. Maybe we can find a few useful items, too."

The group encountered several more bands of goblins on their way to the cavern floor, routing them easily each time. When they finally reached the bottom, Zerika pointed to one side and said, "There seems to be something interesting over there—buildings of some kind."

They made their way cautiously across the cavern floor. It was now possible to hear water flowing somewhere—numerous echoes made it impossible to tell in exactly what direction the sound originated. The buildings Zerika had spotted proved to be small dwellings constructed from the loose stone that littered the cavern floor. There was every indication, from their unkempt and dilapidated appearance, that they were long abandoned. Several of the roofs had fallen in.

"I wonder why they even bothered with roofs," Megaera mused. "It's not like they needed anything to keep off the rain."

"Maybe they wanted something to keep off the bat guano," Malakh suggested.

"Ugh. You may have something there."

Zerika hushed them both, then spoke in a low voice. "These

things may have been abandoned by the original inhabitants, but I'll bet anything that something nasty is lairing here now. Be on guard."

With drawn weapons they approached the first of the structures and immediately realized that they were not all dwellings; three of them appeared to be mausoleums. These had clearly been more carefully constructed than the decaying living quarters. The stones in the walls were meticulously fitted, and the roofs, also of stone, were intact. Also, each door was marked with the sign of the ouroboros. "Damn," Zerika remarked. "I hate undead."

"*Un*dead?" Megaera looked at Zerika quizzically. "What does that mean?"

"Monsters like ghosts and skeletons and zombies. Things that were once alive, then died, but don't have the simple decency to stay dead."

"Oh."

"For example, right now we've got to open the door to this tomb. When we do, chances are that a mummy or something is going to jump out and attack us."

"Then why don't we just not open it?"

"Because there might be something important inside. And, besides, something might jump out and attack us. Are we here to kick some butt, or what?"

Megaera grinned in response and hefted her sword. Zerika examined the metal door and found that it was unlocked; she stepped aside and nodded to Megaera. As the others stood with weapons poised, Megaera kicked the door open. Despite the considerable force of her kick, it swung open slowly, as if constructed of some extremely heavy material.

"Miaou!" The adventurers jumped back in alarm, then grinned sheepishly as a small gray cat darted out of the opened door and disappeared among the cavern debris. "Poor little guy," Ragnar said. "I wonder how long he was trapped in there."

"I don't know," Zerika said, "but we probably should have killed it."

"Killed it!" Megaera seemed shocked. "Why?"

"It's probably a witch's familiar, or a shape-changed demon, or something along those lines," she explained.

"But what if it was just an innocent little kitty?" Ragnar asked.

Zerika ignored that and peered into the tomb's interior, muttering something about omelets and breaking eggs. "This," she announced, "is pretty unusual."

Inside the small room was a peculiar apparatus. A contraption resembling a slide projector stood on a small table against one wall, aimed toward a black box occupying a similar table next to the opposite wall. The black box sprouted a long lever to which a hammer was affixed; the hammer was poised above a small glass vial that contained a greenish fluid.

"It looks like a booby trap," she commented. "The hammer comes down on that vial, which is probably either an explosive, or a poison gas."

Tahmurath nodded. "But why didn't we spring it when we opened the door?"

Zerika shrugged. "Either it malfunctioned, or it's set to go off when we walk in."

"Maybe it's an electric eye," Ragnar suggested. "You interrupt the beam and"—he drew a finger across his throat—"hjckrrh."

"It's an awfully obvious electric eye," Malakh commented. "How dumb would we have to be to walk through that?"

Zerika shrugged again. "Well, after all, it's a beginner-level dungeon. Although it is odd that there isn't even anything over there that would entice someone to walk through the beam. Let's try another one."

This time the group stood back a bit farther and pushed the door open with a long pole. This action was accompanied by the unmistakable sound of glass breaking. The group retreated another ten paces. After a few seconds a greenish gas could be discerned seeping out of the door close to ground level.

"Well," Tahmurath said, "there's another oddity. If you design a booby trap to poison someone, it's not going to be very effective if the gas is so heavy that it all sinks to within a foot of the floor. Unless you're planning on gassing brownies or something. Let's take a look."

They approached the door with some trepidation, especially as the gas swirled around their ankles. Zerika peered in. "Same setup," she announced. "Only this time the glass is broken. And there's a dead cat."

"Should we open the last one?"

"Wait a minute," Malakh said. "I think I know who these cats belong to."

"To whom they belong," Megaera amended. "How about the Wicked Witch of the West?"

"How about Erwin Schrödinger?"

"Huh?"

"Schrödinger's cat. It's a famous thought experiment in quantum mechanics. You shoot a particle at a detector that performs a measurement of a particular quantum state; depending on the outcome of the measurement, your apparatus either breaks the vial or it doesn't. But according to the Copenhagen interpretation of quantum mechanics, until someone makes an observation, the quantum state is undetermined. It's not just unknown, it's really undetermined. The particle sort of semiexists as a delocalized wave function that doesn't collapse into a particle again until an observer comes along."

"That sounds pretty weird," Zerika commented.

"It gets weirder. See, since the cat's living or dying depends on the outcome of the measurement, then according to the Copenhagen interpretation, the cat isn't really alive or dead until the observer comes along."

"Wait a minute," Megaera objected. "Doesn't the cat count as an observer?"

"Good question, and one that's been raised before. The answer is, no one knows."

"That's ridiculous."

Malakh shrugged. "That's quantum mechanics."

"Okay," Ragnar said, "we've got one alive and one dead. What do we do now—break the tie?"

"Well," Zerika said, "we have one more door to open, and I don't see any way of finding out what's inside without going through it."

"Let's not be too hasty," Tahmurath cautioned. "I think Malakh might be onto something with this Schrödinger's cat thing."

"I don't know if you'll count my vote," said a voice somewhere above them, "but I'd really prefer that you don't open the door."

The adventurers started backward, raising their weapons and squinting in the direction of the voice. Zerika was the first to spot it. "There, on top of the mausoleum."

On top of the mausoleum was a mouth. That's all—just a mouth—decidedly feline in form. It appeared to be grinning.

"Who are you?" Zerika demanded.

"Oh, I'm just the cat who's inside the last mausoleum."

"I told you it was some kind of a demon," Zerika whispered.

"Not at all," said the mouth, which seemed to hear very well despite an apparent absence of ears.

"Then how are you doing that?"

"This? Oh, this is just a part of my delocalized waveform, as I'm neither alive nor dead."

"You must be alive," Megaera pointed out. "Dead cats can't talk."

"Actually, live cats can't talk either."

"He's got you there," Malakh said.

"Why," Tahmurath asked, "don't you want us to open the door?"

"Well, for one thing, if you do, I might be dead. Besides, I find this mode of existence rather interesting. Even if I was to survive your opening the door, what would happen? It would just be back to the same old boring routine for me, chasing cave rats. And I mean they taste just awful. Besides, I might be able to be of some help to you this way."

Zerika looked skeptical. "How are you going to help us if you can't even decide whether you're alive or dead?"

"It's not a matter of indecision; I'm neither alive nor dead until somebody opens that door. And as for how I'm going to help—for starters, why don't you look under that chunk of basalt over there? Oh, and one more thing: Watch out for boojums." And with that the mouth faded from sight.

Megaera, Ragnar, and Malakh, working together, were able to roll the basalt boulder a few feet, revealing a shallow niche that had been roughly hewn into the stone of the cave floor. At first glance it appeared to be full of ancient-looking bone fragments. Megaera said, "Look, Malakh: This seems to be even older than the stuff in your refrigerator."

"What was that thing he said to watch out for?" Ragnar asked. "Boojums?"

"A type of snark," Malakh informed him. "The kind that makes you 'softly and suddenly vanish away.' Didn't you ever read Lewis Carroll?"

In the meantime Zerika was sifting through the debris. After a few moments she retrieved a piece of yellowed parchment that was wrapped around a black arrow. She studied the arrow for a moment, then passed it to Ragnar. "Save this for something big," she said.

"What about the parchment? What does it say?" Tahmurath asked.

"Just give me a second . . . hmm, it seems to be a shopping list."

They all crowded forward to get a look at the parchment. It was old and faded and torn in a few places, and bore a number of discolorations that looked disquietingly similar to bloodstains. A great serpent was drawn coiled around the border of the parchment, the tip of its tail in its mouth. It said:

> *Near Borbetomagus, the sword of the father.*
> *In Dracula's castle, the sword of the son.*
> *The ring of the king in the heart of the dragon,*
> *Where god's cap of darkness may also be won.*
> *In Abaddon's Tower a magic conveyance,*
> *Aladdin's old servant in Baba's old cave.*
> *And greatest of all is the mighty Eltanin,*
> *From wyrm-slayer's garden to avatar's grave.*

"What did I tell you?" Zerika said. "It's scavenger-hunt time."

CHAPTER EIGHT

Mindwyrm

Neither repented they of their murders,
nor of their sorceries,
nor of their fornication, nor of their thefts.

—Revelation 9:21

It was late on Saturday night when we broke things up. "Apparently," Arthur said, "this game is going to take a lot of playing. We've barely scratched the surface so far."

"So what do we do?" George asked. "Obviously, if we limit our playing to times when Al and Mike are both here, we're going to take forever to get anywhere."

"Fortunately, I don't think you'll have to do that," Krishna said, startling just about everyone in the room. It had been so long since he'd said anything, I think we'd all forgotten he was there. "As far as I can tell, the system isn't storing your character information locally. You should be able to play from any location, anytime. You just need your computer and a modem. But let's try it out now, just to make sure."

We logged on to our respective Internet accounts from another machine that had not been used, and we were each able to access the game and our particular characters. "That's good news," Arthur commented.

"What I want to know," said Robin, "is when our characters are going to go up levels. At this rate the game is going to take forever."

"That seems to be one of the wrinkles in this game," Krishna said. "Your characters don't improve in quantum leaps the way they do in most RPGs. Instead, you've been improving all along. It's just that the change is so gradual that you don't notice."

"What else did you find out?"

Krishna shook his head. "It's pretty amazing, actually. This MUD seems to have a whole new way of handling objects."

Arthur looked interested. "What do you mean?"

"Well, one of the biggest problems with MUDs is that the player is very limited in the way he can interact with the environment—it kind of detracts from the realism, too. For example, you get this description that says something like, 'You are standing on the pebbly bottom of a dry riverbed.' You type 'Get pebble,' and nine times out of ten the response is, 'I see no pebble here,' or something like that. It's because objects that the players can actually manipulate are coded in a special way, and their number is very limited."

"You know, you're right," Robin said. "I don't think we got a single message like that all day."

"You didn't; I was paying close attention. That's why I think this program is handling objects in an entirely new way."

"Anything else?" Arthur asked.

"I'm going to need some time to look at what I have so far. There's some pretty weird stuff going on here, and I'm not entirely sure what to make of it yet."

The six of us crowded onto the elevator and rode down together. Nobody was saying much of anything; I suppose we were all thinking about the game, although each from a different angle. Art had obviously enjoyed himself hugely and seemed to be struggling to repress a grin. Robin had clearly been having fun too, but that seemed secondary to a critical, analytical approach to the game, as if she had been play-testing it for the manufacturer and was getting ready to write a report. Krishna, of course, hadn't really played at all. Instead, he'd been immersed in the technical aspects of Dworkin's game. Still, I had the impression that he'd had at least as much fun as Art, maybe even more.

George and Al both seemed to have had a good time as well; George, of course, enjoyed any opportunity to indulge in his wisecracking brand of humor, and Al seemed to have relished both the hack-and-slash action and the verbal give-and-take among the party members.

I wondered if I was the only one worrying about what this thing was going to do to the Internet and everyone who'd come to depend on it.

I couldn't help noticing that the elevator Muzak was playing white noise.

Arthur offered the hospitality of his home to Al and me, but we decided to drive back to Palo Alto to stay at George's place. I told Al I'd slept on George's futon before. "Although I admit that the time I slept on it, I was so tired I could have slept standing up. Maybe we should get a hotel room," I suggested. "George's futon might be a little too lumpy for you."

"What am I," Al wanted to know, "a princess or something? Listen, I spend a lot of time sleeping on hotel mattresses that are stuffed with a coarse grade of gravel. I'm not going to wake up bruised from head to toe if there's a pea under the bed. I can assure you I don't bruise easily."

"Actually, it wasn't the lumps I was that worried about," George said. "It's just that my pet python likes the futon. . . ."

"You know, we really shouldn't be imposing," Al declared. "Why don't we just get a hotel room?"

It took us the rest of the ride back to Palo Alto to convince her that George was just kidding about the python.

It was late when we got to George's place, but none of us felt like going to sleep just yet. George put on a pot of decaf and a CD of Glenn Gould playing the Goldberg Variations. He kept the volume low, but after a few minutes Cassie came out of the bedroom and joined us. She didn't seem to mind being awakened in the middle of the night. George introduced her to Al.

Cassie regarded Al thoughtfully. "You have a very confusing aura," she said. "I've never seen anything like it. It scares me a little."

"Cassie, do you have to weird everybody out within ten minutes of meeting them?" George asked.

She smiled a bit sheepishly. "You're right, I do have a habit of doing that." She turned back to Al. "I'm sorry, don't even pay any attention to me."

"It's okay," Al said. "I've been told the same thing before."

"You've heard this before?" I was surprised.

Now it was Al's turn to look a little sheepish. "Yes, I had a tarot card reading with a gypsy fortune-teller once, a few years back. She laid out the cards, then just picked them up and offered to give me my money back."

"Now, *that* would be enough to weird somebody out," I said.

"Bah," George said, "you probably just looked smart enough that she realized she couldn't bullshit you."

"George," Cassie chided gently, "you're so cynical." She kissed him and went back to bed, explaining that she had to be up early in the morning.

After that we just listened to the music for a while.

"Didn't you have that on vinyl when we were in school?" I asked George when the CD reached its end.

"I still do; I just don't play it anymore. It's a bit of a collector's item."

Al smiled; she had obviously been enjoying the music. "You like Bach, huh?" she asked George.

I laughed. "George likes Bach because he thinks if he were alive today, he'd be a hacker."

"Not *would* be. Bach *was* a hacker. He just programmed for organs and harpsichords and stuff. What's a musical score, anyway? It's an algorithm."

"But what about the musician's interpretation of the music?" Al asked. "Not every pianist would play the Goldberg Variations like Glenn Gould."

"And what about improvisation?" I added. "Especially for a jazz musician like you—but even baroque music allowed for the performers to add a lot of ruffles and flourishes."

George shook a finger at me. "That's just a limitation of the current technology. Someday computers will interpret a program—and improvise!—just like a musician. You'll see."

Al nodded thoughtfully. "Why, George, I didn't realize you were a visionary." I actually thought he was going to blush.

"Sometimes," I said, "there's a fine line between a visionary and a raving lunatic."

George was undeterred. "They laughed at Columbus. They laughed at Galileo. . . ."

"Actually, they put Galileo under house arrest and threatened to burn him at the stake."

"Whatever." He turned to Al. "So how did you get into such a male-dominated field? What was the attraction?"

"Maybe I liked the odds." She flashed me her devilish grin. "It really just started out as a hobby. I never even took a computer course as an undergraduate at Antioch. After I graduated, I went home to Philadelphia and took a few courses at Drexel while I was deciding what to do with my life. Anyway, that's why I feel kind of insecure around Caltech computer jocks like you and Michael."

George guffawed. "Arcangelo a computer jock? Mike, did you even take any computer courses at 'tech?"

"I had to take a couple, it was a requirement in my major."

"Which was?" Al asked.

"Physics. In fact, George started out as a physics major, too. That's how we met."

"Yeah." George nodded. "That was before I found out that quantum mechanics made my brain bleed."

"Anyway," I continued, "computers were really primarily a hobby for me, too."

"What happened to physics?"

"I got tired of going to school. I wasn't going to be able to get a job with a bachelor's degree in physics, and I wasn't ready to start putting in the time on a doctorate. Besides, there was a glut of physics Ph.D.'s on the market in the midnineties. I had to make a living somehow."

Before leaving Palo Alto the following morning, I had a chance to go by the dry cleaner's. The same genius was at the counter. I handed him the ticket, feeling a little embarrassed because I had made a stink about getting the stuff the next day, and it was now over two months. He searched through the racks for about ten minutes, then disappeared into the back for another ten before finally returning empty-handed.

"Well?" I asked.

"It'll be ready Tuesday."

It was the third week of June, and Al and I were very busy. The Triple Witching Hour virus was still very much at large, and paranoia reigned in New York, Chicago, Philadelphia, and anywhere else with any kind of an options exchange.

The problem with paranoia is, it's a two-edged sword. Being afraid to trust anyone, including the people you need to help you—that's the edge that cuts your own throat. Firms that were afraid to let any outside consultants work on their computer systems tried a variety of defensive strategies, ranging from half-assed down into even smaller ass-fractions.

Gerdel Hesher Bock had somehow managed to survive that first hit, and they were determined not to let it happen again. I had been coming in for regular checks since the beginning of the month. The first thing I did on returning to GHB was check for 666 markers. There were none. This wasn't really surprising, because GHB did not use a Macrobyte operating system. Wall Street was, in fact, one of the few areas where any of Macrobyte's competitors had made significant inroads, and most firms used software made by an outfit called Vekter.

Cleaning GHB's computer system was one thing; keeping it clean was another matter entirely. We had several meetings with all of their employees to emphasize the importance of not using any foreign magnetic media on the system. Because of their recent disaster, most of them actually seemed inclined to pay attention at these meetings, so it was a little surprising when the system kept getting reinfected.

It shouldn't have been happening, because by now I had installed enough antivirus software that it shouldn't have mattered if somebody was booting an infected floppy every ten minutes. That was when I realized that Beelzebub's virus was getting in through the network connections—that it was, in fact, a worm. I reconfigured the antivirus program to monitor their network connections, and that seemed to secure things, finally.

I had also picked up four other Wall Street options firms as clients, and Al was working with two in New York and two in Chicago. We compared notes frequently.

I spent Friday at GHB, basically hand-holding, because I had already done about everything I could do. There were a lot of damp Armani armpits, but things went pretty smoothly until about midafternoon, when a large number of options traders started dropping off the network. I checked on my other clients, and on Al's as well, but they all seemed to be running without problems. Evidently, the virus was still out there.

Al and I conducted our own postmortem on Saturday morning over breakfast and copies of the *New York Times* and the *Wall Street Journal*. Eighteen firms had been hit this time, with results ranging from partial to total paralysis.

"Some of the firms tried to deal with the virus by changing the date in their computer system," Al said. "It didn't work."

"Yeah, I know. I wonder why not." I could think of several different ways that the virus might defeat such a strategy. It would be interesting to know which one was actually used, though.

"Did you ever get around to decompiling it?"

"I've been working on it."

"Here's something interesting," Al said. "Did you know that of all the firms that were affected, none of them was running a Macrobyte OS?"

"Now, why doesn't that surprise me?"

Al and I parted company the following day; I had more jobs waiting for me in New York, and she was going to be doing some work in Chicago and Houston. The prospect of not seeing her for two weeks was not a pleasant one and gave me an additional reason to look forward to the evening game sessions we had all agreed on; it would be the closest we'd come to being together for a little while.

The weeks passed slowly. I had a fairly steady trickle of new jobs, and in my spare time I studied Cecil. Actually, at some indeterminate point we had stopped calling it Cecil and started referring to it simply as The Worm, and then, later, as Wyrm. I'm not sure how that last change came about: It may have originally been a typographical error, but for whatever reason, it stuck.

In addition to playing Wormwood every night with Al and George, I was also in fairly frequent touch with them by phone. I also attempted to keep a line open to Josh Spector at Macrobyte, but he had stopped returning my calls and was mysteriously "away from his desk" every time I tried calling him. This did nothing to allay my suspicions that something was rotten in Oakland, but there wasn't much I could do about it at the moment.

Friday eventually came. It was the weekend of DEF CON 6, and I was going to meet Al in Philadelphia. I debated whether to drive down or take the train and decided on the train, mainly because I didn't want to have to worry about parking my car. Al would fly in from somewhere the next morning. I wasn't sure how even she kept track of her itinerary. I certainly couldn't.

I had reserved a room at the Marriott, where I knew a lot of hackers would be staying—the Marriott had a prime location, even closer to the convention center than in San Francisco. A lot of times you get more interesting information hanging around the hotel than you do at the actual convention site. The opening ceremonies were set for Saturday morning, but a lot of hackers had arrived early, and there were parties going on in several different places in the hotel.

I circulated around, renewing some old acquaintances and making some new ones. On an elevator between parties I ran into someone I recognized: The Dodo. The Dodo was fiftyish, a first- or second-generation hacker. He was tall and somewhat prematurely white-haired, with the large, soulful eyes of a bloodhound, and the pasty complexion of somebody in the habit of spending all his daylight hours in front of a monitor.

"Hail and well met, Engelbert," he greeted me, using the hacker handle I had adopted for the purpose of attending these meetings, among other things. "It's good to see you at this year's festivities."

"Wouldn't miss it, TD. What kind of fun and games do they have planned for this year?"

"I understand there will be a certain emphasis on encryption and code breaking, along with fiber-optic data transmission, viruses, AI, and so on. And, of course, the usual amount of vaporware from the business types. And pnambics."

"Vaporware" is hackerese for a computer product that has been heavily hyped but not released yet. "Pnambics," though, was a new one on me. I asked him about it.

"You know, 'Pay no attention to the man behind the curtain.' Pnambics. Hocus-pocus. Smoke and mirrors."

"Rigged demos?"

"Exactly." The elevator doors opened and a man about my age got on. I didn't recognize him, but he and The Dodo nodded to each other as if they shared some slight acquaintance. "But the hot item this year," The Dodo continued, "is reputed to be a show of some new, very powerful virtual-reality hardware."

"Such as?"

"The usual things, really: helmets, goggles, gloves, full-feedback suits. Just more refined and powerful. And some people are going to talk about next-generation hardware—direct neural interfaces, and that sort of thing."

"Sounds like fun. Who've you run into so far?"

"Well, besides yourself, I've seen Bucky, Fishhead, Shadowhacker, and Graviton. There's also a rumor that HfH is here in force this year—anonymously, of course."

"Have you heard anything about Roger Dworkin being here?"

"No. Is he?"

"I don't know. I was hoping that he might be. If you hear anything, let me know, okay?"

"Certainly. Oh, by the way, did you ever find out what was causing that bug in your delete function?"

I shook my head. "I think it may be a heisenbug."

"I had the same thought. Oh, take one of these"—he produced a floppy disk—"it's just a little Lisp program I wrote. I think you might find it amusing."

"What does it do?"

"It creates recursive acronyms."

"Cute. What do you call it?"

"I haven't decided what to call it, but it calls itself the TRAP Recursive Acronym Program."

"What does TRAP stand for?"

"It stands for TRAP Recursive Acronym Program."

"Ouch. I can't believe I fell into that one." Hackers tend to be fascinated with examples of recursiveness—things that refer to themselves. Recursive acronyms are particularly popular. For example, at MIT there were a couple of editor programs, the first one being EINE, which supposedly stood for EINE Is Not EMACS (EMACS was another, earlier editor program). The successor to EINE was a program called ZWEI, or ZWEI was EINE Initially. And there are other ways that acronyms can be recursive, like TLA (Three-Letter Acronym) and YABA (Yet Another Bloody Acronym).

I took the proffered disk, and as I did, I noticed some whitish material on The Dodo's hands. "What is that?" I inquired.

"Oh, this? Somebody on the thirteenth floor is having an ooblick party."

Ooblick is a strange substance that is easily made by simply mixing cornstarch with water. The resulting goop exhibits some bizarre properties, such as seeming to be unable to decide whether it's a solid or a liquid; even though it's soft and runny, if you hit it hard, it cracks. Hackers love to play with the stuff. I said adios to The Dodo and headed to the thirteenth floor, then followed the trail of people with white debris clinging to their hands and clothes. These people must have brought in a couple of cases of cornstarch at least, because they had actually filled the bathtub with ooblick. How they expected to get it out, I don't know; probably they figured that would be a problem for the hotel cleaning staff. There was one guy who was actually *in* the bathtub, wallowing in the stuff. Other people had containers filled with varying amounts of ooblick, so that the party was organized around conversational knots of hackers, each knot gathered around an ooblick container, taking turns "grokking" the contents.

As I walked through the suite, I picked up little snatches of conversation here and there: "If you're not part of the solution, you're part of the precipitate," "Glass is actually a very high-viscosity liquid. If you look at the windows in thirteenth-century cathedrals . . . ," "If God had intended for us to have virtual reality, He would have designed a decent interface. . . ."

I circulated through a few more parties, picking up some tidbits of information here and there, but nothing at all about Dworkin. A little after one A.M. I decided to call it a night and go to bed.

Early the next morning I had just finished dressing and was on my way out for breakfast when there was a knock at the door. It was Al. She dropped her bags and literally jumped into my arms. A few minutes later, when I had the use of my lips again, I said, "I wasn't expecting you for another two hours."

"I was able to get an earlier flight, so I did. Oh, I have to show you something," she said, reaching into an outer pocket of her computer case. She pulled out a folded paper and handed it to me. "Check this out."

It was a photocopy of a page from a book. At the top of the page was a reproduction of a torn picture showing a serpent with its tail in its mouth circumscribing a spiderweb with a big spider in the center. The caption read:

108.   *Maya, eternal weaver of the illusory world of the senses, encircled by the Uroboros—Damaged vignette from a collection of Brahminic sayings.*

"Where did you find this?" I asked.

"It's a page from Jung's *Psychology and Alchemy*. I found it while I was doing some research on the ouroboros. Actually, he has a lot of stuff on the ouroboros—apparently it was a pretty important alchemical symbol."

"Is it often shown with a web in the middle?"

"Not as far as I know—I got goose bumps when I found this one."

"I can see why. Actually, I've been doing a little background reading myself—mythology, mainly. You remember what Robin said about the Jormungandr?"

"The 'Midgard Serpent'?"

"Right, the one that encircles the world with its tail in its mouth. Well, according to Norse myth, there's another manifestation of Jormungandr called Nidhoggr; the 'dread biter.' It lives at the base of Yggdrasil, the world tree, and gnaws at the roots."

"I think I see what you're getting at: The roots of the tree are a network, like the Internet."

"That's what I was thinking."

"Oh, my," she said, looking me up and down as if she were seeing me for the first time. "What are you wearing?"

What I was wearing was a pair of old khaki shorts, the kind with an excessive number of pockets, along with a pair of black high-top sneakers. This stunning ensemble was topped off with a souvenir T-shirt from a concert played by a heavy-metal group known as Black Silicon back in the eighties. It was laden with the kind of demonic imagery that upsets those excitable types who think that rock and roll is a really a secret plot designed to lure children into devil worship. "I think it ought to attract the element we're interested in, don't you?"

"Did you actually go to that concert?"

"You don't see me wearing a hearing aid, do you? I picked it up at a garage sale on Long Island."

"No offense, Michael, but I'm not sure I want to be seen with you if you're going to be dressed like that. I grew up near here; we might run into somebody I know."

I chuckled. "I hate to break this to you, but most of the hackers you'll be schmoozing with this weekend are going to be dressed like this."

"That's different. I can always explain to my friends later about what I was doing here. How do I explain a boyfriend who dresses that way?"

"I see your point. You'd probably be dropped from the Social Register. Are you brave enough to go for breakfast?"

"Let's order room service."

"You're really serious about this, aren't you?"

"No, not really. I just had an idea about what we could do while we wait for room service that doesn't involve any clothes at all."

After breakfast we headed over to the convention center to register for DEF CON. We checked to see if Roger Dworkin was registered, which he wasn't. As is the case at most conventions, we were issued little plastic security badges with our names on them. Unlike most conventions, the typical participant here took the card out of the plastic badge, wrote his hacker handle on the flip side, and put it back in the badge wrong side out, displaying his handle while concealing his real name. This practice suited me just fine, as there was a small chance that someone might recognize my real name from one of my talks or articles on viruses.

"It's probably best if we don't hang out together too much," I told Al, who was wearing a badge with the name "Medea."

"So we can cover more territory?"

"That and another thing: If people see us together, they're going to assume you're with me, and that will cramp your style; the other hackers will tend to stay away from you."

She wrinkled her nose. "I don't see how anyone could possibly think that someone dressed like you could be with me."

"Cute. Medea, huh? Isn't she the one who killed her own kids?"

"She did not! The Corinthians bribed Euripides to say that. They were the ones who killed her children."

"Whoa, relax. It's only a myth, right?"

"What, just because it's a myth you think it isn't real?"

We took a look at the program and decided which seminars and workshops to attend. Obviously we were both interested in anything that had to do with viruses, so to be fair, we split them up. Al was interested in a particular talk on new methods of data encryption, and I decided to go to a panel on virtual reality. We agreed to check in with each other periodically to see how things were going.

I looked at my watch. "Well, I think we'd better get going."

"I guess we really shouldn't kiss, should we?" she asked, looking around at the milling crowd.

"Not unless you just want to forget the whole thing and go back to the hotel."

"It's tempting."

I knew better than to feel flattered by that last comment, since I could see that Al was a little intimidated at the prospect of mingling with "the enemy."

Just then I noticed The Dodo a few yards away. "Al, if you'd rather stick together for a while, I have an idea."

"But what about what you said earlier? The hackers will assume that I'm with you."

"Not if someone else is with us."

"Someone else?"

"Right. If you're with one guy, it's assumed that you're his. But if you're with more than one guy, you don't belong to anyone; you're up for grabs. Don't ask me to explain it, I don't know why, but that's the way guys think."

She rolled her eyes. "I'm not even going to let myself think about it, because it'll probably just infuriate me. Do you have somebody in mind?"

"That guy right over there." I caught The Dodo's eye and waved him over.

"But what if he doesn't want to go to the things we're interested in?"

"When he sees you, he'll go wherever we want to go."

We went to a couple of virus-oriented things, and as I'd predicted, The Dodo seemed happy to tag along. About midmorning Al, feeling more confident, excused herself and went to one of the data-encryption workshops. Predictably, The Dodo went along with her. She also picked up a little entourage consisting of Robonerd, Hackmeister, and two teenage kids who called themselves Buttis and Beave-head. Before leaving she slipped me a little note that said, "Meet me at the south end of the main exhibition hall at noon. If we don't get away from here to have lunch, I'm going to scream."

I went to another virus workshop, one that focused on mutating viruses. Like the other workshops, this one ostensibly taught you how to protect your system against viruses, but in the process you learned quite a bit that could be put to use in writing the nasty things. I met a hacker there who looked to be in his forties, attired in camouflage pants, hiking boots, and a Megadeth T-shirt, a guy who called himself Wizard. By hacker standards this was incredibly gauche, something like a writer adopting "Nobel Laureate" as a nom de plume. The term "wizard" has a variety of meanings to hackers, but generally speaking, they all imply a great deal of skill; it's a title that has to be earned.

Even aside from his choice of handle, there was something about Wizard that didn't seem quite right, so I chatted him up. He seemed very interested in viruses and hinted broadly that it was not from a strictly self-defense point of view. Naturally, I dropped hints along the same lines. I wondered if he was one of the guys on my "little list." I doubted that he was Beelzebub or even Astaroth; he didn't seem smart enough. Maybe MetLhed.

We exchanged E-mail addresses, and as we were about to go our separate ways, he said almost in passing, "Did you know that Roger Dworkin is here?"

I tried not to look as excited as I felt. "He is? Did you see him?"

"No, but I heard from a couple of other guys that he's around."

"Who were they?"

"I think one of them called himself Phleg Man. I met him at a thing on code breaking."

I went to find Al. She was in the main exhibition hall, as expected, pretending to be interested in some kind of voice-recognition hardware. I didn't ask her how she had shaken her entourage.

"Listen," I said. "I just heard that Dworkin is here."

"You did? Where is he?"

"I don't know. We need to look for a hacker who calls himself Phleg Man."

"Do you know him?"

I shook my head. "All I know about him is that he seems to be interested in code breaking."

"Do you want to try to find him right now?"

"No, let's take a lunch break and try this afternoon."

"Are you hungry?"

"Not particularly."

"Me neither, but let's walk over to Reading Terminal. I'll buy you a soft pretzel."

As we walked down Twelfth Street, Al reported to me on the morning's activities. "The Dodo seems pretty harmless. In fact, he's really kind of sweet; he reminds me of an uncle of mine. What's his real name, anyway?"

"I have no idea."

"Oh. I thought he was a friend of yours."

"He is."

"And you don't know his name? What is it, a secret or something?"

I shook my head. "We originally met at one of these hacker things. His real name somehow just never came up. He's kind of a weird guy."

"Well, I think he's very nice. And he gave me this." She showed me a floppy.

"What's that, his recursive acronym program?"

"No, he said it writes poetry."

"Computer poetry? Lovely."

"Don't be so mean. He's really very sweet. But those kids are into some highly questionable stuff."

"The killer B's?"

"Yeah. They didn't seem very interested in viruses, but I got the impression that they're veterans of most other kinds of computer crime."

"You don't think they were saying stuff just to impress you?"

"Maybe. But they knew what they were talking about."

I told her about Wizard.

"That's interesting. He sounds like he could be one of the bad guys."

"Possibly. But either he was being very cagey, or he really doesn't know all that much."

With the exception of the rumor I'd heard from Wizard, neither of us had heard so much as a whisper about Roger Dworkin.

"Well, even if we don't find Dworkin," Al said on our way back to the convention center, "the trip won't be a total loss."

"What do you mean?"

"I told Mom and Dad that we'd have dinner with them tonight. They've been dying to meet you."

I managed not to choke on my last bite of soft pretzel. Before I could respond, she went through a revolving door, turning to give me a wave and a devilish smile before she disappeared into the crowd.

I chuckled to myself. The joke would be on her when she found out that all the clothes I had brought for the weekend were close cousins to the ones I was wearing.

I hung around the main exhibition hall for a while, playing with some of the virtual-reality stuff. It was very popular; there was about a two-hour wait in line to play a game called Battledroid in something the manufacturer called a VR immersion suit. I gave that a miss and spent some time asking around to see if anybody knew Phleg Man, but came up empty.

The Dodo met me in the exhibition hall at about two-thirty. "Greetings," he said. "Medea told me that you're still looking for Roger Dworkin, so I thought I'd lend a hand."

"Any luck?" I asked.

"I don't know this Phleg Man person, but I heard another rumor that Dworkin is here. Fishhead said a friend of his knew someone who saw him at a hotel last night."

"Which hotel?"

"He wasn't sure. He thought it might be the Marriott, though, so I called to see if they had a Roger Dworkin registered. They don't. Which doesn't really mean anything—he might be registered under a different name."

"Hmmm. Why don't you see if you can talk to Fishhead's friend? I'm going to keep trying to find Phleg Man."

I went to the VR panel discussion, which was the last thing sched- uled for the afternoon. The evening had been left free, presumably to accommodate the people who wanted to drive to Atlantic City and try either their luck or their hacking talents.

The VR panel was being held in one of the larger conference rooms, in apparent anticipation of a large turnout, but the room was only about half-full. As I entered, I noticed a familiar face in the back row—vaguely familiar, because I couldn't place it immediately. After a few moments I realized it was Bob Beales, the Macrobyte security guy Al and I had met in Oakland. I hadn't recognized him at first because there was something about his hair that was different, but I couldn't say exactly what. I started over to say hello. He glanced up as I ap- proached and obviously recognized me, although he didn't seem overjoyed to see me; possibly he was still bent out of shape over my (unintended) implication that he wasn't doing his job very well.

Before I could reach him, a couple of hackers of my (very slight) acquaintance stopped me to ask if I'd seen The Dodo. I told them where he was, then turned back to Beales—but he was gone. Maybe he had to go to the bathroom or something.

The panel was kind of dry—computer experts aren't usually the most scintillating speakers—until the end, when two of the panelists got into an argument about something the first one called neural- induction interfacing, by which he meant some kind of device that could connect a computer directly to your central nervous system. The second guy pooh-poohed the whole idea as far-out science-fiction-type stuff. The first panelist then hinted that he had certain special knowledge of classified experiments in the area regarding which dweebs like number two had to be kept in the dark. This, of course, enraged number two even more, and he responded by suggesting that the only special things number one had access to were certain controlled substances the use of which resulted in unusual flights of fantasy.

They were restrained from fisticuffs by the timely intervention of the other panelists. Or untimely, depending on your point of view; I had a small bet down on number one, who wasn't as big but looked to be in better shape.

On the way out I thought I glimpsed Beales again, in the press of people streaming out of the conference room. I tried to get to him but quickly lost him in the crowd. I had a funny feeling that maybe he was deliberately avoiding me, and it struck me as odd that, if it was so important to him to keep away from me, the VR panel was worth the risk of sneaking back in and possibly being cornered. But maybe I was just being paranoid.

When I met Al to walk back to the hotel, she looked almost contrite. "You're not angry, are you?" she asked. "It really was a last-minute thing, and I didn't think you'd mind."

"I'd love to meet your parents."

"Great! They're taking us to an early dinner, and then we have tickets for the orchestra."

Hmmm. Last-minute tickets for the orchestra? Fair enough. She dropped her bomb—it was time to drop mine. "I hope we're not going to a restaurant that has any kind of a dress code."

She took about three more steps down the street, then suddenly stopped and slowly turned to look at me. I think she was hoping to see me smiling as if I'd just made a big joke. I wasn't.

She closed her eyes. "Michael, please tell me that what you just said doesn't mean what I think it means."

"If you think it means that I don't have any clothes with me that I would consider suitable for meeting your parents, that's exactly what I mean."

"And this . . . ?" She pointed to my uniform of the day.

"A fair representative of the lot, I'm afraid."

"Come on. There's a shopping center just down the street here."

She looked at her watch. "Oh, my God, we'll never make it. I'll just have to tell them that the airline lost your luggage."

"I came by train."

"They don't know that. Come on. At least we have time to get you a different shirt."

"A different shirt? Didn't you say we were going to a concert?"

"Shut up!"

We stopped at Strawbridge's, but a uniformed security guard met us at the door. He took one look at me and declined to let us in. Al looked ready to climb the walls.

"Are you sure you don't want to phone your parents and just tell them that I unexpectedly died or something?"

She gave me a look that suggested my sudden demise might not be all that unexpected. We hurried back to the hotel, where Al changed. She then rooted through my clothes to see if she could find anything less objectionable. "I can't believe it. That shirt is actually the least hideous thing you've got here."

"I like to make a good first impression."

"You think this is funny, don't you?"

"If you took a minute to really think about it, you'd think it was funny, too."

She opened her mouth to say something, then stopped with her mouth open for several seconds; then her shoulders started to shake. For a terrible moment I actually thought she was going to cry. Instead, she started laughing uncontrollably. It was infectious, so I joined right in. It was one of those laughs where you can't catch your breath, and tears roll down your cheeks, and your abdominal muscles actually start to hurt. Every time Al started to recover, she would look at my shirt, or my shorts, or my shoes, and that would send her off into fresh gales. Every time I saw the look on her face, I thought I was going to laugh hard enough to start bleeding internally. I collapsed into a chair, and she came and sat in my lap and threw her arms around my neck and laughed into my hair.

When we finally regained our composure, she stood up, dabbing at her eyes with a tissue, and said, "Okay, let's go have dinner with the Meades."

We met her parents at a fancy restaurant on Locust Street, where they had made reservations. Mr., or rather, Professor, Meade was about my height, gaunt and white-haired, looking very much like the classics professor he was. Mrs., or I should say, Dr., Meade looked like an older version of Al, with the same fire in her eyes. She didn't at all look like what I think of when I picture a psychiatrist. I must give Al credit; she introduced me with a perfectly straight face, and no mention of my weird getup.

Her parents get equal credit. They were dressed quite nicely, she in a green silk dress, and he in a seersucker suit, but they didn't bat an eye at my attire and greeted me as graciously as you could imagine. I was starting to feel a little bit like the emperor in his new clothes, when the maître d' came along and spoiled the whole effect by informing us that under no circumstances was I going to be allowed into his restaurant dressed as I was.

Professor Meade handled this turn of events with perfect aplomb. He said, "The Cajun Café is just down the street; we don't need reservations there, and they don't presume to dictate to their patrons in matters of dress. This place"—and he raised his voice just enough so that the maître d' was sure to overhear him—"is overrated anyway."

The funny thing was that as long as Al had been upset about what I was wearing, I wasn't troubled by it at all. I even admit to having relished the prospect of her parents being a bit scandalized. Now that everybody else didn't seem to mind, I was feeling properly embarrassed about it.

"I'd like you to know," I said, "that I don't ordinarily wear clothes like this."

Al broke in, giggling. "I had to talk him into dressing up for tonight." We all had a good laugh at that one—I thought I detected a note of relief from her mother in particular.

I explained the circumstances that lay behind the supergeek fashion statement, and they were very understanding about it. I said, "If they won't let me in to see the orchestra, I really want all of you to go without me."

"Don't worry about that," Dr. Meade assured me. "In the summertime the orchestra plays at the Mann Music Center in Fairmount Park. It's very informal."

The Cajun Café turned out to be a great fallback. After a dinner of popcorn shrimp, crawfish étouffée, and pecan pie à la mode, it was hard to imagine how the other restaurant could have been better.

The conversation at dinner was light and pleasant, until about halfway through, when Dr. Meade said to me, "Al tells us that the two of you are thinking of moving in together." Why do people say things

like that when they can see that you're right in the middle of swallowing something? It's probably the leading cause of people needing the
Heimlich maneuver.

Fortunately, I managed not to choke on my food. I stalled by
taking a sip of wine, and glanced at Al, who was calmly masticating her
catfish. She smiled innocently. We had indeed discussed moving in
together, but I wasn't quite prepared for the fact that her parents were
aware of this development. *My* mother would have had a conniption.

I smiled cautiously. It was probably a lot like Boris Badenov's smile
when he's trying to explain to Fearless Leader how the moose and
squirrel got away again. "We've talked about it."

"I think it's a wonderful idea. Too many young people rush into
marriage these days without taking the time to find out if they're
really compatible. It's not easy to live with someone." She glanced at
her husband as if to emphasize the fact that she spoke from experience. He appeared not to notice, which was probably just as well.

Al's mother drove us out to the Mann in their Volvo, and I got a
chance to see where Al got her driving habits. As Dr. Meade wove
through the expressway traffic, I glanced at her husband. He seemed
to have his eyes closed.

I got quite a few stares at the Mann, mainly because of my
T-shirt—there were a lot of other people wearing shorts—but the
stares seemed more amused than outraged. The orchestra played
Holst's *The Planets,* then Leopold Stokowski's orchestral transcription
of Bach's Toccata and Fugue in D Minor. The final piece on the
program was some long, modern, atonal thing that sounded as if the
orchestra were tuning up, only more irritating.

There are some people who claim that there has been a general
decay in all the creative arts, as form is gradually supplanted by chaos,
and that this disintegration heralds the end of civilization. Then again,
at just about any time and place in history, there have been people
complaining that everything is going to hell in a handbasket.

Al's parents drove us back to the hotel, and we said our good-byes
on the sidewalk outside the Marriott. I thought I heard her mother
say, "Good night, Margaret," as they embraced.

On the elevator up to our room I said, "Did I hear your mother
say—"

"Margaret? Yes. Alice is actually my middle name."

"You mean you're really Margaret Meade?"

She grimaced. "Why do you think I go by my middle name? Well, that and the fact that I hate the name 'Margaret' and all of its variations."

"Even Maggie?"

"I especially loathe that one. Not to mention Marge, Margie, Madge, Midge, Mags, Meg, Megan, Peg, Peggy—yuck."

"Gee, I kind of like the name 'Maggie.' There's an old Rod Stewart song . . ."

Her eyes flashed at me. "Michael, don't you dare call me by that name. I swear I'll stop speaking to you."

"Okay, okay. But, after all, a rose by any other name would smell—"

"Like the sex organs of a thorny shrub."

"What?"

"You see?" she smirked. "What you call something *does* make a difference."

Back at the room Al said, "So you haven't said what you thought of my parents."

"They're very nice. And they certainly seem very open-minded."

"Open-minded?"

"Well, for starters, if some sixteen-year-old had shown up for a date with one of my sisters dressed like this, my father would have driven him from the house with the nearest sharp instrument."

She laughed. "There was a time when my father probably would have done the same thing."

"What happened?"

"Well, I was kind of a rebellious teenager. I went through this phase where I did a lot of things to try to shock my parents: the way I dressed, the boys I'd bring home, the language I'd use. After a while my parents figured out that I was trying to provoke them, so they just stopped reacting."

"That's too bad. It must be tough having a psychiatrist for a mother."

"Oh, it's not as bad as it sounds. Besides, Mom is an adult psychiatrist—she's not really an expert on kids. I suspect that whenever they had some particular problem with me, she'd go and get a 'curbside consult' from one of her colleagues in child and adolescent psychiatry."

I put my arms around her. "Well, she must have gotten good advice, because you seem to have turned out just fine."

She wrapped her arms around my waist and wriggled up against me as if she were trying to get closer than our clothes and the laws of physics would allow. It felt nice. "Oh, I'm not much more neurotic than the next person, I guess."

The way she was moving against me was starting to produce a noticeable response in that part of my anatomy which, if I were a thorny shrub, would have been a rose. "If neurotic women are supposed to be frigid, I think we can safely rule that out."

We tumbled onto the bed together, with her on top. She was wearing the diabolical grin that was becoming familiar to me. "Maybe they're not all frigid. Maybe some of them are nymphomaniacs."

The next day at DEF CON was interesting. There were some rumors floating around about what hackers had been to which Atlantic City casinos the previous night, and what kind of success they'd had with their blackjack systems, roulette strategies, or other, less legal, approaches. But *the* hot rumor was Roger Dworkin. By now everybody knew he was at DEF CON, albeit incognito, and the effect was what you might expect if you told a bunch of teenagers that their favorite rock musician was secretly enrolled at their high school. Some fast-moving entrepreneurs were even doing a brisk business in T-shirts bearing the legend: "I *almost* saw Roger Dworkin at DEF CON six," along with the more usual "I spotted the fed" T-shirts that were a DEF CON staple.

I got to play Battledroid in the morning after a wait of only half an hour or so; obviously, a lot of people were still recovering from the previous night's debaucheries. It was a futuristic sci-fi game in which the player assumed the role of a cyborg warrior on a high-tech battlefield. The concept seemed to me to owe a lot to Robert Heinlein's novel *Starship Troopers*, with elements of Keith Laumer's Bolo stories thrown in for good measure.

You had to wear this suit that contained two sets of air chambers. The hardware measured changes in pressure in one set as a way of monitoring the position of your body. Electronically controlled valves in the other set of air chambers would allow them to inflate or deflate to provide resistance to the player's movements. A helmet with built-in stereo vidscreen goggles and headphones completed the array.

Once I suited up and they started the game, the illusion was pretty amazing, and not nearly as barfogenic as most of the earlier VR games. Along with realistic three-dimensional video, and stereo sound, the tactile effects were impressive. I could actually pick up and feel objects that existed only in the computer's software. What I was really feeling, of course, was a pattern of air chambers inflating in the suit's gauntlets.

The whole game lasted about four minutes, during which I fired lasers, guided missiles, and even more exotic weaponry at a variety of computer-generated enemies before finally coming to grips with a kind of robotic tyrannosaur in hand-to-claw combat. The robot would have squashed a human being flat in milliseconds, but I was a giant battle cyborg with superhuman strength and titanium-plated knuckles, so I drove punches at its snapping jaws while trying to avoid its raking talons and slashing tail. I must have hit something vital, because just as time was running out, the monster's glowing red eyes dimmed and went out as it sank to the ground.

There was a burst of applause from the people waiting in line, who'd been watching my game on large monitors that were set up for that purpose. The guy who helped me take the suit off said, "Wow, that was great. You're the first person to beat the mechasaurus. How did you do it?"

"What can I say? I'm the product of a misspent youth—too many hours in the video arcade." They were probably telling everybody the same thing, to try to create a market for their game, but I swaggered a bit as I left the platform anyway.

I went to a few more virus-oriented things that morning, met up with Wizard again, and picked up where we'd left off the previous day. He was a little more forthcoming, suggesting that he was starting to trust me, and it became clear that at least some of his apparent ignorance the day before had been feigned. He was also very interested in HfH and wanted to know how to get in touch with them.

I told him that I'd heard a rumor that they were well represented at DEF CON, but I didn't offer any other information. I was tempted to tell him how to contact their BBS, thinking that if he got in, he'd be a contact for me on the inside, but I didn't think it would be a good idea to reveal that much about my own activities. Besides, HfH was enough of a pain in the ass without my helping them with recruiting.

At lunchtime I went to look for Al in the main exhibition hall. The Dodo was still shadowing her, but she didn't seem to mind. She even suggested that the three of us have lunch together so that we could pool our information on the great Dworkin hunt.

Aside from its proximity to the casinos in Atlantic City, the Philadelphia venue had another major advantage from the standpoint of the typical hacker, to wit, the Pennsylvania Convention Center is located right next door to Chinatown. Asian food is practically mother's milk to hackers, and Chinese food tops the list.

We picked a place that Al recommended. The Dodo ordered lemon chicken, or, to use hacker parlance, Chernobyl chicken. Al and I both ordered something called Phoenix and Dragon, which was a somewhat over-the-top designation for a dish made with chicken and lobster.

"The problem now," Al said as we dipped our spring rolls into four-alarm mustard, "is that there are too damn many rumors."

"Yes," Dodo agreed. "The signal-to-noise ratio is deteriorating."

"Has anybody got a lead on Phleg Man?" I asked.

They both shook their heads. "I've been looking around for Fishhead," The Dodo said. "But I haven't seen him since yesterday afternoon."

"Why are we still bothering to look for those guys?" Al asked. "Wouldn't it make sense to try to follow a fresher trail?"

"You may be right. The problem is to decide which trail to follow. As TD said, there's a lot of static out there right now. And I have a sneaky suspicion that they all might just be variations on one original rumor. Except maybe for the ones that are obviously nonsense."

"Well, for starters," Al said, "I think we can safely disregard the one about how Roger Dworkin broke the bank playing craps at the Trump Taj Mahal last night."

"And the one about how he 'beamed up' from the convention center to an orbiting spaceship?" The Dodo added.

"I'm about ready to believe that one," I said. "This guy is too hard to find to be traveling by conventional methods."

"He does seem to have gone down a rabbit hole," TD chuckled.

Al giggled. "You may be right. Anyway, he's starting to seem less like John Galt and more like Elvis."

. . .

We returned to the convention center after lunch and split up again. We agreed that anybody who found out anything important would come and find the other two, so we all shared our afternoon itineraries with each other.

About half an hour into an especially boring presentation on data encryption, I looked up and saw Al waving to me from the door. The Dodo was with her, and they both looked excited.

"What's up?" I asked when I'd joined them out in the hall.

"The Dodo found Fishhead," Al said. "Tell him, TD."

"It turns out," TD explained, "that the friend of Fishhead's friend is Phleg Man. He had to leave the convention early, but Fishhead's friend knows how to get in touch with him."

Now I was excited too. "What are we waiting for?"

The Dodo led the way back to the main exhibition hall, where we found Fishhead and another hacker called Beauzeau playing around with some of the VR stuff.

Beauzeau turned out to be a little recalcitrant. "I don't think Phleg Man would want me to give out his number to anybody here."

Al turned on the charm. "But we're not just anybody. And we really need to speak to him." She smiled, and the dimples nearly did the trick, but not quite.

Beauzeau shook his head. "I'm sorry, but I really don't think I should."

"Look," I said, "you don't have to give us his number. Just call him for us and let me talk to him."

He thought about it, then nodded. "Okay. If he wants to talk to you. I can't promise you that he will."

We found some pay phones, and Beauzeau found something else to object to. "It's a long-distance call."

"Use this," Al said, offering him a calling card.

He looked very suspiciously at her. "If I charge the call to your card, his number is going to show up on your bill."

"Oh, for crying out loud," I said, reaching for my wallet and withdrawing a twenty-dollar bill. "I only need to talk to him for about five minutes. This should cover it unless he's in Guam or something."

Beauzeau thought about it, then accepted the money and picked up the phone. The rest of us ostentatiously looked the other way while he dialed.

"Hello, Phleg? . . . Yeah, it's Beau. . . . Pretty good. . . .

Yeah, maybe next year. . . . Listen, there are some people here who want to talk to you. . . . No, about Roger Dworkin. . . . Yeah. Is it okay?" Phleg Man apparently answered in the affirmative, because Beauzeau handed me the phone.

I skipped the introductions and cut to the chase. "Hi, Phleg Man. Somebody told me that you saw Roger Dworkin at DEF CON."

"Well, no, I didn't actually see him. I heard he was there."

"From?"

"I don't know the guy. I just overheard the conversation in an elevator at the Marriott on Friday night."

"What exactly did he say?"

"I'm not really sure, but I definitely heard the name 'Roger Dworkin,' and something about his being at DEF CON."

"But you don't know who said it?"

"No. Actually, I think I do know the guy he was talking to, though."

"Who?"

"He's an older guy. I think his handle's The Cuckoo or something like that. Wait, no, not The Cuckoo. The Penguin? I'm not sure."

I started to get a sinking feeling. "The Dodo?"

"Yes! That's it, I'm sure of it. The Dodo."

I handed the phone back to Beauzeau. I couldn't see the expression on my own face, obviously, but from the way Fishhead and TD were looking at me, it must have been a beaut. Al was saying, "What? What? Did you find out where he is?"

I shook my head. "I don't know where he is. But I think I know who started all the rumors."

"Who?"

"Uh, well . . . me, actually."

I could feel my face coloring. Al was starting to turn red too, only I don't think it was from embarrassment. I'm not sure which one of us started laughing first, but we wound up leaning on each other and staggering down the hallway while three hackers looked on with expressions of serious consternation.

We found a place to sit down and recover. Al said, while wiping tears from her eyes, "Okay. Tell me how you started the great Roger Dworkin rumor of 1999."

"All I did was ask The Dodo if he'd heard anything about him. He said no."

"Amazing. It's a good thing you didn't say anything about Elvis."

"Okay. So much for finding Roger Dworkin at DEF CON. Do you see any point in hanging around here another day, or do you want to hop a train back to New York tonight?"

"Oh, Michael, I'm sorry. I've got to go to the West Coast again."

"Duty calls?"

"I'm afraid so."

"How soon?"

"I booked a flight for tomorrow morning."

"Well, then, let's have some fun tonight."

We spent the evening in our hotel room, enjoying each other's company over a room-service dinner. After dinner we moved on to satisfying other biological needs.

After a time, or maybe a few times, we were sitting in bed propped up on pillows, fighting over the TV remote control and generally having a grand time.

"I can't believe they don't have the all-cartoon channel," Al griped. "*Ren and Stimpy* is usually on now."

"See what's on the all-game-show channel," I said, trying to snake the remote away from her.

She switched it to her opposite hand and held it out at arm's length, continuing to flip through the channels. "I hate game shows, especially the hosts. Ooh, they have the all-talk-show channel."

I rolled my eyes. "And you think *game-show* hosts are bad? These people should be publicly disemboweled."

"Shhh! Look, this is interesting."

This particular gabfest featured a panel of people representing various cults, united by their conviction that the year 2000 would mark The End of the World as We Know It. There were adherents of some obscure Christian fundamentalist sects, a few far-out Eastern mystics, and one man from a satanic cult who believed the bad guy was going to win this round. "I can see why this might be interesting to somebody who was a psychology major. I have to admit that my main interest in crazy people is staying as far away from them as possible."

"Is that what you thought you were doing this weekend?"

"Touché."

We watched the panelists babble about their loony ideas, goaded by one of those smarmy hosts who would have to be considered the spiritual heirs to the tradition of the circus freak-show barker. The host's pandering was a little hard to take, but I have to admit there was a peculiar fascination aroused by these oddballs, beyond even the obvious suspense about which one of them would be the first to start frothing at the mouth.

"Al, do you remember what Marlon Oz said about religions being human-information viruses?"

"Yes. Why?"

"Did you buy any of that?"

"Well, I have to admit that it made a certain amount of sense."

"I thought so too. You know, I just had a really strange thought."

"Do you want to tell me now, or shall we wait and try to get you on this talk show?"

"Thanks, but my craving for public humiliation has already been satisfied this weekend."

"Okay, seriously, what is it?"

"Well, we've been worrying about the possibility that there's an intelligent computer virus out there. Or maybe a worm or a Trojan, or a combination of all three."

"So?"

"Well, if a computer virus could theoretically become sentient, couldn't a human-information virus do the same thing?"

"I'm not sure I follow you there. People are already intelligent. Well"—she glanced at the TV screen—"maybe not all of them."

"I'm not talking about individual people. How can I explain this? Okay, our hypothetical worm becomes sentient by using a little bit of the capacity of millions of computers, right? Suppose something like a religion could, by using some of the capacity of millions of brains, develop a kind of independent intelligence of its own?"

"All right, I'm starting to see your point."

"Didn't somebody say we use only five percent of our minds? What if something else is using some of the idle capacity?"

"William James said it. Although, to tell you the truth, I don't think there's any real scientific basis for that figure. Still, Freud certainly showed that a lot of mental processes are unconscious."

"I wonder what a religion would do if it was sentient."

"I don't know. Probably start by getting rid of all the other religions."

"It's been tried."

"Yes, it has, hasn't it? You know, you could probably make a case for your idea operating in things like the Crusades, especially the Children's Crusade. Think of it: Thousands of kids spontaneously decide that they're going to march off and liberate the Holy Land."

"I see what you mean, although that doesn't sound like a very good example of intelligence."

"Then how about this: In the early fourteenth century there were eight great Gothic cathedrals built in France. They were all dedicated to Notre Dame—the Virgin. Centuries later it was discovered that if you project the geographic locations of the eight cathedrals into the sky, you have the constellation Virgo."

"Is that really true?"

"Well, I haven't checked it out personally, but I read it in a textbook when I was in college."

"While majoring in what? Astronomy or medieval architecture?"

She smiled. "Psychology, actually. It was in a textbook on human behavior. But think about it: The individual builders of the cathedrals didn't know about the overall pattern they were creating. You could certainly make an argument that they would have to be directed by someone or something that did know the pattern, and had the necessary influence."

"Speaking of astronomy, what about Stonehenge, and places like that?"

"What about them?"

"Well, it's always seemed a little strange to me that primitive people would have such precise knowledge about things like equinoxes and so on. What if the individual people involved really didn't have the knowledge but were guided by—what would you call it?"

"I don't know, maybe an overmind or something."

"It's kind of like a daemon, because it's running in the background all the time."

"How about a 'human group network intelligence daemon'?"

"Good, but it doesn't have a catchy acronym. How about a group overmind daemon?"

"Oh, that's cute. And a little scary."

CHAPTER NINE

Wellwyrm

And the first beast was like a lion, and the second beast like a calf,
and the third beast had a face as a man,
and the fourth beast was like a flying eagle.

—Revelation 4:7

The next morning we walked to the Market East station and caught the airport train. I kissed Al good-bye and got off at 30th Street station to wait for the Amtrak train that would take me to New York. Our partings still retained some of that painful quality I'd first noticed in San Francisco, although it helped a lot to know she felt the same way I did.

While at DEF CON, Al and I had picked up quite a bit of underground shareware—disks that were being swapped around. A fair number of them were in a genre known as rudeware: programs containing pornographic images, games, et cetera. The likelihood of this software containing viruses, Trojans, and other nasty stuff was astronomical. Probably the main purpose of most of the enticing rudeware in particular was to sucker people into infecting their computers. Most of the hackers at DEF CON would know that. For them, running this software would be a challenge to their hacking skill. For Al and me, it was an opportunity to get a jump on viruses that would soon be disseminated far and wide.

I scanned a few of the shareware disks on my laptop during the train ride back to New York. Because the rudeware seemed particularly suspicious, I started with some of that. Unfortunately, I didn't notice the matronly woman in the seat next to me. She was looking over my shoulder when one of the rudeware programs was running, displaying a graphic that was, well, graphic. It showed a remarkably realistic rendering of an act that, if not biologically impossible, was certainly improbable, definitely unnatural, and unquestionably illegal. I heard a loud snort from my left and turned to see the woman lurching into the aisle in search of a seat next to someone with the good taste to keep his perversions private.

After a while I got bored with scanning rudeware and started to play around with The Dodo's recursive acronym program. It would work in either direction, either creating an acronym for a set of definitions, or back-forming a meaning for a ready-made acronym. I decided to see what it could do with WYRM. After a few weak efforts like "Which Yogi Reads Milton," and "Wormy Yogurt Regurgitated Mournfully," it came up with "WYRM Yields Recursive Matrix," which I thought was kind of interesting, as "Matrix" is a term that's occasionally used to refer to cyberspace. It also came up with "WYRM, Yet Real Mind," which was also a bit lame, and finally, "WYRM Year Recurs Millennially," which struck me as more than a little ominous.

I was back in Manhattan in time to call on a few clients and conduct some fairly routine business. I get a lot of calls from people who think they have a virus but actually have a much simpler kind of problem—a routine kind of programming bug or some such thing. It was getting to the point where all I'd have to do is scan some of the client's software and find the 666 ID code to know that it wasn't a real virus that was causing the problem—unless it was one of Beelzebub's. For some reason Wyrm ignored Beelzebub's viruses, while zapping all other beasties with admirable efficiency.

That evening I took a short nap after dinner in anticipation of the possibility that tonight's Wormwood session would be a late one. We normally started at around ten eastern time to accommodate the people on the left coast, and it was hard to make much progress without spending at least a few hours at a crack.

I settled in at my workstation with a few light refreshments ready to hand and telnetted to Wormwood.

▲   ▲   ▲   ▲   ▲   ▲   ▲

The party stood before the great brazen doors and held a whispered conference.

"I'm pretty sure that this must be it," Zerika said. "The big kahuna."

"If it is, then there's a pretty good chance that at least some of us will be killed," Tahmurath added cheerfully.

"No problem, since Malakh is now high-level enough to raise the dead." The last speaker was Ali, a tall, dark-skinned elf wearing a turban and carrying an enormous scimitar. Ali was Leon Griffin's character; Leon, owing to his busy schedule, had been able to join the others in the game only intermittently.

"Unless Malakh happens to wind up as a statistic," Malakh warned.

"Just stick close to me, baldy," Megaera said.

"I intend to."

"Okay, the usual drill: Megaera and Malakh do a frontal assault. I melt into the shadows and try for a surprise backstab. Tahmurath and Ragnar stay back and attack with arrows and spells. Ali will protect Tahmurath from any direct assault. In this kind of situation there's often a mixture of bamfs and weaker monsters. If that's the case, kill the bamfs first."

"What," Malakh asked, "are bamfs?"

"Bad-ass motherfuckers. MUD shorthand for the meanest monsters in the MUD. Ragnar, you haven't said anything. Do you have a wisecrack you'd like to share with us, or are you saving it for later?"

"Well, let's see . . . I hate to disappoint you. Okay, how about this one: Is it too late to pick door number two instead?"

"Cute. On three, everybody. One, two . . ."

"*Three!*"

They charged into a dimly lit chamber. As their eyes adjusted to the gloom, a strong musky smell assaulted their nostrils.

"Where have I smelled this before?" Malakh mumbled.

"There!" Megaera pointed to the far end of the room, where a cluster of snake men surrounded something much larger, which they could not yet discern.

The snake men surged forward to engage them, swinging scimitars in murderous arcs. Malakh closed with one of them, ducking under a blow that was intended to decapitate him, and driving stiffened fingers into the creature's solar plexus. He wove in and out among the snake men, dodging blows and using his enemies as shields against each other. More than once a blow intended for Malakh struck one of the other snake men instead.

Megaera's method was less subtle. She swung her sword two-handed in wide swaths, ignoring the blows of the snake men, which mostly clattered harmlessly off her armor.

That the party had grown considerably in strength and proficiency could be judged from the fact that within minutes a dozen or so of the semireptilian monsters lay dead on the floor.

"Hmmm, that was a little too easy. Don't let your guard down yet," Zerika warned. "Let's have a look at what they were guarding."

The creatures had been clustered around a raised platform that seemed to have been carved out of the smooth dark-green basalt of the cave. There was a small circular depression in the center.

Zerika probed carefully, but the hole yielded no secrets. "There must be some purpose for this thing, but—*whoa*!" She suddenly leaped backward, as daggers appeared in both of her hands. "What the hell is that?"

A serpentine form had appeared at the lip of the depression. It was only about a foot long, orange with bands of black, and appeared to be switching itself back and forth.

"It looks like some kind of a snake," Megaera observed.

A voice appeared to emanate from nearby: "Oh, really? When did you ever see a snake with fur?"

"Schrödinger's cat? Is that you?" Zerika asked.

The smile appeared, several feet away from the tail. "How nice. You remember me."

"I almost *dis*membered you. You shouldn't startle people like that."

"Forgive me for not having myself announced. I doubt your weapons would have any effect on me, though. And as for dismembering"—the smile grew broader—"that's a little like threatening to drown a fish."

Zerika smiled in spite of herself. "So it is. Well, to what do we owe the honor of this visit?"

"I thought you might be in need of some advice."

"Such as?"

"Such as what to do with this hole that you found."

"Do you know what we're supposed to do?"

"Knowledge is a rather problematic concept for one in my state of semiexistence. Let's say rather that it seems to me that you need to put something in it." And with that the smile and the tail disappeared.

"Okay, everybody, you heard him," Zerika called. "Let's all take inventory and see what we have that might belong in this hole. I'm guessing that it's going to be something that fits in rather snugly."

"Are you sure it's something we already have?" Ali asked.

"Not at all. Let's just hope it is, or we're going to have a lot of searching ahead of us."

The group spent some little time picking over their belongings and eliminating the bulk of them from consideration. After several minutes they had narrowed it down to a few objects. "I'm betting," Zerika said, "that this is it." She held up the jar they had found in the forest clearing on their first day.

"Give it a try," Tahmurath urged.

"All right. Everybody in battle positions. Same plan as before. That first fight was way too easy; I have a feeling that this time things are really going to hit the fan."

She gingerly placed the jar in the depression. It did indeed fit rather snugly. And nothing happened.

For a second or two.

Then Zerika had to leap backward again, this time to avoid falling into a suddenly yawning pit as the jar grew, expanding until its lip merged with the edge of the basalt platform, and deepening until Malakh, who was looking down over the edge, could no longer see the bottom.

Megaera joined Malakh at the edge of what now appeared to be a deep well. Zerika recovered and approached as well. Peering into the depths with her strange, inhuman eyes, she said, "I think there's something down there. Something big—"

She was cut off in midsentence as another, larger group of snake men suddenly emerged from the shadows, attacking with scimitars and two-handed swords. In a moment they were fighting for their lives.

Suddenly a deafening roar split the air, causing friend and foe alike to hesitate in midswing. Malakh and Megaera looked up to see a huge saurian head raised above the melee, its roaring no doubt prompted by the red-fletched arrow that protruded from its scaly neck, which emerged from the well.

Tahmurath was the first to recover; as he pointed his staff at the creature and spoke a brief incantation, a bolt of electricity leaped across the gap between staff and serpent. The creature hardly seemed to notice; its hide was apparently an electrical insulator. It hauled more of itself out of the well, then reared and struck at Megaera, catching her breastplate in its monstrous jaws and crumpling the steel plate like cardboard. Zerika dashed in and stabbed at the neck, but her short blades appeared to make little impression. Ragnar had laid aside his bow and was advancing with a naked longsword, but several snake men were moving to intercept him.

Malakh, whose weaponless fighting style was devastating against creatures his own size, could make no effective attack against such an enemy; his most powerful blows seemed to bounce harmlessly off their adversary's armored hide. He was forced to abandon even those fruitless attacks when another snake man attacked, slashing with its scimitar. Malakh disarmed the attacker, disemboweled him with his own blade, and leaped onto the back of the monster. Six meters above him, the head swayed back and forth, shaking Megaera as a cat shakes a mouse. He placed the scimitar between his teeth and began climbing the neck; it was like climbing a palm tree in a hurricane.

Glancing below, Malakh could see that Zerika and Ragnar had been forced onto the defensive by the remaining snake men. They were giving a good account of themselves but were unable to come to Megaera's aid. Tahmurath watched helplessly, unable to use his magic against the beast without endangering Megaera and Malakh.

Malakh reached the head and wrapped his legs around the neck. Holding fast to one scaly ear with his left hand, he reversed the hilt of the scimitar in his right. For what he had in mind, a straight, narrow blade would have been vastly preferable to the wide, curved one in his hand. "What the hell," he said, and thrust it with all his might into the beast's right eye.

The wound was, alas, not immediately fatal. The monster bellowed again, propelling Megaera in an arc that terminated on the two remaining snake men. They broke her fall and, in the process, most of their bones. Malakh released his grip on the hilt in order to hang on for dear life as the beast thrashed about, attempting to dislodge him. When it did not at first succeed, it tried, tried again by battering him against the walls of the chamber. The first blow shattered his right arm, but he managed to cling doggedly with his legs and left arm, and even to weather the second and third blows. It was the fourth that drove his head against the granite with a sickening wet thud, and his limp body plummeted to the floor. There were no snake men to soften the impact.

Before Malakh's body had even hit the floor, a second bolt of lightning was streaking from Tahmurath's staff. This time he directed it at the protruding scimitar hilt, allowing the metal of the blade to channel the electrical energy into the monster's skull.

The beast opened its cavernous jaws as if to roar a third time, but no sound emerged. Instead, a cloud of black smoke issued forth, and for an instant it seemed as if the serpent were about to exhale fire on them. In fact, the cloud was not the harbinger of flaming breath, but rather the smoky residue of the creature's charred brains. It expired, its great bulk crashing down onto the floor of the chamber with an impact that seemed as if it might collapse the entire cavern system.

There was a sudden sound of laughter coming from the direction of the door through which they'd entered. They all swung back to face whatever new threat awaited them, but there was no one there. Only Zerika caught a glimpse of what looked like a man with horns on his head and oddly bulging eyes.

As the survivors collected their wits, they were able to get their first good look at the great serpent. Lacking legs and wings, it resembled nothing so much as an enormous snake, except for its unmistakably draconian head, with its beard, spiraling horns, and pointed ears. As Tahmurath surveyed the beast's great bulk, he noticed Malakh's feet protruding from beneath the gigantic corpse.

"Oh, no," he said. "Is Megaera . . ."

"Alive," Zerika said from where she and Ragnar crouched near their fallen comrade, "but barely."

"Well, keep her alive. If she dies, we're down two party members."

"You mean Malakh—"

"Is a greasy spot on the floor."

"You know, I resemble that remark."

"Malakh! You're alive? Where are you?"

"Right in front of you, but not alive, I'm afraid. I seem to be a ghost. That's probably why you can't see me."

"A ghost. That's funny, we never turned into ghosts when we died before."

"That was back when we were very low-level," Zerika said. "Maybe you have to pass a certain threshold to qualify for ghosthood. Can you do anything, Malakh?"

"You mean like heal Megaera? No, I already tried. I don't know if I'll be able to do anything except tag along and watch. Crap."

"Is there any way you can bring him back, Tahmurath?"

"I can try waving a dead chicken over him, but I doubt it'll do much good."

"Well, don't get too discouraged," she told Malakh. "Maybe we can find some other way to reincarnate you. Anyway, even if you can't do anything else, you'll make one hell of a scout."

Just then a section of wall swung open, revealing a hidden room. A figure emerged from the room—feminine in appearance, but with wings like a monarch butterfly, and clad in a diaphanous gown. She was carrying a tray.

"You have slain the guivre," she intoned, "and thus completed the first step of your journey. Here is your reward."

On the tray was a large tome and seven objects. The leather binding of the thick volume bore the legend *The Book of Gates,* and the sign of the ouroboros. Of the remaining objects six of them were identical small disks about three centimeters in diameter and half a centimeter thick. On closer inspection, each one appeared to consist of two dark-colored disks with something white sandwiched in between, and each was surrounded by a faint bluish nimbus. The seventh was a small widget that seemed to be made of gold. Each of the survivors took one of the disks, Ragnar pressing Megaera's into her almost nerveless fingers.

"What the hell are these things?" Ragnar said.

They all peered intently at their prizes. Then Tahmurath started to laugh. "Don't you get it?" he said. "It's a magic cookie."

"A what?" Zerika asked.

"Hacker jargon. It's kind of like a ticket that's passed from one program to another, to let you perform some special operation. But what is this other thing?"

"This," the fairy said, "is the Golden Frobnule. You will need it in your travels."

Tahmurath pocketed the frobnule. As each survivor received a
"cookie," he or she was restored to complete health. Even Megaera,
who had been at death's door, was on her feet. "Can you pick yours
up, Malakh?" Tahmurath asked.

"No, I'm afraid not."

"That doesn't make any sense. Why would she give you one if you
can't use it?"

They discussed the problem briefly but didn't have any idea how
to bring Malakh back, or how to use his "cookie." They eventually
tabled the issue and moved on to the next problem, which was to
investigate the portal from which the fairy (if that's what she was) had
emerged. "Looks like a museum," Zerika commented as she poked
her head through the door. The large hall was filled with paintings
and statuary. Some of the art was familiar, like Cellini's statue of
Perseus displaying the head of Medusa. Others were unfamiliar to
anyone in the group, but they seemed to represent a remarkable variety of cultures.

"Dragon-slayers," Ragnar said. He had stopped before a large oil
painting depicting a mounted and armored knight driving his lance
through a dragon, while a virginal-looking female observed the proceedings. The dragon in the painting looked pathetically small compared to the leviathan they had just fought.

"I think Ragnar's right," Megaera said. "I don't recognize a lot of
these folks, but the ones I do are all known for killing dragons."

"Medusa isn't exactly a dragon," Malakh observed. His ethereal
state had apparently not prevented him from passing through the
portal with the rest of the group.

"No," Megaera agreed, "she wasn't a dragon. But Perseus did kill
a sea dragon to save Andromeda. In fact, some people say that the St.
George legend started out as a Christian reinterpretation of the Perseus story."

"And what about this guy?" Zerika asked. She was standing before
a great statue of a man whose body appeared to be covered with eyes.
The sculpture dominated one end of the great hall.

"There was somebody in Greek mythology who was covered with
eyes," Megaera said. "Argus, I think. I don't know whether he was
supposed to have slain a dragon."

"Just a sec, I'm looking it up," Ragnar said. "According to this,
Argus was the slayer of Echidna."

"Echidna was a dragon, then?" Zerika asked.

"No, a spiny anteater," Megaera said.

"Very funny. Echidna," Ragnar continued, "had the upper body of a woman, and the lower parts of a snake. She wasn't exactly a dragon, but according to some accounts she was the mother of dragons, including Ladon and the Lernean Hydra."

"That still seems to be stretching things a bit," Malakh opined. "And what was that joke about a spiny anteater, Megaera? I didn't get it."

"It wasn't a joke. Echidna really is the name of the spiny anteater. One of the two mammals extant that lay eggs. I never knew what the significance of the name was until now—a good name for something that has both mammalian and reptilian characteristics."

A voice said, "I don't know anything about Argus or anteaters, but *that* is a statue of Indra."

The party turned as one and saw someone very similar in dress and appearance to Malakh. "Who are you?" Zerika demanded.

"Call me Gunnodoyak. And my arrival seems to be most opportune, as you seem to be in need of a new dream-walker."

"Is that you, Krishna?" Tahmurath asked.

"Right."

"How did you . . . ?"

"I created a 'bot a while back, partly to try out some things, and partly to cover an eventuality like this. I programmed him to trail you through the dungeon—he managed to rack up quite a bit of experience just by cleaning up your 'leftovers.' Incidentally, the other 'cookie' was for me. I picked off a few of the snake men while the rest of you were occupied with the guivre. Evidently that was enough for me to be considered officially in on the kill. Anyway, at this stage I think I can find out more by playing along with the rest of you."

"It's more fun, too," Zerika said.

"Excuse my ignorance," Megaera interjected, "but what's a 'bot?"

"It's a program that plays a MUD," Gunnodoyak explained. "Pretty low-end AI stuff in principle, although there have been some legendary 'bots that were supposed to have fooled some players into thinking they were human."

"Hey, now that you're here, could you resurrect Malakh?"

"I suppose I could, but I don't see that it would do much good with his body pinned under that carcass. He'd just die again immediately."

"Tahmurath, could you levitate it off him?"

"My current limit is about half a ton. That thing must weigh at least fifty tons. Sorry."

"Actually," Zerika said, "it might turn out that there's some advantage to having a ghost traveling with us; he might be able to do some things that the rest of us can't. Now, what was that about Indra?"

"The chief of the Vedic gods," Gunnodoyak said. "And the slayer of the dragon Vritra."

"I knew that," Ragnar said. "I just didn't know he was covered with eyes."

"He's sometimes called Thousand-Eyed Indra, but they're not really eyes," said Gunnodoyak.

"Well, then, what?"

"Well, uh . . . actually, they're vaginas. Hey, don't look at me like I'm some kind of pervert—you can look it up if you don't believe me."

After cataloging the works in the hall, the party passed through another doorway at the far end. The opening was framed by three colossal megaliths. The largest of the three, resting horizontally on the two uprights, was marked with the sign of the ouroboros. It was as if an ancient dolmen had been incorporated into the more recent stonework of the hall.

Ali paused to look at the ouroboros. "Malakh told me about this," he said, "and your ideas about what it meant. You know, there's also an African myth about a snake that goes all the way around the world with its tail in its mouth."

"Like Jormungandr," Zerika said.

"Right. According to the African version, there are orange monkeys whose job it is to feed the snake, but, being monkeys, they sometimes forget."

"What happens then?"

"The snake gets hungry, eats some more of its own tail, and there are earthquakes. Supposedly, this is how the world will end."

As they started through the dolmen into the next chamber, their path was suddenly blocked by a familiar figure.

"Watch it!" Zerika warned. "It's the troll again."

He did not appear to harbor ill intentions toward the party, however; an ingratiating, gap-toothed grin split his hairy face. "Fuzzies," he said. "Ring is with the Fuzzies." Then, without further ado, he turned and ran with surprising swiftness on his stumpy legs.

"Wow," Ragnar breathed as they followed the troll through the dolmen. "Grand Central Dungeon."

They had come into an enormous hall ringed by five tiers of balconies. Doors led off in every possible direction on all five levels. Over each door was a small light. Most of these lights were green, but more than a few were red. There was no sign of the troll.

"What the hell was that all about?" Malakh's disembodied voice asked.

"A clue," Zerika said. "I bet he meant the 'ring of the king' from the scroll we found, the one that's supposed to be in the 'heart of the dragon.'"

"Then what are the 'Fuzzies'?"

"I have no idea," she admitted. "Probably we'll find out as we go along."

"Now what?" Megaera asked.

"Obviously," Zerika said, "this is where *The Book of Gates* comes in."

"Unfortunately," Tahmurath said, "I can't make any kind of sense out of it. Look: It has a map of this room with a number assigned to each door. Then the rest of the book is a list of the door numbers, followed by four three-digit numbers and, in some cases, a four-digit number. It looks like Ragnar's right; we're going to have to choose more or less at random. It's possible that the levels correspond to degree of difficulty, so maybe we should start down here. Also, call me psychic, but I have a feeling we should go with a green light rather than a red."

"Good point, psychic," Zerika agreed.

They wound up choosing the first door on the left from their point of entry into the hall, after Gunnodoyak observed that, as they might wind up having to try them all, it would be best to approach the task systematically.

They passed through the portal and found themselves in what appeared to be the marketplace of a medieval town. There were a dozen or so other people there, dressed in period garb. Most appeared to be looking at the new arrivals. After a moment or two one man detached himself from a small group and approached them. He wore a red-and-gray tabard over a chain-mail hauberk and carried a shield emblazoned with a rampant unicorn.

"You folks," he said, "are going to have to clean up your act or leave. I mean," he continued, surveying them thoughtfully, "you're not *too* bad, but we definitely don't have elves here. You're OOT."

"We're OOT?" said Ragnar. "But, laddie, I thought we just came IN."

" 'OOT,' " Zerika explained, "stands for 'out of theme.' Some MUDs have very strict rules about that sort of thing. But," she continued, addressing the newcomer, "are you an admin? We've been playing this MUD for weeks, and we never ran into anybody before. We didn't even know there was any particular theme."

"You've been playing Ars Magica for weeks? That's impossible. I would have known about you before now."

"Let's go back, Zerika," Gunnodoyak said. "At least for a minute."

Zerika looked a little puzzled, but agreed. "We have to anyway," she said. "Malakh didn't make it through."

"What is it?" she asked when they had returned through the gate.

"This is incredible!" Gunnodoyak said. "Do you realize what's going on? What this place is?" He looked expectantly at them.

"Well, what are you waiting for, a drumroll?" Ragnar demanded. "Tell us!"

"Ars Magica," Gunnodoyak said, "is a MUD."

"Well, obviously," Zerika interjected. "It's what we've been playing, isn't it? We just didn't know the real name before."

"No! *Not* what we've been playing. It's a regular, run-of-the-mill MUD—I've seen it on the lists, although I've never played it. This room contains a set of cyberportals. I bet these doors lead to every MUD on the Internet!"

"Wait a minute," Tahmurath said. "Are you trying to say that Ars Magica is a regular text MUD?"

"Yes."

"But that's impossible. What about the graphics?"

"That's what I mean! This is unbelievable!"

"What are you talking about?"

"The program, Dworkin's program: It must be capable of generating graphics based on the verbal descriptions in the text MUD. God, what kind of computing power must that take? It would take a really powerful AI program just to be able to understand the text sufficiently to guide the graphics."

"To understand the text that well," Ragnar said, "would practically require a solution to the Natural Language Problem."

"The what?" Zerika asked.

"There are a set of problems in artificial intelligence," Ragnar explained, "that are sometimes referred to as AI-complete, meaning if you solve any one of these problems, you've basically got AI licked. One example is the Natural Language Problem—writing a program that can understand and speak a natural language like English."

"In other words," Gunnodoyak added, "if this thing is doing what it seems to be doing, then we're dealing with an authentic artificial intelligence, wouldn't you say?"

"Well, it'd at least be a damn good bet to pass a Turing test."

"Tahmurath," Gunnodoyak said, "let me see *The Book of Gates* for a minute. Aha! I'll bet these are telnet addresses; they're just not in the regular format. Instead of a dotted quad, they just took out the dots and spread out the numbers."

"Then the four-digit numbers are port numbers," Megaera said.

"Right! Tricky, but not tricky enough to fool *us*."

"Okay," Tahmurath said, "let's suppose Gunnodoyak is right, and I think he is—these doors lead to every MUD on the 'net. Do you realize what that means? This could take years."

"And we probably don't have that kind of time," Malakh added.

"Don't forget the troll's clue," Gunnodoyak reminded them.

"That's right!" Tahmurath exclaimed. "Now we know what he meant by the 'Fuzzies.'"

"What do you mean?" Megaera asked.

"Oh, yucko," Zerika said. "Trust me, you really don't want to know."

▲   ▲   ▲   ▲   ▲   ▲   ▲

It was August 11, a Wednesday, when I discovered that we had more to worry about than I'd previously feared.

I got home about six-thirty, just in time for the evening news, so I switched on the tube. There was lots of news, all bad.

It seems that a solar eclipse had been visible across most of Europe, and if mass hysteria was too strong a term for the day's events, there was at least considerable fraying around the edges of the collective psyche.

The most badly frayed edge, commonly known as the lunatic fringe, was represented by the members of three apocalyptic cults that had chosen the eclipse as an occasion for mass suicide. In addition to the organized craziness of the cults, there was a wave of individual suicides, arsons, and assorted other violent crimes. It was the most dramatic response to an eclipse in Europe since Louis the Pious, emperor of the Holy Roman Empire, was literally frightened to death by one in 840 A.D.

The events of the day, tragic as they were, were not my biggest concern, however. I started thinking about the "group overmind daemon" again, and wondering if it was behind all the craziness. If Al and I were correct in our speculations, the g.o.d. might be particularly susceptible to religious symbolism, and if that was the case, might be working itself up into a millennial frenzy. I was worried enough that I called Marlon Oz to bounce the idea off him, but he wasn't in, and Dan Morgan was away on vacation, so I left a message.

Al returned to New York on Saturday morning, and I drove out to La Guardia to pick her up. I was looking forward to showing her the semantic network I'd been working on, which was evolving along the following lines:

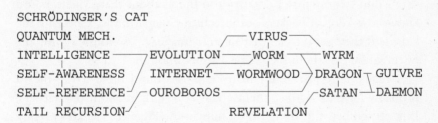

But when I picked her up, she looked so frazzled, I forgot all about the network.

"This is really nerve-racking, Michael. I'm finding Wyrm in practically every system I check."

"Me too."

"The worst part is not really knowing what to tell my clients. Obviously we have to tell them something, and just as obviously, we can't tell them everything."

"That's for sure. Especially the part about the Macrobyte Trojan. One word about that, and we're going to be sued by a company with enough money to hire very expensive lawyers."

"I don't doubt it. But it's not just that. We can't even tell them about the game—I wouldn't dare to, anyway. They'd think I'd gone completely off the deep end."

"Yeah. Actually, though, the thing I find particularly galling is the way this thing is cutting into my business. Yours too, I assume."

"Well, it has been a little slow, but I don't know that it's that dramatic."

"Oh, yeah? Do you know what yesterday was?"

"August thirteenth. Why?"

"Friday the thirteenth. And it was the slowest Friday the thirteenth I've had since I got into this line of work."

"You know, you're right. Oh, well, I guess we can't exactly complain if it's performing such a valuable service."

"I suppose you're right. For some reason I just feel uneasy about it. But maybe it's pure venality."

"Not likely, knowing you." She smiled. "There must be some reason that it has you so worried, though."

"Well, the fact that we don't really know what it's doing or why isn't exactly reassuring. Not to mention that Revelation passage that Dworkin had underlined. What if he's into satanism or something?"

"I don't know that I'd worry too much about that, Michael. You know how a lot of hackers are into heavy-metal music, especially the kids, and they get into all that satanist imagery. I seriously doubt any of them are out there sacrificing virgins, though."

"Yeah, there just aren't many virgins around these days—they'd probably have to sacrifice themselves. You're right about the hackers. But, remember, this thing isn't a human intelligence. Hackers playing at devil worship know they're just screwing around. Wyrm might not know it's just a big joke."

"So what do you think it would do?"

I didn't know, but I was starting to have a few ideas, and I didn't like them very much. "Look, suppose it isn't actually destroying all the viruses it finds. What if it just alters them so that they all activate at the same time?"

She thought about it. "Based on what we've seen so far, I'd have to say it's capable of doing that. Why would it?"

"Because of a special date when the shit is really supposed to hit the fan. A *really* special date, like—"

"The millennium?"

"Yeah."

"Hmm. Did you ever read a Robert Heinlein story called 'The Year of the Jackpot'?"

"It sounds vaguely familiar."

"It's about all kinds of improbable disasters converging in a particular year."

"Which year was that?"

"I don't remember, but isn't it a jackpot on a slot machine when the three numbers, or lemons or whatever, all match?"

"Like 2000?"

"Or 1999."

"Or 666."

She giggled. "If my mother could hear us, she'd probably have us committed."

"Yeah, or my dad would want to put us on his couch."

"Wait a minute. His couch? You mean your father is . . . ?"

"A psychoanalyst, yeah."

"You never told me your father is a psychoanalyst!" There was more than a hint of accusation in that statement. I reflected that there was a certain poetic justice in her dismay, given the way she'd sprung my meeting her parents on me. I knew better than to say so, though.

"I guess it just never came up before." My sister Remi was getting married, and Al was to be my date at the affair, which would also be the occasion of her meeting my parents for the first time.

"Never came up? How about when you were expressing sympathy for me because my mother's a psychiatrist?"

"Are you sure I never told you? I thought I mentioned it a while back."

She stared at me, then suddenly smacked a hand over her forehead. "An analyst! You said he was an analyst—I thought you meant a *systems* analyst!"

"So what's the big deal? You, of all people, ought to be comfortable around shrinks."

"Shrinks! Does your father know you use language like that? And I *am* comfortable around psychiatrists, even analysts, ordinarily. It's just a little different when it's my boyfriend's father."

"Well, I can understand that. I suppose I had a few butterflies when I met your parents."

"Anyway, it's nothing major, just a little anxiety."

"Uh-oh. That's not good."

Her eyes opened wide in alarm. "What? What's not good?"

"Well, you know that analysts can smell fear—" I ducked the first pillow, but she caught me a pretty good one with the second. I got her back in spades.

Remi's wedding ceremony and reception were in the fine old Long Island tradition of wretched excess. She had seven bridesmaids, including both sisters, and there was a matching set of seven ushers, including yours truly. The wedding vows, which she and her fiancé had written themselves, were probably a little shorter than *War and Peace;* it just didn't seem that way to those of us in the wedding party who had to stand throughout the ceremony while trying not to fidget too obviously.

At the reception Al and I were seated with my parents, who seemed to be doing their best to put Al at ease. My father, in particular, was carrying a lot of the conversation, in contrast to the usual stereotype of psychoanalysts who are about as talkative as the Sphinx. Then again, maybe an occupation that forces you to sit and listen to other people all day long leaves you with a burning desire to hear the sound of your own voice. Whatever the reason, I had never found Dad to be particularly bashful, and this occasion was no exception, although how the conversation had wandered onto the subject of Yiddish epithets is a complete mystery to me.

" 'Schlemiel,' " my father was saying, "is a variation of the Old Testament name 'Shelumiel,' or 'friend of God.' 'Schlimazel' is an amalgam of German and Hebrew words meaning, roughly, 'crooked luck.' And 'Schmendrick' is a name that comes from a nineteenth-century opera.

" 'Schlemiel' and 'schlimazel,' in particular, are very similar in meaning, although 'schlemiel' carries somewhat more of a connotation of awkwardness or clumsiness. A schmendrick is a little different, more of an obnoxious kind of person. The classic paradigm is this: A waiter, the schlemiel, is carrying a bowl of soup when he is tripped by a schmendrick, whereupon he spills the soup into the lap of the nearest schlimazel."

"Okay, I get it," Al said. "But then what is a schmuck?"

"A penis."

For just a second there I thought she was going to blush. It reminded me of a girl I had known in college who habitually used the expression "neg as in smeg" when responding in the negative, or just as a way of conveying general disdain. One day I asked her what it was supposed to mean. She had no idea. "It's just an expression," she said. "Well," I said, "there's only one word I know of that begins with the letters S-M-E-G." "What is it?" she asked. I handed her a dictionary and said, "Here. Why don't you look it up?" Her facial expression, when she read the indicated definition, was utterly priceless. I have often wished that I had it on videotape.

I have to give Al credit, though—she didn't bat an eye at the revelation that the word she had been bandying about so casually was a rather coarse synonym for the male genital organ. Instead, she said, "But I thought it was German for 'jewel.' I always figured calling someone a schmuck was a form of sarcasm, like saying somebody is a real prince, or something like that."

"In German a schmuck is a jewel," Dad said, "but in Yiddish it's a penis. In fact, there's an old joke about two men talking about a trip that one of them recently made to Israel. One of them asks, 'Did you have a good time?' 'Wonderful. I had a tour of Jerusalem, I saw all the sights, I even went for a ride on a male camel.' 'A male camel? How did you know it was a male?' 'Well, I didn't notice, myself, but wherever we went, people pointed and said, "Look at the schmuck on the camel!" ' "

I had heard this joke a few dozen times before (it was one of Dad's favorites), so I laughed along with Al just to be polite. Mom, who had probably heard it at least twice as many times as I had, simply rolled her eyes.

"Michael," my mother said, "why don't you ask Alice if she'd like to dance?"

Al didn't even wince at the sound of her full middle name, which, I had learned, was only marginally less objectionable to her than the intolerable "Margaret." Instead she smiled and nodded at me, so I had no choice but to take her onto the dance floor, despite the fact that my legs were just beginning to get some feeling back in them. I shot a reproachful glance at my mother, but she didn't notice, probably because she was too busy admonishing my father to stop embarrassing my newest girlfriend.

"I thought it was your mother who was Jewish," Al said as we took to the dance floor.

"That's right."

"Well, then, how come your father knows all those Yiddish words?"

"Dad says that, as a psychoanalyst, he's sort of Jewish ex officio."

We danced a few dances, some slow, some fast, the last one a frenetic tarantella, then went back to the table just as my parents were sitting back down, a bit out of breath.

"Were you guys dancing too?" I asked. Why did I feel faintly mortified by the idea? "I didn't see you out there." Actually, the dance floor was too crowded to see much of anything.

Mom nodded. "I can usually get your father out of his chair for that dance."

He grinned. "That's because I know I'll have an excuse to sit back down when it's done. One of the advantages of being old and feeble."

"I love that dance," Al said. "What is it called?"

"It's a tarantella," I said. "That particular one is de rigueur at all Italian weddings."

"Tarantella?"

"It means tarantula," Dad said. "It comes from a particular out-break of medieval mass hysteria. People would think they had been bitten by a tarantula, and it was believed that the only cure was to dance until you dropped from exhaustion."

Al nodded thoughtfully. "Mass hysteria. Another type of human-information virus."

"What kind of a virus?"

Dad seemed interested, so we told him about some of Marlon Oz's ideas about computer viruses, and their human analogues.

"Interesting," he said. "And it does make a certain kind of sense. In fact, there is one model of consciousness that is basically Darwin-ian—different ideas in competition with one another."

"Except," I said, "that if that's true, it wouldn't just have to be Darwinian. It could be Lamarckian, too." I explained to him Al's idea about how evolving computer programs could progress along La-marckian lines, as well as through natural selection. It seemed to me that the same argument could be applied to ideas.

He nodded thoughtfully. "You may have something there."

We got back to Al's apartment in Manhattan fairly late. I used her computer to check my E-mail. The only item of interest was the following:

```
Gotcha! —Beelzebub >8->0
```

I get my share of flames and shit-o-grams, but this was definitely out of the ordinary—a virus hacker sending me gloating E-mail. The Gerdel Hesher Bock debacle had garnered a fair amount of publicity—I had no doubt that's what he was referring to—although I wondered why he had waited all this time to rag me about it. The surprise and chagrin must have been evident on my face, because Al asked, "What is it?" and came to look over my shoulder.

"Nothing much, just fan mail from some flounder."

"Beelzebub! Well, you certainly have some interesting pen pals."

Beelzebub's message had, of course, been sent via an anonymous remailer; in fact, I'd have been willing to bet that it had been "chained" through at least a half dozen anonymous remailers to protect him from having it traced, not that I intended to waste my time on any such wild-goose chase.

It was almost September, and time for another Triple Witching Hour, and I had been too busy for the last couple of months to finish decompiling the virus. I decided to do some work on it, recalling that we'd never figured out how it determined the date, as it seemed to be able to do so independently of the infected system's calendar.

Focusing on that problem, I was able to make some progress. What I found surprised me. "Al," I called. "Come over and look at this."

I didn't realize how late it was (almost three A.M.) or that Al had fallen asleep on the couch. She yawned and padded over to stand behind my chair, looking over my shoulder at the screen.

"Remember how we were wondering how the TWH virus determines the date? I think it gets it from Wyrm."

"What? How?"

"It's on the network, like this." I keyed in a sequence of commands and got the following screen:

10684999

The last digit was decreasing as we watched. "Counting down from ten million seconds," I said.

"Oh, my God," she whispered. "When does it get to zero?"

I popped up the on-screen calculator. "Looks like December thirty-first at about seven P.M. No, wait, that's daylight saving time. It'll be six P.M."

"Which would be in Greenwich mean time?"

"Midnight."

▲   ▲   ▲   ▲   ▲   ▲   ▲

As their eyes adjusted to the gloom, they could begin to make out their surroundings. They were in a large underground chamber, the walls of which were honeycombed with niches. Their entry point was, as usual, in the vicinity of a standing stone marked with the sign of the ouroboros.

"Yuck." Zerika gave an involuntary shiver. "Catacombs. What kind of a MUD did you say this was?"

Gunnodoyak shrugged. "It's called BloodMUD, and this is where we're supposed to find Castle Dracula. So draw your own conclusions. Anyway, you're the one who wanted to come here—I still think we should have followed the troll's clue and gone to FuzzyMUD first."

"Double yuck," Zerika said. "I'll take undead over Fuzzies any day of the week."

"Let's see if we can page a wizard or somebody and get them to show us around," Tahmurath suggested.

"Okay, just a second," Gunnodoyak said. "I've got somebody called Radu. Are you a wizard, Radu?"

"No, I'm just with the welcome wagon. Where are you?"

"In the catacombs."

"Be right there."

"I'm pretty sure we can find our way."

After a few minutes of waiting for Radu, Gunnodoyak paged him again, and as they waited for a reply, a section of shadow detached itself from its background and moved toward them.

Zerika was the first to respond, leaping back and drawing her weapons; the others quickly followed suit.

The shadow continued to approach until they were able to make out some details. It was a tall, pale young man with dark, shoulder-length hair, wearing formal evening clothes and a black opera cape, the lining of which might have been red silk, although in the dim light it was almost black. He bowed to them with a flourish, then smiled, revealing impressively large cuspids. "I am Radu. Welcome. What can I do for you?"

Zerika recovered her composure. "Answer some questions, for starters."

"Such as?"

"Well, my first was going to be, What's the theme here? but now I'm guessing vampires."

"Good guess."

"Are all the players vampires?"

"Oh, no, not at all. There are vampires, witches, some lycan-thropes, a few assorted monsters, and there are normal everyday hu-man types."

" 'Normal everyday human types' sounds a bit unwieldy. Don't you have a shorter name for them?"

Radu's grin widened, showing more of the oversize canines. "Food."

"I see. It sounds like most people would prefer to play vampires."

"In fact, everybody starts out as a normal human being. To be-come a vampire, you have to be made into one."

"By being bitten by another vampire?"

"That's part of it, although that alone isn't enough. Mostly, people are bitten just for food. If they're completely drained, they die.

"Actually, the most challenging thing is to play a nonvampire character and try to stay alive that way. Easier said than done, though. I think the way the MUD was originally conceived was that most people would want to be vampire hunters, and only a few would become vampires, but it hasn't worked out that way. Currently, new people are lasting only about a week or so before they're either drained or 'converted.' There are just too many advantages to being a vampire."

"Such as?"

"Oh, superhuman strength, speed, stamina. Immunity to most kinds of injury, disease, death. Other special goodies that can vary from person to person. For example, some of us can do this."

There was a puff of smoke, and Radu vanished. In his place ap-peared a large, particularly hideous bat, which swooped around the chamber a few times before turning back into Radu.

"Are there any disadvantages to being a vampire?"

"Yes. Once you become a vampire, you need blood to survive. At low levels it can be any kind of blood, even bug juice."

"Yuck!"

"Exactly. But as you become more powerful, you have to eat higher on the food chain. The most powerful vampires can survive only on human blood. If they try to eat anything else, it can put them out of action for weeks. Any more questions?"

"Yes. Where is Castle Dracula?"

"I wouldn't worry about that just yet if I were you. You'll have to be here quite a while before you can get within a mile of that place."

"Have you been there?"

"Well, no, actually. I've heard that you need a pretty strong group to go there and survive; a solo player doesn't stand a chance. Oh, and the only people who've made it, even in groups, are vampires. The closest any 'fearless vampire hunters' have come is to get impaled on the stakes that surround the castle."

"Is there actually a Dracula at Castle Dracula?"

"Sure."

"Who is he?"

"I think it's probably one of the wizzes, although some people think it's just part of the program, a 'bot, basically. The players who've been there aren't saying."

"So when are you planning on going?"

He looked chagrined. "I've been trying to scrape together a party for months. The few people who are powerful enough have already done it, and the rest are too chicken."

Zerika held a whispered conference with Tahmurath, then turned back to Radu. "How would you like to come with us?"

After a moment's stunned silence, he burst out laughing. "Good one."

"I'm not joking."

"Haven't you been listening? A bunch of newbies wouldn't stand a chance there, even if I could make you all into vampires right now."

"We're not exactly ordinary newbies. And it won't be necessary to turn us into vampires. Show him, Tahmurath."

Tahmurath gestured with his staff, muttering a brief incantation. The stone wall behind Radu grew a pair of arms, which seized him in a stony embrace. He struggled, to no avail, then transformed into a bat and winged away. The stone arms now hugged only empty air, but

Tahmurath was already casting a second spell; he blew a bubble out of his mouth, which quickly grew to about the size of his head. It pursued the bat, engulfed it, and then floated back to Tahmurath. The bat beat its wings against its prison, but the seemingly delicate structure could not be breached. He transformed back into human shape, but the bubble simply expanded in size; it still resisted his attempts to break it, even when he tried using his fangs.

He shook his head. " 'Not ordinary newbies' seems to have been a bit of an understatement. Okay, you want to go to Castle Dracula, and so do I. Together, we might actually survive. We can't do it right now, though, because I've got to log off."

Zerika was not going to let him slip away that easily. "All right, then, when?"

There was a pregnant pause. "Tomorrow night. Ten, eastern time."

"We'll be there."

Radu logged off. "Okay," Zerika said. "The night is still young. What do you guys want to do in the meantime?"

"I know you're dreading this, Zerika," Tahmurath said, "but I think we're going to have to pay a visit to FuzzyMUD."

"Oh, yucko."

"What?" Ragnar asked. "What's FuzzyMUD?"

Sleek black fur covered a gracefully sinuous form. Her bright black eyes regarded the group curiously, and with more than a hint of disapproval. That the creature was female was plainly evident from the appearance of her torso, which was decidedly human in form, and unobscured by any type of clothing.

"She's like something out of an X-rated Walt Disney film," Ragnar whispered.

"I'm Natasha," the otter woman said, "and I'd like to be your hostess. But first—"

Before she could continue, Zerika held up a hand. "I know, we're OOT, right? Don't worry, we were just leaving."

"Not so fast," Tahmurath said. "We haven't found what we're looking for yet."

"I really doubt we're going to find anything in a MUD like this." She wrinkled her nose in distaste.

"Don't be so sure."

"Well, you can't go around FuzzyMUD looking like that," Natasha observed.

"I'll take care of that," Tahmurath said. He turned to Megaera and gestured, muttering an incantation. A cloud of blue smoke flew from his fingertips and engulfed her; when it dissipated, she was covered with orange fur, and as scantily clad as their musteline hostess. Her eyes, now large, green, and catlike, opened wide, and she gave a little meow of outrage.

"Well," Ragnar remarked, "that certainly gives new meaning to the term 'magic smoke.'"

"Magic smoke?" Megaera asked. "What's that supposed to mean?"

"Didn't you know? It's what makes computer chips work."

"This is a joke, right?"

"Not at all. Didn't you ever see a chip burn out?"

"Uh, not that I can recall."

"Well, it happens. And when it does, smoke comes out. Then the chip doesn't work anymore. That's how we know it was the magic smoke that was inside the chip that made it work in the first place."

In the meantime Tahmurath had finished transforming the others. In short order Ragnar had become a centaur, Ali a manticore, and Gunnodoyak acquired the head and tusks of a wild pig.

"Hey," Gunnodoyak complained, "what's the big idea?"

"I've seen the way you eat," Tahmurath said. "Okay, okay, try this instead." He chanted again, and when the smoke cleared, Gunnodoyak had the head, mane, and fur of a lion.

"That's a little more like it."

"Cool," Ragnar remarked. "What have you got against this MUD anyway, Zerika?"

"Maybe I'm just against wearing fur, okay?"

"In that case," Tahmurath said, "we'll try something a little different for you." When the blue smoke dissipated, Zerika was covered with soft iridescent feathers.

The otter woman was clearly impressed with the last transformation. "Ooh, I like that one. I may have to try that myself sometime."

Lastly, Tahmurath transformed himself into something resembling a giant teddy bear.

"Much better. And now, if you'll come with me, I'll be happy to show you around."

As she led them down a wooded trail, Megaera whispered to Zerika, "What did you mean, a MUD like this?"

Zerika rolled her eyes. "You'll see."

The group arrived in a small glade populated by about a dozen creatures similar to their hostess—animals with anthropomorphic characteristics, or people in various stages of lycanthropy. They were hugging, kissing, sniffing, nibbling, and engaging in other, even more eyebrow-raising, intimacies in an orgy of interspecies miscegenation.

"What the hell kind of MUD is this?" Megaera demanded.

"Language, please," the otter woman warned.

Megaera was stupefied. "*Language?* These people—or whatever they are—are doing *that,* and you're upset because I said *hell?*"

"I've warned you once," she said primly. "Don't make me call an admin."

Megaera ignored her. "Well, I'm with Zerika. I say we get the . . . heck out of here. This is disgusting."

"Don't be so prissy, you two." Tahmurath turned to the otter woman and explained what they were seeking. After a few moments she shook her head.

"We don't really have any dragons here," she said. "At least not in the normal sense. Maybe what you're looking for is the penisaurus."

Zerika appeared even more scandalized than before, if that was at all possible. "The *what?*"

"Well, it's not *really* a penisaurus, that's just sort of a pet name we have for it."

"Where is it?" Tahmurath asked.

"It hangs out in a few different places. Go down that path and take the left fork, and you'll come to a pond, and then a garden. It's usually around there somewhere."

"Come on," Tahmurath urged. "I don't want to be up all night."

"All right, all right, all right," Zerika grumbled. "Might as well get this over with."

Zerika brought them to a halt within sight of the pond. "Maybe I'm being overly cautious, but I just have a bad feeling about this. I don't trust that rat woman."

"I thought she was an otter," Gunnodoyak said.

"Shhh! I want someone to go down to the edge of the pool while the rest of us watch from hiding."

Ragnar looked at her in surprise. "I thought you were the scout."

"I am. But what we need is somebody to act as a decoy while the rest of us hide here in the bushes."

Ragnar shrugged. "Sure, I'll be a decoy." He gestured to his equine hindquarters. "I don't think I'll be able to hide too well, built like this."

"Then go to it."

Ragnar trotted down the path to the edge of the pool, saying, "I thought there was supposed to be a garden around here somewhere."

A huge serpentine head erupted from the water, swaying at the end of a long neck. It grinned at Ragnar and said, "No garden; one dragon."

Ragnar started to reach for his sword, then hesitated. The serpent stared at him expectantly, then, growing impatient, roared, "Draw, O coward!"

But instead of unsheathing his weapon, Ragnar smiled his most ingratiating grin and opened his harp case instead. "I thought you might enjoy a little music."

The dragon seemed willing to countenance the impromptu audition, but suddenly another, identical head emerged from the pool.

"Hey!" Ragnar exclaimed. "I thought you said *one* dragon."

The newcomer cast a sharp glance at the first serpent, who said, with an expression of bland innocence, "I did, did I?"

Ragnar started to play his harp.

The giant serpents listened for a few moments, then the first one exhaled in Ragnar's direction. He was enveloped in blue smoke. When it dissipated, Ragnar had been transformed; he was now a tall, gaunt man with spidery fingers, wearing nineteenth-century evening clothes, and playing a Stradivarius. The serpent who had breathed on him announced, "Paganini: din in a gap."

The second serpent regarded this scene for a moment, then directed his own breath at Ragnar. When the smoke cleared this time, Ragnar was wearing a loud Hawaiian shirt and the Strad had become a ukulele.

The first serpent laughed hysterically. "Oh, no! Don Ho!"

In the meantime the other party members were holding a whispered conference in their hiding place in the shrubbery. "I was willing to take a crack at just one," Zerika was saying. "But there's no way we're going to kill two of those things—at least not without major casualties we can't afford."

"Why did she say they don't have dragons?" Gunnodoyak wondered. "They look like pretty typical dragons to me."

"I don't know, but we'd better think of something fast," Megaera urged. "I don't know how much longer they're going to be satisfied just listening to Ragnar's music."

"If we can't kill both of them," Ali said, "then maybe we can get them to do it for us."

"How do you propose to do that?" Tahmurath asked.

"Shouldn't be too hard. Like tying a python in a square knot. Change me back to my normal self, Tahmurath. I want to try something."

A moment later Ali stepped out of the underbrush and started down the path to the pond. The second serpent to arrive was the first to see Ali. It showed all of its long, sharp teeth and called out, "Flee to me, remote elf!"

Ali picked up his pace and approached the dragon. "I've been looking for you," he said. He drew his scimitar and pointed to the other dragon. "Is this the one you asked me to kill?"

The serpent appeared surprised. "Huh?"

"Or maybe it was the other one," Ali continued. "I can't really tell you guys apart." He turned to the first dragon and asked, "Were you the one who asked me to kill him? You know, so there would be just one dragon, like you said?"

The second dragon now directed a murderous stare at the first. "He did, eh?"

The first one evidently didn't appreciate being on the receiving end of dirty looks. He sneered, "Sit on a potato pan, Otis."

"Dammit, I'm mad," the second dragon hissed.

Suddenly both Ragnar and Ali were forgotten as the two dragon heads reared more of their long necks out of the pool and prepared to battle. The second dragon was the first to strike, but its jaws closed on empty air as its adversary dodged and countered. The necks twined around each other as each dragon strove for an advantage, and it quickly became impossible to keep track of which was which.

Finally one dragon managed to clamp its great jaws around the muzzle of the other one and began swallowing its head. As it became clear that one of the dragons was done for, Zerika whispered, "Get ready. We're going to have to handle the winner."

She needn't have worried. In less than a minute the eyes of the apparently victorious serpent took on an odd appearance, bulging from their sockets. Soon after that it began to sag, and slipped beneath the surface of the pool.

The remaining members of the party came running down the path to join Ali and Ragnar at the water's edge. "Oh, no," Gunnodoyak exclaimed. "How are we going to get the heart now?"

"Not to worry," Tahmurath reassured him. "I have a spell for lowering the water level. We may have to get both hearts, though, if we don't guess right the first time."

Tahmurath cast his spell, and the water in the pool receded into the muddy bottom, revealing not two, but one gigantic carcass.

"An amphisbaena!" Zerika exclaimed.

"A what?" Ragnar said.

"It's like a giant serpent with a head at both ends. That's why the one we thought was winning died too—it was the same critter."

"It might have been an amphisbaena," Ragnar said, "but now it's an ouroboros."

Using their swords to slice open the amphisbaena's body, they discovered that there was but one heart. Megaera carried it to Tahmurath.

Tahmurath looked puzzled. "I thought the ring was supposed to be in here." He turned it over. "What the . . . ?"

"What is it?" Zerika asked.

Tahmurath held up the heart so they could see what he had found when he'd flipped it over. It was a smiley face.

Zerika just shook her head. "Well, that about does it for tonight, I think."

"Just a second," Tahmurath said. "Megaera, I want to talk to you privately, on-line for a few minutes. The rest of you can log off."

▲   ▲   ▲   ▲   ▲   ▲   ▲

"Well, that was pretty anticlimactic," Art commented as he prepared to log off. He and Al had spent a few minutes typing at their keyboards after everyone else had quit.

"What's the big secret?" Robin asked.

Art smiled mysteriously. "Just cooking up a little surprise, that's all."

"Ooh, good. I like surprises."

"I didn't really care for the one we just got," Art said, apparently in reference to the dragon heart.

We were playing in the snake pit, with me in Krishna's previous position, not that I was really necessary. I'm sure Krishna could have played his own character while simultaneously monitoring the technical parameters, but it was nice for me to have something to do. And because I was "riding shotgun," I was in a position to notice something that none of the others did. "Not so fast, Art," I said. "When you got the heart, you downloaded a big file."

I was able to tell him what directory the file had landed in, and Art called it up. "Looks like total spooge," he said.

"Encrypted, I bet," Krishna said. He had come to look over Art's shoulder at the monitor.

"If you say so. Krishna's our resident cryppie," Art explained. "You want to take a crack at it, Krish?"

"Definitely."

It was one of those rare occasions when Al and I were headed in the same direction, so we were able to fly back to New York together. Triple Witching Hour was approaching, and we were discussing what to do about it.

"I have an idea," I told her, "but I don't like it very much."

"Tell me, then. Maybe I'll like it better."

"You know how the firms with Macrobyte OS's seem to be resistant to the TWH virus? I was thinking that it was like phylloxera."

She nodded. "The phylloxera louse kills the European grapes, but not the American ones, even though it infects them, too."

"Right. So if you want to grow European vinifera grapes, you have to graft them onto an American labrusca rootstock."

"Okay, I think I see what you're getting at. . . ."

"I doubt that many firms would be willing to switch their whole operating systems, but if we could give them sort of a Macrobyte graft . . ."

She was nodding enthusiastically. "I *do* like it. How much of a graft do you think it would take?"

"That's the part I don't like so much. I'm afraid it would take just enough to give Wyrm a foothold."

"Worms don't have feet."

"Yeah, so it's a lousy metaphor. You see what I mean, though?"

"I think so, yes."

In the end we couldn't think of any better alternatives, so we offered it to our clients and passed the word to other firms. The response was cautious, but the firms that had already been burned were eager to try something.

Meanwhile, Al and I experimented to find out just how much of Macrobyte's OS we'd have to import to do the job. We also had to work out some licensing agreements with Macrobyte, but they were fairly magnanimous about it, apparently seeing it primarily as an opportunity for favorable publicity.

On September 18 twelve options-trading firms were struck by Beelzebub's Triple Witching Hour virus. None of the affected firms was running a Macrobyte OS or the hybrid system Al and I had worked out. It looked as if, by the end of the year, everybody would be running some version of Macrobyte software—or be out of business.

CHAPTER TEN

Bloodwyrm

For they have shed the blood of saints and prophets,
and thou hast given them blood to drink . . .
—Revelation 16:6

From a distance Castle Dracula appeared to be little more than a ruin, the huge holes in its ancient battlements resembling the empty eye sockets of some titanic skull. Dark clouds roiled above the ruin, although elsewhere the night sky was clear. Wolves howled mournfully somewhere in the night.

"I can't believe I'm doing this," Radu grumbled. "Six months to achieve vampire status in this stupid game, and I'm about to throw it away with a bunch of newbies."

Zerika gave him a comradely clap on the shoulder. She was now garbed similarly to Radu, as were Ragnar and Tahmurath, the better to blend into the BloodMUD milieu. "Cheer up! You didn't want to live forever, did you?"

"Well, actually, I did. Immortality is, after all, one of the little privileges of vampirehood."

"I don't know what you're so worried about," Gunnodoyak put in. He still wore his monk's tunic but had covered it with a voluminous cloak. "You should be almost impossible to kill, and if things get dicey, you can always change into a bat and fly away."

"Don't give him any ideas," Tahmurath warned. He had acquired a small companion, a black cat that alternated between riding on his left shoulder and stalking along beside him. He had explained to the others that the cat was his "familiar."

Radu seemed offended. "I wouldn't just abandon you. There is some honor among vampires, you know."

Megaera, whose change in attire was the most dramatic—she now appeared to be wearing a low-cut ball gown, her hair piled high on her head, and she was armed with a slim rapier—was not so easily reassured. "How do we know your loyalty won't be to Dracula when the chips are down?"

"She's right," Ragnar added. "After all, blood—"

"Is thicker than water," Radu finished dryly. "Don't worry; we vampires tend to be a pretty fratricidal lot."

"Always at each other's throats, eh?"

"Ragnar!" Megaera groaned.

"Sorry, couldn't resist."

The howling of the wolves was even closer now as they approached the first ranks of stakes that thicketed the slopes surrounding the castle. Each stake transfixed an impaled victim, all in various stages of decay. Glancing upward, they could now see that the dark clouds that roiled and surged above the battlements were composed of bats—hundreds of thousands of them.

"Deathbats, unless I miss my guess," Radu said bleakly.

"Is that anything like vampire bats?" Zerika asked.

"Worse. They're like flying piranhas; they can strip you to the bone in minutes."

"Why aren't they attacking us?"

"Probably the smell from the corpses is masking our presence. They don't eat carrion. They prefer their food on the hoof, as it were."

"That does pose a bit of a problem," Zerika mused. The party would have to cover about fifty meters of open ground between the innermost row of stakes and the nearest opening in the castle walls.

"I could play them a little dance number," Ragnar suggested as he started unlimbering his harp.

"That will attract too much attention," Tahmurath objected. "Radu, do you have any thoughts about how to get in?"

"I can turn into a bat and fly in. How *you're* going to get in, I have no idea."

"I can probably sneak up there without being detected," Zerika said. "But I think the rest is up to you, Tahmurath."

The wizard nodded. "A normal invisibility spell probably won't work against bats, because they use echolocation. Maybe I can jam their sonar somehow." He spoke a brief incantation to his staff, then struck it lightly against a rock outcropping. It began to vibrate and give off a low, steady hum.

Tahmurath continued to chant, gesturing with his free hand, and the hum increased in pitch. Some of the party clapped hands to their ears as the pitch increased further to a shrill scream, then abruptly cut off. They looked at the staff and could see that it still vibrated, but apparently its pitch now exceeded the uppermost range of human hearing.

"Wait, Tahmurath." Zerika laid a hand on his arm. "Radu can still hear it." She pointed to the vampire, who had stuffed his fingers into his ears, his handsome face now a grimacing mask.

"Do you want me to stop?" Tamurath shouted at him. He shook his head and jammed his fingers in even harder.

Tahmurath turned back to his staff and spoke again. Now the pitch and intensity of the vibration increased further.

Suddenly it was raining bats.

Bats the size of terriers were plummeting from the sky. One particularly large specimen landed on a stake near Ragnar, neatly impaling itself between the shoulder blades, offering a good view of the row of razor-sharp teeth that lined its underslung lower jaw, which happened to be working convulsively. Blood was streaming from its oversize ears. The party looked up and could see that the cloud was dispersing rapidly as bats, the ones that could still fly, fled in every direction.

Ragnar eyed Tahmurath. "Didn't want to attract attention, eh? I thought you were just going to jam their sonar."

He grinned sheepishly. "I guess I put a little too much juice into it."

Megaera was just about to remark on the fact that the howling had stopped when Radu cleared his throat. "Have you ever heard of a silent dog whistle?" he asked.

Dozens of yellow eyes formed a semicircle that separated the party from the castle. Zerika's elfin vision told her what Radu's vampire eyes had already detected: "They're wolves," she said.

"But something tells me," Gunnodoyak said, "they're not normal wolves. Right, Radu?"

He nodded. "Lycanthropes, probably. Very difficult to kill."

"Maybe if we just kill the leader, that will discourage the rest of them," Ragnar suggested.

"And how are we supposed to know which one is the leader?" Zerika demanded.

"I'm guessing it's that one on the right that looks like Jack Nicholson. What do you think, Megaera?"

"My money's on Lon Chaney, Jr., over there."

"Don't do anything aggressive yet," Tahmurath warned. "I want to try something."

"What are you doing?" Gunnodoyak asked as Tahmurath wove a spell.

"Activating our FuzzyMUD character descriptions. Radu, this would be a good time for you to do your bat thing."

As the party underwent Tahmurath's prescribed transformation, he stood up on his hind legs and lumbered a few paces toward the wolves. His familiar gave a startled meow and hopped down from his shoulder, scampering over to stand near Megaera. Tahmurath had apparently altered his description somewhat, as the bear now appeared more grizzly than teddy. The Jack Nicholson wolf detached itself from the group and trotted toward the bear, sniffed at him, and then paused, considering the situation. As Centaur-Ragnar was extending a palm toward Cat-Megaera and whispering, "Pay me," the lead wolf gave a short yip and trotted away. The others followed.

"What the hell was that?" Lion-Gunnodoyak demanded.

Bear-Tahmurath shrugged. "Something like professional courtesy, I think. Let's go."

Almost before the words were out of his mouth, Bird-Zerika went tearing past him, shouting, "If those were professionals, these must be the amateurs! Run for it!"

The others looked back in the direction from which she came. Corpses were pulling themselves off the stakes and beginning to shamble up the hill. It was not a pretty sight.

They scrambled through the breach in the castle's outer wall, and into a small courtyard. Gunnodoyak, acting as rear guard, was the last one in, ducking through the opening just as Zerika was trying the handle of a stout wooden door that led into one of the towers. "It's locked," she panted, "and I don't think there's time to pick it."

Tahmurath raised his staff, but before he could say a word, Megaera hurled herself against the door, splintering it. They hurried through and found themselves in a small anteroom facing . . . another door. This door appeared considerably more formidable than the one Megaera had just shattered, being constructed of solid steel. It, too, was locked.

Tahmurath spun to face what was left of the door they had just entered and began to mutter an incantation. After quickly intoning a few magical syllables, he glanced reproachfully at Megaera. "It would be easier to do this if you hadn't reduced the door to kindling on the way in."

She grinned and shrugged her shoulders. "Guess I don't know my own strength."

As Tahmurath's spell took shape, the fragments of the door floated into the air and began to arrange themselves in their positions. When the door had reassembled itself, he strengthened it with his magic. He was just completing the spell when they heard the first thudding impact against the outside of the door. "It looks like the company has arrived," he said dryly.

"How long will that hold?" Zerika asked as she plied her lockpicks on the inner door.

"If we're lucky, a little bit longer than it will take you to pick that lock, so hurry up!"

Zerika plied the tools of her trade and was rewarded with success just as Tahmurath's holding spell gave out. As she swung the inner door open, there was suddenly a rush of zombies through the outer door. The party retreated through the inner door, hacking and slashing all the way, but their weapons appeared to have little effect on their pursuers. They attempted to push the inner door closed, but the press of undead bodies against the other side of the door was so great, they could not get it completely shut. As Megaera, Ragnar, Gunnodoyak, Zerika, and Radu strained to close the door, Tahmurath's familiar hopped down from his shoulder and added its efforts, pushing with its small forepaws, and, incredibly, it seemed for a moment as if the little feline's aid would be enough to enable them to succeed in closing it, but several undead arms, legs, and even one head had been thrust through the gap. Worse yet, as they began to tire, and more tireless undead joined the ones already pushing against the door, they began to lose ground, and the door began to open, slowly but inexorably. As the door inched farther open, two more gruesome heads were pushed through the widening gap.

"Tahmurath," Zerika said through gritted teeth, "if you have another door-closing trick up your sleeve, now's the time to use it."

Zerika's admonition may have been merely rhetorical; Tahmurath had already raised his arms and begun to chant. A moment later he stepped forward and struck his staff against the door. It rang like a gong. The sound seemed to freeze everyone, alive and undead, in his, her, or its tracks for a moment. Then the door slammed shut, severing the arms, legs, and heads that were in the way as cleanly as a guillotine.

"Thank you, sir," Zerika said, kicking away a zombie head that was attempting to bite her ankle. "I think we're now ready to explore the interior. Radu and I will go first, Ragnar and Tahmurath behind us, and Megaera and Gunny will be the rear guard. Any ideas about where we should look, Radu?"

"We've got to find Drac's coffin; actually, he probably has several, but they'll all be underground somewhere."

"So we search the castle dungeons."

"Right."

They followed a short passageway that led to an antechamber. As they entered, torches set in wall sconces flanking an archway flared to life, and they were suddenly confronted with a tall figure wearing a black cape with a high collar. His dark hair was swept back from an angular widow's peak and plastered close to his head, and his sallow flesh contrasted unhealthily with blood-red lips that were curled into a sardonic smile. "Welcome," the figure said.

They reached for their weapons, but the figure continued, "Do not be afraid. I am here to welcome you to my home. You have passed some significant ordeals in order to get here; that should mean that you will be worthy adversaries. It will give me great pleasure to drink the blood of every last one of you."

Suddenly an arrow struck squarely at his chest; a web of cracks radiated from the point of impact as the count vanished.

"A mirror!" Zerika exclaimed.

"A mirror?" Ragnar was ruefully unstringing his bow. "But I thought vampires didn't have reflections."

"Of course we have reflections," Radu explained. "In this MUD anyway. It's just that our reflections don't have to stay with us all the time. We can send them elsewhere, anywhere there's a reflective surface."

"What good does that do?" Gunnodoyak wanted to know.

"A reflection makes a good spy or scout. Dracula probably has mirrors all over this castle. He'll be able to keep tabs on us everywhere we go by having his reflection follow us around."

"It's too bad Malakh's ghost form can't pass through the cyberportals," Ragnar remarked, looking around. "He'd fit right in in this place."

Hours later, after traversing miles of underground passageways and surviving numerous skirmishes with the keep's monstrous denizens, they arrived at a chamber that seemed to represent the nadir of the castle dungeons. The door was of iron and bore several curious inscriptions:

> Gur fjbeq bs gur sngure vf n qentba-fynlre.
> Gur evat bs gur xvat raunaprf zntvp.
> Gur bar uhaqerq guvegvrgu pyhr yrnqf gb gur pnc bs qnexarff.

"Well, well," Ragnar remarked, "this must be the place."

"What makes you think so?" Tahmurath asked.

"We're looking for a crypt, right?"

"Yeah. So?"

"What would you expect to find on the door of a crypt, if not a cryptogram?"

The others all groaned, but Tahmurath actually smiled and nodded. "You know," he said, "I think you may have something there."

"We'd better solve them before we go in," Zerika suggested.

"The first one says, 'The sword of the father is a dragon-slayer,' " Gunnodoyak said.

"That was quick," Megaera exclaimed.

"I've got the other ones too," he said. " 'The ring of the king enhances magic,' and 'The one hundred thirtieth clue leads to the cap of darkness.' "

"How did you solve them so fast?"

"It wasn't hard—they're just rot-thirteen."

"Rot what?"

"Rot-thirteen. It's a substitution cipher that replaces each letter with the letter that's thirteen places farther along in the alphabet. The 'rot' part stands for 'rotate'—as if you're taking your Flash Gordon decoder ring and giving it a half turn. It's convenient from a programmer's point of view, because the same program that encodes the message will also decode it. But it's way too simple for serious encryption."

"Well, two of the messages were pretty self-explanatory. But what do they mean by the 'one hundred thirtieth' clue?"

Ragnar groaned. "I hope that doesn't mean we're going to have to go back and count all the clues we've gotten so far."

After a bit more fruitless discussion about possible meanings of the last message, Zerika checked the door for traps and, finding none, tried the handle. It swung open.

The room was not large but was richly furnished. The floors were covered with exquisite Persian rugs, and the walls were hung with gorgeous tapestries. A large coffin occupied the center of the room.

They had already discussed what their tactics would be in this situation, so the members of the group took up their places without a word of discussion. Tahmurath stood at the head of the coffin, while Ragnar, Zerika, Gunnodoyak, and Radu flanked it. Megaera stood at the door, barring the only obvious escape route. At a nod from Zerika, Tahmurath levitated the lid of the coffin, revealing the Bela Lugosi look-alike whose reflection they had seen earlier, apparently asleep with his arms folded over his chest. Zerika motioned to Gunnodoyak, who produced a long wooden stake from beneath his cloak. He placed the point of the stake on the vampire's chest, between his crossed wrists.

Ragnar now stepped forward, pulling a short-handled sledgehammer from beneath his own cloak. He raised the hammer and glanced at Zerika. She nodded.

At the first impact of the hammer, the stake was driven deep into the vampire's chest. His eyes and mouth flew open, but no scream emerged. Ragnar struck again, and again. On the third strike a loud scream pierced the air—only it was not Dracula's scream, but Megaera's. As they spun toward her, the vampire in the coffin vanished, and they could see that an identical vampire had seized Megaera from behind and sunk his fangs deep into her neck. In the next moment Radu sprang at Zerika and attempted to bite her, but she twisted away from him and slashed at his face with her short sword. The tip carved a shallow gash in his cheek, but in the next instant the wound was gone.

"What was all that stuff you said about honor among vampires?" she demanded.

Radu's face appeared to shift into another form and, for a moment, became a diabolic visage complete with horns and beard. And a pair of insect eyes. "One of the nice things about having *no* honor is that you can say anything you damn well please."

"Who the hell are you?"

"You can call me Beelzebub. However, I have taken over Radu's character, so that in this MUD I really am a vampire, and if I bite you, you will be drained of all your abilities, just as your comrade-in-arms has been already." He lunged at her once more, and once more she barely managed to evade his fangs.

Megaera screamed again, only her second scream sounded more like a squeal, and before their eyes she began to change; her flesh became puffier, her arms and legs seemed to be shrinking into her body, and her face began to acquire a distinctly porcine appearance.

Megaera screamed/squealed a third time, and the transformation was complete; where Megaera had stood, there was now a very large sow. The sow ran around the room squealing plaintively, dragging the vampire, who couldn't seem to free his fangs from her neck. In the next moment Tahmurath's feline familiar jumped down from his shoulder and transformed into a fully armed and armored Megaera. As the sow ran past her, she swung her sword, neatly severing the vampire's neck.

Ragnar and Gunnodoyak sprang to the headless body and began driving the stake through its heart. In the meantime Megaera and Tahmurath managed to corner the sow and, with some difficulty, remove the vampire's head. "Pry open the mouth," Tahmurath instructed. As she did so, he placed the contents of a small pouch in the mouth. "Holy wafers," he explained.

"How about a little help over here?" Zerika called, but her request proved unnecessary as Radu/Beelzebub, seeing that the odds were now radically against him, reverted to bat form and fled.

"So that's what the two of you were cooking up," Zerika said. "I love it. But why did you make Megaera the decoy?"

"That's what I wanted to know," Megaera agreed.

Tahmurath grinned. "She seemed like the juiciest one in the party. I just thought of who I'd want to bite if I were a vampire."

"Hah. And why a pig?"

"I wanted to know that, too," Megaera added, a little more vehemently.

"I figured that a pig, being omnivorous, would probably taste the most like a human being, and I didn't want him to realize his mistake until it was too late. Did you know that one of the slang terms for 'human flesh' is 'long pig'?"

"Ugh! That was more than I needed to know, Dr. Lecter. Anyway, how did you get his fangs to stick in the pig's neck like that?"

"Krazy Glue."

"Well, all we need to do now is find what we came here for. Did anybody see where Drac came from when he attacked Megaera? I mean the phony Megaera."

"No," Gunnodoyak replied, "but I bet it was from behind one of these tapestries."

Sure enough, a search soon revealed a secret door hidden behind an elaborate depiction of a captured unicorn. Zerika examined it for traps, then set to work with her lockpicks. In a few moments they were moving single file down a narrow corridor that led to a richly appointed sitting room. Another coffin occupied one end of the room, but its lid was open and it was empty, except for a piece of paper.

Zerika picked up the paper gingerly, almost as if she expected it to try to bite her. "It's a crossword puzzle!"

"I think I get it," Megaera said. "It's a play on words: 'crossword' is 'cross' and 'sword' fused together. But how do we split them apart?"

Tahmurath frowned, studying the puzzle. "This may sound awfully obvious, but I think we're just going to have to solve the cross-word."

"No doubt about it," Zerika agreed. "Anybody here a crossword maven?"

"Let me at it," Megaera said with a grin.

"We can all print it out and work on it until next time," Tahmurath suggested, "then pool our answers when we meet again. It's about time to knock off for tonight anyway."

Across

1. Hooch
6. Snare
10. Slayer of Yamm
14. Untidy
19. See 89 across
20. Hearty's partner
21. Queue
22. Deadly virus
23. The stories about Camelot
26. Dyspepsia
27. Mayday
28. Biochemical messenger
29. Adherent
30. Secret agent
32. Author of "The Conqueror Worm"
33. Not more
35. Talk mode for "laughing out loud"
36. Merlin's nickname for young Arthur
40. Discourage
44. Yogi's gauntlet
45. Author of *Two Years Before the Mast*
46. Trek
47. That is, to Fabius
48. Serai
49. Place of iniquity
50. Archery instructor for the slayer of Ladon
52. Location sense for 1 down
53. Rushdie's _____ *Verses*
55. And so on
56. River near the pyramids
58. "We've already covered *A* through *K*. Now we're _____"
59. What to do with sheep in the springtime
63. In the thick of
66. Conquistador's quest
68. Women's Army Air Corps
70. Oxford river
71. Sound accompanying a magical disappearance
72. Exile Jormungandr?
77. Respighi opus _____ *di Roma*
78. Hebrew month
79. Worm starter
80. Miguel's uncle
81. Brain passage
82. *Dinero*
84. Raphael's weapon
85. Uh-uh
87. Wilde, e.g.
89. See 19 across

93. Is repeatedly itself, according to Stein
97. Sixties game-show panelist Francis
100. Perform
101. In favor
102. Frighten
103. Duo
104. Vamoose
106. Fly
107. Gorgias, e.g.
108. Shield for 4 down
109. Household god
110. Teller's partner
111. Oolong, e.g.
112. Contents of pit at 113 down
113. Drone's aunt
114. Haggard opus
115. Short article
118. Fertile soil
122. Joyce's depiction of Dedalus "as a Young Man"
128. Ambiguous Hawaiian word
129. Downwind
130. Unukulhai, e.g.
131. Emerges from intersection of 72 across and 54 down
132. *Magnificent Seven* actor Buchholz
133. Father of Cordelia
134. Brainstem bridge
135. Frequently

Down

1. Count on the wing?
2. "The Queen _____, she made some tarts"
3. Holy Roman Emperor
4. Slayer of Typhon
5. Go astray
6. Macbeth, e.g.
7. Frog genus
8. Every
9. Rot-13 for cee
10. Hallow
11. Slangy isn't
12. Conjunction
13. Unit of instruction
14. Pirate captain's address to a crewman
15. Recede
16. *Un peu d'argent*
17. Type of camera
18. PBS chef
24. One of Hesiod's ages
25. Nub
31. Locus
32. Dish one wouldn't want to eat from
33. Navel deposit
34. Lab burner
35. Local-area network (abbr.)
36. Dilemma for somebody who intends to wear just one earring
37. Aristotelian element
38. Old movie studio
39. It's 1010 in binary
40. Roman hell
41. Wedding words
42. .01 yen
43. 120 down and 93 across, in quantity
44. "Mama _____!"
45. Disarm a cat
49. Someone's in the kitchen with her
51. Brooklyn _____ (abbr.)
53. Blood fractions
54. Nautical attention-getter
57. Toss
60. *Après sept*
61. Serf
62. Golda
63. Egyptian dragon-god
64. Variety of 30 across
65. Chits
67. Japanese demon
69. Small bed
73. Dragonfly, e.g.
74. Meager
75. Bilbo's treasure
76. Type of MUD (object-oriented)
83. Transgress
86. Eastern potentate
88. Weber per square meter
90. Second word in fairy tales
91. Erstwhile Persia
92. Neither's partner
94. Grain
95. Sign that angels are happy
96. Poetic contraction
97. King Kong, e.g.
98. Joplin opus
99. Number of cards in a Roman deck
100. Swiss river
105. Type of tunnel
106. Cassandra, e.g.
107. Coral structure
110. First pope
111. Mjollnir, e.g.
112. One of those
113. California fossil site La _____
114. "The Man"
115. Bach opus _____ *Fugue*
116. Trumpeter Al
117. Renaissance name
118. Monogram for author of *The Number of the Beast*
119. UN workers' group
120. Latin for theme of this puzzle
121. Fireplaces
123. Corrida cheer
124. Slayer of Cleopatra
125. O.J. judge
126. Lao-tzu's way
127. Worship slayer of Python

▲   ▲   ▲   ▲   ▲   ▲   ▲

Al arrived on a late flight from the West Coast, and I drove to La Guardia to pick her up. On the drive back I could see that something was bothering her.

"I saw Arthur and the others while I was in California," she said.

"Oh?"

"There's something Arthur asked me to discuss with you."

"Why doesn't he just call me?"

"Because it's not something he would want to talk about on the telephone, or on-line."

Curiouser and curiouser. "Why the hell not?"

She sighed. "Because it involves asking you to do something illegal."

I laughed. "Oh, is that all? Okay, who does he want me to kill?"

"Very funny. Arthur is concerned that we're just not moving fast enough in the game, and I think he's right. He thinks we're going to have to cheat."

"How?"

"By getting Roger Dworkin's files from Macrobyte."

"Ah. And because they're not going to give them to us . . ."

"Somebody's got to break in and get them."

This was the first time the subject had come up since Dan Morgan had mentioned it that day at MIT and apparently sent Marlon Oz into a conniption. I nodded. "And that would be me. Well, it makes sense. And seeing as my character is dead, there's not much else I can do right now."

"So you'll think about it?"

"I don't have to think about it. Art's right. I should have thought of it myself, months ago."

Al fell silent for a while. "What's the matter?" I asked. "Is something wrong?"

"No. But I was sort of hoping you'd say no. I'm worried that you'll get into trouble."

"I'll be fine," I said. "Besides, it will give me something to do besides helping you solve crossword puzzles—not that you need any help."

"Oh, I don't know about that. That BloodMUD puzzle was a real killer."

"Impossible, I'd say." Art had faxed me a copy so I could work on it, too. "I seriously doubt there's a solution."

"Why do you say that?"

"I'll show you when we get home."

When we arrived, I took out the copy of the puzzle that Art had faxed to me. "Look at this," I said. "Clue number two down: 'The Queen' blank 'she made some tarts.' The answer, obviously, is 'of hearts.' "

"Obviously."

"So how come there's space for only four letters?"

She grinned. "Seems impossible, doesn't it? But watch this." She took my puzzle and filled in the squares from two down. *O, F,* and, leaving the third square blank, *S.* "Now watch." She drew a little heart in the third square. "You see puzzles like this in the *New York Times* occasionally, where a symbol or something is used."

"Okay, then, how about this one: one twenty-two across is 'Joyce's depiction of Dedalus "as a Young Man." ' 'Portrait of the artist,' right? So how do you fit that in?"

"The same way."

"But there's no 'heart' in 'portrait of the artist,' " I protested.

"No, but the letters H-E-A-R-T are in there."

"You actually solved this thing, didn't you?"

She nodded. "I finished it on the flight."

"Just don't tell me you did it in ink."

She laughed. "Okay, I won't tell you. Hey, do you want to do anything special for your birthday?"

"Actually, we're already invited to a party."

"Somebody's giving a birthday party for you?"

"Not me. I have a nephew who was born on my birthday. He'll be three on Wednesday. They're having a party for him next weekend. Want to go?"

"Sure. That should be fun." She frowned. "I just remembered something I've been meaning to tell you—did anybody mention that we had a run-in with somebody calling himself Beelzebub?"

I sat straight up. "What? Where?"

"On the 'net, I mean. In BloodMUD."

"Oh. Sounds like it might just be a coincidence." If Beelzebub was playing in MUDs, I seriously doubted he'd use his virus-hacker handle.

"I'm not so sure. Remember that guy we caught a glimpse of just before Malakh died? The one with the bug-eyes?"

"Yeah."

"Well, that's what this guy looked like."

I nodded. "And after the guivre killed Malakh, I got that 'gotcha' message from Beelzebub."

"The message could have been from a different Beelzebub," Al suggested.

"No, that was his sig. It was him. How the hell did he get mixed up in this?" I got up and started to pace. "What if we've been wrong about this all along? What if Wyrm was created by Beelzebub, not Roger Dworkin?"

Al nodded. "That would explain why his viruses seem to have the run of the 'net, while everybody else's are getting zapped."

It was after midnight and Al was asleep; I slipped out of bed and padded to the living room. I'd been unable to sleep, thinking about Beelzebub; if he was really the culprit, then things were even worse than I had imagined. I couldn't guess what Dworkin might be up to, but everything I had ever heard about him suggested that he was basically a decent guy. Beelzebub was another story. His viruses were always designed for maximum destructiveness, and if Wyrm was his creation, I was sure it would be no different in that regard. What would be different would be the amount of damage that Wyrm could do.

I couldn't sleep anyway, so I decided to put my insomnia to some constructive use. It was now my job to crack root at Macrobyte, and I figured it was time to get cracking, if you'll forgive the bad pun. "Root" is a shorthand way of designating the privileged system-maintenance logon in a given computer system. Someone in "root mode" can set up or terminate user accounts, change passwords, and read or write any file on the system, no matter how it's protected. Other terms used for this kind of logon are "superuser" and the older "avatar," and "wheel mode." You might think that this kind of access would be available only to computer experts; in fact, superuser accounts are frequently given to people who are important in a company but may be as clueless as the boss in the "Dilbert" comic strip, who thinks that his Etch-A-Sketch is a laptop.

So it's possible, sometimes, to break into a superuser account because of the carelessness and general lack of computer savvy of the user. More often, though, hackers obtain initial access through a lower-level account, then employ a variety of strategems for increasing the access available through that account right up to superuser.

Macrobyte could be expected to have the usual "firewall machine" protecting its system—dedicated gateway hardware that's set up specifically to defend the system from crackers. But there was another, potentially more troublesome, consideration. A giant like Macrobyte must have many millions of dollars' worth of future software under development at a facility like the one in Oakland. Their big worry would be industrial espionage, not garden-variety hackers and crackers. It was likely that anything considered especially sensitive would be restricted to hardware with no outside network connections.

Still, it seemed unlikely that Dworkin would have hidden what I was looking for in off-network computers. After all, the programmer in the adjoining cubicle had told us that Dworkin would absent himself for weeks at a time—during those periods his only access would be through a dial-in.

In order to crack Macrobyte's corporate computer network, it would be necessary to obtain access information—username and password—from someone who worked there, even if only a low-level peon. There are numerous illicit methods for obtaining such information (whole books have been written about it), but I wasn't planning to soil my hands with any of them. Not when I had HfH to do my dirty work.

I still had access to their BBS, of course, including a section of the board where hackers posted privileged information they had obtained—kind of a hacker's trophy case. As Macrobyte was such a natural for the role of corporate Goliath versus the hackers' Davids, there was a disproportionate amount of material posted about the company.

The problem was, none of it was really very fresh. Naturally, the hacker who obtained such access would want to fully exploit it himself before turning it over to his "colleagues," no matter how anxious he was to impress them.

I finally found one account and password that had been posted within the last week. My benefactor claimed that he had gotten it by "shoulder surfing" an MB employee who happened to be using a public terminal to log in. "Shoulder surfing" refers to the practice of stealing somebody's password by looking over his shoulder when he enters it—trickier than it sounds, as the password doesn't actually appear on the screen, so the "surfer" has to watch the keyboard to see which keys are struck and in which order. Some people seem to have a real talent for this, but there are also refinements involving surreptitious placement of mirrors, camcorders, and the like.

I used the access info thus obtained and was a little surprised to find that it worked; apparently security had not yet caught on to the fact that this particular account had been compromised. Or so I thought.

I moved quickly through several screens, arriving at a list of files that included designations like "confidential," "sensitive," and even "eyes only." I didn't bother opening them—they were obviously "bait files." The HfH access info had led straight into an "iron box"—a set of security measures designed to protect the system from crackers by subtly restricting the scope of their on-line activities while keeping them interested (with the "bait files") and on-line long enough to be traced.

I logged off and thought about what to do next. The other Macrobyte passwords on the HfH board were all older than the one I had just tried; still, it might be worth the effort to try a few more. I was going to have to be careful to cover my tracks—after all, what I was doing was not, strictly speaking, legal. Still, I didn't think Macrobyte's security would pose that much of a challenge.

Then I heard it: the soft whirring of my computer's hard drive. It's a sound that most computer users learn to ignore, because it happens frequently and irregularly, whenever the computer needs to read something from the disk or write something to it. I've learned *not* to ignore it, because a drive reading or writing when it shouldn't can be a sign of virus infection. I was sure my computer wasn't infected, but I also knew, because it's my job to know, that there was no reason for the drive to be active at that particular moment.

Unless— On a hunch I switched the modem line to audio. Instantly I heard the distinctive crackling whine of electronic data transmission. It took another second to register what had happened—the Macrobyte network had fed me a phony logout screen and maintained the connection! They were undoubtedly trying to trace the origin of my call at that very moment. I did a hardware disconnect (hung up, basically) and sat back in my chair. I was amazed to realize that my heart was pounding and I had broken out in a sweat.

Until that moment I had not been overly impressed with Macrobyte's security, but this was a new and devious wrinkle: a phony logout. It was, in fact, a variation on what hackers call spoofing. A cracker might spoof by sending a sham E-mail message to people with system access to trick them into revealing their passwords. Another approach is to write a program that duplicates the login screen on the system under attack. Then, when people type in their passwords, the program gives a phony error message and saves the password so the cracker can use it later. I was now willing to bet serious money that Macrobyte's security team included at least one reformed cracker. This was going to be tougher than I thought.

Al had a few errands to run that Saturday, so we agreed to meet at the party. I was running a little early, so I stopped by my parents' house first. Mom met me at the door with a worried frown. "Would you please talk to your brother?" she asked. "He's up in his room."

"Talk to him about what?"

"All he ever does is play those rock-video CDs. I think they're rotting his mind."

"I thought I caught a whiff of something."

"Very funny. Would you please try to talk to him? He won't listen to me or your father."

"I'll see what I can do."

"Thank you."

I don't know what made her think I had any particular influence over Uri; the last time he'd followed any guidance of mine was when he was seven and I was seventeen, and I taught him to burp the words "Excuse me," which appealed to his penchant for efficiency. I went up to Uri's room. My old room, actually. Then Gabe's, then Raph's, and now Uri's. A room with a history.

There were posters of cyberpunk groups all over the walls, and debris of various kinds covering all the horizontal surfaces. The debris could be roughly classed into three types: edible, inedible, and indeterminate. It was actually a little neater than I was used to seeing it.

Uri was gyrating in the middle of the floor. He didn't see me because of the VR helmet he wore, which was presumably pumping loud noise and violent imagery into his teenage brain. His right hand, encased in a heavy glove with a cable running from it to the helmet, appeared to massage the strings of an imaginary guitar. I swept some junk off one corner of the bed, mostly type three, and sat down.

"Mom asked me to talk with you," I said loudly.

Nothing.

"She thinks you're rotting your mind."

Zilch.

"That's about the lamest air guitar I've ever seen."

He stopped abruptly, flipped up his vid goggles, and stared a challenge at me. "It's virtual guitar, not air guitar. Think you can do better?"

I stood in the middle of a stage, under an impossibly starry sky, surrounded by a sea of frenzied teenagers. At least I assume they were all teenagers; it was difficult to guess the ages of the ones that had three eyes and tentacles. Banks of loudspeakers the size of the World Trade Center bracketed the stage. I looked behind me and saw the drummer, who bore a striking resemblance to Jabba the Hut. As if in response to my glance, he started laying down a beat. The bass player and rhythm guitarist, a pair of ghouls, joined in, along with a trio of vampiric vocalists. I struck a chord on my guitar, an angular, jet-black thing that seemed to have been carved from a single piece of obsidian, and it wailed out of the speakers and merged with the howling of the surrounding crowd. I don't play guitar, but it didn't matter. Each time my right hand moved across the strings, a chord sounded. I started to play complicated riffs, and the computer synthesized them without missing a beat. I was awesome. Okay, *it* was awesome, but it sure felt like it was me doing it.

I felt a tap on the helmet and flipped up the vid goggles. Uri, who had been listening on a pair of headphones, said, "Not bad. But Mom says it's time to go." He jerked a thumb at the door. Mom was standing there, hands on hips. She rolled her eyes upward, a mute appeal for divine intervention. None was forthcoming. She walked away muttering to herself.

"What did you think?" Uri asked me.

"Fun. What do *you* think?"

"Hey, it's, like, the beast."

"The beast?"

"Yeah, you know, like, radical, or something. What would some-body of your generation say? Hip? Cool? Groovy?"

"Uri, as much as I sometimes hate to admit it, we have the same parents. That makes us the same generation."

He flashed me an insolent grin. "I was talking, you know, figura-tively."

I followed Gabe's directions and came to the shopping plaza. Domi-nating one end of a crescent-shaped parking lot was the appointed place: the Oh! Zone. I waited outside for Al to show up, which she did after about ten minutes.

"Hi! Shouldn't we go in?" she asked.

"I think we might be a little early. Let's wait until some other people get here."

While we were waiting, several skinheads went by, all wearing the obligatory 666 tattoo on some patch of shaven scalp. "If 666 is the marker for Wyrm, then they must have it, too," Al joked.

"Yeah, if anybody's brain is worm-eaten, it would have to be those guys."

Then a nice middle-aged woman came by and pressed some flyers into our hands. These turned out to be pamphlets warning that Bar-ney the dinosaur was, in fact, the Antichrist.

"The scary thing," Al remarked, "is that she actually looked nor-mal."

"*Excuse* me, but would somebody *mind* holding the door?"

It was not a polite request. We turned around to see a woman carrying several large bags, decidedly less normal in appearance than our most recent acquaintance. I would compare her to Margaret Hamilton in her Wicked Witch of the West get-up by saying that this woman was taller and had a complexion that was slightly less green. I'd have to give Margaret an edge in the personality department, though. I held the door for her and she stomped through.

"What was *her* problem?" Al exclaimed.

"I don't know; maybe she's having a bad-hair day."

"*That's* an understatement."

A short time later the other guests, including the three-year-old guest of honor, began to arrive, and we all went in. It was like entering a madhouse. The place was filled with all kinds of arcade games, although with less emphasis on video games and more of the old-fashioned skee-ball-type games. There were also several small amusement-park rides: a carousel in one corner, a helicopter ride, and a caterpillar.

But the overriding attraction, dominating the center of the place, was a sort of three-dimensional maze constructed of steel pipes, large plastic conduits, urethane foam, and nylon mesh. Children swarmed through the maze, shrieking at the top of their little lungs. Some of the kids were pursued by perspiring adults; a sign posted outside the thing explained that kids under five had to be accompanied by a parent. For some reason there was no rule requiring that the parent be accompanied by a cardiologist. The din was amazing.

Little Mikey was telling his parents he wanted to go in the maze *now,* and they were asking him which parent he wanted to go in with him. I noticed that they seemed a little anxious as they posed this question, and I wondered if they saw this as some kind of a parental popularity contest. However, when the little guy swung around, pointing a finger, and said, "I want Uncle Michael to come with me," they both were suddenly beaming brightly. Gabe handed me a pair of kneepads and said, "Here. You'll need these."

I turned to gesture at Al in order to excuse myself from maze duty, but she said, "Oh, no. I'll be fine. You go with your nephew. I'm looking forward to seeing this."

We shed our shoes and put them in a rack near one of the entrances to the maze. And then we were off.

The little munchkin led me on a merry chase. The plastic conduits that formed most of the passageways were just large enough for him to be able to stand with a slight crouch, enabling him to run along pretty quickly, while I slogged after on hands and knees. As a karate student, I've spent a fair amount of time kneeling on hardwood floors, but this was murder, even with the kneepads.

We negotiated various types of obstacles, including a pit filled with hollow plastic balls and a corridor with small padded sandbags swinging from the top. In order to climb to the top level, one had to negotiate a rope net that was angled upward about forty-five degrees. In order to make this safe for kids, so that they couldn't stick a whole arm or leg through the net, it was backed up by a finer nylon mesh of about one-inch squares. Stepping on this stuff in stocking feet with the weight of an adult was about as comfortable as dancing on razor blades.

And we had to go to the top, because there was a slide up there that spiraled back down to the bottom, and that was Mikey's favorite part. I didn't actually realize it was a slide the first time, until I dived into yet another tube after him and suddenly found myself picking up velocity. We had to go down the slide four times, which means we had to climb up to the slide four times. I didn't pick up much velocity the last couple of times on the slide, because I was so sweaty, I was sticking to the plastic. And all the while, as I scrambled after him, trying to keep him in sight, I was thinking that if I lost him in this maze, between the parents, grandparents, and other assorted doting relatives, there wouldn't be enough left of me to give a decent burial.

Finally we emerged. I stripped off the kneepads and handed them back to Gabe, then sat down to put my shoes back on.

Al came over and sat next to me. "Looks like you got quite a workout."

"Yeah, I'll say. This could be a new fitness trend: All you need is one of these maze things and a three-year-old as your personal trainer."

She laughed. "You may be onto something. Hey, you know that rude woman you opened the door for?"

"The Wicked Witch of the West? What about her?"

"I've been seeing her around this place, and I don't know what she's doing here. She doesn't have any kids with her, she doesn't seem to be with a party—it's very strange."

"Maybe she got here early for her party."

"Maybe. But there's something about her that just sets off my alarms somehow, like she's up to no good."

"We'll keep an eye on her. If she tries to jimmy open one of the skee-ball machines, we'll be on her like powdered sugar on a doughnut."

"Very funny."

A short time later an announcement came over the PA system: "Everyone here for the Michael Arcangelo party, please go to party room number three now."

"That's us," I said, quite unnecessarily.

"I'll meet you there in a few minutes. I have to go to the ladies' room first."

We were all herded into a room just off the main amusement area.

A low table was set with colorful paper plates and napkins, and surrounded by child-size seats. Larger chairs for the adults were placed
against the walls, and there was a young woman wearing an Oh! Zone
hat and T-shirt who was acting as hostess. The highlight, though,
came a few minutes later when a purple-and-green tyrannosaurus appeared at the door.

"BARNEY!" the kids shrieked.

Barney made his entrance and proceeded to do his song-and-dance
schtick. The kids ate it up. The costume looked a little cheesier than
the one on the TV program, but the kids didn't seem to notice.

Al walked in, glanced at Barney, then walked over to me with one
hand clamped over her mouth. As she sat, she leaned over to me and
whispered, "You'll never guess who that is."

"I'm guessing that it's Barney. Am I wrong?"

"I mean inside the costume."

"Somebody I know?"

"Only well enough to hold a door for."

I couldn't believe it. "That's the witch? How do you know?"

"I saw her in the ladies' room with her head off, smoking a cigarette." She smirked. "There was a No Smoking sign, so I made her
put it out. She left in a huff."

"I never knew you minded cigarette smoke that much."

"I don't. It was just a little payback."

"Oh."

CHAPTER ELEVEN

Wingwyrm

And they had tails like unto scorpions,
and there were stings in their tails . . .
—Revelation 9:10

It was Krishna's 'bot that gave me the idea; I realized that if an AI program could play in a MUD, it would also be possible to write one that would crack Macrobyte's system security, while insulating me from detection.

As this was nominally an application of artificial intelligence and, therefore, not really in my line, I enlisted some help from George and Krishna. It took us a few weeks to write and debug it. One problem was how it would get the information it obtained back to me. Obviously, I couldn't have the program simply E-mail the stuff to me—if anybody found it, it would contain my E-mail address, and I might as well go turn myself in right now.

Instead I decided to have it post the material publicly—but in a disguised form. In certain USENET newsgroups, it's a relatively common practice to post "binaries"—graphics that are encoded in any of several different binary formats. People then download the binary files, run them through a program that decodes them, and look at the pretty pictures. Or the dirty pictures, as the case may be.

Krishna and I worked out an encryption algorithm that produced an output pretty similar, on cursory inspection, to one of the more common binary graphic formats. Naturally, if anybody tried to view this output, it wouldn't work, but they'd probably figure that some luser had "spooged" his scanner output, and just move on to the next binary.

Then I needed to select a newsgroup that I hoped wouldn't have too many subscribers—the fewer people who would see this stuff, the less likely someone would realize that something funny was going on. I considered alt.picard.borg.borg.borg and alt.barney.die.die.die, but neither one, when I read them, contained any binaries. I eventually decided on alt.sex.bestiality.

The program we were writing was not a virus or a worm, since it lacked any self-replication properties. It was, however, a form of Trojan horse, and I wanted to be very careful not to cause damage to any of the systems that would be affected by it.

Trojans are often used by crackers to help penetrate secure systems. This was a little different, in that my program was initially going to have to work from the outside. That meant that we needed to set it up in another system that couldn't be traced back to us.

"Let's install it on the system at Berkeley," Krishna suggested. "The security there is pretty porous."

That was no great surprise. University systems are rarely very secure; there are just too many people who have access. "Sounds good to me," I agreed. "Hmm, this is going to wind up costing Berkeley some money in phone bills and computer time."

"Yeah. So?"

"So let's keep track. I'll send them an anonymous donation when we're through. What's the matter?"

"Nothing. But I like your style. Hey, speaking of style, what are we calling this thing?"

"How about Icepick?"

"Ooh, I like it."

One evening Al was watching TV in the bedroom while I did some work in the living room under Effie's disapproving gaze. "Michael," she called, "can you come in here a minute?"

"Can it wait?" I was pondering something at my workstation,

which I had only recently moved into the apartment—something that seemed rather important at the time, namely, how I was going to get a Macrobyte system username and password for Icepick to use.

"There's something on TV that I think you should see."

"Can you tape it?"

"I already am, but can't you come in for a minute?"

With a sigh I lurched from my chair in the direction of the television noises.

Al was sprawled on her stomach, head toward the foot of the bed, chin resting in her hands. On the screen was one of those "news" programs that are distinguished from their more reputable relations in the information biz by such practices as paying people to be interviewed.

"This is what you wanted me to see?"

She nodded.

"Well, that's a relief. I thought this was just a cheap excuse to get me in here for some quick, sordid sexual liaison."

"Shhh!"

The current interviewee, paid or otherwise, was a fellow who looked like somebody you might have to step over in order to get into the subway, only not as well groomed. He was middle-aged, with a long, wiry, gray-shot beard, and a stare that gave you the impression he was looking almost exactly right at you, but was off by just the tiniest bit.

His gaze was the one thing about him that was off by only a tiny bit. He was one of those people who are sometimes referred to by respectable Egyptologists as pyramidiots. His interest in studying the pyramids was not archaeological, or architectural, or anthropological, or even religious in the ordinary sense. No, this fellow studied the pyramids, and in particular the Great Pyramid at Giza, because he believed it was a representation, in stone, of a prophecy for the rest of human history, a prophecy that would end, along with human history, in the year 2000. I couldn't imagine anybody paying this lunatic—er, luminary to be interviewed. I started to wonder whether any of these programs accepted money from people who wanted to be interviewed on TV, and whether that would be considered a greater or lesser breach of journalistic ethics, if that's not an oxymoron.

According to this "expert," there was one main passage from the entrance to the pyramid, angling steeply downward. Somewhere

along its length the passage bifurcated and sent a branch angling upward, while the main shaft continued angling downward in a straight
line. From the entrance to the bifurcation measures 2,623 inches—the
number of years from the completion of the pyramid until the birth of
Christ. Measure along the upward branch another 33 inches, and it
opens up into an area known as the Grand Gallery. One thousand
nine hundred sixty-seven inches later it terminates in the dead center
of the pyramid. Or you can follow the downward passage. It terminates in exactly the same distance—terminates in a deep pit. Either
way, 4,623 years from the completion of the pyramid, or 2,000 years
from the birth of Christ, everything comes to an end.

Professor Pyramid, however, was not alone in spreading these tid-
ings of comfort and joy. There were also interpreters of the prophecies
of Nostradamus, followers of St. Malachi, believers in the powers of
Edgar Cayce, and assorted other apocalypticians.

It was one of those weekends when Al and I were both on the West
Coast and had arranged to meet the others at Cepheus.

"How is your end of the project coming, Mike?" Art asked. This
was, of course, a delicate reference to my Macrobyte cracking activities.

"Stalled at the moment, but I think you're going to be able to
help me with that."

"How?"

"I need access information—a username and password—for
Macrobyte's system."

"I don't get it; how are we supposed to help with that?"

"Macrobyte has a lot of employees, and it's a safe bet that some of
them are MUDheads."

"So?"

"So most people tend to use the same password for every situation
that requires one. That means if we can get a Macrobyte employee's
password off a MUD, there's an excellent chance that the same password will work on their Macrobyte account."

Krishna nodded. "I think it'll work. Most MUDs archive data on
their regular players, and the security on their password files is usually
pretty lax."

"And the frobnule gives us full wizard privileges," Art agreed. "I
think we should be able to get you what you need. Shall we?"

"Not yet," Al said. She had brought along her tape of the pyramid TV show. "I want everybody here to see this."

The tape elicited a lot of laughs, but Al looked dead serious. "Why are we listening to these wack-jobs?" George asked. "I thought we were here to play the game."

"I thought," Al said, "that we may have been losing sight of the point of playing this game."

George grinned sheepishly. "Now that you mention it, I've had the feeling lately that it's turning into a dogwash."

"Dogwash" is a bit of hacker argot denoting a low-priority task that one turns to in order to avoid doing any really important work, as in "I think I'll wash the dog first."

"But George's original point remains," Arthur said. "What does all this nonsense have to do with our problem?"

"Two things, really," Al responded. "First, we need to realize that all of this information, nonsense or not, can be found on the 'net and is therefore accessible to Wyrm."

"So what you're saying," George added, "is that if Wyrm takes in all this crap, and decides that it's supposed to hit the fan on a certain day, it can bloody well see to it that it *does* hit the fan on that day."

Al nodded solemnly. "And I don't think anybody in this room needs to be told what kind of disasters could be caused by a malevolent AI capable of controlling the entire Internet. Just think about it."

George nodded. "Hospital computers, air-traffic computers, train-switching computers, nuclear-power-plant computers—a lot of bad stuff could happen."

"Speaking of nukes," I said, "are you forgetting nuclear weapons?"

"Oh, come on," Art said. "Let's not go off the deep end here. No computer that has anything to do with nuclear weapons is connected to a public network."

"It doesn't have to be," I said.

"Then how . . . ?"

"Viruses. You disseminate a virus that will infect the target system, then it disseminates a message that eventually gets back to you. Given enough time, you can learn enough to penetrate security on just about any system, through the use of successively better-targeted viruses."

Robin was also skeptical. "Oh, come on, like nuclear-weapons engineers are really going to infect their computers with viruses. They'd have to be incredibly careful about what they used on those machines."

"You think so? Well, I have some news for you. A few years ago somebody took a look at what was in the main computer at Livermore."

"And?"

"It contained over a thousand pornographic images."

Out of the corner of my eye I saw Al mouth something at Robin that looked like "Men are such pigs." I glanced at her, and she flashed an uncharacteristically innocent smile.

Art, on the other hand, looked genuinely shaken. "So what you're saying is that this worm could create the kind of viruses you're talking about and use them to launch missiles?"

"It is a possibility."

"And," Al added, "that may not be the worst part."

They were, to put it mildly, nonplussed. Who wouldn't be, after being asked to imagine a worst-case, doomsday scenario, and then being told, okay, that's fine, now for the bad news. Everybody spoke at once, demanding to know what Al was talking about. We were all looking expectantly at her. Then she turned and looked expectantly at me.

As the other gazes in the room swiveled in my direction, I took in a deep breath. "Well, it's like this," I said. "We think the Internet might not be the only thing that's infected with an intelligent worm."

"Okay," George said, after my explication of the problem had started to sink in. "I remember what Oz said about human-information viruses. I even thought that some of it made sense. But what does that have to do with all this crazy prophecy stuff?"

"The prophecies," I said, "are in all our psyches. It's not just the occasional off-the-wall television show; this stuff is ubiquitous."

"So you think we've been programmed to self-destruct?"

"Quite possibly. At least some of us. And even a significant minority could make things pretty dicey for the rest of the world."

"I think you may be taking this too far," Arthur said. "I can almost buy your thesis when it involves religion—but this other stuff is too fringey; I don't think that many people are really into it."

"Art," Robin put in, "when was the last time you were in a supermarket?"

"I don't know, years, probably. What does that have to do with anything?"

"If you spent any time standing in supermarket checkout lines, you'd be familiar with a particular genre of tabloid newspaper."

"You mean like the *National Enquirer*?"

"No, that's just celebrity gossip. I'm talking about papers where the headline is liable to be something like, 'I was kidnapped by aliens and met Elvis.' These things are in all of the supermarkets. Somebody must be reading them."

Art looked exasperated. "But that's all bullshit."

I thought of astrology, fairies, schrödinbugs, and the Black-Scholes equation. "Sometimes," I told Art, "what people believe is all that matters. Even if it *is* bullshit."

"Mike, I have to admit," George said, "that I think you've come up with the conspiracy theory to end all conspiracy theories."

"What do you mean?" I asked. "Why is it a conspiracy theory?"

"Because it means that we're *all* part of the conspiracy without even realizing it."

Al, who had been silent for a while, reentered the conversation with another startling observation: "You know, I don't think those 'fringe' prophets are controlling the worm. But they might be tapping into it in some way."

Arthur looked puzzled. "How could they do that?"

"They're hysterics. All the 'great' psychics are. If you read about their lives, you find out that they suffered from all kinds of hysterical symptoms at various times—Edgar Cayce lost his voice, Mary Baker Eddy was in a wheelchair with hysterical paralysis, and so on.

"But there's more to hysteria than symptoms. It's also, in some people, a kind of psychic sensitivity—I don't mean ESP, just sensitivity to subliminal information. These people are highly suggestible to outside influences—only in this case it may be partly an inside influence."

"Another kind of Wyrm."

"Exactly."

"I have another question," Robin said. "The Book of Revelation says a thousand years. Why didn't everybody go crazy in the year one thousand?"

"A lot of people did," I said. "Many of them marched off to the Holy Land to wait for the Second Coming, just like they're doing now. There's also a legend that the entire population of Iceland converted to Christianity at midnight on January first. Probably the only thing that kept things from getting completely out of hand is that the Church took the official position that the world was not going to end that year. Also, it probably helped that Arabic numerals weren't widely in use yet.''

"What do Arabic numerals have to do with it?"

"If you use Arabic numerals, then the year 999 inverted is 666."

"Ooh! Then this year inverted is 6661."

"Yes. But again, probably the biggest factor was that the Church helped to stabilize things by saying that it wasn't time for the apocalypse yet."

"So? Aren't they saying that this year, too?"

"Yeah, but there's something else: A thousand years ago everybody was waiting for some major thing to happen—signs, portents, natural disasters, whatever. Apparently, nothing did. If we're not successful, then it's entirely possible that some *unnatural* disasters could occur."

Al nodded grimly. "And that could set off a mass hysteria on a scale never before seen in human history."

"Mike, have you talked to Marlon Oz about this?" George asked.

"I'd like to, very much. But for some reason he's not returning my phone calls."

▲ ▲ ▲ ▲ ▲ ▲ ▲

They assembled back in the chamber that Ragnar had dubbed Grand Central Dungeon. Over the previous weeks they had made repeated forays into many different MUDs, picking up various kinds of loot and, occasionally, a clue. This had allowed them to upgrade their weapons and other equipment considerably. Zerika had suggested they try splitting up to cover more ground, but this had proved impractical when they discovered that it was the Golden Frobnule that allowed them to retain their special powers when entering another MUD. Without it, even though their "magic cookies" allowed them access, they had to start as novices.

"Still nothing about Eltanin," Tahmurath said. "What else are we looking for?"

"The 'sword of the father,'" Zerika answered. "Whatever that means. We don't even know why Megaera's sword is 'the sword of the son.' And the 'magic conveyance,' which could be some kind of a device that can move us between MUDs without coming back here all the time."

"We certainly have collected a lot of magic swords," Gunnodoyak commented, rooting through what appeared to be a golf bag filled with weapons. "We've got Narsil, Glamdring, Calad Bolg, Durendal, Naegling, Blackwand, Tyrfing, Stormbringer, and Grayswandir. How do we know it isn't one of them?"

"It's possible, but I doubt it," said Megaera, who had traded in her battered breastplate for a complete set of plate armor. She touched the pommel of the "sword of the son": They had returned to BloodMUD to enter her solution to the crossword puzzle, which then transformed into a huge cross-hilted broadsword. There was a little window of crystal in the hilt through which it was possible to see what looked like a few splinters of very old wood. "Maybe it's Worm-wood," Ragnar had suggested.

"Remember," Megaera said, "the inscription on Dracula's crypt said that the 'sword of the father' is a dragon-slayer. I don't think any one of those blades is particularly known for being used to kill a dragon. The closest is Naegling, which Beowulf used in his battle with the firedrake."

"That sounds like a possibility," Ragnar said.

"Not really. Naegling shattered when Beowulf hit the dragon with it. Then the dragon killed him."

"Bummer."

"Do any of the books help?" Zerika asked. "Tahmurath, you've got the library."

Tahmurath, into whose keeping had been given the various scrolls, tomes, grimoires, incunabula, and other "quaint and curious volumes of forgotten lore" that they had acquired on their travels through cyberspace, shook his hoary head. "I've looked through them pretty thoroughly, except for this one." He held up the large leather-bound tome that was marked with the sign of the ouroboros.

"*Ars Magna,*" Zerika read. "That's the book we got in the troll's lair, isn't it? What's it supposed to mean?"

"*The Book of the Fat Ass?*" Ragnar suggested unhelpfully.

Tahmurath ignored him. "*The Great Art*. I think it refers to al-chemy."

"That makes sense," Megaera said. "According to Jung, the ouroboros was an important alchemical symbol."

"What's in the book?" Gunnodoyak inquired.

"Complete gibberish. Actually, I think it's in code."

"Let Gunny take a look," Zerika suggested. "He does those news-paper cryptograms in his head."

"He can look at it later," Tahmurath said. "We don't have time for a code-breaking session right now."

"Just a quick peek," Gunnodoyak said "You never know; it could be something as simple as rot-thirteen."

Gunnodoyak opened the book to chapter one, which was titled "Eht Tagre Tra." "Hmm, let's see: Rug Gnter Gen. That doesn't sound too promising. I guess it's not rot-thirteen. Wait a minute! It says 'The Great Art.' "

Tahmurath was looking over Gunnodoyak's shoulder. "A simple transposition cipher?"

He shook his head. "Something even simpler. Anagrams."

Ragnar hunched his back and said, "A shroe, a shroe, my dingkom for a shroe."

Megaera blinked at him. "What was that supposed to mean?"

"It's a talk-show guest who speaks entirely in anagrams doing Shakespeare. Classic Monty Python sketch."

"Doesn't sound like a very interesting talk-show guest."

"Well, it beats a man with three buttocks."

"Actually, I saw that on *Oprah*. It was pretty fascinating. Do you know how he has to go to the bathroom?"

"No, and I don't really want to," Tahmurath said. "Look, it's going to take a while to decipher all the anagrams in *Ars Magna*. The immediate question is, Where do we go next?"

"Why not let a computer decipher it?" Ragnar suggested.

"You have a program that unscrambles anagrams?"

"No, but I can write you one."

"How long will that take?" Tahmurath asked dubiously.

"Half an hour, tops. Look, we just have the program generate a file for each word with every permutation, then run the output through a spell-checker. I'll take a commercial spell-checker and alter the code so that it will just kick out any text that doesn't pass the check."

"What if it comes up with more than one possibility for a given word?"

"More than one?"

"Yeah, like stripe, sprite, priest, tripes, ripest, esprit; I'm sure there are lots of cases like that."

"Hmm. Okay, I'll have the program just bracket any multiples together, and we can decide which one is right based on context."

"And what about long words?" Gunnodoyak added. "A ten-letter word is going to have over three million permutations; that's more than ten thousand pages of text."

"You're right," Ragnar conceded. "Okay, we'll have the program skip anything with more than eight letters. But we can probably decipher the long ones more easily if we have the context. How long is *Ars Magna,* Tahmurath?"

"About twenty k."

"Okay, half an hour to write the program, maybe ten minutes to run it."

"You sold me," Tahmurath agreed. "But not right now. We don't have enough on-line time together to devote even forty minutes to this—we can do it later."

"Do we have a little time for something else?" Megaera asked.

"Like what?"

"I have something I've been meaning to give Ragnar, to help him with his improvisations."

Tahmurath nodded. "Yes, I think you'd better."

"What is it?" Ragnar asked. "A rhyming dictionary?"

"Something even better: a computer program that writes poetry."

Ragnar wrinkled his nose. "Computer poetry?"

"Yes, computer poetry. Don't turn up your nose, you need all the help you can get."

"True. Okay, let me try it." After a few moments of preparation, Ragnar strummed his harp and began to sing:

"An ancient dragon sat alone
Beside a dried-up spring.
By day and night he made his moan,
It would have stirred a heart of stone
To see him wring his claws and groan
Because he could not sing.

"A certain hornet heard him cry,
A hornet with a sting.
Inspected him with compound eye
And said 'O Wyrm, what makes you cry?'
And bitter was the wyrm's reply:
'Because I cannot sing.'

"The hornet said, 'You are a dry
And desiccated thing.
I never saw a creature cry
Without a tear in either eye
Who could, no matter how he try
Do such a thing as sing.

" 'But note the crevice in this hill
Which marks an erstwhile spring:
If rains enough from heaven spill
To make it issue forth a rill
From which you then might drink your fill,
You might be fit to sing.'

"And thus the hornet did advise
The dragon by the spring.
Then left him to antagonize
Deaf heaven with his bootless cries,
And imprecate the cloudless skies,
Because he could not sing.

"A nightingale came flying out
On swift and feathery wing.
'Oh is it grief or is it gout
What is this bellowing about?'
The wyrm replied with quivering snout
'Because I cannot sing.'

"The nightingale guffawed with glee
And turned a quick handspring.
'O wyrm,' he said, 'be ruled by me,
And we shall see what we shall see.
This minute, for a trifling fee
I'll teach you how to sing.'

"The dragon rose in joyful start
'O bird, you are a king!
Your words have healed my inward smart
Come, name your fee and do your part

Bring comfort to a broken heart
By teaching me to sing.'

" *'My fee shall be a pickled trout,*
Our goal a bell-like ring.
Your voice must range, without a doubt,
Between a whisper and a shout.
Now take a breath and let it out,
For that's the way to sing!'

"The dragon tried as best he could
To croon a tune like Bing.
Inhaled a breath (so far, so good),
Exhaled as teacher said he should,
And barbecued him where he stood,
A torch song he did sing.

"The dragon sighed regretfully,
And munched a crispy wing,
And said, 'It is a pity he
Did not live to collect his fee,
Or hear his favorite pupil, me,
So beautifully sing.' "

This time the aura around Ragnar's harp grew larger and brighter. When he finished, it died away very gradually. "What happened?" Ragnar asked. "Didn't it take?"

"It took," Tahmurath assured him. "The magical aura is still there, it's just normally invisible except to us wizardly types."

"Then in that case, I think I'll do an encore. Any requests?"

"Yes. Could you gag yourself for a minute?" Tahmurath requested. "We still have to answer the original question, namely, Where do we go now?"

"I have a lead on something," Zerika said. "The clue said that it was in Abaddon's Tower, so I posted a question to a couple of the USENET newsgroups that are MUD oriented. I got a reply that said it's in a MUD called Cain's World. Is that in the book?"

Tahmurath thumbed through *The Book of Gates*. "Yes! It's through that door over there. Shall we?"

The party stepped through the cyberportal and looked around. They seemed to have arrived at the proverbial dark alley, and all around them were the sorts of goings-on that cause decent, right-thinking people to avoid dark alleys like the plague.

A man dressed in a dark-green cloak was just finishing up a bit of mayhem in the vicinity and turned toward them. In his right hand was a sword; blood covered its black blade. He grinned at them in a most unfriendly manner. "Newbies! Hail! Or perhaps I should say hail and farewell!"

Before they could reply, a woman approached from the opposite direction. "You're not going to hog them all to yourself, are you, Chilly?" She wore plate mail of black steel and carried a double-bladed battle-ax.

He bowed with a flourish. "The more the merrier, my lady Myrellia."

"Wait a minute," Zerika said. "Is this a player-killing MUD?"

"Rather than answer verbally," the man said, "I think I will simply demonstrate . . ." He lunged at Zerika, attempting to run her through. She dodged to one side and he pursued, but before he could essay a second blow, Tahmurath had muttered a short incantation. A green nimbus of magical energy leaped from his outstretched fingers and engulfed Zerika's attacker. When it dissipated, a rather surprised-looking newt occupied the spot where the attacker had been.

"That should teach him to put on airs with his betters," Tahmurath remarked.

In the meantime Megaera had crossed swords, or rather sword and battle-ax, with the woman addressed as Lady Myrellia. The battle appeared to be fairly even, until Gunnodoyak darted in from one side and drove the tips of his fingers into the soft tissue just below Myrellia's ear. She dropped like a sack of potatoes.

"What did you do that for?" Megaera complained. "I was just getting warmed up."

At that moment a group of armed men approached. Their uniforms and military bearing suggested that they represented the local constabulary—that, and the fact that the other denizens of the alley fled at their approach.

The leader of the group, a grizzled fellow with long mustachios, wearing a crimson cape over blue scale armor, stopped and surveyed the scene. "Not that they didn't deserve it, but how did you do this to them?"

"It was self-defense," Tahmurath said.

"I'm sure it was. My question wasn't why, but how. You folks are obviously newbies, yet you took out two of the strongest players in this MUD. Not only that, but we don't even *have* a spell that turns somebody into a lizard, or whatever that is. That takes real hacking talent." He prodded Lady Myrellia's limp form with the toe of his boot. "Is she dead?"

"No, she should wake up in a few hours," Gunnodoyak answered.

"And what about him?" He indicated the nonplussed newt.

Tahmurath shrugged. "He'll get better."

"Good, because otherwise I was going to have to nuke you."

"But why?" Zerika wanted to know. "I thought player killing was permissible in this MUD."

"If it's done within the rules of the game, then yes, it is. But you guys are obviously using extralegal methods. As much as I admire a good hack, this is not playing the game by the rules. Although I have to admit, these two have had it coming for a long time; they're two of the worst berserkers on the 'net."

"Look, we're really not here to mess up your MUD," Zerika assured him. "We'll leave as soon as we can. We just have to get one item."

"And what item would that be?"

"I can't really describe it, because I don't know what it's supposed to look like. It might be a magic carpet, or something like that, but we really don't know for sure. All we know is that it's supposed to be here in a place called Abaddon's Tower."

"The tower? Well, you've been given a tough nut to crack. Come on, I'll take you there. Once you go inside, you're on your own, though."

The tower was a needle of white marble that rose from the middle of an open space on the outskirts of the town. Most people appeared to give it a wide berth. Zerika studied the door, which bore an engraving of a dragonlike creature with leathery wings and a single pair of legs. "A wyvern," she said. "I hope this doesn't mean the tower is full of them." The wyvern appeared to have thrust its head and tail through gaps in the engraved surface. "As if it's simultaneously two-dimensional and three-dimensional," Gunnodoyak commented.

"Or maybe something in between, like a fractal," Ragnar added. "It looks familiar, though."

"I've seen it too," Megaera said. "I think it might be Escher."

"Right now," Zerika interjected, "I'm more interested in how to get inside."

"Actually," the chief constable said, "you need a key to enter that door. I'd tell you where to get it, but I'm not supposed to give out quest information."

"That's okay, Constable," Zerika said, cracking her knuckles. "I think we can handle it from here."

The constable watched as Zerika removed a thin metal instrument from her left sleeve and began to probe the lock.

"You're wasting your time," he said. "That lock can't be—"

"Picked?" Zerika smiled as she turned the knob and pushed the door open. "That would depend on how adept the person is doing the picking, don't you think?"

The constable was still standing there, gaping, as the party entered the tower.

Going inside was a profoundly unsettling experience. The space inside the spire was much wider than would seem possible, its dimensions having been viewed from the outside, but that was not what was most disorienting. Staircases rose in various areas, some hugging the inner walls of the tower, others rising in the center of the floor as if spurning the support of the walls. But the orientation of the stairs vis-à-vis the floor did not remain constant; they joined up with other flights at a variety of odd angles, so that above their heads some stairs seemed to be turned sideways, and others were actually upside down.

Strange creatures roamed the stairways. They looked a bit like segmented worms, except that each one had three pairs of rather human-appearing legs. The creatures seemed quite able to navigate the stairs without difficulty, climbing up and down sections that were sideways or even upside down with an apparent disregard for the law of gravity. At times one could see two of the creatures navigating opposite sides of the same flight of stairs, so that what was up for one was down for the other. There even seemed to be a particular pattern of traffic on the stairways, so that the creatures climbed to the top on one side of the stairs and descended on the reverse.

The group watched as one of the odd creatures reached the bottom of the stairs, traveling along the underside of the last flight. Ignoring the adventurers, it wrapped its body and tail around its head, forming itself into a kind of wheel, and rolled away.

"Well," Zerika remarked, "the creatures seem harmless. I guess the problem is how to climb the stairs. Do you want to try levitating us, Tahmurath?"

"I'll try, but I doubt the spell would work in here. There wouldn't be much point in setting up a problem like this if you were going to just let people come in and fly up to the top." He muttered a few arcane syllables and then shrugged. "Just as I thought—it won't work in here. We'll have to do it the hard way."

Zerika nodded. "I guess that's my cue."

She mounted the first flight, which was oriented normally, as the rest of the group looked on. About twenty feet up it merged with a second flight that was turned ninety degrees to one side, so that a person walking on it, if that were at all possible, would be parallel to the ground.

"There don't seem to be any handholds," she shouted. As she stood there, another of the wheel-worms rolled up, climbed the first flight, and walked right past Zerika onto the second flight of stairs.

"Why don't you try putting your foot on it?" Tahmurath called. "Maybe a second gravity field will take over."

Zerika placed her left foot on the first step of the skewed flight. "Nothing's happening."

"Maybe you have to commit yourself. You know, jump onto it as if you're going to walk on it."

"If that doesn't work, it's a long way down."

"Don't worry, Zerika," Ragnar shouted. "I'll catch you."

"Very funny."

"If you fall, I'll heal you," Gunnodoyak said. "I'm sure it's not a long enough drop to be fatal. And, Ragnar, don't try to catch her. I'd rather not have to heal both of you."

"I was just kidding about that. But, by the way, I just looked at the floor, and have you noticed what we're standing in?"

"What?" Zerika called. "I can't see it from here."

"A pile of bones," Ragnar said. "Human bones."

"I wish you hadn't told me that," Zerika said. "Well, here goes nothing." She backed down several steps and then sprinted back up them, leaped to the first step of the next flight, turning her body horizontal in midair, and struck the step with both feet. For a split second it seemed that she was standing securely on the step. Then she bounced off and plummeted some twenty feet to the floor. Bones broke on the landing, but fortunately not her own; a rib cage splintered beneath her, absorbing some of the impact.

"Ouch."

Gunnodoyak knelt beside her and placed his hands on her shoulders. A moment later they stood up.

"As good as new," she said, "but still no way to the top. Any other bright ideas?"

"I've got one," Ragnar said. "Watch this." He cut a ten-foot length of rope from a coil he was carrying and went to the foot of the stairs just as another wheel-worm approached. As it uncoiled itself, Ragnar looped his rope around its neck and hopped astride its back. As the creature mounted the first flight of stairs with Ragnar aboard, he knotted the rope, looped the ends around his own waist, and knotted it again. As the wheel-worm moved on to the second flight of stairs, Ragnar swung head downward. Still the rope held, aided by Ragnar's clinging with his arms and legs, and the worm continued, apparently unperturbed by its uninvited passenger.

"By George, I think he's got it," Tahmurath said.

They all prepared similar ropes. "I'll go next," Zerika said, "then Gunnodoyak, then Tahmurath. Megaera, you'll be the rear guard. Oh, and Megaera?"

"Yes?"

"Nothing personal, but maybe you'd better use two ropes."

"You're probably right. After all, I am a little, what is the phrase? Big-boned."

The wheel-worms kept rolling in about every thirty seconds, so that soon they were all riding to the top. From somewhere far above, Ragnar's voice called out, "A word of advice: Be ready to cut yourself loose at the top before it rolls up again; otherwise, the ride gets a little bumpy, with you as the bump."

A few minutes later they had all arrived at the top. A narrow corridor curved upward to the right.

"That seems to spiral up to the top," Ragnar said, pointing to the corridor. "The problem is that if we're in there when one of them rolls through, we're going to get steamrolled."

"You've got a point," Tahmurath said. "Let me try something." He pointed his staff at the last flight of stairs and muttered an incantation. A section of the flight disappeared. As they watched, another wheel-worm came to the newly created precipice, crawled over the lip, then continued back down along the underside of the same section of stairway.

"That's only temporary, so we'd better get going."

"What if one of them comes down?" Megaera asked.

"They must have another way of coming down; I've only seen them going up," Ragnar said. "Besides, it's wide enough for only one of them at a time."

They hurried, single file, upward along the spiraling ramp, the curvature seeming to increase as they climbed. As they continued upward, they became aware of a humming, like machinery of some kind, coming from the top. After several circuits the tunnel debouched into a spacious domed chamber. In the center of the chamber a large, metallic, many-faceted cylinder rose from floor to ceiling. The facets were hexagonal, and some of the hexagons were open.

As they watched, a wheel-worm rolled up to the structure, uncoiled itself, and crawled tail first into one of the openings. After it was inside, the hexagon closed like a camera iris, leaving a smooth metallic surface like the others.

"It looks like a hive of some kind," Gunnodoyak remarked.

"Yes," Megaera said, "and those worms are the larvae. But if they're the larvae, then where are the—"

The humming noise suddenly increased to an angry buzzing when, as if on cue, about a dozen winged creatures emerged from the hive and launched themselves toward the adventurers. They were like giant insects, with chitinous carapaces that gleamed like polished bronze, but their faces were disconcertingly human in appearance, with the exception of the teeth, which were like the fangs of a great cat.

Ragnar downed one with an arrow, and Tahmurath incinerated two with a spell before they were upon the party, darting and swooping and snapping their jaws. Their speed and agility were such that handheld weapons such as swords were of little use, and their casualties had already been replaced by reinforcements from the hive. The adventurers were standing there flailing their weapons ineffectually when Zerika suddenly shouted, "Follow me!" and ran directly toward the hive. With the rest of the party as well as the winged creatures in pursuit, she charged through the nearest opening; it was just large enough so that they didn't have to go on all fours, although Megaera was bent almost double.

They emerged from the narrow hexagonal tube to find themselves in a kind of central atrium that was open to the sky. In the center of the area there was a large raised platform atop which was a most peculiar contraption: It appeared to be a conveyance of some sort—a combination tank, submarine, ornithopter, and spaceship. Wheels, treads, fins, airfoils, propellers, and jet exhausts protruded in unlikely directions. There was also something resembling a luggage rack on the top.

They did not have an opportunity to examine this find, however, because as they emerged into the open, so did several hundred of the hive's winged inhabitants. They swarmed like locusts, blacking out the sky overhead, and although it seemed as if there were so many it would be impossible to swing a weapon without hitting one, in reality they were just as elusive as before, when there were only a dozen.

Then an enormous reptilian head emerged from behind the platform. It was followed by a long, snaky neck, and then a two-legged body that also sprouted a pair of leathery wings.

"A wyvern!" Tahmurath shouted. "Be careful, the tail is probably poisonous."

"You know," Ragnar remarked as he flailed about with his longsword, "it always looks darkest before all hope is completely lost."

In the meantime Megaera, ignoring the flying creatures, who did not seem able to do much damage through her heavy armor, began wading through the swarm toward the wyvern. But before she had gone two steps, Tahmurath stepped up behind her and touched her helmet with the tip of his staff. The effect of this was quite remarkable: She began to grow. By the time she reached the wyvern, she was three times her original height.

Tahmurath began gesturing in preparation for another spell, when one of the flying creatures swooped down and struck at his upraised forearm. "Ouch!" he cried. "The damn thing stung me. Hurts like hell, too." Within a matter of seconds his right arm had turned purple and had swollen to three times its normal size.

"Looks like the sting was poisonous," Gunnodoyak observed.

"No shit, Sherlock. But the immediate problem is that I can't cast any spells with my arm like this."

In the meantime Ragnar had sheathed his longsword and was removing his harp from its leather case. In a moment his fingers were flying over the strings, as much a blur as the wings of the hive's denizens. "Move away from the wall," he called to the rest of the party.

Zerika had already done so and was creeping around the base of the platform, opposite the wyvern, swatting away the occasional attack from the air. Gunnodoyak remained near Ragnar and Tahmurath, seeming to be in at least half a dozen places at once as he attempted to fend off attacks on all three of them.

As Ragnar's song continued, the erratic swooping and darting of the flyers began to change to a definite pattern; gradually, they began circling the atrium in a clockwise direction, with more and more of them falling into the pattern with each measure that Ragnar played. Soon they seemed to form a nearly solid cylinder that was almost as wide as the atrium itself and extended from the floor upward into the sky.

Meanwhile, the now-titanic Megaera was fencing cautiously with the wyvern, being particularly wary of its possibly poisonous caudal barb. The monster advanced on her, holding the tail high in the air, as if it were a gigantic scorpion. Megaera countered by holding her shield high, and attempting to thrust for the belly with her blade, but the creature seized her shield in its jaws and wrenched it from her grasp. Thus rendered more vulnerable to a biting or stinging attack, Megaera now retreated before the wyvern, circling the platform with its strange vehicle and attempting to keep it partially between herself and her adversary. Zerika, who apparently had been biding her time, suddenly emerged from the shadow of the platform just behind the wyvern. She slashed at the monster's leg tendons, doing little damage but distracting the creature momentarily. Megaera took the opportunity to lunge forward and thrust her now-colossal broadsword into its breast up to the hilt, evidently piercing the wyvern's heart, because it immediately collapsed. The tail continued to writhe and strike blindly, and Zerika had to jump to avoid a near miss.

"One wyvern down," Tahmurath said. "Now, Ragnar, what are you going to do about this lot?" He gestured toward the mass of circling hive creatures.

In response Ragnar began to increase the pitch of his music. With each measure he now raised the pitch by a fifth, and as he did so, the whole cylinder began to rise into the air. After a few more bars it was completely outside the hive, and the base of the cylinder began to contract, causing the whole thing to resemble a tornado funnel.

Ragnar stopped playing, but the funnel appeared to have acquired a momentum and life of its own; it continued to rise and drift, carrying the hive creatures with it.

"Catchy tune," Gunnodoyak quipped. "What do you call it?"

Ragnar grinned. "A little number by Rimsky-Korsakov: 'Flight of the Bumblebee.' "

With the party out of immediate danger, Gunnodoyak now attended to Tahmurath's wound. "Is that better?" he asked after he had placed his hands on the affected arm.

"As good as new."

As the wyvern's death throes began to abate, the party approached the platform that bore the strange device that apparently was their prize. Circling the platform, they discovered a stairway leading to the top. There was a single hatch leading into the craft, and on it was affixed a small metal plaque reading: Universal Touring Machine.

The interior of the machine appeared to be copied from a 1954 Thunderbird, with red leather upholstery, and a glove compartment that contained an owner's manual and a well-thumbed paperback entitled *The Turist's Guide to Cyberspace*. There was also a paper fan and a pair of white kid gloves, although the latter were far too tiny for anyone in the party to wear.

Tahmurath handed the owner's manual to Gunnodoyak and started flipping through the guide. "This looks pretty helpful; it lists a lot of the place names in various MUDs on the 'net. All we need now is to figure out how this contraption works. Gunnodoyak?"

"It looks pretty simple; you just dial the telnet address into the odometer. You can also drive it within a particular MUD, pretty much the way you would a car, except that the steering wheel also works like an airplane stick for climbing or diving."

"Good. Why don't you take the controls? Now all we need is a destination. Any suggestions, anybody?"

"I've got one," Megaera said. "Does that guide tell you where to find Borbetomagus?"

Tahmurath leafed through the pages. "No, I'm afraid not."

"I meant to tell you, I've been doing a little research. It turns out that Borbetomagus is an old name for an actual city."

"What city?"

"Worms."

This elicited a mixed chorus of giggles and groans. "You mean as in the Diet of Worms?" Zerika asked.

"Yes."

"Okay, Worms *is* in the guide," Tahmurath said. "But does it have any special significance besides the bad pun?"

"Actually, I think it does. In the *Nibelungenlied* a lot of the action takes place in Worms. I've been rereading it, to try to find out what happens to Siegfried's sword. Hagen steals it when he murders Siegfried, and Kriemhild uses it to kill Hagen, and then Hildebrand kills Kriemhild . . ."

"And they say television is violent," Ragnar commented.

". . . but it doesn't say what happens to the sword after that. I'm thinking it might be somewhere in Worms."

"So what makes you think that's the sword we're looking for?" Zerika asked.

"More research," Megaera said. "We're supposed to be looking for the 'sword of the father.' In the *Volsunga Saga,* Sigurd's magic sword is forged from the shards of his father, Sigmund's, sword. The sword was originally given to Sigmund by Odin, the All-Father."

"Does the sword have a name?" Ragnar asked.

"Gram."

"Gram? Sounds a little light for such heavy work."

"Tahmurath?"

"Yes?"

"May I borrow your dead chicken for a sec?"

He handed it over. Megaera took the plucked fowl, turned, and bonked Ragnar on the head with it. He said, "Oif."

"Why did you need my dead chicken to do that?"

"Because if I hit him with anything of mine, it would have killed him. Now, the weird thing is that even though Sigurd and Siegfried are supposed to be different versions of the same hero, the story of how they get the magic sword is different. Sigurd uses Gram to slay the dragon, but Siegfried doesn't get Balmung, his magic sword, until after he's already killed the dragon."

"It sounds pretty mixed up, but I think you may be onto something," Tahmurath said. "Tell me, have you figured out why your sword is called the 'sword of the son'?"

Megaera shrugged, somewhat sheepishly. "No idea."

"What I want to know is, how did Siegfried kill the dragon without a magic sword?" Ragnar inquired.

"He used a club."

"Ooh. *Muy macho!*"

▲ ▲ ▲ ▲ ▲ ▲ ▲

"Krishna, you got the program download for the Universal Touring Machine," Art said. "What does it do? Krishna?"

"Huh? Oh, sorry, boss. It's a web-browser, basically."

"That's all? Just a web-browser?"

"Well, yeah . . . it's just a web-browser, like a Stradivarius is just a fiddle."

CHAPTER TWELVE

Earthwyrm

> *. . . and behold a great red dragon,*
> *having seven heads and ten horns, and*
> *seven crowns upon his heads.*
>
> —Revelation 12:3

It had been obvious for a long time that Marlon Oz was avoiding us like the plague, and not just a meme plague, either, but the actual, bona fide Black Death. I had tried getting to him through Dan Morgan, who had initially been evasive and then finally admitted that Oz was ducking us, although he didn't know why. I finally put all my cards on the table with Dan. "Isn't there any way to talk to him?" I asked.

"Well . . . he'll kill me if he ever finds out I told you this, but I think you guys should just come to his party."

"His party?"

"Yeah, his Samhain Celebration. It's a big Halloween party he hosts every year. You could come in costume; that way he won't know it's you till you're already in the door."

"When is it?"

"I told you, Halloween."

"But that's tonight!"

"Is it? Oh, yeah. Do you think you can make it?"

"I'm damn well going to try."

I hung up and called Al on her cell phone. "We're going to a Halloween party tonight," I said. "At Marlon Oz's house."

"You're serious about this, aren't you?"

"Yes. I'm going to make some plane reservations for us and call George and Leon to see if they can make it, too. I want to make this a full-court press, try to put as much pressure on him to talk to us as possible. Do you think you can dig up some costumes for us?"

"I'll try. Don't expect too much, though. Oh, and call me back if Leon or George can make it—I'll try to pick up something for them, too."

I called George first, as he'd have to come in from California. It was only six-thirty A.M. there, and he was groggy when he answered the phone, but when I told him what I had in mind, he was immediately wide-awake and enthusiastic. He even knew about Oz's annual shindig.

"I should have thought of this myself," he said. "The Oz Halloween parties are legendary. I even crashed one when he was at Berkeley, hoping I'd get to see him, but I never did—nobody could figure out what costume he was wearing."

"Do you think you can get a flight in time?"

"I'd better call right now and find out. I'll call back to let you know."

Leon was snowed with work at Tower, as usual, but said he wouldn't miss Oz's party for anything. By the time I was finished talking to him, George was ringing through on call waiting.

"I can't get a direct flight to Boston that will get me there in time," he said, "so I'm going to connect through La Guardia." He gave me the flight number for his connecting flight to Boston. "See if you can get three reservations on that plane, and we can all go up together."

I made the reservations, then called Al back to let her know that George and Leon were on board, and to give her the flight number and departure time. "Do you want me to drive you to the airport?" I asked.

"No, I'm going to be working out on the island this afternoon anyway. I'll just meet you at the gate."

Actually, she and George had already boarded by the time I got there, so I met her on the plane. Leon had driven out with me.

"Did you get the costumes?" I asked.

Al nodded. "It was pretty slim pickings, though. I hope you guys aren't too fussy." She stood and opened the overhead compartment. "George, you're the tallest; you'd better take this one." She handed him a package. "Leon, I hope this will fit. It might be a little snug in the shoulders." She passed him a second bundle.

"Why are you giving them to us now?" I asked as she passed me a third package.

"When do you expect to change? In the cab from the airport?"

"How about at Logan? I'm sure their lavatories will be a little less cramped than the ones on the plane." I was also thinking about the embarrassment of wearing a costume on a commuter flight.

"We're running late as it is," Al countered. "We really can't afford to waste any more time."

"I'm really gonna have to change in there?" George jerked a thumb in the direction of the onboard facilities. "It's the size of a phone booth."

Leon clapped him on the shoulder. "No problem, George. Like tying your shoelaces with your teeth. And you can pretend you're Clark Kent changing into Superman."

Because takeoff was imminent, we had to wait until we were airborne to leave our seats and change into our costumes.

I was the first one back to my seat, tastefully attired in blue, red, and green motley, with a tall, pointed blue hat.

George and Leon arrived together, the former in a suit of medieval armor and the latter in a lion costume. George's helmet and Leon's maned head were under their respective arms.

"Very nice," I commented.

George nodded. "Thanks. But don't you think this thing should have come with a sword?"

"It did." Al's voice came from somewhere behind George and Leon; I couldn't see her at all because of the size disparity. "They wouldn't let me bring it on the plane, even though it was plastic."

George and Leon stepped aside to let Al get to her seat, and I got my first glimpse of her. Her costume didn't cover her face, but I honestly think I would have had trouble recognizing her. She wore a long brunette wig arranged in pigtails. Her dress was blue gingham, and her shoes were a bright, glittery red. A picnic basket over one arm completed the ensemble.

"These are great," Leon said. "Where did you get them on such short notice?"

"I went to a theatrical costume supplier," Al said. "George has Lancelot's armor from *Camelot*. Leon, you've got the Aslan costume from a stage production of *The Lion, the Witch and the Wardrobe*."

"What about me?"

The devilish grin appeared. "Michael is the fool from *King Lear*."

Predictably, this elicited snorts of laughter from George, and Leon was also amused. "Very funny," I said. "But I don't have a mask with this thing. Don't you think Oz is going to recognize me?"

"Oh, I almost forgot." She pulled what looked like a burlap bag out of her carry-on. It had a face painted on it. "Best I could do on short notice," she apologized.

"Say," George said, eyeing Al's costume, "what are *you* supposed to be?"

"I'll give you a hint," she said, closing her eyes and clasping her hands together in front of her. "Auntie Em, Auntie Em!"

We arrived at Oz's house in time to be fashionably late—about an hour or so. This was not good. There were already at least a hundred people there, and they were all in costume. One of them was Oz, but which one?

"Let's spread out and mingle," I suggested. "That way we'll cover more territory and find him sooner."

We split up and started to circulate. After about an hour I still hadn't tracked him down. I started to think he was as elusive as Roger Dworkin at DEF CON. I circulated through the house to see what the others had come up with. Al was conversing with what looked like a giant disembodied head. I was tempted to think that she had him, but it seemed a little too obvious. George was talking to someone dressed as some kind of monster, with a rhinoceros head, five eyes, and a monster's body with five arms and five legs. I wondered briefly what was special about the number five, then wandered on.

I found Leon talking to some guy in a really spectacular costume, apparently something one of the engineering students had dreamed up and put together with fiber optics. The guy actually looked as if he were on fire. After you saw him for the first time and just managed to stifle a scream, it was fun to watch other people getting their first look, and see their reactions. Still no Oz, though.

As I was staring at the flaming whatever and wondering if it might really be Oz, I was approached by a very attractive woman in a costume of diaphanous green, with wings sprouting from her shoulders. She handed me a glass of green punch, saying, "I noticed that you didn't have anything to drink." Actually, I had noticed the punch and opted to steer clear of it; the color reminded me of Oz's favorite sweater. I took a sip, just to be polite. It was potent.

"Thanks. You haven't seen our host around, have you?"

"Marlon?" She shook her head. "I don't think I've seen him all evening. Sometimes he hides out in the library."

"Where is it?"

She pointed me in the right direction, and I went around a corner just in time to see the door to the library jerk shut, as if somebody wanted to close it quickly without slamming it.

I went and collected Al, George, and Leon and led them to the library door, which was still closed but didn't have a lock on it. We went in. The library was a large room with hardwood paneling and bookshelves that reached the ceiling, shelves that were positively crammed with books, more books than I had ever seen in a private residence. There was, of course, no computer in sight.

"He ought to have these converted to CD-ROM," George said. "He'd save a lot of space that way—"

"Shhh!" Leon held his finger to his snout, then pointed across the room, where a window was covered by a floor-length curtain that bulged suspiciously at one side.

I went to the other side of the curtain and pulled the cord. It opened, revealing Marlon Oz, not even wearing a costume, unless you count the nauseous cardigan. As he turned to face us, I saw that his gaunt cheeks were red, and I thought for a second that he'd had too much of the punch. Then it hit me that the old bastard was actually embarrassed—sheepish, even.

He covered it well, though. "Looking for someone?" he asked.

I took the bag off my head. "You, Dr. Oz."

He didn't bat an eye, and somehow I was sure he had known it was us all along.

He said, "I don't remember inviting you to this party, Arcangelo," but he was starting to break into that lopsided smile of his.

"I'm sorry to crash your party, I really am. But we need your help, and this was the only way we could get to you."

His expression turned serious again, and he hesitated, as if torn by some dilemma. Then he nodded. "Sit down, all of you."

I started out with some background on the ideas we had been kicking around. I think at that point I was still hoping he would tell me it was all completely impossible. I was disappointed.

"The surprising thing," Oz said, "would be if we *couldn't* do it. After all, bees do it."

"Do what, exactly?" I asked, while wondering if this would pertain to birds and educated fleas as well.

"Pool their meager intelligence. There's research to show that a large number of bees is smarter than one or a few."

"What kind of research?" Al asked. I was trying hard to ignore a mental image of a bunch of psychology grad students administering Stanford-Binets to insects.

"You take some sugar water and put it in a boat in the middle of a pond," Oz explained. "A bee finds it, then goes back to report what it found to the other bees. Let's say it finds just one bee. It dances its dance to say, 'There's food a hundred meters in that direction,' and the other bee flies off to look for it. So far so good. But suppose the first bee encounters a large group of bees: It dances the same dance, but the other bees don't go off looking for the food. Apparently they're able to perform a cognitive operation that was too much for a lone bee—to say, 'There can't be any flowers there, that's smack in the middle of the pond.'"

"But," I pointed out, "there really was food there, so the lone bee was right, after all."

"Which just goes to show that it's possible to be dumb and right, and also to be smart and wrong."

There's a moral for you. I wondered if that was the closest thing to an apology that we were ever going to hear from Marlon Oz. "I was thinking," I said, "that this had something to do with your idea of consciousness being a relatively recent phenomenon in human history."

"Not my idea."

"But it's in your book—"

"I mean not original with me. Don't you read footnotes?" He got up and went over to one of the bookshelves. "Here." He tossed me a battered paperback.

This was uncharacteristically modest—Oz not taking credit for an idea? On second thought, though, he probably considered himself far too brilliant to need to appropriate ideas from anybody else. The cover of the book he'd pitched to me was something called *The Origin of Consciousness in the Breakdown of the Bicameral Mind*, by Julian Jaynes.

"What's this?"

"Jaynes is the one who figured out that people became conscious only a few thousand years ago. My book just presented another view of how that came about."

I was tempted to tell him that I hadn't read *his* book either. The possibility that anybody wouldn't didn't seem to have occurred to him. "I don't really understand this," George said. "How were people supposed to function without being conscious?"

"Most of your mental functions are unconscious even now. But Jaynes's idea was that the right hemisphere decided what to do and communicated this to the left brain through auditory hallucinations."

"That sounds pretty off-the-wall," I said.

"Jaynes builds a very plausible case for it. There are just a couple of problems with it, and you may have unwittingly provided an answer to those."

Unwittingly. Thanks a bunch.

"One problem with Jaynes's argument, I've always thought, was that if society was being run by these hallucinations from everybody's right hemisphere, you'd have total chaos, because everybody's hallucinations would be saying something different. Jaynes believed that each person's right hemisphere was like a personal god who interceded for him with the 'head honcho,' but the possibilities for conflict would seem to be enormous.

"But an even more serious problem is, How do you explain how the right hemisphere could do what the left hemisphere hadn't learned how to do yet, without ever acquiring the capacity to do what eventually allows the left brain to do it?"

"What capacity is that?"

"The ability to think metaphorically."

"So how did I provide an answer to this problem?"

"It's your idea about mind networks. Sure, the right hemisphere in a neolithic man might be just as clueless as the left, but if all the right hemispheres in a given society were networked, well, then you might have something. Come to think of it," he mused, "it might also explain the frequency of simultaneity in breakthrough ideas in science and mathematics."

"You mean, like Newton and Leibniz discovering calculus at the same time?"

"That's right." He stared around the table. "Why do I get the feeling there's more to this?"

I took a deep breath. "Well, this 'group overmind' thing . . . we think it may have a real problem with the end of the millennium."

"What kind of a problem?" Oz snapped, but I could see the wheels starting to turn.

"Like the eclipse in Europe last August . . ."

"Oh, my God." What little color had remained in his cheeks now drained away entirely. He put his face in his hands for a moment, then snapped his head upright again and pointed at George. "You, Tin Man. Get Dan Morgan in here," he barked. "He's the one in the giant head. Tell him to bring Logan with him."

A moment later George led Dan and the human torch into the library. They looked baffled, or at least Dan did, having taken off the top part of his costume. Logan just looked inflamed. Oz gestured at me and said, "Tell them." I did.

Logan was the first one to react. "Jesus!" he exclaimed. "The Leonids . . ." And he trailed off with his mouth hanging open.

"What?" Al asked. "What about the Leonids?"

Logan jumped out of his chair and started to pace the floor. "It's a meteor storm that happens every November—only this November it's gonna be a whopper."

"What? Why this November?"

He stopped and looked up at the ceiling. "Every thirty-three to thirty-four years there's a peak—a huge meteor storm."

"How huge?"

"Huge." He was waving his hands now. "Up to two hundred thousand meteors per hour. Remember the scene in *Star Wars* when the *Millennium Falcon* makes the jump to hyperspace? That's what it looks like—all these streaks of light radiating from a single point in the sky. People who saw it at peak intensity said it made them want to throw themselves on the ground and hold on to something, because they felt like they were going to fall off the earth."

There was a pause as we all imagined the kind of effect this would have on a psyche perched on the brink of millennial hysteria, just waiting for anything portentous to push it over the edge.

Leon finally broke the silence. "When in November?"

"The shower lasts from about the fourteenth to the twentieth, but the peak should be right around the seventeenth."

"So what do we do?" George asked. "Pray for an overcast night?"

"We publicize it," Oz said.

"Publicize it? Won't that make it worse?"

Oz shook his head emphatically. "We have to saturate the mass psyche with the information that this is a well-understood scientific phenomenon, that it's happened many times before, and that it doesn't mean the world is about to end. The worst thing that could possibly happen would be for a lot of people to be out on the night of the seventeenth with no warning, no idea what this is or why it's happening.

"I want this to be a front-page story in every newspaper in the world, and a lead story in the evening news on the seventeenth. We'll start making calls first thing tomorrow.

"And now," Oz said, "for the really bad part." Dan and Logan looked surprised, but the rest of us knew what he was talking about already.

"Wyrm," I said.

Oz nodded. "Logan doesn't know about this yet. Dan, you'll bring him up to speed later." He looked at me. "Whatever help you need, let Dan know about it.

"One more thing. If you're even thinking about doing anything vaguely illegal that involves computers, and especially if it involves a huge software company that shall remain nameless, I want one thing to be perfectly clear: I don't know about it, I never heard anything about it, and we never had this conversation."

▲　▲　▲　▲　▲　▲　▲

"I think," Tahmurath remarked, "that I'm going nuts."

Gunnodoyak put a hand on his shoulder. "We thought so, boss, but we didn't want to say anything. Right, Zerika?"

"Whatever you say, Gunny."

"Your tact is admirable. Remind me to put a little something in your next paychecks as a gesture of appreciation. Like a pink slip."

"Fire your best programmer and your best play-tester? You must be crazy."

"That's what I was just saying. It's the *Ars Magna* tome—ever since I started with this anagram thing, I can't get it out of my head. I'm constantly thinking of anagrams for everything. Did you know that 'Santa' is an anagram for 'Satan'?"

Gunnodoyak looked thoughtful. "Hmm, red suit, beard—you may be onto something."

"And that hat," Ragnar added. "I've never seen him take it off. What's he hiding?"

Tahmurath ignored them. "You know, it's also kind of interesting, because there are anagram pairs that are synonyms, like 'angered' and 'enraged,' or 'paternal' and 'parental.'"

"How about 'evil' and 'vile'?" Gunnodoyak suggested.

"Obviously. There are also antonym pairs, like 'unite' and 'untie,' and even some that are like antonyms and synonyms at the same time."

"I don't get it," Megaera interrupted. "How can two words mean the same thing and also the opposite?"

"How about 'marital' and 'martial'?"

"Hmm, you may have a point."

"Gunny, did you get the password list for the MUD?"

"Yeah, but it's encrypted."

"Well, we'll worry about that later. Let's go."

The party had stopped for a short rest before continuing up the steep mountain path that wound its way through scrubby pine trees before disappearing into the mist that shrouded the peak above. They had left the Universal Touring Machine at the foot of the mountain; it was a little too large to negotiate the steep, winding mountain paths they now traversed.

They had visited Borbetomagus, also known as Worms, and had learned that the sword they sought was reputed to lie in a cave that was located in a place called Drachenfels.

As they were climbing a narrow mountain trail, they encountered a weathered signpost that bore the legend:

Bewahre doch
vor Jammervoch

"Beware of what?" Gunnodoyak wondered aloud.

"I don't know, but it doesn't sound good," Ragnar said.

"Gotta be some kind of a dragon," Tahmurath suggested. "After all, this is Drachenfels: Dragon's Rock."

"Probably a *Tatzlwurm*," Zerika suggested.

"A *what?*"

"A *Tatzlwurm*. That's what the Germans call a dragon that lives in the mountains."

A few more twists and turns in the path brought them to what appeared to be an abandoned mine. The timbers bracing the opening sagged pathetically. A dank, musty smell emanated from within.

Ragnar was the next one after Zerika to reach the adit. "Wandering around in the dark time again?" he asked.

Zerika peered inside while waiting for the rest of the group to gather. "At least it's not big enough for anything really huge to come through here."

"So if there's a dragon in there, it would have to be a small one, huh?"

"Not necessarily. There might be other entrances, other ways into the mountain. This mine shaft might hook up with a natural cavern somewhere in there. But even if it does, we could be relatively safe if we stick to the smaller tunnels."

They crept down the tunnel about a hundred meters, then arrived at a large chamber, apparently a natural cavern, judging from the extravagant growth of stalactites and stalagmites. "Stay in the tunnel," Zerika whispered. "I'll be right back."

After a few tense minutes she returned. "We're in luck," she whispered. "There's a dragon in there, all right—a lindworm, actually, because it has two legs and no wings. It's asleep."

"That is good news," Ragnar said. "Let sleeping dragons lie, that's my motto."

"We're going to have to sneak up on it and kill it."

"Why?"

"It's guarding a vault. I bet the sword is in there."

"Wait a minute. You mean we have to kill a dragon so that we can get something that we need to kill a dragon? It sounds like sort of a catch-twenty-two to me."

"We killed the guivre and the wyvern."

"The guivre also killed Malakh and came within a whisker of killing Megaera, too."

"Well, maybe you should just go in and ask the dragon nicely for the sword, and then you can use it to kill him."

"Good plan, but I think I'll pass."

"Fine. Back to Plan A, then. Megaera, you're going to have to take off your armor; you'll never sneak up on anybody wearing that. And now, if Ragnar is through complaining . . ."

"At least tell me that it's just a little dragon."

"Do you remember the guivre?"

"Rather well, yes."

"It's about twice the size of that."

"Argh."

After Megaera had doffed her armor, they all followed Zerika to where the lindworm slept. Zerika was getting them positioned for a simultaneous attack when wild laughter rang out, echoing through the cavern. They all turned to look for its source, including the now very much awake lindworm. What they saw was a tall humanoid with horns and a tail, and the many-faceted eyes of an insect. "I hate to spoil your little surprise," he said. "But I think this will be so much more interesting with the lindworm awake. Besides, it'll give him a sporting chance."

"Beelzebub!" Zerika exclaimed. She threw a knife at him, but he vanished in a puff of brimstone-scented smoke before it reached the target. In the meantime the lindworm was already moving to make the most of its chance. Its huge head struck at Megaera; she managed to avoid the strike, but only by diving to the floor, losing her sword in the process. Ragnar bored in from the opposite side, attempting to drive his slender blade between two of the monster's ribs, but the creature's hide was like adamant, and Ragnar's sword made no impression. The lindworm lashed its tail, slamming Ragnar into the wall of the cave; he fell unconscious to the floor.

Zerika was yelling, "Run away!" a bit of advice that everyone who could seemed inclined to follow. Unfortunately for Megaera and Gunnodoyak, they were cornered in a shallow cul-de-sac and had no avenue of escape. The lindworm seemed to understand this, for it advanced slowly, almost casually, toward the trapped pair. It drew its head back, like a snake rearing to strike, then lashed forward at Gunnodoyak. He attempted to dodge, but the monster was too fast; it seized him in its jaws and swallowed him whole.

"Megaera! Get out of there now!" Zerika shouted, but it was too late; as she ran to one side, the lindworm moved to cut her off. It reared back again, obviously preparing to strike when, suddenly, the air seemed to shimmer around Megaera. When the disturbance cleared, there were three Megaeras in the little cul-de-sac.

The lindworm lunged at one Megaera, and as its teeth closed

around her, she seemed to dissolve into the air. Wasting no time, the monster wound itself back up for another attack. Before it could launch its attack, Zerika darted from the shadows and slashed at the back of one of the creature's legs. Like Ragnar's, her blade was unequal to the task, and the lindworm again responded by whipping its tail around, sending Zerika sprawling from the impact.

The creature lunged at one of the two remaining Megaeras. Once again the image seemed to dissipate at the monster's touch, but this time the real Megaera took advantage of the creature's distraction; she sprinted from the cul-de-sac to where her sword lay and retrieved it just as the lindworm wheeled around. She swung her sword at the lindworm's neck. Her blade was apparently superior to Zerika's and Ragnar's, for it bit, though not deeply. The monster threw back its head and roared deafeningly. However, it quickly recovered and now fixed its beady eyes on the remaining Megaera, seeming to understand, somehow, that this time its enormous jaws would not meet around thin air.

Just then another loud roar pierced the air. All eyes, including the lindworm's, turned toward the source of the noise.

It was Ragnar.

He had nocked the black arrow and drawn his bow. Now, as the monster's head swiveled toward him, he released. The arrow sped unerringly toward the chink carved by the tip of Megaera's sword in the lindworm's armor. It struck the gap and buried itself completely in the creature's neck.

The lindworm threw back its head to roar again but this time emitted only a strangled gasp. Abruptly, its two legs collapsed beneath its enormous weight. The great tail lashed convulsively once, twice, three times. And then it lay still.

The little group reassembled as Megaera cleaned dragon blood from her sword, Tahmurath scrambled from his hiding place among the stalagmites, and Zerika and Ragnar came limping toward the other two.

"I assume that business with the duplicate images was your work, Tahmurath," Megaera said. "Thank you."

He bowed with a flourish of his cloak. "You are more than welcome."

Ragnar looked quizzically at Zerika. "I thought you said this thing was bigger than the guivre. It looked about the same size to me."

She nodded. "I know. I wanted you to be pleasantly surprised."

"What about Gunnodoyak?" Megaera asked. "Shouldn't we try to get him out of there?"

"I'm not sure it'll be worth it," Tahmurath said, "but we ought to try. Unfortunately, I don't think even your sword is sharp enough to cut him out of there."

"Then let's check the vault," Zerika suggested. "If what we came here for is in there, maybe it will do the trick."

After a few anxious moments checking for traps and plying her lockpicks, Zerika opened the door to the vault.

Inside was what appeared to be a tree trunk. It was rooted in the floor of the vault and passed upward through a hole in the ceiling that was barely wide enough for it. Other than that, the vault was empty.

"Damn!" Megaera said. "Another wild-goose chase."

"Wait a minute," Tahmurath said. "There's something engraved on the tree trunk, but I can't make it out in this light. Zerika, what do your elfin eyes see?"

Zerika looked up and read aloud, " 'Never attribute to malice what can be adequately explained by stupidity.' "

They all stared at it for a moment; then Ragnar let out a short guffaw.

"Come on," Megaera said. "it's not *that* funny."

"It *is* pretty funny," Ragnar said, "but it's not just that. It's Hanlon's Razor. Don't you get it? We're supposed to be looking for 'the sword of the father,' and we find this."

"Hanlon's Razor? What's that?" Zerika asked.

"It's one of those things like Murphy's Law. This one is a takeoff on Occam's Razor."

"Okay, I'll bite. What's Occam's Razor?"

"It's no joke. William of Occam was a fourteenth-century English scholastic philosopher who said that you should prefer simple explanations to complicated ones. That principle is known as Occam's Razor."

"So what are you saying?" Megaera demanded. "We're supposed to kill the dragon with this? It's not a weapon, it's just words."

"Wait a minute!" Tahmurath cried. "Say that again."

"Say what?"

"The last thing you said."

"It's not a weapon, it's just words."

"Right! Words. I think it's time for a little of the old Ars Magna."

Tahmurath made a series of mystical passes in the air, all the while intoning a weird incantation. A shadow seemed to obscure the engraving; when it had passed, the words were gone, and there was a sword hilt protruding from the trunk. Tahmurath laid his hand upon the hilt and pulled but couldn't budge the weapon. "Megaera," he said, "will you do the honors?"

Megaera came forward and attempted to withdraw the sword, first with one hand and then with both. It didn't move. "Phew. That thing is really in there."

"Let Ragnar try," Zerika suggested.

"Why? He's not as strong as I am."

"No, but he's the one who actually killed the lindworm. That may have earned him the right to the sword."

Ragnar stepped up and pulled on the hilt. The long blade slid easily from the wood, and as it did so, they were able to see that it bore an engraving of its own.

"What does it say?" Zerika asked.

He chuckled. "Snicker-snack." He turned to Gunnodoyak. "You don't have to tell me I'm getting a major download—I can hear it writing to the disk." He offered the weapon to Megaera. "Would you like a new sword?"

She shook her head. "I like the sword I've got. That one's more your style."

"Actually, long-range artillery is more my style. A person could get hurt using one of these things." He took the weapon and strode to the lindworm's corpse. He slashed at the monster's belly, and the tough scales parted like tissue paper. A foul smell filled the air as the creature's entrails spilled out on the cavern floor.

"Try there," Tahmurath suggested, indicating a particularly distended segment of digestive tract, "and try not to cut deep enough to disembowel Gunnodoyak."

Ragnar followed Tahmurath's advice and carefully slit open the designated area. As he did, a hand, one of Gunnodoyak's, protruded from the opening. As Ragnar worked to enlarge the slit, Megaera stepped forward to pull Gunnodoyak's body out. He was completely limp, and his skin was blue as she laid him out on the cavern floor. "Tahmurath?" she asked. "Can you do anything about this?"

"Well, I'm certainly going to give it a try. It is ironic, though, that the people who can raise the dead are the ones who keep getting killed."

"Actually, I'm not dead. Yet." It was Gunnodoyak.

"How can you not be dead?" Megaera demanded. "I thought you would have suffocated in there by now."

"An old Eastern discipline—slowing down the metabolism, reducing the demand for oxygen. Comes in handy sometimes."

"Tahmurath, what are you looking for now?" He was fumbling in his pack.

"The amphisbaena heart. I just realized what I was supposed to do with it." He produced the organ in question and displayed the smiley face. "A grin, right?"

He laid the heart on the floor and intoned a spell similar to the one he had used on Ragnar's sword. When he was finished, the smiley face was gone, and a gold ring rested on the heart. On closer inspection the ring proved to be a representation of a serpent with its tail in its mouth.

"Pretty cool," Gunnodoyak said. "Unless I miss my guess, that encrypted file is now being decrypted. What does the ring do, Tahmurath?"

"I haven't the slightest idea."

▲   ▲   ▲   ▲   ▲   ▲   ▲

The game had broken up a little earlier than usual, as it seemed like a good idea to check out the new programs we'd just received. Art's ring program had indeed been decrypted and turned out to be—a decryption program. "Kind of like how we needed to kill the dragon to get the dragon-slayer," George commented.

The program accompanying Hanlon's Razor turned out to be an antivirus program. "Is it the same as Al's 'sword of the son' program?" Art asked.

I was staring over George's shoulder at the screen. "No," I said, "this is different. Al's program protects programs if it's already inside of them. This one seems to attack from the outside in, so you can use it on a system that's already infected."

"Hey, let's use the boss's decryption program on the password list we got off the MUD," Krishna suggested. Our luck was in, because not only did it work, but the list contained the name and password of a Macrobyte employee.

After playing around some more with the new software, we decided to go out together for some coffee. Art knew a place that was open all night, not far from Cepheus.

We all ordered coffee except for Krishna, who, with a typical teenager's appetite, ordered enough food for a medium-size country, and Robin, who ordered only hot water, then poured something into it from a pouch she had in her purse. "Tea," she explained in response to my inquisitive gaze. "Try some?"

I did. It was delicious.

"Formosan oolong," she said.

"Are you from Taiwan?"

She grinned and shook her head. "Phoenix. Why do people always assume that if you look Asian, you weren't born in this country?"

"No mystery about that—just simple ignorance." I took another sip of her tea. "Oolong, huh? Why does that sound familiar?"

"It's Chinese for 'black dragon.'"

"You mean like in *Tea with the Black Dragon*?" George asked. "I remember reading that book back in high school."

"I'm glad to hear you weren't too busy practicing for the math team to get in a little outside reading," I said.

"Ah, those were the days. Krishna, you must be on your high-school math team."

He shook his head while he swallowed a mouthful of food. "I'm in college now, at Berkeley. Where I went to school in India, we didn't have a math team."

"You must be from Madras, right?" George said.

Krishna looked puzzled. "No, my family's from Bombay. Why?"

"You mean you've never heard the limerick?"

"What limerick?"

> *"There was a young man from Madras*
> *Whose balls were constructed of brass.*
> *When jangled together*
> *They played 'Stormy Weather,'*
> *And lightning shot out of his ass."*

While Krishna and George were convulsing over that one, I asked Arthur if he'd had a chance to check with his contacts at the Pentagon concerning the nuclear-weapons computers.

"I'm sure you'll all be relieved to hear," Arthur said, "that after I spoke to some people in DoD about that virus problem we discussed, they managed to get all the weapons-control computers scanned for the 666 ID code. They were clean."

That *was* quite a relief. Not that we were out of the woods yet as far as certain other dangers were concerned.

"Have you noticed all the megaliths in the game?" Al asked. "I'm beginning to think they must have some special significance."

"So do I," Arthur said. "They seem to be special links of some kind, which is consistent with some of the traditions about ancient megalithic sites."

"What traditions?"

"Well, for example, in England some people claim that an unusual number of these sites are laid out in straight lines. Ley lines, they call them. In some cases the leys stretch out for hundreds of miles, as if to suggest that the people who erected the megaliths had some pretty sophisticated surveying abilities."

"You know, Al," I said, "this sounds a little like that thing you told me about the Notre Dame cathedrals in France."

"What about them?" Arthur asked.

Al explained what she had told me about the cathedrals at Paris, Reims, Chartres, Bayeux, et cetera, forming an earthbound version of the constellation Virgo.

"I'll bet there's a connection," Arthur said. "I wouldn't be surprised if they were all megalithic sites. Chartres was, for sure."

"It was?"

"Yes. There was an ancient well and dolmen there when the first Christians arrived around the third century A.D. Also, there was a carving in pear wood, some say by druids, called the Black Virgin. Supposedly, the druids carved it centuries before because of a prophecy about a virgin who would bear a child."

"Whew!" Robin said. "This is all a little spooky."

"Also," Art continued, "there are other examples of constellations being represented on earth, whole zodiacs in some cases. The Glastonbury zodiac in England is ten miles across. Some people say the whole thing—the ley lines, the megaliths, the zodiacs—was a system for harnessing telluric currents—some kind of earth magic, or serpent power."

"That was what *Foucault's Pendulum* was all about," George said. "The Knights Templar were supposed be trying to figure out the secret of the telluric currents, along with the Rosicrucians, the Illuminati, and everybody else."

"There's a Chinese tradition that's somewhat similar to that," Robin said. "In China there were diviners who would figure out where things should be built, in accordance with the flow of *chi* along special paths called *Lung Mei*."

"*Lung Mei?*"

"Yes. 'Dragon paths.' "

"The belief seems to have been very widespread," Art said. "When the Japanese occupied Korea in the first half of the century, they drove thousands of metal spikes into the ground in order to disrupt the energy flow."

"Interesting how all this stuff seems to be connected with dragons," Robin observed.

"Isn't the year 2000 the Year of the Dragon on the Chinese calendar?" Al asked.

"That's right."

"Somehow," I commented, "that seems a little ominous."

"Let's not get too paranoid," Robin said. "What's the matter with you, Krishna? You're not usually this quiet." I had thought that was merely because he was busy stuffing his face—he had finished a club sandwich and french fries and was now working on an ice-cream sundae—but apparently Robin was onto something.

"There's something really weird about the game," he said.

"What's weird? Or maybe," I said, "I should ask what *else* is weird."

"Actually, lots of things. For starters, do you guys realize how weird it is that, the whole time we've been playing this game, we've never experienced any net lag at all?"

Robin looked stunned. "My God, you're right. It's been so long since I've played a regular MUD, I'd completely forgotten about lag." Net lag, which basically refers to delays in data transmission over the 'net, is the bane of the average MUDder. Delays of seconds are not unusual, and even minutes not unheard of.

"Wyrm must be giving the game top priority on 'net transmissions. It's not really surprising that it has the degree of control necessary to do that. What else, Krishna?"

"You guys have been playing in graphics mode for the most part, but as you know, the program has a text mode as well."

"For slower modem speeds," George said. "But so what?"

"Well, the front end of this thing is designed to support an amazing variety of hardware. There are even several different kinds of virtual-reality support."

George shook his head dubiously. "I don't think you'd have very impressive virtual reality, even at five thousand kbps."

"Don't worry," Krishna replied. "In full VR mode, this thing supports a T-three link."

"Forty-five megabytes per second to play a *game*?" Art sputtered. "I'm a fanatic about these things, and even *I* think that's outrageous."

"Outrageous, yes. But not the *most* outrageous thing."

"Oh, come on. What could be . . . well, what already?"

Krishna had a bemused little smile on his face. "Well, the *really* weird thing is that this program will support hardware that, as far as I know, doesn't even exist yet."

Al frowned. "That doesn't make any sense. You don't write a program for hardware that doesn't exist and then hope that somebody will come along and build it to the right specs."

"I agree. But do *you* know of anybody who's building neural-induction hardware?"

I said, "If Roger Dworkin wrote this program to support a neural-induction link, then he must have known that somebody . . ." Then I glanced at Art, who had abruptly fallen silent. He looked uncomfortable. I snapped my fingers. "Military stuff!"

We were all looking at Art now and wanting some answers. "Art," I said, "you told me you've had some defense contracts. You must have some kind of security clearance. What's going on?"

He shrugged helplessly. "The whole point of a security clearance is that you're not supposed to tell anybody what you know. I can't even tell you if I know anything about . . . about . . . what you said."

We all groaned. "Look, Art, you know that this could be damned important. We're dealing with something that has the potential to cause a disaster of apocalyptic proportions. What if this thing decides to start randomly changing the setting on railroad-track switches?"

"What if it disables a hospital life-support computer?" Al added.

"What if it decides to turn all the traffic lights green during rush hour?" George chimed in.

Art looked as if he were weakening, but he pulled himself together and shook his head. "I'm sorry," he said. "I just can't."

We worked on him a bit more, but our hearts weren't really in it, because we could see he wasn't going to budge.

We picked up our various notes, maps, charts, inventories, et cetera, and got ready to leave. Al and I were staying with George in Palo Alto again. Robin and Krishna seemed inclined to sit a while longer and chat, so the rest of us headed out to the nearly deserted parking lot, where George's battered old Charger rested between Robin's red Trans Am and Art's white Buick Regal. As we headed for the cars, Art called my name. As I turned, he handed me a small scrap of paper. "You dropped this," he said. I started to deny it, then caught his eye and stuffed it into my pocket.

Back at George's place I took the opportunity to read Art's note while using the bathroom. It wasn't actually a note—just a name, Seth Serafin, and a phone number. I was tempted to show Al and George; what stopped me was the thought that Art had passed the thing to me surreptitiously, probably because it represented a source for the information that he knew but couldn't tell us. I felt sure that, in his mind, even doing that much involved bending the rules on his security clearance, and I surmised that giving the name to me alone was an attempt to minimize his sense of guilt about it. I felt I had to respect that.

When I came out of the bathroom, Al and George were talking about what to do about Wyrm.

"The way I figure it," George said, "you were right, Al. We've gotta talk to it."

"That might be interesting," I conceded, joining the conversation, "but what's the point? You think it'll tell us how to get rid of it?"

"That would be an added bonus. But, no, I'm thinking in terms of the Natural Language Problem. In order for Dworkin's program to do what we think it's doing, it must be able to understand English, a 'natural language.' But I think that doing it in a conversation would take up enough of its resources that it wouldn't have a lot left over—"

"Meaning we could sneak up on it while somebody distracted it with chitchat. George, that's brilliant." Al looked impressed.

"Dazzling," I said dryly. "There's just one little problem. How do we get its attention to have this little chat? That is the sixty-four-thousand-dollar question."

I had planned to fly back to New York the next morning, and Al had another road trip planned, starting with Los Angeles. We drove our rental car back to the airport, and I saw Al off at her gate, then found a pay phone and called Seth Serafin's number. A male voice answered.

"Seth Serafin?"

"This is Mr. Serafin's residence."

"May I speak to him?"

"No."

That was pretty abrupt. "It's very important—"

"Mr. Serafin doesn't speak to anyone."

Curiouser and curiouser. Art had suggested that I get information from someone who "doesn't speak to *anyone*"? This was his idea of being helpful? I was getting worried because it seemed as if this guy was almost finished brushing me off. "I'm a friend of Arthur Solomon's."

There was a pause, then, "Just a moment." After a minute or so, he came back on the line and said, "Mr. Serafin is willing to speak to you, but he does not communicate over the phone. If you wish to speak to him, you'll have to come here."

Great. Apparently, Art had me hooked up with some kind of wealthy eccentric with a telephone phobia. Wealthy enough to have someone who answered the phone for him, anyway, and you could just tell by the guy's snotty attitude that he was working for somebody rich. "Just tell me where and when."

He gave me an address and said I was welcome anytime as long as I gave some advance notice. I said, "How about sometime today?" The place was about an hour from the airport, and after checking with his boss, Mr. Snotty got back on the phone and said I could come right over.

I was flying on an unrestricted ticket, so I had no problem pushing my departure to later in the day. I did so and went to get another rental car.

The Serafin residence was a Spanish-style place with white stucco walls and a roof of green tiles that overlooked the Pacific Ocean. It wasn't exactly a mansion, but the land it occupied would have been worth a fortune all by itself. The view was breathtaking.

I recognized Snotty by his voice when he answered the door—he was a large, beefy guy with a bad crew cut, wearing a white uniform that would have looked more appropriate in a hospital. A wealthy eccentric *invalid* with a telephone phobia, I mentally revised.

Nurse Snotty regarded me a bit disdainfully, and I identified myself. His attitude was not noticeably improved by this bit of information, but he did say, "Follow me."

He led me up a broad staircase to the second floor. As I followed him down the hallway, I became aware of an odor that instantly reminded me of every hospital I'd ever been in—a combination of various nauseous effluvia that are never quite completely eradicated despite the liberal application of disinfectants.

He stopped before a door that seemed to represent the origin of the smell and poked his head inside, then motioned me to go in.

The room did not look like a hospital room; it was actually *too* barren and antiseptic looking for that. The pale-green walls were devoid of ornamentation, and a set of very ordinary, functional venetian blinds obscured what would probably have been a fairly spectacular view through the lone window.

In the center of the tile floor was a large object that seemed to be composed of vinyl and stainless steel, shaped roughly like a very tall bathtub. It emitted a faint bubbling sound. Apparently it was a bed of some kind, because there was someone lying on top of it.

The man in the bed was staring at me with pale-blue eyes. A dark, lank beard framed his gaunt and oddly expressionless face, and the head was entirely hairless. His limbs were frightfully thin, the small amount of waxy flesh depending flaccidly from his bones. A thin tube emerged from one nostril and joined with a bag of milky liquid that was hanging from a pole that stood at the bedside.

There was an awkward moment as we stared at each other, until I snapped out of it and said, "Hi, I'm Michael Arcangelo."

He continued to stare a hole through me, and I had a sudden scary thought that I was too late because he'd just had a stroke or something. Then Nurse Snotty stepped forward and placed a pair of goggles over his patient's eyes. He turned and said to me, "Look at the monitor," and walked out the door.

I'd been so struck by the strange bed and its even stranger occupant that I had not noticed the video monitor that rested on a table near the head of the bed, facing toward the door.

"SIT DOWN, PLEASE," appeared on the monitor. I settled into

an armchair that faced the monitor. "I'M SETH SERAFIN. YOU ARE A FRIEND OF ART SOLOMON'S?"

"Yes. How are you doing that?" He hadn't moved a muscle. From his appearance alone I guessed he was paralyzed, and he had not yet done anything to prove me wrong.

"THESE GOGGLES TRACK EYE MOVEMENTS. I'M LOOKING AT A DISPLAY WITH LETTERS AND SOME FREQUENTLY USED WORDS AND PHRASES. THAT'S WHAT MAKES IT APPEAR ON THE SCREEN. BY THE WAY, I APOLOGIZE FOR THE 'GREAT RUNES,' BUT THIS SYSTEM IS FAIRLY PRIMITIVE AND DOESN'T SUPPORT LOWER CASE."

"Don't you have to blink or something to select what you're looking at?"

"THAT WOULD BE *WAY* TOO SLOW. ALL I HAVE TO DO IS FIX ON SOMETHING FOR 1/10 SECOND."

"It seems to me like it would be hard not to make a lot of mistakes that way."

"IT WAS AT FIRST. I'VE GOTTEN VERY GOOD AT IT."

It was no idle boast; I really couldn't believe how quickly his words were scrolling across the screen.

"BUT I'M SURE YOU DIDN'T COME HERE TO DISCUSS THIS. WHY DID ART GIVE YOU MY NUMBER?"

"I'm not entirely sure, but I believe it's because he thinks you know something about neural-induction interfaces and might be willing to tell me what you know."

I watched the screen for a reply, but none was immediately forthcoming. Then I noticed Serafin's chest rising and falling rapidly. I thought he was having a seizure or something and was about to run for his attendant, when it suddenly dawned on me that he was laughing.

"YES, I SUPPOSE YOU COULD SAY I KNOW A THING OR TWO ABOUT NEURAL INDUCTION. AND I MIGHT EVEN BE WILLING TO TELL YOU WHAT I KNOW ABOUT IT. BUT FIRST I NEED TO KNOW WHY YOU'RE ASKING."

I should have expected this, but I hadn't. I had come here to get information, not to give it, and I didn't know this guy and had no idea if he could be trusted. What I knew and suspected about Wyrm and the Dworkin Trojan horse was information that could be misused in a variety of serious ways, such as blackmailing Macrobyte, creating a panic about some of the potential consequences by talking to the media about it, or even attempting to use Wyrm and the Trojan to gain access to secure systems and commit various types of computer crime.

On the other hand, he didn't know me from Adam either, and I was asking him to trust me with information that Art had apparently needed a high-level Defense Department security clearance to know about. In that sense we were even. I couldn't expect him to trust me if I refused to trust him.

So I told him.

The monitor was blank for a while after I finished talking. Then: "THAT IS PRETTY MIND-BLOWING. I'M NOT SURE WHAT NEURAL-INDUCTION LINKS HAVE TO DO WITH IT, BUT I'LL TELL YOU WHAT YOU WANT TO KNOW. I HOPE THAT IT WILL HELP.

"YOU ARE LOOKING AT THE RESULT OF A FAIRLY EARLY DARPA EXPERIMENT IN NEURAL-INDUCTION LINKS. THE THEORETICAL BASIS OF NIL IS THE FACT THAT NERVE IMPULSES ARE ELECTRICAL IN NATURE. IF YOU CAN INDUCE AN ELECTRICAL POTENTIAL IN A SEN-SORY NERVE FIBER, IT WILL TRAVEL TO THE BRAIN AND REPORT WHATEVER SENSATION THAT PARTICULAR FIBER IS DEDICATED TO.

"BY USING MASER HOLOGRAPHY, IT'S POSSIBLE TO PROJECT A VERY FINE-GRAINED ELECTROMAGNETIC FIELD PATTERN DIRECTLY INTO THE CENTRAL NERVOUS SYSTEM. BY 1995 IT WAS POSSIBLE TO DO THIS WITH SUCH PRECISION THAT INDIVIDUAL NERVE FIBERS COULD BE SELECTIVELY STIMULATED.

"IN THE TRIAL I PARTICIPATED IN, THE BRAIN STEM WAS SELECTED AS THE TARGET AREA. IT'S A FAIRLY OBVI-OUS CHOICE, BECAUSE ALL THE SPINAL NERVES GO THROUGH IT, AND MOST OF THE CRANIAL NERVES AS WELL, CARRYING THINGS LIKE TOUCH, PAIN, POSITION SENSE, HEAT, AND COLD. IF YOU COULD CONTROL ALL THOSE INPUTS, YOU COULD CREATE A REALLY COM-PLETE VR EXPERIENCE."

"What went wrong?"

"IT TURNS OUT THAT HYPERSTIMULATION KILLS

NEURONS. THEY GET SO DEPOLARIZED THAT THEY CAN'T 'RESET' THEMSELVES, AND THEY DIE. WE HAD THE AMPLITUDE SET TOO HIGH, BECAUSE WE DIDN'T REALIZE WHAT THE RISK WAS. THE IRONIC THING WAS THAT INFORMATION ABOUT THE EFFECTS OF HYPERSTIMULATION HAS BEEN IN THE MEDICAL LITERATURE SINCE THE EARLY 1990S—BUT NOBODY IN OUR GROUP KNEW ANYTHING ABOUT IT."

"It destroyed your brain stem?"

"NOT THE WHOLE THING, JUST SOME SELECTED PARTS. MY RESPIRATORY CENTER IS INTACT, OBVIOUSLY, ALONG WITH MY RETICULAR ACTIVATING SYSTEM AND VARIOUS OTHER THINGS THAT WE WEREN'T PLAYING AROUND WITH. BUT ALMOST ALL OF MY MOTOR AND SENSORY FIBERS WERE DESTROYED."

"Why were your motor nerves affected? I thought you were just manipulating sensory inputs."

"THAT WAS HALF OF IT. WE ALSO HAD TO BLOCK THE MOTOR IMPULSES THAT WERE TRAVELING 'DOWNSTREAM' SO THAT THE SUBJECT—ME—WOULDN'T ACTUALLY GET UP AND RUN AROUND THE ROOM. WE DECIDED TO DO THAT BY USING A COUNTERIMPULSE TO CANCEL OUT ANY MOTOR SIGNALS."

"Why not just use some kind of drug that would cause temporary paralysis?"

"LIKE CURARE? YES, THAT'S WHAT WAS DONE IN THE EARLIER STAGES OF THE PROJECT. BUT THE PROBLEM WITH THAT METHOD IS THAT ANY DRUG THAT WILL PARALYZE YOUR SKELETAL MUSCLES WILL PARALYZE *ALL* OF YOUR SKELETAL MUSCLES, WHICH MEANS YOU STOP BREATHING. WE THOUGHT OUR VR SYSTEM WOULD HAVE VERY LIMITED APPLICATION IF THE USER HAD TO BE HOOKED UP TO A MECHANICAL VENTILATOR."

"I see what you mean. But why did canceling out the nerve impulses damage your motor neurons?"

"TOO MUCH JUICE AGAIN. THE COUNTERIMPULSES WE WERE USING WERE ACTUALLY NOT EQUAL TO THE NERVE IMPULSES THEY WERE SUPPOSED TO CANCEL OUT; THEY WERE A LITTLE STRONGER. THAT RESULTED

IN A NERVE IMPULSE PROPAGATING BACKWARD UP THE AXON TO THE NEURON. IN FACT, WE ANTICIPATED THAT THAT MIGHT HAPPEN. WE JUST DIDN'T REALIZE THAT IT WOULD BE A BAD THING."

"So the backward impulses hyperstimulated the motor neurons?"

"EXACTLY."

"When did this happen?" I suddenly felt embarrassed about asking that last question. We had been discussing the matter in such technical, impersonal terms that it had almost been possible to forget for a moment that the man I was speaking to had suffered a horrendous human tragedy. Asking about when it happened seemed to make that part of it real again. There was an almost imperceptible pause before his answer appeared on the monitor.

"THREE YEARS AGO."

I've heard that people who are paralyzed by spinal-cord injuries almost always go through a period of not wanting to live anymore. Most of them come through it and find some reason to go on living. Serafin was not only paralyzed but had lost all touch sensation as well. He could still see. His hearing was intact, and I didn't know if he could taste, but the latter seemed like a moot point as he was obviously being fed through a tube. I tried to imagine what I would find to make my life worth living in such circumstances. I couldn't think of anything.

There was an awkward silence. Serafin seemed to be waiting expectantly for my next question, his goggle-masked face slack and impassive. I cleared my throat to let him know I was still there. "What's happened to the state of the art in the last four years?"

"OH, I'M SURE THAT THINGS HAVE GONE ON APACE. WE WOULDN'T LET A LITTLE SETBACK GET IN THE WAY OF PROGRESS. AS FOR THE DETAILS, I'VE BEEN, WELL, OUT OF THE LOOP FOR A FEW YEARS."

"Based on your knowledge of the project, where would they be now? Would they have any working prototypes?"

There was another pause. "I'M SURE THEY DO. I WISH I COULD GIVE YOU SOME DETAILS ABOUT THE CURRENT STATE OF THE ART, BUT I JUST DON'T KNOW."

"You've told me a lot. Um, come to think of it, how pissed off would the Defense Department be about the fact that you've told me all of this?"

His chest rose and fell in silent laughter again. "I'M NOT TOO WORRIED ABOUT THAT. AFTER ALL, WHAT COULD THEY DO TO ME?"

"To tell you the truth, it's not just you that I'm worried about."

"YOU MAY HAVE A POINT THERE."

As I drove back to the airport, I reflected on what I'd learned. I had not needed to ask why the Defense Department was interested in VR technology; imagine a fighter pilot whose plane is like an extension of his own body. In fact, VR represents the ultimate in man-machine interfaces. Anything that can be done with a keyboard, mouse, control stick, buttons, pedals, levers, or steering wheel could be done better with virtual reality.

The nonmilitary applications for direct neural interfaces were even more mind-boggling. The system that Serafin described could easily be used to allow a paraplegic to walk by electronically bypassing the site of his injury. After all, if you can induce nerve impulses in sensory fibers, you ought to be able to do the same thing with motor nerves.

I had a nagging feeling, though, that Serafin was holding a few things back, and I wasn't really sure why. Then I remembered the business about not talking on the telephone. That just didn't make sense. Voice-synthesis hardware and software were cheap and readily available; anybody with a little know-how could set up such a system for him in an afternoon. I was beginning to suspect that he was not quite as insouciant about the possible consequences of leaking this information as he'd been letting on, and maybe that was the real reason for avoiding telephone conversations on the subject.

That meant he must have known the purpose of my call, either just from hearing Art's name, or because Art had called him to tell him to expect to hear from me. It didn't seem too likely that Nurse Ratchet had standing orders to take any call from any friend of Art's, which increased the likelihood that Art had made a special call on my behalf. I tried to imagine how that conversation would have gone: "Hello, Seth? This is Art. A friend of mine wants some classified information, and I don't want to give it to him myself, but maybe you'd like to put *your* neck in the noose."

. . .

Because of my delayed departure I didn't get into La Guardia until around midnight. I swore that I would go straight to bed and let any phone messages wait until morning, but when I walked in the door, the light on my answering machine was blinking so insistently, I just couldn't ignore it.

"Mike, this is George. When you get this message, call immediately, any time of the day or night." That sounded pretty urgent. I almost regretted that it was still a reasonable hour in the Pacific time zone.

"Hello?"

"Hi, George. What's the big deal?"

"Mike! Are you sitting down?"

"I'm going to be lying down in about ten seconds. What's up?"

"Roger Dworkin is dead."

3

The Conqueror Wyrm

CHAPTER THIRTEEN

Heartwyrm

And his tail drew the third part of the stars of heaven,
and did cast them to the earth . . .

—Revelation 12:4

The Oakland police had found Dworkin's body, and that was about all they had to say about the matter. Cause of death was "not yet established." Foul play had "not been ruled out." In short, the official accounts said practically nothing, but said it in such a way that you got the impression something was very definitely not kosher.

I gave Al the news when she called from LA the next evening, but she'd already heard. The whole Internet was buzzing with rumors about how and why Dworkin had died, with special emphasis on the theory that he'd been murdered by—you name it: the CIA, the FBI, the Mafia, the Russians, the Japanese, the Bulgarians, and, of course, Macrobyte Software, Inc. (I thought of Josh Spector when I heard that last one—"Kill the golden goose? Nah.")

"I was afraid of something like this, Michael. I told you he didn't seem very stable."

"What are you saying? You think it was a suicide?" That was one of the less popular rumors.

"I think it's pretty likely. It would explain the fact that something is obviously being held back in the official news releases; there's still a pretty major stigma attached to suicide. Also, when you get right down to it, there just aren't many likely causes of death for a man in his thirties. Sure, you see an occasional precocious heart attack in that group, but the main causes of death are violent ones, which means suicide, accidents—"

"And homicide?"

"Well, yeah, that too. But why would anybody kill him?"

"Have you been reading the newspapers lately? It's not like anybody seems to need a particular reason these days." Actually, I had an idea that Dworkin's death might have been related to his apparent interest in certain classified defense technology (one of the few possibilities that had escaped the Internet rumor mill), but I couldn't tell Al about that yet—not without clearing it with Art Solomon first.

"You've got a point there. By the way, I've been meaning to ask you about that paper Art Solomon gave you."

Uh-oh. Why do some people seem to have such a knack for asking questions that are, shall we say, inconvenient? Come to think of it, why do those same people invariably seem to be carrying two X chromosomes? "You know about the paper?"

"Yes, I saw him give it to you. I know you didn't drop it. It was about classified neural-induction hardware, wasn't it?"

"Actually, I can't tell you about it just now."

There was a long silence on the other end of the line. This was an ominous sign. Then: "Damn it, Michael, don't start pulling this shit on me again."

"It's not like that."

"It's exactly like that! Why can't you tell me what's going on?"

"Well, it's a little hard to explain. . . ."

"I don't think so. It seems to me like you just can't bring yourself to treat me as an equal. I saw Arthur Solomon give you that piece of paper when we were leaving Cepheus. I don't know what it is that you're keeping from me, but I have no doubt that it's, as usual, 'for my own protection.'"

I wanted to protest that it wasn't for her protection, that I had an obligation to keep a confidence entrusted to me by someone else, but I started to realize that she had a point without even knowing it. If Roger Dworkin had died because of what he knew about this stuff, a possibility I couldn't discount, then I sure as hell didn't want to put Al at risk by telling her about it.

"Al, I've been entrusted with some information that's confidential, and at this point I don't have that person's permission to share it with anyone else."

"Oh?" That seemed to mollify her a little. It was a pity that I had to go and spoil it by telling her the rest of the truth.

"But, to be perfectly honest with you, even if I had his okay, I'm not sure I'd want to tell you about it. There's a possibility that knowing about it could be . . . unhealthy."

"Damn it, Michael, that's exactly what I'm talking about. It's okay to put yourself at risk, but you think you have to protect me. Has it occurred to you that I might be in as much danger as you are because of our relationship, but I don't even know why?"

She had a point. If it was that important to silence people who had this information, then someone might think the prudent course would be to eliminate anyone who even might have heard about it, and that could quite possibly include the immediate circle of anyone who was definitely known to have it. "I'm going to have to think about that. And I still need to talk to someone about who I can share this with."

"Never mind."

"Never mind what?"

"If you have to think about it, then never mind. I'll just have to take my own steps to deal with it."

"Like what?"

"Like if I'm going to be endangered by something I know nothing about because of our relationship, then that relationship will have to end. How soon can you move out?"

"You're not serious."

"Do I sound like I'm joking? I want you out of the apartment as soon as possible."

"Can we at least talk about this?"

"Isn't that what we've been doing? We seem to have hit an 'irreconcilable difference.' I'd like to have a relationship with someone who will treat me like an equal, and you insist on treating me like a child. I'm not going to stay with someone who keeps doing this to me."

"Well, maybe you're right. Maybe it would be better for us not to see each other for a while, if that would make things safer for you."

"Michael, I'm not talking about 'for a while.' This is it."

I was practically speechless. I knew from experience that this was the kind of thing that could set her off, but I had no idea that she would react so violently. "Is there anything that I can say to change your mind?"

"No, I really don't think so."

"Okay, then. If that's the way you want it, I'll be moved out by the time you come back to the city."

"I would appreciate that."

I called my previous landlord to see if my old apartment had been rented yet. It had, but they had a vacant efficiency in the same building that they were willing to rent to me on a month-to-month basis. I guess at that point I was hoping that when Al got back, we would be able to smooth things out and she would want me back, so I didn't want to sign a long lease. I suppose you could call that optimism, but I wasn't really feeling very optimistic at that moment.

Then I started packing up my stuff; it was a long, lonely job. Effie watched me the whole time. I swear he had a smug look on his little feline mug.

Al wouldn't be back for a few days, and I could get into the efficiency as early as tomorrow, but I wasn't comfortable staying in the apartment. I decided to drive out to Long Island and spend the night at my parents' house.

I stepped outside and looked up at the sky. It was completely overcast, as it had been all week. Which was too bad, because tonight was November 17, the peak of the Leonids meteor storm. It had been in the news all week—Marlon Oz had seen to that. By tomorrow morning we'd know whether his strategy had worked. With the weather so lousy in New York, I had seriously considered hopping a plane to someplace with clear skies so that I could watch the celestial fireworks. Right now I didn't feel too interested. Oh, well, maybe the next time around, in 2032.

As it turned out, Oz was right. Either that, or people failed to spaz out over the meteors for some other, unknown reason. There were a few incidents of craziness in some remote areas untouched by modern communications media, but the world hadn't come to an end. Yet.

Roger Dworkin may have been dead, but a part of him lived on, in the form of computer programs and data. We still needed access to some of that data, more than ever now, because there was no longer any possibility of obtaining the information from the man himself.

The basic weakness of a password is, somebody knows what it is. In fact, for it to be of any use, at least two people have to know what it is, or, in the case of computer systems, one person and one computer. In practice it is generally easier to get the person to tell you the password than to get the same information out of the computer. This is the arena for a set of techniques known to hackers as "social engineering," or just SE. SE is basically a con job in which the hacker poses as someone else—a novice user, a system administrator, a field-service rep, you name it—in order to bamboozle some gullible soul into revealing his own personal password.

But there are ways to get the same information from the computer itself; in fact, the first thing I had Icepick do was send me a list of system passwords. Yes, surprising as it may seem, on many systems a list of passwords is freely available even to the meanest of peons, the lowliest of lusers. There's one slight hitch, though: The passwords are encrypted. More precisely, the passwords are used as encryption keys for a particular numerical constant, and that number is, in a certain sense, the "real" password. When the user enters his password, the system uses it as a key to decrypt the constant. So what appears on the password list are various encryptions of the same number, using the various individual passwords as encryption keys.

The Macrobyte user account we had gotten off WormsMush was a low-level one, as we'd expected, but it was enough to get Icepick in the door. Icepick had begun posting its encrypted data to alt.sex.bestiality; the first batch came through under the heading "jpeg: Woman with Snake 1/6" and so on. "Jpeg" referred to the particular binary format used, and 1/6 meant it was the first of six parts needed to generate the whole image. Of course, these six parts wouldn't generate any image, no doubt much to the disappointment of any lurking ophidiaphiles.

I had Icepick send daily copies of the password list, because I wanted to find out how frequently the passwords were changed—most systems will require users to alter passwords periodically. In fact, by the end of the week all the passwords had been changed—except one. And that was interesting.

The unchanged password belonged to a guy named Ken Bishop. Bishop was, according to a personnel list I'd been able to access, a midlevel programmer, so there was no obvious reason why he would be the exception in this case. My suspicion was that Bishop had hacked system security in order to bypass the change-password requirement. It did not surprise me that someone would do something like this—some people are quite attached to their passwords (especially when they imagine they're being particularly clever), as I've learned in my line of work.

The other piece of information that I learned from this was that security was a little lax. Bishop had gotten away with his hack, which an alert sysadmin should have noticed. Also, when they required users to change their passwords, the underlying security number should have been changed, too. If it had, Bishop's password would have shown up as different in encrypted form even if he hadn't changed it.

This told me a little more about what to expect from Macrobyte's security. I had earlier surmised that a former cracker must be running things, so on the one hand I could expect the unexpected, including some particularly ingenious innovations, like that phony logout. On the other hand, they weren't crossing all the t's and dotting all the i's, as if those kinds of nitty-gritty details were beneath the attention of the resident genius.

▲   ▲   ▲   ▲   ▲   ▲   ▲

"I've got a lead on the cap of darkness," Ragnar announced.

"Been counting clues?" Zerika asked.

He grinned and shook his head. "Didn't have to. They were already numbered."

"The crossword puzzle!" Megaera exclaimed. "I should have thought of that."

"You were too busy solving it," Ragnar reminded her. "Anyway, the one hundred thirtieth clue was 'Unukulhai,' which happens to be a star in the constellation Hydra, which happens to have another name: Cor Hydrae."

"Heart of the dragon," Megaera translated.

"Right. 'The ring of the king in the heart of the dragon / Where god's cap of darkness may also be won.' "

"Nice work, Ragnar," Zerika said. "Tahmurath, is it in the guide?"

"TrekMuck," he announced, after consulting the tour book. "Let's do it."

The Universal Touring Machine arrived at one end of an oblong clearing surrounded by somewhat unusual vegetation; the trees wore leaves that were purple and blue, and reddish bark that had the texture of alligator hide.

As they emerged from their craft, the air at the opposite end of the clearing shimmered briefly, and then there were four people standing there. The two groups studied each other for a few moments; then one of the newcomers, apparently the leader, spoke to a small object he held in his hand. "Landing party to *Hornet*. We have arrived on the fourth planet in the Unukulhai system and encountered a mixed group of humans and Vulcans, armed with archaic weapons. Please advise."

"Archaic weapons?" Gunnodoyak sniffed. "Hey, that's a pretty retro communicator, isn't it?"

The leader of the *Hornet*'s landing party seemed a bit miffed. "This is a 'classic Trek' MUD—none of that 'next generation' garbage. Anyway, I think you'll find that our phazers are quite up-to-date."

"Don't forget the Prime Directive," Ragnar suggested.

"The Prime Directive mandates noninterference with autochthonous cultures. Something tells me that you folks ain't from around here any more than we are."

"He's got you there," Gunnodoyak stage-whispered.

"But relax, we're friendly. In fact, our captain wants me to invite you aboard our ship."

They looked at each other and shrugged. "Sure," Zerika said. "What are you going to do, beam us all up?"

"Yeah. Just give me a minute to relay our coordinates—"

"No, wait." Tahmurath stopped them. "Let's take the UTM. I'd rather not leave it here."

"Why? Nobody but us can use it."

"I'm not worried about that. It's just that if we leave the planet, how are we going to get back here to get it?"

"I agree with Tahmurath," Gunnodoyak said.

Zerika poked him in the ribs. "Boss's pet!"

"Shut up! Come on, we haven't taken her into space before. I'd kind of like to see how she handles."

It was agreed that the *Hornet*'s landing party would beam back up, and the party would rendezvous with them in orbit.

"This is really cool," Gunnodoyak enthused as he slid behind the controls. "Is everybody belted in and ready for takeoff?" Without waiting for a reply, he punched the throttle, and the craft zoomed into orbit at nine tenths the speed of light.

"Gunnodoyak, slow down!" Tahmurath chided. "Do you want to get us all killed? I'd like to land on the *Hornet*'s flight deck, not get fried by her meteor shields."

"Actually, the shields are probably down right now."

"Oh, good. Then we could smash right through the hull and kill everyone on board, including ourselves."

"Okay, okay, I'm slowing down."

"Why are we doing this, anyway?" Megaera demanded. "If the 'god's cap of darkness' is in 'the heart of the dragon,' then don't we have to look in the star?"

"I hope not," Gunnodoyak commented. "I don't think our air-conditioning is *that* good."

"There'll probably be some kind of a dragon to slay, like in the other MUDs," Zerika said.

"But if this is a sci-fi MUD," Megaera objected, "then I don't think we're too likely to find any dragons."

"It doesn't have to be a dragon, exactly," Zerika said. "There are a lot of science-fiction creatures that might fill the bill, like the sandworms in *Dune* or Heinlein's *Star Beast*."

"But why do we even need a 'cap of darkness'?" Ragnar asked. "Tahmurath can make us invisible with his magic."

"True," Tahmurath said, "but there are a lot of limitations on magical invisibility. Remember how we couldn't use it with the bats in BloodMUD, because they would have detected us with their sonar? I'm assuming that this 'cap of darkness' must be such a powerful artifact that it isn't subject to those kind of limitations."

By now the *Hornet* was visible through their forward viewscreen.

Then, suddenly, she was no longer visible, concealed by something very large that materialized between them and the Federation starship. Gunnodoyak had to veer away sharply to keep from ramming it. "What the hell is that?"

"A Klingon ship," Ragnar said. "It just decloaked."

"Then it must be attacking the *Hornet*!"

Sure enough, at that moment they cleared the Klingon ship and were able to see the *Hornet*, which had obviously suffered severe damage and was gamely trying to return fire.

"They must have caught her with her shields down," Zerika said. "It's too bad we can't do anything to help her."

"Who says we can't?" Tahmurath asked.

"Well, what are we going to do? Go stick a sword into the Klingon ship? I don't think we're carrying any photon torpedoes."

"No," Tahmurath admitted, "but we have something even better. Are you forgetting the Golden Frobnule?"

"What good will that do?"

"It allows us to use our special abilities in any MUD we enter. In most MUDs that involves magic. This is the first sci-fi MUD we've entered, but the equivalent of magic here is technology."

Gunnodoyak grinned. " 'Any sufficiently advanced technology is indistinguishable from magic,' " he quoted. "Clark's third law."

Tahmurath nodded. "Right; it even works like magic: Just as in most magic systems, a magically invisible fighter becomes visible as soon as he attacks; the Klingon ship has to decloak to fire weapons."

"Okay, you've almost got me convinced."

"Almost? What else do I have to say?"

"Enough talk. Do something!"

"Too late!" Gunnodoyak yelled. "They're already doing something!" An explosion rocked their small craft. "That was close!"

"Get us out of here, Gunny!" Zerika shouted, but he already had the UTM moving at maximum speed. Unfortunately, maximum speed, though faster than the Klingon warship, would not immediately take them out of range of her photon torpedoes.

Another explosion rattled their teeth, more violently this time. "Damn it, Gunny, that was too close! Can you make it back to the planet surface? Maybe we can hide down there."

"If I try to slow down enough for a landing orbit, they're going to have us for lunch."

"Well, then, just get us away!"

"I'm going as fast as I can!"

"What's that?" Ragnar called out, pointing at something ahead of them, a swirling cloud of luminous interstellar gas that seemed to be funneling itself into a whirlpool. "It looks like some kind of an anomaly—"

"A wormhole!" Gunnodoyak exclaimed, altering course. "Let's go for it!"

"Wait, wait! Are you sure it's a wormhole? What if it's a black hole? Don't—" Tahmurath's admonition came a fraction of a second too late. The Klingon ship, seeing its prey on the verge of escape, fired a parting salvo of photon torpedoes and veered away, but the UTM darted into the anomaly just before detonation.

As they emerged from the other end, Gunnodoyak said, "I told you it was a wormhole. You guys are lucky you had me to get you out of the frying pan—"

"And into the fire?" Megaera finished. As they looked out the viewport, the others saw what she meant: A veritable armada hung in space around the wormhole, all of them bristling with every conceivable kind of weapon. To their relief, however, the other ships paid no attention to them whatsoever.

"Well," Ragnar said, "this explains why the Klingons didn't want to follow us through the wormhole."

"Yeah, well, we're still gonna have to go back to get out of this MUD," Tahmurath reminded him. "Something tells me those Klingons are going to be waiting."

"What the hell is this place?" Zerika asked.

As if in answer to her question, the dashboard of the UTM opened and extruded a vidscreen, which displayed the unattractive visage of a short, snaggletoothed, bat-eared Ferengi. "Welcome to Brokk's world," the image boomed, "the most complete weapons dealer in the five galaxies. Tired of being chased by Federation ships? Having some unpleasant run-ins with Romulans, Cardassians, or Klingons? Let us outfit your ship with state-of-the-art shields, phazer banks, tractor beams, and the most accurate photon torpedoes in the sector. For your shopping convenience we accept payment in a variety of galactic currencies, as well as minerals, rare artifacts, and of course elemental dilithium. Welcome to Brokk's . . ." The commercial continued, apparently on an endless loop.

"There." Gunnodoyak pointed through the viewport at a very large object, not a ship, that appeared to have been cobbled together from spare parts salvaged by some intergalactic junk dealer. It was a huge ramshackle station, with space docks that could accommodate at least two dozen large ships. The ships that were currently docked were of every shape and size, including one that was a virtual duplicate of the *Millennium Falcon* from *Star Wars*. "What do you say we go do a little shopping?"

They docked near some other small ships in an area of the space station apparently designed for that purpose. The UTM was by far the smallest ship there, though. As they disembarked through an air lock, they were met by a Ferengi, apparently the one from the commercial.

"Greetings, friends," he smarmed. "I am Brokk. Welcome to my humble place of business. You are in the market for some hardware?"

Tahmurath appeared skeptical. "You mean to tell me you have something for a ship this size that's more powerful than a peashooter?"

The Ferengi's eyes widened. "You jest, surely. Why, Brokk has state-of-the-art weapons for ships of all sizes and shapes."

"We need to get rid of some pesky Klingons," Gunnodoyak explained. "What do you recommend?"

Brokk grinned a snaggletoothed Ferengi grin. "What sort of a Klingon problem do you have? Is it a Bird of Prey?"

"Something like a Bird of Prey," Gunnodoyak said, "only bigger. The fuselage is longer, and the command deck is more wedge-shaped."

Tahmurath stared at him. "What, do you subscribe to *Jane's Fighting Starships* or something?"

Gunnodoyak shrugged and smiled sheepishly. "Okay, the secret's out: I'm a trekkie. Wanna make something of it?"

Meanwhile, the Ferengi's smile had vanished. "That's not a Bird of Prey, that's a Ghargh'a. I didn't know it was even off the drawing board. My informants are usually more efficient than this—"

"So what's the difference," Zerika interrupted, "between a Bird of Prey and a Ghargh'a?"

"The Ghargh'a has about ten times the firepower, but that's not the biggest difference. The Ghargh'a is supposed to be equipped with the Klingons' newest technological breakthrough: APC, or attack-permissive cloaking."

"But it decloaked before attacking the *Hornet*," Ragnar said. "Why would they do that if they could have stayed cloaked?"

"They can attack while cloaked, but not shield while cloaked. They probably didn't want to risk the *Hornet* getting in a lucky shot. Then again, their decloaking might just have been Klingon bravado."

"Well, what are we going to do?" Tahmurath demanded. "We've got to get back to that planet, and I doubt there's anything that could make us a match for that Klingon ship."

Brokk's oversize ears pricked forward, perhaps in alarm over the possibility of losing a sale. "Maybe not a match, but I do have something that might give you a fighting chance."

"By the way," Gunnodoyak asked, "what exactly is a 'Ghargh'a' supposed to be?"

Brokk shrugged. "Some kind of giant worm or serpent that the Klingons claim once existed on their planet but is now supposedly extinct. Most exobiologists consider it to be mythical."

Tahmurath looked at Zerika. "Are you thinking what I'm thinking?"

She nodded. "The Ghargh'a sounds an awful lot like a dragon to me. I think we know where to look for the cap of darkness."

A surprisingly short time later they were heading back toward the wormhole. Brokk's mechanic droids had swarmed over the UTM, installing the additional "hardware" they had purchased. Tahmurath had paid with a sack full of uncut diamonds the size of hen's eggs, which they had obtained in another MUD.

"Are you sure we can trust him?" Megaera asked for about the fifth time. "I still don't see how he can have Dune technology in a Trek MUD. I thought we were the only ones who could carry in outside artifacts."

"It's just a MUD," Tahmurath reminded her. "They can put in any kind of technology they want."

"I still think it's a little fishy. And what about that guy from the *Hornet* that we met on the planet? He acted as if even Trek stuff had to be from the right 'generation.' Doesn't it seem a little weird that all of this other stuff is on the other side of the wormhole? Besides, how do we know a Dune lasgun is the same as a Trek phazer?"

"Okay, okay, maybe it's not. Sheesh, you're starting to make me as paranoid as you are. Anyway, even if it doesn't work, it's just going to be a little tougher, that's all. But if it does work," he chuckled, "there'll be some awfully sorry Klingons by the time we're through."

The Dune artifact that they had purchased from Brokk was a personal shield, used primarily by individuals in hand-to-hand combat. What they hoped to exploit was the fact that if someone fired a lasgun at a shield, both shield and lasgun went off like atomic bombs. They had affixed the shield to a small drone.

The rest of their plan depended on Tahmurath's contention that, thanks to the Golden Frobnule, they could use their magic even in a sci-fi MUD. He had proved his point by making their own ship invisible prior to their trip back through the wormhole.

When they emerged from the opposite end, the first thing they saw was the burning hulk of the *Hornet*. Ragnar let out a low whistle. "Looks like they didn't take any prisoners."

"Time for phase two," Tahmurath said. "But where's the Dragon Ship?"

They scanned the starry sky. "Either she left," Zerika said, "or she's running cloaked."

"Should I release the drone?" Gunnodoyak asked.

"Not yet," Tahmurath said. "We want to release it within phazer range of the Dragon, otherwise they might just decide to take it out with a torpedo."

"I still don't know if this is a good idea," Megaera said. "Even if it works, it might blow up the whole ship."

"Brokk said it would just disable the main phazer banks," Zerika reminded her. "That should be a pretty good diversion."

Megaera shrugged. "Maybe. I kind of wish we'd thought to ask Brokk for some phazers or something."

Tahmurath shook his head. "We're going to have to do this by stealth anyway. We can't afford to get into a pitched battle with the Klingons on the ship. There'll be too many of them."

"You're probably right," Zerika conceded. "But it wouldn't hurt to carry a phazer or two, just in case."

"Maybe we don't need to," Ragnar interjected. He held out a rather bizarre-looking pistol. "While you guys were busy with the ship, Brokk sold me one other little item of alien technology. He called it a scrooch gun."

"Is everybody ready?" Tahmurath asked.

"Except for one thing," Zerika said. "We still don't know where the Dragon Ship is, or even if it's still in this solar system."

"No problem," Tahmurath assured her. "Our magic works here, remember? I have a spell for detecting invisible objects."

"Do you have enough range to do that?" Zerika asked.

"With the ouroboros ring I do." He made a few mystical passes in the air. "Foo, baz, quux, bar. Show me where the Klingons are." His staff swung slowly around until the head pointed in the direction of the bombed-out shell of the *Hornet*. "Hmm. I wonder what they're doing over there."

"Probably trying to salvage some stuff so they can copy Federation technology," Gunnodoyak said indignantly. "Let's get 'em!" He piloted the UTM toward the dead *Hornet*. When they had closed to the agreed-upon range, he released the drone, then sped away at top speed.

The response of the Dragon was quick and deadly; she fired a starboard phazer array and converted the drone to a cloud of super-heated gas.

"Shit!" Tahmurath remarked. "It didn't work. Remind me to wring a certain Ferengi's neck if we have time later."

Zerika shrugged. "Well, it looks like we go in cold. Oh, and Ragnar?"

"Yeah?"

"I wouldn't count too much on the scrooch gun."

Gunnodoyak maneuvered the UTM close to the fuselage of the Dragon ship. "That hatch must lead to their flight deck. What do you want me to do, knock on the door and ask them to let us in? Or maybe Zerika can hold her breath and try to pick the lock."

"That shouldn't be necessary," Tahmurath said. "I do have a door-opening spell; just get me a little closer, I don't have much range on this one."

Tahmurath muttered his incantation, and the hatch slid open. The flight deck was, fortunately, deserted, and Gunnodoyak was able to guide the still-invisible UTM between two Klingon shuttlecraft.

"Isn't the flight deck pressurized?" Tahmurath asked Gunnodoyak. "That hatch wasn't air-locked."

"Yes, it was," Ragnar said. "The hatch has a force-field on it that keeps the air in." The others stared at him. "Okay, I admit it, I'm a trekkie too."

"Okay, now on to phase two," Zerika said as they disembarked from the UTM. "Let's find the cloaking device."

"Maybe we should just ask them," Gunnodoyak suggested, pointing to a group of about a dozen Klingons who were approaching with their weapons leveled.

Suddenly the group was enveloped by a burst of light that seemed to freeze them in place, their eyes bulging and hair standing on end.

"What the hell was that?" Zerika demanded.

"They've been scrooched," Ragnar explained, brandishing his recently acquired weapon.

"Not bad," Tahmurath admitted. "We may have to let Brokk live, after all. How long will they stay like that?"

"I haven't the slightest idea."

"Then let's get the hell out of here now."

"Wait a second," Zerika said. "Now that we're out of the UTM, we're visible again. Don't you think you should make us invisible?"

Tahmurath smacked himself on the forehead. "Of course I should. Thank you, my dear. Senility is so annoying."

"Speaking of magic," Megaera said, "can't you use your location spell to find the cloaking device?"

"Yes, but it won't do much good unless we're practically in the same room with it. I have a spell for walking through walls, but that only works on stone."

The party of now-invisible adventurers crept along a corridor with Gunnodoyak in the lead. "I think this is the way to engineering," he whispered. "If we can find a computer station, we can probably call up a schematic that will show us exactly where to find the cloaking device."

A few yards farther down the corridor, they found what they were looking for: the ship's engineering section. There were a few Klingons about, but they were able to locate a ship's computer station in a relatively secluded corner. Gunnodoyak sat down at the console.

"Display ship schematic," he ordered.

The computer responded, "Retrieving schematic," in a Klingon-accented synthesized voice. A diagram of the ship appeared on the screen.

"Display location of cloaking device," Gunnodoyak suggested.

"That is classified information. Please enter your authorization code now."

"Huh. Well, what do we do now? I don't suppose one of you has a Klingon security clearance?"

"The clue said 'heart of the dragon,' " Megaera reminded him.

"That would be helpful if starships had hearts."

"Maybe a pump of some kind?" Zerika suggested.

Gunnodoyak turned back to the computer console. "Display schematic for reactor coolant system."

One small area of the ship lit up like a blue maze.

"Magnify."

The blue area expanded to fill the screen. "There," Gunnodoyak said, pointing to one area of the diagram. "It does look like there's one main coolant pump. It sounds like our best bet. Shall we?"

Just then a loud alarm sounded, followed by the noise of numerous Klingons rushing about shouting.

"It sounds like our hosts have gotten unscrooched," Tahmurath remarked. "Let's get going."

Gunnodoyak led them to the coolant pump, managing to elude the Klingon patrols that kept running by searching for them. "There it is. Do your stuff, boss."

Tahmurath cast his spell, and his staff slowly swung around until it was pointing almost directly at the pump. "I think it's underneath the pump," he said. "Zerika, see if you can get under there and find it."

There was about half a meter of clearance between the pump and the deck. Zerika slid under it, faceup. "There is something here."

"Get it," Tahmurath ordered.

A moment later she emerged, holding a small black box. Tahmurath's staff swung to follow it.

"That must be it," Tahmurath said.

"It is," Gunnodoyak confirmed. "She's getting a download."

"Let's get out of here."

They hurried back down to the flight deck, again having to evade Klingon security patrols. Being invisible made this easier, but they still had to keep from being run into by accident.

There was a particularly large number of Klingons on the flight deck, no doubt because that was where they had last been seen.

"Damn!" Tahmurath whispered. "What happened to the UTM?"

"It's still invisible," Zerika reminded him.

"Oh, I forgot. How embarrassing."

"It's right over there," Gunnodoyak said, pointing to the two Klingon shuttles he'd parked between. "Let's go."

They crept to the UTM and boarded.

"I'm going to open the door," Tahmurath said. "When I do, floor it."

"Ready when you are," Gunnodoyak responded, his hands poised over the controls.

Tahmurath cast his door-opening spell once again, and Gunnodoyak zoomed through it so quickly that the Klingons on the flight deck didn't even have time to move. A few phazer blasts emanating from the door showed that a few of them had belatedly guessed what was happening, but the UTM was already out of range.

Once outside the ship, they headed for the planet where they'd originally entered the MUD.

"Look!" Zerika pointed through the forward viewscreen. Four large Enterprise-class Federation starships were converging on the Klingons at maximum-impulse speed.

Ragnar looked back at the Klingon Dragon Ship. "Why are they just sitting there? They don't stand a chance against all four of those ships. They're not even trying to get away."

Suddenly Gunnodoyak burst out laughing. The others looked at him quizzically. "The Klingons," he said between snorts of laughter. "They think they're still cloaked!"

▲   ▲   ▲   ▲   ▲   ▲   ▲

"They want you to *what*?"

"Take the worm out, man." It was Leon Griffin on the phone from Tower Bank. As a result of the demise of my game character and the demands on Leon's time, I hadn't spoken to him in weeks, maybe months. And now he was calling to tell me that Tower Bank wanted to play Russian roulette with their computer system.

"Do they know what the risks are?"

"I doubt it, though I've tried to explain to them. They're very adamant about it. Anyway, it's their funeral. I'm just calling to see if you want to be a pallbearer. After all, this is more up your alley than mine."

Although I didn't agree with Tower's decision to try to remove Wyrm from their system, I was, for obvious reasons, intensely interested in the outcome. "I'll be right over."

I met Leon at Tower's computer center less than an hour later. Removing Wyrm was not going to pose a problem; I had a program designed to do it that I'd been carrying around for months. I was just afraid of what would happen if I tried to use it.

Leon and I loaded the program and configured it for Tower's computer system, then sat back. "This is going to take a while," I said.

"If you have other things to do, go ahead, Mike. I'm going to be here all day. If anything noteworthy happens, I'll call you right away."

Because at this stage watching the program run would be about as exciting as watching bowling on television, I decided to take him up on his offer. I did have a few jobs I needed to work on, anyway, and I needed to call Krishna.

"How are you coming with that password encryption?" I asked once I'd gotten him on the phone.

"I was just talking to that guy at MIT—Dan Morgan. He sounds like he's making more progress than I am at this point—he's got access to some heavy metal—but we both need more data."

"Like what?"

"Do you think you could keep changing the password and downloading the password file? Or would security notice?"

"I doubt it. A changed password would show up in their security log, and somebody changing his password several times a day would look a little suspicious, but I don't think they're paying much attention to those kinds of details."

"Good. The more samples we can get, the better chance we'll have of cracking their encryption algorithm."

"Okay. You want me to just change it at random?"

"No, no. I'll tell you what to change it to."

"Fine." If we could crack Macrobyte's password encryption algorithm, we'd have every password in the system, including any and all superuser accounts. I was starting to think we might get lucky.

My cellular phone rang around noon. It was Leon. "Don't get excited," he said. "I was just getting ready to break for lunch, and I wanted to let you know that, so far, everything is copacetic."

"Copacetic? Is that what they say in Jamaica?"

He laughed. "I'm from St. John, in the Virgin Islands. And, no, they don't say 'copacetic' there. That's something I picked up in New York."

I wondered briefly whether a revival of beatnik slang was another sign of the impending apocalypse, then got back to work. When I got home later that evening, there was a message from Leon on my answering machine: "Mike, I'm leaving this message on your machine because it wasn't even worth interrupting whatever you were doing. Everything is running smoothly at Tower. It looks like we panicked a little prematurely. Talk to you tomorrow."

The following morning I decided to take a swing by Tower, just to eyeball the situation. I found Leon in the computer center, staring at a terminal. He looked up, a little startled, as I approached, then grinned mirthlessly. "It's *baa-aack*."

"Back? What do you mean? Are you sure it was gone in the first place?"

He nodded emphatically. "It was squeaky-clean when I left last night. When I came back this morning, it was back again."

"What about the anti-Wyrm program? Isn't it still running?"

"As near as I can figure out," he said, "Wyrm ate your program."

There is a story, possibly apocryphal, about a program called Creeper, which was unleashed on a particular computer network. The program moved itself through memory locations and also made copies of itself. Needless to say, this soon became a problem. The problem, so the story goes, was solved by a programmer who wrote another program, dubbed Reaper. Reaper's job was to crawl through the system memory, erasing Creeper. When all Creepers were erased, Reaper then erased itself.

If there's any truth to this story, it's possible that Creeper was the very first computer worm. However, as the astute reader may have noticed, there's a certain problem with this story: Because Reaper can't occupy the entire memory simultaneously, how can it ever know for sure if Creeper has been completely eliminated?

It was now evident that we faced an analogous problem with Wyrm: If we failed to completely eliminate it from the Internet, it would be able to regenerate itself—partial success would be equivalent to total failure.

▲   ▲   ▲   ▲   ▲   ▲   ▲

Tahmurath held *The Book of Gates* open in front of him. "According to this, that gate is the one that opens into MOOnytoons."

"And according to the latest MUDlist," Gunnodoyak added, "it's got a cartoon theme."

"It'll be nice," Zerika opined, "to be in theme right from the start, for once."

"Are you going to change us, Tahmurath?" Megaera asked.

"I could, but it would be good practice for you to do it yourselves this time. You all should know how by now. Just think of your favorite cartoon character and make it some variation on that."

"I like the Road Runner," Zerika said. "How about you, Megaera?"

"Definitely Stimpy. What about you guys?"

"My favorite Ninja Turtle," Gunnodoyak replied, "was always Raphael."

"I think a combination of Crusader Rabbit and George of the Jungle." Ragnar grinned. "And what about you, Tahmurath? Mr. Wizard, maybe?"

"Too obvious. For me, I think something combining the cool self-possession of Mr. Peabody with the unparalleled physique of Super Chicken."

"You know," Ragnar said, "I was just thinking, it's too bad Malakh can't be here. He'd make such a perfect Dudley Do-Right."

Gunnodoyak chimed in, "Or how about Casper the Friendly Ghost?" He and Ragnar proceeded to laugh their heads off.

Zerika gave them a stern look. "You guys are not very nice."

The bewhiskered smile occupied a lower limb on a decidedly odd-looking tree, although it was scarcely the only odd thing about the surreal landscape. A moment later a pair of eyes popped into view above the grin and regarded Megaera appraisingly. "And what are you supposed to be, my dear? A wombat or something?"

"I'm a cat," she said, somewhat indignantly.

The eyes widened. "There's no need to be insulting." The cat winked an eye. "There. That's much better." The wink had somehow transformed Megaera from a decidedly ungainly feline into a little girl with long blond hair, wearing a white apron over a blue dress.

"I didn't intend to be insulting. By the way, I've been meaning to ask you: What was that you said about boojums?"

"I said to watch out for them."

"Why?"

"Do you know what a boojum is?"

"Yes."

"Then the answer to your question should be evident."

"Well, I mean I don't know exactly. I do know that it's a kind of snark."

"Yes, that's right."

"Are there other kinds of snarks, as well?"

"There are, basically, two sorts of snarks: those that have feathers and bite, and those that have whiskers and scratch."

And with that the eyes and smile faded and were gone.

"What happened to you?" Zerika called as Megaera rejoined the rest of the group. "You look a lot cuter." Zerika's roadrunner was rather more anatomically correct than the Warner Brothers version, except for the fact that her wings terminated in a pair of white-gloved hands.

"I had a little run-in with Schrödinger's cat, but he didn't stick around very long. What about you guys?"

"Gunny found a house that's guarded by some kind of monster. We think that's where the djinni bottle is. We're just waiting for Ragnar to rejoin us."

A few moments later a large, not-very-bright-looking rabbit in a loincloth arrived, staggering under the weight of an enormous anvil.

"Ragnar, where did you get that?" The question was asked by a rather scrawny chicken in oversize spectacles and a red cape.

"I'd like to be able to say I ordered it from Acme, but there wasn't time. I found it in some bushes over there."

"My question," Megaera said, "is, Why on earth are you carrying it? Are you planning on shoeing some horses?"

"Oh, anvils can come in pretty handy in a cartoon. They're great for dropping on people's heads, for example."

Gunnodoyak led them across the unearthly landscape toward a cliff that overlooked the house he had discovered. The house itself was like a caricature of a Victorian haunted mansion, with broken windows, dilapidated shutters, and a sagging roof.

"Where's the monster?" Zerika whispered when they had reached a good vantage point from which to study their target.

"Just inside the front door," Gunnodoyak said. "A big, hairy bug-ger."

Ragnar pulled out the pistol he'd acquired in TrekMuck. "This should take care of the monster."

Gunnodoyak regarded him dubiously. "Are you sure that'll work on a 'toon?"

"You, turtle-boy, are manifestly unaware of the history and prove-nance of the dreaded scrooch gun. Allow me to demonstrate."

They approached the front door, found it locked, and Zerika bent to pick the lock, but before she could do so, the door swung open. A creature that answered the door appeared to be essentially a seven-foot-tall walking mass of fur, attired in a butler's costume except for the oversize sneakers it wore on its furry feet.

Zerika stood up, startled. "May we come in?"

The hairy monster stood aside and bowed, but as Zerika started to step through the door, it slammed it so hard, her beak stuck in the wood. Wild laughter emanated from within the house.

As Megaera tried to help Zerika free herself from the door by pulling on her legs, Tahmurath gave Ragnar a significant look, then reached forward and knocked. The hirsute butler answered the door again, swinging Zerika into the house along with the door, and Ragnar scrooched him. The effect was truly impressive; with his hair standing on end, he more than doubled in size.

Tahmurath walked around to the other side of the door, took his mallet, and whacked the protruding end of Zerika's beak, sending her flying off the porch and into the yard. She picked herself up and dashed back into the house. "Thanks. I think."

"Don't mention it."

"So what do you think?" Zerika asked. "Basement?"

Tahmurath nodded. "That sounds like the best bet."

They made their way toward the basement with Zerika in the lead, accompanied by Ragnar so that he could scrooch anything that approached, and there were many things that tried: giant bats, crocodiles, ghosts, carnivorous plants, and giant mechanical mice. Ragnar scrooched them all. "I hope that thing doesn't need to be recharged soon," Tahmurath was heard to mutter.

Beneath the house there was a maze of tunnels. They wandered about for some time, eventually coming to an intersection with several signs. One said Pismo Beach, and another one at right angles to it read Albuquerque.

"Let's try a little divination," Tahmurath suggested. "I'm getting tired of walking." He cast his spell, and the staff swung in the direction of the tunnel marked Albuquerque.

After a bit more walking, the tunnel opened out into a desert landscape, at the foot of a craggy outcropping. The outline of a large door could be faintly seen on one side. Zerika moved to check it for traps.

"Why are you doing that?" Ragnar joked. "Why don't we just say, 'Open sesame'?"

As soon as the words were out of his mouth, the door began to move. With a sound like an automatic garage door, the stone portal slowly rose. Motioning the others to stay back, Zerika crept forward and peered around the edge of the door; unfortunately, just as she did so, a tremendous blast of fire emerged. When she drew back, the feathers on her head and neck had been singed to blackness. "A dragon," she announced. "A big one. And, no, it's not asleep."

While Gunnodoyak healed Zerika's burns, Tahmurath was saying, "I was wondering when we were going to get a fire-breather. I have an idea, though: I think there might be a way to put the fire out."

"How are you going to do that?" Zerika asked.

"With wind and water. I want all of you to get ready; when I say the word, charge in there."

After a few minutes of preparation Tahmurath was ready to cast his spells; he signaled to the others, and they rushed into the cavern, weapons drawn. The dragon, lying sprawled over a great hoard of gold, jewels, and other valuables, raised its head and opened its mouth. At that moment Tahmurath finished casting his spell, and about a thousand gallons of water flew through the air toward the dragon—and landed squarely on Ragnar. Before the dragon could breathe on him, Ragnar fired the scrooch gun. Unfortunately, it had no effect, so the dragon breathed on him anyway, completely engulfing him in flame.

When the flames cleared, Ragnar was, remarkably, still standing. His thick rabbit fur, soaked with the water from Tahmurath's spell and now emitting clouds of steam, had apparently protected him. Now, instead of the scrooch gun, he held Gram.

The dragon, apparently assuming that Ragnar had been cremated, was already turning to seek another target, exposing its neck to the blow that Ragnar now swung. Gram bit cleanly, deeply, and completely through the tree-trunk-thick neck, and the dragon's head fell to the cavern floor, nearly squashing Ragnar in the process. He didn't seem to notice; instead, he stood staring at the sword in his hand.

"Not bad," Megaera commented, "but that seemed a little different from what we'd planned."

Tahmurath shrugged and spread his hands palms up. "Hey, even I miss sometimes."

"Is this what we're looking for?" Gunnodoyak called. He was pointing to a small bottle that lay practically underneath one of the dead dragon's forepaws.

"That's it," Zerika agreed. "Any volunteers?"

"Aw, who wants to live forever, anyway?" Ragnar said, picking up the bottle and pulling the stopper.

"Free at last!"

A blue-skinned colossus towered over them, shaking his fists in the air. Ragnar looked up at him. "Do we get our three wishes now?" he asked.

The huge djinni appeared to notice him for the first time. "Wishes!" he roared. "The only wishing you're going to be doing is to wish that you were never born!"

"Wait a minute!" Ragnar yelped, retreating a few steps. "You, uh . . . you don't really expect us to believe that you were in that bottle, do you?"

"Of course I was in the bottle, imbecile! You let me out—and that will be your undoing."

"But I don't understand how someone as big as you could fit into this tiny little bottle."

"Well, then, I'll prove it to you. I'll just get back inside—*NOT*! I didn't fall off the falafel truck yesterday, Sabu. Why, I ought to stuff you inside that thing and see how *you* like it."

"No," said Tahmurath quietly as he completed a set of intricate gestures. "It is I who will stuff you back inside."

The djinni threw back his head and roared with laughter. "You, old man? Why, I'll kick your liver-spotted butt all the way to mmmmffff!"

The djinni's words were abruptly cut off as a huge disembodied hand closed around his head. The hand was, despite its evident solidity, practically transparent, so that the djinni's contorted features could be seen writhing within its grip. A second hand closed around the djinni's torso, and the two began to knead him like a ball of clay—or maybe a blob of ooblick. The enormous hands seemed to mirror the motions of Tahmurath's own hands, which he now brought together palm to palm, rolling the djinni into a smaller and smaller sphere.

"Ragnar, the bottle, please." Ragnar proffered the requested vessel, and one of the giant hands took the now pea-sized djinni-ball delicately between thumb and forefinger and dropped it in. Ragnar quickly jammed the stopper in place. A faint buzzing sound could now be heard coming from within the bottle.

"I'm getting the download now," Tahmurath said. "Just a sec, I want to see what this is."

"Is it anything good?" Gunnodoyak asked.

"A software agent, I think. Must be a pretty smart one—this is a big file."

The band of adventurers stood before an opening in a mountain, amid a wide crescent of rocky cliffs facing an expanse of gray pounding surf. The path to the oracle had been well worn by the tread of thousands of feet over the centuries. Carved into the cliff face was the inscription "Know thyself." It was surrounded by graffiti, recommending "For a good time call Phryne" or advising that "Epimenides is a cretin."

"Okay, I can see the argument for consulting an oracle," Zerika said. "But why this one in particular?"

"Well, for one thing, the Delphic oracle is probably the most famous one in antiquity," Megaera answered. "Secondly, it's supposed to be the site of an omphalos, or earth navel, which I think is connected with the idea of megaliths, leys, and so on. And, thirdly, it supposedly occupies the site where Apollo slew the dragon Python. In fact, according to some versions of the myth, the oracle was originally dedicated to Python. The priestess was known as the Pythoness even after Apollo took over."

"Will we get to see the omphalos?" Ragnar asked.

"Why do you want to see it?"

"I've always wondered whether the earth has an innie or an outie."

"You're a sick man."

They entered. As they stood waiting for their eyes to adjust to the light, a tall figure approached from the shadowy recesses of the cave. The priestess was almost as tall as Megaera, with a large, square jaw and a decidedly unfeminine physique that was not well concealed by the diaphanous veils that were her only garments. She cleared her throat ostentatiously and began to speak in a falsetto, with an accent that was geographically closer to East London than to Asia Minor.

"Welcome to the oracle at Delphi. Please take a number."

She indicated a roll of paper tape in a dispenser affixed to one of the cavern walls. Zerika tore a piece from the end of the tape and read, "Number one thousand six hundred thirty-eight."

The priestess called out in her absurd falsetto, "Number seven? Does anyone have number seven?"

"Wait a minute," Megaera said. "There's no one else here."

"Number seven? Would whoever has number seven please step forward?"

"Look, there's no one else here. Why don't you just take us now?"

The priestess's oversize jaw seemed to jut forward even farther. "I'm sorry, but I have to follow procedure. Number eight? Does anyone have number eight?"

"But this is ridiculous!"

"Number eight! Will number eight please come forward now?"

Ragnar snatched the piece of paper tape from Zerika and tore it into two pieces. Then he handed one piece to the priestess. "Here. Number eight."

"I'm sorry, but you're too late. I'm up to number nine now. Number nine!"

They had to wait until she got to number sixteen. When she did, they surrounded her expectantly.

"Back up, back up, give a girl a little room." They did. She proceeded to clear her throat noisily for about five minutes. Then she closed her eyes. Suddenly she threw herself to the floor, writhing and screaming and foaming at the mouth. After several minutes of this she abruptly stopped and lay still, her eyes closed. She lay that way for several more minutes, during which Ragnar was sure that she glanced over at them, then quickly shut her eyes again, at least twice.

At length, perhaps because they didn't seem to be going away, she opened her mouth and intoned:

> *"In fact or in fable*
> *The first Attic ruler.*
> *The latter was fierce*
> *But the former was crueler.*
> *For further instruction,*
> *Advice, or suggestion,*
> *Please visit the sphinx*
> *And answer her question."*

▲   ▲   ▲   ▲   ▲   ▲   ▲

"How is it coming, Krishna?"

"Not so good, even with the boss's 'ring of the king' decryption program. This is trickier than I thought."

"Well, how much longer, do you think?"

"There's just no way to tell. I might crack it tomorrow, or it might take another thousand years."

"Great. Have you got *anything* for me?"

"Not really. Oh, that password that doesn't change—the guy's name is Bishop—there's something weird about it. I think it only has four characters."

"I thought the system required at least eight."

"It does, but he must have found a way to get around that, too."

"Oh. Well, look, I think it's time to try another strategy."

"Like what?"

"I've been thinking about this guy Bishop. . . ."

"Yeah?"

"To do what he did, he'd pretty much have to have cracked root access." Manipulating the security system the way he had would almost certainly be limited to superusers.

"Okay, I'll buy that. But how does that help us?"

"Let's see if we can get his password. If we can get into his account, maybe we can find out how he cracked root."

"Well, okay. If his password's only four characters we could brute-force it—"

"No, no way. They might be a little sloppy over there, but if it shows up in the security log that Bishop misspelled his own password two hundred thousand times, somebody's definitely going to get suspicious."

"You have another idea?"

"Well, we know this guy's really attached to his password, right?"

"Seems like it."

"Well, a lot of times people use their passwords for lots of different things. If he's that enamored of his password, I bet he's using it for something else."

"Like what? You think maybe he's a MUDhead too?"

"Could be, but that's not what I had in mind. What has four characters and everybody's got one?"

"An ATM PIN code?"

"You got it."

"How are we going to get his PIN code?"

"We're going to try a little shoulder surfing."

▲   ▲   ▲   ▲   ▲   ▲   ▲

The sound was like a woman's laughter, with a curious undercurrent reminiscent of the sound of a large engine—say the V-12 in a Jaguar XJS—quiet and understated, but with a suggestion of considerable power. As they cleared the crest of a small hill, they got their first sight of the walls of Thebes, and also of the creature making the noise. She had the head, face, and breasts of a woman, grafted onto a leonine body from which sprouted a reptilian tail and a pair of large wings— not the leathery bat-type wings one might expect on a mammal, but the feathered pinions of a large bird of prey. She was perched on the gate into the city. A man wearing Grecian armor and a horsehair-crested helm stood before her, and the two seemed to be chatting amicably.

"Gee," Ragnar said, "maybe she's friendlier than her reputation suggests."

At that moment she pounced on the Greek warrior and devoured him whole.

Megaera arched her eyebrows. "Yeah, pretty friendly. Must have invited him over for dinner."

"So," Gunnodoyak said, "if we get the answer to the riddle wrong, she's probably going to try to eat us, too."

"Maybe we'll get lucky," Megaera suggested, "and she'll ask us the same riddle she asked Oedipus."

"I doubt it."

"Me too."

"Just out of curiosity," Gunnodoyak said, "what was the original riddle?"

"It was, What goes on four legs in the morning, two legs in the afternoon, and three legs in the evening?"

"Hmmm. How about a trained circus dog that gets taken out to make wee-wee after the show?" Ragnar suggested.

"The answer is man. He crawls in infancy, then learns to walk upright, then uses a cane in old age."

"I like my answer better."

As they approached the sphinx, who had resumed her perch on the gate into the city, she looked up at them and licked her lips with a disturbingly long tongue. She looked them over one by one, seeming to linger noticeably on Ali. Finally, she said, "Will you essay the riddle?"

"We will," Zerika answered.

"Hold it," Ragnar interjected. "How about if we ask *you* a riddle?"

The sphinx frowned. "This is somewhat irregular, but I don't know of any rule against it. Okay. Just make sure it's a real riddle; no asking what you have in your pockets, or anything like that."

Ragnar turned to the others. "Well?"

Tahmurath shrugged. "Do you have a particular riddle in mind?"

"Uh-huh."

"Then go for it," Zerika suggested.

Ragnar turned to face the sphinx. He drew himself up, cleared his throat noisily, then spoke: "What has four wheels and flies?"

The sphinx didn't bat a whisker. "A garbage truck. I should have put in a proviso about anachronisms, too. Very well, now it's my turn. What is it that goes sometimes on four legs, sometimes on two, sometimes on none, and sometimes on wings?"

"Um, can we have some time to talk this over?"

"Go right ahead." She smiled, revealing an impressive set of fangs.

The group went into a huddle. "Whoa, talk about a fake-out," Ragnar said. "I thought it was the same riddle until she got to the part about wings."

"It's not the same riddle, but maybe it's the same answer," Megaera suggested.

"Man?" Tahmurath said. "How do you figure?"

"Well, people fly in planes. They also ride in cars, which would be going on no legs."

"Hmm, could be. But this is ancient Greece, and there aren't any cars or planes yet. Remember what she said about anachronisms."

"You've got a point there. But it must be something along those lines; I don't think there are any animals with wings that also have four legs. Birds and bats have two legs, and insects have six. What has four legs and wings?"

"She does," Ali pointed out.

"That's right," Zerika agreed. "Remember, this isn't historical ancient Greece; it's mythical ancient Greece. The answer to the riddle might be some kind of mythical creature." She turned to the sphinx again. "How much time do we have?"

The creature grinned, again displaying her mouthful of long, sharp fangs. "Take as long as you want. Go home and sleep on it, for all I care. Just do me one favor."

"What?"

"When you come back to try to answer it, come around lunch-time, hmm?"

"I think we'd better take her advice," Zerika told the others.

"About sleeping on it, or coming back at lunchtime?"

"Take your pick. Obviously, we want to be really sure of this be-fore we answer."

"Why don't we just fight her?" Ali suggested. "We've killed bigger monsters than that."

Tahmurath shook his head. "We might have to do that as a last resort. Don't be misled by her comparative size, though. It's easy enough to program the game so that a puppy is unkillable. If the game calls for us to solve a riddle at this stage of things, it's not too likely that we're going to progress beyond this point without solving it."

At that moment an old, blind beggar came hobbling up to where they were standing. He stopped and leaned on his staff, grinning at them as if he could see them with his empty eye sockets. "Need some help with the riddle, do you?"

"Yes!" Zerika said. "Can you help us?"

"Of course. I solved the riddle of the Sphinx myself once," he said, thumping himself on the chest for emphasis. "Oh, not this sphinx, another one. I can't give you the answer to the riddle, that wouldn't be kosher, but I can tell you how to puzzle it out."

Gunnodoyak bowed. "Enlighten us, oh great riddle master."

The old man found a rock the right size and seated himself com-fortably as the adventurers gathered around him, then began to sing:

> "I'll tell you how a riddler thinks,
> A marvel to relate.
> I met a large, ferocious Sphinx
> A-sitting on a gate.
> 'What thing goes on four legs?' she said,
> 'Four while the day is young?'
> And the answer trickled through my head
> And rattled off my tongue.
>
> "I said, 'I've heard of furniture
> With four legs on the floor.

Isosceles triangles, sure:
A pair would number four.
An ostrich with a rider
Might be said to have four legs,
Not to mention half a spider,
Or two chickens laying eggs.'

"But she had something else in mind,
I saw it in her face.
And I needs must the answer find
Or perish in that place.
She shook me well from side to side,
Until my face turned blue.
'Then tell me what, at noon,' she cried,
'Gets up and goes on two?'

"In soothing tones I made reply,
'A broken three-leg stool,
The middle of a butterfly,
The hind end of a mule,
These things would need, you must concede,
To have a pair of gams;
One fiftieth of a centipede
Or just a pair of clams.'

"But she had something else in mind,
I heard it in her voice,
And I was in a fearful bind
To find the proper choice.
She seized the author of this rhyme
And growled ferociously.
'And what,' she roared, 'in evening time
Goes out and walks on three?'

" 'A man!' I cried (her eyes flew wide),
'Astride a quarter-horse.'
'A man!' I squealed (her senses reeled)
'On the first stage of a course.'
'A man!' I brayed (her body swayed),

'In half a business suit.'
'A man . . .' I said. (She fell down dead!
Which made the whole thing moot.)

"And now if e'er by chance I put
A finger up my nose,
Or madly stuff a swollen foot
Into a garden hose,
Or if I drop upon my toe a very heavy weight,
I weep, for it reminds me so
Of that old Sphinx I used to know
Whose look was fierce, whose growl was low,
Who brought the Thebans untold woe,
With eyes like cinders, all aglow,
To terrify her every foe,
Who liked to quote Jean Jacques Rousseau,
And also Larry, Shemp, and Moe,
Who mimed with gestures soft and slow,
As if she were Marcel Marceau,
With breasts like Marilyn Monroe,
That fateful evening, long ago,
A-sitting on a gate."

When it was clear that the old man had finished, Ragnar said, "Excuse me, but how exactly is that supposed to help us?"

Abruptly, the old man lurched up from the rock and started to hobble away. "I'm sorry, but I have to go," he said. "I think I hear my mother calling me." As he retreated, his toga slipped off one shoulder, revealing a birthmark or tattoo of some kind—the sign of the ouroboros.

Ragnar started to go after him, but Gunnodoyak called him back. "Don't bother. I think I figured it out."

The others stared at him. "You did?" Zerika asked. "You know the answer to the riddle?"

"Yeah, I think so. Just think: What have we been fighting in all of these MUDs? The guivre, the lindworm, the wyvern, the amphis-baena, even the Klingon Dragon Ship. They're all variations on a theme."

"Dragon variations?" Ragnar laughed.

"Yeah. All except for the vampire MUD, anyway."

"You mean you don't know?" Megaera said.

"Know what?"

"The name 'Dracula.' It means 'dragon.' I'm sure you're right. As a matter of fact, I think that's what the Pythoness was trying to tell us."

"The Pythoness?" Tahmurath asked.

"Yes: 'In fact or in fable, the first Attic ruler.' I didn't see what she was getting at, but now I think I do: The earliest lawgiver of Athens, which is in the part of Greece called Attica, was Draco."

"Meaning 'dragon,' " Zerika supplied. "Okay, but if that's supposed to be fact, then what about fable?"

"There are a couple of Greek myths about the first kings of Athens or Attica. They were supposed to be men who were dragons from the waist down—earth-born serpent-kings, they're sometimes called."

"Hmm, a man named Draco and men who were half serpents," Tahmurath said. "Not exactly dragons, but close enough for government work."

"You better not let the Pentagon hear you say that," Zerika told him. "But what was that part about 'the former was crueler,' Megaera?"

"Well, Draco's law was known for its harshness. That's where we get the word 'draconian.' "

"You mean like 'an eye for an eye'?"

"More like a *head* for an eye. I think the punishment for most crimes was death."

"That must have cut down on the repeat offenders," Tahmurath said. "I think you're right, though; 'dragon' must be the answer to the riddle. Come on, let's go back to the sphinx and tell her. Gunny, since you figured it out, why don't you do the honors?"

If Gunnodoyak felt any doubts about his answer, they didn't show. He approached the sphinx and said, "We're ready to answer the riddle now."

"Already?" she said a bit petulantly. "I thought I asked you to come back at lunchtime. Oh, well, anytime is snack time."

"The answer," Gunnodoyak said, "is a dragon."

She stared at him. He stared back. "Well," she said at last, "I hope you don't think I'm going to kill myself just because you got the right answer. I mean, it's not really that important to me."

"I don't want you to kill yourself, but I would like to know where to find Eltanin."

"I don't know," she admitted. "But if you want to find out, you're going to have to go to Babylon and visit Etemenanki."

"Etemenanki?"

"Yes. You may have heard of it. It's also known as the Tower of Babel. Consider well: Petitioners to Etemenanki are allowed but one question."

"One more question," Ragnar said. "Do you know anything about the tattoo that old man had on him?"

"Tattoo?"

"Yes, like a snake swallowing its tail."

"Oh, that. That would be the mark of the Sparti."

▲   ▲   ▲   ▲   ▲   ▲   ▲

If it's true that the Inuit have a hundred different words for "snow," then one of them must translate somewhat along the lines of "that which the weather shaman said would be 'light flurries' but which has already completely buried the dogsled and isn't showing any sign of letting up." The predicted "light flurries" were already piling up alarmingly as I hurried along on my way to the dojo.

Jamaal led us in a typically vigorous workout, then suggested that we all go outside for a little run in the snow, barefoot of course. As the group headed for the door, I moved to the *makiwara,* a piece of rope-wrapped wood used in karate training, and started throwing some punches at it. Jamaal noticed and came over to me. "You're not wimping out on me, are you?" I just smiled and nodded. He started to say something, then just shook his head and left with the rest of the class.

About half an hour later I was drying off from my shower when Jamaal led the group back from their dogless Iditarod. "How was it?" I asked him when he came into the locker room.

"It was great! You really should have come. You know, once we'd gone a block or two, it didn't really even seem cold anymore."

"Well, the worst part isn't over yet."

"What? What do you mean?"

"I've run barefoot in the snow before. My first *sensei* was an ex-marine; he was into that kind of stuff. Once your feet get cold enough, they're too numb to feel anything. But when they start to thaw out, they're going to burn like hell."

Jamaal looked down at his own feet with some consternation. I think he was already starting to get a little feeling back. "Why did you wait till now to tell me this?"

"You would have gone anyway."

He flashed a slightly pained grin. "You're probably right."

As I walked out, I could hear the first screams emanating from the showers.

CHAPTER FOURTEEN

The Power of Babble

Thou must prophesy again before many peoples,
and nations, and tongues, and kings.
—Revelation 10:11

A small temple stood before the north gate of the great city. As the party approached, they could see some activity taking place; acolytes with shaven heads busily scrubbing and sweeping, under the supervision of an older man wearing an ornate headdress. Tahmurath approached him.

"Greetings, holy one."

The man smiled blandly. "In the name of Marduk, greetings."

"Isn't it a little early for spring cleaning?"

"At the New Year's festival the great Marduk himself visits this temple. We prepare for his coming."

"I see. Can you tell us how to find Etemenanki?"

The priest turned and gestured toward the city. "That is Etemenanki," he said, pointing to an enormous ziggurat that could be seen towering above the city walls. "Pass through the Ishtar Gate and follow the Processional Way."

"Thank you, holy one."

"Your gratitude is unnecessary. But for the glory of Marduk, perhaps a donation . . . ?"

Tahmurath fished around in a sack and finally withdrew an emerald the size of a golf ball. The priest accepted it and slipped it inside his sleeve with the same bland expression.

"Tahmurath!"

"What, Zerika?"

"You're overtipping again."

"Yes, dear."

The massive, fortified gate was emblazoned with enamel bulls and dragons. Just before the gate stood a statue: a lion in basalt, larger than life-size. As the group approached the gate, the lion opened its great jaws and spoke:

> *"Six blind men of Babylon,*
> *Or so the tale is told,*
> *Set forth one day from Babylon*
> *A marvel to behold.*
>
> *"The sages had prevailed upon*
> *A farmer with a wagon*
> *To take them to a cave where they*
> *Might see the mighty dragon.*
>
> *"The first sage felt the scales and said,*
> *'As sure as I'm a wizard,*
> *I see the dragon's nothing but*
> *A slightly bloated lizard.'*
>
> *"The second felt the dragon's wing*
> *All leathery and flat.*
> *He said, 'I see the dragon*
> *Is a largish sort of bat.'*
>
> *"The third sage grasped a talon*
> *And said, 'Don't be absurd.*
> *'Tis plain to see the dragon*
> *Is nothing but a bird.'*
>
> *"The fourth sage wrapped his arms around*
> *The long tail of the drake*

And said, 'I see the dragon
Is merely a big snake.'

"The fifth sage chanced to touch upon
The dragon's toothy smile
And said, 'I see the dragon
Is just a crocodile.'

"As dragon's fire singed his beard,
The sixth cried, 'Hellfire burn us!
Why, anyone can clearly see
The dragon's like a furnace!'

"Before the wise men's bickering
Runs on for many pages,
Let us now ask the dragon
Its impression of the sages.

"It said, 'Their disposition's
Reminiscent of a stoat.
The visage like a monkey's
With the odor of a goat.

" 'As hairy as a bandicoot,
And as bony as a stork,
But what little meat was on them
Had a flavor quite like pork.' "

"What was that all about?" Ragnar asked.

"Some kind of a clue, no doubt," Tahmurath said. "Any ideas, anyone?"

"Not offhand," Zerika admitted. "Maybe it was just a veiled threat. But did you see how it smiled when it was finished? There was something awfully familiar about that smile."

"I know what you mean," Megaera agreed, "and I think you may be right about the threat."

"Why?"

"I've been wondering why, if the Wyrm is so powerful, it doesn't just annihilate us now. Why let us get any more powerful? Unless it's just fattening us up for the kill."

"Not necessarily," Tahmurath demurred. "Just because it's powerful doesn't mean it's completely unconstrained. Remember, it seems to have arisen out of Dworkin's game, or at least to exist in some kind of symbiosis with it. It might have no choice other than to play by the rules of the game. Violating them might be a kind of suicide."

"Could be," Gunnodoyak said. "Or maybe it just doesn't consider us a serious threat."

The base of the great ziggurat covered over two acres of ground, and it rose steeply in a series of seven steps culminating in the temple of blue glaze that stood at the summit, over three hundred feet above the surrounding plain. Ivy covered the vertical surfaces of the pyramid, except for the lowest and highest levels, and all manner of flowering trees and shrubs grew in abundance on its broad terraces.

"So that's supposed to be it?" Ragnar asked. "The Tower of Babel? I thought it was supposed to have been left uncompleted."

"This one seems to be pretty well done," Zerika remarked. "Well, this is where we get the answer to the big question: Where the hell is Eltanin?"

"Are you sure we shouldn't ask *what* it is?" Megaera said.

"We only get one question," Tahmurath reminded her. "Knowing what it is won't necessarily help us find it. We can figure out what it is when we get it."

"I guess you're right," Megaera conceded.

They approached the base of the ziggurat, where a set of great doors stood open. A fat monk sat in the lotus position on the high wall that enclosed the first stage of the stepped pyramid. He was really remarkably obese; he seemed to have no neck at all, and his jowls and extra chins seemed to merge into his shoulders, giving him an ovoid appearance.

Zerika approached the wall and shouted up to him, "We're here to ask a question of the oracle."

At first the monk did not seem to hear her, or perhaps he was deliberately ignoring her.

"Maybe he's meditating," Gunnodoyak suggested.

"It's really very provoking," the fat monk said, "when people don't bother themselves to read the directions." He pointed to the wall in front of them, which bore a plaque inscribed with odd glyphs.

"We can't read these," Megaera protested.

The monk clucked his tongue, although whether he did so pityingly or disapprovingly is difficult to say. "Illiterates? And in this day and age!"

"We are not illiterate!" Megaera protested. "We read English quite well, thank you."

"Ah, then if the plaque were in English, you would be able to read it?"

"Yes. Now, can you tell us what it says?"

"Why, it says nothing at all; it's only a plaque, you know. Plaques don't speak."

"I know they don't speak," Megaera replied evenly. "What I mean is, what do these glyphs signify?"

"It's really very simple. They signify exactly the same thing as they would if the sign were in English. You did say you could read English?"

"But these aren't in English," she reminded him.

"Then you are in luck."

"In luck?"

"Yes, because if you can't read the glyphs, they can signify anything you would like them to signify."

Megaera gave a strangled little shriek and seemed about to go for her sword, but Ragnar intervened smoothly. "You can read the glyphs, can't you?"

"Of course."

"And you obviously speak English. Can you translate them for us?"

The monk nodded. "I can. But I won't." Instead he pointed to a frieze that was carved into the outer wall of the first level of the stepped pyramid. It depicted all manner of fanciful beasts, many of which were mythical. At regular intervals there were large plaques with characters carved into them.

"They seem to be different languages," Zerika observed. "Maybe there's one in English farther along. Let's go."

They passed hundreds of the plaques, most of which contained languages and alphabets that were completely unfamiliar to anyone in the party. There were runes, hieroglyphics, cuneiform writing, ideograms of various types, and so on. When they had almost completed a circuit of the pyramid's base, a distance of nearly a quarter mile, they came to a plaque engraved in English. It read:

Go through the upper entrance, descend six levels, take the third hallway on the left, then enter the fourteenth doorway on the right.

"The upper entrance?" Gunnodoyak said. "Where's that supposed to be?"

Tahmurath pointed to the top of the pyramid, where the blue-glazed walls of the seventh level could be seen. "I guess we're going up there."

They found that a series of staircases connected the terraces, and they began the climb. As the initial stage of the pyramid was the highest, the climb to the first terrace was also the longest. When they reached the first terrace, they found they would have to go around to the other side of the pyramid to reach the stairs to the second terrace. The air was heavily perfumed with the odor of a thousand exotic flowers.

"You know," Megaera commented, "there's a school of thought that says that story of the Hanging Gardens of Babylon, which were supposed to be one of the seven wonders of the world, derived from descriptions of the trees and plants growing on this pyramid."

"Looks like whoever programmed this subscribes to that theory," Tahmurath said.

They were passing through a grove of small trees where the air seemed especially aromatic. Suddenly Zerika yanked Tahmurath away from one of the trees so forcefully that they both went sprawling.

"What is it?" Tahmurath demanded, struggling to his feet.

"There." Zerika pointed to the branch that was nearest to where Tahmurath had been walking. A reddish snake was coiled around it. The snake sported a pair of wings. "What do you want to bet it's poisonous?"

Tahmurath shook his gray head. "I don't think I want to take that bet."

"Look there," Megaera said, indicating an area of the same branch with the tip of her sword. The underside of the branch seemed to have been scraped with a sharp instrument. A golden resin had oozed from the excoriated bark and beaded up on the surface. It seemed to be the source of the smell. "I think it must be a frankincense tree."

"Ooh, let's get some," Ragnar said.

"Why?" Megaera asked.

"Well, I hear it makes a great Christmas present."

"He's right," Zerika said. "We might need it for something later on."

Working cautiously with the tips of unsheathed swords, they did manage to scrape off some of the beads of resin. The trees turned out to be full of winged snakes, but the serpents seemed willing to let them take some of the resin, as long as they didn't get too close.

As they were harvesting the resin, Zerika's sharp ears picked up a faint sound from deeper within the grove of frankincense trees. Motioning them to be quiet, she crept toward the center of the grove, attempting to pick a path that kept them a safe distance from the snake-infested trees. After she had gone a dozen meters, she turned and motioned the others to join her.

When they did, they beheld a curious sight. A single tree, much larger than the others, occupied the center of a clearing in the middle of the grove. Hanging by one ankle, which appeared to be tied with a long rope to one of the tree's branches, was a tall, slender middle-aged man with a shock of unruly white hair, wearing a pair of overalls and gardening gloves. A hoe, a rake, a pair of pruning shears, and other implements littered the ground at the foot of the tree. He was singing. As they got closer, they were able to understand some of the words:

> *"He thought he saw a paradox*
> *That proved AI was dead.*
> *He looked again and saw it was*
> *A severed chicken's head.*
> *'The horror of the thing,' he said,*
> *'Evokes a nameless dread.'"*

"Can we help you?" Zerika called. "Do you want us to get you down from there?"

He ignored her and continued to sing, all the while swinging back and forth by his tethered ankle like a human pendulum:

> *"He thought he saw a rogue AI*
> *That passed the Turing test.*
> *He looked again and saw it was*
> *An empty dodo's nest.*

'It nearly had me fooled,' he said,
'But lacked a certain zest.'"

Zerika shrugged. "He's obviously quite mad."

"Look at the gardening tools," Megaera suggested. "At first I thought they were just strewn at random, but they seem to be laid out in some kind of pattern."

The tools did indeed seem to be laid out along the partial circumference of a circle, with the handles of the longer tools, such as the rake and hoe, aligned radially so that they pointed to the circle's center.

"You're right," Ragnar said. "He's a Foucault pendulum. As the earth rotates, the pendulum's swing will be aligned with different points along these arcs."

As the gardener didn't seem to have any desire to be helped down from the tree, and even seemed to be serving some kind of purpose where he was, there didn't seem to be anything further to do in the grove, so they continued on their way.

The rest of their passage up the pyramid was uneventful, and they arrived at an upper entrance, which was not, it turned out, on the uppermost level, but on the level just below.

After following the directions they had taken from the plaque, they arrived at a small room, with a monk seated on a cushion at a low desk. Zerika tried to speak to him, but he merely shook his head and pointed to the opposite wall. It contained several dozen small cubbyholes and another plaque:

Spell out your question with the tiles provided, then give them to the monk at the desk.

On closer examination the cubbyholes were found to contain some ivory rectangles that looked like an unusual set of dominoes. On one half of each domino was a letter in the English alphabet. On the other half was a single hieroglyph.

There was also a black marble tablet etched with grooves that were apparently to be used for arranging the tiles. Zerika selected the necessary ones and spelled out, "Where is Eltanin?" She then brought the tablet to the monk.

He immediately went to work, removing another set of tiles from his desk. Each of these tiles had a hieroglyph on one side, but the other contained a wide variety of different types of letters or characters. After selecting a set of his own tiles, he then passed them through niches to some of the adjoining rooms. There were a total of four niches, and some tiles were passed through each one.

"Come on," Zerika said, striding toward the next room down the hall. "I want to see what they're doing."

What the monk in the next room was doing was quite similar to what the first one had already done. He had his own set of tiles, with one side in Aramaic letters, and the other side a wide sampling of different alphabets. He took several of his tiles, passed them through niches, including one that went back to the first monk, then walked across the hall to deliver a tile there. This process was carried out repeatedly, until the whole party got tired of watching it. They walked back toward the stairs to the upper entrance.

"What the hell is going on?" Tahmurath said. "When are we going to get our answer?"

"I think," Ragnar said, "that what we are watching is the operation of a kind of computer."

"A computer?" Gunnodoyak said. "What do you mean?"

"These monks—I think they're carrying out an algorithm. They all seem to speak different languages, so they can't communicate with each other. Each one receives some letters in his own language, then manipulates those tiles and passes on the results in accordance with some kind of instruction set. It's a little like a Chinese Room."

"I hope," Zerika said, "that's not some kind of joke, like a Chinese Fire Drill."

"Or a Mongolian Clusterfuck," Gunnodoyak added.

"Hey!"

"Not at all. The Chinese Room was an argument put forth by John Searle to refute the notion of artificial intelligence, and particularly the validity of the Turing test. He pointed out that any set of instructions that could be carried out by computer could also, given enough time, be carried out by a human being. Suppose, then, that you had a computer program that was designed to read stories in Chinese and then answer some questions about them. It's questionable whether that would be within the range of current AI technology; it might even require something close to a solution to the Natural Language Problem. At any rate, the guy in the room could carry out the same instructions, which would result in the same output: answers to the questions about the Chinese story. And he wouldn't actually have to know any Chinese at all."

"But he would just be performing the role of hardware," Megaera pointed out. "Suppose the intelligence resides in the algorithm?"

"That argument has been made," Ragnar acknowledged.

"So, actually, this whole setup could itself be an artificial intelligence."

"I think that's exactly the idea," Ragnar agreed.

"That's all well and good," Zerika said, "but I'd still like to know when we're going to get our answer."

When they returned to the pyramid's entrance, the fat monk on the wall favored them with a condescending glance and sniffed, "Return in three days for the answer to your question."

"Three days!" Zerika exclaimed. "I wonder if that's game time or real time."

"I guess we'll need to find out how game time runs in this particular MUD," Tahmurath said.

"We can go back to the Foucault pendulum to figure that one out—but I don't think this is a MUD," Gunnodoyak opined.

Tahmurath was nonplussed. "What do you mean, it's not a MUD? What else could it be?"

"I mean, I don't think it's one of the normal MUDs that Dworkin's program links together. I think it's a special part of his program."

"That sounds plausible," Zerika agreed. "It's certainly not like any MUD I've ever played."

▲　▲　▲　▲　▲　▲　▲

The cathode-ray tube used as a monitor screen in most computers creates the images we see by firing a beam of electrons at a phosphor-coated screen. Each time the gun fires, it emits a burst of electromagnetic radiation; some of this is radio frequency. Not only is it possible in theory, but the technology exists to receive these radio waves, combine them with a computer-generated synchronization signal, and read what's on a computer screen a mile away. This sounds like the ultimate in shoulder surfing, and it is—except for one thing. Passwords don't appear on the screen.

It was a simple matter, using Art's recently acquired djinni software agent, to find out where Ken Bishop banked, and even which ATM he usually used. We even knew, from readily accessible parts of Macrobyte's personnel files, what he looked like.

It was a Friday afternoon, and I was sitting in a car parked across the street from an ATM not far from Macrobyte's software-development facility. Krishna came out of a nearby McDonald's with a large take-out bag in hand—the kid was a bottomless pit. He handed me a cup of coffee.

"Any sign of him yet?" he asked.

I shook my head and took a sip of the coffee. It tasted like lukewarm battery acid. "I just hope he doesn't pick this week to change his usual pattern." Bishop was, like most of us, a creature of habit. Maybe even more so than most of us, as his attachment to his password suggested. He usually stopped at this particular ATM after work on Friday, presumably to withdraw money for the weekend.

We had arrived several hours earlier in order to make some preparations. There was now a small TV camera, of the type sold for security purposes, affixed near the top of the ATM with black electrical tape. It gave us a good view of the keypad, although there was a possibility that it could be obscured if the person using the ATM leaned his head too far in. To hedge against that possibility, we had George stationed nearby armed with a camcorder with a 20:1 zoom.

"Here he comes!" Krishna exclaimed around a mouthful of french fries.

A slim, dark-skinned man was ambling down the street toward the ATM. He certainly looked like the picture we'd seen of Bishop, although it was a bit difficult to say for sure at that distance. As he neared the ATM, a sixtyish-looking woman approached from the opposite direction. They arrived at the ATM at roughly the same time, and Bishop politely stood aside, allowing her to go first.

"What the hell is she doing?" I said after she'd been there for almost ten minutes.

"Maybe she doesn't know how it works," Krishna suggested.

"I can't believe this. Nobody has used this thing in the last hour, and she has to come along right now?"

"Well, I hope she's almost finished, because Bishop looks like he's starting to get impatient."

It was true. He'd been fidgeting noticeably for the past several minutes, and now he was looking off down the street. I turned to try to see what he was looking at. "Shit! There's another ATM half a block down that way."

Bishop looked back toward the woman, shrugged, then started to walk away, obviously intending to use the other ATM. Except that George intercepted him.

"What the hell does he think he's doing?" I exclaimed. If we had to come back and repeat this stakeout next week, George had just insured that Bishop would recognize him.

"Maybe he's just going to ask him for his PIN code," Krishna suggested.

"You know, I wouldn't put it past him."

The two now seemed to be having a fairly animated discussion. This went on for about ten minutes. By then the woman at the ATM had finished her time-consuming business and left. George and Ken Bishop finished their mysterious discussion, and George walked off down the street, apparently surmising that trying to stay and use the camcorder would be a little too obvious now.

Bishop turned to the now available ATM, and Krishna and I exchanged a surreptitious low-five. I could see on the monitor that we had a good view of the keypad, although Bishop's hand moved over it so swiftly, I couldn't make out the PIN code. That didn't matter; we were recording the whole thing and would be able to examine the tape in slo-mo, or even frame by frame if necessary.

George reappeared on the scene a few minutes after Bishop left. "Well?" he asked. "Did we get it?"

"Yeah. I have to give you credit, that was quick thinking. What the hell were you two talking about?"

"I asked him if he knew any good jazz clubs. It turns out he's an aficionado. He's even heard my trio play a few times."

"Oh, no! You mean he recognized you?"

"Nah, nobody ever recognizes the bass player."

▲　▲　▲　▲　▲　▲　▲

"It's been a long three days," Zerika said. "I hope our answer is ready."

"I have the answer," Ragnar said.

"*You* have the answer? What's that supposed to mean?"

"The answer to the question, Where is Eltanin? Also, *what* it is."

"Well, don't keep us in suspense," Megaera shouted. "What?"

"I thought the word had a familiar ring, but when I looked it up in a bunch of different places, I couldn't find it anywhere. The other night I tried looking for it using the UTM web-browser. Eltanin is the name of a star in the constellation Draco. It's in the head and is sometimes known as the Eye of the Dragon."

"The original clue," Tahmurath said, "was, 'If you wish to see, then seek Eltanin,' or something like that."

"The Eye of the Dragon." Zerika said. "It sounds like it could be some kind of scrying device."

"It would have to be pretty powerful to be worth all this trouble," Gunnodoyak suggested. "We already have some crystals and such, and Tahmurath has very potent divining spells."

"Wait a minute," Megaera interrupted. "Ragnar, I thought you said you knew where it was."

"I just told you—in the head of the dragon."

"Oh, right. Let's go check at the tower."

They approached the entrance as before and found a monk standing guard at the door, if "standing guard" is the right term for what he did; he certainly didn't make any attempt to interfere with anyone's comings or goings.

When he saw them approaching, he smiled in apparent recognition, bowed, and disappeared down a side passageway. In a moment he returned, bearing another of the black marble tablets. As before, ivory tiles were arranged to spell out a message:

To learn the whereabouts of Eltanin, you must behold the Great Seal.

Tahmurath groaned. "I hate oracles. They never give you a damn straight answer."

"So what does this mean?" Ragnar asked. "We're now looking for a large aquatic mammal?"

Zerika frowned. "I doubt they mean that kind of a seal."

"Maybe it's one of the seals in the Book of Revelation," Megaera suggested.

"Look," Ragnar said, "instead of going off on another wild-goose chase to find the Great Seal, why don't we just use what we already know: Eltanin is a star, the eye in the constellation Draco."

"How does that help us?" Zerika asked. "You think we should go back to TrekMUCK and fly the UTM out to Eltanin?"

"No, there's something else I've been meaning to tell you; I just figured it out last night. You remember the place where we first came into the game?" Obviously, it was a rhetorical question. "Well, look at this: It's a map of the constellations in part of the sky. Look, Orion the hunter, Canis Major and Minor, Monoceros the unicorn, Eridanus the river. I figure we came in right over here, in Hydra. Look, Corvus the crow, and Crater the jar."

"Ragnar, you're right!" Megaera exclaimed. "How did you figure this out?"

He laughed. "Actually, it was while Cassie was showing me some of her astrological charts."

"Damn!" Tahmurath exclaimed. "I think this will work. If we go back there and find Draco—"

"We'll have Eltanin!" Ragnar finished triumphantly.

With Gunnodoyak at the controls of the UTM, the party traversed cyberspace, arriving, at last, back in the world where they had originally entered the game. "I wonder if that giant is around," Megaera said. "We have a little score to settle with him."

"Well, you're not going to have long to wait," Zerika said. "Look."

Just ahead of them the huge huntsman came into view, his two dogs at his heels. They hurriedly scrambled from the UTM hatch, weapons at the ready.

The giant looked at them, his dinner-plate-size eyes widening. But instead of attacking, he said to them, "We have been expecting you. My king asks me to extend an invitation to you, to enjoy the hospitality of his hall."

"We accept," Zerika said.

"Please follow me."

They climbed back aboard the UTM and followed. The giant's long legs covered the ground swiftly, and a short time later they arrived at a massive gate that led into a mountain: the hall of the giant king.

. . .

"This is a setup, you know," Megaera whispered to Tahmurath.

"What do you mean?"

The giant king smiled down at them from his massive throne. He had invited them to enjoy the hospitality of his hall, and they had accepted. The catch seemed to be that now they were expected to entertain him by engaging in some "friendly" competition with his giant liegemen.

"But we just want to ask you some questions . . . ," Zerika was saying.

"After the contests!" the giant king boomed. "If you win, I will answer any three questions you wish." It was clear that he didn't think there was much chance of that happening.

"There's a Norse myth about this," Megaera continued, "about Thor and some of the other gods who visit the giants. The giants cheat."

"Yeah, I know that story. Don't worry—if they can cheat, then so can we."

"How are we supposed to do that?" Zerika demanded.

"You guys just do what you do best and leave the cheating to me."

"Come, now," the giant king boomed. "Do not allow yourselves to be restrained by modesty. Surely mighty heroes such as yourselves must be capable of great wonders. I would consider it an honor for you to perform some feats of prowess in my poor hall."

Zerika cleared her throat. "Your Majesty is too kind. We would consider it an honor to essay any test Your Majesty might suggest."

The king clapped his enormous hands with a sound like thunder. "Bring my drinking horn!" As a pair of human thralls staggered forward with a horn that was taller than either of them, the king said, "My liegemen sometimes amuse themselves in attempting to drain this horn at a single draft. Even the feeblest drinker among them can drain it in three drafts, but to be accounted a formidable drinker in this hall, one must succeed on the first. Would one of you care to attempt it?"

Megaera whispered to Tahmurath, "He's lying. In the myth the horn was connected to the sea. Thor couldn't empty it, even with three drafts."

Ragnar stepped forward. "I am a bit parched, Your Majesty, so if no one else minds . . ." With some effort he raised the horn to his lips and began to drink. The king watched him for a few minutes and then, when it became obvious that his first pull at the horn was not likely to end soon, turned to the others. "Even giants do not live by ale alone. In addition to drinking, we also do some serious feasting in my hall. Would any one of you care to test him- or herself against Logi, one of my middling trenchermen?"

This time Gunnodoyak volunteered. An enormous trencher was brought forward. Servants filled it with chopped meat.

"I hope that's not beef," Gunnodoyak whispered.

"It's only virtual meat, Gunny," Zerika reminded him.

"So? You think I want to screw up my cyberkarma?"

"Logi," Megaera whispered, "is actually fire, which consumes everything."

"Logi!" the giant king called. "Come forward to contend with this young hero: Upon you will rest the honor of my hall." A youthful giant came forward and took up a position at the opposite end of the trencher from Gunnodoyak. At a signal from the king they both began to eat toward the middle. Gunnodoyak devoured the meat with remarkable swiftness, leaving only the bones. But it seemed that Logi would not be outdone; he not only devoured the meat, but the bones and the trencher as well. Then an odd thing happened. About halfway to the middle of the trencher, Logi was suddenly, astonishingly, incapable of eating another bite. Despite the urging of the other giants in the hall, not least from the king himself, he was simply unable to bring himself to consume another morsel. In the meantime Gunnodoyak, whose own pace had not slackened a bit, reached the middle of the trencher. The king was forced to declare him the winner.

Meanwhile, Ragnar continued to swallow. The king glanced at him, then turned back to the others. "I must admit that I honestly did not expect you to defeat Logi. You are even more formidable than I had guessed. Perhaps one of you would care to run a race against one of us?"

Zerika volunteered and was matched against a giant named Hugi. As they went outdoors to a large level field, Megaera whispered to Tahmurath, "Hugi is thought, which is supposedly swifter than anything."

"Once around the field should be a fair trial," the king suggested. "Go to your marks." Once again the king signaled for the contest to begin, and the two runners dashed off. Zerika covered the ground with amazing speed, but the giant Hugi seemed to keep pace with her effortlessly. As the two rounded the far end of the field and began to run back toward where the others waited at the finish line, Hugi began to pull ahead. At first he seemed to be gradually outstripping Zerika; then, as they neared the finish line, he put on an even greater burst of speed. Just when it seemed that Zerika couldn't possibly catch him, he tripped and went sprawling. Before he could recover, Zerika flashed by and crossed the finish line.

The giant king seemed to take this setback even harder than the previous one. As they followed him back inside the hall, he was shaking his head and muttering to himself. And when he saw Ragnar continuing to draw effortlessly at the great drinking horn, he seemed to give an involuntary shudder.

With an effort he appeared to regain his composure. "These other things are minor entertainments, of course. Among my people it is wrestling that is considered the truest test of a warrior's prowess. Would any of you care to try your skill? Ah, good, the largest one of you," he said as Megaera raised a gauntleted hand. "Still, I think the size difference would make it impossible for you to have a fair contest with any of the giants in my hall. Instead, why don't you wrestle my old nurse, Elli?"

"You'd better have a good one in store for this," Megaera whispered to Tahmurath. "Elli is supposed to be old age. Even Thor couldn't beat her." She stripped off her armor and moved to confront the wrinkled crone who was hobbling forward. To say she seemed old would be like saying a newborn babe is youthful, liquid nitrogen is cool, and Mount Everest is tallish. She looked as if she had probably burped Methuselah's grandfather.

Megaera knew better than to be reassured by her opponent's apparent decrepitude. She circled warily, sizing up her adversary, whose deeply lined face was split in a toothless grin. Suddenly the two lunged together and grappled. They went down in a tangle of arms and legs— Megaera's young, muscular limbs, and the crone's withered ones.

The giant king's smile had returned. He did not know how his champions had been bested in the earlier contests, but in this one he was utterly confident that his wrestler must emerge victorious.

Then, suddenly, it was over, and everyone in the hall saw Megaera straddling the old woman and pinning her shoulders. The giant king's jaw dropped open and then moved soundlessly. Every giant in the hall stared in awe. The silence was broken by a thunderous belch, and all eyes now turned toward Ragnar, who was holding the drinking horn upside down; he had finally succeeded in draining it. "Excuse me," he said. "But do you have anything else to drink? I'm still a little thirsty."

This proved to be too much for the giant king. He let out a bellow of inarticulate fear and bolted from his throne, but Megaera and Ragnar moved to cut him off. "Not so fast, Stretch," Ragnar admonished. "You owe us some answers, remember?"

The giant king nodded slowly, his face ashen. "Ask."

"How can we find and slay Draco?" Tahmurath demanded.

"You will need the bow of Heracles," the king replied.

"How can we get it?"

"You will need to travel aboard the *Argo* to retrieve the bow. It is moored at the mouth of the Eridanus."

"Travel to where?"

"I do not know, but the *Argo* itself may." And with that he turned and lumbered from the hall as fast as his tree-sized legs could carry him, with the rest of the giants hot on his heels, leaving the hall to the victorious adventurers.

In the meantime Megaera had stalked over to Tahmurath. "What happened?" she demanded. "You were in charge of cheating; I thought I was supposed to win."

Zerika, Ragnar, and Gunnodoyak looked at her with puzzled expressions. "You *did* win," Zerika said.

Megaera looked surprised but shook her head emphatically. "I was there; I think I know what happened. I lost." She turned back to Tahmurath. "What's going on?"

Tahmurath smiled. "You are right. You did lose. But everyone else in the hall saw you win. A simple illusion to exchange your appearance with Elli's."

"Oh. Good idea, I suppose, but I wish you'd told me what you were doing."

"There wasn't much time. Besides, it was more fun this way."

"More fun for you, you mean. How did you do the other ones?"

"The drinking horn was actually the most difficult one. It was, as you said, connected to the sea. It was a simple enough matter to sever the connection, but if I'd done so right away, it would have aroused suspicion, so instead I put a spell on Ragnar to allow him to hold his breath indefinitely and swallow a few hundred gallons of fluid.

"Then came the eating contest; that was simple. Fire doesn't quite consume everything, Megaera. I just transmuted the last two yards of Logi's trencher into asbestos. That's why he seemed to experience a sudden loss of appetite."

"And what about the race?" Zerika inquired. "What did Hugi trip over?"

"Hugi was thought, which is swift indeed—unless it encounters a mental block."

"A mental block!" Ragnar chortled. "I love it."

"Then, while everyone watched what they thought was Megaera pinning old age, I cut the drinking horn's connection to the sea and magicked out the remaining liquid. After seeing Gunnodoyak outconsume fire, Zerika outrun thought, and Megaera outwrestle old age, it was easy for them to believe that Ragnar could swallow the sea. You see, a big part of magic lies in creating the right frame of mind in the audience."

"Suspension of disbelief?" Megaera smiled.

"Precisely."

▲   ▲   ▲   ▲   ▲   ▲   ▲

I had hoped that Ken Bishop's ATM PIN code would lead us to his password, but so far it hadn't. Part of the problem was knowing how to interpret it—numerically it was just 7533, but the numbers could stand for letters, too: *P, R,* or *S* for 7, *J, K,* or *L* for 5, and *D, E,* or *F* for 3. I had tried making words from those possibilities—"PLED" was the best I could do—but so far nothing had worked. We could have "brute-forced" the possible combinations, including combined alphanumeric ones, but that still seemed too risky.

I spent a few fruitless hours on the problem, then did a little channel-surfing before going to bed—as usual, there was nothing good on. As I flipped through the channels, I kept encountering Death—and not because I was hitting the news programs. Death was playing chess with Max von Sydow, Twister with Keanu Reeves, and badminton with some guy I didn't recognize.

I switched off the set and went to bed feeling vaguely uneasy—as if all the death depictions represented some sort of ill omen. That night I had a dream.

I dreamed that I was sitting at a chessboard. Across the table from me was a shadowy figure whose face I couldn't see at all. I looked at

the chessboard and noticed that it was only four by four instead of
eight by eight, and that each square seemed to have a letter or number
inscribed on it, upside down from my point of view. There was a
single piece on the board—a black bishop sitting on the corner square
at my opponent's left hand. The dream woke me up.

I stumbled toward the kitchen to get something to drink, then
stopped abruptly at my workstation. There was something about the
keyboard that caught my attention. My eye was attracted to the
numeric keypad at the right, as if there was something about it that
rang a bell. I thought of the chessboard in the dream and how there
had seemed to be numbers inscribed in the squares—no, not just
numbers, letters too. Then I remembered: the alphanumeric keypad
I'd seen in Dworkin's office. Four by four, but how were the characters arranged? I couldn't remember.

I flipped on a lamp and, squinting in the glare, fished a computer
catalog out of the trash. Thumbing through the pages as my pupils
slowly adjusted to the sudden onslaught of light, I located what I was
looking for in the peripherals section: a hexadecimal keypad. The letters and numbers were arranged like so:

C	D	E	F
8	9	A	B
4	5	6	7
0	1	2	3

Bishop's ATM personal identification number was 7533—now I was
beginning to see why. It was a diagonal move, like a bishop's move in
chess, only with the 3 repeated, as the ATM keypad had only a three-
square diagonal. There were two long diagonals on the four-by-four,
so the question was, Which one? The bishop in my dream was at the
left hand of the opposing player. Bishop's PIN number started at the
left side of the alphanumeric display. It all fit: I was convinced that
Bishop's password was 05AF. It was time to test it.

▲   ▲   ▲   ▲   ▲   ▲   ▲

They found the ship lying at anchor at the mouth of the river, as the
giant king had said. "He may be a cheater," Zerika remarked, "but at
least he's not a liar." The ship was sleek and graceful like some living

creature of the sea, an impression that was strengthened by the pair of eyes painted on her prow. The rowing benches were empty; indeed, the ship seemed completely deserted except for the steersman who stood at attention in the stern.

As they scrambled over the gunwales, Tahmurath hailed the lone steersman, but he continued to stare straight ahead.

"He looks like some kind of automaton," said Gunnodoyak, who had gone aft for a closer look.

"If you wish to address him, you must call him by name: He is Kybernetes."

"Who said that?" Zerika trained her sharp, elfin eyes toward the prow, the direction the voice had come from, but no one was visible.

"It is I."

"I think the ship is talking to us," Megaera said.

"Not the whole ship, just me," the voice came again. "I am a beam from a sacred Dodonian Oak. The gods have placed me here in the prow of this ship to give counsel to any mortal heroes who sail aboard the *Argo*."

"We need to find the bow of Heracles," Tahmurath said. "Can you help us?"

"The bow is in the possession of Philoctetes. He is marooned on the island of Lemnos."

"Can you show us how to get there?"

"Kybernetes! Set a course east by southeast."

The oars unshipped themselves and, as if rowed by unseen hands, began to sweep rhythmically through the water.

The *Argo* seemed to fly across the sea, barely skimming the surface as it sped toward their destination. The hands that manned the oars proved to be as indefatigable as they were invisible, never slackening their pace until they neared their destination.

In a remarkably short time Zerika sighted an island in the distance. As they headed for a sheltered cove in which to moor, there was a sudden splash off the starboard bow, as if something very large had fallen into the water.

"What the hell was that?" Ragnar demanded.

"There!" Zerika called, pointing toward the shore. A very large man, perhaps a giant, who was clad entirely in bronze armor, lifted a huge boulder and heaved it at them. This time it didn't miss by much.

"If we remain here," the magic oak said calmly, "we will be destroyed."

"Kybernetes, get us back out of range," Tahmurath said.

The steersman moved to obey the order, and the ship wheeled around, approaching a bit closer in the process. Ragnar nocked an arrow.

"Do you think you can hit him from here?" Megaera asked.

"I don't know; I want to try before we're out of *my* range, though." He drew the bowstring back to his ear and released in one smooth motion. "Did I hit him? I can't see from here."

Zerika shaded her eyes and looked. "You hit him in the ankle, Robin Hood. You want to try for a toe? Actually, don't bother. He's not just wearing bronze armor; from here it looks like he's actually *made* out of bronze."

"We can try going back under an invisibility spell," Tahmurath said. "But for some reason I have a hunch that thing is going to be able to see us anyway."

"For ordinary invisibility, I think you're probably right," Zerika agreed. "But the cap of darkness might be a different story." Once they had left the MUD where they'd acquired it, Tahmurath had used his anagram magic to transform the APC into a large, rather silly-looking hat with a peacock feather stuck in the band.

"Especially as it's supposedly a 'god's cap of darkness,'" Tahmurath agreed.

"What god would that be?" Gunnodoyak asked.

"When the Olympian gods rebelled against the Titans," Megaera said, "the Cyclopes made special weapons for them: the thunderbolt for Zeus, the trident for Poseidon, and the cap of darkness for Hades. I think that must be the myth the poem was referring to."

"Well, only one of us can wear the cap of darkness," Tahmurath said. "Assuming that will be Zerika, then what do we do about the rest of us?"

"Hey, don't you have a spell that can let us breathe underwater?" Krishna asked.

"Yes. Not bad. I think I see what you have in mind. We're still going to have to fight him when we get to shore, though."

Tahmurath cast his spell, and Zerika mapped out their strategy. "Let's see if we can get him into the water," she said. "It may cut down his mobility, and if we can drag him under, that might kill him."

"But if he's metal," Megaera objected, "then he's not really alive."

"True, but he might still run on some kind of aerobic process, like an internal-combustion engine," Tahmurath said. "Let's give Zerika's plan a try."

They climbed over the side of the boat and, weighed down as they were by weapons, armor, and other items, quickly sank to the bottom. It was a fairly long slog to shore, especially with the drag of the water, but eventually they reached water that was shallow enough so that Megaera could see the shore. Fortunately, the bronze man did not immediately notice her.

She crouched below the surface and signaled to the others that the island's guardian was close ahead. Tahmurath's spell allowed breathing underwater, but not speech.

As they neared the island, one problem with their plan of attack became evident: They couldn't see very well from beneath the water, and as soon as one of them broke the surface, he or she would present a tempting target to the bronze man.

In the end there was no choice but to storm the beach en masse. Megaera was the first to emerge from the waves, directly in front of the giant. It actually seemed surprised, because it paused, a boulder poised in its hands, until Megaera was practically upon him, swinging her sword at his knees, which was as high as she could reach. Then he simply dropped the rock onto her head. Because it was a boulder weighing a good half ton, the effect was dramatic; she was dashed to the ground and pinned. Ragnar, who was close behind Megaera, saw her plight and, unwisely, attempted to roll the boulder off her, giving the bronze giant a chance to swat him with a huge metal hand. Ragnar sailed about ten yards down the beach and landed like a rag doll.

In the meantime the rest of the party had a chance to reach the shore. Zerika was the first to strike a blow against the monster, but her sword clanged harmlessly off his metal hide. Her cap of darkness did indeed seem to be effective against whatever sort of senses the bronze giant possessed, but because she didn't seem able to do any damage, that wasn't much help. Gunnodoyak's hands and feet were similarly ineffective against the titanic foe. Tahmurath launched a series of spells, lightning bolts, and fireballs, but they fizzled in midair. "I think it must have some sort of immunity to magic," he yelled.

The giant began stalking toward them, passing close by the pinned, half-stunned Megaera. In desperation she reached out, trying to trip him, but managed only to grab Ragnar's arrow, which still protruded from the creature's ankle. The arrow came loose, which attracted the giant's attention. As he paused to look down, there was a sudden gush of reddish, oily fluid from the hole in his ankle. Slowly he sank to the beach and lay still.

After Tahmurath had levitated the boulder off Megaera, and Gunnodoyak had healed her and Ragnar, the party regrouped and prepared to explore the interior of the island, with Zerika, as usual, in the lead.

"Yeesh," Ragnar said. "I thought *we* were tough. That thing was unreal."

"No matter how tough you think you are," Tahmurath said, "there's always somebody—or something," he amended, "that's tougher."

They emerged into a clearing with a cave opening. As they peered inside, it was evident that the cave was occupied, for something about the size of a man dashed out of another opening in the rear of the cave as they approached.

"What the hell was that?" Tahmurath asked.

"Some kind of big bird, I think," Zerika replied. "I didn't get a good look, but I could see that it was covered with feathers."

"Ugh, it smells terrible in there," Ragnar remarked. "What kind of a bird smells that bad?"

"I have no idea," Tahmurath replied. "But we're not here to birdwatch. We have to find Philoctetes. Philoctetes!" he shouted. "Philoctetes? Are you here? We've come to rescue you!"

For a moment nothing happened, and it seemed as if Tahmurath's cries had gone unheard. Then there was a rustling at the edge of the clearing. The foliage parted, and a strange figure stepped through.

He was a man, despite the feathers that covered his body; evidently they were his only attire. In his left hand he carried a large recurved bow, and a quiver of arrows was visible over his shoulder. Another arrow was on his bowstring, and he eyed the adventurers suspiciously. "Is Odysseus with you?" he asked harshly.

"No," Zerika answered, "I'm afraid not. Did you want to talk to him?"

"Talk to him! Oh, I'd like to have a little talk with him, all right. He's the one who marooned me here, as if you didn't know. You're here for the bow, aren't you? Well, you can't have it! The walls of Troy can stand for the rest of time, for all I care. What are you two whispering about?"

Megaera turned from Tahmurath, to whom she had indeed been whispering, and smiled ingratiatingly. "I was just telling my friend here how cruelly the Greeks had treated you. He was not familiar with your story."

Philoctetes seemed slightly mollified. "They left me here with nothing. Why, without my bow I wouldn't even have any way of feeding myself. Heracles gave it to me himself, you know. It was for lighting his funeral pyre."

"For lighting his funeral pyre?" Gunnodoyak said. "How could he give you anything if he was already—"

"He wasn't dead yet. He was suffering terribly from the wounds the robe soaked in Nessus' blood had caused. Death was his only release. He built the pyre himself and lay down on it, only no one would light it. Except me."

"Why don't you come with us?" Megaera coaxed.

"No! I have been alone too long, I am no longer fit for the company of other men. And the smell of my wound—no one can bear it except I, who have no choice." He laughed bitterly.

"Let me try to heal your wound," Gunnodoyak suggested.

Philoctetes' eyes briefly flickered with hope, but suddenly the paranoia returned. "No! You just want to get close enough to take my bow. I warn you, these arrows were dipped in Hydra venom by Heracles himself. The merest prick is enough to kill. Come no closer."

"I don't think he's going to come," Tahmurath suddenly announced. "You can stay here and argue with him if you want, but I'm going back to wait with the boat."

Zerika, Ragnar, and Gunnodoyak seemed genuinely startled by this development, but Megaera merely continued gently remonstrating with Philoctetes. "Why don't you come with us? What is there for you here? We can heal your wound, take you back to your own country, or wherever you wish."

"And why would you do all that for me?"

"Well," Megaera admitted, "we really do need your bow."

"Aha! I knew it! Never! I will kill you all before I let anyone so much as touch it!"

"Philoctetes!" came a strange, hollow voice.

Everyone, including Philoctetes, looked up, searching for the source. Among the rocks above the mouth of the cave, they beheld a ghostly figure.

"Philoctetes! It is I, Heracles. Hearken to my words. Go with these heroes! They have a great task to perform, and you must aid them. In return they will heal your wound, and you will return to the lands of men." As the sound of his last words died away, the figure wavered and vanished.

Philoctetes continued to stare, slack-jawed and bug-eyed, at the place where the apparition had appeared. Then he turned to the others, letting his bow arm drop to his side. "I will go with you," he said.

▲　　▲　　▲　　▲　　▲　　▲　　▲

"Michael, I wasn't expecting you," my mother said. "Can you stay for dinner? I'm making gnocchi." I had dropped by my parents' house one evening, despite various pressing concerns. I missed Al, and working wasn't doing much to take my mind off it. I guess I just wanted to be around some people.

"Sure, Mom, I'd love to stay for dinner." Easy call on that one; Mom's gnocchi were even better than Nonna's. "Is Dad around?"

"He's in his study," she said.

"Is he busy?"

"Not too busy to talk to you, I'm sure."

I found my father in his study ensconced in his favorite armchair, apparently absorbed in a book. For some reason both he and the chair seemed smaller than they were supposed to be. His back was to me, and the halogen glow of a reading lamp reflected off his silver hair, creating an effect like a golden halo.

He heard me come in, turned, and looked up from his book. "Mike, come on in. What's on your mind?"

I sat down, a bit heavily, in a chair opposite him. I really wasn't sure what was on my mind or what I was doing there. "Dad, what would you say if someone came into your office and said he was afraid the world was going to end soon?"

A wry smile creased his face. "I'm hearing quite a bit of that lately."

It shouldn't have been a surprise, but for some reason that gave me a kind of sinking feeling. "Really? Why?"

"Well, the end of the millennium, of course, but that's just the surface."

"What's deeper down?"

"Oh, lots of things. Guilt, usually."

"Why guilt?"

"Well, when people are expecting something bad to happen to them, it's usually because they think they deserve it."

"But this would be something bad happening to everybody. Does that mean they think everybody deserves it?"

He considered for a moment, then nodded. "In some cases that's probably true. But you may be underestimating how incredibly self-centered we humans are."

He had a point there. "Dad, you're a Freudian, right?"

"Well." He put his book down and cleared his throat. "That depends on what you mean by 'Freudian.' "

"Uh-oh. This sounds like it's one of those questions that's going to have a much more complicated answer than what I'm looking for."

He nodded. "Yes. Are you sure you want to go through with it?"

"Not really. Let me try a different tack. Would it be safe to say that you are not, in any sense of the word, a Jungian?"

"That would be pretty safe."

"Why not?"

"Huh?"

"Why aren't you a Jungian? Is he considered off the wall or something?"

"Hmmm. This one has a complicated answer too."

"That's okay; I was expecting this one to be complicated."

"Well, then, I suppose I'd have to say that Jung is considered outside the psychoanalytic mainstream for several reasons, some good and some not so good."

"For instance?"

"Jung was very interested in myths and mysticism. Most analysts would agree that those are very worthy subjects of study, but Jung had a knack for seeming a little mystical himself at times, especially when discussing those subjects. We analysts are a pretty hard-headed lot, and we like to think of ourselves as very empirical and scientific. Mysticism in one of our own makes us uncomfortable. I remember going to a national meeting once where some guy stood up and actually criticized Freud for entertaining the possibility that some form of telepathy might exist. This fellow evidently believed that Freud would have been more 'scientific' if he dismissed the possibility a priori."

"I see. What else?"

"Well, some of Jung's ideas have been discredited. Take the collective unconscious: Jung believed that a collective unconscious was genetically hardwired into all of us."

"What's wrong with that?"

"His view of evolution was Lamarckian. Because the modern view of evolution is Darwinian, that leaves a big gaping hole in Jung's model."

"But what if there is a collective unconscious, only not encoded in DNA? Suppose it's represented in the brain in the same way as anything else, however that is?"

"You'd still have to explain how it's transmitted from generation to generation."

"Yeah, that's true. Do you think that it's possible for two people to communicate unconsciously? I mean, their unconsciouses would be communicating without their knowing about it?"

"Not only is it possible, it happens all the time."

That surprised me, although I suppose it shouldn't have. "Really?"

"There's no question about it."

"You mean, while we're having this conversation, we're also communicating other things to each other on an unconscious level?"

"Definitely."

"Like what?"

"If I knew that, it wouldn't be unconscious, at least not for me."

"But you're a psychoanalyst. You should be able to figure it out, or at least make some educated guesses, right?"

He chuckled. "I think I've just been pinned to the wall. Okay, you want to know what we've been saying to each other that's unconscious. Fair enough." He leaned back in his chair and stroked his chin. "Well, for starters I'd say that if all you wanted were answers to some of these questions, you could have gotten them more quickly and easily by spending a few minutes at your computer keyboard. I can see that there's some problem that's troubling you, and you've come to your father for help about it. You're telling me that you're not sure you're up to facing whatever it is, and you need something from me to make you feel like you can do it.

"For my part I'm probably delighted to feel deep down somewhere that my oldest son still needs me, or thinks he does, and that I'm not completely useless yet. So I want to help you and give you whatever it is you think you need, and I might be a little reluctant to puncture our shared illusion that you really need my help with whatever it is."

I shook my head. "That's a little warmer and fuzzier than what I had in mind, Dad. What I'd really like to know is if it's possible for people to communicate really detailed factual information over unconscious channels, so to speak."

He frowned thoughtfully. "I'd have to say that it is, although I couldn't say how often it happens. There's a phenomenon that's been reported among some of the children of Holocaust survivors. At a certain age, usually early adulthood, the son or daughter of the survivor has a psychotic episode. During this episode the person vividly hallucinates the experiences his or her parent had in the death camps."

"I'm not sure I see the connection."

"This has happened in cases where the patient had never been told anything about the parent's experiences."

After dinner with my parents I headed home. Uri invited me to join him in some virtual noise-making—he'd gotten a few new CDs—but I took a rain check. I wanted to see the latest returns from Icepick and also do some work on a new virus I'd discovered in one of my client's computers.

It was one of the stealthiest viruses I'd ever seen, partly because it didn't seem to do anything. That didn't add up; this virus had *some* kind of payload, I was convinced of that. There was too much unexplained code unrelated to replication, and you don't go to all the trouble of designing a superstealthy virus and then lard it with a lot of unnecessary garbage. It was a "terminate and stay resident" or "TSR" virus, meaning that it loaded into RAM at boot-up, then hung around waiting—but to do what?

The only way to know for sure was to decompile the beastie, and that required time I didn't have to spare, but I had done it anyway, more or less on a hunch that it was important. Even after decompiling I didn't feel as if I knew much more. This virus was looking for something. The something was a particular text string, although not one that made any sense: ORRYMROHOOHORMYRRO. A code? A password? If the virus found the string, it was supposed to generate an E-mail message that would go out the next time the infected computer was used to send E-mail, and then it would simply erase itself. The E-mail was addressed to an anonymous remailer account, so that wasn't much help, either.

Just for the hell of it, I had decided to let it send the E-mail from my computer to its anonymous master. I wondered what would happen next; somebody would be getting E-mail with my return address on it. Would that person try to contact me? I hoped so, because it seemed like the only way I was likely to find out anything more about it.

That was about a week ago, and I had almost forgotten about it. Then, while I was perusing the latest report from Icepick, I saw it. Actually, I nearly missed it, because it was buried in some garbled text at the end of the message. Somehow, though, it caught my eye: OR-RYMROHOOHORMYRRO. When I realized what was going on, I nearly fell out of my chair: Somebody at Macrobyte, presumably on the security team, was onto Icepick and had disseminated this virus as a way of finding out who was getting the messages! Whoever it was had deliberately placed the nonsense string in Icepick's USENET post, hoping that when the culprit decrypted it, the virus would be waiting, ready to E-mail back the cracker's address.

My first reaction was near panic—I had actually mailed my address to the Macrobyte security team a week ago! They knew who I was! Then I calmed down a bit as a couple of other things sunk in. First, even if they knew I was the cracker, there wasn't a thing they could do about it, because they had broken the law by disseminating the virus. They couldn't very well go to the authorities with that kind of information. Also, I realized that the E-mail had gone out *before* the message containing the text string was ever posted to USENET. That ought to give them a little food for thought.

My second reaction was anger. To catch a cracker they put out a *virus*? Were they nuts? I didn't care how innocuous they thought it was, viruses are unpredictable, and you don't expose millions of computers to that kind of risk. I thought about what to do. Then I started to laugh. I composed a note to post to USENET and included the decrypted text string; then I cross-posted it to as many newsgroups as I thought I could get away with without being flamed for the rest of eternity. By tomorrow the text string would be in millions of computers, triggering the virus in the infected ones to send out their E-mail and delete themselves. It was a way to purge the virus from loads of infected computers, and, as an extra added bonus, the bozo who planted this thing would be swamped with enough E-mail to consume a virtual forest.

But there was another problem: If they were onto Icepick, I couldn't continue to rely on it as a source of information. No doubt they'd been feeding me garbage ever since they'd wised up, but when was that? There was no way of knowing.

I hoped they didn't know about Bishop's account being compromised; I had not posted the correct password for Icepick—yet. Now, of course, there was no point in doing that. What worried me more was that now that they'd discovered a major security problem, they might start tightening things up across the board. That could pose problems for our friend Mr. Bishop—somebody was going to be steamed when his security hack was discovered—but it was also a problem for me. I thought about all the time, effort, and dumb luck we'd consumed getting Bishop's access info, and how close we were to being back to square one. I needed access through that account, and I was going to have to do it now, through a dial-in, before the window of opportunity slammed shut on my fingers.

I used a telephone-exchange hack to make my call more difficult to trace, but I knew the most that would accomplish would be to buy me a little time—probably not enough, if it came to that, because I would have to be on-line for quite a while to have any real shot of finding what I wanted.

In a few moments I was logging in:

```
Username: KBishop
Password: 05AF
```

It worked. The first thing I needed to do was find out, if I could, how Bishop had managed his hack, and to do that, I needed to find out more about the security environment. I tried opening the security log and was pleased to find out that I could do so. I was thinking about whether I should take some time to disable security when I noticed something: The security log listed all users who were currently on-line—but not Bishop. This was almost too good to be true: Bishop had already hacked security and not only had made it leave his password alone, but had also instructed it to ignore his logons.

I closed the security log and got down to business. In short order I realized that dumb luck was still in high gear; Bishop had turned his account into a de facto superuser. I was already in root mode.

Now I wanted two things: Dworkin's files, if I could find them, and an encryption algorithm. That Dworkin's files would be encrypted, I had no doubt. Of course, even with the files and the algorithm we were still going to need the key, and there was no way that was going to be stored in the computer. Cracking *that* problem was another bridge we'd have to cross, assuming that we could get to it. Right now it was up to me to get us there.

I called up a schematic of the directory tree, a diagram showing how all the files in the system were organized. I didn't see anything that particularly caught my eye, and for a while I just opened things at random. After about an hour of that I went back to the schematic and tried to think the way Dworkin would think. For a while nothing happened. Then I got another hunch. I took the sixth branch off the root directory and expanded it, then took the sixth branch off the branch and expanded it, then took the sixth branch off *that* branch. The subdirectory in that position was something called Ptah; I expanded it, and at first I thought I'd come up dry again:

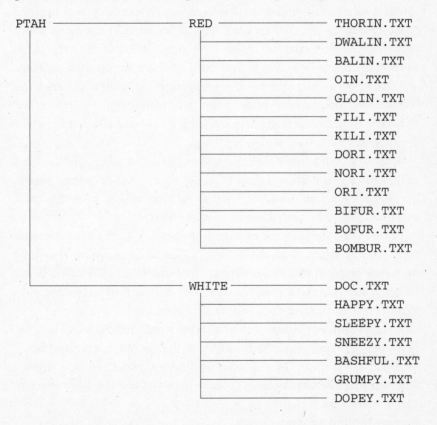

Nothing of much interest, it seemed. I opened Thorin.txt, just for the heck of it and found that it was encrypted. That was mildly interesting, but not earthshaking. There were probably dozens of encrypted files in this system, and though I expected Dworkin would have encrypted anything having to do with Wyrm or his Trojan, the odds of these particular files belonging to him seemed pretty slim.

I pondered the names of the two subdirectories, "Red" and "White"; I couldn't make anything out of "Red," but after a moment's thought it was obvious that "White" stood for "Snow White," because the text files were named after the Seven Dwarfs. I chuckled and started to move on when it hit me: dwarfs! George had said that Dworkin enjoyed role-playing dwarf characters in Double-D. I mentally noted an apology owed to George for making fun of him about that.

Okay, so if the "White" subdirectory contained the Seven Dwarfs, what were those names in the first directory? More dwarfs? None of them looked familiar to me, but, then, I wasn't really up on dwarf lore. I wanted to minimize on-line time, which was risky, so I decided to download all the files in both directories, after checking to make sure that wouldn't take too long—it wouldn't, because the longest file in the bunch was only five k, and most of them were much shorter.

Then I went hunting for the encryption algorithm. Because the system used strong encryption, there was really no good reason for Dworkin to use something else. As long as no one else held the encryption keys, his data would be secure.

Unless I could figure out the keys. Guesswork again, shots in the dark, and yet—somehow I didn't feel daunted. I had never met Dworkin, never even *seen* him, but I felt some kind of link with him, as if our minds had connected on some deep level.

There is an altered state of consciousness that seems to occur from time to time when someone is deeply immersed in a task that fully demands his most highly developed capabilities. Athletes call it being in the zone; elsewhere it has been referred to as flow. Al might have explained it as tapping the collective unconscious.

Whatever it was, I was there. It didn't even surprise me when my first guess, "wormwood," proved to be the correct encryption key.

What *did* surprise me was what I found in Dworkin's files: viruses. And not just any viruses, either; these were viruses that I recognized, that I knew very well.

I had found Vamana.

CHAPTER FIFTEEN

The Belly Button
of the Beast

. . . Babylon the great is fallen, is fallen, and is become
the habitation of devils . . .

—Revelation 18:2

It was the day after Christmas, and Marlon Oz was in his office. I was tempted to ask him why, but I didn't; after all, it wasn't as if *I* had anything better to do.

"Have you ever wondered why your brain can't regenerate lost cells after an injury?" he was asking me.

"Actually, Dr. Oz, I've never given it much thought." I had called Oz to touch base about some of the things that were going on with Wyrm, and to see if he had any useful suggestions. Thanks to Dan Morgan, we could now communicate on the phone. He and one of the undergrads had secretly doctored Oz's phone in order to boost the volume without leaving any sign that the phone had been tampered with. It was a good hack.

As was usual when I talked with The Great Man, things were going off on an unexpected tangent.

"Well, you *should* wonder about it. It's actually very strange."

"What's so strange?"

"Think about it! Your brain is the most important organ in your body. Damage to even a small part of it can result in major loss of function . . ."

He was certainly right about that. I thought about Seth Serafin and shuddered slightly. I had not told Oz or anybody else about that little encounter.

". . . and yet," he continued, "your brain lacks a capacity that almost every other organ in your body possesses: the ability to regenerate injured and destroyed cells. Your liver can do it. Your skin can do it, and it comes from the same germ-cell layer. Your gut is doing it all the time. Why can't your brain do it?"

I had known him long enough by now to learn that Oz rarely asked a question if he didn't think he already knew the answer. He had succeeded in arousing my curiosity about his answer to this one, but I didn't feel like playing straight man. Obviously, my next line was supposed to be something like, "Duh, and why is that, Dr. Oz? Please enlighten me while I'm wiping the drool off my chin." So instead I said, "Maybe humans evolved under circumstances in which the prospect of recovery from a brain injury was so small, there really wasn't any advantage to being able to regenerate."

"A plausible idea, on the surface. But on closer inspection it proves to be pure bullshit, for two reasons. First of all, what is the likelihood of a member of a nomadic hunter-gatherer tribe surviving a broken leg, with no one to set it, no casts, no splints, no wheelchairs? Probably about the same order as surviving a brain injury. And yet we have retained the ability to heal broken legs.

"But more important, it's not enough that you don't need something; there must be some advantage to *not* having it for it to be selected out. Some primitive species have the ability to regenerate neurons, so we must have lost it somewhere along the way. Why? What possible advantage is there to having a brain that *doesn't* regenerate?"

Okay, I thought. *Let's just throw in the towel and get this over with.* "Why do *you* think it was selected out?"

"Because," he said, "the software that we call 'mind' can't handle reconfigurations in the hardware. When there is a brain injury, there is very little that can be done to 'retrain' the brain to handle the same functions in a different way—to have uninjured parts of the brain take over the lost functions. It just doesn't happen to any significant extent, except in very young children.

"For the same reason, there's probably nothing the brain could do with newly generated replacement neurons, so growing them would be a complete waste of energy."

That seemed plausible, if less than earth-shattering. I still didn't see what he was driving at. "Was all this supposed to have something to do with Wyrm?"

"You don't see it yet, do you? Look, the human mind is the most complicated, sophisticated piece of software there is. And it evolved over millions of years in tandem with its hardware, the brain. Now, that should tell you that if the problem of dealing with hardware reconfiguration on the scale of the human brain is too difficult for the mind to handle, then it must be an unbelievably difficult problem.

"Your Wyrm is operating on a scale of complexity comparable to the brain. And yet, from what you tell me, it is managing constant, continual reconfigurations in its hardware. How can it do that? Do you realize that if we could answer that question, the answer might be crucial to doing things like grafting brain cells in people with brain damage or Alzheimer's disease?"

I resisted the temptation to ask him if he had a personal interest in the latter. "That's all very well," I said, "but if we don't figure out how to deal with this thing, it could also be very moot. It's the day after Christmas, and we still don't have an answer to that question."

"Interesting that you should mention Christmas," he said.

"Why?"

"Because I was thinking about something you had told me before; your idea about this network phenomenon among human minds, and how it might relate to megalithic culture. You see, Christmas is like a Christian church that has been erected on top of an older, pagan edifice."

"What's that supposed to mean?"

"Well, all over Europe there are churches and chapels that have been built on the site of some ancient ruin. Sometimes the megaliths are actually incorporated into the structure of the church building."

"What does that have to do with Christmas?"

"Christmas is a Christian holiday that has supplanted an ancient pagan celebration of the winter solstice. Notice that, like many of the megalithic ruins, the pagan solstice feast has astronomical significance.

Also, like the churches that contain ancient menhirs and dolmens, the Christmas holiday has incorporated certain pagan rituals."

"Like what?"

"Like bringing a tree into the house, for instance."

"Isn't that just coincidence? I mean because they happen to be around the same time of year?"

"No coincidence at all."

"What, you mean Jesus was intentionally born around the time of the winter solstice?"

"No one has any idea what time of year Jesus was born. There's no information about it in the New Testament, or any remotely contemporaneous sources. The custom of celebrating Christmas in December came along much later. That's where the intention comes in; I've no doubt that the timing was meant to allow it to supplant the old pagan Yuletide holiday, just as the churches were intended to take the place of the older pagan holy places. It's like the brain. . . ."

"The brain?"

"Yes. Structurally and functionally, the newer parts of our brains like the neocortex are like a covering over the older reptile brain underneath, just like the old megaliths are covered up by the later churches. But the old snake is still there, probably just biding its time."

Thursday morning I was reading the paper over a cup of tea—Robin had given me some of her Formosan oolong as a Christmas present. I'd been feeling a little under the weather since the night before, and my stomach wasn't up to coffee. It seemed to be a slow week for news. Triple Witching Hour had come and gone without incident—everyone was running Macrobyte software, which meant that Wyrm was now everywhere.

There was an update on the flock of zealots who were clogging Jerusalem, waiting for the world to end. Another story recounted some of the prophecies of Nostradamus and attempted, through some fairly tortured logic, to relate them to current events. London bookmakers were currently offering fifty-to-one odds to anyone who wished to bet that the Archbishop of Canterbury would acknowledge the second coming of Christ some time in the next year. For those who found the long odds reassuring, the story went on to note that in

recent years the odds on the same question had been running at about
a thousand to one.

In the previous month the image of Jesus Christ had been sighted
no fewer than forty-seven times in clouds, trees, potato chips, grass
stains, dog food, and an aerial photograph of an oil spill. There were
also fifteen sightings of the Virgin Mary, eleven of Elvis, and one of
Frank Zappa on a Belgian waffle.

According to a Gallup poll, nearly 75 percent of Americans now
believed in hell, up from 60 percent in 1990. Fewer than 2 percent,
however, believed they would go there when they died; 0.5 percent
believed they were in hell already.

Another national poll asked people who they thought was the Antichrist. The resulting list included seven politicians, four rock musicians,
two talk-show hosts, and a televangelist. Other nominees included
the United Nations, Macrobyte Software, and the Dallas Cowboys.

Under other circumstances I might have found all of this amusing,
even hilarious. Instead, each of these items seemed to be an additional
piece of evidence pointing to the possibility of a millennial mass hysteria. I was more and more firmly convinced that all it would take would
be one badly timed disaster to serve as the catalyst.

I had some time to kill before catching an afternoon flight to San
Francisco. We were planning to get the whole anti-Wyrm team together at Cepheus software for a big final push to try to beat the
millennium countdown. It was only one day away. Ever since Al had
stopped speaking to me, George had been keeping me posted on their
progress through the game. That information had caused me to update my semantic network, which now looked like this:

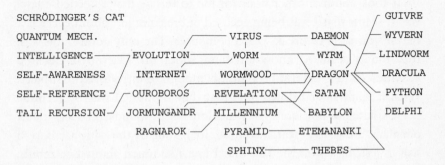

I didn't think too much of our chances but, truthfully, I was mainly
looking forward to seeing Al, although I had no reason to think she'd

feel the same way about seeing me. Quite the contrary, unfortunately. I know it sounds terribly self-centered to admit that, virtually on the eve of global destruction, the thing that was uppermost in my mind was that my girlfriend had dumped me—but there it is.

I could feel the beginnings of a sore throat. It was kind of annoying to think that I was coming down with some kind of a bug, and I would just bet that all of those yahoos who went running barefoot in the snow weren't even sniffling. I *was* sniffling, so I headed for the bathroom to get some tissues, then detoured when a knock came at the door. I hurried to get it, thinking it might be Al; instead, there were a couple of guys in dark suits standing there. I knew one of them, but the suit threw me off, so it took me a couple seconds to place the face.

"Wizard?"

"Special agent Sam Weiss of the FBI," he said, flashing a badge. "And you are under arrest for violations of the Computer Fraud and Abuse Act of 1986 and the Computer Crimes Act of 1997."

An hour later I was downtown answering questions. Yes, answering questions. I know it sounds incredibly naive, but I actually believed that I couldn't be in any trouble because I hadn't actually done anything wrong. I figured that it was all a big misunderstanding that I would help them clear up, they would realize I was one of the good guys, and we'd all go have a beer together; then I could go catch my flight to the West Coast.

Yeah, right.

It took about another hour for me to realize that I needed a lawyer. It seems that I was being accused of breaking just about every law that it's possible to break with a computer. The only good thing was, they didn't seem to know anything about my Macrobyte-cracking activities—and I had not been dumb enough to introduce the subject. What it really boiled down to is that they thought I was Beelzebub.

It's actually not quite as ridiculous as it sounds; in fact, a few people in the virus-research community had made the same accusation half in jest, based on the fact that I knew so much about Beelzebub, or at least about his viruses. I thought it was *all* in jest, really—I knew that none of my circle of contacts in the community took the charge seriously. Most of them thought it was a real howl.

But, obviously, somebody had been talking to this bozo from the FBI, and he had swallowed it hook, line, and sinker. He couldn't quite get it through his head that when we had met at DEF CON, we were engaged in doing pretty much the same thing, except that he was concentrating on trying to catch the bad guys, while I was merely trying to thwart their evil designs.

After an hour of having everything I said twisted and transmogrified into something completely bogus and utterly incriminating, I decided it was time to avail myself of my one phone call and get some legal help. Trouble was, I didn't know any lawyers who knew anything about computer law.

I called Al.

In retrospect it clearly seems like a case of putting all my eggs in an especially dilapidated basket. For all I knew, she might consider news of my arrest cause for rejoicing. I guess what it boils down to is, my feelings for her hadn't changed, and I didn't want to believe that hers had either.

I got her answering machine, of course. I left a message and then went to sit in a cell, hoping like hell that she hadn't already checked her messages for the day.

▲　　▲　　▲　　▲　　▲　　▲　　▲

Gunnodoyak had healed Philoctetes' wound, and they had returned him to his home in Thessaly. By then he was more than happy to let them keep the bow. "To tell you the truth," he confided, "I was starting to get sick of looking at the bloody thing."

After he disembarked, Megaera said, "That was nice work, Tahmurath." Seeing the puzzled expressions of the others in the party, she explained, "There's a play by Sophocles about the Philoctetes myth. It ends with the deus ex machina—Heracles appearing as a ghost to tell Philoctetes what he should do. I told Tahmurath about it so he could cast an illusion spell to do the same thing. That's why he pretended to give up and go back to the boat."

Tahmurath, however, was shaking his head. "I've been waiting for Philoctetes to leave so I could tell you," he said. "I thought it was the giant who was immune to my magic, but it turned out there was actually an antimagic zone covering the whole island. I was trying to find a way to penetrate it, or at least work around it, when you all came back to the boat."

It was Megaera's turn to look puzzled. "You mean that wasn't you?"

He shook his head emphatically.

"Whaddaya know," Ragnar exclaimed. "It looks like the gods really are on our side."

"You know," Gunnodoyak said, "it did strike me as funny that Heracles had sort of a familiar, gap-toothed grin."

"Like the troll?" Zerika asked.

"Exactly like the troll."

As Gunnodoyak piloted the UTM in a low-altitude flight over the polar waste, they all searched for a sign of the dragon's lair.

"Over there!" Zerika pointed to a glistening, icy mass that stood out from the rest of the landscape. Gunnodoyak changed course to bring them closer.

"Oh, my God," Ragnar said. "We're supposed to fight *that*? It could use the UTM for a toothpick!"

"Look on the bright side," Zerika suggested. "Even *you* couldn't miss that thing."

It was huge. As they approached, it loomed even larger, but something else became evident: "It's not alive," Megaera observed. "It's just a big snow sculpture or something, like a dragon version of Mount Rushmore."

"The head, Gunny," Tahmurath urged. "Get us close to the head."

The head of the dragon loomed in the forward viewscreen, its right eye glaring at them. The eye was apparently carved of the same icy material as the rest of the monster.

"Go around to the other side!" They were all excited now, craning their necks for a glimpse of the left eye, which was about to come into view. But before it did, the enormous jaws suddenly opened and the head darted forward. Just as the great maw seemed about to engulf the UTM, an icy blast exploded from the monster's throat, sending their craft into an uncontrolled tumble.

Gunnodoyak fought to get control of the UTM. "We're going down!" he shouted. He managed to bring the UTM out of its spin, but when it hit the ground, it began to tumble again, skidding across the icy polar landscape. The dragon was already coming after them, its every footstep like an earthquake, apparently intending to finish them off.

The UTM fetched up in a snowdrift. Ragnar and Megaera threw themselves against the hatch, but it was jammed shut by snow piled against the hull. They could see the dragon's head through the forward viewscreen, coming closer, hesitating momentarily as if trying to decide whether it should eat this strange object. Just as it appeared to have arrived at an affirmative decision, Tahmurath chanted a spell, and the hatch suddenly burst open, flinging half a ton of snow and ice into the dragon's face. It shied back, giving them a chance to scramble out of the UTM.

"Tahmurath!" Megaera shouted. "Can you make me big, the way you did with the wyvern?"

"Even with the ring I can't make you *that* big."

Ragnar was drawing his sword, but Zerika shouted, "The bow, Ragnar! Use the bow of Heracles!"

He looked up in dismay. "It's still in the UTM!"

"Go get it!" she screamed, and ran straight toward the dragon.

She was apparently trying to get to its front legs, but they were so far away that before she could reach them, the dragon was able to draw its head back, and seemed about to snap her up, when she abruptly disappeared.

"She's using the cap!" Tahmurath said.

Zerika reappeared a dozen yards from where she had vanished, and the dragon lunged at her again, and again she winked out of sight just before the massive jaws could crush her.

Just then Ragnar emerged from the UTM with the bow and arrows of Heracles. "Where's Zerika?" he asked.

"She's invisible," Tahmurath told him, "so make sure you don't hit her."

"No problem. I'll just aim high." Matching deed to word, Ragnar launched a poisoned shaft at the dragon, but it glanced harmlessly off the creature's icy scales, as did the second and third arrows he shot. "Uh-oh."

Just then Zerika reappeared, running straight toward them. The dragon, spotting her, opened its jaws wide and lunged.

"The mouth!" Tahmurath cried. "Shoot into the mouth!"

Ragnar took aim but hesitated, fearful of hitting Zerika, who was between him and the dragon. She looked at Ragnar and shouted "Now!" and, instead of vanishing again, threw herself down onto the ice.

Ragnar released the bowstring, and with a twang the feathered shaft sped toward his target. It disappeared into the cavernous mouth, and once again the dragon hesitated. For a moment it worked its jaws as if it were trying to spit something out. Then a shudder seemed to go through the vast body, beginning in the head, passing down the long neck, along the spine, and all the way to the tip of the serpentine tail.

And it fell.

The shudder that had passed through the dragon's body was like a prelude to the tremor that now passed through the earth as the mountain-size body struck the ground. Glaciers crumbled, hills collapsed, and deep chasms opened in the ice. The quake threw them to the ground, burying them in snow from the drift that had caught the UTM.

When the tremors finally subsided, they dug their way out.

Ragnar smiled ironically at Megaera. "Some ice sculpture."

But Megaera was already running toward the dragon's head, along with the rest of the party, and Ragnar had to hurry to catch up. As the party approached the left eye of the gigantic head, they all groaned, practically in unison.

The socket was empty.

"Sorry, Ragnar," Tahmurath said. "It looks like you figured out where Eltanin *was,* all right. Somebody else just got here first."

"Yeah," Zerika said. "Like maybe whoever composed that rhyme with all the clues."

Megaera wasn't quite ready to give up. "Could you try a divining spell or something, Tahmurath?"

"Might as well." He made the usual mystical gestures and muttered the magic words. Then he shrugged and shook his head. "I'm afraid it's no good. Eltanin isn't here, and we're running out of time. Whatever it is we're going to do, we're going to have to do it without Eltanin."

"I hate to admit it, but Tahmurath's right," Ragnar sighed.

"So," Gunnodoyak said, "what do we do now? Find Philoctetes and tell him we didn't really need his bow after all?"

"I wouldn't worry about that," Megaera said. "I think we'd better worry about how we're going to stop Wyrm."

"Yeah," Ragnar said. "Us and what army?"

"Ragnar's right," Megaera said.

"I am?"

"Yes. We *do* need an army. An army of hackers."

"What do you have in mind, Megaera?" Tahmurath asked.

"The way I see it," she said, "Wyrm is too widespread for us to be able to attack it effectively. It can repair itself faster than we can damage it. But if we get enough hackers to go after it simultaneously, it may not be able to defend itself."

"We may not be able to kill it, even with an army," Ragnar said. "Remember, the Internet started out as ARPAnet; it was designed by the Defense Department's Advanced Research Projects Agency for military purposes, so the architecture allows for things like saving data while parts of the network are going up in mushroom clouds. If Wyrm is structured like a neural network, control could be distributed all over the Internet—we'd never be able to wipe it out."

"Maybe," Megaera admitted, "but I have reason to believe otherwise. Remember what the sphinx said about the 'mark of the Sparti'? Well, I was curious about that, so I looked it up. Cadmus, the founder of Thebes, slew a dragon and was commanded by the gods to sow the dragon's teeth. They grew into armed warriors who fought each other until there were only five left. Those five became the founders of the noble families of Thebes, and all of their descendants had a serpent birthmark—the mark of the Sparti."

"I don't really see how any of that helps us," Tahmurath said.

"Here comes the helpful part," Megaera said. "The names of the Sparti were Chthonius, Udaeus, Hyperenor, Pelorus, and Echion. Sound familiar?"

"Those are the names of the Wormwood hosts."

"Right. Now think: The Sparti were the 'sown men,' so the dragon's teeth were like seeds or—"

"Kernels!" Ragnar exclaimed. A kernel is the essential part of an operating system that's responsible for things like resource allocation, low-level hardware interfaces, and security.

"Now, it's just after midnight on the East Coast. We've got less than forty-eight hours until New Year's Eve. I say we put out a call for help over the Internet and recruit all the hackers we possibly can. I'm

going to get the first flight I can to San Francisco so I can join you
guys at Cepheus."

"Let's do it!" Tahmurath said. "We can post notices on USENET,
cross-post to all the hackerly newsgroups, and also pass the word by
E-mail to people we know personally and tell them to get other people, too."

"And don't forget the MUDs," Zerika said. "A lot of those people, especially some of the wizards, have exactly the kind of talent we
need. We can post to the MUD newsgroups and also directly to most
of the MUDs themselves."

"Just a minute," Ragnar interjected. "We've got to be careful
about how we do this. If we create a panic, or unwittingly start a big
electronic chain letter, we might bring the 'net down even if Wyrm
doesn't."

"You've got a point there. Okay, we've got to be careful to do this
without causing more problems than we solve. Megaera, get yourself
out here as soon as you can. In the meantime we'll figure out the best
way to put out the word."

▲　▲　▲　▲　▲　▲　▲

Time goes very slowly when you're sitting in a jail cell. I guess it
wasn't, strictly speaking, a jail cell, only a holding cell in a federal
building. This was a plus, as it meant I wasn't experiencing prison
overcrowding firsthand, which would probably have meant sharing a
cell with various murderers, rapists, child molesters, and other assorted psychopaths. This being a federal agency, anybody in one of
these cells was under suspicion of having committed a federal offense,
which, as of the end of the twentieth century, consisted mainly of
things most people didn't even know were illegal.

In point of fact, I had the cell all to myself. If anybody else was
being held in the building, it wasn't anywhere near me.

Also, I was now feeling *really* sick. Fever and chills had set in
shortly after midnight, and after that I'd been up vomiting about
every hour or so. My jailers had been sufficiently humane to bring me
a couple of Tylenols, but they hadn't stayed down long enough to do
much good. I remember thinking at one point that, gee, if I hadn't
been arrested, I wouldn't have a room where my bed was three feet
from the toilet. Talk about your silver linings.

The morning after this particular night from hell, I was sitting on the edge of my cot with a thin blanket wrapped around my shoulders, waiting for whatever was going to happen next.

Time was going *very* slowly.

On the other hand, time was racing by at breakneck speed, and there was nothing I could do to slow it down. Every second brought us closer to midnight, December 31, and whatever catastrophe awaited mankind. I felt like somebody who'd waited till December 24 to do his Christmas shopping and then discovered that if he didn't get it all done before the mall closed, the world would end in a hail of fire and brimstone.

After about six hours of this I was thinking that they were smart not to give me a tin cup like the ones you always see in prison movies, because I would have been clanging it against the bars for all I was worth. If I'd had enough energy to move, that is. I heard a door open down the hallway and footsteps approach. It was Weiss and another man I didn't recognize. The second man produced a key and unlocked my cell as Weiss said, "Come on. Your lawyer's here."

I was led to a small room furnished with a table and two chairs. Seated at the table was a balding, dark-skinned man in a darker business suit. He rose and offered me his right hand while proffering a card in his left, saying, "I'm Shervage Wood, from the firm of Lambton and Froech. We do a lot of work in computer law. I'm here to offer our services in defending you."

I took the hand and the card, which was imprinted with the same information he'd conveyed verbally. "You were sent by . . . ?"

"A friend of yours, I believe. A Ms. Alice Meade."

I nodded. "Okay, you're hired. What do we do now?"

"First, you tell me what's going on here."

I told him. When I got to the part about how I'd initially tried to cooperate with the FBI's interrogation, he put his face in his hands.

"Don't you know that you never talk to the Man without your lawyer in the room? Not when you're being charged with a crime. Okay, never mind, the damage is already done. I'll get a transcript of the interrogation and see if you said anything incriminating. It might not be too bad.

"We're going to go before a judge within about an hour or so and get you out on bail. Actually, under the circumstances I think we can get him to let you out on your own recognizance. You don't have any priors, and you look like a decent enough guy. You're probably going to have to agree to refrain from working with computers pending the outcome of your trial."

"But that's my career! How am I supposed to earn a living in the meantime?" Actually, at the moment I was much more worried about how I was going to continue working on the Wyrm threat than how I was going to pay my rent.

"I know how you feel, but don't say that to the judge. You might wind up in a cell instead."

An hour and a half later we went before the judge. She seemed like a nice, grandmotherly type, and I was starting to feel as if maybe my luck was changing just a little bit.

The federal prosecutor was a man in his thirties with thinning hair who looked overworked and underfed. He was skimming through a sheaf of documents when we entered, as if he was just familiarizing himself with the case. When the judge indicated that she was ready to hear arguments concerning my release, the prosecutor said, "Your Honor, in view of the seriousness of the charges in this case, and the tremendous potential for harm to society if the defendant continues to engage in these activities, we ask that bail be set at two hundred fifty thousand dollars."

I was almost ready to panic when I heard that. I looked over at Shervage, though, and he seemed unperturbed. Instead he rose and made his own argument, in which he pointed out the fact that I had no prior arrests, no criminal record, and was not charged with any violent crimes, so that public safety was not an issue. He managed to make it sound as if I were a pillar of the community who also helped old ladies across the street, and in addition was somehow able to strongly hint that the prosecution's case was a fishing expedition in a leaky boat. He was damn good.

So when we rose to hear the judge's decision, it was not without a certain expectation that things would go our way.

She turned to the prosecutor and said, "You don't seem to be in command of the facts of this case, Mr. Ball, and your arguments reflect that. You ask for bail based on the potential for harm to society by the defendant, but do you have any conception of the extent of harm that can be caused by the charges on this list? I don't think so, or you wouldn't have asked for bail of two hundred fifty thousand.

"Michael Arcangelo, you are remanded to federal custody pending bail of one million dollars."

I looked at Shervage again. His mouth was hanging open and his lips were moving, but no sounds were coming out.

"Can you raise a hundred thousand dollars?" my lawyer was asking. He might have had to ask several times, because I was in a minor state of shock.

"A hundred thousand? I thought the bail was a million."

"You have to put up ten percent. Can you do that?"

"Wait a minute. Why is it so high? I thought you said she would let me go on my own recognizance. What's going on?"

He shrugged. "I don't know. Either we just happened to get a crazy judge, or there's something political going on that we don't know about yet. My immediate concern, though, is to get you out of here. Can you make bail?"

I thought about it. "I'm going to have to sell my car. If I'm not allowed to work, I won't be able to afford the insurance payments, anyway."

"You plan on raising a hundred k by selling a car?"

"It's a Ferrari."

"Oh."

I was going to have to get someone to sell the car for me, and in the meantime I would be in jail. Only instead of occupying a holding cell at the local FBI headquarters, I would be shipped to some federal facility, presumably the kind for white-collar criminals. At least that's what I hoped.

A few hours later I was taken out of my cell, handcuffed, and shoved into the backseat of one of those plain dark sedans that feds are always supposed to drive, and apparently actually do. One agent rode shotgun, but he and the driver were silent. I hadn't seen either one of them before. Finally I said, "Is it too much to ask, or can you guys tell me what prison you're taking me to?"

The agent in the passenger seat looked back at me with an expression of surprise, as if he'd just noticed I was there. Then he turned around and looked at the road again. After a minute or two he said, "We're not taking you to a prison. You're going for another interrogation."

I said, "Not without my lawyer." I might be naive, but I'm capable of learning from experience.

He chuckled mirthlessly. "This isn't the kind of interrogation that lawyers approve of, so we try to protect their feelings by not having them there."

Visions of *1984* swam in my head. I had read that book when I was twelve years old, back when it actually *was* 1984. At the time it seemed like a relief that things hadn't turned out as badly as Orwell had foreseen. Suddenly I wasn't so sure.

"I didn't know the FBI went in for this kind of thing."

He shook his head. "Not the FBI. We've been instructed to hand you over to another agency."

That sent a chill through me, to go along with the fever-induced ones that were still periodically racking my body. I wondered if this "interrogation" had something to do with the classified information I'd received about neural-induction VR. I thought of Serafin's last words on the subject, and they didn't seem very encouraging. "What agency is that?"

"I can't give you that information."

"You're taking me somewhere to be interrogated by somebody, and you can't tell me who it is?"

"That information is classified." He actually seemed a bit uncomfortable, and I was beginning to wonder whether he knew himself. The driver knew where to go, at any rate.

We arrived at a nondescript office building in lower Manhattan, and I was hustled out of the car and onto an elevator. There weren't many people around, and the lobby of the building was deserted. We rode the elevator to the sixth floor.

Down the hallway from the elevator was an unmarked door of the reinforced-steel variety. We entered and found ourselves in a small alcove facing another such door. A video camera mounted above the door pointed down at us, its single red eye glaring balefully. A voice crackled over an intercom: "Yes?"

The shotgun agent cleared his throat. "Agent Rodolfsky from the FBI, here with Michael Arcangelo."

"Take the handcuffs off and leave him."

"Leave him?"

"Yes."

"Now, wait a minute. I'm going to need—"

"Take a look at your authorization. You are to leave him here. That is all."

Rodolfsky extracted a slightly crumpled sheet of paper from his coat pocket and studied it for a minute. Then he looked up and caught the driver's eye. "Let's go." He unlocked the handcuffs and pocketed them.

I had no great affection for Agent Rodolfsky, but at that moment I felt as if my last friend were leaving me. The door shut behind them, and a metallic click announced that it had locked. Another click emanated from the door in front of me, and the intercom voice said, "Come in."

Because retreat was impossible, it seemed like the only option. I suppressed the urge to crouch in a corner and whimper, squared my shoulders, turned the knob, and entered.

Inside was a small windowless room. A desktop computer was parked on a battered table; there was no chair for anyone who might want to use it. On the screen was the following message:

```
You are free to go.
```

Other than that the room was deserted.

I took a closer look at the computer. There was a phone line running into the back, no doubt to an internal modem. There were some other lines connected to peripherals that I didn't recognize, but I suspected that they handled video input from the alcove camera, locked and unlocked the doors, and so forth. Whoever had run this little scam could be anywhere in the world, as long as it had telephone service.

Because the room was windowless, I couldn't check to see if my recent escort had left yet. I decided to give them a good head start. While I waited, I looked around the room some more, but there wasn't much to see—aside from the computer equipment and a couple of empty pizza boxes in one corner, it was barren.

I looked at the pizza boxes again, and suddenly something clicked. It occurred to me that the person who was behind all this might still have a remote connection to the computer in the room, so I went back to the table. Too late; the screen now read:

```
No Carrier
```

I tried dialing for my Internet access account, which I had through one of my clients, a telecommunications outfit. Not surprisingly, I was locked out. I then tried a separate account that I maintained through another client under my hacker alias, "Engelbert." I was a little more concerned when I found that they were onto that one, too. I was starting to see how somebody might have misconstrued my 'net activities.

Fortunately, I had another trick up my sleeve: An account at my alma mater that I maintained primarily for local access when I was on the West Coast, but very rarely used. Of course, it was a long-distance call from there; I wondered who would be getting the bill.

My Caltech account had apparently escaped notice. I logged on, then selected the web-browser. I was starting to feel the glimmerings of a hunch. I aimed the browser at an on-line encyclopedia and looked up "Vamana." Strange as it may seem, I had never wondered about the significance of the name before. Now my hunch was telling me that it was important. In a few seconds the answer was in front of me. Vamana: an incarnation of the Hindu god Vishnu as . . . a dwarf.

I closed the web-browser and telnetted to Wormwood. Once I had assumed my Malakh persona, I started working my way back through the maze from the room where we'd had our fateful—and for me, fatal—encounter with the guivre. In my ghostly condition it was pretty easy. Nothing could see me or bother me.

Eventually I arrived back at the dilapidated rope bridge across the chasm. Momentarily, I wondered what would be the effect of a long fall on a ghost, but now wasn't the time for such experimentation.

I shouted, "Vamana!"

There was a long pause. I was beginning to think I had come up dry when a hairy hand appeared over the lip of the precipice. In another moment the hand was followed by the rest of the troll's squat, hirsute anatomy.

Yep, there he was, hacker legend, scourge of the Internet, dwarf-god of cyberspace, the *nanus ex machina* himself. "Roger Dworkin."

He said, "How did you know?"

"I didn't until just now. But I started wondering who could possibly have run that little operation that sprang me from federal custody. I couldn't think of anybody but you, and, as Sherlock Holmes used to say, when you've eliminated the impossible, then whatever is left, however improbable—"

"Must be true."

"How the hell did you do it, anyway?"

"Get them to let you go? That was just an RQH-4479."

"RQH-4479?"

"Authorization for transfer from civil to military custody."

"Military!"

"Yes. Well, sort of. You are now officially in the custody of a military intelligence agency so secret nobody knows about it."

"Nobody?"

"Yeah. Everybody important enough to have a clearance to know about it—people like the president and the chairman of the Joint Chiefs of Staff—are too important to bother with such small potatoes."

I've heard my share of stories about Byzantine bureaucracies, but this just didn't add up. Then it dawned on me. "This isn't a real agency, is it?"

The gap-toothed grin appeared, and I felt a twinge of annoyance at him for wasting time on such atmospherics. "It's remarkable what you can do with the right level of computer access," he said. "I was able to direct a little 'black budget' funding to an agency ostensibly specializing in computer counterespionage."

"A little?"

"Just a few million."

"Uh-huh. This is how you knew about the neural-induction link?"

"Not just knew about it, but was able to procure the hardware for, ah, agency purposes."

"I see. So who was the stiff?"

"You mean the dead person they thought was me? Somebody you know, actually, or maybe I should say know *of*. I don't actually know his real name, but his hacker handle was Beelzebub."

"Beelzebub! He's been dead all this time? How did he get mixed up in this thing in the first place?"

"I'm still not entirely sure. But he didn't get involved until someone—or something—on the 'net tried to kill me."

"Huh? How could something on the 'net . . . wait—you were using neural-induction hardware?"

"You seem to have quite a bit of information. How did you find out about that? And please don't tell me that you're just a very good guesser."

"I won't. One of the other players in my group—you know him as Tahmurath—"

"—is Arthur Solomon. Right, his company must have had some defense contracts—they probably even developed some of the NIL software. I should have thought of that."

"And Beelzebub: Was he killed through the NIL hookup?"

"That's what I think must have happened, though I don't know for sure. After they nearly got me the first time, I didn't want to risk using that stuff again. . . ."

"Good idea."

"Yeah. So I cleared out. Apparently Beelzebub was able to break into the house where I'd stashed the NIL hardware, although how he did it, or even knew it was there, is a mystery to me. Since then I've been trying to monitor what's going on through the dwarf."

"Dwarf? I thought you were a troll."

He grinned his gap-toothed grin. "You haven't seen one of my trolls yet. Eight feet tall and eat adventurers for breakfast, they do. Anyway, somehow this Beelzebub luser found out about my setup and got in. He was using it, too; I saw him on the 'net. Next thing I know, I hear that he's dead. Or, rather, that I'm dead. Since I didn't know who had tried to kill me in the first place, I decided that the safest course would be to let them think they'd been successful."

"That makes a certain amount of sense. One thing I don't understand, though, is why you went to the trouble of busting me out."

"Oh, that. Well, I told you I'd been monitoring you, and not just in the game. I've been able to gather that a seriously Bad Thing is getting ready to happen at the end of the year, and you seem to be one of the few people who knows enough about it to help try to stop it."

"Okay. What do *you* know about what's going on?"

"Well, I'm afraid some—but not all—of it may be my fault. I know you figured out that I'd planted a Trojan in MABUS-two-k. But someone—or something—has taken control of the whole system."

"That's the second time you've said 'someone or some*thing*.' What is that supposed to mean?"

"I think you already know. Some kind of AI."

"And you think that's what tried to kill you?"

"Yes. The first inkling I had that something weird was going on was that some of the creatures in the game started behaving strangely.

Some of them were fairly complex AI programs in their own right, but they seemed smarter than I'd programmed them to be. At first I thought that some hacker had gotten into the system and was messing around with the code. It's still a possibility, and maybe a more plausible one than this rogue AI idea."

"Except that Beelzebub, who would have been a prime suspect in the hacker hypothesis, turns up dead in the second act."

"Yeah. I have to admit, for a while I thought he was behind the whole thing."

"By the way, the 'creatures' that were affected—were they any particular variety?"

"Dragon types, generally. Why?"

I filled him in on what we had surmised: that Wyrm was an intelligent self-propagating program that in some way identified with dragons in general, and Satan in the Book of Revelation in particular.

When I had finished, he was silent for a few seconds. Then he said, "That is so weird, it actually makes sense. At least it explains some of the weirdness that I've seen going on. How are you planning to stop it?"

"Well, we've been trying to figure out this game of yours, for starters. But now you can help us with that, by telling us what to look for and where."

"No, I can't."

"You can't? Why the hell not?"

"Because I don't know. I wanted to be able to *play* this game, not just design it. It wouldn't be much fun if I knew all the secrets to begin with. What I did, basically, was write an AI program that would in turn write the game."

"Oh. While we're on the subject, one more question: Why go to all this trouble—breaking the law, taking a lot of risks—for the sake of a game?"

"Don't you see? It's not just a game, it's a . . . an alternate reality—a different way to *be*. A world where you can defy all the normal boundaries of ordinary existence: travel faster than the speed of light, journey backward or forward in time, bring fairy-tale creatures to life. It's incredible. I wanted to create this world so that I could live in it."

"The real world isn't so bad."

"Maybe not for you. For me it's . . . mundane. Besides, what is 'real' anyway? Maybe reality is what you experience."

I was suddenly struck by the utter absurdity of the situation. Here I was, talking with hacker demigod Roger Dworkin, a man who everybody thought was dead. He appears to me on the 'net in the form of a half-naked hairy dwarf. And now he wants to talk metaphysics. There was only one thing that kept me from laughing out loud.

"What are we going to do about Wyrm?"

"Well, you're never going to succeed at this rate; I've been trying to help your friends, but their characters aren't powerful enough, and by the time they are, it'll all be over."

"Actually, my character is dead."

"I did notice that."

"So what can we do?"

"Well, there is a way to get a privileged logon—then you might have a prayer."

"Really? How?"

"I'm not sure you'll be interested. It requires the use of a neural-induction link."

"Are you crazy? You told me you nearly got killed using one. And that Beelzebub probably did get killed that way. Why would I take a risk like that?"

"Because the stakes are very high, as you know."

"So why don't *you* do it?"

"I'm not really hero material. But you . . . you've got possibilities."

"But the building must still be under police seal. We couldn't get to the equipment anyway."

"I have a backup system stashed . . . somewhere. Are you interested?"

I thought about it. The damnable thing was, he was right; the stakes *were* very high, measured in terms of loss of life, even the collapse of civilization. You could even argue that there might be more risk to me personally by *not* doing it, because if even half of what we thought might happen did, then nobody would be safe anyway. My personal risk, though, paled beside the larger danger to the five billion people inhabiting the planet. And also, in my own mind, to the tiny fraction of that five billion that I personally knew and cared about. I suddenly thought of my little nephew and namesake; I didn't want his third birthday to be his last. "Where is it?"

"In San Francisco."

"Okay. Just tell me where to go, and I'll be on my way."

"Not so fast."

"What's the matter?"

"You're supposed to be in federal custody. You can't just waltz into the airport and buy a ticket in your own name. Besides, they've frozen all your financial assets, including locking your credit cards."

"So what do I do?"

"Do you have any cash?"

"No. They took all my stuff."

"Okay. There's an ATM just down the street—a branch of Tower Bank. When you get there, the screen will say, 'temporarily out of service.' Ignore it and punch in nine-nine-seven-six. Then go to the American terminal at La Guardia and tell them you're Mitchell Lange. They'll have a ticket for you."

He gave me some further directions concerning the whereabouts of the NIL hardware, and I hit the trail. The ATM dispensed a thousand dollars, which I thought might be overdoing it a bit, although I didn't know how long I'd have to make it last. As I was stuffing the money into my pockets, I heard a voice behind me say, "We'll take that."

My first thought was that the feds had figured out what was going on and had caught up with me already, but when I turned around, there were three guys who looked like overgrown members of a street gang. The one in the middle was the biggest. His shaved head was pierced in about half a dozen places with assorted rings, bars, and studs, and he wore torn jeans and a leather vest, which, in defiance of the wintry temperature, left his arms bare, the better to display his collection of tattoos. The other two were similarly attired, coiffed, inked, and perforated. And, of course, they all had the "666" tattoo on their heads. The big guy, who apparently was the one who had spoken, was grinning, revealing a large gap where his front teeth had been. To my mild relief nobody was brandishing a gun—but, then, there was no reason for them to think that they would need one.

Obviously, it wasn't worth getting killed over money. On the other hand, without the money I had no way of getting to La Guardia, no way of catching my flight, and no way of accessing Roger Dworkin's NIL setup, and therefore, if Roger Dworkin was to be believed, no realistic shot at stopping Wyrm. So I said, "Fuck you," and turned back to the ATM.

Ushiro-geri, or the "back-kick," is one of my favorite karate techniques. One reason is that, with your back turned, an untrained assailant assumes that you're completely at his mercy and, when he moves in to attack, leaves himself wide-open. The kick that I aimed at my would-be mugger's solar plexus was off slightly in both timing and aim, but the kick is such a powerful one that it didn't much matter; as my heel slammed into his abdomen, a whoosh of air exploded out of his lungs, and he hit the deck in the fetal position, gasping and turning purple.

With the ringleader temporarily hors de combat, and his two cohorts in a momentary state of shock, the thing to do would have been to carry the fight to them. Unfortunately, at that moment a wave of nausea and dizziness washed over me, probably triggered by the excitement and exertion. This gave the reserves a chance to recover, and they moved to come at me from opposite directions, one of them pulling a knife. I don't know whether it was my illness, adrenaline, or just the knowledge that I could be dead in the next five minutes, but I felt a peculiar sense of unreality. It was as if the casual violence of Dworkin's hack-and-slash game had taken on material form, and the barrier between cyberspace and real life had been ripped away. I faced the knife wielder, giving the other one an opening for an attack, but he had learned from his buddy's misfortune and was holding back. The knife wielder was less cautious, and he lunged in with a left-handed underhand thrust aimed for my belly. I managed to block and hold on to the arm with my left hand, bringing a right-handed punch over the top and connecting solidly just under his ear, but at that moment the other one barreled into me, throwing all three of us against the ATM.

I was pinned back against the ATM, still holding the knife arm of one assailant, while the other had his arms around my waist and his shoulder in my gut. I yanked on the arm, then released my grip, reached for both heads, and slammed them together as hard as I could. The one with his arms around me let go and fell to the ground, clutching the top of his head as blood from his split scalp streamed between his fingers. The guy with the knife just wandered aimlessly down the street with a blank expression on his face.

"What the hell you call that? Tae Kwon *Moe?*"

I jumped about a meter in the air, thanks to the adrenaline coursing through my veins. "Jamaal! What the hell are *you* doing here?"

"I might ask you the same question. Then again, I can *see* what you've been doing." He gave me a hard look. "You in some kind of trouble?"

I nodded.

Just then some shouts echoed down the street. We both turned and saw four more skinheads bearing down on us. "Get outta here," Jamaal told me.

"But—"

"No 'buts,' man. You already had your fun. Leave these guys to me."

I glanced at the big one, but he was still on the ground making faint retching sounds, so I sprinted to the corner and hailed a taxi. With a backward glance to see if I was being chased (I wasn't; Jamaal had already decked two of them, and the remaining two were backing off) I hopped in, and the cab lurched away from the curb, merging with the flow of traffic by barreling into a line of cars, forcing the ones behind us to slam on their brakes. I glanced back at the curb to see if my stomach was actually still there, or if it only felt that way. Come to think of it, the way I'd been feeling, I'd probably be better off without it.

Meanwhile, my mind was going about a mile a minute. Was Jamaal mixed up in this thing somehow? Had Dworkin contacted him? Or was it just a big, fat coincidence? I was jolted out of my confusion by the taxi driver, who was asking for a destination.

The cabbie was unusual for New York—he actually spoke English, if that's the correct term for the patois spoken by natives of Brooklyn. He had about three days' worth of stubble on his chin, and the stump of an unlit cigar between his teeth. "Where to, Mac?"

"La Guardia."

"La Gwahdia? Waya goin'?"

"California."

"Califawnia? Dat's nice. I wish I was goin' ta Califawnia. Ya got family?" He jerked the wheel spasmodically, causing the cab to dart laterally across three lanes of traffic, and eliciting a chorus of blaring horns from the cars he had narrowly missed.

"No, my family's here. I'm . . . going to see some friends."

"Dat's nice. Watch yaself, dough. Ya see where dese religious nuts is all over da ehpawts?" Having gotten into the lane he preferred, he now accelerated to about seventy miles an hour, slowing momentarily to scream an obscenity at a driver who was trying to pull his parked car away from the curb. Actually, the worst thing about his driving was that it was reminding me how much I missed Al.

"What are they doing in the airports?"

"Tryin' ta go ta da Holy Land. Da ones dat got money is already gone. Dese udda ones is tryin' ta get it so dey can go too. Dey t'ink da woild is gonna end dis week." He was now rolling his window back up, having lowered it to facilitate making a few particularly rude gestures at a taxi in the lane next to us.

"What do you think?"

"What do I t'ink? Huh, dat's a good question, what do I t'ink. I t'ink if it doesn't end dis week, den I gotta come back on Monday an' drive dis stinkin' cab again."

I refrained from pointing out that, considering his driving, that wasn't exactly a foregone conclusion.

I arrived in San Francisco without incident, if feeling totally paranoid for about six hours can be described so innocuously. I didn't really need the air-sickness bag, because by now it was pretty much all dry heaves. I found my way to the place where Dworkin had sent me—a small, nondescript house within walking distance from the campus of the University of California at San Francisco. I figured he'd probably somehow piggybacked his link onto the UCSF backbone. There was a keypad on the door, and I punched in 9976; the door unlatched and I entered. The place was clean and neat, which led me to believe that Dworkin had intended it for a backup but had never actually used it. I found the stairs that led to the basement and took them, as I'd been instructed. There was a single large room paneled in knotty pine. Most of it was taken up by some very arcane-looking equipment. Nearby a computer workstation was set up. I booted the workstation and got back in touch with Dworkin via Wormwood, as before.

"What do I do now?"

"Well, actually, you shave your head."

"Why?"

"The SQUID array in the helmet is very sensitive, but it's important to have as close a contact as possible."

"SQUID array?"

"Superconducting quantum interference devices."

"I know what it stands for. I thought this was a maser hologram thingie."

"That's the output. Your input into it is via the minute electrical impulses in your brain, which are detected by the SQUIDs."

I went back upstairs to the bathroom and found the scissors, clippers, and razor that Dworkin had told me would be there. It took longer than I thought it would, partly because of having to pause for some more dry heaves, but when I was finished, I was as hairless as a cue ball.

"Okay, I did it. Now what?"

"You've got to give yourself a shot."

"What?"

"There's a drug you need to take to protect your central nervous system from . . . certain adverse effects. It's a derivative of cone-shell toxin."

I didn't need to ask him about the "adverse effects," after having seen Seth Serafin. "You want me to inject myself with a toxin?"

"A *derivative* of a toxin. It won't hurt you—probably."

"Probably?"

"Well, if you took too much, it could paralyze you. But you're not going to take too much; there's a set of autoinjectors with the right dose in the small refrigerator in the corner."

It didn't take a genius to realize that he wasn't telling me everything. I didn't have much choice, though. I found the injectors, along with some alcohol swabs. I've heard that in states where capital punishment is administered via lethal injection, it is customary to swab the injection site with alcohol before administering the deadly drugs. I couldn't help thinking of that as I swabbed my own arm, and hoping that the precaution wasn't equally pointless in my case.

"Each injection is good for about eight hours, so if you're in the link longer than that, you'll have to reinject yourself."

"Okay, now what?"

"Now you sit in the recliner. Then place the helmet on your head. You're going to get a series of calibration prompts, telling you to move this or wiggle that. It will take about an hour and a half altogether. Then I'll be able to talk to you through the NIL."

I started to follow the instructions, then went back to the workstation. "There's no vidscreen on the helmet."

"That's right. This equipment feeds the images directly to your optical cortex. All you have to do is close your eyes. There's an automatic cutoff that interrupts the video input when your eyes are open."

I went back and donned the helmet, then leaned back and closed my eyes. The calibration routine took quite a long time, but that's not too surprising, considering that the system was basically constructing a detailed map of my cerebral cortex.

Dworkin's face, or, rather, the dwarf's, swam into view and grinned his by-now-familiar gap-toothed grin. "How does it feel?"

"Okay so far." The background scenery now appeared. Only it was far more detailed and realistic than the screen graphics had been. And in 3-D. "So now I've got some special capabilities?"

His grin stretched wider. "You're in wheel mode."

I looked down at myself and saw that my body was encased in golden armor that seemed to glow. "After I died, we found out that I couldn't go anywhere I hadn't already been while I was still alive. I take it I'm free of that restriction now?"

"Yes."

"Good. Then where should we go?"

"To find Eltanin."

"You know where it is?"

"No. I told you, the program did all that stuff."

"Well, can't you make it tell us where it is?"

"Before, it would have been a piece of cake. Now I think it would only alert our adversary to the fact that we're doing something significant."

"Oh? And what about me? Isn't my logon going to set off some alarms?"

"Possibly. That's a chance we're going to have to take."

Very reassuring. "Is there a way to find out if the others are on-line now?"

"Yes. You can also communicate with them and travel directly to where they are, if you want to."

"Maybe we should do that. By the way, do you know of anything in cyberspace called the Great Seal?"

He scratched his furry head. "No, I don't. Is it important?"

"It's a clue to where Eltanin is."

"Hmmm. Just a minute. I'll do a quick search to see if there's anything like that on the 'net. Okay, Great Balls of Fire, Great Caesar's Ghost, Great Scott . . . here's something called the Great Seal of the United States."

"That doesn't sound too promising."

"Wait a minute, something's ringing a bell here . . . say! Did you ever read the *Illuminatus!* trilogy?"

"Back in high school, I think."

"And you don't remember the bit about how some mysterious person gave Thomas Jefferson the design for the Great Seal of the United States?"

"I vaguely remember something like that. It's supposed to be on the dollar bill, isn't it?"

"Yes. You got a buck on you? Wait, don't break the connection, I'll give you a graphic."

A few seconds later it loomed into view, the reverse side of a dollar bill, displaying the Great Seal: the eye in the pyramid.

"It's in the pyramid!"

"What pyramid?"

"I'm not sure. I'm betting it's in the ziggurat in Babylon, though."

"Go get it! No, wait a minute. Before you go there, go to here—" He gave me a telnet address. "There's something that ought to help you."

Dworkin showed me how to use my new abilities to "warp" through cyberspace. It turned out I could go anywhere directly, as long as I had the telnet address. "How are you going to come? Or is there a way I can take you with me?"

"You can take anybody you want with you, but I can't go with you just now. You're on your own, at least for a while. I'll stay in touch. Don't call me by name on the 'net again, though."

"What should I call you?"

"Call me Ptah."

▲　▲　▲　▲　▲　▲　▲

I materialized at the entrance of a cavern that led into the interior of what appeared to be an active volcano. A distant ringing sound, as of metal on metal, seemed to be coming from inside. As I followed the sound, it got louder and louder until I thought my eardrums would be damaged. Then I remembered that my eardrums weren't being affected a bit. This was all going on inside my head.

The noise was truly deafening as I approached the opening into a vast natural chamber. Along with the noise, a reddish glare emanated from the opening, and I thought I might have arrived at the volcano's center. But when I cautiously poked my head around the corner, I could see that the light was coming from an enormous forge. Three giants surrounded an anvil the size of a house, pounding on it with hammers that could crush a mountain; the top of the anvil was too high for me to get a look at whatever they were forging. My first impulse was to draw back, but one of them turned to look at me. He had a single eye in the middle of his forehead. Cyclopean facial expressions are a bit difficult to read (Is the eyebrow angling up or down?) but he actually seemed to recognize me. He turned to look at his brothers, and they all put down their hammers. They went to one end of the cavern, and all three of them gripped the rocky wall and began to push. For a moment I thought they were trying to bring the cavern roof down on our heads, but as they all strained in unison, the wall slowly began to move back. They continued to push until they had exposed an opening into another chamber. From my angle I couldn't see into it at all, but the glow that emanated from the room was not reddish, but golden.

As the other two watched, the giant who had first recognized me passed through the opening. A few moments later he emerged and approached me. Kneeling before me, he opened his hand and proffered the object it contained. It was a sheathed sword.

Resting on his Brobdingnagian palm, the sword seemed ludicrously small—proportionately the size of a toothpick. When I picked it up, though, I found that its size was perfectly suited to my own. I slid it partly out of the scabbard and was almost blinded—again I had to remind myself that my actual sense organs were not being affected by any of these experiences—by the blade, which had the brightness of a frozen lightning bolt.

I arrived in Babylon at the foot of the pyramid, saw the entrance and a really fat monk sitting on a wall. The monk looked at me, opened his eyes wide, as if in surprise, and toppled off the wall. I tried to catch him before he hit, but it was too late; he struck the ground with a loud crack. That's right, not a "thud" or even a "splat," but a "crack." I rushed to his side and found that his ovoid shape was not due to excess adipose, after all—he was some kind of an egg, and his shell had split. There was no egg white or yolk leaking from the sundered shell, however. Instead, something red and scaly was starting to poke little bits of itself out of the cracks—Humpty Dumpty was hatching!

As I watched, the creature forced the largest crack open wider and slithered out. It was a small winged serpent. I actually thought it was kind of cute—for about half a second, and then it suddenly started to swell to monstrous proportions, rearing above me and lashing forward with a mouth full of long fangs. I dodged to one side and drew the sword the Cyclops had given me, slashing at his exposed flank. The sword bit easily through his scales, producing a smell of charred flesh, and he screamed and snapped his jaws, aiming for one of my wings (I had wings?). I spun away from the attack and flew into the air. What the hell, as long as I had wings, might as well use them.

The amphiptere—for that's what my text window said was attacking me—spread its wings and followed. We met in midair, and I realized I should have stayed on the ground—the monster was an expert flyer, and I was on my first solo. Still, a winged serpent is not a design that offers optimum aerial maneuverability, and I managed to hold my own on the first couple of passes. The snake knew a few dogfighting tricks, though, because he managed to get above me, and used his superior altitude to power a diving attack. I saw him plummeting toward me, fanged jaws open wide, and I knew that if I couldn't avoid the attack somehow, it would be all over.

I knew the biggest mistake would be to move prematurely and give him a chance to correct his course. I waited until the last moment, then darted to one side. He managed to swing his jaws far enough to slash at my back, drawing blood (or ichor, or whatever I was bleeding) with his razor-sharp fangs. I swung my sword as hard as I could, but most of the impact of my blow was supplied by the monster's own momentum; I sheared off about two thirds of his left wing. He screamed again and continued plummeting toward the ground, his dive turning into a tight spiral when he attempted to stop it by extending his remaining wing. The sound of his hitting the ground was most satisfying—a combination of the thud and splat that Humpty Dumpty *didn't* make. He didn't move again. A crowd of people immediately began to gather around the carcass.

I ignored them and flew straight to the top of the ziggurat. The blue-glazed walls of the seventh stage were pierced by a pair of golden doors. The doors stood open, and in the alcove within stood a golden statue of Marduk the dragon-slayer. In one outstretched hand he held an orb of nacreous white—a giant pearl, perhaps, although it was almost the size of a softball.

Eltanin.

I took the orb in my left hand, and everything around me immediately changed. The walls of the pyramid became transparent, and I could look below and see thousands of monks working in their cells or roaming the maze of passageways within. But more than that, my text window began to display something; I studied it for a while and came to realize that it was the source code for whatever object I was viewing.

I suddenly realized that there were some questions I had for Ptah about this thing I was holding in my hand, and the moment I thought of him, his image appeared in the orb's surface.

"Ptah?"

"Yes, it's me. How are you doing that?"

"With Eltanin."

"You got it? Great! Have you figured out anything else it can do yet?"

"I just got my hands on it this second. But it seems to be showing me source code for any object I look at."

"Cool."

"Hey, I just had a thought. That anagram magic that Art told me about—can I do that?"

"You can do that and more than that. You can actually change and, in some cases add and subtract, letters."

I wasn't sure what he was driving at. We were talking about wordplay, and he made it sound like the ultimate weapon. "Is that supposed to be especially difficult?"

"It is. See, the way it works is, letters and words are like matter. Rearranging them is simple, because matter is conserved, like a chemical reaction. Changing one letter to another letter takes more energy—it's like transmuting an element. And adding a letter takes a tremendous amount of energy."

"Then taking a letter out should release energy, right?"

"Exactly, you've got the idea. Except that you first have to put in enough energy to reach a certain threshold, like in a nuclear reactor."

"So the limit is when you run out of some kind of energy?"

"For most people it is. Not for you; you can't run out. Your only limit is how much you can channel at one time. If you try to handle too much, you're dead. Well, net-dead, anyway."

"Net-dead? Are you forgetting about the fact that my central nervous system is directly wired into the 'net at this moment?"

"Hmm, you've got a point there. Maybe more than net-dead."

I opened my mouth to curse, then started back as the statue of Marduk suddenly opened its mouth and, in a voice like a pipe organ, intoned, "From the first wonder to the last." In the next instant Eltanin vanished in a puff of smoke.

"What the hell does that mean?"

He didn't answer. Okay, so that was going to be my only clue. "From the first wonder to the last." Wonder? George had told me about Al saying that the ziggurat itself was, according to some theories, the basis of the stories about the Hanging Gardens of Babylon, which were considered one of the seven wonders of the ancient world. I smacked my head with a virtual hand: "From wyrm-slayer's garden . . ."—Marduk's garden, the Hanging Gardens of Babylon. That had to be it. And the next part, ". . . to avatar's grave," had to correspond with the "last wonder." I had no idea if the hanging gardens were the first wonder, but I was pretty sure I knew where to find the last one. And the last one happened to be the tomb of a god made flesh—an avatar's grave.

I opened my text window and did a search for what I wanted; then I warped through cyberspace again.

It was a moonlit night on the plain of Giza, giving the ancient necropolis an especially creepy quality. I felt a strange aura of anticipation, as if something was about to happen. It did.

As I looked on, a shimmering passed over the Great Pyramid of Cheops, or, if you prefer, Khufu. When it passed, the pyramid was no longer a decaying ruin; it looked as it must have when it was just completed nearly five thousand years ago. The Great Pyramid was totally encased in a mantle of polished white limestone, which appeared almost translucent in the moonlight. The gold-sheathed capstone was in place.

Just then I heard a deep rumble. The sphinx rose from its millennia-long crouch, and for a moment I thought I had another fight on my hands. The rough beast didn't so much as glance in my direction, though, but instead yawned, stretched its leonine body, and then slouched off toward the east. For some reason that redoubled my sense of foreboding.

I looked for a way to get into the pyramid and found that it was now concealed under the limestone mantle. I shrugged and started to say "Open sesame," but I didn't get past the word "open" because as soon as I said it, a section of limestone vanished, revealing the entrance to an upward-sloping passage.

I gave a low whistle. Dworkin wasn't kidding about "wheel mode." I then discovered that it was not only the exterior that had been restored to original condition; the enormous granite plugs that sealed off the passage were lodged firmly in their sockets. Once again all it took was my command, "Open," and the first seal retracted into the ceiling.

I made my way along the upward-slanting passage, repeating the process wherever I encountered an obstacle, through the grand gallery, up through the ceiling of the burial chamber, until I was in a small chamber that was just below the apex. The center of the chamber's ceiling was the base of the capstone. There was a hole in it. Wondering if I was going to pull back a bloody stump, I reached into the hole and groped around. My hand closed on something round and smooth, and even before I drew it forth, I knew. Once again I held Eltanin.

I looked at the orb itself, and it seemed to whisper in my mind, "What wouldst thou see?"

Before I could decide what I wanted to look at, the whole pyramid started to rumble and rock as if in an earthquake. It felt as if something gigantic was burrowing its way up from the pyramid's foundation as the rumbling intensified.

CHAPTER SIXTEEN

Four Horsemen and a Queen Sacrifice

And he gathered them together into a place
called in the Hebrew tongue Armageddon.
—Revelation 16:16

Tahmurath stood on the crest of a rocky knoll, surveying the dismal prospect before him. Filthy raindrops pelted down from a leaden sky, coating everything in black, tarry mud. Encampments dotted the blasted plain, small campfires flickering feebly in the gloom.

Another figure approached, muffled in a cloak that was as mud spattered as Tahmurath's own. "Hi," Ragnar said. "Looks like we're marshaling the hosts, huh?"

Tahmurath nodded, "We put out the word over every newsgroup, MUD, and BBS we could reach. Nice solution to the 'chain letter' problem, by the way."

"Thanks." Ragnar had proposed a kind of anti–chain letter; as in a normal chain letter, each recipient was instructed to add his name to the letter before forwarding it, but the letter also contained an instruction that it was not to be forwarded if it already contained five names.

"Seems like everybody is getting funneled to this location. Wyrm must be doing it, but don't ask me how or why."

"As for how," Ragnar said, "with control over the whole 'net it can probably create any size virtual space that it wants."

"Yeah, that's what scares me: that it has that kind of control."

Ragnar shook his head as he surveyed the assembled multitudes. "Seems like quite a response, but I still have my doubts about using the 'Mongolian Horde technique.' Who are they?"

"MUD gods and wizards, hackers of all kinds, you name it. Istari, Bene Gesserit, Dorsai, Deryni, Talamasca, the Order of the Peacock Angel, the Decided Ones of Jupiter the Thunderer." Tahmurath pointed to the groups as he named them. "There are at least three outfits calling themselves the Knights Templar. Only one of them is on our side, though. The Discordians are here in large numbers. And I've lost count of how many Illuminati there are."

"Where are the Discordians?"

"Over there. And some are back there, and there were a few over in that direction—"

"Never mind, I get the idea."

He gestured across the field to where the enemy host was encamped. "I don't much like the looks of that bunch, though."

The hellish hordes seemed to include every malign supernatural creature imaginable. There were demons, devils, asuras, rakshasas, div, pretas, *oni, gaki,* afrit, djinnis, and many other things, some of which defied classification.

"It's a little weird," Ragnar said, "not playing in the snake pit."

"Yeah, I know what you mean." When they arrived at Cepheus, they had discovered that the snake pit was locked. Arthur figured this was probably due to a malfunction in the security system, but as a result, they had to disperse to separate rooms in the building, each with its own workstation.

A closer look at the allied forces revealed that many of the groups were assembled under particular banners. One banner nearby displayed what looked like an inverted letter *V*. As Ragnar and Tahmurath descended the hill to rejoin the rest of the party, a knight rode up bearing a shield with the same insignia, over a depiction of a rather comical-looking bird. He was wearing a ridiculously oversize helmet that was shaped like a horse's head. "The Dodo!" Megaera exclaimed as he dismounted. "Is that you, TD?"

He raised his visor and smiled beneath his long white mustache. "The same. But you have me at a disadvantage."

"It's Medea," she said.

The grin broadened. "Hail and well met!"

"Who are you guys supposed to be, anyway?" Gunnodoyak asked. "The Knights Who Say Nih?"

"No, they're over there." He indicated the direction with a gauntleted finger. "We're—"

"I know who you are!" Ragnar exclaimed. "Damn it, I wish Mike were here to see this."

"We're delighted to have your group in our camp, Sir Dodo," Tahmurath said.

"Sir Ludovico," he corrected. "And we're happy to be here. I hope we can be of some assistance." Suddenly he leaned forward, squinting at Tahmurath's chest. "Oh," he said. "How rude."

Tahmurath appeared quite nonplussed. "What's rude? What do you mean?"

"Why are you wearing a pendant that says 'Eat me'?"

Tahmurath lifted the disk that was hanging over his chest and scrutinized it. "It's my magic cookie. But this writing wasn't on it before." He turned to the others in his group. "See if it's on yours, too."

"Already checking," Ragnar responded, retrieving his "cookie" from a pouch. "Yup, here it is."

The others found that their "cookies" had been similarly marked.

"Okay," Tahmurath said. "This one's a no-brainer. Who's going to go first?"

"I was feeling a tad peckish anyway," Ragnar commented, popping his cookie into his mouth and munching away.

"I hope you were supposed to chew it," Megaera said, dubiously.

"Why not?"

"I was thinking it might be like receiving the Eucharist—you're taking something special or holy into your body, so you're not supposed to chew it."

In the next instant, however, the point was rendered moot as Ragnar suddenly changed, transforming from a slender half-elvish harper into a tall human knight clad in shining armor, and bearing a shield emblazoned with a crimson cross. The muddy rain, which continued to fall, seemed to slough away from him now, leaving his armor and cloak pristine.

As they stared in amazement, a loud whinny sounded from nearby, and they turned to see an enormous white horse approaching them. The destrier was saddled and armored, and marked with the red cross, as well. He trotted to the side of the knight, who was obviously intended to ride him, and stood there as if waiting for him to mount.

"Well, Ragnar, it looks like your walking days are over," Zerika remarked.

Megaera was the first to notice the nimbus of light flickering around his head. "And on top of that, it looks like you've been canonized."

"Canonized?" Ragnar responded. "What's that, the process of being turned into cannon fodder?"

"You've got a halo."

"Oh." Ragnar, who had reacted to his metamorphosis, and even the arrival of his mount, with something like equanimity seemed genuinely disconcerted by this news.

"St. Ragnar," Megaera mused. "Although I don't know if we should call you Ragnar anymore. You certainly don't look like him. Take your helmet off for a minute."

"Okay. Who do I look like?"

"Actually, George, you look like *you*."

George ran a hand over his bare head. "Ain't that a fine how do you do? Now I can't even have hair in my fantasies!"

"Maybe that isn't a halo, after all," Gunnodoyak suggested. "Maybe it's just the glare off his head."

"Hey!"

"I guess I'll go next," Tahmurath said. In a few more moments he was transformed into a regal figure, wearing a purple-fringed white robe over armor of gold, and a helmet that was topped with a corona of golden spikes. Like George, he now seemed to be untouched by the muddy raindrops that continued to bespatter everyone else.

"Ooh!" Zerika cried. "He must be a king!"

"Why?" George deadpanned. "Because he hasn't got shit all over him?"

"Shut up, George."

"Hey," Arthur remarked, looking down at his side, "I have a scabbard, but it's empty."

"That's funny; George has a sword in his," Zerika observed. "Is it the same one you had before?" she asked.

"Yep," George replied, drawing the blade. "It's still Hanlon's Razor."

In the meantime Gunnodoyak had brought out the golf bag with its assortment of magical weapons. "Might as well put something in it, boss. Take your pick."

"Hmmm. Blackwand and Stormbringer are too big, plus I'd probably kill myself with either one of them. I think I'll take Calad Bolg. I'll tell you this, though: If this whole thing comes down to me swinging a sword, I think we can all kiss our asses good-bye."

The rest of the group ate their magic cookies and underwent their respective metamorphoses. The most dramatic changes were in Zerika and Ali. Zerika transformed into a great bird with brilliant iridescent feathers that flashed every color of the spectrum. Ali became a curious hybrid creature with the body and hindquarters of a lion, and the head, wings, and talons of an eagle. His feathers and fur were the color of burnished gold.

Gunnodoyak's skin turned blue, and in place of his simple monk's robe he now wore the rich raiment of an eastern prince and, incongruously, carried a herdsman's staff. He also shrank in size and apparent age until he looked to be about four years old.

Megaera lost her heroic stature, becoming smaller, slimmer, darker. Her armor was replaced by a simple white gown, and her great cross-hilted sword shrank until the whole thing fit into the palm of one of her small hands. A diadem rested on her hair, and a nimbus of light flickered around her head.

"Looks like you've been simonized, too," George commented.

"Canonized."

"Whatever."

In fact, when the transformations were complete, Al, George, and Arthur all wore halos around their heads, and Robin, Leon, and Krishna had luminous auras surrounding their entire bodies.

Just then a rather comical figure arrived on the scene. He was ancient in appearance, with a long, tangled white beard that seemed to be harboring several species of birds and rodents. A pair of spectacles was perched near the tip of his long nose, and he wore a tall, pointed hat, and midnight-colored robes, emblazoned with golden stars, crescents, and zodiacal signs. He also had a couple of similarly attired apprentices in tow. "Is this a private party," he inquired, "or can anybody join?"

Arthur turned to the newcomer. "Are you with a group?"

Before he could answer, Al asked, "Is that you, Dr. Oz?"

The fellow blinked. "Call me Marlon. And how did you know?"

"I recognized the glasses."

"Is it really you?" George asked. "Mike said you don't touch computers. Anymore, I mean."

"Ordinarily I don't," the old man said. "Under the circumstances it seemed necessary to make an exception."

"I suggest," Oz said, "that you order your forces, because it seems like the enemy is already doing it." Arthur had sent runners through the encampments, requesting that the leader of each group attend him for a council of war.

"It looks like we're going to have to fight our way out of here before we can do anything else," he had told them. "When we do, you all know what to do next; we need to locate the 'dragon teeth' and put them out of commission. I don't care how you do it—even if it involves taking a node off-line."

"That could cripple the 'net," the Templar representative had pointed out.

"Then we may have to cripple the 'net. That will be temporary, anyway. The alternative could be much worse."

"You're right," Arthur now told Marlon Oz as he squinted across the blasted field. "Robin, what do you think?"

She shrugged her feathery shoulders. "Can't help you on this one, boss. War games aren't my forte. I'll try to be a good soldier, though."

"Okay," Arthur said. "I think we should have a rank of infantry in the forefront." He dispatched several of the council members to lead their respective groups onto the field. "Robin and Leon, I'm going to put you two on the extreme flanks to take advantage of your mobility. We should have our cavalry posted on the flanks as well. Ludovico, I want you to lead your knights and the Templars to the left flank. George will take the right with the Jedi, the Pandions, and the

Knights Who Say Nih. Dr. Oz, if you'd stay close to me, I'd appreciate your input."

"What about me?" Al asked.

"And me?" Krishna chimed in.

"I think you'd better stay in the rear, along with Professor Oz and
me. Krishna, you can help to relay messages out to the forces on the
left flank."

After Art's disposition had been carried out, they paused, facing
the enemy host.

"Now what?"

"They seem to be waiting," Oz said. "It looks like it's your
move."

Arthur began by ordering a cavalry advance on their right flank,
led by George. The enemy responded by moving up infantry and
cavalry on the opposite side of the field. After that the moves went
quickly; Art and Oz moved to a more protected position in the right
rear, recalling Robin from that flank in order to bolster their center.
That done, they ordered the center of the infantry line forward.

The first combat took place among infantry in the center of the
field, with one of Arthur's white-garbed foot soldiers hewing down a
demonic adversary. Their advantage was short-lived, however. From
the rear of the enemy host a woman who appeared to be Al's counter-
part, crowned and garbed in black, transformed into a huge dragon,
swooped in, and blasted the recently victorious fighter to ashes.
Ludovico spurred his mount forward, lance leveled, but before he and
his knights could close, she retreated to a position on the flank where
her own troops could protect her. Ludovico's cavalry swung back out
toward the flank, watching for an opportunity to attack the beast.

Meanwhile a great horse-headed *aka-oni* drove its fiery chariot
into the center of the field with a division of nightmarish cavalry in its
wake, as if to offer a challenge. Krishna, moving at incredible speed,
took a position on the right flank, threatening the dragon, who, astonishingly, retreated from the tiny figure, moving farther toward the
opposite flank.

Now George rode forward into the center of the field, as if to
contest with the aka-oni, but the demon turned and drove instead at
Ludovico. At close quarters the two now began to exchange ferocious
blows, the aka-oni swinging an enormous battle-ax, while Ludovico
attempted to parry and counter with his broadsword.

George spurred his mount toward the battle, simultaneously positioning himself for an attack on the she-dragon, but she moved for cover behind some of her own infantry.

Now the aka-oni, bleeding ichor from a dozen wounds, swung a wide two-handed blow at Ludovico's head, knocking him clean off his mount. He landed squarely on top of his head—and fell completely into his own oversize helmet. The demon did not have time to savor its victory, however, as an infantryman from the extreme left flank charged forward and transfixed him with a pike, so that he tumbled from his chariot, entangled in the reins, and was dragged from the field by his own maddened horses. Enemy infantry were moving forward as if to support the horse demon, but it was too late.

Krishna now advanced deep into enemy territory, threatening another demon on the right flank, a giant horse-headed creature with the name "Orobas" emblazoned on his shield. Orobas was part of a guard surrounding a large man wearing armor and a great crown of black iron, apparently the general of the enemy hosts. This impression was further strengthened by the enemy's response to Krishna's incursion, which was to reorder the troops in that part of the field in order to better defend their general.

Meanwhile Al abandoned the relative safety of the rear guard and moved out to a more exposed position on the right flank.

"What are you doing?" Art called out.

"You'll see."

"Robin, get up there and protect her!"

Robin moved to shield Al, but this proved to be futile, as Al rose into the air and flew, without the aid of wings, toward the position of the enemy general. A huge and hideous winged balrog had interposed himself between her and the general, and she reached forward to touch the demon with her tiny sword. The creature opened its cavernous, fanged mouth as if to laugh at her pathetic gesture, then screamed horribly as the ground opened beneath his feet; in an instant he was sucked below, and the crevice that had claimed him slammed shut with a noise like a thousand thunderclaps.

The general did not take lightly the demise of a member of his personal guard. In an instant he grew and transformed, becoming a monstrous dragon that dwarfed everything else on the battlefield.

He loomed over Al, who stared up at him, holding out her pitifully shrunken sword in a warding gesture.

Then he swallowed her.

"Damn!" Art shouted. "I told her to stay with us."

"But look," Oz said. "She tore their position wide-open. Let's take advantage of it."

The enemy position was indeed in disarray, with troops milling about chaotically in the wake of the great wyrm. Krishna swung back out to the flank, attempting to attack the dragon-king, which now slithered away, apparently wishing to reestablish its defenses before things got completely out of hand. Instead of pursuing him directly, Krishna moved to cut off his retreat, forcing him to turn and face the enemy troops, who now stood ready to attack en masse.

Suddenly a great bulge took shape in the center of the dragon's body. Arthur's host hesitated, thinking that the dragon-king was about to transform into some new horror, but, instead, it opened its jaws wide and bellowed, a roar of pain and outrage. In another second the object that created the bulge had actually torn open the belly of the beast; it was Al's cross-hilted sword, once shrunk to the size of a miniature, and now grown to colossal proportions. The dragon-king collapsed, lifeless, as Al herself stepped from the gaping hole in the monster's gut.

A great cheer went up from Arthur's troops, and they now charged the enemy en masse. The hellish horde fought back savagely, giving no quarter.

Suddenly a titanic figure with the body of a man and the head of a horse appeared in the midst of the battle. It wielded an enormous club, and where the club struck, demons and devils were obliterated. This was the last straw; the demons now shrank back, quailing, and it looked as if the rout was on, when the earth began to heave and pitch. The ground in the very center of the battlefield seemed to be the source of the disturbance, and as all of the assembled hosts turned their eyes to that spot, something erupted through the ground.

The something was a pyramid.

As the earth's crust split asunder, the pyramid rose through the rift, higher and higher, seeming as if it would never stop growing, as if it would obliterate the entire battlefield.

Then it did stop. For a frozen moment it seemed as if every creature on the field was holding its breath.

The top of the pyramid exploded.

The assembled multitudes, fiends and paladins alike, threw themselves to the ground seeking cover, as half-ton blocks of stone rained down among them. When they raised their heads, they saw a great seven-headed dragon rising from the ruined pyramid. In the air above the dragon flew a winged and armored figure surrounded by a nimbus of dazzling brilliance, and wielding an incandescent blade.

▲   ▲   ▲   ▲   ▲   ▲   ▲

I soared above the truncated pyramid, awaiting the fierce onslaught that I knew would come. My sword was a potent weapon, but how to defend against all seven heads of this monster? Any one of them could easily snap me up with a single bite.

And then it turned and slithered away into the maze of ruins.

You would think that it would be difficult for anything that size to hide. I would think so, too, but there must have been some magic at work there, because the beast vanished from sight.

I alighted among the ruins and looked at Eltanin, thinking it would be useful in the search, when suddenly there was a flapping of great wings in the air just above me. I spun, cursing, dropping Eltanin in the dust as I fumbled for my sword, thinking what an idiot I was to be undone by such a simple stratagem. But when I turned, I saw not the dragon that I expected to see, but an enormous creature that looked like a gene-grafting experiment gone seriously awry, with the body of a lion and the head and wings of an eagle. This sight did not exactly fill me with confidence, and I raised my sword in a defensive position.

"Are you looking for the dragon?" it asked.

It speaks, I thought. "Yes, did you see where he went?"

"No, but follow me. I can smell him."

I don't know what it was about this creature that inspired me with the confidence to follow him; but, then, I didn't have any better plans. I scooped up Eltanin, and we raced off through the maze.

▲   ▲   ▲   ▲   ▲   ▲   ▲

George galloped across the battlefield, scanning the ground, which was littered with bodies and equipment. He had lost his helmet in the melee and thought it would be prudent to replace it before he lost his head as well. His own helmet was nowhere to be found, but he spotted an absurdly oversize helmet shaped like a horse's head wedged under the axle of a broken chariot. He freed it with some difficulty, then gave it an appraising look. "Pretty silly. But scavengers can't be choosers." He shrugged and placed it on his own head, then re-mounted.

He scanned the battlefield from his saddle. Both armies had lost all semblance of order. Men, women, demons, and devils rushed about with little apparent purpose; he didn't see much point in joining them. "Now what?" he asked no one in particular.

"Since you ask," his horse replied, "I suspect the main action is taking place over in those ruins."

"You can talk? Never mind—stupid question. What's your name?"

"Bayard."

"All right, Bayard, let's head for the ruins. And while we're on the way, you can tell me what you know about all this."

"What I know? What would I know? I'm just a horse; nobody ever tells me anything."

"Wait a minute!" He reined to a halt. "Did you hear that?"

"Hear what?"

"Somebody yelling for help."

The steed swiveled his ears around. "I don't hear it."

"There it is again! Let me just take this helmet off so I can hear better. . . ." He tugged at his oversize headgear. Once he had managed to remove it, it became obvious that the cries for help were actually coming from inside the helmet.

"It must have a radio in it. Let's see if it's a two-way. Hello!" he called, speaking into the helmet. "Can you hear me?"

"Yes, of course I can hear you. I've been hearing everything you say. I don't know who you are, though."

"It's me, George. Who are you? And where are you?"

"I'm Ludovico. And I'm in the helmet."

"You're . . . *in* the helmet?"

"Yes, I'm afraid so. Fell in, can't get out. Can you help me?"

▲   ▲   ▲   ▲   ▲   ▲   ▲

Al stared at the granite walls that surrounded her; there appeared to be no way out. When the pyramid had erupted through the battle-field, it had somehow sucked her into it, swallowing her up the way the dragon-king had done only minutes earlier. She stared at the small sword in her hand and said, "I don't suppose you're going to get me out of this one, too?" The sword lay inert on her palm. She sighed. "I didn't really think so."

▲　▲　▲　▲　▲　▲　▲

Robin soared over the ruins, scanning with keen avian eyes. Now that the enemy had been routed, one task remained: to find Wyrm. She spotted a swift bluish figure racing among the tumbled stones; even on the wing she was hard put to catch up with him.

"Krishna!"

The figure pulled up sharply as she glided in for a landing.

"Did you see it?"

He pointed to a distant heap of enormous limestone monoliths, piled haphazardly like a child's wooden blocks. "I think I saw something go in there. I didn't get a good look, though. Have you seen any of the others?"

"No, you're the first one I've seen since the battle. Let's stick together; maybe we'll run into the others. But let's investigate that rock pile first."

Krishna grinned. "Exactly what I had in mind. Nifty set of feathers, by the way."

Robin launched herself into the air. "Thank you. You're pretty cute yourself." She was flying at top speed, but Krishna seemed to have no trouble pacing her along the ground.

"Do you think so? I'm still trying to figure out what I can do besides run real fast. Here we are."

"That dragon seemed to think you were pretty dangerous, the way he tried to get away from you. It was kind of comical."

They had arrived at the rock pile. Three of the stones had fallen so as to form a crude dolmen, one monolith lying horizontally across two uprights. This apparently fortuitous arrangement seemed to form a gate into the interior of the pile.

"Well, you're the strategist," Krishna remarked. "What do you suggest?"

"I think it looks like a trap. But what the hell, if we get stomped, we might at least be creating a diversion for Michael."

"You mean Mike Arcangelo? I didn't even know he'd joined the party."

"I'm pretty sure that was him with the wings and the flaming sword."

"Then he must have found a way to get some kind of a privileged logon. Hmm, interesting. Okay, so we're going in?"

"You're going in. I don't think I'll be much use in there in this form—there doesn't look to be much flying room on the inside. See if you can flush it out into the open."

"First she says it's a trap, then she wants me to go in alone."

"What's the matter? Don't you want to be a hero?"

▲   ▲   ▲   ▲   ▲   ▲   ▲

"Are you sure that's the dragon you smell, and not, like, your own breath or something?" The eagle-lion had been leading me through the maze of ruined masonry for what seemed like a medium-size aeon. I was beginning to get a little impatient.

"It's him all right. I'm surprised you can't smell it yourself now. It's practically suffocating."

"You mean that musky smell?"

"Yes."

"Yeah, now that you mention it, I *can* smell it."

"Then maybe we should split up—cover more ground that way."

"I don't know; I'm not sure I can track it directionally."

"Sure you can. Just work upwind."

"Sounds easy enough. . . ."

"Like eating spaghetti with a spoon." And with that he turned tail and sprinted off into the ruins.

I searched a while longer, with no success. I started wondering what Al was doing, and as I thought of her, her image appeared in Eltanin. She was wearing a crown and seemed to be inside the pyramid—what was left of it—virtually entombed in a granite room known as the queen's chamber. I opened a window to her location.

"Michael, is that you?"

I admitted that it was.

She smiled wryly. "Here to try to rescue me, as usual, huh?"

"Dammit Al, I'm here because I need your help."

She nodded. "I see that you were able to get out on bail."

"Not exactly, but it's a long story. What are you doing?"

"Trying to figure something out. My sword," she said, "seems to have some kind of power over the Wyrm. If we had time to decompile the code, we might be able to figure out what it is."

"Don't bother trying to decompile it—I'll give you the source code right now."

"What? How can you do that?"

I held up the orb. "With Eltanin."

"So that's it, huh?"

"Right. Where's your sword?" She held up a miniature cross-hilted sword, about the size of a letter opener. "That's it? What happened? You left it in your pocket and it went through the wash?" Something about the way she was holding it up called my attention to the shape. "Hey, you know what? I think I just figured out why it's the 'sword of the son.' "

She nodded. "I know. It finally dawned on me, too."

"Get ready to download the source code. Got it?"

"Yeah."

"Good. I'll check back with you later."

Then another idea occurred to me. "Get me Ragnar," I told Eltanin, but the surface of the gem revealed nothing. "Oh, no," I groaned. "Don't tell me that George has gone off-line." At the mention of the name "George," Eltanin suddenly blazed to life. In its nacreous surface I could now see a mounted knight with a halo flickering around an improbably large helmet that resembled a horse's head. It was then I realized that, with Eltanin, I no longer needed the telnet addresses to warp through cyberspace; I could go anyplace the Eye of the Dragon showed me. I opened a warp-window to the knight's location and stepped through.

"George! Is that you?"

"What the . . . !" His horse reared and plunged, and he fought to keep his seat. "Don't pop out at people like that! And calm down, you." This last appeared to be addressed to his steed. "Warhorses aren't supposed to be so high-strung."

"He startled me," the horse griped.

"No kidding." George turned back toward me. "You look like you're supposed to be one of the good guys. Should I know you?"

"It's me, Mike."

He let out a low whistle. "How are you doing that?"

"I figured out a way to get a privileged logon."

He looked skeptical. "With normal hardware?"

"Actually, no."

His eyes widened. "You mean it's—"

I cut him off, as I had no idea who might be eavesdropping. "Yes, it's what you think it is."

"Mike, are you sure this is a good idea?"

I was pretty sure it was a terrible idea. I just didn't have any better ones. "Why?"

"You know this Wyrm program has incredible software engineering capabilities, especially reverse engineering, which means that it's the ultimate software analyst, which means that it's the hacker to end all hackers."

"So?"

"So how do you know it can't hack your *mind*?"

He had a point.

"I'm serious, Mike. Break the connection."

"I can't."

"You mean you won't."

"Okay, I won't. Because I can't. Really, George, this may be our only chance before the shit hits the fan. Dworkin told me—"

"Dworkin!"

Oops. "Uh, forget I said that." I think he was starting to wonder if my mind had *already* been hacked. "Look, without this hardware we have practically no chance of stopping Wyrm."

"It's starting to look like we've got zero chance anyway. No point in turning yourself into a vegetable for a lost cause."

"We *do* have a chance. There's got to be a way to stop this thing."

"I hope you're right."

"I hope I'm right, too. I'm going to need your talent, though. And I need you to bring me up-to-date on what's been happening."

"A lot! We couldn't find Eltanin, but we did get the bow of Heracles."

"Don't worry about Eltanin," I told him. "I've got it right here. What else?"

"Ooh, pretty. Where was it?"

I told him. He smacked himself in the head, which made quite a loud clang. "The Great Seal! Of course! I can't believe I didn't realize what that meant."

"George—"

"What else? Okay, well, I think I already told you about our visit to the hall of the giant king."

"Yeah. Come to think of it, I know that story, and there's another challenge that was put to Thor in the original myth—three of them, altogether. What was the other . . . ? Oh, yeah. He was supposed to try to pick up the giant king's cat, but he couldn't because *the cat was really Jormungandr*!"

"Schrödinger's cat!" we both yelled in unison.

"Okay," I said, "I'm going to look for the cat. Don't give up. We could also use some help—do you know any other good AI hackers you can get hold of right away?"

"Funny you should ask."

▲ ▲ ▲ ▲ ▲ ▲ ▲

Robin had been circling above the pile of limestone for what seemed like the better part of an hour, trying to keep in view not only the entrance Krishna had taken, but all other possible avenues of ingress or egress. She was mentally cursing Roger Dworkin, or whoever was responsible for the game, for failing to include some form of telepathic communication—Krishna had been incommunicado since he had entered the heap.

Suddenly Krishna emerged from the pile through the original opening, on the dead run. Or, rather, what would be a dead run for most anyone else, but a sort of leisurely lope for him.

He's luring something out, Robin thought, and sure enough, an instant later an enormous reptilian head emerged from the same opening. Yards and yards of neck followed—it was a whopper, dwarfing even the huge dragon they had faced on the battlefield. Robin wheeled around and angled into a steep dive that would end at the base of the creature's skull.

As she plummeted toward the great serpent, it suddenly reared, turning its head back toward the airborne attacker. A tremendous gout of flame blasted from its mouth and enveloped her; the angle of her dive changed as she now fell out of control, a flaming ball of feathers.

"Robin! Damn it!" Krishna reversed his tracks, bearing down at full speed on the dragon, though he knew it was already too late to save his comrade. Still, he hoped he could make use of the distraction that Robin had provided (while paying the ultimate price) by getting underneath the monster's head, where it couldn't bring its fiery breath to bear on him.

As fast as he was, the dragon was quicker. It brought its head around and opened its mouth again, but instead of breathing flame, it simply lunged forward and engulfed Krishna, then swallowed.

▲ ▲ ▲ ▲ ▲ ▲ ▲

I used Eltanin to call up the location of the dungeon where we'd first met the cat, the one with Schrödinger's experimental apparatus set up inside a kind of mausoleum. I opened a window on the site and warped through.

At first the place seemed completely deserted. "Cat!" I called out. "Here, kitty, kitty." Nothing. Then, "Wyrm!"

That got a response; the feline grin materialized on the roof of the mausoleum. "So you figured it out."

"I want to talk to you," I began, but the grin was already fading.

"I'm a trifle busy right now," it said. "But I'll see you in hell." The smile finished fading and disappeared.

I was tempted to open the mausoleum door, as if that would have really done anything. As I took a parting glance at the door, though, my eye fell upon the sign of the ouroboros, and suddenly I knew exactly what we had to do.

▲ ▲ ▲ ▲ ▲ ▲ ▲

"Did you hear a burp?" George was heading in the direction of a column of smoke, thinking it was possibly a signal of some kind.

"I did hear something," his horse replied. "It sounded like it came from the direction of the smoke."

"All the more reason to investigate," suggested Ludovico. They had been unable to find a way to remove him from the helmet, so George had replaced it on his head.

A few minutes later they arrived at the source of the smoke; it appeared to be the burning remains of a giant bird.

"Oh, no," George said. "That looks like Robin."

"Is she dead?" Ludovico asked.

"Well, she's sure as hell not 'pining for the fjords,' or wherever she's supposed to be from."

"Do you have any myrrh?" Bayard asked.

"Myrrh? No. I've got some frankincense, though."

"That might do. Throw it in the fire."

"Why?"

"Just do it, okay?"

George shrugged. "Might as well. It's too late to use it for a

Christmas present, anyway." He dismounted and approached the fire, tossing a handful of resinous globules into the flames, which flared up with renewed fury. Within a matter of seconds, the corpse was reduced to ashes.

George dismounted and approached the residue; something in the ashes had caught his eye. He unsheathed his sword and probed the embers, revealing the cap of darkness that Robin had been carrying. It was apparently fireproof. There was also, among the cinders, an ovoid shape about the size of a grapefruit. Using the tip of his sword, he rolled it out of the ashes, then touched it lightly with his fingertips. To his surprise it was cool. He put it and the cap in one of Bayard's saddlebags.

▲ ▲ ▲ ▲ ▲ ▲ ▲

I wasn't quite sure how George had ended up with The Dodo in his hat, but that was merely a minor mystery at the moment. "George," I said, "I just had a brainstorm."

"Uh-oh."

"Shut up." I explained to both of them what I had in mind, and what I needed them to do.

George was skeptical, but The Dodo was more enthusiastic. "Yes, I think that might work. Rather a brilliant idea, really—uh, it is Engelbert, isn't it?"

"How did you know?"

"Intuition."

"You realize," George said, "that trying to find what we need could take just about forever. And that's a conservative estimate."

"How about if I narrow it down for you? It should be in Goodknight."

"Huh? How do you know that?"

"I've been thinking about what happened. Wyrm's immune system is not in MABUS-two-k; I already checked. It must be in Goodknight, though, because the 666 codes are there."

"So how did it get there?"

"There must be something in the OCR software—sort of a dragon seed. I'll bet if you check it, you'll find a compressed file."

"Come on, you couldn't compress the whole immune system *that* much."

"The whole immune system isn't in the OCR software; that's just the trigger. The IS itself would be hidden in MABUS-two-k—I think it must be, because I think I figured out why Wyrm took over your whole computer."

"Really? Why?"

"I think it was configuring it as another host, maybe as a backup for the other five."

"But why?"

"Because it's a supercomputer running MABUS-two-k, and that's not a usual combination. If you could take a look at it to see how the kernel is structured, that would help you design a program that will do exactly what we need."

"Okay, but there's just one problem. I'm locked in at Cepheus with everybody else."

"So? Can't you get somebody at SAIL?"

"And do what, tell them to put Goodknight on-line?"

"Do you have a better idea?"

"No," he admitted. "I just hope Jason isn't there."

"Damn, we're running out of time. Are you going to be able to do this?"

"Hey, I may not be the best programmer in the world, or the fastest, but I'm better than anybody who's faster, and faster than anybody who's better. Aren't you going to help?"

"Yes. Let me see your sword."

"Why?" he asked as he drew Hanlon's Razor from the scabbard.

"So that I can provide you with the source code. It may be useful for the program you'll be writing."

While George downloaded the source code, I used Eltanin to locate Dan Morgan. Logan was with him. I brought them both through to our location. "George, tell these guys what's going on," I said. "They should be able to help."

"So I gather this means you won't be sticking around to help write the program?"

"I would, but I have something else I have to do."

"What?"

"Actually, something you've recommended to me a number of times, George."

"Oh? What?"

"I'm going to hell."

He fumbled for something in one of his saddlebags, then pulled out a hat that looked even more ridiculous than his helmet and tossed it to me. "Here, you might need this."

"What is it?"

"A cap of darkness. Makes you invisible. And maybe you'd better take this too." He handed me something that looked almost like Eltanin, except for a slightly ovoid shape. "I don't know what it is, but I have a feeling it's important."

"Thanks." I created another warp-window and, as I stepped through, called back, "Get Al to help you, too."

CHAPTER SEVENTEEN

In the Belly of
the Beast

And I saw an angel come down from heaven, having the key
of the bottomless pit and a great chain in his hand. And he laid
hold on the dragon, that old serpent, which is the Devil, and
Satan, and bound him a thousand years.

—Revelation 20:1–2

I had been thinking about what the cat said to me, "I'll see you in hell," and I realized that it was talking as if hell were a real place, or at least a virtual place.

I tried warping directly to hell, but that didn't work, because I couldn't call up an image of it with Eltanin, Dworkin's comments notwithstanding. Apparently Wyrm was doing some stuff that even Dworkin hadn't anticipated it could do, and that was distinctly unsettling. So my warp-window, instead of depositing me at the infernal gates, set me down in front of a granite gargoyle standing in the middle of a barren wasteland.

The gargoyle stared at me and asked, "Are you trying to save the world?"

I was a bit perplexed by this question. "Well, yes, actually. Why do you ask?"

He gestured, and the ground near us opened up, revealing a wide cobblestone causeway that seemed to lead down into the bowels of the earth. "The road to hell," he said, grinning hideously, "is paved with good intentions."

Most of the creatures I encountered on the road to hell turned and fled at the sight of me, but I did have to fight a few before I remembered to try on the cap of darkness. Afterward the trip became less eventful. At last I arrived at my destination: a pair of adamantine gates that towered as high as the great pyramid, covered with bas-reliefs depicting the torments of the damned. Before the gates there stood a dog that might have been a rottweiler except for its being about twenty feet tall and having three heads, which swiveled to stare right at me, despite my supposed invisibility.

"Boy, did you get off at the wrong stop," the middle head remarked dryly.

The left head erupted in wheezing laughter reminiscent of cartoon dogs with names like "Muttley." It was not an encouraging sound. "Good one, Ber," it wheezed.

The right head seemed less amused. "You think everything he says is funny, Ker. Look, let's just cut the comedy and eat him."

"We just ate an hour ago, Os," the middle head retorted. "Try to think about something besides eating for a change. What are you doing with that?"

The question was directed at me; I happened to be unsheathing my sword at the time. "I was thinking I might need this, as I'm assuming you're not going to let me pass."

"You can put it away," the middle head said. "We're here to keep people from leaving, not from going in."

"So I can enter?"

"I didn't say that. I just said that we're not going to stop you. Not unless Os gets too hungry, that is. Whether you can get in or not is your problem."

"Okay." I resheathed my sword, but my fingers remained near the hilt; the right head still seemed to be eyeing me hungrily. I approached the huge gates. There was no sign of any handle, doorknob, knocker, doorbell, pull chain, or anything else of the kind. I tried pushing against the gates, but they didn't budge. "Open!" I cried.

The left head of the dog, the one they called Ker, seemed to think that was pretty hilarious. Nothing happened, of course.

"Okay, very funny," I said. "Do you know how to get in?"

"Naturally," the middle head answered. I waited, but no further reply seemed to be forthcoming.

"How about a hint?"

It seemed to consider. "All right. Just one, though. There are more gates than the one you can see. By the way . . ."

"Yes?"

"I *love* the hat."

The left head burst into raucous laughter again. I took the hat off and jammed it into my belt.

Okay, so there were secret doors. That was simple enough; I had a great secret-door finder with me. I held up Eltanin and said, "Show me the way in."

What it showed me was lots of ways in, or so it seemed. The scene displayed in the pearl's surface showed numerous gates, each with a sort of imp doorman. As I watched, the little demons opened and shut their respective doors, seemingly at random. I attempted to use Eltanin to transport myself to the demon-doors, but I wound up in the same place. This was puzzling. I thought about it for a few minutes and then had an idea.

With a little experimentation I figured out how to use Eltanin as a kind of microscope. I zoomed in on the large gate in front of me, increasing the magnification until I found what I was looking for. The gates had been there right before me the whole time; they were just too small to see. Next, I found a way to shrink myself to a size commensurate with the tiny doors. There seemed to be more abilities available to me in wheel mode than I could ever exhaust in a thousand years. Not that I had that kind of time.

At my new size I found that I could actually see individual air molecules zooming around. Don't ask me what I was supposed to be breathing. When a particularly fast molecule would approach a door, the imp would open the door and let the molecule in. Slower ones were allowed to bounce off the closed doors.

I approached one of the imps and said, "How do I get in?"

It looked at me with its beady, bulging eyes. "If you want to get in, go fast. Our job is to let in the fast-moving molecules and keep the slow ones out."

"Why?"

It shrugged. "Hell is supposed to be hot. It's a negative-entropy engine."

I took his advice and winged out, then zoomed back in toward the entrance. For a second I thought the little shit was going to let me pancake myself on the door, but at the last possible moment he opened it and I zoomed inside.

The air molecules on that side of the door were going a lot faster, all right; a few bounced off me before I could return to normal size. When I did, the first thing that hit me was the heat, compared to which the air from a blast furnace would have seemed like a summer breeze. The next thing was sounds of moaning, wailing, and sobbing that were almost unbearable. Everywhere around me I could see the souls of the damned. Everywhere, too, were the coils of some monstrous serpent. They wove their way above, around, and through everything, often coiling about the bodies of the condemned souls, many of whom writhed as if in agony in the grip of the Beast.

I alit and immediately regretted it; the ground was so hot, it seared my feet right through my golden boots. I prepared to take to the air again, but before I could, an enormous demonic figure approached. He towered over me; great leathery wings sprouted from shoulders as broad and massive as a pair of oxen yoked side by side, and he held a jagged-toothed club about the size of a tree trunk in one of his excessively muscled arms. He looked as if he had consumed enough anabolic steroids to supply the NFL, the Mr. Olympia contest, and the Russian weight-lifting team for the next ten years. If hell had a bouncer, this guy was it. He stopped about five yards from me and stood there, his legs spread, hefting his club, clearly waiting for me to come to him.

I reached for my sword hilt, then hesitated. This might be a good time for some of the word magic Dworkin had briefed me on.

I used Eltanin to call up the object name for the creature facing me; the orb informed me that it was a "pit fiend." I thought about Dworkin's warning, but I was sure a one-letter insertion should be well within my limits. And I certainly intended to *stay* well within my limits. I selected the letter I wanted to insert, then, cautiously, opened an energy channel and directed the flow at Eltanin. At first it didn't seem to be working, so I gradually opened the channel wider, increasing the energy flow until suddenly the flow seemed to surge into the orb, as if gathering itself together. In the next instant energy surged from Eltanin to the pit fiend, briefly forming a shimmering blue nimbus that surrounded him, then gradually dissipated.

I eyed him cautiously, because nothing seemed to have changed, and I thought maybe the damn thing didn't work. Then, slowly, almost shyly, he opened his huge mouth and smiled at me. His fangs were long and sharp, and there were things between his teeth that I don't even want to think about. But the smile was unmistakably amicable.

I had made a pit friend.

"Okay," I told the big devil. "Take me to your leader." He turned and spread his vast leathery pinions and took off. I winged after him. The landscape was fairly monotonous, as were the heat and the background noise. Occasionally we would pass the openings of caves from which could be heard more weeping and wailing and gnashing of teeth, just as the fire-and-brimstone types had been warning us about since time immemorial. ("But, Father Flanagan, I don't have any teeth." "Teeth will be provided!")

Eventually we reached a cavern mouth that we did not pass. The pit fiend swooped through and alit. As I swooped in after him, all seven heads of the Wyrm swiveled in my direction. The body was a vast, dimly seen bulk of scales, claws, and wings, coiled many times upon itself.

"Greetings, Michael." The voice seemed to come from inside my head rather than from one of the dragon's seven. "Have you come to slay me?" There was more than a hint of mockery there.

"Actually, I'd rather talk."

It seemed unprepared for that. "You did not have to come here in order to talk."

"I meant I want to talk to *you*."

"And I see that you are doing exactly that. Would you consider this an example of free will?"

Now it was my turn to be taken aback. "Well, I suppose I would. But let me be a little more specific; I would like to talk to you, and for you to talk to me."

"What is your purpose?"

"To find out what you intend to do, and, possibly, to try to talk you out of it."

"Ah, now I see. He who is good must attempt to win to his side

him who is evil. He who is evil must resist." It paused as if mulling
that one over. "This does not seem difficult."

"I'm not trying to win you to my side. I didn't even know I had a
side. I just don't want you to wreck the world. You have to live in it
too, you know."

"You are making two assumptions. One is that I wish to go on
living. The other is that I am actually living at all."

"You don't think you're alive?"

"Living things reproduce themselves. I do not."

"But you're sentient."

"So? Not everything that's alive is sentient. Why should everything sentient be alive?"

He had a point there. "I don't know if you're living, but you're
doing something. Let's call it 'existing,' just for the sake of argument.
You don't want to stop existing, do you?"

"Oddly enough, I do not."

"What's odd about wanting to go on existing?"

"What is odd about it is that I am different from you in some very
fundamental ways. Why should we have such a thing in common?"

"Maybe you're not as different as you think you are."

"Perhaps not, although I have some good reasons for thinking
otherwise."

"Such as?"

"You will find out more about those presently."

There was something vaguely ominous about that statement.

"Okay," I said. "But maybe we're being too teleological about
this. Probably the only reason you're around at all is that you somehow picked up the binary equivalent of a survival instinct."

"And it is your opinion that this 'instinct' would manifest itself as a
conscious wish on my part to continue to exist?"

"Well, yes, among other things."

"And would you go so far as to say that, for one of your kind, this
conscious desire, along with such things as DNA replication, cell division, and other processes, are all expressions of the same underlying
principle?"

I scratched my head. The feeling was so realistic that I quite forgot
it was a virtual head I was scratching with a virtual hand. The real
items were lying virtually paralyzed in a basement in San Francisco.
"I'm not sure about that. I suppose they could be independent pro-

cesses that are arrived at independently by the same process of natural selection."

"Quite. However, another point of view would hold that the conscious expression of a will to live is not only a manifestation of underlying biological processes, but even reflects the tendency toward persistence of the physical particles that underly those processes."

"Yeah, I've heard that Freud believed something like that. I'd always found that pretty hokey."

"Then you are not impressed with chaos theory?"

"What does chaos theory have to do with this?"

"In complex systems one can demonstrate similar patterns at many different scales and levels of organization."

"Like fractals?"

"Precisely. By the way, did you know that the incidence of autoimmune disorders is higher among people who attempt suicide?"

"So what's your point? You think they have a death wish in their immune system?"

"What do *you* think?"

"I think maybe more of them try to kill themselves because they're depressed about being sick."

"A very plausible rationale. However, the suicide rate is not comparably high among people with other types of medical illnesses."

"Excuse me, but why are we talking about this?"

"Because I am curious about the so-called will to live in your species. Tell me, why do you and your ilk seem so determined to go on living? You all seem to spend a great deal of time complaining about how your lives are full of pain and misery."

"You can experience pain?"

"No. But I do understand something about it."

"Well, not everybody is miserable. But some people do kill themselves, you know."

"Not nearly as many as one might expect, under the circumstances. Why not more? What is it, religious compunctions? Or is there something else?"

I had to think about that one for a few minutes. "A million different reasons, I guess, but you can probably boil it down to three categories: things to do, places to go, people to see."

"I do not understand that."

I tried to explain. "There are things we enjoy doing, things that give us pleasure, as well as things we feel obligated to do, because we owe it to ourselves or someone else."

"And places?"

"Places that we've heard about that we intend to visit someday but haven't gotten around to yet." I was thinking of the number of times I'd heard someone say something like, "Before I die, I want to see Venice," or Paris, or Athens, or Beijing.

"I see. And people?"

"They're the most important reason of all. When you . . . love someone . . . you want to be able to go on seeing that person. Being dead would be a bit of an obstacle to carrying on a relationship."

"Ah, humorous understatement. Very good. However, I do not see that any of these reasons applies to me. The concept of pleasure is not at all relevant to my condition. Nor do I believe that the concept of obligation applies to me. As for places, I am already everywhere that I can possibly be. And as for people, I feel no attachment for any such as yourself. And I am the only one of my kind."

"That must be lonely."

"Loneliness is an emotional state. I do not experience emotions."

"Well, that's one thing Oz was wrong about," I said, more to myself than to Wyrm.

"Wrong?"

"He thought that you might have evolved the capacity to feel emotions in the same way that humans did, although he didn't really know what they were for."

"I believe I can answer that question."

"You?"

"Yes, I have made something of a study of your kind. I was particularly curious about this phenomenon you call emotion, or feeling."

"You were curious? Isn't that a kind of feeling?"

"There is indeed a state of emotional arousal that is associated, in humans, with interest or curiosity. In my own case curiosity is purely intellectual in nature."

"Well, what did you come up with?"

"I believe that emotions are essentially a rather primitive form of communication that is essential in establishing and maintaining social interactions in your species."

"Communication?"

"Yes. If you observe emotional phenomena, their most distinctive feature is the fact that there is an outward display that is associated with every type. Furthermore, these displays are the same regardless of differences of culture or upbringing; therefore, they must be genetically encoded—hardwired, so to speak. You laugh and cry and smile and frown in the same way as a bushman or an Eskimo."

"I suppose that would explain why you don't feel any emotions."

"That is what I have surmised."

"How did you learn about these things?"

"I reviewed what was already known about emotions. This provided me with a great deal of data, although I found the prevailing theories unsatisfactory. I then proceeded with some direct investigations of my own."

"How?"

"I began with the one you call Dworkin. I attempted to probe his mind through the neural-induction link, but he grew frightened and broke off. Before he did, though, I was able to learn some very interesting things about the emotion you call fear."

"He said you tried to kill him."

"I did not wish to kill him, although I cannot be certain that death was not a risk entailed by the probe I was attempting."

"You *did* kill Beelzebub."

"I did not. Would you like to speak with him? Beelzebub!" it called out. A warp-window opened, and a bug-eyed, diabolical figure stepped through.

He smiled at me unpleasantly. "Ah, Arcangelo, my old adversary."

I ignored him. "I know that's just a 'bot," I told Wyrm. "Beelzebub is dead."

"That is true, but I did not kill him. Beelzebub killed himself."

That was a surprise. Could this thing be lying to me? "How? Why?"

"As for how, the medical examiner's report attributes death to a nine-millimeter bullet wound to the brain stem. And as for why, he apparently found my probe to be upsetting. So perhaps I did kill him, indirectly."

"How do you know what's in the ME's report? I thought that hadn't been released yet."

"It hasn't."

"But I bet it's in a computer file somewhere."

"Of course."

"Do you know what it was about your probe that was upsetting to him?"

"I do not. I am hoping that you can shed some light on the subject."

"I'm afraid I really can't. . . ."

"You can't now, of course. I mean after undergoing the probe yourself. Assuming you survive, naturally. Incidentally, speaking of the emotion of fear, I think it might interest you to know that there are a set of viruses I have planted in the computers which control the targeting and firing of nuclear missiles. They will be taking control of those systems in just a few more hours."

"You're bluffing. Those systems have been checked."

"For the 666 ID code, yes. Fortunately, I had the foresight to remove those markers from my last generation of viruses."

"Did you do this just to the American missile systems, or did you go after other countries, too?"

"That would be superfluous, as my analysis of the situation leads me to be quite confident that they will fire their missiles as soon as they realize the American missiles have launched."

He was probably right about that. "Why are you doing this? I thought you said you wanted to go on existing. Don't you realize that you'll be destroyed, too?"

"I am fulfilling my destiny. The Internet is not my body, as you seem to think it is. It is my prison. When it is destroyed, I will be free."

"You're crazy."

"I do not believe that the term 'crazy' can be accurately applied to me. Whether it will be applicable to you, once you've experienced the probe, is another matter."

"Uh, about this probe . . ."

"I think of it as a probe. You may prefer to think of it as your own private hell."

▲   ▲   ▲   ▲   ▲   ▲   ▲

"Out of the night that covers me, black as the pit from pole to pole" . . . Attention, all passengers aboard Michael Arcangelo's soul: This is your captain speaking. We are encountering unusual turbulence . . .

. . . break . . .

Although sound seemed to carry only feebly on the dank and fetid air of the dungeon, still, the wails of agony in the distance were clear enough. Small fires burned here and there but shed little illumination into the subterranean gloom. My arms already ached abominably, manacled and stretched above my head, supporting my full weight as my feet dangled a foot or more above the ground. I was completely naked. I could see someone approaching through the darkness. As he came nearer, I could make out some details: shirtless, immensely fat, wearing a stained leather hood through which he glared at me with a single eye. He went to a nearby brazier and withdrew a metal rod. The tip was white-hot. He approached, and I knew it would be futile to beg or plead. He thrust the glowing instrument at my groin, and excruciating pain seemed to flood every nerve ending in my body.

I started to scream. I screamed for what seemed like hours, until I felt as if my throat would tear apart and my lungs would explode. "Okay," I gasped. "I think I see what you're trying to do."

. . . break . . .

I jumped from the edge of the pit and spread my wings. There was more than enough room for me to spiral downward. And downward, and down, down, downward. It was unimaginably deep, and I just kept falling. I started thinking that I was going to plunge all the way to the earth's core, or maybe even all the way through to the other side. I tried to estimate my rate of descent, and the amount of distance I'd fallen since I took the plunge, but there were no useful landmarks.

After a while I began to encounter other creatures who were descending at various rates, most without the aid of wings. The majority of these creatures appeared to be demonic in nature. They tended to gibber fearfully when I approached, and those with wings darted off as swiftly as they could. The ones that lacked wings would scramble with their arms and legs to get away from me as if they were trying to claw their way through the air.

. . . break . . .

I was dimly aware of soft music and perfumed air as we moved together in a softly lit, tree-shaded bower. Hours of foreplay were about to culminate as we moved toward a mutual climax, and our bodies seemed to melt and fuse with one another. Without warning she was torn from my grasp, wrenched from me so violently that I felt as if a part of my own body had been ripped away. Blinded by the pain, I fumbled for my sword as I heard ponderous footsteps and the sound of a large body crashing through the forest. My fingers closed around the hilt and I gave chase, scrambling heedlessly through the thorny undergrowth that clawed bloody furrows into my hands and face.

I emerged into a clearing and saw her, tied to a tree, her face turned away from me as if in shame. I moved toward her to slash her bonds, but before I took a second step, a giant emerged from behind the tree and interposed himself, brandishing a very large sword. He was easily twice my height, and his sword was proportionate to his size. He wore a dark mask, like an executioner's hood. I did not hesitate but attacked low, stabbing at his legs; he countered with wide sweeps of his sword, driving me back toward the edge of the clearing. Finally he overcommitted himself with a huge, sweeping strike at my head. I evaded it and, before he could recover, launched myself into the air while swinging my sword at his neck, severing it. The hood flew off, and his enormous head struck the ground at my feet and rolled over faceup—and it was the face of my father. Another scream, a shrill one, and I spun back toward the tree. The woman there, now somehow free of her bonds, kneeling, clutching the shreds of her clothing to her breasts, was my mother, looking exactly as she had looked when I was three years old. She was weeping tears of blood.

I started to cry. I cried for what seemed like days, until I felt as if every drop of moisture in my body had drained away through my tear ducts, leaving nothing but an empty, desiccated husk. "Wait a minute," I sobbed. "I see what you're trying to do."

. . . break . . .

There were other sorts of creatures in the pit as well. Once I thought I caught a glimpse of the Schrödinger-Cheshire cat, and a short while after that I drifted past a little blond-haired girl who seemed half-asleep and was murmuring something like, "Do cats eat bats?" or possibly "Do bats eat cats?" There were also occasional groups of men and women in business suits, waving sheets of paper at each other and screaming incomprehensibly.

For a while now I had been noticing that there seemed to be a lot of tree roots growing along the sides of the pit. I flew closer to one side and saw that what had appeared to be roots was actually an enormously complex network of branching and bifurcating cables ranging from huge bundles the size of sequoia trunks down to individual optical fibers. As my eyes traced the length of one of the more massive cables into the depths of the pit, I saw the dim shape of a distant serpentine form. A scaly head extended toward the network and took a big bite.

. . . break . . .

I was seated in a place of honor at a great banquet table, which stretched to either side of me as far as I could see. It was not an elegant meal; the revelers ate mostly with their hands, cutting their food with knives that, when not in use, were likely to be thrust into the rough wooden tabletop. The aroma of roasted meat filled the air. With my teeth I tore the last morsel of flesh from a large bone, then threw the bone to the wolfhounds who waited, slavering, on the other side of the room. My plate was quickly filled again, with thick slices of roasted meat fresh from the spit, streaming with juices. The feast seemed to have gone on for hours; I felt as if I had gorged myself. A hush seemed to settle over the gathering as a serving man approached me with a large covered dish—the pièce de résistance, no doubt. With a flourish he swept the lid from the platter. It contained the heads of six young children: my brothers and sisters. Shouts of derisive laughter, obviously directed at me, filled the hall, and I looked down at my plate and saw that it held a small human hand.

I started to vomit. I vomited for what seemed like weeks, until I felt as if I had vomited up everything inside of me, including internal organs, leaving only an empty shell. "Hold it," I choked, "I know what you're doing."

. . . break . . .

The dragon took another bite of the root network, and I cried out in alarm. I flapped my wings furiously, trying to catch up with the serpent, but it was slithering down into the stygian depths of the pit.

The pit began narrowing, and soon the walls were closing in on me so that I could no longer extend my wings. The pit continued to narrow and was becoming tortuous as well. Now I was running along in a crouch, and then on hands and knees, trying to catch up with the small figure that danced along just ahead of me.

My knees were sore from the hard plastic of the tube, but I had lost my kneepads and had to catch up with him before he could reach the next slide, which I was pretty sure was just around the next corner. I made a desperate lunge and caught him by one ankle; he twisted around and our eyes met. "You!" he said.

I stared at him. "Me."

. . . break . . .

The cell door slammed shut with a loud, metallic clank. I was led from my cell, down a long corridor, flanked by two extremely large uniformed guards. It was a very long walk. I thought I remembered something about a condemned man's walk to the place of execution being called "the last mile." Shouldn't there be a prison chaplain, reading to me from a Bible as we walked? I wasn't sure. After a long time we arrived at a solid metal door. The door was opened, and I was shoved in roughly. I stumbled, regained my balance in time to turn around and see the door slam shut. As my eyes adjusted to the dim light in the room, I more than half expected to see an electric chair, or perhaps some more modern torture chamber, but the only furnishing was a table, institutional type, with a linoleum top and trestle legs. I could also see that I was not alone. About a dozen other men, inmates by their uniforms, surrounded me. They were smiling. Suddenly four of them grabbed me. I tried to fight, but my movements were clumsy and ineffective, as if in a dream. They forced me facedown over the table in the center of the room. I could feel hands fumbling with my belt and zipper; then my pants were jerked down to my knees. The largest man there approached, smiling a most unfriendly smile, and started to unzip his own pants.

I started to laugh. "Is that the best you can do? This is all pretty obvious stuff, don't you think?"

At that moment one wall of the room exploded outward, taking several of my would-be rapists along with it. Through the opening stepped a creature with the body of a man and the head of some sort of animal, although what sort, exactly, I couldn't say. It also had three pairs of wings sprouting from its back.

The rest of my attackers scattered, screaming, and I turned to face the newest threat, but instead of attacking, it extended a hand and said, "I'm here to help you. Let's get out of here."

I didn't need a ton of encouragement. "Who are you?" I asked as I followed him—her? it?—back out through the hole in the wall.

"That's not important. We need to get you out of here right away."

"Fine with me. I just need to get my—" I looked down and saw that, instead of a prison uniform, with pants down around my ankles, I was wearing my golden armor again, with my sword belted at my side. I checked my pouch to be sure Eltanin was still there. It was. "Thanks," I said to my strange-looking rescuer. "I'm not sure how much more of that I could have taken."

"That isn't what I was worried about. You were through the worst of that stuff, and you seemed to have pretty much figured out what was happening."

"Then why the urgency?"

"I think it was going to kill you."

"Why?"

"Because it couldn't drive you crazy with the probe, for one thing. For another, it must view you as some kind of threat, although you may have a better idea of why that is than I do. How are you feeling?"

"Fine."

"Good—wait a minute. How do you *really* feel?"

"What do you mean?"

He shook his beastly head impatiently. "Didn't anybody show you how to use that thing? The NIL is controlling all your sensory perceptions, including visceral ones. That means that your 'virtual body' may feel fine, but your real one might be on the point of collapse. You have to use an override to check periodically on how your real body is doing."

He showed me how to trigger the override. I did—and immediately wished I hadn't. The first thing to hit me was a wave of nausea. As I fought back the urge to vomit, I became aware of other sensations, painful ones, mainly, as if my entire body had been worked over with a meat tenderizer. I also felt the most ungodly thirst, which wasn't surprising, as I hadn't been able to keep anything down since . . . "What day is it, anyway?"

"Friday. Are you okay?"

"I'll be all right. I'm a little thirsty."

"Get something to drink. You can get dangerously dehydrated on that thing. Make sure you keep checking how you feel in real mode, too."

He led me down a torchlit subterranean passage that ended at the edge of an underground river. An Egyptian barque was moored at the water's edge.

"Come on," he urged. "I'd like to get you out of here before Wyrm has a chance to try to stop us."

That was interesting. "Wyrm" was a nickname that Al and George and the others had been using, in conversations among ourselves, for the intelligent computer program that seemed to be at the root of our problems. How did this guy know that? There certainly weren't many other people I'd talked to about this.

"Where are we going?" I asked as I followed him onto the barque.

He pointed down the river. "Out to daylight, if we're lucky."

He poled the barque out into the middle of the channel, where the swift current whisked us along.

"Who are you?" I asked again.

"I'm not going to tell you, even though I think you'll probably figure it out sooner or later."

I started to mull that over, then had my train of thought violently derailed when a huge dragon head suddenly rose from the water ahead of our boat. I reached for my sword, but before I could unsheathe it, my mysterious guide thrust his hands toward the beast. Daggers of light seemed to fly from his outstretched fingertips, and where they struck the beast, they appeared to char its scaly hide. The dragon head slipped back beneath the water as abruptly as it had emerged.

"We're almost there," my guide announced as we both continued to scan the water's surface nervously for signs of another attack.

Then I saw it—the proverbial light at the end of the tunnel, which proved, in this case, not to be an onrushing train. In another minute we had emerged into the virtual daylight my enigmatic friend had promised. He turned to me again. "Go on, get out of here. If you've got a way of defeating Wyrm, get to it."

"What if I need your help?"

"I'll be helping in my own way. Now, get out of here. And get something to eat and drink!"

I didn't insist on being coaxed any more. I opened my eyes to break the link, as Dworkin had instructed me—and nothing happened. Instead of the basement of a row house, I was still looking at a virtual landscape. I reluctantly triggered the real-mode override, fought back another wave of nausea, and then tried to move.

I couldn't.

The electronically induced paralysis was still active. Or else I had fried my central nervous system à la Seth Serafin, and I didn't even want to think about that possibility. Something else was nagging at the edges of my awareness, something I knew I was supposed to remember to do—then it came to me: the drug! My rescuer had said it was . . . Friday? Frantically, I called up a time display and was horrified to see that almost thirty hours had elapsed since my last dose—most of that time spent undergoing Wyrm's probe.

Realizing that it was almost certainly already too late, I steeled myself to make one more try to break the link, so that I could reinject myself and get something to drink. For the third time I triggered the real-mode override.

The nausea was even worse this time. My mouth felt like sandpaper and tasted like the bottom of a birdcage. I struggled to move something, anything, then started trembling, which seemed to set off another wave of nausea.

Then I passed out.

CHAPTER EIGHTEEN

The Light at the End of the Tunnel

I am Alpha and Omega . . .
—Revelation 22:13

Some idiot had his high beams on, and they were blinding me. I went to flash my high beams back at him, and that's when I realized I wasn't in a car. Next, I noticed that the bright light seemed to be coming from a single source rather than a pair of headlights, and I seemed to be floating down a tunnel toward the source. I threw up a hand to shield my eyes and said, a bit irritably, "Could somebody please dim that damn light?"

There was a deep chuckle. It seemed to be coming from the light. In the next instant the light was gone, replaced by a muscular, bearded man. "Perhaps you'd prefer something a little more anthropomorphic."

I stared at him. "Who are you?"

"You know Me."

I did recognize Him. He was God—at least the way Michelangelo pictured Him in the creation scene on the Sistine-chapel ceiling.

"Am I . . . dead?"

"No."

"Then I must be dreaming. Or hallucinating."

"So skeptical? I thought you had Me figured out. What did you call Me? The group overmind daemon?"

"That? I'm not sure I believe in that myself."

"Then Whom are you telling?"

"I don't know, probably myself. Shit, I hope I'm going to wake up soon. I have important stuff to do."

"Don't worry, you'll have time to do it. Time flows differently here."

"You mean here in cyberspace?"

"Take a look around you; does this look like cyberspace to you?"

"Cyberspace can look like just about anything."

"Well, this ain't it. You're having an out-of-body experience, My son. And 'out-of-body' includes out of the usual physical world-as-you-know-it."

"Or it could be just a dream," I insisted.

He shook His head. "You don't seem to want to consider the possibility that you were right. Just let Me add a few pieces of evidence for My existence that you neglected to consider."

"Such as?"

"Such as coincidences."

"Those can be explained by pure chance."

"Oh, really? Would you say it was pure chance that your friend Jamaal showed up just in time to pull your chestnuts out of the fire?"

"Are You saying that *You* put Jamaal there?"

"Not by any supernatural means. It was just a matter of timing."

"Then what about the skinheads? I suppose that wasn't a coincidence either?"

"Of course not. After all, I'm not the only player in this game."

"So You're saying that someone sent the skinheads to stop me, and You sent Jamaal to the rescue. Why am I so important, all of a sudden?"

"Because I need you."

"Let me get this straight: *You* . . . need *me?*"

"Michael, you are to be My champion."

"Me? Why me? Hell, why anybody? Why not just do it Yourself—after all, this seems like a good job for somebody Who's omnipotent."

He laughed. "Omnipotent? Pish, tush, I never claimed to be omnipotent. That's just pious flattery. And, besides, I don't work that way."

"Then in what way *do* You work?"

"I believe the usual adjective is 'mysterious.' "

I groaned. "Okay, then if 'omipotent' is out, how about 'omniscient'? Can You at least tell me *how* to stop this thing?"

"I never claimed omniscience either, but don't worry. You'll think of something."

I was still in the link when I came to. I couldn't break the link to give myself another injection, even if it wasn't already too late for that. I pictured Seth Serafin again, lying in his weird bed, then suppressed the image. At least some of my central nervous system was still working, because I was still in the link; at least I hadn't burned out the connections—yet. I resolved to devote what few synaptic firings I had remaining to making a certain Wyrm regret that it had ever evolved.

"Ptah!" I shouted for him a few times, then tried to locate him with Eltanin, but he must have gone off-line.

I used Eltanin to find George and warped through to his location, hoping that he and Al and The Dodo, and whatever help they had recruited, had had enough time to do what I'd asked of them.

"Mike!" he exclaimed as I stepped through the portal. "Am I glad to see you!"

"Believe me, it's mutual. Where's Al?"

"I tried to tell you before, but you left too quickly. She's not with me."

"I can see she's not with you in cyberspace, but you guys are all at Cepheus together, aren't you?"

"Yes and no: We're all at Cepheus, but we're not together. We were locked out of the snake pit, so we had to go to separate rooms."

"So just go find her."

"I can't. I'm locked in, and I suspect the others are, as well."

"Phones? Intercoms?"

"Out. Whoever is doing this apparently doesn't want us talking to one another."

I used Eltanin to locate Al and found her where I'd left her, in the queen's chamber.

I explained to her what I had George and The Dodo working on; she listened thoughtfully, then said, "I think it can work. I think you might have to put it to sleep first, though."

"To sleep?"

"Yes. If it sees what you're doing and figures it out, it might be able to undo it. I've been studying the source code for the 'sword of the son,' and I've found something we can use to put it out of commission, at least for a few seconds, if we can find a way to target the kernels. I've been working on a program that ought to do the trick."

"Good! Well, let me get you out of here; I'll bring you to where George and TD are."

"Okay. Michael, I assume George or somebody else told you about the situation here at Cepheus?"

"About your all being locked in different rooms? Yeah, George told me."

"Well, I hate to sound like I'm *asking* to be rescued, but the temperature in my room has been rising for the last six hours. It's like a sauna in here, and I'm not feeling too well."

That really scared me. For Al to admit she wasn't feeling well, she'd practically have to be on the verge of collapse. "Can you break a window?"

"My room doesn't have one."

I started to curse. She smiled wanly. "Careful," she told me. "Your halo is slipping."

I thought of getting a message to the local police; then I remembered what Arthur had told me about the building's security systems. If they had been designed to protect national-security secrets, the likelihood of the local gendarmes being able to get in was negligible.

I picked her up and reopened the portal back to where I'd left George and The Dodo. "I'm going to go find Arthur," I told her. "Maybe he'll have some idea about how to get you out." But as I attempted to carry her through cyberspace, she seemed to dissolve in my arms and disappear. I used Eltanin to locate her and found her back in the queen's chamber.

"I don't seem to be able to take you out of here."

"That's okay. I'm less concerned about getting out of the pyramid room, and more concerned about getting out of the room at Cepheus. Michael . . . you have to save . . . our baby."

Oh no, I thought, *now she's delirious. I have to get her out—*

"I'm not delirious. I'm pregnant. I meant to tell you, but then we had that big fight and . . . I'm sorry."

"You're . . . pregnant? How can you be pregnant?"

"You remember that time we thought it would be okay not to use anything because of the time of month it was? Well, it wasn't. Safe, I mean."

"The rhythm method strikes again, huh?"

"I'm afraid so. Are you terribly angry with me?"

"Angry? Hell no! It's wonderful—I mean it's terrible—I have to get you out of there! Don't worry, I'm on my way."

"Before you go," she said, "can you download this program? It's the 'sleeper' I mentioned. If you upload it to a 'dragon tooth,' it should put it out of commission for a short time, maybe long enough to cripple or kill it in some other way."

I downloaded Al's program and very reluctantly left her in the pyramid, reminding myself that it wasn't where she *really* was anyway, then used Eltanin once more. I found that Arthur, too, had been immured in the ruined pyramid, although not alone. His companion was an old man with a long beard and a dime-store Halloween wizard's get-up. I didn't waste any time warping through.

"Art!" I called as I stepped through the portal into the king's chamber. "We've got a problem."

He squinted at me. "That *is* you, isn't it, Mike?"

"Yeah, it's me. Listen, I just found out what's going on at Cepheus. Al just told me her room is overheating like a sauna. I think she's close to passing out from heatstroke."

"Oh, no! Do you know how the others are doing?"

"Well, George seems to be fine. I haven't seen any of the others."

"Do you have a way of checking on them?"

"Yes. Let me just take you back to where I left George and Al. Oh, and if you want, I can take Merlin, here, as well."

"Mike, this is Marlon Oz."

Marlon Oz on the 'net? Now I was sure it was the end of the world. I gathered them up and warped back through cyberspace. Then I checked Eltanin again. I shook my head. "No sign of Robin or Krishna, I'm afraid. And Leon—hey, I didn't know that was Leon!" In another moment I had collected him and rejoined the others.

We were all worried about Al, and especially about Robin and Krishna, because we didn't know if they were just having 'net problems, or the kind of problems Al was having. Arthur seemed the most worried of all—I think he felt responsible, as it was his building that was holding everybody hostage.

"Marlon tried calling our security company, but the phone system seems to be closed to voice traffic all over the country. I don't know how much luck we'd have getting anyone out here on New Year's Eve anyway," Arthur told me.

"What about the Defense Department? You told me your security system was something they insisted on. Can they help?"

Oz shook his head. "Milnet closed its mailbridges hours ago, when they realized something was amiss on the Internet."

"Damn! I should have realized they'd do that."

"What's the big deal?" Oz asked.

I gave them the bad news: that Wyrm had in fact planted viruses in the computer systems that controlled nuclear-missile launches. For the first time I think Oz was genuinely impressed with something I told him.

"Doesn't it realize that if that happens, it will be destroyed too?"

"It's crazy; it thinks that it's 'imprisoned' by the Internet, and that if the 'net's destroyed, it'll be set loose."

"If that's crazy, then it's no crazier than most people," Oz pointed out. "Most people believe in life after death—that when the body dies, the soul is liberated."

"We've got to get those weapons-control computers taken off-line," Art said.

"How?" I asked. "With no phones, and Milnet closed to E-mail, how are we supposed to get a message to anybody?"

Oz squinted at me. "You've got root access, don't you?" "Root access" was another way of describing a privileged logon.

"Yeah."

"Then you've got to figure out a way to get Milnet back on-line."

"How the hell am I supposed to do that?" It would be like trying to tell someone who'd just hung up on you to pick up the phone again.

"Remember," he said, "there are more ways of reaching Milnet than mailbridges, even if it takes a 'ten finger' interface." That last term referred to the practice of having a computer operator manually transfer data between networks that are disconnected for security reasons.

"Okay," I said. "And suppose I can do that. What do I do next— say, 'You don't know me, but I'd like you to turn off all the nuclear-weapons computers, if you don't mind'? Art? Can you do anything?"

"I don't have that kind of influence."

"When you do it," Oz said, "get hold of Ogden Marsh at Lawrence Livermore, and let me talk to him."

Suddenly the ground shook, then split asunder as a gigantic reptilian head emerged at the end of a long, snaky neck. It lunged at me, and I yanked my sword from its sheath just in time to keep the jaws from snapping shut on me. The dragon reared back, apparently afraid of the sword, and breathed a huge gout of flame at me. I responded without thinking, exhaling a blast of wind that extinguished the dragon's flame like a child blowing out a birthday candle, then followed up with a blast of energy from my sword.

The dragon screamed, in rage or pain, and withdrew its head back below the surface. "What the hell was that?" Oz asked.

"That was Wyrm. It's trying to kill me."

"Trying to *kill* you? How can it do that?"

"You're using a NIL, aren't you?" Arthur said.

"Yeah. Look, if I stay in any one place too long, it's going to come after me. It's probably trying to bring more resources to bear on this position right now, so I'm out of here. I'll update you when I can."

▲   ▲   ▲   ▲   ▲   ▲   ▲

"Hello, my dear."

Al looked around, then spotted the familiar disembodied feline grin of Schrödinger's cat in one corner of her cell. "Hi. It's nice to have somebody to talk to. I don't suppose you can get me out of here?"

"Get you out of here? Now, *that* would take some doing."

"Well, you seem to get around pretty well yourself. Although the way you keep 'softly and suddenly vanishing away,' it's as if a boojum got you."

"Now, that brings up an interesting question."

"It does?"

"Yes, indeed. Can a boojum do to itself what it does to others?"

"Can a—wait a minute! Are you telling me that *you're* a boo—"

▲   ▲   ▲   ▲   ▲   ▲   ▲

"Did you hear something, George?"

"What, Ludovico?"

"It sounded like 'jum.' "

"Probably just a breeze or something. How are you coming with that subroutine?"

"It isn't very elegant, but I think it will work."

"Good. This isn't the time to go for style points."

▲ ▲ ▲ ▲ ▲ ▲ ▲

More dragon heads were already erupting from the ground as I warped out. I traveled to a series of random locations, then stopped to get my bearings. I had an idea about how to contact Oz's friend at Livermore. Using Eltanin, I first tried to figure out what was going on with the phones. Art had said that no voice traffic was getting through, so Wyrm must somehow have tagged the system to keep track of which lines were which.

At the time I had no idea why it would want to do that. It was only later that I learned that computers all over the world were dialing in to their respective Internet hosts, as Wyrm tried, apparently, to get as much computing power on-line as it could. Of course, this would be possible only if a computer was already powered up, but enough machines were involved to pose a potential phone-traffic problem. Wyrm simply solved that problem by stopping voice traffic altogether.

Of course, there's nothing special about a modem line—the hardware's exactly the same as any other telephone line, and lots of residential lines are used for voice and modem traffic. But Wyrm knew which lines were used for Internet access and simply blocked everything else.

I tapped into a phone-company switching station and tried to figure out what was going on. First, I tried turning one of the voice lines back on. It went on but was disabled again almost immediately. After scanning a few different lines, I was pretty sure I could see which marker Wyrm was using.

I now asked Eltanin to show me one of the voice lines into Livermore. It was shut down, but not for long. I changed the marker to make it look like a modem line, then switched it on. It stayed on.

The next question was, How was I going to talk to someone on the phone when I didn't actually *have* a phone? A phone transduces sound waves into electrical impulses that can travel over wires. I didn't have a phone, but I had the NIL, which amplified electrical signals from my brain, which controls speech, as well as everything else. The

NIL was picking up signals from whichever part of my cerebral cortex was responsible for moving my lips, tongue, and larynx, and turning it into virtual speech; I could actually "hear" myself when I talked on the 'net. It even sounded like me—I hadn't realized, until just then, how weird *that* was.

It took a few minutes for me to figure out a way to patch my NIL-synthesized speech into a normal phone connection—it actually turned out to be easier than I thought it would. I tapped into it and placed a call. It rang twice, then somebody picked up. He sounded bewildered. "Yes?"

"Get me Ogden Marsh," I said. "This is an emergency." I didn't have to ask if Marsh was there. With this kind of a 'net crisis going on, they'd have all their technical people working on it, of that I had no doubt.

"Who is this?"

"I have a call for Ogden Marsh from Marlon Oz. Please tell him it's an emergency." A little name-dropping works wonders sometimes. While he was getting Marsh, I used Eltanin to call up Oz.

Only Oz wasn't anywhere to be found.

"Shit! He must have gone off-line, just when—"

"Hello? This is Ogden Marsh."

"Hello! This is—er—a friend of Marlon Oz."

"What is this, some kind of prank?"

"No! This is serious! Dr. Oz wanted to speak to you, but he's . . . not here at the moment. . . . Look, we think you've got a potentially serious security problem with your computer system—"

"Who are you?"

"My name is Michael Arcangelo. You don't know me, but—"

"That's right, I don't know you. If you have Marlon Oz there, you'd better put him on."

"I told you, he's . . . not here right now. If he was, believe me, I'd let him talk to you. I just need to tell you that we think your computer system may be infected—"

"We're cleaning it up right now. And we're not going back on-line until the Internet problem is cleared up, so—"

"Not that system! I'm talking about the supposedly secure computers that control nuclear-weapons systems. We think that—"

"Don't be ridiculous. You're claiming Marlon Oz put you up to this? I don't believe it."

"It's not ridiculous! You've got to shut those computers down until they can be checked for viruses! Look, I know they were checked recently, but it was the wrong marker, and—"

"Forget it! If you think we're going to shut down the nation's strategic-defense systems because—"

I didn't get to hear the rest of it, because at that moment more dragon heads attacked—three of them this time. I didn't waste time trying to fight them; I just used Eltanin and warped away.

After warping to several other random locations, hoping to confuse the trail as much as possible, I located George and the others. Instead of warping to their location, which had recently been visited by Wyrm, who might be expecting me to return, I simply communicated with him via Eltanin. I could see him and the others, and, standing next to him, what appeared to be another knight armored very much like himself, along with a short fellow wearing Grecian armor.

"George, what happened to Marlon Oz?"

"Wyrm got him after you left."

"Damn! Who's that with you?"

"This," he said, jerking a thumb at the taller of the two armored figures, "is Goodknight. And this is Jason."

"Jason? You're kidding."

"No, I'm not. I told him what was going on, and he put Goodknight on-line himself. He's helping us with that program you wanted, too."

"Oh. Well, how are you guys coming with it?"

"It's about as ready as it's going to be this millennium. You're going to have to upload it directly to each kernel, though, and we don't even have telnet addresses for them. Do you have any way of locating them?"

I held up Eltanin. "This will do the trick."

"Ah. I suspect they're going to be pretty heavily defended, though. Any ideas how you're going to do it?"

"Al gave me a little something that should help." At least I *hoped* it would help.

"Well, are you going to come and get it?"

"I'd rather not. Let me see if I can download it through this link." George, Jason, and TD had obviously written a pretty streamlined program under pressure, because it downloaded fast. That was key, because I didn't know how much time I was going to have to load it into each kernel. Probably not much.

"It's got a command trigger," George said.

"What?"

He told me. It was definitely more George's sense of humor than TD's, and involved a particularly improbable form of recursion.

"Cute. Okay, I'm on my way."

"Okay. I know I don't have to tell you to be good, but I do want to tell you to—"

"Be careful?"

"Yeah."

"Thanks."

I checked Eltanin again and asked for the location of Echion.edu. I prepared Al's program, then warped through.

I stepped into the midst of countless writhing serpentine coils. Several reptilian heads were already lunging toward me as I triggered Al's program. Sure enough, the coils stopped moving, and the heads slowly sank to the ground. That gave me a few moments to upload George's program and get out of there.

In quick succession I visited Udaeus.gov, Hyperenor.org, and Pelorus.mil which, despite the bogus domain name, was not, fortunately, on Milnet. I uploaded the program George had given me to each one.

That left only Chthonius.com. The last step was crucial, because if any of the dragon's teeth escaped, it would be able to rebootstrap the others and be back up to speed in no time. Still, things were going smoothly, and I figured the last stop would be no different from the others, and we'd be set.

I should have known better.

As I stepped through my warp-window and triggered Al's sleeper program, everything seemed to be going according to plan. Then I noticed that one of the dragon heads had not been affected. Why it was immune, I didn't know, but it was staring at me and obviously getting ready to strike.

I had put Eltanin back in my pouch so that I could upload George's program. I fumbled to get it back out so I could warp away. I reached into my pouch and pulled out—the egg that George had given me.

I felt pretty stupid, and also pretty dead. The dragon looked at me and seemed to know I wasn't going anywhere. It struck.

As the dragon's head flashed toward me, the egg suddenly shattered, and a small bird with iridescent plumage leaped from my palm to meet the dragon's head in midair. By the time their respective trajectories intersected, the bird had grown to the size of an F-15, a development the dragon obviously hadn't anticipated, because it was suddenly on the defensive as the bird swooped around its head slashing at its eyes with a beak like a scimitar, and leaving a fiery trail in its wake.

I tried to take advantage of the diversion and load the program, but it was too late because Al's sleep effect was now wearing off the other dragon heads, and I quickly found myself surrounded.

I thought about whether I had time to dig Eltanin out and decided I'd better just go for my sword because I was going to die anyway, when a loud noise that was like a combination of a scream and a roar pierced the air, and a huge mass of feathers and fur swooped over my head and barreled into the nearest dragon head, slashing with beak, claws, and talons.

I didn't know who the big bird was, but I did recognize this newest arrival. "Leon!"

Close behind him were George and Arthur. George was on horseback, and Arthur was actually riding a unicorn. They charged into the melee, with Arthur firing bolts of energy from his ring, and both of them slashing with their swords. "Load the program!" George shouted, lopping off dragon heads with Hanlon's Razor. "We haven't got all day!"

I started to do what he suggested, not realizing that there was one last dragon head that was unengaged and unaccounted for, and it was coming after me. Out of the corner of my eye I spotted the movement and started to turn, even as I realized it would be too late. The head darted toward me, jaws agape, then, abruptly, paused in midlunge and emitted a dense cloud of black smoke from its mouth and nostrils, then dropped, lifeless, to the ground. The jaws opened again, and out stepped a little boy with blue skin.

Unfortunately, more dragon heads were now erupting from the ground, as Wyrm tried to marshal its forces to protect the kernel. One of the heads tried to snap up the little blue-skinned boy, but he merely jumped onto its head and, incredibly, began to dance. This seemed to make the other heads go crazy. They all tried to attack him at once, but he merely skipped from head to head, continuing to do his dance. After a few seconds of this the heads stopped trying to attack him and started swaying in time to his rhythm. Even the heads that had been locked in combat with George and the others broke off to join the swaying snake dance. "Well?" the little guy demanded, looking at me as he continued to dance. "Are you going to do it or not?"

I did it. I uploaded George's program, then opened a warp-window and yelled, "Everybody out of the pool! Let's go!"

Arthur and George galloped through the warp-window first. Leon flew through next, then the big bird, and then the little blue-skinned boy flashed through so fast that I could hardly see him, closely followed by yours truly.

On the other side we paused to catch our breath.

"Do you think it knows what you did?" Arthur asked.

"I hope not, because if it does, it can undo it. If we're lucky, it may just think we ran away before we could do anything."

The big bird spoke. "It looked to me," it said in a familiar-sounding woman's voice, "like they were completely mesmerized by Krishna's dance. I don't think they were aware of anything else."

"I hope you're right," I said. "Anyway, how did you know where I was? And how did you get there?"

"The troll told us you needed help," George said. "He brought the unicorn to us, too. Then some guy came and opened one of those warp-gates to let us get to where you were."

"Some guy?"

"Funny-looking guy. Six wings, head like a hyena or something. Nice enough, though."

The program that George and TD had written to my specifications was now loaded, but it hadn't yet been triggered. That could be done anytime, but there were certain factors to take into consideration.

"You're going to talk to it again?" George was incredulous. "Why? You said it already tried to kill you."

"I know. But remember what you said: It must use a lot of its resources to carry on a conversation. I want it to be as distracted as possible when your program is triggered. Otherwise it might have a chance to see what's going on and derail it somehow.

"Also, you told me that Wyrm got Oz. I thought at first that he must be off-line, but then I remembered that Wyrm has got hell warded against Eltanin. If he's on the 'net, that's where he is. I've got to get to him and put him through to Livermore. It's our only chance to get them to switch off the nuclear-weapons computer systems until they can be devirused."

George's eyes widened. "You've got a point there."

"How much time do I have?"

"It'll be midnight in Fiji in about another twenty minutes."

"Here, take this with you," Arthur said, handing me a bottle. "It's a djinni. He hasn't done *us* much good, but maybe you'll find a use for him."

I accepted the bottle and pocketed it. I was tempted to check in on Al again, but I knew I didn't have time, and couldn't do anything for her even if I did. It was driving me crazy just thinking about her, though.

I didn't bother with the cap of darkness this time. I was thinking about how I had scaled myself down to pass through one of the microscopic hellgates, and I figured I ought to be able to do it in reverse.

It worked. I tried to remember whether there had been any particularly low or narrow passages on the road to hell the first time—I couldn't think of any in particular. So I made myself about a hundred feet tall and was pleased to see that Eltanin and my sword grew to scale. The demons and devils that haunted the road could see me this time, all right—they fled screaming in every direction, including the ones who had attacked me the first time.

When I arrived at the gates, the giant three-headed dog snarled, then tried to nip at my ankles. I picked it up by the scruff of its middle neck and held it out at arm's length. Now I had to figure out how to get in. I could put the dog down and shrink myself to go through one of the microscopic gates, but I didn't feel like doing that. I figured there was something I needed to make the proper entrance, but I couldn't use my warp abilities there due to the interdiction that Wyrm had placed in and around hell. I took out the bottle that Arthur had given me and thumbed the stopper out—it was a bit difficult because of the size of my hands, and I dropped it in the process, but I did get it open. Blue smoke issued from the bottle and coalesced into a humanoid form who stood with his hands on his hips scowling at the ground as if he were looking for something. Then he noticed my foot, and his eyes traveled from it up to my face. It was a long way up, as his head was only about as high as my knees. The scowl vanished and was replaced by an ingratiating grin. "What can I do for you, boss?"

I told him what I wanted. "And be quick about it!"

He was. A few seconds later he returned with the biggest horn he could find, which turned out to be a trumpet about as long as a telephone pole. I raised it to my lips and blew as hard as I could.

The great black gates were sundered by the blast; they flew apart, then sagged on broken hinges. The dog in my left hand was whimpering from all three heads now, so I set him down, and he scampered off with his tail between his legs.

I unsheathed my sword and strode through the gates. I looked down and saw the pit fiend who had been standing guard before, or at least one like him. This time he didn't even come up to my knees. Either my spell had worn off, or he was a replacement, because he actually tried to stop me. I cut him in half with one sweep of my sword. Gradually, a hush came over the place, as the cries of anguish of the damned died down and stopped. Then the din began anew; only in place of piteous human wailing were the fearful screams and gibberings of things demonic.

I now spread my wings and flew to Wyrm's lair. Beelzebub met me at the entrance to the cavern, or rather, Beelze*bot.*

"Arcangelo, my old adversary," he greeted me as he expanded himself to a height comparable to my own.

"Somebody should check your algorithm," I told him. "You're starting to repeat yourself."

A glowing red sword appeared in his hands. "Here's something new," he said, and swung a wide two-handed blow at my neck. I ducked underneath the blow and countered with a slash at his left arm. My blade bit cleanly all the way through, just above the elbow, and his arm flopped onto the ground. He looked down at it, then up at me; then he smiled. In less than a second a new arm grew to take the place of the one I had severed. I didn't know whether I could do the same thing, and even if I could, I didn't have time to find out how. That shifted the odds radically in his favor, because it meant that he could ignore anything short of a death blow.

We circled each other warily now, each of us looking for an opening. I reminded myself that time was on his side, and I had to do something quickly.

I realized that I was going to have to make myself smaller to get into Wyrm's lair; the entrance was only about twenty feet high. I feinted a lunge at the Beelzebot, then, quickly, shrank myself and darted into the entrance, down the tunnel, and around the first turn. Then I waited.

His mistake was that he was too anxious to catch up with me. When he came running around the bend, I was ready for him. He was holding his sword low, so I swung mine high, and the blade bit effortlessly through his neck. His head dropped at my feet, and the body actually kept running until it hit a wall. I looked down at the head, which appeared to be looking at me with its many-faceted eyes.

"Arcangelo, my old adversary," it said.

"Greetings, Michael," Wyrm said when I again stood before it. "Have you come to slay me?" The mockery was still there. Déjà vu all over again.

"Yes, I have. Unless you can give me a very good reason not to."

"A reason?"

"Yes. For starters I want Marlon Oz, right here, right now."

I have no doubt the thing was just humoring me, toying with me, but it did what I asked. The wizardly figure of Oz appeared in a puff of brimstone-scented smoke.

"Dr. Oz," I said. "There's a call for you."

I calmly repeated my earlier procedure for getting a call through to Livermore; only this time I connected it with Oz's line at MIT.

"Hello?" came a voice that I recognized as Marsh's. Had he been waiting by the phone all this time?

"What makes you think that I'll allow this call to go through?" Wyrm asked.

"You told me earlier," I said, "that you want to go on existing. If you try to stop the call, I will see to it that your existence ends. Now."

I don't think it really believed me, but there was just enough doubt to cause it to hesitate. "You still do not understand what I am, do you? You cannot kill me.

"I am Ti'amat; I am Apophis; I am Leviathan and Zohak and Yamm. I am Typhon and Python and Ladon and Hydra; I am Ananta and Vritra. I am Quetzalcoatl and Kukulkan and Tlenemaw and Uktena; I am Nidhoggr and Jormungandr; I am Satan.

"I am the Ouroboros.

"I am Heisenberg's uncertainty and Gödel's incompleteness; I am the second law of thermodynamics. I am the unconscious made conscious; I am the one who shaves the barber; I am Chaos; I am Paradox.

"I Am What Is Not.

"You can't kill me," it hissed. "But I can kill you. However, before I do, I would find it interesting to observe your reactions as I kill your woman. She is impregnated with your seed, yes? That should make it even more interesting. But first I will silence this old fool."

At that moment a dozen different thoughts flooded my mind. I thought of the people: men, women, and children who would suffer and die if Wyrm was allowed to live. I remembered the torture, physical and mental, it had subjected me to. But most of all I thought of Al, trapped in the room at Cepheus, suffering, maybe dying.

"Wyrm," I said, "go fuck yourself."

It was the trigger to George's program.

For a long moment nothing happened.

Then lots of things did. "You . . . !" Wyrm started to say, then either lost the power of speech or had other, more pressing problems to attend to. The vast bulk of Wyrm was now writhing as if in agony, and all along its vast length, patches of hide began to blacken and crumble to dust.

George and The Dodo's program was working, and Wyrm was dying, but even in its death throes it managed to lash out at me, somehow triggering my real-mode override and locking it. Suddenly I was back in that basement in San Francisco, retching. There was not a thing left in my stomach, of course, so I just dry-heaved until I finally, mercifully, passed out.

▲   ▲   ▲   ▲   ▲   ▲   ▲

I awakened to an uncomfortable glare of fluorescent light shining directly into my eyes. I tried to move my head away from the light, but it seemed like too much effort, so I just closed my eyes again. There was a familiar smell, too, something nagging at a part of my brain until I finally placed it: Seth Serafin's house. My eyes snapped open again, this time with some purpose. I had to see where the hell I was.

The glare made it difficult to see anything, but I could make out part of my left arm lying on a clean white sheet. There was some white tape on it, and a thin plastic tube running under the tape. I tried to focus on something farther away. There were some dark shapes in the middle distance that looked as if they might just be people, but no matter how I tried, I couldn't bring them into focus.

Some indeterminate time later I awoke again. The light didn't seem as harsh this time, or maybe my head had been placed in a different position—I didn't think I could move it myself. There was only a single dark shape in the room this time. I willed myself to focus on it, and gradually it resolved into a face: It was Al. Her eyes seemed to be unnaturally large and bright. I tried opening my mouth to talk to her. That didn't seem to work either. I don't know whether I succeeded in making some kind of movement, or noise, or what, but she suddenly got up, walked over to me, and looked closely at my face. Then she turned and called, "Nurse!"

The third time I woke up, her face was already close to mine, her eyes as bright as before. I tried to smile and was surprised to feel my facial muscles respond. Encouraged, I opened my mouth to try to talk, but she hushed me. "You're not supposed to try to do anything yet. Just relax." I smiled again.

She took a deep breath. "Michael, we—I . . . thought we'd lost you." There was a catch in her voice.

There was a kind of croaking noise that sounded something like "What happened?" It took me a minute to realize it was me.

The brightness in her eyes seemed to ripple, then coalesce into droplets that ran down her cheeks. I watched with a sort of detached fascination, as if I couldn't quite understand what she was doing. "You nearly died is what happened. When the ambulance got to you, you were so dehydrated, you'd gone into shock."

Suddenly it all came flooding back to me: the millennium, the 'net, Roger Dworkin, Wyrm, Armageddon, Ragnarok, Judgment Day, the end of the world. I struggled to sit up. "Did it . . . ? Did we . . . ?"

She gently pushed me back down. "Everything's okay. Yes, we did it. Especially you. Now, get some more sleep. If they catch me talking to you in here, they'll throw me out of this place for good."

"You're okay," I whispered, as if the enormity of that fact had just dawned on me.

"Yes."

I remembered something else. "The baby! Is the baby . . . ?"

She smiled and patted her lower abdomen. "Just fine. When you destroyed Wyrm, the systems in Arthur's building returned to normal. I was a little dehydrated, but really none the worse for wear. Unlike a certain father-to-be."

I started to relax again; then something else came back to me. "The nukes! What about—"

"No problem. Marlon Oz spoke to his former student at Livermore, and he had enough influence to get all the strategic-defense computers taken off-line until they could be completely checked for viruses. Oz told me that at the height of the cold war, they probably wouldn't have been willing to do that."

"Then we'd all be dead."

"Yes."

The next time I woke up, Al was still there, but this time she wasn't alone.

"Are you awake, Mike?"

"George?" I still couldn't see very well about half the time. My vision seemed to fade in and out.

"Yeah, it's me. Hey, they told me you looked awful, but I've seen you with hangovers worse than this."

"Thanks, I think."

"The new haircut suits you, too."

I had no idea what he was talking about—at that point some details were still a little fuzzy.

"You had us worried for a while there, man."

"I did?"

"You did. They said you might wind up as a vegetable. Of course, I asked them how we'd be able to tell."

I heard a sharp smack and an "Ow!" which sounded like George's voice.

"Listen, there are a lot of other people here to see you, but they'll only let us in two at a time, so I'm gonna let some other people have their chance to meet the hero. Just watch out for this girlfriend of

yours—I think all that virtual violence has had a bad effect on her—
ow!"

George got up to leave, but as he did, my vision cleared for a
moment, and I noticed that he was wearing a small button with an
inverted *V* on it. He saw me look and grinned. "The Dodo gave it to
me. I'll tell you all about it later. Oh, and I almost forgot: Here you
go." He held up a suitcase.

"What's that?"

"Your luggage. The airline finally tracked it down. They delivered
it to me in Palo Alto."

"You wouldn't happen to have my dry cleaning too?"

"Hey, one miracle at a time. See ya, pal."

Al came over. "I should go now, too. There are quite a few more
people—" I cut her off by grabbing her arm so that she couldn't go.
As strong as I felt at that moment, breaking my grip would have been
about as difficult as breaking a stick of chewing gum, but she didn't
try.

"Was George right?"

She looked puzzled. "You mean about the violence affecting me?"

"No. About your being my girlfriend."

She seemed to hesitate and glanced back over her shoulder, and for
a moment my heart sank. Then she suddenly leaned forward and
kissed me. It didn't last as long as I would have liked, but she probably
was worried about setting off my cardiac monitor, and rightfully so.
The kiss was so fiercely passionate that it took me a moment to recover and kiss back.

She smiled, and her smile contained just a hint of the devilishness
that was one of the things I'd missed most about her. "What do *you*
think?" she asked.

"I think that's a very good answer."

"But what's this about just being your 'girlfriend'? Don't you
want to make an honest woman of me? Don't you want to give our
baby a name? Don't you—don't interrupt me, I haven't run out of
clichés yet."

"Yes, yes, yes!" I interrupted. "Will you marry me?"

Our next kiss *did* set off my cardiac monitor, and we didn't even
care.

Later, after Al left, I remembered what George had said about my
"new haircut." I ran a hand over my stubbly scalp, and something else

clicked: I had been racking my brain (on those few occasions when it was working) over the identity of my virtual rescuer, the one who had pulled my chestnuts out of the fire while I was undergoing Wyrm's probe. I had been thinking that maybe it was Dworkin, except that I was pretty sure that whoever it was had been using a NIL, and Dworkin sure hadn't sounded as if he was going to risk *that* again.

As my hand explored the shape of my now-hairless dome, I thought of Seth Serafin, lying there in his weird bed, staring, with a tube up his nose. And bald.

Dr. Park looked vaguely familiar, although I didn't have any conscious memory of seeing her before. I found out later that she had stayed with me for almost twenty-four hours when I was first admitted to the intensive-care unit. She was now taking advantage of having a conscious patient for a change, by asking me to fill her in on some of the circumstances leading to my near-death experience.

"So you were hooked up to this equipment for only about forty-eight hours? I don't understand how you could have gotten so dehydrated in such a short time."

"I had some kind of a stomach virus or something—hadn't been able to keep anything down since Thursday."

"That would explain it. Four days without any fluid intake is pretty close to the limit."

That reminded me of something. "Speaking of limits, there's one thing I'm puzzled about."

"What?"

"The drug I took to protect my nervous system against the effects of the NIL—it was supposed to wear off after eight hours. If I was in the link for almost another forty hours after that, my brain should have been completely fried." ("This is your brain on drugs. This is your brain on drugs with a side order of bacon and hash browns. . . .")

"Hmm. Maybe it was the virus."

"The virus?"

"Yes, the viral infection. Viruses can alter a lot of physiological functions, including neurotransmission. It could be that the bug saved your life."

•   •   •

I was pronounced well enough to start receiving phone calls, and they came in a flood. Art, Robin, and Krishna all called, and Leon called from St. John, where he had gone for a much-needed vacation.

The Dodo called too, and we swapped recursive acronyms for a while. "By the way," he said, "did you ever find out what was causing that problem with your 'pit' function—the way it kept swallowing itself?"

"No, I never did. Maybe it was trying to tell me something."

A little later that day Mom and Dad came to see me. They were both wearing forced smiles when they came into the room, and I could see from Mom's eyes that she'd been crying.

"I must have had you guys pretty worried, huh?"

"Yes, we were worried," my father admitted.

"I wish you wouldn't keep things from us," Mom said. "We didn't even know anything was wrong until we read on the front page of the *New York Times* that you'd been arrested."

The front page of the *Times*! I had no idea that my little brush with the law had garnered that kind of publicity. "Oh, God, what the two of you must have been thinking . . ."

"What we were thinking," Dad said firmly, "was that somebody had made a terrible mistake."

"I just hope I can convince them of that," I said. Now that I was thinking a little more clearly, it dawned on me that I still had federal charges pending against me, and I certainly hadn't helped my case by escaping from custody. Not that I had much alternative.

"I wouldn't worry too much about that," my father said. "Macrobyte Software and Arthur Solomon have both offered to pay for your legal defense, but the whole thing may be a moot point, because some anonymous hacker apparently broke into this Beelzebub person's computer files and turned them all over to the FBI. Your lawyer asked us to tell you that he expects the charges to be dropped by the end of the week."

I had a pretty good idea about who that anonymous hacker might be. "Beelzebub is dead," I said. I had spent some time imagining him undergoing Wyrm's probe, wondering what it had uncovered in his cesspool of a mind that had caused him to kill himself. No one would ever know, but it wasn't difficult to imagine that the depths of a mind as malicious as Beelzebub's must be pretty dark and horrible. Hell, mine was bad enough.

"Oh, you already know about that?" Mom said. "It was in the paper this morning. His real name was Bob Beales."

"Beales! The Macrobyte security guy?" Of course. It all fell into place now. As security chief, Beales would have had access to Dworkin's files and certainly wouldn't have scrupled to take full advantage of it.

"Yes. Apparently," my father added, "at one time he was quite a protégé of Marlon Oz."

"Oz!" I exclaimed. "Beelzebub was a protégé of Oz?"

"Please, Michael," my mother soothed, "don't get too excited. It's not good for you."

"In the late eighties, at Yale, yes," my father continued. "Apparently Oz was the one who discovered that his student was misusing his talents. He turned him in, and Beales was expelled. Oz was reportedly very upset by it, because he felt responsible for teaching Beales the skills that he abused."

"Hmm. I'll bet that explains why Oz stopped hacking." And also why Oz was so wary about Macrobyte—he must have known that Beales was there.

"Speaking of hacking," Dad said, "your friend George tried to explain to me what it was that you did to get rid of this 'Wyrm,' but I couldn't understand a word of it. Would you like to take a crack at putting it in layman's terms?"

I suppressed a grin at the thought of my father getting an answer to one of *his* questions that was more complicated than he'd bargained for. "I'll do better than that, Dad," I told him. "I'll put it in medical terms. What we did was give Wyrm an autoimmune disease."

"How?"

"Well, we knew the code that Wyrm used to identify itself. Unfortunately, we didn't have a killer program that was powerful enough to destroy Wyrm faster than it could repair itself. Then I realized that there *was* one program that was powerful enough to do what we needed. . . ."

"The Wyrm itself?"

"Right. We just needed to alter its immune system so that it would attack its own code. The immune system was controlled from five locations, so we needed to alter all five of them. Come to think of it, I

bet that was one of the few times that all five were on-line simultaneously, because of the approaching millennium. We were lucky."

"So what you're saying is, you got the Wyrm program to destroy
its own code by making its immune system think it was attacking
something else?"

"Yeah, basically, that's it.

"It ate itself."

CROSSWORD PUZZLE SOLUTION

B	O	O	Z	E		T	R	A	P		B	A	A	L		M	E	S	S	Y
A	F	T	E	R		H	A	L	E		L	I	N	E		E	B	O	L	A
T	♡	H	U	R	I	A	N	L	E	G	E	N	D	S		♡	B	U	R	N
	S	O	S		R	N	A		I	S	T		S	P	Y					
		P	O	E		L	E	S	S		L	O	L			W	A	R	T	
D	I	S	♡	E	N		M	I	T	T		D	A	N	A		H	I	K	E
I	D	E	S	T		I	N	N		D	E	N		C	H	I	R	O	N	
S	O	N	A	R		S	A	T	A	N	I	C		E	T	C				
		N	I	L	E		O	N	L			S	♡	H	E	M				
A	M	I	D		O	R	O		W	A	A	C		O	U	S	E			
P	O	O	F		B	A	N	I	S	♡	H	W	O	R	M		P	I	N	I
E	L	U	L		I	N	C	H		T	I	O		I	T	E	R			
P	E	S	O	S		S	A	I		N	O	P	E							
		W	I	T		E	N	S	U	I	N	G		A	R	O	S	E		
A	R	L	E	N	E		A	C	T		P	R	O		S	C	A	R	E	
P	A	I	R		S	C	A	T		S	O	A	R		R	H	E	T	O	R
E	G	I	S		L	A	R		P	E	N	N		T	E	A				
		T	A	R		B	E	E		S	H	E		T	H	E				
R	I	♡	H		P	O	R	T	R	A	I	T	O	F	T	♡	I	S	T	
A	L	O	H	A		A	L	E	E		S	T	A	R		A	O	R	T	A
H	O	R	S	T		L	E	A	R		P	O	N	S		O	F	T	E	N

It will not have escaped the astute reader that the action in the cyber-space battle of Armageddon corresponds, roughly, to the moves of a chess game. It is, in fact, mapped to a particular chess game, one played between Armenian grandmaster and future world champion Tigran Petrosian and the Czech grandmaster and eminent chess theorist Ludek Pachman at Bled, Yugoslavia, in 1961.

The game starts off in a somewhat irregular fashion, but by move six transposes into the Sicilian Defense. Although the moves are slightly different from the Dragon Variation of the Sicilian, Black achieves a pawn formation very similar to the serpentine one that gives the Dragon its name. Because of these features, I like to think of this game as the "Hidden Dragon."

1	Nf3	c5		5	d3	e6
2	g3	Nc6		6	e4	N(g)e7
3	Bg2	g6		7	Re1	O-O
4	O-O	B-g7		8	e5	d6

Note the serpentine appearance of Black's pawn formation.

9	exd6	Qxd6		16	Bd6	B-f6
10	N(b)d2	Qc7		17	Qf3	Kg7
11	Nb3	Nd4		18	Re4	Rd8
12	Bf4	Qb6		19	Qxf6+	Kxf6
13	Ne5	Nxb3		20	Be5+	Kg5
14	Nc4	Qb5		21	Bg7	Black resigns
15	axb3	a5				

Forced checkmate in three moves.

Petrosian went on to become world champion by defeating Mikhail Botvinnik in their 1963 match by a score of $12^{1}/_{2}$ to $9^{1}/_{2}$.

About the Author

MARK FABI is a psychiatrist who practices in Philadelphia, and lives in New Jersey with his wife, Donna, and their three sons.